SECRET

FOR THE TRUSTING

TO: Catherine, Lindy-Loo, Jo, Colin, Maureen, Paco, Mo,
Kayleigh, Theresa, Vonni and Geoff.
Who helped to set a spirit free.

AND THE TOLLERANT

FOR: John, Danny, Jay, Zak and James—my sons.
Sandra, Mum, Paula, Steph, Laura, Natalie, Leah and Esmy.
Who'd have thought it, eh?

SECRET
WHAT'S YOURS?

SECRET

JAMES HAYDON

Library of Congress Control Number:		2013908045
ISBN:	Hardcover	978-1-4836-3609-2
	Softcover	978-1-4836-3608-5
	Ebook	978-1-4836-3610-8

This book was printed in the United States of America.

Rev. date: 06/04/2013

To order additional copies of this book, contact:
Xlibris Corporation
0-800-644-6988
www.xlibrispublishing.co.uk
Orders@xlibrispublishing.co.uk
306535

Contents

For James.

Died February 1982

Preface

In the autumn of 1888, an entity struck terror into the East End of London. To date the assailant has never been identified, though many have been offered up as suspects. The victims have been recorded as many as ten and as less as five; Fairy Fay, Emma Elizabeth Smith, Martha Tabram, Mary Ann Nichols, Annie Chapman, Elizabeth Stride, Catharine Eddowes, Mary Jane Kelly, Annie Farmer, Rose Mylett, Alice McKenzie, [possibly] Lydia Hart and Frances Coles. The general consensus is five, beginning with Nichols and ending with Kelly. All were prostitutes who lived in roads off Commercial Street; three at least in Dorset Street. Despite their occupation and the close proximity in which they lived they had nothing in common, and it has never been ascertained as to whether they knew one another; certainly there are no existing records that hint any two were friends. It was therefore impossible for the police to affix a motive to the crimes. What made the murders so shocking was the way in which the killer dispatched his victims; strangulation, cutting the throat, disembowelment, and with the last two, slashing the face beyond all recognition. With the killing of Mary Jane Kelly the murders suddenly stopped, but the search continued. What made the protagonist(s) unique was not only in the way the victims were mutilated but how he evaded capture and continued the onslaught under the very noses of a substantial police presence. As well as striking fear into the populous of East London, it also fuelled the media, who used the diabolical crimes as a way of condemning both the police and government for failing to bring the murderer to justice. A name was being whispered on the streets: Jack the Ripper. The spate of atrocities did not herald Jack the Ripper as the first serial killer; there had been a handful before who had individually racked up six times as many victims—but he was however the one who remained in the public conscience, and to this day is synonymous with everything we regard as evil. On the other hand, the repercussions of those shocking deeds brought to the world's attention the plight of London's poor, assisting in the development of the Metropolitan Police Force to a higher standard, better street lighting, better living condition, redevelopment and the demolition of slum tenements, and the registration of prostitutes. Historians and researchers alike agree that the victims were picked at random, but some are of the view that the murders of Eddowes, Kelly, and certainly Stride, differed from Nichols and Chapman and were not executed by the same hand. Was Jack the Ripper one man—one monster, or was he more than one?

Imagine, if you will, making the discovery as to the Ripper's identity. Imagine that this man was not a monster but something completely different—that he was a good, caring man, revered by his peers and someone who brought about not death but change for the better; to such a degree that not one man thus far had ever achieved alone. Like it or not Jack the Ripper is our heritage, our legacy. Welcome.

Introduction

Sir,—Will you allow me to make a comment on the success of the Whitechapel murderer in calling attention for a moment to the social question? Less than a year ago the West-end press, headed by the St. James's Gazette, the Times, and the Saturday Review, were literally clamouring for the blood of the people—hounding on Sir Charles Warren to thrash and muzzle the scum who dared to complain that they were starving—heaping insult and reckless calumny on those who interceded for the victims—applauding to the skies the open class bias of those magistrates and judges who zealously did their very worse in the criminal proceedings which followed—behaving, in short as the proprietary class always does behave when the workers throw it into a frenzy of terror by venturing to show their teeth. Quite lost on these journals and their patrons were indignant remonstrances, argument, speeches and sacrifices, appeals to history, philosophy, biology, economics, and statistics; references to the reports of inspectors, registrar generals, city missionaries, Parliamentary commissions, and newspapers; collections of evidence by the five senses at every turn; and house-to-house investigations into the condition of the unemployed, all unanswered and unanswerable, and all pointing the same way. The Saturday Review was still frankly for hanging appellants; and the Times denounced them as 'pests of society.' This was still the tone of the class Press as lately as the strike of the Bryant and May girls. Now all is changed. Private enterprise has succeeded where Socialism failed. Whilst we conventional Social Democrats were wasting our time on education, agitation, and organisation, some independent genius has taken the matter in hand, and simply by murdering and disembowelling four women, converted the proprietary press to an inept sort of communism. The moral is a pretty one, and the Insurrectionists, the Dynamitards, the Invincibles, and the extreme left of the Anarchist party will not be slow to draw it. 'Humanity, political science, economics, and religion,' they will say, 'are all rot; the one argument that touches your lady and gentlemen is the knife.' That is so pleasant for the party of Hope and Perseverance in their toughening struggle with the party of Desperation and Death!

To the editor of 'The Star' September 24th 1888.

G. Bernard Shaw.

Chapter One

A Backwards Glance

The rain had been relentless since my father's funeral; pouring without abatement for twelve days, and I stood under the portico of the station watching the soaked pedestrians scurrying up and down the silky streets, covering their heads with anything that came to hand; umbrellas, newspapers, briefcases and even parcels. Rivers had formed in the gutters of Fleet Street, which owing to its incline, had picked up considerable momentum and flowed out into Ludgate Circus like a sewer-pipe spewing into open water, meeting with the torrent cascading down Ludgate Hill, turning the Circus into a mucky pond, steadily rising to curb level. And there I remained for a while, appraising the scene from my dry confine, occasionally making room for anyone who surrendered to the elements and, perhaps, looked upon me with an air of jealousy, opting for dryness instead of total saturation. Londoners had a new preoccupation—the sky. Even with the variants of head-coverings, and the likes of umbrellas, newspapers, briefcases and even parcels were slightly tilted back so as the human eye could roam the dark skies in search of planes. The city traffic rendered every one of us deaf, leaving us devoid of warning, so now we constantly searched the heavens and made ready to seek out the nearest underground. I think that Churchill was much like the city—defiant in the face of adversity, continuing business despite constant bombardment and increasing destruction.

A woman, young and pretty pushed between myself and a fat gentleman to my right, flapping the residue from her umbrella out onto the pavement much to the displeasure of the passing pedestrians who were already wet enough. I flinched and turned my head away as the spray caught my face, and when I slowly turned to express my own dissatisfaction, she had frozen in position, in mid-flap, and she stared directly at me with a look of surprised satisfaction. "I am so-so sorry," she said with a smile that threatened to develop into raucous laughter. I shook my head and smiled, relieved that her beauty had suppressed my intended anger. "Really, it isn't a problem," I said. I looked up to the black, rolling clouds. "It doesn't look like stopping," I added. I returned my stare to the busy street and heard her curse. She was looking down at her rain-sodden shoes and the splashes of mud on her calves, and turning each ankle slightly she endeavored to assess the backs, crooking her head to the left of her shoulder and then the right, and then she emitted a stifled scream. "Tell me that isn't a ladder," she gasped as she turned her calf towards me. I passed it a cursory glance and confirmed her suspicion with a nod. "I'm no expert but I think so. I think it is." She sighed huffily and shook her head. "This is awful!" she exclaimed. "I'm late for an interview; wet, covered in mud and I have a ladder in my stocking." I smiled at her and for a moment was lost in her brown eyes. "I don't think anyone will notice," I said.

The downpour was not about to cease; it hadn't for almost a fortnight so why should it now? And I myself was late to meet with the family solicitor, Mr. Lothby of Lothby & Sons whose offices were in Paternoster Square in the shadow of St. Paul's Cathedral. The young lady was now stooped slightly, tending to the muddy splashes on her legs with a handkerchief, which she moistened with her tongue. She straightened, and turning each ankle alternately again assessed her work. "Have you the time?" she asked me. I glanced at my watch. "A little after eleven," I replied. She appeared then agitated and suddenly her umbrella flared open and she stepped onto the pavement. "Could you tell me how long it would take to walk to Angel Street?" she asked, hurriedly. At that moment a cab pulled up before the station sending a shallow wave of dirty water onto the pavement, and a gentleman got out of the rear and walked to the window to pay the driver. In a moment I considered the possibility of the rain stopping and affording me a dry walk to Paternoster Square, and realizing the prospect was highly unlikely, I walked to the cab. "It's a short walk from where I am going. We can share," I said. She appraised me with doubt, slightly obscured by the droplets of rain that hung from the rim of her umbrella, and her doubtful stare turned to one of curiosity. As I stood with the taxi door half open she remained quite still underneath her makeshift canopy. "I ain't got all day, mate," grunted the cab driver. "Last chance," I said to her. With the moments passing and the cabbie muttering profanities, I decided to abandon her and climbed inside. "Paternoster Square, please." As the cab waited for a chance to pull out into the traffic, the door suddenly opened and she pushed inside. "Move over."

Strange that under the canopy of the station the young lady behaved like a woman devoid of any inhibitions but now, in the confines of a small, dark cab, she behaved like a frightened child. She said nothing as the taxi climbed slowly up Ludgate Hill and slowed to a stop in heavy traffic, no doubt induced by the torrential downpour. She was petite with dark hair that fell in ringlets either side of her face and her large, brown eyes appeared to dominate her perfectly formed features. "You read about things like this, don't you?" she said as she looked out at the wet streets, "the beginnings of love affairs; two people thrown together by unusual circumstances." I laughed, more out of embarrassment than amusement and she turned to face me with a look of astonishment; that what she said were simply thoughts and never meant to be audible. Her face blushed and she looked away. "You're quite safe," I said, brightly, "I'm a married man and you, I see," I gestured to her hand, "are a married woman." Her reddened cheeks returned to their normal colour and she looked at her left hand, her fingers extended and separating, emphasizing a thin band of gold. "He's in France—somewhere," she said, thoughtfully. I nodded but seeing the sadness in her eyes decided not to dwell on the subject. The cab began to move slowly towards Cannon Street and she snapped from her reverie. "So, why aren't you fighting the war?" she asked. It was a question I had often asked myself, every time I saw a newsreel at the local picture-house or picked up a newspaper, but the truth of the matter was my father, eminent physician and due to be knighted William James.

I can't say the relationship between my father and me was a particularly good one. In fact I think I was a source of disappointment for him. His ways were deeply entrenched in Victorian values; a medical tutor and lecturer at Bart's Hospital, Fullerian professor of physiology and Honorary doctorates at London, Oxford, Cambridge and Edinburgh. He lived and breathed medicine his whole life, which sadly expired three weeks ago. It was his wish for me to follow in his footsteps, to become just like him, even taking me to view autopsies when I was barely twelve years old. Protests from my mother fell on deaf ears and he continued to fill my head with everything medical. Inevitably I rebelled, to seek out my own destiny instead of accepting one prefabricated for me. Our father-and-son relationship was steady until then; until my mother died twenty odd years ago and I renounced the medical profession entirely. My mother's death was to mark the end of us as a family. Within two years my elder sister Caroline moved to Canada, and later I married and moved out of London, but my father, being the great physician he was and a key figure within the Masonic fraternity, kept me out of the war. It was never my request and he would never admit to being part of it but I knew he was responsible. Should I be grateful? Perhaps.

As we rounded St. Paul's Cathedral I gave my stock answer; the same reply I always gave whenever I was asked why I wasn't serving my country. "They wouldn't have me; too old." The young lady was looking out of the window, taking in the magnificence of Wren's masterpiece and the skeletal, burned out and broken buildings around it. "Too old?" she said, without turning. "Slightly," I returned. We were closing on our destination and obviously I would never see this woman again. "So you have an interview?" I said. She turned her gaze to her feet, as though her wet shoes and muddy calves reminded her of why she was sitting in a cab with a total stranger. "Accountancy," she said, quietly. "Well, clerk actually but for an accountancy firm. Since David left it's been difficult, and I have a part-time job at my local book shop but it isn't enough." She opened her handbag and passed me a small business card. "Fishers Book Shop in Blackfriars Road; do you know it?" she asked. I shook my head and looked out of the window as the cab drew to a halt at the mouth of Paternoster Row; once a narrow lane of aged bookshops which had fallen foul of the

Luftwaffe with hardly a building standing. "Here we are," I said. After paying the cab driver she offered me half the fare which I declined and she thanked me. "Have you far to walk? You'll get wet," she said as she held her umbrella over our heads. "No; just into the square to my solicitors. I pointed her then to Angel Street just across Newgate Street. "Good luck," I said. She smiled and disappeared into the rain and crowds of Cheapside.

At the entrance of Lothby & Sons, I removed my raincoat and shook it vigorously on the steps before entering and was at once met by Mrs. Metcalf, a family friend who had been in the employment of Lothby & Sons for as long as I cared to remember. Despite being almost an aunt she always addressed me formally. "Mr. James," she cried as she approached. "How are you?" I handed her my wet raincoat which she placed on an old-fashioned hat-rack. "Forgive my lateness," I said. "Nonsense, it's a wonder you're here at all, what with the rain falling and bombs dropping everywhere. Mind you, there haven't been any bombs for a while. The papers say that the Luftwaffe have given up bombing us; did you read that?" I assured her I had but only what I had read in the newspaper on the way here." She swung the door open of Mr. Lothby's door and expressed a smile. "I'll bring tea," she said. Like Mrs. Metcalf, Mr. Lothby was a family friend, having known my father since they were in their twenties; my father a struggling doctor and Mr. Lothby a humble clerk for a city company of solicitors. If I looked upon Mrs. Metcalf as an aunt I certainly looked upon Mr. Lothby as an uncle and his two sons as cousins. Perhaps it was a reminder of betrayal for my father that I had forsaken the medical profession and taken up that of Mr. Lothby's, his best friend. "Welcome, Michael," he said with a beaming smile. "Please take a seat."

We passed a few moments with trivialities—the weather, the ever-increasing unemployment and our mutual hatred for Adolf Hitler, until Mrs. Metcalf brought in tea and a side-plate of biscuits. "To business, then," said Mr. Lothby. "We are here for the reading of the Will of your father William James, who passed away on the evening of August 4th, of this year 1941. May I once again extend my condolences to you and your family. Unfortunately this wretched war has prevented your sister from attending both this reading and the funeral itself; a copy of the Will was sent to her immediately after your father's death."

"I have spoken to her on the telephone; she read it to me," I said.

The old gentleman smiled. "So you are aware of its contents?"

I nodded and returned the smile.

"So you agree that the estate, including your father's house, is to be sold and shared equally between Caroline and yourself? You have no disputes?"

"None whatsoever."

Mr. Lothby turned in his chair and opened a small safe behind him and removed a parcel wrapped in fading brown paper and tied with coarse string, and placing it on the table he reclined in his chair, lacing his fingers across his stomach.

"Then dispensing with formalities it leaves me only to give you this," he said.

I studied the parcel from my position; obviously a book where the wrapping was so old it had shaped itself around its form.

"It's a book," I said with a shrug of my shoulders. "What is it?"

"I have no idea; a ledger, perhaps? Maybe your father was a budding novelist as well as a great physician. Oh, and by the way, despite his death your father is still to receive a knighthood—posthumously."

"That is good news," I returned, my eyes still fixed to the parcel, "but why leave me a book?"

The old gentleman raised his teacup from his saucer.

"Your father brought it in thirty-five years ago; on the very day you were born. It was entrusted to this company on the proviso that should your death proceed his own it was to be destroyed—unread."

My father was never one for exchanging gifts in any shape or form. The purchasing of presents was a task reserved for my mother, and with her death such signs of affection ceased. In the years that followed birthdays and Christmas were considered days much like any other. But then, and as Mr. Lothby had pointed out, my father bequeathed the book thirty-five years ago when he was still considerably young and his attitude to life had not yet been tainted. Still, I considered it strange and it reminded me of an occurrence that happened at my father's funeral.

"Mr. Lothby, you knew my father for many years," I said.

The aging solicitor nodded his head and smiled sadly.

"Indeed. We are . . . or were the same age," he replied. "It was shortly after my twenty fifth birthday when we met at an infirmary in London. Back then he gave one day a week tending to the poor, and I was visiting a patient whose wife had recently died. William was very helpful and we left the infirmary together, stopping on the way home for a tipple. It was the beginning of a life-long friendship."

"Have you ever heard the name 'Jonathan Sandpiper'?"

The old man thought for a moment and slowly shook his head.

"An interesting name and one I would remember," he said. "I can't recall ever hearing it until now."

There was a considerable gathering at my father's funeral; perhaps seventy-five or eighty people, consisting mainly of physicians and surgeons, fellow lecturers and even a few patients my father had struck up friendships with over the years. Indeed, it was difficult for all of them to encircle the grave without standing on the surrounding ones. And it was at the moment when the priest closed his Bible after a considerably lengthy reading that the heavens opened up and so began this endless storm. We dispersed from the graveside in fractured groups, seeking out shelter under the many cluster of trees within the cemetery. My wife and I stood under a large Elm just within a few yards of the church as the rain cascaded down, where all around the ground appeared to come alive, like sand on a drum, the raindrops bouncing off the grass and pavements. It was then a gangly, elderly man emerged from the rear of the tree, dressed casually as opposed to mourning wear, and he smiled warmly at me and extended his hand. Reluctantly I shook it and appraised him curiously. "Michael?" he said. He cut a pathetic figure, and though a true effort had been made concerning his attire, I at once noticed the frayed shirt collar and cuffs of his shirt. But he had a kindly face and an endearing way about him.

"You'll forgive me for not announcing myself earlier, but I didn't want to trouble you in your hour of grief. I'm very sorry," he said. He turned his stare to my wife and again extended his hand. "And you must be Sarah," My wife shook his hand with a courteous smile and then looked at me. "Michael, I'm going to make a run for the church," she said. "It was nice to meet you, Mr . . ." she added. "Sandpiper," replied the old man. "Well, it was very nice to meet you, Mr. Sandpiper. Perhaps you'll join us at the wake?" The gentleman took on an air of embarrassment and shook his head. "Thank you, ma'am, but I come here today only to pay my respects," he said. Expressing another smile my wife scurried out into the rain towards the church, and I watched her until she reached the entrance and waved back at me. Mr. Sandpiper was staring back through the rain towards my father's open grave and I waited patiently until he turned towards me; I was certain I could detect tears in his eyes.

"I knew your father very well;" he said, "as well as any man could know another. We were students together. Has he ever mentioned me? Did he ever mention the name Jonathan Sandpiper?"

I shook my head and curiosity took me completely.

"No, he never did," I replied with an air of certainty.

Suddenly I became suspicious of the stranger. As a litigator with my own firm, I had heard of such people, so-called friends of a recently bereaved family, who scan the obituaries for a victim, claiming to be a long-forgotten associate or friend in order to scam the family who felt duty-bound to give a hand-out to someone who had fallen on hard times. And this man certainly did not look like a doctor; neither were his threadbare clothes befitting someone who was associated with such a man as my father.

"So where did you meet my father?" I asked matter-of-factly.

"As I said: we were students," Mr. Sandpiper reiterated.

"And where was that?"

The old man smiled and looked away again, back to my father's grave.

"You're testing me," he said without turning. "But William James and Jonathan Sandpiper are bound by an incident that happened a lifetime ago. Within the next few weeks you will come to know of it. I am not a scrounger, and I neither want your money or your friendship; I want nothing from your family, least of all anything from William James. Please forgive my bluntness, but soon you will become familiar with all the facts. It is enough you know I am alive. What you choose to do with that knowledge is up to you. I say this without the slightest exaggeration—that you hold what little of my life is left in your hands. Good day to you, Mr. James."

The old gentleman casually walked out from under the tree seemingly without concern for the driving rain and walked directly to the main gate. I was moved to call after him, for him to explain himself fully, but I simply watched him leave.

Mr. Lothby listened intently to my story and then expressed a sympathetic smile.

"Sadly the world is full of such people," he confirmed. "In this time of war, this time of despair, many have lost their families, have lost their dignity. A man like Mr. Sandpiper may be a victim. Perhaps one of Hitler's bombs has left him with no one—without family, without friends. They need to be attached to someone. They stake their claim to a dead person in the mere hope the surviving family will take them in. I have witnessed it! Why, just a few months ago a man walked into this very office and sat in that very seat and claimed to be a long-lost brother of a recently departed client of ours. He had all the relative information and to a point some proof. He said that he and his brother had been separated when they were young and taken to separate orphanages, and for some weeks we believed his story; the family even took him in. Unfortunately for him the real brother came forward after hearing the news from a distant relative. Simply the imposter was a sad soul—a man who had lost his job and inevitably his family. He sought another family; the insatiable desire to belong to someone—even if it is bogus."

We spoke a while longer about my firm and the cases I was working on, and after signing the necessary papers I left Mr. Lothby, bade Mrs. Metcalf goodbye and took my coat from the hat-stand, preparing to brave the weather outside. But on opening the door the rain had stopped and the sun was struggling behind the grey clouds. Before me, on the other side of the square, stood the young lady I had shared the cab with, and just as I was about to step onto the pavement Mrs. Metcalf came up behind me holding the brown paper parcel. "You've forgotten your father's legacy," she said with a smile. "However do you win cases when your mind has more holes than Swiss cheese?" I thanked her and took the book and walked across the square to the young lady.

"I take it you had your interview," I said.

She smiled and nodded. "It was brief but the job was practically mine anyway. A friend works there and put in a good word for me," she replied. "The manager took one look at my legs and told me to start Monday. It's only part time but it will help."

There followed an awkward silence, a moment I took to survey the clearing skies, and when I returned my stare the young lady was peering down at her feet with considerable interest.

"So," I began, drawing the word out slowly, "why are you here? Why are you specifically standing here—outside my solicitors?"

"Well, that's the thing," she said with an embarrassing smile forming on her mouth. "When I left Angel Street it was still raining. You paid for the taxi here so I thought you could share my umbrella on the way back. Just my luck it would stop raining the moment I got here."

I laughed aloud. She was a nice person, kind and, perhaps, a little lonely, and her face flushed again as I looked at her. I asked her if she liked coffee and she nodded and we walked back to New Bridge Road and a coffeehouse on the corner of Pilgrim Street. On the way there she spoke about her husband and of her six-year marriage and that she had no children. From what I gleaned, her mannerisms and her appearance, I put her age at about thirty-two, and she spoke intelligently though sometimes appeared foolish as if it were a trait men admired. In the coffeehouse we sat in the far corner away from the window that was striped with tape in case a nearby bomb blew the glass through. Outside the sun was penetrating the wet streets, inducing ghostly wisps of steam from the pavements and cars. I had placed the coarsely wrapped book on the table before me, which she turned towards her with her slender fingers, and after a brief study of it she looked up at me quizzically.

"My father left it to me," I explained with a shallow shrug of my shoulders. "He died recently. He was a surgeon, well respected and soon to be knighted, I added with an element of pride."

Her look of astonishment returned again.

"I don't wish to be insensitive but he's dead," she said, emphatically. "What purpose would be served by knighting him?"

"Acknowledgement, I suppose," I returned with the same half-shrug. "He was a great physician and deserved the honour."

Her stare dropped back to the raggedy book and the look of surprise remained fixed.

“So if he is to be knighted and being a physician, he was obviously wealthy,” she stated.

“Not to any great extent,” I replied. “In his later years he was a lecturer. There isn’t any money in talking.”

“My point is,” she continued, raising her eyes to mine, “is this great physician, this man who is to be knighted, left you a crumby book.”

I laughed again and shook my head.

“He left his estate to be shared with my sister,” I explained.

She nodded slowly and the book was no longer of any interest.

Perhaps through a bout of nervousness she fired questions at me in quick succession; my name, age, occupation, my home, and finally she settled on my wife.

“Describe her to me,” she asked, but then she held her hand up. “No, no, let me guess. She’s five feet, two or three inches tall, thin but well proportioned and she has long, black hair which more often than not she wears up. And she wears expensive clothes; all the new fashions, but her choice of jewelry is limited. She doesn’t overdo it. She is a woman of taste. Oh, and she helps out at the local church.”

She stared at me for approval and I smiled back at her.

“Not bad,” I nodded. “But she has fair hair; short fair hair, and she isn’t one for jewelry or churches.”

I could not control the smile as I appraised her across the table and her face began to blush again and she looked away.

“I know, I talk too much,” she said, sulkily. “It doesn’t mean you have to laugh at me.”

I leaned forward and patted her hand in an attempt to console her.

“Forgive me, but you know everything about me except my shoe-size. I don’t even know your name.”

At last a smile broke on her face and she nodded her head, and then she bent and looked under the table and when she reemerged she said, “Nine!”

I looked at her in bewilderment.

“Your shoe-size-nine,” she grinned broadly.

"Ten, actually," I confirmed.

"Rachel Porter," she said.

With a second cup of coffee brought to the table she rambled on about her own life, answering the same questions she had asked me, and her life appeared much greyer than my own. The city frightened her; loneliness frightened her, the nightly bombers frightened her.

"I think I need to leave London," she said with an assertive nod. "I never go to the underground when the sirens sound. I know it's the safest place to be but imagine what would happen if one took a direct hit; being buried alive with thousands of others."

"Then why stay here?" I asked. "You could move outside London and commute, as I do."

"Michael, your life is very different from mine. Yours is church fetes and cucumber sandwiches. Mine is being mauled by drunks and dodging bombs. Besides, I would be lonely in the country. At least here I meet a lot of people."

"Your bookshop is that busy, is it?"

"Three nights a week I work in a pub in Southwark; hence being constantly mauled. Why do men think that because you work behind a bar you are their property, to do as they please? I hate it! I've never told them my husband is away but it doesn't stop them. Strange, though, but I feel safe when I'm there. The difficult part is walking home. That's when I feel most vulnerable."

"Perhaps you should befriend one of the locals," I suggested. "Strike up a platonic relationship with someone you can trust; someone who will watch out for you and walk you home."

Her thin eyebrows rose high on her head and she stared at me in total wonderment.

"Michael, you have told me you own a successful law firm in the city," she said with utmost patience, "and I think there is something I need to ask you. Have you ever won a case? Men do not have platonic relationships with women!"

"I think you'll find they do," I replied. "That is why they call it 'platonic'."

She shook her head, drank the last of her coffee and rose from her seat.

"I really have to go. I'm late for the bookshop," she said as she rounded the table.

"And I have to go to work," I said, rising from my seat.

We walked out of the coffee shop and she turned on the pavement.

"It was nice to meet you, Michael," she said. "And if I've been over inquisitive it is only because I'm naturally nosy. I need to be reassured that people are living normal lives out there."

"The pleasure was all mine. Goodbye, Rachel."

-2-

A lunatic had taken over the asylum, and with his inmates laid waste Europe. It was everywhere to be seen in the city, the devastation and destruction. Two years ago Hitler marched on Poland and so endeavoured to take the rest of Europe, and at this time and place he looked like he would be successful. In 1940, he moved west and shortly after set his sights on England. Between the months of September and December the Luftwaffe executed no less than seventy-six bombings on the city, destroying the docks in and around Silvertown and, indeed, the capital itself. Such was the extent of the fires the water ran out and London was left to burn; the flames could be seen as far as sixty miles away. And only in June of this year he invaded Russia. My offices in Aldwych had survived the bombings though many very close by had not, and in those months of intense bombings we traded little and was in fear of going under. But London smiled in the face of adversity and shops with windows blown out and doors little more than splintered kindling boasted signs 'OPEN FOR BUSINESS AS USUAL', and it was that defiance that influenced me to remain as a business and open at every opportunity and, it has to be said, reap whatever opportunities fell to me.

Many—too many—businesses were abruptly terminated with the pull of a lever, and many directors arrived in the city to find their offices and shops little more than a pile of rubble at the edge of a bomb crater. As more and more law firms fell, more and more cases were brought to me and, ironically, we flourished where all around floundered. The trains kept running as best they could, and barely three weeks ago I left my safe-haven of the country and arrived in London. Stepping out of the station everyone appeared to be walking in the same direction—towards a plume of black smoke that twisted up to the sky and hovered above Farringdon Street. With a brief look up Fleet Street, my intended route, I followed and soon came before a large crater where once stood a terrace of houses. Without concern Londoners, men women and children, scrambled into the massive hole and started clawing away at the rubble and charred timber with their bare hands. A woman was pulled out, barely alive, but still alive. I removed my suit jacket and threw it on top of my briefcase and followed. At the end of the day fifteen people were still breathing due to our hard-earned efforts. It was the most fulfilling day of my life.

On September 3rd 1939 Neville Chamberlain announced that we were at war with Germany, and it has to be said that no one was particularly surprised. Germany had been threatening the peace of Europe for months, and with their invasion of Poland—a country we vowed to protect—we had little choice but to intervene. Britain had already been making plans as early as March with the Conscription Bill; registering young men for call-up once the inevitable happened. Coastal defence plans were drawn up and twelve Civil Defence commissioners were appointed to govern certain areas should they be cut off from central government in the event of an invasion. That said, we—the British—were a little mystified by it all and cavalier to the point of believing that it was never going to happen; we were going through the motions for the sake of it. Air raid shelters were delivered by the thousands and women and children were evacuated to the country, miles of barbed-wire was thrown up all over the city and the blackout became law, but still there was no invasion; no planes, no bombs, no threat. So we listened to the radio to hear how our young men were faring abroad, as if they had gone to another planet to fight and not less than fifty miles away. Certainly we lived in a constant state of anxiety but it was a temporary state of mind and its consistency soon gave way to normality and our usual mundane way of life. By the Christmas of 1939, the women, the children, the babies and the infirm returned home, believing the threat of an invasion to be nothing more than that—a threat.

On September 7th 1940, it came. It was beautiful sunny day and everyone in the city was going about their business in the typical London way. For us the war was being fought somewhere else and by someone else, and updates informed us that Germany was busy elsewhere so we, as a nation, were safe from the possibility of any invasion. The tranquillity of both that day and our minds was rudely interrupted. It wasn't like we hadn't been warned. We had! We just refused to accept it. Hundreds of incendiary bombs were dropped, mostly on or around the docks, and their fires became beacons for the nighttime invasion which spread across the East End. By daylight 430 human beings were dead and 1600 injured; the areas bombed were devastated. What followed was fifty-five days of relentless bombing, a period aptly entitled the Blitz, and throughout September and October the city casualties rose to 13,000 killed and 20,000 injured. During this time Britain had learned to fight back and the Luftwaffe restricted their raids to nights having lost too many pilots and planes during their daytime assaults. Not that this mattered because on Sunday, December 29th, London suffered its worst indignity yet. 10,000 incendiary bombs were dropped on the city along with high explosive parachute mines at the beginning of the raid which severed the water services. The Thames was at its lowest ebb and London was ablaze. Twenty thousand fire-fighters fought the uncontrollable fires which threatened to engulf the city entirely, and without any water 2,300 pumps had to be deployed to take water directly from the river.

People harbour a macabre interest in destruction, be it a car crash, a collapsed building or even a corpse; they are enthralled by such sights. I have never seen anybody walk past a bomb-crater without looking into it, and one can only wonder what they expect to see. Shortly after the Blitz began I walked back to the office from Edgware Road, and in Oxford Street firemen were playing their hoses on John Lewis's department store, the flames extinguished but bellows of steam escaping from the rear windows and the exposed side of the building; the bricks and ornate masonry strewn across the road. Most of its frontage was blackened by soot and not a pane of glass remained, and the goods, clearly visible through its large arched window openings were nothing more than dark, grotesque shapes of no recognisable form. A crowd were gathered on the pavement, pointing and grinning with excitement, wringing their hands and clapping whenever more masonry or more roof-tiles crashed to the ground. I surveyed the scene with a deep sense of regret and sadness. These buildings were grand, architecturally splendid and beautiful by design; remnants of great British workmanship never to be seen again. Whatever would replace them; a dreary, bland, characterless obstacle that has no right resting on the foundations of its predecessor?

When I was looking for an office, I contacted Bernard Mansall, an old school friend, and later college buddy. Originally we set off in on the same course but Bernard, being the wiser man of us both, realised at an early age that money could be gained for practically doing nothing, and promptly moved into the world of buying and selling properties, selling or letting office space, and letting houses and flats. He was a podgy adolescent with a fat, round face who had grown up to be a podgy adult with a fat, round face who, despite some of his past shady dealings, was totally trustworthy and reliable. In 1932, we met and I explained with enormous enthusiasm of my new business venture and that I required an office. "No problem, Mike," he replied casually. One had to be specific when consulting with Bernard or one might end up with an office on a remote island off the coast of Scotland. "Not just anywhere, Bernie. In the city," I emphasized. He stared back cautiously, his eyes beginning to narrow. "Where in the city—exactly?" he asked, his hopes of fobbing me off with a room somewhere in the Outer Hebrides fading. "The Stand. I want an office in the Strand. Nothing else will do."

And so it was several weeks later that I was summoned to Aldwych, to a street close to Drury Lane, looking at a detached department store and wondering if I had been given the wrong address. Suddenly Bernie appeared, pulling himself out of his car with a broad grin and clutching his briefcase under his arm.

"How's things, Mike?" he said, slapping me on the shoulder. "Still an alligator?"

"Litigator, Bernie. It's litigator. And things are fine. You?"

"Ah, you know, still wheeling and dealing. Hey, listen, you still interested in history?"

A strange question, I thought, but I nodded. "Of course."

"Then have I got the office for you! You'll love this."

My eyes slowly climbed up the five-storey building and fixed on the very top floor.

"Tell me you don't intend to put me up there, amongst the beds, drapes and linen departments?"

Bernie was stooped, rummaging in his briefcase, and suddenly pulled out a bunch of keys and a large torch."

"Not quite," he replied, walking to the right of the main entrance.

"Hardly the Strand, is it, Bernie?" I said as I followed.

He stopped in front of an insignificant door; an entrance I believed that must lead to a stairway of some kind and would take us up to a floor of offices.

"Don't be pedantic, Michael," he returned as he inserted a key into the lock. "Pigeons can't get ledge-space in the Strand—it's the closest I could get. Technically, though, this particular location has a Strand address."

The door opened to reveal little else but a black void.

"As soon as you get inside, stop! I don't want you hurting yourself," he warned. "Give me a chance to get the lights on."

He flicked the switch on his torch and entered the blackness, and as ordered I followed and stopped. The beam of light swept across the floor that appeared to be a staging of some kind—scaffold boards—and then rose up the wall to a fuse-box and back down again following a yellow cable that dropped away into the darkness. "Ah, good!" said Bernie, his voice lost in the acoustics of whatever place we were in. His hand groped the fuse-box and jerked upward and I heard a loud click; the void remained black. "Shit!" The torchlight touched what appeared to be the top of a ladder, and placing down his briefcase, he swung his leg around and over and began to sink, the beam flashing overhead, erratic and shaky in his moving hand, revealing heavy drainage and water pipes spurring off in all directions and suspended from a concrete ceiling. Clutching the top rung of the ladder, I gingerly peeked over the top, watching the torchlight submerge into the inky blackness and feeling the vibrations as Bernie shuffled downward. After a while the vibrations stopped and I could see the light sweeping back and forth across a red-brick floor far below, until it found a thin strand of yellow coiled a few yards from the foot of the ladder. "Won't be a minute," Bernie's voice echoed up. "I hope you realise how much trouble I've gone to." The beam of light flashed around again and located a black strand snaked across the floor, caught in the mantle of Bernie's torch. The beam suddenly fell still, placed down on the ground, highlighting the shadowy joints between the bricks, and I could make out Bernie's hands, one grasping the yellow strand, and the other the black, and suddenly the two came together. A string of lights suddenly illuminated the area far, far beneath me, and what I thought was just a ladder, was in fact a double extension ladder. Bernie was looking up some thirty feet below. "You all right getting down, Mike?"

I submerged into the abyss, unsettled by the rhythmic bounce of the wooden ladder and doubting its strength with every movement. Lower, the smell of damp and mould filled my lungs and I paused to look around me. Both the walls and floor were made up entirely of red bricks, punctuated only by rows of purposely made vertical holes every six feet or so and also running along the length of the expanse of the floor on both sides and approximately the same distance apart. The only other feature was a discarded door lying flat at the far end of expanse. Simply it was a large room some forty feet long and thirty feet wide, constructed of bricks, devoid of windows or entrances save for the one thirty feet above us.

"Have you completely taken leave of your senses, Bernie?" I growled as my feet touched the floor and I heaved myself away from the ladder.

Bernie walked deeper into the dimly lit room, swirling his arms about and smiling back at me for approval. "What do you think? Great, eh?"

"What do you mean, what do I think? It's a hole, Bernie; a square hole in the ground!"

My voice bounced off the walls as I reprimanded my friend.

"It's more than that, Mike," Bernie replied with a wink. "This is history, my friend."

He moved to the centre, still brandishing a smug grin.

"Go on then—enlighten me," I sighed.

He purposefully took a moment, setting off from the middle of the room and walking halfway round its perimeter, his fingers gently trailing the walls as if it were a precious monument.

"Welcome to Aldwych Gaol, Michael," he said, stopping in the very place from which he had set off.

"What?" I gasped, disbelieving his claim and laughing. "Aldwych hasn't got a gaol! Are there no lengths you'll go to in order to make money?"

"You are of course right," he smiled. "Aldwych does not have a gaol, but it did in 1171. And this is it, Michael, all one thousand, four hundred and eighty-five square feet of it. You are now standing on medieval ground."

Bernard was not a historian by any stretch of the imagination; incapable of remembering what happened last week, let alone several hundred years ago. His reference to the date and medieval period induced me to believe he may be telling the truth. The city once had many prisons and lock-ups, and though many were deliberately torn down without a trace—Newgate, Tyburn, Fleet, King's Bench—some survived or were rediscovered by excavation. Clink Prison existed in medieval times and can still be viewed today in all its morbid glory, attached to the Anchor Inn at the rear of Borough Market, Southwark. Lock-ups such as the Clink were traditionally used to get drunks or unruly miscreants off the streets, either to be let out in the morning without charge once they had sobered up, or to face the judge. Gaols such as these were commonly known as compters. The original compter, built in 1555, was the infamous Wood Street Compter in Mitre Court in the city, and could house up to seventy prisoners at one time, and was also used as an overflow for Newgate Prison when it was full. The Compter had three sections; the Master's side for the affluent; the Knight's side for those of some or little means, and the Hole for common people. Those incarcerated in the Hole were subject to disease, such as typhoid and cholera. The Compter fell fowl to progress and was consumed by redevelopment, assumed lost, but the underground cells were rediscovered early in the twentieth century. The dungeons of The Hole can still be seen today, as part of a wine merchant's, utilized as storage cellars.

I began to view the room differently now. The vertical holes in the walls were in alignment with the holes in the floor running off the walls, squared by holes that run the floor the entire length of the area on either side. They were fixing holes for a construction; cells, cages.

"They discovered this place in late 1873," Bernie explained; "before they built that monstrosity above us and tried to turn us into Americans.

Above here used to be a pub but it began to subside and was closed down by the authorities. They shored it up with planks and scaffolding and no one did much about it for a while. Eventually they knocked it down and dug out the cellar, ready to lay new foundations; obviously stronger foundations for the building they planned to put up; they had to dig deeper . . ."

"And under the original foundations they found this," I anticipated.

"Not straight away. This place was filled to the brim with mud and clay. Experts were called in, believing they had stumbled upon some ancient Saxon or Roman settlement. It was screened off from the publics gaze, and for months they excavated, supervised by archaeologists and historians. At the same time a connection was made with this room and a nearby building under construction."

Bernie was grinning back at me, as if I should know the answer, and he began to wander again in a wide circle, casting long shadows on the brick walls.

1873? A nearby building under construction?

There were literally hundreds of buildings under construction in the area at that time. It was an age when the city authorities succumbed to the rules of nature; that where there was filth there was disease. Entire streets were pulled down, Newgate Prison and its vile reputation was levelled in 1901, giving up its ground to the Old Bailey; rookeries were wiped away, and even the Thames River underwent a major restoration, cleansed of floating debris and sewage; the authorities imposing laws of heavy fines and imprisonment to anyone caught dumping rubbish in her waters. The date of 1873, however, began to link itself with the most prestigious building in the Strand.

"The Royal Courts of Justice?" I said.

Bernie's eyebrows raised and his grin broadened. "Bravo, Michael."

"So what?" I said with a shrug. "In 1873, The Royal Courts of Justice went under construction and at the same time they found this place—it's the only connection."

Bernie was pacing to the far end of the expanse. "Look around you, Michael," he said over his shoulder. "What's missing?"

I followed unsteadily, my feet slipping on the brick floor occasionally.

"No doors or windows. I noticed," I said, my head swinging left and right.

Bernie dropped into a squat. What I believed was a discarded door from my precarious position on the ladder was, in fact, a hatch; a horizontal entrance set into the brick flooring. "Give me a hand here will you, Michael?"

Bernie fished out a large iron ring set flush into the large oak slab, and together we began to pull upward. Three long rusty hinges embellished with squared studs fought against us, but slowly it yielded, groaning like a troubled ghost until it fell flat with a heavy thud. The stench of a thousand years wafted up from the black hole and I turned my face away. Worn steps descended downward, disappearing into darkness.

"Are you telling me that this entrance is somehow connected to the Royal Courts?" I said. "That's got to be eight hundred yards away."

Bernie was standing with his hands on his hips staring into the dark void. "Four hundred and twenty-five, actually," he replied. "This is the entrance to a passage that leads directly to the courts, off which are a dozen rooms exactly the same—some of them considered unsafe, filled with concrete and sealed up."

"Holding cells?"

Bernie shook his head grimly. "In medieval times Aldwych Gaol occupied the site where the Royal Courts now stands. According to historians, it was a small, unassuming building. No one knew what lay beneath it."

Hearing that a passage run a quarter of a mile under the busy streets of the capital did not surprise me; London has more tunnels than any other city in the world. What was beginning to manifest in my mind was an old legend—a story that had never been substantiated, an old wives tale; fragmented claims dating back to the same period devoid of substance or proof. Numerous books, especially those up to the sixteenth century, mention a network of tunnels and vaults somewhere under the city used for the purpose of torture and extracting information called the Spider's Web; an English equivalent to the Spanish Inquisition. It was said that Heretics, traitors, anarchists and even witches were taken *to a house of authority in a quiet street and were never seen again.* Where exactly this house was, no one knew. Neither was the quiet street divulged if, of course, it was ever known. What was known—or at least claimed—was that *all who were taken there perished at the hands of their inquisitors and their bodies, or remains, were disposed of.* Few books, if any, give the story a mention after the sixteenth century. Simply the legend was consumed by doubt and lost forever.

Was I actually standing in one of the many torture chambers the legend spoke of?

I was looking down at the hatch, its underside now facing up and blackened with soot, the result of braziers and torches that once warmed and illuminated the passage.

"Is this what I think it is?" I asked cautiously.

My friend shrugged his shoulders, averted his stare and began to walk away.

"Believing they had found something of historical interest," he explained, "the mud and clay was not removed until the walls were encased in three feet of concrete—you know, to prevent collapse. Once that was achieved, they removed the earth from the inside, washed down the walls and flooring and made ready for a grand inspection. It was of little or no interest to anyone; no Roman or Saxon settlement; no precious artefacts—just a brick room. A search of the vaults leading off the passage held no interest either; they were just rooms—empty and barren. While this area was being excavated, they found the entrance of the tunnel in the grounds of where the Royal Courts was to be built. It's still there—concealed behind panelling of an anti-room. At the time they believed it may serve some purpose—had it been some incredible historical discovery. Anyway, the local authorities stepped in and ordered its immediate closure and had a three feet concrete lid put on it." Bernie was staring up at the ceiling now. "They even had their own contractors reroute the drainage and water system, leaving enough access for maintenance purposes."

I was eyeing my friend with suspicion now, as he stood before me with hands buried in his pockets and his head tilted back.

"Bernard," I said, "how did you come by this? I'm taking it that the government denied all knowledge of its existence."

"Well, they would. They would hardly admit to being part of a secret fraternity that administered torture on the behest of the King of England, would they?"

"Why not?" I argued. "The Newgate Chronicles blatantly boast about their antics in the art of torture. Our history books are filled with references as to how we lopped off the heads of our enemies and any conspirator who dare conspire against the royals or the government. We would decorate London Bridge with their heads impaled on spikes. We would burn innocent people to death believing them to be witches and leave those we hanged to dangle until they were just skeletons. As a nation we excelled in torture and took great pride in it."

"And who am I to make sense of it all? I know only that they regarded it as an embarrassment and disassociated themselves of all rumours."

"Then why not just bury it—fill it with concrete and forget it ever existed?"

"How could they when they had already denied all knowledge of its existence? It wasn't theirs to do as they pleased. And had they, wouldn't their accusers grow more suspicious? Wouldn't burying it confirm their guilt? Bearing in mind, Michael, that these chambers were allegedly still in use up to just one hundred years ago, wouldn't the rest of the world reach the conclusion that we—the greatest empire in the world—were nothing more than barbarians?"

His argument was sound, but in a moment of impulse I seized the torch Bernard had left by the side of the hatch and began to descend the steps down into the rancid, damp stench and utter darkness. The incline of the treads were steep and the passageway deeper than I anticipated. Above me Bernard had hurried to the hatch and was peering down. "Michael, have you gone nuts? Get up here before you kill yourself." My feet touched the passage floor with a splash and I felt a rush of cold, the beam from the torch shining down the arched corridor as far as its power would allow. It disappeared into infinity, in a perfect straight line and shaped like an arrowhead, the torchlight glistening on the water-streaked walls and shimmering on the liquid surface of the floor as it rippled away from me.

All who were brought here perished. So what of the corpses? What of their remains?

Standing in the darkness, with the beam of the torch circling the narrow passageway, I attempted to fathom the geography above me. I believed the room I had just hurriedly left was once above ground. Why else would an underground passage be necessary? Besides, it stood on higher ground than the Royal Courts, and clearly the long corridor, although straight and meticulously constructed, run steadily downhill; a sweet but toxic smell hung in the dank air. The places of torture were the vaults leading off the passage, and the room I first entered was where the prisoners were incarcerated—a waiting area—so to speak. How many died down here? How can you lose eight hundred years of tortured corpses? Wait! The nearest church was St. Mary Le Strand, standing at the top of its namesake, the Strand. Its location was strange enough in itself, actually standing in the middle of the road, in the shadow of the Royal Courts, where the traffic would move left and right of it. It has no graveyard. But once it did. Built in 1712, St. Mary's had a small graveyard in which bodies were tightly crammed into the depth of eight feet. Coffins were brought there at an alarming rate and, inevitably, the graveyard ran out of room, or room was made while the rotting corpses were left on the pavement. By the late 1840s, the government intervened and had the graveyard cleared, and in the process widened the road. During the mass-exhumation, they made an astonishing discovery. Sealed vaults run beneath the church and the entire length of the graveyard, and when they were breached hundred of bodies were found. There were so many that the stink of gases from the decomposing corpses was so bad that the area had to be cordoned off for several weeks.

Was that the answer? Was there a passage that led to the vaults under St. Mary's? Was the discovery of hundreds of unaccountable bodies the reason why the torture chambers were suddenly dismantled, leaving no trace of its existence save for the walls and floor? Both dates coincided.

I could hear Bernie's voice commanding me to return. What troubled me was how he knew the history of this place when most believed it was simply legend. I began to ascend, until he came into view, bent with his hands on his knees and smiling back at me with relief.

"Are you trying to give me heart attack?" he moaned.

I passed him silently and walked further back into the chamber, standing beneath the string of lights.

"Still got one trouser leg rolled up, Bernie?" I said, coldly.

I was spitefully referring to his first initiation—his induction into the brotherhood.

Masonic influences dominated Bernie's bloodline, and had since time immemorial. Every adult male family member had been initiated, and his own father had reached a high degree within the brotherhood and was both influential and powerful in the world of banking.

My friend stretched himself, his smile straightening and his eyes flashing a warning that I had ridiculed something very dear to him.

"You had your chance—several times," he rebuffed.

"And I declined—several times, didn't I, Bernie? Does this have something to do with your . . . friends?"

He hesitated as my eyebrows began to arch higher.

"Inadvertently, yes," he burbled. "I was asked."

"By whom?"

"Now, now, Mike, you know better than to ask me that. It came down the line, from one mason to another and then another . . ."

"And finally to you," I intercepted with a smile. "Isn't that a little like laundering?"

Bernie shook his head, his tolerance fading fast.

"Look! Do you want it or not? I'm offering you five thousand square feet of prime land in the heart of the city, and you're picking holes in it."

"Picking?" I returned sharply. "Has it crossed your mind that I might be a little bit choosy as to who I share my office with; ghouls, ghosts, the living dead? And who collects the rent—the Prince of Darkness?"

"And that," said Bernie, slapping me on the shoulder and smiling again, "is the cherry on the cake, Michael. No rent, no rates—just your word."

Now I was confused, and my friend fell serous again.

"Truth is, Mike, is that this place actually belongs to someone or some organisation," he said. "And before you ask, I don't know who or what. I am but a messenger; entrusted to find someone trustworthy to occupy it and . . . to retain its secret—its original purpose. The building above us is nearing the end of its life, and although the city authorities have no idea what this chamber is part of, it is inevitable that the area we are now standing in will be lost come redevelopment."

"Are you suggesting that all the so-called historians that came here when first it was discovered had no idea what it was?"

Bernie looked silently back, hardly blinking.

I shook my head. "Christ! How powerful are you people?" I said. "They knew! Or at least they surmised."

My friend crooked his head and began to look around the vault.

"I was thinking of a staircase coming down there," he said, sweeping his hand down from the ladder to the floor; three or four offices over there, a waiting area in the corner, a reception area in the centre. And this . . ." he said, pacing back toward the hatch and outstretching his arms, "This can be your office, Michael. An office in the Strand! Imagine that."

The potential was there. I stared up at the ceiling, at the countless galvanised pipes, and cast-iron drainage as thick and as heavy as a tree; nothing a false ceiling could not camouflage. And a staircase, with oak treads and a wrought iron banister could sweep down from the doorway above us to the brick ground. Perhaps a scattering of large paintings here and there to cover up the holes that once secured the cells to the walls. And large terracotta pots housing looming greenery would kill the monotonous red, especially in the reception area. A row of partitioned offices could run the full length on one side, with storage facilities. Those areas of course would have to have false floors and carpets. A toilet and washroom could be constructed at the top of the stairs—by the entrance. Certainly electrics and plumbing presented no problem. Then there was the fact that it was a part of history—a lost and sinister part of history—and it was almost in the Strand.

"You said something about 'My word,'" I said.

"You'll have it?" smiled Bernie brightly.

I shrugged and expressed the vague suggestion of a nod. "My part of the bargain, Bernie?"

He placed his hand on my shoulder, as if the deal had been finalised.

"You tell no one what this place was—no one, Michael," he said. "You take care of the furnishings—we'll take care of everything else."

As he walked back towards the ladder I stopped.

"Why didn't you give this place to one of your own?" I asked.

There was that same look again—eyes staring into nothingness and barely blinking.

"Disassociation?" I proffered.

The smile returned on Bernie's face and his eyes came to life.

"We'll take care of the builders. You pay," he said.

The offices were located in a narrow street and a short walk to Covent Garden, and consisted of three solicitors and myself, two secretaries and one filing clerk. The premises boasted five medium-size offices and a reception area reserved for the filing clerk. Kenneth Banner, a junior partner, often remarked that I must have foreseen the war coming for renting a basement, even though we set up business seven years prior to the lunatic taking over the asylum. Despite his title as 'junior partner' Kenneth Banner, or Badger as we called him, owing to the light and dark hair colouring, was twenty years my senior, but he was an excellent litigator and took some convincing to join the company, but he was a jolly man who enjoyed the company of others. Tom Grieves and Andrew Pitt were both my age given a year or two either way, and in the main worked well together. They were tenacious and methodical in their research and assets to the firm, but we enjoyed a good-working relationship as well as a friendly social life.

The girls, Penny Albrook, Sylvia Tibbs and Joyce Turner, worked well but were apt to talk about their sexual conquests during working hours and had to be constantly reminded, usually by Badger, that the munitions factories were looking for girls just like them and they should apply. With the exception of Joyce, who tended to dress somewhat frumpish, Penny and Sylvia were floosies and the same age, twenty-four; Joyce was a little older and obsessed with being left on the shelf and dying a spinster. "What if all the men die in the war; what will do then?" she once said. "Become lesbians, I suppose," said Badger as he passed by. It was a banter that worked well in the office place. When I started the company I was quite militant, insisting that everyone was addressed by their full title; Miss Albrook or Mr. Banner, and I wouldn't allow idle chit-chat, but the war forced me to re-evaluate the situation and, besides, people work better in a friendlier environment.

Sylvia considered herself to be somewhat of a glam-model, like the ones on the front pages of those magazines she constantly read, fashioning herself on film stars like Betty Grable and Rita Hayworth. Her peroxide hair was as white as virgin snow, her eyes dark as ebony, and her choice of lipstick the colour of blood, and her clothes were designed to enhance her perfectly shaped form to the full; pencil skirts and tight blouses, loose enough to move but tight enough to draw stares from any nearby men. Sometimes she would sit at her desk and tease the likes of Tom Grieves and Andy Pitt by placing a pencil between her lips and slowly pushing it in and out in a most sexual manner, and when she had their full attention she would look at them and laugh cruelly. Her dream was to be a war bride, probably marrying a war-hero, but her relationships—and there were many—survived no more than two or three months. By her own admission she was not monogamous and never likely to be, and as one courtship ended so another began; she accepted it without question—a way of life. But she was funny and trusting, and somewhere beneath those heaving bosoms that had been half-incarcerated in a bra designed to squash, increase and exaggerate, beat a heart of gold.

As I descended the steps into the reception Sylvia moved from her office, her usual bright smile shining, partly exposing her perfectly shaped and brilliant white teeth.

“Afternoon, Michael,” she said, softly. “I expected you before now. You missed your 1.30 appointment with Mr. Randall.”

“The rain slowed me down,” I said as I walked toward my office. “Send Mr. Randall my apologies and reschedule.”

“I have. Tomorrow at 10;” Sylvia replied as she walked along side of me, “tea or coffee?”

“Tea. Thank you, Sylvia.”

I sat at my desk, and like every other day set about deciphering Sylvia’s reminder notes, all of which resembled a doctor’s prescription or a five-legged spider that had been paddling in an ink-well and had wiped its feet on my notepad. Sylvia returned and set a cup of tea on my desk as I strained my eyes in the hope of making out one English word.

"Have you ever considered a job in the War Department?" I asked her after my eyes had lost focus and my brain began to wander. "Perhaps you could be a decoder, you know, secret messages and such."

Sylvia exuded another smile and a brief flutter of her eyelids.

"Did they never teach you at school that when you write more than one word you're supposed to leave a gap? Certainly your way saves time but it's hell on the reader," I added.

She took the notebook from me and read the messages with crystal clear clarity, and then setting it back before me began to stroll from the room.

"Sylvia," I said. She turned at the door to face me. "Have you ever had a platonic relationship with a man?"

She considered the question and leaned against the doorframe.

"My brother," she replied.

"No, Sylvia, not family; an unrelated person of the opposite sex!"

She took on a pensive refrain and her eyes began to aimlessly roam the office, and after some considerable time had passed, and is if struck by a revelation, she clicked her fingers.

"You!" she declared.

"But I'm your boss," I explained. "You couldn't have a relationship with me—platonic or otherwise—in fear of jeopardising your own position within this company, and had we a relationship, sooner or later it would come to an end and the tension between us would be such that you would be forced to leave."

"Correct me if I'm wrong but wasn't Sarah your secretary?"

"She was," I agreed with a nod, "but we were compatible from the outset; we both knew it."

"And Sarah knew from the start that you would be the one she would marry? When she ensnared you do you think she gave a second thought to the consequences had the relationship failed?"

"Probably not," I returned, "but that was not the question."

She moved slowly back into the office expressing a sultry look and sat on the edge of my desk, her skirt tightening and the button of her suspender forming on her thigh. She smiled as my eyes made contact with it and leaned forward.

"The nearest I have come to a platonic relationship is with men I have already sampled but, I guess, that doesn't qualify. So, the answer to your question is 'no'. As for you, well, what can I say? I pigeonhole men, and you are in the same box as my father, my uncles and brother; you are taboo. Furthermore you are married and, I might add, married to someone I know. And finally I don't find you sexually attractive."

She expressed a sweet smile and walked from the office, slowing at the door to pout and flutter her eyelids at me once again. I sat for a moment considering her answer that swiftly manifested into brooding, and I sprung from my chair and walked to her office.

"And why—may I ask—am I not sexually attractive?" I demanded to know indignantly.

Sylvia grinned mockingly and walked to the filing cabinet.

"You might be to someone else, just not me," she replied. "I mean, you're obviously attractive to Sarah; why else would she have married you, but you look . . . well, you look married."

"You can tell?"

"Certainly," she said as she opened the filing cabinet drawer. "Your suits are immaculate, shirts pressed with creases down the sleeves, and never a hair out of place."

"But women have affairs with married men. The history books are full of it."

Sylvia removed a file and gently closed the drawer, and then she turned, assessing me curiously with a knowing smile expanded on her mouth.

"You've met someone, haven't you?" she laughed. "My squeaky clean boss and loving husband has had his head filled with lewd thoughts and now you're curious." She walked to her desk and sat down, crossing her legs provocatively. "The problem is you're devoted to your wife and you're wondering if you could have a platonic relationship with this stranger without messing it all up."

I stood stock still, failing to give a reply and musing how she could possibly know these things.

"You have to understand one thing," she continued. "Men and women think differently. A man will accept his woman is having a platonic relationship with another man, but a woman would never accept that her man is having a platonic relationship with another woman. Why? Unfortunately for you—for mankind—you have been unjustly labelled as the hunters—the stronger sex. The reality of the tale is far simpler. If a woman says no then it's no. I seldom say no. If I want a man I'll have him, but there are certain rituals that must be adhered to. If I see someone who takes my fancy I'll pass him a smile, and if I don't get the right response I might walk past him and make eye-contact and smile again. When I have his attention I will let him do all the running, but never once will I let him know that I want him naked in my bed. You see, I look this way for gain. I dress this way for gain. I act like this for gain. And if a man wants to shower me with gifts then I welcome them with open arms; it makes them feel good. Like it or not we are all prostitutes. Your lady-friend is simply weighing you up; she wants the full story before she goes in for the kill. If you want my advice—and by asking me in the first place you must be—I suggest you fuck her and get it out of your system. Whether it's true or not, Sarah would never accept that your relationship with this mystery woman is platonic."

Without another word being said I returned to my office. I had never heard Sylvia swear to such an extent, but it occurred to me that the word 'fuck' to her had little or nothing to do with profanities but was simply a byword for sex. Within the hour she returned with a file.

"This has been passed to us and I don't know if you want to take it," she said.

"What is it?" I said looking up.

"The Henderson case."

For a brief moment the name meant nothing, but suddenly I jerked back in my seat.

"George Henderson, the 'Blackout Butcher?'" I cried.

"The very same," Sylvia smiled. "You have to hand it to Fleet Street. However do they come up with those names?"

The answer to that was pure and simple. At the beginning of the war England was expecting a heavy bombardment that never happened for some months, and in that time London and the surrounding counties were cast into a dark abyss by the blackout. George Henderson, a 45 year old train driver, used those dark months to murder and butcher eight women, both in the street and in their homes; his choice of weapon being a cutthroat razor. He raped and tortured five of the women—the younger women—and so, as the papers said, bled them to death. It was never clearly ascertained as to whether he had sex with them after death, but many of the newspapers certainly hinted at the possibility of necrophilia.

"Where's Badger?" I asked.

"A meeting across town."

Sylvia was now looking at my father's book on the edge of my desk, gently running her fingers over the aged brown-paper wrapping.

"Tom and Andy?"

"In court; the Driscoll case," she murmured. "What is this?"

"A book of some type," I replied.

"Clearly, but what is in it?"

"I have no idea; as you can see it's wrapped and tied with string. Do you honestly think I opened it, read it and wrapped it up again?"

She frowned a little and smiled and held out the folder.

"And this?" she asked.

"Leave it with me. I'd like Badger's advice before I make a decision. Multiple murderers are a bit out of our league, but the media attention it will receive could put us on the map. I'll let you know tomorrow."

With a nod Sylvia walked from the office but stopped mid-way and swung round.

"So, who is she, this mysterious woman?" she asked.

I had taken the 'Henderson' file from her and opened it and a name caught my eye, Inspector Carlisle; but when she asked the question I closed it again.

"I'm not sure," I said. "I met her this morning; we shared a cab together. When I came out of my solicitor's she was waiting for me, and we had coffee and talked."

I explained everything Rachel had told me about her life—everything I could remember—and Sylvia listened intently, occasionally nodding her head and sometimes smiling. When I finished I reclined in my chair and shrugged my shoulders. "That's it," I said.

Sylvia's suspicious smile turned into one of concern.

"Can I ask you something, Michael?" she asked.

I nodded.

"Do you love Sarah?" I know you did but do you still?"

Without hesitation I replied. "Of course I do. Of course I still love her."

"Then why are you letting some strange woman get under your skin?" she continued. "There probably is no husband, and the ring is more than likely a prop, her mother's or something she bought herself. Some girls do it to fend off unwanted predators; it's a safeguard!"

I rolled my eyes to the ceiling and glared at her.

"I asked you one question, and that was about platonic relationships. That's all I asked," I said.

"And I have answered honestly," replied Sylvia, innocently. "Does she know where you work?"

"I shook my head. "No, I don't think I mentioned it."

"Good!" Sylvia said, firmly. "Then best forgotten; put her to the back of your mind."

I grinned as she left. In the past we had had many heart-to-heart conversations; sometimes concerning me and sometimes concerning her. Despite her appearance and her cavalier attitude towards sex, she excelled at being an agony aunt and appeared to thrive on giving other people advice. Despite her need to untangle everyone else's problems, she appeared stumped when it came to her own. Two years ago she fell in love and it took her completely; she shone brighter then and, perhaps, believed in love a tad more than she did now, but her own precociousness could not be shackled. Inevitably, and in the shortest time she had worn her lover down and he abandoned her. I remember that for three weeks she was inconsolable and I tried desperately to show her a future. She sat in my office quietly staring at the wall, tears running down her cheeks and shaking her head from time to time whenever I attempted to plan her life, as though it was over. Eventually, and after many days, I talked her round, and not long before war reared its ugly head I took her for a meal in a small restaurant off Covent Garden.

"I've behaved childishly," she said as she sipped from a glass of wine. I'm sorry, Michael; I've let you down."

I registered her sadness and smiled. "These things happen from time to time, but we need to talk."

Slowly she lowered her glass and an expression of horror washed over her.

"Oh, no! You're firing me, aren't you? That's why you've brought me here."

I shook my head.

"Yes, it is," she continued. "I've embarrassed you and you're firing me."

She leaned forward and squeezed my hand and tears filled her eyes.

"Give me another chance, Michael. I won't let you down again; I won't! I'll dress differently and I'll be better; I promise I'll be better."

Sylvia was a master in the art of jumping to conclusions, and the slightest rumour, the faintest whisper would send her into a blind panic and for me, to see her in such frenzy, was not so much a revelation as nostalgia.

"I haven't brought you here to fire you, Sylvia," I said, slipping my hand from her gentle grip. "I simply brought you here to talk. Certainly we could speak in my office but then it would just be like employer and employee. I thought here we could talk as friends. Can you understand that?"

She appeared to breathe a shuddering sigh of relief and raised a napkin and dabbed her eyes.

"Thank you," she said.

The method in my madness was simple. Sylvia was a friend of Sarah my wife, and to terminate her employment would certainly affect my own, both at home and in the office. Furthermore, we had four important cases and I could ill-afford my secretary's preoccupation with the male-gender to jeopardise their outcome. Assured her job was safe Sylvia spoke of her weaknesses concerning men and her insecurities concerning her future, and the wine induced honesty within her and, sometimes, graphic images of her bedtime fantasies. She promised me there and then that such an incident would never happen again and to date, it never has. What troubles me still is the effect the conversation of that day must have had on her, for I have never seen her tearful since, nor speak of someone she had fallen in love with. I looked on it then and, perhaps, still, as a form of bullying; that her role as my secretary came before her own precious feelings.

My concern for her wellbeing was reciprocated when my father died. If there was sadness—and I'm sure there was—it was purely selfish. My father and I had rarely seen each other in ten years, and when we did meet the conversations were stilted and minutes passed like hours, but there were times, in a silent moment, I would catch him looking at me as if he had something important to say, and only when he acknowledged my stare did he turn away and the moment was lost. Sylvia knew I was distant from my father, but she also knew I admired him immensely for all his achievement. Her only comment on his death was 'sorry' and her smiles, which more often than not appeared false, were warmer the day he died and she purposefully spoke of anything and everything as long as it wasn't him. If I delved deeper into our relationship, I think I would have to admit that Sylvia had taken place of my sister Caroline, and if platonic relationships existed then surely ours was one.

Alone in my office I briefly read through the George Henderson file and considered whether the case was worth taking on, but my eyes wandered to my father's book and taking out a pair of scissors from my desk-drawer, I gingerly cut the string and unfurled the crisp, brown paper that enveloped it. Before me was an Oxblood, leather-bound ledger with gold inlay, and the pages within were discoloured brown and darker at its edges; the writing on the pages small and neat and definitely my father's. It appeared, as I suspected, a chronicle of his life, starting at med-school back in Victorian England and, no doubt, terminating some thirty-five years ago when he handed it over to Lothby & Sons for safe keeping. As much as medicine left me cold I began to read the first page.

APRIL 1888:

It was raining hard the first day I arrived at The London Hospital and I shall never forget the feeling of exhilaration the moment I walked through the entrance and saw the other students gathered in the foyer. I stood, separated from the others with my bag at my side which held a few books and an assortment of clothes, and after some time had passed I was approached by a tall, thin man with a black beard and shiny hair. There was nothing pleasant about his manner and his role today appeared to be put upon him which he undertook with a spiteful air. He asked my name to which I replied and he checked a list that appeared fused to his hand, and then without hesitation he said "39 New Road. Left out of the hospital and second left. Be back here by 10 o clock." This address was to be my lodgings for the duration of my stay at the hospital, and I lifted my bag and strolled towards the main entrance. At the doors the man called after me and when I turned he was in the company of another student who appeared somewhat emaciated and pale. "This boy will be sharing with you. You can go together and introduce yourself to the landlady. And never forget she is to be treated with the utmost respect; we have a reputation." I was moved to protest. It was not my intention to share with anyone, least of all a child who looked as though he was a deaths door, but I nodded and replied, "Yes, sir," and beckoned the young student to accompany me.

My new companion struggled with his bag; it was far too big and far too heavy, and his frame was thin and lanky, and as we walked down Whitechapel Road in the drizzle, he constantly stopped to regain his energy, much to my annoyance. In comparison I was a broader man, a stronger man, and my baggage was both lighter and smaller, and on the corner of New Road I placed my bag on the pavement and proposed a simple question. "We should swap bags," I said. The young waif stared at me and asked "Why?" There was a need for me to get to my location and remain as dry as I could and I was eager to achieve it. "My bag is lighter," I explained. "You, however, have apparently packed everything, including the grand piano." He stared curiously at me, and as I released the grip on my bag, so we exchanged. I heaved it up with considerable effort and moved forward. "God, boy, what is in here?" I gasped. He smiled back, holding my bag with little effort as we turned into New Road. "My mother packed it for me. I won't know what she has packed until I open it."

We moved slowly down the tenements, me with considerable effort and he with very little. "What do they call you?" I asked. He stopped again, a moment I appreciated, for it was my chance to rejuvenate. "Pip," he returned. "They call me Pip."

I lifted his bag and continued onward. "So, your parents like Dickens, do they?" I quipped. He stopped and dropped the bag to the wet pavement. "Why would you say that?" he asked. I continued, leaving him behind me. "Great Expectations!" I returned. He picked the bag up and followed me hurriedly. "I haven't read it," he said. I strode onward and smiled back at him over my shoulder. "You should, if only for your name. But I must say that you look more of an Oliver." Perhaps he had never read Oliver Twist, but if he had he made no comment, only to say some few moments later, "And what do they call you?" At number 39 I stopped, first facing the modest house and secondly facing him. "William. You may call me William." I appraised him and slowly began to circle his gangly, slouched frame. "And how old are you, Pip?" I asked with a smile. He stretched himself to his full height. "Nearly eighteen," he replied. I looked back to the house and hoisted up his large bag. "Then that settles it. I am nearly twenty which makes me the senior student. Come, Pip, let us inspect our palatial abode."

The landlady greeted us at the door without so much as a smile, assessing us both disapprovingly and drying her hands on her stained apron. She was, perhaps, forty-five but life had unjustly contributed an additional five years. Her hair was mousy and her cheeks were red and blotchy, but I thought that once, and not so long ago, she was a handsome woman. "Good morning, madam. We are here to . . ." I began. "From the hospital. Students." she said, cutting me short. She stepped to one side, and with a nod of her head allowed us entry into a short, dull hallway. "Your room is up the stairs, first on the right," she explained as she looked to the staircase. "You get one evening meal a day; anything else is at your cost." I took it to speak on behalf of Pip as well as myself and point out her mistake. "My good woman, has it gone unnoticed that there are two of us? We require a room apiece and a hearty meal at the end of the day." I placed my hand on Pip's shoulder and gave the landlady an assertive nod. Rather than acknowledge her error and my air of authority, she looked me up and down with some distain and folded her arms and took on a brashness befitting her appearance. "You will share the room," she hissed. "That is all the Hospital Board requires of me. And be warned, my bedroom is in the back downstairs parlour and is strictly out of bounds, as is my kitchen." Pip and I exchanged puzzled glances and obviously this vitriolic woman had dealt with many students in the past and would not be trifled with. For the time being I let the matter of the additional room rest. "Then are we to inform you of our choice of evening meal in the morning so you can purchase the necessary ingredients and prepare it?" I asked. She sneered at me and shook her head and walked off towards her beloved secret kitchen. "Choice!" she groaned. "The only choice you get is whether you eat it or not."

Surprisingly our room was light and airy, sparse in furniture and somewhat garish in décor, but two large windows gazed out solemnly into the back yards towards Turner Street which was befitting the contrast as to the gloomy interior of the house as a whole. There were two single beds and a bedside cabinet between, a large wardrobe and a chest-of-drawers on which sat a china bowl and a pitcher of water. I set down Pip's bag and walked straight to the window. "Be it ever so humble," I said. My room-mate appeared nervous, if not a little frightened. Clearly it was his first time away from home and the vastness of the city and this new home reminded him he was very much alone. "Which bed would you like?" he asked, quietly. I turned to face him and smiled brightly. "Whichever one you desire; you make the choice," I said. He lifted his bag and with all his strength tossed it on the bed and began to unfasten the buckles and, likewise, I did the same. Our clothes were allocated to the appropriate locations and Pip's mother had packed enough medical journals to fill a hospital library. I had brought few books, and those I had had little or nothing to do with medicine. Pip piled his collection under his bed and I placed mine on the bedside cabinet.

It was barely 9 o'clock and we weren't required back at the hospital for another hour and we both lay on our beds acclimatizing to our new and humble surroundings. In a quiet moment Pip lifted my collection of books and passed them through his hands, pausing every now and then to stare at me cautiously. He singled out a book entitled 'Myths and Legends' and began to leaf the pages, chuckling to himself as he read out aloud the title of each story. "Bigfoot; The abominable Snowman; Wolves and Vampires; Arabian Knights," and slamming the book closed he turned on his side grinning broadly at me. "You believe such stuff and nonsense, William?" he asked. I was lying on my back, my hands behind my head and my eyes roaming the cracked and blistered bedroom ceiling. "I do, Pip, I do," I replied, earnestly. "Or should I say I am taken by the notion that we want them to exist even though we know they don't; they live on forever when there is not one shred of evidence to suggest they ever existed in the first place. We want them in our world."

Pip swung his legs round and sat on the edge of his bed, his elbows on his knees and hands cradling his face; he was intrigued and I continued. "You see, Pip, sometimes in a dark room we see and hear frightening things; ghosts and ghouls, even monsters, yet we know for certain they're not actually there.

Under such conditions our minds revert to a dark side; a world beyond our own. I believe it's a madness we all possess yet most have learned to harness and control. Take Darwin for instance; was he mad?" Pip shook his head vigorously. "How could he be?" he said. "He proved that mankind descended from apes!"

"Thus denouncing God and all his believers! Darwin categorically proved, beyond a shadow of a doubt, that God is a lie, throwing religion into turmoil. But did they stop believing in him? No! We see them every Sunday, filling our churches and praying to someone who isn't there, and some of these people, Pip, are of the highest standing; they run our country, our schools and pass laws, yet they continue to worship a myth. Not so long ago Devil worshippers were drowned and burned at the stake for their beliefs; they were tortured and butchered with impunity. But if some have the right to believe in God, then surely others have the right to believe in the Devil, even though both are simply myths. Do you believe in God, Pip?"

He raised his head from his supporting hands. "I may have when I was younger," he said, "but not now. Knowing Darwin's theory how could I?"

"Exactly," I agreed. "But God as an entity, or whatever he is, continues to live in the minds of millions of people, and the church continues to prosper. God is a legend, and the foundation to any legend is the written word. Can you imagine those wizened old men with pen and parchment translating fables into the Bible? They must have roared with laughter at the absurdity of such stories; seas opening and voices booming from the skies. The gullible are convinced. Why? Because it is written. We believe what we read in the newspapers simply because it is written though hardly a word is true, and it is a fact of life that our minds store the written word rather than the verbal; those who penned the scriptures knew it, the monks knew it and the church knew it. It is a form of brainwashing. God doesn't exist! He is pure invention!"

It was time to leave for the hospital and at the bottom of the staircase the landlady appeared, still wearing her mucky apron. "I take it the room is to your satisfaction?" she asked sarcastically. I did not rise to the remark and turned to face her. "It will suffice, my good woman," I replied. Obviously irritated by the title of 'good woman' she scowled at me and through gritted teeth said, "Mrs. Steere. My name is Mrs. Steere, and you'd be well advised to remember that it's my roof you're under." As formidable as her expression looked and as harsh as her warning was delivered, I conveyed a pleasant smile and looked over her shoulder, towards the kitchen and the back parlour. "And is there a Mr. Steere residing in this splendid rabbit-hutch?" I asked. Her reply came in the form of a glower that wished me dead. "Are you being funny?" she growled. "Apparently not," I replied as I moved to the front door. "My associate and I look forward to dinner on our return," I continued. "May I be so bold as to enquire as to what delicious slop you intend serving up?" Her face did not twitch in the slightest and she delved her hand into her apron pocket and thrust a key at me. "Let yourself in," she spat.

Outside Pip and I laughed heartily. He was impressed by my pompous attitude towards the dragon landlady and tears of joy run down his face and he held his stomach with both hands. "You have to be assertive, Pip. If people are to take you seriously, you must let it be known that you are stronger than they are," I said. Pip straightened as his laughter subsided and he wiped the tears from his eyes. "Really?" he replied. I put my arm about his shoulder and we strolled up New Road. "Be assertive in your attitude and your appearance," I said. "You are about to embark in the life of a doctor and people will look to you both for strength and guidance. May I make a criticism of you, Pip?" He nodded his head and he looked at me and we stopped on the pavement. "You slouch, Pip," I said placing both my hands on his shoulders, "and that just will not do. Straighten up and walk tall. First impressions count." He pulled himself up to his full height and pushed his chest out but appeared just as puny as he had before. I appraised him with a trace of sympathy. "Perhaps we could work on your verbal assertiveness," I suggested.

Suddenly Sylvia was standing in the doorway with her coat on and her handbag hanging from her shoulder. "Are you staying the night, Michael?" she asked. I looked to the clock on the wall and closed the book; time had slipped by me, and then there were the blackout rules to adhere to, even though we were in a basement and lacked the luxuries of windows. "Interesting?" she asked, nodding towards the book. "My father's early days at medical school," I replied as I placed the book in my desk-drawer. Every night Sylvia and I would walk to the station, and if my particular train was postponed, we would have coffee in the same coffeehouse I went to with Rachel. Other times we may stop off for a drink in a small pub off Fleet

Street, in Wine Office Court, called Ye Old Cheshire Cheese. For my sins I was a history buff and walking into the Cheshire Cheese was like stepping back in time. In 1666 the Great Fire had destroyed Old St. Paul's and many houses in Fleet Street. The Cheshire Cheese public house survived and its interior, furniture and even pictures on the wall had been unchanged for two hundred years. In that space of time its patrons consisted of some of the most remarkable men in history; Sir Arthur Conan Doyle, Charles Dickens, Mark Twain and even our Prime Minister Stanley Baldwin.

On this particular evening—and whether the trains were running on time or not—I walked straight into Wine Office Court and Sylvia remained by my side. I had often thought, but had never asked, why such a beautiful and sensual woman as Sylvia had no better way to spend her time and would want to waste a precious hour with someone she had spent most of the day with. There was one table in particular I always sat at or, at least, tried to. Even if it was occupied I would stand at the bar until it was vacated and take it up at once. It was in the corner by the door, in a small room opposite the public bar, and Charles Dickens spent many a long evening sat at that very table, no doubt considering his next masterpiece. On this evening we were fortunate and took our positions at the table. For me it had been a strange day, a day of reflection, of the future, of the present and, perhaps, new horizons never considered before, but it had left me distant and thoughtful. Sylvia, in her typical caring way, realised it at once.

"So, what do you intend to do about the Henderson case?" she asked in an attempt to break me out of my shell.

I was casually surveying the busy pub, slowly filling with lawyers and bankers, slightly obscured by a mist of blue cigar smoke. Seated at the table where the great Dickens once sat, I felt the connection with my father and his reference to 'Great Expectations' and his new found-friend Pip, and I smiled sadly to myself. I had never had the time to grieve, but on consideration I lacked the emotion to do so; then and now. I can't remember ever being close to him though I believe he made a true effort to make it so, but once I decided to be a lawyer the void between us widened. He deplored the profession and condemned their very existence, and his opinion of them never wavered. "*They're nought but arrogant parasites,*" he blasted the day I told him of my choice. "*And their trade union—The Law*

Society—ensures their work is minimal and their fees are exorbitant." I could not put up an argument at the time and I would not attempt to today; surveys throughout history have always voted Lawyers among the worst professionals, second only to journalists.

"Michael, are you listening to me?"

I turned slowly to face Sylvia staring intently back at me.

"Tell me you're not considering taking on the Henderson case," she continued. "We deal in swindles, frauds and divorce! We are not experienced enough to defend a multiple murderer."

I raised my beer and sipped the froth off the top and gently placed it back down.

"Did you know this pub once had a famous parrot?" I said. "She was called Polly and, by all accounts, extremely eccentric yet intelligent and possessed the requisite skill to mimic anything she heard, but she could also be rude to anyone who didn't take her fancy. In 1918, at the end of the First World War, Polly imitated the sound of Champagne corks popping no less then four-hundred times before falling off her perch with exhaustion; she was known all over the world. She died in 1926 and her obituary appeared in a staggering two hundred newspapers."

Sylvia was staring back at me in disbelief, but she knew also that whenever I shied away from a particular subject, I would spout certain historical facts in order to fill a silent void, but her stare remained fixed and she slowly shook her head.

"Polly was just a bird, Sylvia!" I said. "She achieved greatness by just being a bird. She took risks and was recognised for it."

My devoted secretary continued to shake her head rapidly and emitted an exhaustive sigh, but after a moment she composed herself and leaned forward with her arms resting on the table.

"What is troubling you, Michael? Is it the strange girl you met this morning, the meeting with your solicitor, the Henderson case?"

The question wasn't open for consideration for I knew it had nothing to do with what she had listed. Simply I contributed my frame of mind to a mild form of melancholia, that the meeting with the family solicitor this morning had somehow reminded me that I was very much alone in a country under siege and under threat. At sometime during the day I had taken comfort with the images of Sarah, but even that relationship was somewhat strained. I had never mentioned it to anyone, least of all to Sylvia who was a friend to my wife, even though I knew she could be trusted with whatever information I entrusted her with. When war broke out Sarah begged me to stay home, suggesting that we convert the guest-room into an office, but I categorically refused; I was uncomfortable enough knowing my father had spirited me out of the war; I wasn't about to abandon my company or the city. My persistence to fight the good fight had slowly but surely began to cut rifts between us. The trains rarely run to time and sometimes they never run at all, and I would either spend the night in a small hotel on the embankment or curled up on my office floor; in the Blitz I would take to the underground with thousands of others. In that time I rarely went home, knowing the bombers struck only by night and not by day; business continued as usual. But with each return home the greetings were a little colder, and though Sarah attempted to play the doting wife, her casual conversations were sparse, her enquires minimal and her touch scarce.

Like any good husband I would ask what was wrong but the answers were always short and excuses fabricated; tiredness, the war; I knew a lie when I heard one. And one evening, not so long ago, I was sat alone and played a game of role-reversal. What if I was home safe in the Kentish countryside and Sarah was in London, sometimes for weeks at a time; the answer was literally in front of me—Sylvia. Friend or no friend Sarah knew of Sylvia's mania for sex and companionship, and she knew we often went to the pub together after work. She was convinced that an illicit-relationship had flourished between us even though one never had nor, for that matter, was ever likely to. Sarah had never mentioned or even hinted at the possibility but once, before the war, she would always ask how Sylvia was; now she never mentioned her name.

"I'm not sure what to do anymore, Sylvia," I said as I stared into my beer. "Maybe I'm re-evaluating my life; you know, reassessing what I am. I will never be the great man my father was, and nor would I wish to be, but . . . but I think I need something more than I have. Does that make sense to you?"

Not by any stretch of the imagination had I cornered the market on human suffering, for there was not a soul in the city that did not harbour the same feelings. At this present time England stood alone. On May 26th of last year, half a million British and French soldiers faced defeat on the beaches of Dunkirk, and had it not been for the calm seas they would have undoubtedly suffered annihilation by Hitler's approaching armies; any vessel that could float crossed the channel to bring our boys home, but France made a decision to opt out of the war; we considered Dunkirk as utter defeat. Churchill called it 'Their finest hour.' In November 1940, we faced the wrath of the Luftwaffe. Coventry was first to be bombed and two million homes were destroyed; all major cities followed and, inevitably, our children were evacuated abroad or to the countryside, and recently Earnest Bevin had introduced conscription for women. Our once uniformed streets were now scenes of devastation and mile upon mile of coiled barbed wire strewn the city and the skies filled with floating and bobbing barrage balloons. But what gave Londoners strength were the Londoners themselves. They continued regardless with a smile and an air of adventure.

"I can't ever imagine you feeling lonely," I said.

Sylvia turned her face away and her eyes remained on the crowded bar as if to give herself time to construct a witty anecdote, but when she turned back I was still awaiting a reply.

"I get lonely," she replied quietly. "It isn't all ballroom dancing and Martini's. Besides, stockings are hard to get these days; what choice do I have but to stay in?"

She tried to make light of it, but I could see in her dark eyes that she was genuinely hurt, and that troubled me even more.

"Tell me, how could anyone like you ever be lonely?"

She sat in silence for a moment, her head slightly lowered, staring into her glass of wine as if it possessed an answer, but she pulled herself back and forced a smile.

"I live from day to day, and one is much like any other. I have a few friends but I don't see them as much as I used to; they have boyfriends now, but sometimes we meet on a Friday and Saturday night. I'm a grown woman, a legal-secretary, and I still live with my parents; imagine that! It's only a matter of time before I'm conscripted into some munitions factory or the

Land Army or a bomb drops on our street. It's having no one that worries me. If I'm to die I'd like it to be in the arms of someone who loves me."

I looked at her in wonder and began to laugh.

"You're a hopeless romantic, Sylvia," I said. "Come on, drink up, I have a train to catch."

-3-

Our railway station was nameless now. In an attempt to dupe any invading Germans, the War Office decided to remove all signposts or anything that may aid the enemy reaching a particular location, and though many took the matter very seriously, I could not help but smile every time I got off the train. It was a little after 7.30 and I walked down the incline from the station and turned into the leafy avenue where I lived. It was still light and the warmth of the day was only beginning to recede, and children on bicycles sped down the quiet street with arms outstretched, impersonating Spitfires and imitating the sound of machine-gun fire; in these green and pleasant surroundings, it was difficult to believe we were in the midst of a war at all. My home was a three-bedroom, white-washed semi, set in a road of identical houses, and like any good neighbour I would stop sometimes and talk, passing a few moments on the day's events that nowadays more often or not concerned the war. Commuting by train was always a good way to keep up on the war-effort, for my fellow strap-hangers were always considerably more informed, and I would pass this information on to any neighbour I may happen by thus giving the impression that I actually cared, but on this evening I was spared any interruption and moved straight to my front door.

Sarah greeted me in the hallway, as she always did when she heard the turn of the key in lock, and our once long kisses were now little more than a brief brush of the lips and, as always, she would turn on her heels and set off for the kitchen while I entered the lounge.

"Did you get caught in the rain this morning?" she asked, her voice sounding through the serving-hatch. "Strange how it's turned out such a beautiful evening."

"I took a cab to Mr. Lothby's," I replied as I unlaced my shoes.

Her face was suddenly framed within the serving-hatch.

"Any changes?" she asked.

"No. It was as Caroline said; straight down the middle."

With my shoes off I reclined in my easy chair and took the newspaper from my briefcase.

"He left me a book," I added.

"What kind of book?"

"About his early days at medical-school."

I unfurled the newspaper and looked to the hatch which was now empty, but suddenly Sarah appeared at the door.

"Why would he leave you a book?"

"Perhaps it's his way of letting me know what I missed out on," I replied. "But he left it with Mr. Lothby the day I was born so how could he have known I wouldn't grow up to be a doctor?"

My wife shrugged her shoulders and left the room and I dropped my eyes to the newspaper, but suddenly she reappeared again, a concerned expression on her face.

"Why would he do that?" she questioned. "Why, on the day you were born, would he go to his solicitor and leave a book for you to inherit when he died?"

I shook my head and continued reading.

"Your father could be very strange sometimes," she said as she vanished again.

We sat and ate dinner and she told me of her day and the local gossip. In the morning she had gone into town to collect some groceries and met with her friend Patricia, who was married to Gerald—a tedious, whiskey-swilling bigot—who worked in government in one capacity or another and who had told his wife that rationing was soon to be introduced. My response was dull surprise; the story had been bandied around the national newspapers for months. In the afternoon she had gone to see Sheila Bishop who lived in the next road and whose husband was one of those stranded at Dunkirk and was lucky enough to make it home. By all accounts he never remained in England for long and was shipped off abroad to an undisclosed country; she suspected Belgium. Mrs. Carver, at number 17 had lost her cat, and Mr. and Mrs. Driver at 54 had just received news that their only son had been lost in action, presumed dead. She continued speaking but I hardly heard a word and it was with some relief that someone knocked on the front door. "I'll get it," I said. Sarah was up before I placed down my knife and fork and was heading out of the room. "Finish your dinner," she said.

In her absence I thought of what she said about my father leaving the book the very day of my birth, and then Rachel came to mind and I wondered what she was doing at this particular time and if she had yet struck up a platonic relationship with one of the locals in her pub. Sarah had gone but a few minutes and she returned to the table and continued with her dinner.

"Well?" I asked.

She looked at me briefly and dropped her stare back to her food.

"I saw Mr. Fletcher today and he was saying he could do with someone to help out at the shop; I offered to help," she said. "And that was him."

I turned and looked at the clock on the mantelpiece.

"It must be urgent. Why would old Mr. Fletcher be walking the dark streets at this time of night?"

She rose and picked up my plate and headed off to the kitchen.

"It was Billy," she said. "He just needs me a few hours a day."

I moved to the comfort of my easy chair and resumed reading. Billy was the son of Mr. Fletcher the local grocer and rather than work in the shop, he could be seen walking the streets with a barrow filled with vegetables touting for business. For the elderly, who found the walk into the town too tiring, Fletcher & Son was a Godsend and well appreciated.

"It'll do you good; get you out of the house," I said.

"Do you mind?"

"Like I said; it'll do you good."

The town was a place I rarely ventured, as the train station was in the opposite direction and anything I needed I purchased in London. I had only seen Mr. Fletcher three or maybe four times, but I had seen his son Billy on many occasions and often spoken with him. He was pleasant enough and in his early forties, muscular and possessed with a certain charm I could not quite define. He would call, usually on a Saturday, and while Sarah made her choice from his display on the barrow we would talk but not about anything specific. His wife had absconded years ago taking two children with her and had not been heard of since, though the children sent him cards every Christmas. He was extremely hard working and his father was in ill health, and before he went on his rounds he would stock the shop so as his father did not exert himself lifting heavy crates. I could understand his need for someone to help out in the shop.

By the time Sarah entered the lounge I was reading through the sports pages. There was a pent-up anger about her that was becoming more familiar with the passing days, as though she had grown accustomed to my absence and now resented my presence. Every move she made appeared deliberate and executed with frustration. She moved to the settee and lifted a book from the coffee table, thumbing the pages noisily and finding the passage where she left it.

"So, how was your day apart from your meeting with Mr. Lothby?" she asked so coldly I sear I could see her frosty breath.

"We've been offered the Henderson case," I replied.

"Who?" she asked.

"George Henderson, the murderer."

"The butcher!" she shrilled with horror.

"I doubt I'll take it though. We're not experienced enough."

"Good!" she said expressing a shudder. "You surprise me sometimes, Michael, you really do. Why would you want to defend such a monster?"

I dropped the newspaper to my lap and stared back at her.

"It just fell on my desk," I snapped. "I haven't decided to take it yet; I need to speak with Badger."

She shook her head and returned to her book.

"Well, tell Badger you don't want it," she grumbled. "What would people say, knowing my husband is defending a maniac?"

"You can tell them I'm doing my job—the job I'm paid to do," I returned with an edge in my voice.

She shot me one of her loathing stares, the look that always precluded a vitriolic reprimand in one shape or form.

"Play all the games you like in the city, Michael, but I have a reputation to uphold in this town, and how am I going to look when everyone knows you intend to defend a murderer? Do you never consider my position?"

I was in no mood to argue and shook my head.

"Okay, I won't take the case," I said.

"Good!"

"Fine."

I awoke in the early hours in semi-darkness, still in my easy chair and the newspaper in a pile at my feet. Sarah had gone to bed and extinguished all the lights in the house but the hallway, leaving me in my slumber. I cursed myself because I had done it so many times before and it was just one more excuse for her to reprimand me at the breakfast table; one more excuse to highlight my insensitivity; one more excuse to question my role as a husband. At a little after 5.30 I gently closed the front door and walked slowly to the station as morning broke, like a cowardly thief steeling to safety; a guilty man running from the authorities, a fox escaping the gnashing jaws of the pack. An absurd comparison, perhaps, but one I had grown accustomed to over the years and one I had learned to live with. Once I would sit at the breakfast table enduring Sarah's verbal onslaught, but more often than not I found myself retreating from the house with an excuse of an early meeting or blaming the sporadic train timetable, and with every carefully executed escape, and the sense of freedom that exhilarated me with every step towards the station, I knew the same subject, the same onslaught and the same belittlement would be waiting for me at our next meeting in the kitchen.

I was not without blame, or to be more precise, I was probably totally to blame. Sarah was my first secretary when I started the company, in the days when Badger and myself had dreams of greatness, of being a law firm to be reckoned with, and with hard work came the rewards which inevitably led us to a house in the country, and with this achieved, procreation was the next stop on the merry-go-round and one I shied away from. Sarah and I were divided on the subject. Her view was to have children before the paint had had a chance to dry in the new house, and although I was not adverse to having children, I could not see the point when my work-load was such that I would never get a chance to see them grow up; the outbreak of war only strengthened my argument but left my wife of six years feeling utterly betrayed. Thus the divide between us grew even wider and she never allowed the matter to rest, but as much as I despised Adolf Hitler he had provided me with a foolproof excuse. "Do you really want to bring children into a world that's at war?" I would say to her. Sometimes she would listen to reason and sometimes she would regard it as just another lame excuse and, for that matter, sometimes so would I.

And so I arrived early in the city and the streets were empty by comparison, and I strolled up Fleet Street with the sun on my face, breathing clean air that had yet to be contaminated by the impending traffic, and I stopped and purchased a copy of The Times from old Sid the newspaper vendor on the corner of Aldwych and even had a short conversation with him. His kiosk was like a large wardrobe, a weather-beaten, temporary structure set within an ornate archway of a building that rounded the corner of Surrey Street. On its exterior were literally hundreds of photographs of missing people, placed there by loved-ones during and after the Blitz. New photographs were added to the collage on a daily basis, with a sparse description, their name and age, and recently, despite the cessation of bombings, more pictures appeared, usually of young women. "Who are all these people?" I once asked him as I studied the board. Old Sid sat on his usual fishing seat, counting his money and wearing his fingerless gloves. "Runaways; young women coming to London looking for fame and fortune," he explained. "God only knows what has become of them."

I submerged from the brightness and the sounds of the city into the silent darkness of my office, groping for the light switches at the bottom of the staircase and then moved straight to my desk. And there I sat with nothing before me but the Henderson file which could wait for Badger's consideration, but if by instinct I pulled open the drawer and took out my father's book and turned the pages to where I left it yesterday.

Our first day and, indeed, the first two weeks were relatively easy for me as a medical student though Pip, my room-mate was having difficulties. My father was Charles James, a well respected MD, and he had instilled in me much of his knowledge over my short life and enthusiastically enticed me to become familiar with the profession by way of borrowing me his own personal journals, and he would ask me questions, usually at dinner, and for every correct answer I was rewarded with a small token; as a student I was probably advanced by two years. Pip, on the other hand, studied vigorously back in our room and constantly asked me questions to which I rendered my assistance whenever I could. His relentless studying at night was becoming almost an obsession and it affected him by day; usually with bouts of dozing during lectures. We agreed we would study together for two hours every night but two hours only, and during that time I would help him to the best of my ability. "I admire your tenacity, Pip, but you must learn to separate the student from the man," I told him. "You'll be no good to anyone if you cannot concentrate at lessons."

We witnessed our first corpse on the second day. Twenty or so medical students were ushered into the morgue in the basement of the London Hospital and our tutor, Dr. Spence stood beside a slab of marble on which lay the body of a recently deceased woman covered with a white sheet. Dr. Spence was rather plump with a head of wild hair and a mottled beard of grey and black, and he had a tendency to sweat without exerting the slightest effort; fellow students attributed this affliction to vast alcohol consumption and habitual acts of masturbation. He removed the sheet with all the panache of a magician who had spirited his female assistant from one box to another, and there before us lay a dead, naked woman the colour of alabaster. Spence was on the lookout for reaction, shock, horror or stifled schoolboy tittering; not one of us made a sound or expressed the slightest facial alteration.

"Her name is Emma Elizabeth Smith," explained Dr. Spence. "She was a forty-five year old prostitute working the streets of Whitechapel. By her own account she was attacked in Brick Lane at a little after midnight on April 2nd, by three youths who raped and robbed her; she died here on April 5th. Is anyone familiar with the case?"

His eyes roamed across our vacant faces while all our eyes were fixed to the cadaver's sagging breasts and pubic bush, but Pip gingerly half-raised his hand to which Dr. Spence nodded. "A blunt instrument was forced into her vagina which tore the perineum and after falling into a coma, she died of peritonitis," said Pip in a shaky voice. Dr. Spence raised his eyebrows high, forcing a trickle of sweat out between the creases of his forehead which weaved its way down his cheek and finally became entangled in his beard. "Very good," he said. "Keeping up with events in the East-End may serve you well when evaluating a patient's condition. There are literally thousands of prostitutes in this vicinity and most will pass through this hospital or the infirmary at one time or another; diseased or the victims of pimps and so-called clients. Many are found dead and the perpetrators are rarely captured; as in the case of this poor unfortunate woman."

Back in our room Pip and I lay on our beds, he reading a book on the human anatomy and me engrossed in Jekyll & Hyde, but I paused to look at him. "How did you know about that woman in the morgue?" I asked. He continued reading and without looking back at me, he said, "I read it on the train the day we arrived; such things interest me." It occurred to me then that Pip possessed a dark side; a macabre interest in death or, perhaps, in the way it is administered, and as the moments passed he could feel my eyes burning into him and he placed his book down and turned to see me grinning back. "So we do have something in common," I said. Pip shook his head furiously and raised his eyes to the ceiling. "We have nothing in common!" he said, emphatically. "Yours is a fascination with ghouls and ghosts. Mine is with the real world—real life." He raised his book as if there were no more to say on the subject and continued to read, but I was not about to let the matter rest. "So tell me why such things interest you." He stubbornly refused to detach his eyes from the written page and I returned to my book. "Inevitably they will catch those responsible for killing the whore," I remarked casually in an attempt to coax him out of his silence. "Not necessarily," he returned spontaneously. "There are thousands of unsolved murders in the city, especially in reference to prostitution; they're worthless, you see."

It was my intention to ease my companion into conversation gently but before I could pose my next question he rested his book down. "We consider them vermin," he said. I pretended to be engrossed in my own book and muttered, "Who?" He half-rolled on his side with a clenched fist under his cheek, dispensing with his medical journal completely. "Why, prostitutes, of course! They're troublesome creatures and a source of contagion. The police are reluctant to act on their behalf because they know they consort with the lowest and most vicious criminals, and should one be found dead, then it's just one less prostitute that can contaminate us." Pip had a sparkle in his eyes when he spoke, for although I may have been more advanced as a medical student, he was talking about a subject he knew well. "I wanted to be a detective," he said, "but my father wanted me to become a doctor but, I suppose, it's a means to an end. Detectives save lives, don't they? I hope one day to be a police surgeon, to assist the police in apprehending the murderer." I lowered my book and folded my arms across my chest. "And how could that be achieved?" I asked, giving him my full attention. "You'd be surprised," he returned. "A police surgeon can determine whether the killer is left or right handed, and in such cases when a knife has been used, he can even gauge the killer's weight and height."

Over the following weeks we engaged in debates. He fought on the side of reality and I fought on the side of fantasy, and on one night—in the early hours—we lay in our darkened room and I asked him if he had ever heard of Jesse James, the notorious American outlaw. "No, I never have," he replied. In an effort to bolster my argument for legends I began to explain. "He was a thief and a murderer, and some years ago he was shot in the back by his cousin. Just imagine, a fearsome gunfighter like Jesse James being shot in the back by a cowardly relative." Pip made no reply at first but after a moment he said, "What is your point?" Till now my defence for legends had been somewhat weak, consigned to the imaginations of Stevenson, Shelly and Poe, but now I was offering a living and breathing person or, at least, living and breathing until April 3rd 1882, when he was hanging a picture and his cousin terminated his life. "Jesse James was a legend; in life he was a legend! Some people have to die first before they achieve that immortality. His cousin was jealous of that status; that's why he killed him. After he killed him he was packing American theatres, reliving those final moments in a vein attempt to convince the world that he was a bigger hero than Jesse James; that he was a bigger legend."

"So what did Jesse James do—exactly?" asked young Pip. I pondered for a moment and hunched my shoulders. "I'm not sure, exactly. He just killed people," I returned with uncertainty. "But you admire him!" said Pip. I frowned immediately. "I don't admire him as a person," I retaliated. "I admire him for the legacy he created; the legend. That isn't to say he created the legend on purpose; it just happened."

"But he was a killer!" Pip argued.

"Yes, he was, but in the eyes of many he was a hero; you know, an American outlaw of the Wild West. What I'm trying to say is that Jesse James as a person wasn't the legend; the myth that surrounded him made him a legend, and it wasn't a myth he intentionally created."

Suddenly the room illuminated bright with the sound of a match being struck, and Pip lit the oil-lamp on the bedside cabinet between us and sat up.

"So, what makes a legend?" he asked.

"Mystery, Pip, mystery," I replied enthusiastically. "Most legends are lies, cobbled together by fishwives and penny-a-liners over many, many years; so-called facts that can neither be neither substantiated nor supported. Was Jesus a real person or was he someone manufactured by Christianity to promote their faith? It's the written word, Pip! Mankind is gullible and will believe anything they read; famous or infamous." I lifted my book from the bedside cabinet and shook it. "Take Dr. Jekyll; utterly boring as an individual, but with Mr. Hyde—well, it's a phenomenal read. Hyde is the myth. Hyde gives the tale a whole new dimension, and it's the monster that makes the story; every other character pales into insignificance."

Pip raised his knees and rested his head upon them, looking thoughtful and turning my analogy over in his mind.

"The individual does not create his own legend—we do; the public creates it." I continued. "The stories about them are twisted and exaggerated until the original concept is lost."

"So, can anyone be a legend?"

I shook my head. "No, but anyone can create a legend; anyone can create a myth."

My concentration was broken by someone moving down the stairs, and after a brief sound of rustling paper and faint murmurings Sylvia appeared in the doorway, resplendent in her tight clothes and her overall immaculate appearance. Her smile was brighter than her usual well-rehearsed morning smile and her dark eyes twinkled and glistened with recollection of a previous night's passion. I reclined and appraised her with a knowing grin.

"So—who is this one?" I asked.

"Just someone," she said, desperately trying to exude coyness, "a friend of a friend. Tea?"

"Tea would be fine, Sylvia. So when did you meet him?"

She was eager to tell me the whole story; well, as much of the story that worked in her favour and did not depict her as a man-eating doxy, hell-bent on feminine world domination. She moved directly to the chair in front of my desk and sat down, crossing her legs and leaning her arms on the table.

"When I left you at the station I met my friend Rose," she began. "Rose is working nights in a factory at the Elephant and Castle, and she was with Harold, this dishy carpenter from Camberwell, and after Rose caught her bus he asked me if I wanted a drink. Well, of course I said no and made an excuse I was tired, but then I thought 'what harm can it do?' and off we went to Blackfriars where Harold met a friend of his; Dennis, I think his name was. Anyway, Dennis works for a removal company in Camberwell and had to take the lorry back to the yard for the night and asked Harold if he wanted a lift home . . ."

"And you went along for the ride—literally!" I broke in.

Her eyes fell away from mine and she started doodling invisible shapes on the desktop with her index finger.

"Sylvia, would I be correct in assuming that Harry and Rose are not related?" I asked.

She continued her make-believe abstract and shrugged her shoulders sulkily.

"So Harold is Rose's boyfriend! Your night of unbridled lust was with your friend's lover!"

With her imaginary masterpiece complete she folded her arms and looked at me.

"It doesn't make me a bad person," she said almost in a whisper.

I shook my head and sighed with exasperation.

"No, Sylvia it doesn't. It just makes you a very stupid one. Can I have coffee instead? I think I need one."

She rose suddenly, tossed her head as a form of rebuke and paced from the office indignantly.

"Don't forget your 10 o'clock appointment with Mr. Randall," she grunted.

"Ah, yes, Sylvia, perhaps you can enlighten me as to who exactly Mr. Randall is."

She turned and frowned at me like a teacher might at an unruly child.

"Don't you read my reminder notes?" she said, her eyebrows perched high on her head and with more than a hint of sarcasm in her tone.

"Actually, no I don't. It isn't that I haven't tried—I can't, you see," I rebuffed.

"The Henderson case!" she said as if to coax me into her world of understanding. "He was the man who brought it to us; from the Director of Public Prosecutions Office," she added impatiently.

As she stomped from the office I lowered my eyes back to my father's book.

It soon became apparent, within the first week of our arrival, that our contemptible landlady Mrs. Steere was an incorrigible drunk and, to make matters worse, prostituted herself on a nightly basis. Sometimes she would have up to four callers a night which she speedily and quietly led down the hallway to the back parlour, her bedroom. Pip was quite impressed by her timing, in that one client on his way out did not bump into another on his way in, and as our room was directly above her, little was left to the imagination; obviously this poor, depraved woman needed to supplement her income from the hospital by lying on her back. "Rather them than me," I said to Pip. Imagination or not, the water-closet roof was outside our window, and besides that was an upturned water-barrel and Pip and myself would sometimes scamper down to view Mrs. Steere exercising her rights through the chink in the curtains. Of course we would be on our best behaviour if we passed her in the hallway in the morning, and only erupt into uncontrollable laughter once we were outside on the pavement. Apart from furnishing us with a room and an evening meal, Mrs. Steere was accountable to The London Hospital Board, for not only did they look upon her as a landlady but also as our guardian, and it was her role to ensure that we behaved as gentlemen and did not go gallivanting all over the East End procuring loose women and getting drunk.

In our second month as students we were taken to the Whitechapel Workhouse Infirmary, a formidable looking building of three tiers which incorporated four floors of endless sinister looking arched windows as well as a basement. Indeed, the building took up the length of the street, and from one end it was difficult to see the other. It had stood here in the Mount and Mountfield since 1752, but it was originally established in 1740 in a meagre house in Featherstone Street and was simply called The London Infirmary. I admit to feeling uneasy when I entered, and for good reason. There had always been distance between myself and poverty, and the few times I viewed the poor at close proximity was usually from a passing carriage window. Pip however was eager to be part of it and pushed forward through the mass of other students to the front. Dr. Morgan was the nameless doctor I had met the first day I went to the hospital and who had placed Pip into my care, and neither his attitude nor his permanent scowl showed any signs of improving.

He stood before us planning out the route we were to take; from the top floor down. Dr. Morgan was an obstetrician and as the sign at the entrance stated that particular field of medicine was in the basement, I knew it would be our last port of call. As he spoke I was looking nervously about me, at those entering and leaving or just those stationary around us, most of them dirty in appearance, wearing clothes that weren't fit for the fire. A constable was stationed outside the main entrance which I thought unusual and he appeared unconcerned at the noisy drunks and complaining harridans at the desk. My wandering eyes had caught Dr. Morgan's attention and he paused and pointed directly at me. "You! Your name?" he asked pointedly. "William James," I replied, meekly. "You may want to pay attention, Mr. James. I may say something important." I expressed a smile of apology and was doubtful whether he was capable of saying anything important at all. I concentrated for a moment but my eyes were drawn to a woman sitting on a seat in the hall to the right of us. Her face and clothes were dirty as though she had fallen in mud and her eyes were wide and staring and a smile played on her lips throughout. She was perhaps thirty but obviously a vagrant.

When Dr. Morgan had stopped talking he pointed to the staircase and walked towards it, and as to his instructions, we followed, but as we moved off the woman on the seat rose and started moving towards us, her right hand rummaging through a clutch-bag but her eyes and menacing leer focussed on Pip who was seemingly oblivious to her presence, and as she was almost upon him she pulled out a knife and lunged forward. From the back I rushed closer and cried 'Pip!' and at that moment he noticed her and held his arms up in front of him in defence. The blade caught his forearm at the very second I struck her with my fist and she collapsed to the floor, after which I sat astride her and would have struck her again had I not been constrained by my fellow students. Dr. Morgan walked casually back and appraised me with a knowing grin. "That is why you have to pay attention," he said. The constable was now through the doors and manhandling the woman to her feet, taking her knife and placing it in his pocket. "Anyone hurt?" he asked. Pip had taken his arm out of the sleeve of his jacket and Dr. Morgan was assessing the damage; a cut perhaps two inches in length, and he looked to the constable and shook his head. "Come on, Lillian, to the cells with you," said the policeman. As the woman passed she grinned broadly and then blew me a kiss.

After Pip was attended to we continued our walk of the infirmary, through the wards of the living and of the dying, of those who were literally starving to death, of those beaten and robbed and of those who came with bogus complaints because they had nowhere else to go. And I followed almost in a trance, astounded by the attack on my friend which the doctor, the hospital authorities and indeed the arresting policeman considered to be nothing more than a meaningless fracas, and Dr. Morgan noticed my indifference and on the staircase into the basement he stopped me. "Her name is Lilly Stone, a prostitute of the lowest order," he said. "She had no intentions of killing your friend, but the very act will get her a few days in a nice warm cell or better, prison for a month or so; food, clean blankets. If you're to work in East End hospitals, Mr. James, you had better get used to it; you will see much worse." We continued our descent into the bowels of the infirmary and as we stepped out of the stairwell, the corridor was lined both sides in the main with women, most, if not all prostitutes and their heads turned, and we—fresh-faced young men—were subjected to all manner of sexual innuendo. According to Dr. Morgan these wretched specimens of womanhood were all casualties of venereal disease yet all were still plying their trade.

Dr. Morgan led us into an anti-room, no more than a large storeroom, a warehouse for Obstetricians and Gynaecologists, where every available space was racked out with shelves on which sat innumerable glass jars of various shapes and sizes. Inside each were specimens preserved in surgical alcohol, and each jar was labelled with the specimen's history; its disease, its advancement, even its age. Most were uterus's infected by syphilis, discoloured of their rich pink and now grey in appearance, ulcerated and grotesque. While my classmates shivered with disgust, I felt I had entered a kingdom few had ever ventured into, and I gazed in wonder at newborn infants who had been pickled for posterity, who were so grossly deformed they defied belief, or were the work of some madman who had cobbled together a human-being from remnants of others, like Frankenstein had achieved with help from grave-robbers. I chuckled cruelly as one of my colleagues' vomited at the hideous sights. These tiny, subnormal beings incarcerated in their glass cells and hidden away from the world were not the work of any crazed professor. They were the invention of whores, of the present social conditions, of the constant self-abuse of alcohol consumption during pregnancy, of syphilis and even of incest.

'Slumming it,' is a term used by the toffs, the hierarchy; society people who, in the main, frequent the West End clubs and fine restaurants, but every now and then, and for their amusement, they would traverse from the West to the East to view and sample the life of the poor; occasionally throwing a handful of coins in the air and watching the needy fight over them. Pip had never heard it used before, and one lonely, Friday night in our room I proposed we should go. "What does it entail?" he asked nervously. I was combing my hair in the mirror and Pip was lying on his bed fully clothed. "It doesn't entail anything. We just visit a few pubs and have a drink," I replied to his reflection. "We should see first hand what and who we are dealing with; how they live." Young Pip's eyes opened wide and a look of horror washed over him. "But what if I'm attacked again," he said. I took my jacket from its hanger and placed it on. "You won't be attacked, Pip, I promise you. Besides you're with me. No harm will come to you," I said. He was reluctant, but I threw his jacket at him. "Come on, look lively,"

I said as I slid the sash-chord up. "We'll go out the servant's entrance." Pip was off his bed, threading his arms into the sleeves of his jacket. "But what about Mrs. Steere; she'll report us?" he said. I was out of the window and standing on the water-closet roof. "She'll do no such thing," I whispered back at him. "She's either drunk, in the passionate grips of a frustrated sailor—or both. Come on!"

We walked down the Whitechapel Road and turned into Commercial Street; my strategy being that it would not be wise to partake in such a past-time locally in case we were seen by somebody associated with the hospital, and Pip agreed. Our first port of call was The Princess Alice, on the corner of Wentworth Street. It was busy, and one wondered how these destitute creatures were still able to find money for alcohol, but we made the best of it and ingratiated ourselves into the company. An old man with a half-cocked flat cap played an accordion and people sang along; the dockers, the market traders, sailors of all nationalities and, of course, the prostitutes plying their trade. There was no reason to be fearful, for at first we may have received the odd concerned glance, but we soon became part of the crowd. It was Pip's wish to stand by the open door for a number of reasons. The smoke was dense and attacked his eyes the moment we entered, causing them to tear, and quite heavily at first, and also he still harboured a wariness when around whores; the open door was his assurance of a hasty retreat should it be necessary.

It was only a matter of a time before we were accosted. A girl, perhaps in her mid-twenties, walked in off the street; pleasantly pretty with green eyes and a fine head of ginger hair that reached nearly to her waist. She passed me only a fleeting glance at first and Pip even less, but she stopped and set her eyes on me. "You're new," she said with a flirtatious smile. "Are you students?" Pip had receded behind me almost completely and he looked at the woman over my shoulder. I grasped my lapels and pushed my chest out. "My fine lady, we are not students! We are doctors." I said, haughtily. Her smile remained fixed as she shook her head in disbelief. "You look very young," she replied. "It is a curse I've learned to live with." She raised a hand to her mouth and began to laugh and looked behind her through the open door. "Have you a name?" I enquired. "I'll wager it's as beautiful as your appearance. Perhaps I can buy you a drink." She turned back and her smile was a little warmer. "Mary Jane," she said. Before I could introduce myself she glimpsed behind her and suddenly walked to the bar and a stocky man walked through the doors and immediately accompanied her, gently kissing her cheek and sliding his arm around her waist to stress ownership. "Obviously her husband," said Pip as he emerged from behind me. "Or her pimp," I replied, my eyes fixed on the couple. "God! You mean she's one, too?" I patted my companion gently on the head. "Undoubtedly Pip, undoubtedly."

With our first drink under our belts we moved on to The Queen's Head on the corner of Fashion Street; the ambience much the same with an elderly woman playing an upright piano, its top covered in glasses and empty beer bottles. At the bar a tall woman with blond hair and high cheek bones argued quietly with an irate stocky man, and despite the loudness of the dreadful piano playing, a young man was asleep at a nearby table where all around everyone danced and sang. Here was a multitude of different cultures, different races and skin colour, different classes and, sometimes, impenetrable language barriers. And music was the key to breaking that barrier, for Poles and Russians sang in perfect English even though they could not understand a single word, and for a brief moment in time they were no longer alienated by creed or colour; they were simply part of a moment. Pip was sceptical and wary of the surroundings, but I sucked it in like inhaling the smell of freshly mown grass on a summer's day, and though I may have had my reservations at first, now I endeared it with a morbid curiosity. "Welcome to the dark side, Pip," I said.

Within half an hour we were walking towards Spitalfields, crossing the road and standing at the mouth of Dorset Street. "I've read about this place," I said to Pip; "one of the most dangerous streets in the East End; a rookery." Pip stared at me nervously anticipating an explanation. "A rookery is a place where thieves and beggars reside; a place the authorities dare not go," I said. "Fagin lived in a rookery at Saffron Hill with the Dodger and Oliver Twist. Murderers and vicious criminals live in these houses, Pip." We were standing next to a public house called The Britannia, though colloquially it was known as 'The Ringer's' after the landlord and landlady, and outside were forty or maybe fifty women wandering aimlessly up and down, sometimes talking amongst themselves and sometimes pushing and hissing at one another. Across the road outside Christchurch there were more, leaning against the railings, and further up the road was the Ten Bells where maybe another sixty were gathered, searching out their prey. "Look at them, Pip, so many; disease, spreading whores—dregs of society," I whispered. Pip run his eyes over the mob and slowly shook his head. "Can we go now?" he asked. I patted him on the shoulder and nodded. "Yes, I believe we've had our fill for one night."

'Scarlet women' sounds somehow romantic, mysterious and creates an illusion that every man succumbs to sooner or later, but on our way back we passed many so-called women of the night, and none neither looked mysterious or romantic; they simply existed to offer a service, to extract money. It is a myth that most were forced into prostitution by present social conditions; they chose the profession willingly. It was easier than working in the many sweat-shops in the area, or working below stairs or standing in the cold and rain selling off a market stall. Have no doubts that these women had choice, and theirs was the path of least resistance. On our way back we saw many, moving towards the city in groups or gathered under shop-awnings touting for trade, and it was from one of these canopies that a young girl stepped out of the shadows and moved directly to Pip. She was petite and small, and by the gas lamp on the corner of Union Street, I could see the heavy make-up she—or someone—had applied to her face; I estimated her age at no more than eleven years old. She asked Pip if he cared to go somewhere; "sixpence," she said. Pip gave no reply, only to look at me, but I was peering into the greyness of the sheltering canopy where three women were looking on. "Which one of you is the mother?" I asked tersely. One angrily paced forward and pointed to the young child. "Do you want her or not? Sixpence!" I spat at her feet and we continued walking.

The route for our night-time excursions was to pass New Road and into Turner Street, where between Walden Street and Varden Street, we would enter an alley at the rear of our lodgings, and with a simple manoeuvre onto the upturned barrel, the roof of the water-closet and raising the sash-chord window, we were back in our room. Pip sat on his bed, silently studying the scar on his arm, courtesy of the prostitute at the infirmary, and I continued reading Jekyll and Hyde. "How could a mother do that?" he mumbled quietly. "How could a mother put her own daughter on the streets?" I looked up from my book and sighed. "She won't be the first, Pip, or the last," I said. "The sad thing is, is that girl probably won't live to see her twenty-fifth birthday. If syphilis doesn't kill her first, then she has the brutality of the clients and the pimps to look forward to, and with over eighty thousand prostitutes in London it's extremely difficult to police; it's an age old problem." Pip agreed with a nod. "I hate them!" he snarled. "They're vermin. Do you know in medieval times we drove them out of the city beyond the London wall, and tried to impose laws upon them but without success? They should be driven off the streets." I pondered for a moment, looking down at my book but not reading a word, and then I looked back to Pip. "Do you know the only thing people react to is fear? They should be killed," I said. Pip looked back at me, pensively at first but then he burst out laughing and fell back into his pillows. "You can't kill eighty-thousand prostitutes!" he cackled. I shook my head. "Not all of them, Pip, just enough to scare the others; enough to scare them off the streets."

Alcohol is the thief that steals all reason. Pip and I stayed up all night talking about prostitutes and tried to propose a plausible explanation for their miserable existence, and with every proposal we were confronted with the undeniable truth—there wasn't one. "So, what is your great plan?" Pip asked me. I was reluctant to explain but I sat on the edge of the bed and attempted to outline my theory as best I could. "Do you agree that these women are the scourge of the earth and that they serve no purpose whatsoever being on this planet?" I asked. Pip dropped his stare to the scar on his arm and nodded in agreement. "What would you do with a lame horse, Pip? What would you do with a rabid dog?" I continued. "Put them out of their misery," he stated firmly. "Correct, Pip, correct. So how do we get this scum off our streets?" Pip's glazed eyes began to roam the room and he shrugged his shoulders. I was on my feet and pacing up and down in front of him, as if I were constructing some major strategy that will serve mankind for all eternity. "You've seen the syphilis wards, Pip; you've seen dead bodies and you've assisted with autopsies! Did it bother you when you plunged the scalpel in to a cadaver's torso?" Pip shook his head. "They were already dead," he rebuffed.

Clearly my room-mate was not convinced. We were now ten days into August, and over the last four months we had seen many disturbing cases. We had even witnessed the naked and grotesque form of Joseph Merrick, known as the Elephant Man, who was rescued from a freak show by one of our very own members of staff, Dr. Treaves. Now we considered death in a casual manner; an inevitable event from which no one was exempt. We had walked the morgue where on either side lay the dead and decaying, most infants. And here we were in the greatest empire the world had ever seen and Queen Victoria with all her power continued to ignore the fact that one in five children starved to death before they reached the age of five, while she simply wallowed in her misery for the death of her beloved Albert.

Just three days ago on Bank Holiday Monday, a prostitute called Martha Tabram was found dead in George Yard Buildings; she had been stabbed no less than thirty-nine times and it was unlikely the perpetrator or perpetrators would ever be captured. "Tell me your fears, Pip," I asked him as I sat down before him. "You could be a legend. I could make you a legend," I added. My companion grinned broadly as he stared into my wide eyes. "How?" he asked with a wary tilt of his head. "Metaphorically, how could it be done?" I smiled slyly and lifted my copy of Jekyll and Hyde and handed it to him. "We create a myth, a legend; we create a monster, Pip. We search out our prey and execute them . . ." Pip opened his mouth to interrupt but I held a finger up. "But the executions must be so terrible, so diabolical, so atrocious that they could not possibly be the work of a sane, human-being," I continued. My companion's eyes were locked with mine and then he raised the book. "You're talking about Hyde, aren't you?" he said. "I am, Pip; the allusive monster that myths and legends are made of."

I was grinning broadly when Sylvia entered with my coffee and I closed the book and placed it back in the drawer of my desk. If my subtle reprimand concerning her behaviour had wounded her in any way it certainly wasn't apparent now. "Are you still laughing at me?" she asked as she placed the cup down on the desk. "No. Sorry, Sylvia, I was reading about the exploits of two drunken students with aspirations of creating a bogie man," I said. She laughed and turned to leave. "Sylvia, do you know why Mr. Randall brought us the Henderson case?" I asked inquisitively. She stopped and shook her head. "Not really," she replied thoughtfully. "He just said that as his designated solicitors we were entitled to the option of accepting or declining the case." I stared back blankly and suddenly gasped, "Designated! Why would Henderson designate us?" Sylvia continued walking and looked back over her shoulder. "Perhaps we represented him at one time or another." Suddenly I was struck by a revelation with the same force as a bolt of lightening. Back in the early days we had represented a Mr. Henderson who had been dismissed from the Great Eastern Railway for continuous absence from work, but Henderson was able to furnish good reason with a report from his doctor and verification from his local hospital, and to my recollection the case was settled out of court with a modest sum of money and reinstatement. "Jesus Christ! George Henderson is our client!"

When Joyce Turner put her head around the door she found Sylvia and me rummaging through countless boxes in the storeroom in a quest to find the original Henderson file. As best I could remember it was not long after I set up the company so my estimate was around 1934 or 1935, long before Sylvia or Joyce joined us, but she joined in the search vigorously. "Why the urgency to find a file on something that happened so long ago?" she asked as files passed through her hands like large playing cards. "Because Henderson is our client," I grunted as I lifted another box down from the shelf. "And he's important, is he?" she asked. "The Blackout Butcher," said Sylvia; "killed and raped eight women; you must have read about it." Joyce's mouth fell open and her eyes opened so wide they were in fear of popping out of their sockets. "What!" she shrieked as she snatched her hands back from the box of files. "Can we just keep looking? I'll explain later. Try 1935," I hissed impatiently. It was at that point Badger arrived standing in the doorway in his usual black and white pinstripe and his snowy white hair with a shock of black shot through the temples. Sylvia would always remark that he looked like a negative. "Looks fun," he said as he observed the three of us climbing over one another in the small, cluttered room. Suddenly Sylvia shrieked aloud, "Found it!"

The original file dated back to 1933, and after taking a brief look at it, Badger picked up the file in which contained Henderson's arrest sheet, a dozen or so grisly photographs of the victims in situ and a signed statement taken by the arresting officer Inspector Carlisle, to which George Henderson confessed to all the murders and bore his signature. Badger studied the gruesome photographs for a few moments and then looked at me.

"Why would you want to take this, Michael?" he asked. "Henderson mutilated eight women and walked into the nearest police station and gave himself up. He's guilty as hell. What is there to defend?"

"I thought it may be good for the company," I replied.

"It could also be catastrophic. We are not criminal lawyers. Why would you want to defend a killer who by his own admission is guilty?"

"You agree he'll hang?"

"Undoubtedly!" said Badger emphatically.

I turned the folder on the desk, flipped over to the written statement and pointed to the name of the arresting police officer.

"I read in the newspaper that Inspector Carlisle was suspended," I explained. "At present he's under investigation for perjury and fabricating evidence. We may be able to get Henderson's sentence commuted to life."

Before Badger had a chance to make any reply, a tall gentleman wearing a charcoal grey suit and with a clean complexion entered the office. He was perhaps nearing sixty years of age and slightly balding with grey hair, and looking to the desk and the open file he smiled. "I see you're prepared," he said.

I glanced at Badger and then to Sylvia who was standing in the doorway, who silently mouthed, "Mis-ter Ran-dall."

I shook his hand and motioned him to a seat at my desk and introduced Badger by his correct title Kenneth Banner, and then ordering Sylvia to bring tea we all sat down to address the matter at hand.

"You're familiar with the case?" asked Mr. Randall, taking in Badger and myself alternately.

"Everyone in the western world must be," said Badger with an assertive nod. "He raped and murdered eight women; it isn't something you forget."

Mr. Randall agreed with a faint smile and a fainter nod of his head.

"And Inspector Carlisle?" he asked.

"I know he's corrupt," I said. "He's been under investigation for several weeks."

The official looking gentleman shook his head.

"Not several weeks. Several months," he returned. "Carlisle was something of an icon in the Metropolitan Police Force and had solved many cases, but at the age of forty-nine he had only made it to the rank of inspector. Some attributed this lack of promotion to his arrogance, others to his continuous success with meagre evidence. On information from an associate, who for obvious reasons shall remain nameless, Carlisle was put under surveillance and was found to be receiving pay-offs from the money-lenders and the pimps, though none would swear to it in a court of law in fear of repercussions. In order to gain promotion, which in turn would give greater rewards, he was found to be framing certain suspects by fabricating evidence and perjuring himself in court. The Met. tried to keep it under wraps, but the story was leaked to the press; we think by one of Carlisle's associates who was recently dismissed for accepting bribes."

Badger and I exchanged puzzled glances of which Mr. Randall acknowledged.

"Did you know George Henderson is illiterate?" he asked.

"But he signed his own confession!" Badger stated, tapping the folder with his finger.

"It was something he learned to do; something he had to do. As a train driver he would have to sign for his wages, but he could neither read nor write. Given the situation Carlisle would have had to have read the statement back to Henderson before he signed it, but as both his character and integrity is open to question, it renders the statement inadmissible as evidence; Carlisle could have read back something completely different from what he had written and Henderson would have believed it. What makes the situation more problematic is the evidence accumulated against Henderson; simply there is nothing, and what little there is may well be questioned once Carlisle's conduct comes into question. In the eyes of the law Henderson is an innocent man although, and apparently from his own lips, he's completely guilty."

At that point Sylvia brought in tea on a tray, set it down on the desk and promptly left the room, and while I spooned in sugar for our visiting official, Badger studied the file a little closer.

"Are you saying that despite murdering eight women there is not one single shred of evidence against Henderson?" he asked, looking directly to Mr. Randall.

"Very little," returned the official as he leaned forward and took a cup of tea. "You must understand that this was Carlisle's case from the outset, and not only is the evidence against Henderson circumstantial, it's now completely worthless when set against his dubious conduct."

"No fingerprints, footprints, bruising?" I asked.

"Certainly, there were all the tell-tale signs associated with murder but nothing of any importance. Henderson was a meticulous killer, always wore gloves, but on three occasions bloody footprints were discovered on the floors, but closer scrutiny exposed them to be nothing more than smears.

The only common denominator was woollen fibres found under the fingernails of six of the victims, and from this discovery it was concluded that the killer wore a balaclava, and the few witnesses we have who claim to have seen him before or after a murder make it impossible for a positive identification."

"But wouldn't the wearing of a balaclava single Henderson out as the murderer had he been seen by—as you say—a few witnesses?" suggested Badger.

"Mr. Banner, Henderson's reign was in the middle of winter; the wearing of balaclavas is quite common. Never at any murder scene were any hair fibres found belonging to Henderson . . ."

"Hence the balaclava theory?" I broke in.

"Indeed," replied Mr. Randall with a nod. "After he gave himself up Henderson's house was searched but nothing was discovered; nothing woollen to match the fibres found, no balaclava and no gloves."

"Perhaps some of the victims put up some kind of defence. Wasn't Henderson checked for cuts, bruises, abrasions?"

"Henderson gave himself up five weeks after the last murder occurred; any marks would have disappeared."

"What about semen?" Badger asked. "He raped his victims, right?"

Mr. Randall tilted his head slightly and smiled.

"Despite the grim character the media have painted him to be over the past year, George Henderson is a devoted husband and loving father to five children. He would have never left it to chance of contracting a venereal disease and passing it onto his wife. And had he done so, he would have been that much easier to find. As to his state of his mind, he has undergone psychiatric examinations and has been found to be quite sane. Any defence would have problems proving temporary insanity, especially as the murders happened over a five week period."

Mr. Randall smiled politely, indicating that he had completed his address and slowly sipped at his tea.

"Correct me if I'm wrong, Mr. Randall, but can't Henderson simply give another statement?" my colleague suggested.

"He could but won't," returned the official. "You see, I think when Henderson turned himself in he was consumed by a brief moment of guilt;

he admitted that he didn't want any more to die. And I think it was in his mind to confess and be taken directly to the gallows, and had that been the case I believe he would have gone willingly. But for the past year he has sat in a six by eight cell, probably thinking about his wife and his children, the aftermath of his crimes and how it will affect them once he goes to trial; how they will suffer being the family of a mass murderer. Without doubt the investigation into Carlisle has postponed Henderson's trial, and now he's had time to reconsider; he'll never confess again. Certainly any prosecutor worth his salt could hint at the contents of the original confession, but a defence would have any such reference struck from the record."

Badger, certainly more experienced than myself in the field of criminal law, appeared utterly confused and one could almost hear his mind turning as he tried to make sense of what Mr. Randall had explained. I too was trying to pull together the loose threads of the scenario and, perhaps, managed to do so slightly quicker than Badger.

"So this is total role-reversal!" I said. "Once the prosecution had so much but now has nothing, and the defence has a very good chance of proving a self-confessed murderer innocent . . ."

"I'm confused," Badger interrupted, finding his voice. "Carlisle could not have taken the statement alone; there must have been another officer present; someone who can substantiate Henderson's original statement."

The official's face fell quite still and after a brief moment of turning his eyes from Badger to me and then back to Badger again, I detected a slight cringe beneath his calm exterior.

"I'm guessing that there was another officer in the room," I said. "I'm also guessing that he was the officer accepting bribes and who allegedly leaked the story of Carlisle's guilt to the press."

Mr. Randall reluctantly nodded his head and expressed a feigned smile by way of appreciation for my correct analysis. He said no more on the subject but rose from his seat and placed down his cup and saucer.

"You have a modest law firm, Mr. James, but criminal law is obviously not your forte," he said, looking down on me. "You may wish for a referral, to farm it out to someone more experienced in this field; that choice is yours. Either way you have ten days before Carlisle goes to trial, of which I'm assured will last but a week. Thank you for your hospitality, gentlemen."

He turned to walk to the door.

"Why were we not informed before now?" asked Badger tersely.

Mr. Randall slowly turned and looked down on Badger somewhat indignantly.

"Are you saying you were not aware that Mr. Henderson was your client?" he asked.

I held up the 1933 file as a form of defence but the official continued.

"Obviously you were not aware that Mr. Henderson was the same Mr. Henderson who slaughtered eight women. Why should you? There were never any photographs published, and it was as I explained earlier. When he walked into the police station he had a death wish; he wanted to die for his sins and offered neither a defence nor the name of his solicitors; now he has had a change of heart. I trust you will inform me of your decision."

-4-

The subject simmered throughout the duration of the day, intermittently and calm and sometimes heated to boiling point, and when we closed the office Sylvia, Penny, Badger and I strolled down Fleet Street under a clear blue sky, bobbing and weaving the pedestrian traffic and still debating the intricacies of the case. We convened like a hung jury around Dickens's table with Badger airing his views and offering only negative conclusions, and I, intrigued by its complexities, was at least willing to give it further consideration. For their part the girls simply sat and listened, eyeing up the incoming men with surreptitious glances at one another or foot nudging beneath the table, which at times could be distracting. Penny's sensuality was in direct contrast to Sylvia's; a natural beauty with long, shimmering, chestnut brown hair and green eyes, whose choice of fashion was immaterial as she looked good in anything. Her annoyance was her tendency to raise her hand to her forehead whenever she saw a man that took her fancy; an unconscious reaction to a small scar she apparently received as a child of which she was very self-conscious, and one that induced her to fashion her hair in such a way her fringe obscured it. The office had perhaps unjustly paired Sylvia and Penny together, labelling them as floosies, but I sometimes mused as to whether Penny was influenced by her friend and exchanged the details of her sexual conquests simply to boost her own self-esteem; I seriously doubted if she had undertaken any of the exploits she spoke of.

Despite his expertise as a lawyer and his calm demeanour when undergoing an examination of a witness, Badger could be brutally blunt, especially when two or three brandies had warmed his gullet. A wise man once said to me, '*Never put your name to anything that may fail*' and so with that advice in mind I called my company 'Cross Associates,' and as a present Badger gave to me two cross swords that now take pride and place on the wall behind my desk. It was his humour; a warning to those who dare cross swords with us; an emblem of the cross Jesus carried; cross as a form of anger and cross-examination. That wise man was Badger.

"Don't you find this case intriguing?" I asked. "Doesn't Carlisle's conduct give you food for thought?"

Badger lit a cigarette and disappeared behind a veil of white smoke, and as it dissolved he stared down his slender nose at me, intentionally taking a moment to gain the composure he had lost several times during the day.

"Carlisle is corrupt and probably embellished Henderson's statement to his own ends, but it doesn't detract from the fact that it was Henderson who gave himself up and admitted to all the murders," he said in a patient tone. "There are no less than nine pages of his statement, all of which go into minute detail as to how he executed those murders. Carlisle may have fabricated the statement but he couldn't have choreographed the outcome; to wit, Henderson giving himself up. The bastard should hang!"

"You believe in fairness?"

Badger rolled his eyes and shook his head. "Of course. Hanged, drawn and quartered would be fair."

Obviously he wasn't to be moved and his tenacity and stubbornness sometimes obscured his reasoning.

"Don't you tire of the cases we defend; insurance swindles, petty criminals and fraud? Badger, this is our chance to make an impact; to be something more than we are," I argued.

"You're out of your depth, Michael," he returned tiredly.

"Perhaps I am, but at present we're not moving forward. We're not going anywhere."

My junior partner drew on his cigarette and blew smoke towards the ceiling and looked back at me with a mocking grin. "And you think Henderson is your meal-ticket? You think this killer will bring you notoriety? Michael, Henderson was a train driver with a large family; there are no rewards in fighting this case."

I swallowed the remains of a large scotch and held up my hand to gain the barman's attention and gestured with the other hand a circle around the table; same again.

"The Blackout Butcher is the most notorious killer of this century," I continued, "and his exploits—no matter how ghastly or horrific they are—have captured the imagination of the western world. There isn't a newspaper or magazine that won't be clamouring for the story; it's an open chequebook, Badger."

"So it might me, but some of us have integrity," he rebuffed sharply. "I would imagine that when I die I won't have achieved much. I only know that I wouldn't want the knowledge of freeing a known killer on my conscience until then."

Although Sylvia's eyes relentlessly searched out a new victim—preferably one with tight buttocks—Penny appeared to have given up and was now engrossed in the conversation between Badger and myself.

"Does Sarah know about this?" she asked in her usual husky tone.

Badger's eyes moved slightly towards her as she spoke and his smile broadened.

"I—I've mentioned it," I stumbled with a hapless shrug.

"A-n-d?" she continued, drawing the word out, accompanied by doubting narrowed eyes.

Badger's eyes turned to mine.

"And she doesn't like it. She doesn't want me to take it on," I said.

"You should heed her words," muttered Badger.

The barman signalled that our drinks were waiting and scribbled down the cost on a notepad; an account we paid monthly, and Sylvia and Penny left the table to collect them, though Sylvia had an ulterior motive and moved directly to the first handsome man she saw.

"She wants you, you know that, don't you?" said Badger, leaning forward and dropping his voice to a whisper.

"Sylvia?" I said, turning towards the bar.

"Not Sylvia. Penny, you idiot!"

I looked to Penny at the bar, gathering a large scotch, a large brandy, a white wine and a gin and tonic on a tray and signing the barman's receipt, and I began to laugh.

"And how did you reach that conclusion?" I asked, a little flushed, either through alcohol consumption or embarrassment.

"I've heard her talking. I've seen the way she looks at you. Girls are attracted to successful men and they like the idea of them being successful and married; they regard it as a challenge."

Penny returned and placed the tray on the table, taking up her place next to Badger who expressed a knowing wink at me, and I appraised her for a moment in her emerald green two-piece suit and considered the prospect for the briefest of moments as she busied herself distributing the glasses to the rightful consumer. There had been a change in her since first she joined our firm. Her choice of dress then was conservative and her make-up sparse, but she was deeply influenced by Sylvia, and over the following months her hemlines gradually climbed and her blouses became a little more revealing, but unlike her friend, Penny knew her limitations; how much she could drink before becoming embarrassing; how much she could flirt before endangering herself, and how to conduct herself at all times. I peered into my glass, "No ice," and Badger looked into his; "Me neither." And while I picked up both tumblers and headed off in search of the nearest ice-bucket, Badger swung round, his arm stretched down the back of his seat. "You know he's mad about you, don't you?" he said to her. Penny's head jerked back in surprise. "He talks about you all the time; what he'd like to do to you." Her eyes opened wider and a smile appeared, accompanied by a slight trace of embarrassment induced, no doubt, by flattery, and when I returned I immediately continued the debate on Henderson.

"Listen to me, Kenny, I'm not proposing we take the case, but can we at least look at it?"

Badger swung about to face me and sighed exhaustively.

"What are you working on at the moment?" I continued relentlessly. "To my knowledge you have two cases, both of which will never go to trial and will be settled before the ink dries. I promise you that if you don't think this case worthy, we'll decline it, but I can't go back to the D.P.P. without at least giving it consideration."

Badger sat brooding for a while, sipping his brandy and screwing out his cigarette into the ashtray, and I sat silently awaiting a reply. Suddenly he gulped down his tipple and slowly nodded his head. "You're the boss, Michael," he said in a throaty voice, "but I'll hold you to your word. If I don't like it I'm out. Drink anyone?"

As Badger headed off back to the bar, I smiled with pride. The times I had won him over were few and far between and, in all honesty, his instincts were usually correct, but we had ten days to play with this case and I was willing to go with whatever he decided once the deadline was reached.

"Are you happy now?" asked Penny.

She was looking at me with her piercing green eyes, a clenched fist beneath her chin and a playful smile dancing on her lips.

"I'm a lawyer, Penny; unscrupulous," I returned with a grin. "What more can I say? Liar—Lawyer; sounds the same and means the same."

Penny had been with us barely two years and was recommended by her best friend Sylvia; they had grown up together, went to the same school and, no doubt, shared the same boyfriends, and for a while she worked for a small insurance company but found the work tedious. To be fair she came to us as a clerk, but she proved herself to be more than adequate within the first few months and she was made secretary to Tom Grieves and Andrew Pitt when Joyce was employed as a filing clerk a little over a year ago.

"Do you really consider yourself to be unscrupulous?" she asked.

My smile broadened and I nodded my head. "All lawyers are mercenary bastards, and anyone who tells you different is a liar. We believe we're a law unto ourselves because we invent them, because we're responsible for writing new laws. Our arrogance is renown throughout history. Back in

1668 we took umbrage when Nicolas Barbon, a property developer, bought a piece of land that we now know as Red Lion Square. The lawyers at Gray's Inn were affronted at the prospect of having a housing development practically outside their front door and took Barbon to court. As then, like today, possession and property is nine-tenths of the law and the developer won. Undeterred several hundred lawyers brandishing sticks and clubs ascended on the site when the foundations were being dug and the workmen run for safety; the lawyers filled in the foundations. But Barbon played them at their own game and hired new workmen, which consisted in the main of thugs, and when the lawyers returned they met their match and Red Lion Square was completed. Can you imagine that?"

"Still spouting historical jargon, Michael?" said Badger when he returned. He looked at Penny with a sly grin. "Keep your hand on your ha'penny, sweetheart, that's how he seduces them all, by spouting historical facts."

Penny smiled warmly. "I find it interesting," she said.

Badger passed me another long, suggestive wink.

"I suggest we contact Henderson's wife and workmates at the Great Eastern," I said, chinking my glass with his. "After which we make arrangements to interview Henderson himself in prison."

Badger shook his head wearily. "I can see this turning into the Great Jennings case."

"Who?" asked Penny as she raised her gin and tonic to her lips.

"Oh, my God, no!" sighed Badger, realising he had unwittingly played my stooge and I was about to launch into another historical reference.

"Ever read 'Bleak House' by Dickens, Penny?" I asked smirking at my junior partner's frustrated expression.

Penny shook her head and leaned in a little closer.

"He satirised the Great Jennings case with his own interpretation of the Jarndyce and Jarndyce trial. It was a great legal scandal and only served to highlight the contempt the public have for lawyers—and for good reason. Dickens was only seven years old when the trial began in 1819 and it didn't end until the year he died in 1870 . . ."

"The trial lasted fifty years!" Penny gasped.

"Fifty-one. You see, the lawyers involved didn't want it to end—they were all earning a fortune, so nobody made any real effort to conclude it, and it only reached a conclusion when the money ran out. As I said: all lawyers are unscrupulous."

Sylvia called out to us and waved, and then locking her arm in her newfound companion's disappeared out the door.

Badger swirled the ice around in his remaining brandy. "She should be thankful sex isn't fattening; she'd weigh a ton by now," he said, and then swallowing the contents he looked at his watch and rose to his feet. "Time I was leaving. Besides I don't think I could take anymore history lessons." And with another wink he too left.

It was later than I had anticipated and Penny, who was bound for Southwark, accompanied me to the station which, to my horror was closed, with a chalk board outside boasting the obvious, and maybe a hundred commuters were gathered outside gawping at the static turnstiles beyond the caged shutters as if, by some miracle, the authority that had closed it may have a sudden change of heart. "All the stations are closed," I heard someone say. "Perhaps we're in for another bombing." I cursed under my breath and then cursed louder when I saw the length of the queues waiting at the taxi rank and bus stops. It was reminiscent of last year when I either slept in my office or at the seedy hotel down on the embankment, and as I stood there debating which luxurious surroundings to opt for, Penny made a suggestion. "You can stay with me," she said, timidly. "I mean, if you want to. I can cook you something." I appraised her through bleary eyes, the result of which were several large scotches, and by simply taking a step back, she came into sharper focus. "I promise I won't seduce you," she smiled. I absorbed her beauty for a brief second, the sheen of her hair and her dazzling, green eyes. I would decline her offer. Of course I would. I was happily married and loved my wife passionately, and no matter how arduous or how long the journey was to take, I would make it home. "That's a very kind offer, Penny . . ." I began. "Good!" she interrupted. "Let's go."

We followed the other disgruntled commuters across Blackfriars Bridge, all moving like a raggedy trail of refugees under a fading blue sky shot through with flecks of red, where beyond the skyline the darkness began to rise like a black apparition, and then turning into Southwark Street and down several short roads, we arrived in Union Street before a tall Victorian styled house. It was strange, because we had passed at least three phone-boxes and I never once considered stopping at any to call my wife and tell her that I wouldn't be home. What would I say? "Hello, darling, won't be home tonight because there aren't any trains running. Love you. Oh, and by the way, I'm staying with my secretary." Besides, Sarah and I had a code. If I wasn't home by 9 o'clock, she would phone the station and know the reason why, and she knew that on occasions such as these, I had tried many times to beat the consequences of the war only to end up stranded in Croydon or Clapham. Penny's flat was in the rafters at the very top where three large dormers looked out towards the river, and as we climbed the stairs I asked if there was a Mr. Penny in her life, to which she just laughed. Inside, the flat was surprisingly roomy with a varnished wooden floor exposing the original boards and a scattering of rugs here and there, and reproductions of landscapes hung in the hallway in perfect alignment and all the same size. At its end it opened up into a lounge area where an unused, Victorian fireplace with tiled cheeks centred the room, on which the mantelpiece housed a multitude of ornaments strategically placed into a uniformed order. Around the walls were various side-tables supporting a variation of plants, and a long, leather settee stretched beneath one of the large dormers that met the angled ceiling. "Very nice," I said as I surveyed the room with an approving smile. "Very nice indeed." Penny moved directly to window and pulled down the heavy blind to mask out the light from the outside world, and then unbuttoning her jacket and tossing it on the settee, she moved out of the room. "I'll make tea . . . Or would you prefer coffee? You've had a lot to drink," she said.

I heard her clattering around in the kitchen while I sat on the settee surveying the room, and on one of the tables sat a wireless which I was tempted to turn on, if only to find out why I was sitting in my secretary's flat and not in my own home. The walk had cleared my woozy condition and both my mind and my eyes were clear, or as clear as I could hope for, and I found myself sitting on the edge of my seat—to the point of slipping off—until I could view the hallway in its entirety, counting the doors of each room and wondering which represented what. It was my attempt to establish whether it was a one or two bedroom flat and was curious, if not a little anxious, to know where I would be sleeping tonight. I straightened the moment Penny came back and handed me a mug of black coffee, to which I stared into with disapproval, due to its lack of colour and obvious absence of milk. “Well, there’s a war on,” I said. Penny sat herself at the end of the settee, a mug of coffee on her lap that was considerably lighter in colour than mine. “I have milk, pasteurised and powdered, but that will do you good.” I took a short sip and visibly grimaced at the taste that bordered on toxic. “It will?” I shuddered. She laughed at my show of discomfort and nodded her head. “You need to have a clear head tomorrow,” she said. She was referring to ‘Henderson’ that, quite frankly, was already beginning to trouble me and one, for that day at least, I was tiring of speaking about, and before I had a chance to give a reply, the lights flashed three or four times—a signal from the power station—and I looked at her for an explanation. “I’ll get the candles,” she said as she hurriedly left the room.

In less than a minute the room plunged into total blackness, but a pathetic, yellow light emerged in the hallway and grew brighter as it closed on me, and Penny set down two candles on two of the side-tables and returned to the kitchen for more. I helped, placing candles on saucers, hot wax acting as adhesive to stabilize them, and in no time no less than two dozen tiny beacons decorated the apartment, throwing frightening shadows across the ceiling that were also somehow romantic. It was reminiscent of my father’s descriptions, before electricity was reserved only for industry and government buildings and not yet distributed amongst the people. “Do you think we’ll win?” asked Penny as she resumed her seat at the end of the settee, accepting the situation with complete normality. “The Henderson case?” I returned. “The war,” she said. She was sitting quite still, the candlelight dancing upon the shine of her hair, and her eyes turned towards the ceiling, as though awaiting a mass of bombers to pass overhead at any moment. While I spent my summer evenings sitting in the garden or drinking warm beer at the local, she sat alone in the epicentre of Germany’s prize, debating her future and whether she still had one. “I know only this, Penny,” I began. “Britain will never give in to tyranny and neither will Churchill. You have to remember that we are Hitler’s nemesis, the greatest, fighting nation the world has ever known. We’ll never throw our hands up in the air and surrender, and he knows it. For what it's worth, you will never see a German walking the streets of London during wartime; simply we shall wipe them from the globe. As sure as God we will win." To my shame I was reciting someone else's words, an authority I had heard on the radio, and though it wasn't word for word or as passionate, it had a modicum effect, for she nodded and a smile glowed through the dull light.

In the bleakness she told me of the many houses and factories that had been bombed close by and when, during the blitz, she saw the bombers following the route of the Thames, spewing out their loads onto the city beneath until it was just a mass of fire. "That was when I was most frightened," she explained. "I ran to Southwark Underground and stayed there all night with the thousands of others. When we emerged in the morning nothing looked the same—fires and devastation everywhere. When I got home I immediately looked out of the window, and through the smoke I could see the dome of St. Paul's still in tact, but the rest of London looked so sad, so broken." And for the next two hours she continued to tell me about her friends and her family who lived in Putney, who had remarkably escaped after their street took a direct hit, and of her father who was a fire-watcher as well as working for the council and her mother who was a midwife. It occurred to me then that I had spoken to her more in the last two hours than I had since I employed her. There is something about tranquil surroundings that makes people open up and divulge their most treasured secrets or their most terrifying fears, when the demons and angels come out to play and hide amongst the shadows and cause the flames of the candles to flicker, and it was in a moment when the conversation had trailed into a long silence, that we simply sat staring at one another as if we could read each others minds.

Bright light brings with it reality; like the cold light of day after a night on the tiles, and whatever moment is created in the comfortable confines of the shadows, it is lost to nostalgia—sometimes for forever; the lights blinked repeatedly and suddenly found their full potential, illuminating the flat completely, consigning the soft greys and pastel shades back to their own world. And in that artificial brightness and almost clinical surroundings, the cosy warmth that had enveloped us was indeed gone.

"False alarm," said Penny as she blew out the candle next to her. As she gathered up the others and headed off to the kitchen I smiled to myself and murmured, "Was she referring to me or the electricity?" I listened to the noises coming from the kitchen and suddenly she put her head around the door. "I'm going to have a bath why I have the chance," she said. "Chance?" I shouted, though she had disappeared completely. "In case the electricity goes off again." A door closed and I heard the muffled sound of running water.

When she reappeared some fifteen minutes later she looked entirely different, devoid of make-up that only served to enhance her natural beauty, her hair coiled up shabbily on top of her head and wearing a red satin dressing gown that reached to the floor and only slightly revealed the shallow cleavage of her breasts. During the time I had been with her I hadn't felt the slightest pangs of guilt or regret but now, seeing her in her own environment and out of uniform, so to speak, I was suddenly consumed by doubt but tried desperately to hide it. "You like casserole, Michael?" she asked as she moved to the wireless and turned it on. The music was classical, soft and quiet and deserved a better form of expression than that of a crackling, hissing wireless, and as she took her place at the end of the settee I replied, "Casserole would be fine." After a while of listening to the music, sporadically marked by a narrative on gardening that annoyingly drifted in and out from a neighbouring station, I turned to her. "I hope I'm not being too much trouble. I'm sure you have better things to do."

"Don't worry, Michael," she said reassuringly. "I have nothing better to do, at least not tonight. If you want to take a bath, help yourself; there should be enough hot water."

I told her I would make do with a wash and moved straight to the bathroom as she headed off to the kitchen, and stooped over a washbasin I studied myself in the mirror of the bathroom cabinet. A shave would have to wait until tomorrow. The bottom drawer of my filing cabinet was reserved for such emergencies, a razor, soap, toothbrush, two shirts and even an assortment of underwear, but tonight I would have to make do with the bare necessities. As I gazed at my reflection in the mirror I was reassured that any concerns I had regarding Penny were unfounded and were little more than the result of my own misinterpretation of the situation. There was a war on, and she was simply helping her boss. "So why hadn't she in the past?" I thought.

We sat and ate the casserole on our laps and talked about various subjects, mainly work, and when she took my plate she pointed to the door in the hallway, the first nearest the lounge, and said, "Your room is there. Anytime you want to go to bed, just go. I'll finish the washing up." I offered to help but she refused and vanished into the kitchen. The bedroom was nice, tastefully decorated as I would expect from someone as particular as Penny, and I was relieved that her spare room had a double-bed and not a single; a claustrophobic contraption I had not slept in since I was a teenager and had no desire to now. When I turned the light off the room plunged into a black abyss, the blackout screens shutting out what meagre light existed outside, and I lay there looking at the thin ribbon of light that marked the threshold of the bedroom door until sleep consumed me. Exactly how long I had been asleep I can't begin to fathom, perhaps minutes, maybe hours, but either way I was awakened by the sense of warmth next to me, and I could hear faint breathing. "Penny?" I whispered. I moved my hand slightly and touched warm skin and pulled it back immediately. "Penny, is that you?" She lay quite still and silent for a while, and in the darkness she said, "Of course it's me. Where else would I sleep?" I sat bolt upright. "This isn't a spare room?" I said. I heard her laugh quietly, as if she had put her hand over her mouth or buried her face in the pillow. "I only have one room, Michael. Go back to sleep," she said. I began to experience a mild form of panic, something I can only describe as a comfortable fear, like a first kiss or your first clumsy attempt at undoing a brazier, that for all your hard-earned attempts you may as well be wearing boxing gloves, and like all women who are either blessed or cursed with that sixth sense, she began to laugh again. "Don't worry, Michael. I said I wouldn't seduce you," she said, and within thirty seconds she added, "But I didn't say you couldn't seduce me."

I arrived at the office early. Guilt infested me like a disease, preventing me from falling into a deep sleep, and no sooner had daylight seeped through the edges of the blackout screen, I gathered up my clothes and left the apartment as quick as I could. I'm sure Penny was awake as I attempted to execute my plan quietly, only to end up making more noise than the Luftwaffe, but either way she never said a word. I washed and shaved at the office and sat at my desk with my head in my hands, vowing that such an occurrence would never happen again, and dispensing with the Henderson case or any other come to that, I took my father's book from the drawer and opened it.

Pip and I had spent many hours discussing and, indeed, inventing our mythical creature, and after concocting a multitude of images, designed to strike terror into the bravest of hearts, we made a decision that it should not look like anything at all; it should be invisible. "There is nothing scarier than an assailant that can't be seen," I said to Pip as we walked a long corridor in the hospital. "That isn't to say that it shouldn't have an image. First and foremost its role should be specific; the slayer of streetwalkers," I added thoughtfully. Pip agreed with a nod and looked at me. "How do you perceive our myth to be?" he asked. I slowed to a stop, looking on my companion with a pensive refrain, and in a moment a hundred ghoulish pictures passed through my mind of pale-faced, boggle-eyed madmen; of debonair prince's with bloodstained lips; even hairy monsters with gnashing teeth. I put my arm around his shoulder and strolled onward. "I see him as the silent but deadly type," I said. "He should neither be man nor beast, devoid of identity; a faceless avenger similar to the Grim Reaper; cloaked and hooded with no visible part of the anatomy showing to give the slightest clue as to what lies beneath his dark shroud; the ruffled sleeve concealing the hand that holds the weapon of execution." Pip nodded enthusiastically and held up a single finger. "We could call him the Grim Ripper," he suggested with an element of pride. I shook my head. "An interesting play on words, young Pip, and not without further consideration, but I think we might be infringing somewhat on the copyright laws."

It was on one of our Friday night jaunts into Spitalfields—one of many Pip and I had undergone since April, unobserved by our drunken and fornicating landlady—that while drinking in the Ten Bells, I came up with the name of 'Jack' as a form of identity for our creation; it was, after all, a legendary name; Spring-Heeled Jack and Jack Sheppard to name but two, and I thought it apt as 'Jack' was such an obscure title and could be used as an alternative for 'John' and was so often used to address a total stranger; as a name it had no fixed identity. Pip was not completely convinced and asked why our myth had to have a name at all. "It has to have a name, Pip," I explained. "If we are to execute our quest to the full then blame must be assigned to someone or—in our case—something else." My roommate sipped on his ale and looked at me quizzically. "And how do we do that without drawing attention to ourselves?" he enquired. "We do it with whispers, Pip. We do it with rumour," I said, quietly. "In shops, in hallways, in the streets and in pubs, whenever someone talks of the murder we can say 'Jack was responsible'. That's how myths are created, Pip, whispers and rumour." My companion pursed his lips and stared intently back at me and then, with a rapid shake of his head, he said, "It isn't enough! 'Jack' isn't a scary name." After a moment's consideration I had to agree and we both pondered on the subject for a while. 'Jack the whore Avenger' he suddenly suggested. I turned my nose up immediately. "Too theatrical, Pip. Too concise," I returned. A few names came to mind but none worth a mention, and had I done so, I'm certain my young friend would have howled with laughter, but then Pip said quite casually, "If our myth is to have the image of the Grim Reaper, why not call it 'Jack the Reaper'? Suddenly a name evolved befitting our Genesis. "Not Reaper, Pip!" I said, excitedly. "Ripper! Jack the Ripper!"

During the next week we spoke of little else, planning our executions with military precision, but I was never certain, and I'm sure Pip felt the same, that either one of us were actually prepared to go through with it. We constantly questioned one another as to which of us would carry out the first murder and we made a decision that it should be a joint effort, and thereafter we would act as one another's lookout. My doubts towards Pip's loyalty concerning our new-found experiment were laid to rest when he returned back to our room one night and, as always, unpacked his medical reference journals and laid them out on the bed in the order he planned to read them, and that accomplished he pulled out a broad-back knife of six inches long with a sturdy handle from his leather bag and gently laid it on the candlewick bedspread. "Tell me you don't plan to pick your toenails with that," I said, gazing upon the weapon. Pip sat cross-legged on the bed and opened his first textbook; the desired point of reference carefully identified with a bookmark. "It's our weapon of execution," he said as he casually surveyed the passage he was about to read. "I purchased it from a knife-grinder touting his business in Newark Street. As soon as I saw it I knew it was the perfect choice," he added. I gently picked it up between my index fingers, from point to the handle's end. "My dear deluded child, we are about to embark on the killing of whores, not Rhinos," I said as I considered its overall length. "I will not leave to chance survival," Pip returned as he continued to study. "Do you know how murderers are captured, Willy?" As much as the name 'Willy' made the hairs on the back of my neck stand up on end, I shook my head. Pip looked over the top of his book. "Survivors!" he said. "Unless you are caught in the act red-handed or your partner-in-crime turns tail on you, there's no possible way you can get caught, unless, of course, you leave . . ." He waited anxiously for the answer. "Survivors," I said. My roommate nodded conclusively and continued to read.

And so, it was on the following Thursday, August 30th, when Pip and I was 'Slumming it' that our first victim fell foul to our creation; we were to discover later that her name was Polly Nichols. Pip and I had not left the hospital until 8 o'clock that evening and were both enthralled that we were not expected back until Saturday, and such nights were reserved for our excursions, but first we would have to go through the usual procedure and return to our digs where we would sit in the front parlour, a make-shift dining room, and await whatever culinary delights our landlady may have cooked up. Mrs. Steere had not warmed to me in close on five months and treated me with utter contempt whenever I expressed my dislike for either her cooking or her overall appearance, but she had a place in her heart for Pip, though I often mused whether she had one at all. On this evening she breezed into the room carrying a tray, her face made—up like a Geisha girl and humming a tune that nobody could recognise but her, and it was whenever she appeared and acted this way that we knew that a certain gent—a councillor from the local town hall—was due to pay her a visit. She put our plates before us and said with great pride, "There you are gents, steak and kidney pie." Pip smiled up at her while I poked and prodded the so-called dish disapprovingly with my fork. "You're familiar with the name Sweeney Todd, are you, Mrs. Steere?" I asked. She was not to be provoked, not tonight if Mr. Caplin from the Sewage and Water Department was about call. "Is this actually dead? I wondered because we viewed something very similar to this floating in a bucket in the morgue not an hour ago, didn't we, Pip?" I said. She had taken up a stance reserved for those she wanted to devour; weight resting on one leg, arms folded tightly across those sagging breasts and a stare Medusa herself would have been proud of. "Then go hungry," she replied through clenched teeth that framed a forced smile. She stood for a moment and once she realised she had won tonight's battle, she about turned and left the room.

To be honest Mrs. Steere was actually a very good cook and an excellent housekeeper, but I could not help but tease her at every opportune moment, and her dislike towards me ensured she never—if ever—ventured near our room when we were there. At 9.30 sharp we heard the familiar knock on the door and cracked the bedroom door open to see Mr. Caplin with his withered bunch of flowers and bag full of cheap alcohol standing on the front door step. Mrs. Steere led him directly down the passage to the back parlour and I placed on my jacket and opened the window. "Come, Pip, let us go and fraternize with the locals." Pip gently eased the door closed and went to his bed where he lifted the mattress and pulled out the knife from its hiding place. I was midway out of the window, one leg in and one leg out, and my eyes locked with his and I uttered in all seriousness, "Are you sure you want to do this?" Pip's face never flinched; I can't even recall whether he blinked in that long moment, but eventually he slowly nodded. Until now they had just been words and invention but our illusion was now complete; it even had a name, and now Pip looked on me as the creator and expected to see our creation come to life. I admit to being apprehensive, perhaps a little frightened, but over the past five months I had led this young man to a particular moment and had little alternative but to play my part, if only to save face. He placed the knife inside his jacket pocket but was forced to pierce the lining to conceal the handle, and gingerly he approached and climbed out onto the water-closet roof with me.

We visited our usual haunts up Commercial Street and finally ended up in The Sugar Loaf on the corner of Hanbury Street, a superior public house in comparison, frequented by West End toffs as well as the East End poor, who come to listen to the many musical acts. The bar was smoky and noisy but the atmosphere contagious and Pip and I drank heartily and joined in conversations with practically everyone there. And it was while I stood at the bar, engaged in casual banter with my roommate, that I was tapped on the shoulder and a voice said, 'doctor?' The face was familiar, female, young and reasonably pretty, and I remembered it was the young prostitute I had encountered on our first excursion. "Mary Jane!" I said. She eyed Pip up and down with a menacing leer and a sparkle in her eyes and then turned back to me. "On your own tonight?" I enquired as I raised my glass. "Joe is drinking with a friend in the Ten Bells," she explained. "He will join me soon. He gets very jealous, you know." Pip's animosity towards her was obvious and alcohol had exaggerated his condition tenfold, for he leaned on the bar and simply sneered at her to which, acknowledging his hostility, she laughed aloud. "Your friend doesn't like me," she said. I put my arm around my companion's shoulder. "My friend was once cruelly and unjustly set upon by a woman of your ilk. You must not take it personally, madam," I explained. "Ilk?" she questioned, her mood changing in a trice. "A woman of your reputable profession," I replied, informatively. Her mood lightened again as quickly as it had vanished and she took my arm and led me away from the bar. "Have you money?" she enquired, leaning into me and whispering suggestively in my ear. She was steering me towards the door but I stopped and looked back at Pip who was staring back disapprovingly. "Vast amounts but not on my person, and not one penny of it would I invest in that rat infested, scabby hole that we doctors refer to as a vagina, madam." Her response was not only to spit in my face but slap it as well, much to the amusement of everyone gathered around us, and she promptly vanished.

I suggested to Pip it was best we make a swift getaway, both to save me from further humiliation and the possibility that Mary Jane may return with Joe and crush my scull to dust. It was already late and we walked down Hanbury Street, and the pair of us were worse for ware, and it was on the corner of Baker's Row that I stopped and was looking at a prostitute standing beneath a street light on the corner of Thomas Street. "What about her?" I hissed to my friend. Pip found it difficult to focus. Indeed, he found it difficult to stand, but he gazed up the street through squinted eyes to her lone figure. "We can't just do it," he slurred. "We need strafflegy . . . stratmony." I eased him back into the shadows until he was enveloped in total darkness. "The word you're looking for is 'Strategy,' Pip, and I entirely agree. Furthermore I can't take you back in this condition. You'll probably fall off the roof of the water-closet and break your neck." A brisk walk would do us both good, and we strolled off—somewhat unsteadily—down Old Montague Street and into Wentworth Street. Pip was feeling decidedly ill and vomited into a dustbin in Goulston Street, where after I sat him down on a doorstep. "It's an acquired taste," I said, patting him on the shoulder. My roommate shook his head that was slowly sinking between his knees. "What is?" he burbled. "Bitter." I returned. "Not everyone's constitution can withstand its potency. You, Pip, are obviously one of them." He mumbled an incoherent sentence and slumped against the doorframe, falling into a state of unconsciousness.

Fortunately for us Goulston Street was not renowned for its nightlife. It was an inconsequential road of narrow terraces, warehouses and apartments, which by day was a hive of activity owing to its cloth market, and by night a storage place for the many mobile stalls chained together ready for the next day's business. While Pip dozed, twitched and dribbled on the step, I leaned against the wall, focussed on a prick-pincher a little way down the road, bent over a packing-case while a shadowy figure thrashed away behind her with all the precision-timing of a steam engine whilst murmuring terms of endearment in a Russian dialect. I allowed my room-mate his time in the arms of Morpheus until I spied the unmistakable figure of a policeman loitering on the corner of Whitechapel High Street, and then I shook him awake. My initial concern was should my intoxicated friend's condition attract any unwanted attention, we would have much to explain to the hospital governors. "Look lively, young Pip. Time we were gone." I manhandled him back down the route we had taken, constantly stopping, and by the time we had reached Baker's Row, he had sobered up considerably. "What time is it, anyway?" he asked as we emerged on the Whitechapel Road. "A little after 3.15," I said, registering my pocket watch under the corner streetlamp. "No matter, we can sleep in late tomorrow."

It was then we saw her, sauntering up the high street towards us some fifty yards away, illuminated as she passed under the lamps and disappearing again into the darkness, her steps unsure and wandering. Instinctively Pip and I looked at each other. "Well, Pip, is it time to bring our creation to life?" He looked back in the same direction, until she emerged again under the next streetlamp, closing nearer. "She's drunk," he said, turning back to me. "But still a whore, nevertheless," I returned. "You lose yourself in the shadows and I'll engage her in conversation. I'll lead her to a nearby street. Stay close, and when the time is right stab her." Pip shook his head. "Changed your mind?" I asked. He looked back at her and then to me, and drawing a deep breath, nodded his head and receded into the shadows. She was smaller than I expected, 5 feet, two inches, with greying hair and almost childlike features, and she smiled the moment she saw me, which I found to be quite disconcerting as her two front teeth were missing. "A fine morning, ma'am," I said. "And what brings you up and around so early?" She slowly veered towards me. "I could ask you the same thing," she said, stopping before me. By the light of the streetlamp I could see she had grey eyes and her age to be about forty. "Madam, I am a doctor just off duty," I said pointing towards the London Hospital. "And after a hard day I seek companionship." She was obviously drunk and appraised me for some time, while I searched the streets for any onlookers. There were a few figures milling around outside the hospital, far enough away, but I spied no one else in the vicinity. Feeling the time was right and in an effort to coax her from the main road, I dipped my hand into my trousers pocket. "I have a pretty sixpence to spend," I said, holding it before her. It was enough to convince her that my intentions were honourable, and putting my arm around her shoulder, I led her back into Baker's Row.

There is a smell only whores emit—a stench of dirt, filth and of copulation. It oozes from every worthless pore of their skin and is a stark reminder of what they represent both to womanhood and mankind. And there's no whore so worthless as a drunken whore who expels the odour of rancid food and cheap gin with every breath she exhales, and their every clumsy act of sultriness is designed to entrap and prey on the weakness of man. Sex is a form of currency and, to some degrees, a form of revenge; the only power they possess, that for a moment rewards them with the equality they desire; that they believe they deserve. She was wavering and if she told me once about her new bonnet she told me a hundred times, and as she spoke I was constantly on the lookout for anyone approaching, for any face at a window, or a policeman walking his beat; I saw no one. We turned into Buck's Row, a bleak narrow lane, and I constantly looked behind me to see if Pip was following. "Something wrong, dear?" she asked. I feigned a confident grin that she probably couldn't see given the deficit of light. "Not at all, ma'am, but one has to be careful. I am a doctor, after all." Suddenly, from the corner of my eye, I saw something move in the shadows a little in front of me. I was impressed by Pip's cunning, that he was not following from behind but from the front, and reassured that my friend was there, I stopped the woman before a stable entrance and she leaned her back against the gates. "Here?" she asked. "Here would be fine. Turn around,"

I said. No sooner had she turned than I clasped my hand around her mouth and nose, pulling her head back and lifting her body off the ground, her hands and legs flaying around in a desperate attempt to break free, and the breath I drew when first I grabbed her was the same breath I exhaled when all her fight abandoned her and she hung lifeless in my arms.

Pip suddenly emerged from the shadows, like a ghostly apparition, his eyes wide and staring, his face shiny with sweat, induced by fear that had not yet developed into droplets. I released my grip and let the limp body fall to the floor. Despite all my exertion and all the effort that left me breathless, I felt remarkably calm. "No survivor's, Pip!" I said. He nodded, drew his knife and sunk from my line of sight. When I looked down he was straightening her body out, like a morgue attendant might do, and I stooped, picking the feather from her bonnet and slowly ambled a short distance away, leaning up against the wall of the Board School located in the centre of Buck's Row, surveying it with great interest while Pip set about silencing her forever. The next few minutes passed quickly and I can only recall looking over at my companion once, knelt beside the body, his back to me, the dull streetlamp rendering him practically invisible. And then he was before me again, like a returning dog that had been thrown a stick, staring at his master for approval. "Are we done?" I asked as I continued to appraise the feather. Pip nodded assertively, his expression stern and serious. "Then let us retire," I said. "We shall sleep in late and in the afternoon read of our exploits."

We moved from the bleakness of Buck's Row into the well-lighted thoroughfare of Whitechapel High Street, and standing beneath a street lamp was a shadowy figure of a small woman. I appraised her briefly as we passed, poorly dressed and probably drunk, giving the impression of a vagrant. She mumbled something incoherent, and while Pip and I waited at the roadside for a dray to pass by she began to close on us, and in moments her face was so close to ours I could feel her rancid breath on my face. Pip's nervousness, combined with his adrenalin almost compelled him to run in front of the oncoming dray if only to escape the inquisitive woman, but I held him fast by his arm and faced her sternly. "Be good enough to go about your business, madam. Have you no home to go to?" I growled. The dray passed and Pip lurched forward. On the other side of the road I turned but the woman had disappeared into the night. "She's seen us, she's seen us," said Pip as he walked speedily to our destination. "Pay her no mind." I replied, calmly. "She's just a drunk; probably won't remember anything when she wakes up."

The next morning I was back. I had slept soundly enough but awoke at 9 o'clock and leaving young Pip beneath his pile of blankets, left the house and headed straight up New Road to Whitechapel Road. I could see many people gathered in Baker's Row and strolled brazenly onward until I was amongst them, and in Buck's Row the crowd was denser, but I pushed my way through until I reached a thin line of policemen strung across the cobbled street like a human rampart. The body had gone from outside the gates and for a brief moment I considered the possibility that Pip had not done his job to the full and the whore had simply got up and walked to the nearest police station. "Whatever has happened here, officer?" I asked a young policeman who was part of the human chain." "A woman killed last night. Nothing for you to see. Be on your way and clear the street," he demanded. I expressed a concerned expression. "If only I could, sir, but I come to visit my aunt who lives in this very street," I explained. "Not today!" he snarled back at me. "Off with you and let us do our job." I backed away from the cordon and surveyed the street that looked very different in daylight than it did but a few hours ago. Its appearance was unpleasant, grimy, and the two-storey terraces had long-ago forsaken their state of disrepair and were now moving swiftly on to a state of decay; the once red brick facades now black, the windows screened with a heavy veneer of city grime. The surrounding warehouses and factories were very much in the same condition, dilapidated but still functioning as businesses, and the people gathered in the streets were very much like them; downtrodden and filthy.

Constables appeared to be outside every door interviewing the occupants who, when asked if they had seen or heard anything, simply shook their heads. The stables, warehouses and factories had been turned out; their employees standing in the street accounting for their whereabouts in the early hours, and the insides and outsides were being searched for any clues as to who the killer may be. I sidled up to a young reporter ambitiously jotting down notes in his notepad. "Do you know what happened to the poor woman?" I asked him. He shrugged his shoulders and continued to write. "Cut to pieces, by all accounts," he explained. "No one saw or a heard a thing. She was just a prossy and probably had it coming, much like that Martha Tabram at the beginning of the month. It's my guess they're connected in some way, you know, both cut up. I reckon it's probably a pimp doing it, that or the money-lenders." I complimented him immediately and patted him on the shoulder. "How remarkably astute of you. Perhaps you should inform the police of your thoughts." He closed his notepad and took on a confident refrain. "I like to help the police whenever I can," he said. I smiled and bade him farewell, grinning broadly as I walked back through the crowd, and at the end of Buck's Row I turned and looked back at the busy policemen. "Idiots!"

It was then I saw her, the same vagrant woman who stepped out from beneath the streetlamp last night. Now she was standing on the corner of Baker's Row, apart from the throng gathered in Buck's Row, observing the activity with great interest, and as I emerged from the crowd her eyes fixed to me, and as I moved so her head slowly turned in my direction. I stopped in the exact same spot on the high street, waiting to cross the road and could feel her eyes burning into the back of me. I wouldn't turn around. I mustn't turn around. I walked across the road, purposefully ambling on the other side, giving the impression there was no urgency in my mission and certainly no reason to make a hasty retreat. She was a drunk, a whore; she knew nothing.

I slammed the book shut and jumped from my seat simultaneously, staring at it in absolute horror. I can't remember if I stopped breathing just then, but if I did it was only my body's natural instinct for survival that started my lungs moving again. My heart beat fast and heavy as if it were about to burst. Had I really read what I had? Had I just discovered the identity of Jack the Ripper—my own father? I moved without purpose, pivoting in no particular direction, out into the reception and then to Sylvia's office and then back into my own, still staring at the leather-bound book. "Fuck!" I cursed. "Fuck, fuck, fuck, fuck!" I was consumed entirely, my mind racing to no specific conclusion or opinion, and then a voice spoke. "Michael?" I was just staring at the book, waiting for it to come to life, waiting for it to do something. "Michael, are you all right?" The book just lay there, appearing like an innocent, inanimate object, but its contents had a totally different meaning. A hand touched my shoulder and startled me to such a degree I actually screamed. "Michael, whatever is up with you?" said Sylvia.

"Nothing! Nothing is up with me. What should be up with me?

"I don't know, but you look . . . Well, you look like . . ."

"I look like what, Sylvia? How do I look?" I asked impatiently.

"Shit. I was going to say you look like shit. What's happened?"

I sat in my chair, trying to regain some composure and shook my head.

"Have you seen that girl again?" she asked suspiciously and planting her hands on her hips.

"Girl? What girl?"

"Miss Bookmark; the one who fills your head with lewd thoughts."

"No, Sylvia. Could you get me a strong coffee?"

My stare was enough to let her know I was in no mood for talking, and with a toss of her head and a weary sigh she left the room.

I quickly swept the book up and slammed it in the desk drawer, and as I sat pensively considering my father's confession, Tom Grieves and Andrew Turner suddenly appeared.

"Our case is in trouble," Andrew explained.

"What case?"

"The Driscoll case; the one we've been working on for three weeks."

"Ah, yes, the Driscoll case," I said, collecting my thoughts. "What kind of trouble?"

"The prosecution has conjured up two key witnesses out of thin air without notifying us. The rumour is that their evidence will swing the case in their favour."

"But till now we were ahead of the game?"

"Certainly," interposed Tom. "We were hoping to close it today but it could drag on for another two weeks."

"Demand a deferral and find out exactly what these two witnesses know."

"Prosecution would object to the suggestion of a deferral; the witnesses would be considered as rebuttal witnesses and the judge will allow it."

"Then, gentlemen, your case is not in trouble; you just never saw it coming. Your only option is to discredit them. Who's first in the chair?"

"I am," said Andrew.

"Then go fishing, Andy. Hook them and slowly reel them in. And you, Tom, prepare the next onslaught of questions while the prosecution carries out his examination; predict what these two witnesses know; the prosecution may inadvertently help you if you play it right. Other than that you're on your own."

My answer was the best I could give, given the circumstances, and I pulled the Henderson file in front of me and pretended to read it. I was hoping they would leave me with my thoughts but they remained silent just within the doorway.

"Are you still here?" I said, abruptly. "You've just finished telling me that you're on the verge of losing an important case, and you're standing here like a couple of shop mannequins."

They disappeared at once only to be replaced by Sylvia with my coffee. I rolled my eyes to the ceiling.

"I heard the trains weren't running again last night," she said. "Why did you sleep here and not your usual hotel?"

"And who said I slept here?" I sighed wearily.

"Whiskers and shaving soap left in the basin."

I took my coffee and expressed a shallow smile. Somewhere between closing my father's book and now, I reached the conclusion that the confession was a facetious joke, a student's prank, and tried desperately to push it to the back of mind. But then I saw Penny descending the staircase through the open office door and a whole new set of problems occupied my mind. Not six hours ago she was writhing beneath me, and now all I wanted was to do was turn back the clock, to sleep in my office or the seedy hotel on the embankment. "Morning, Michael," she said as she passed the door. I gave no reply and Sylvia stared scornfully back at me. "Penny said good morning," she said. "Didn't you hear?"

"Did she?" I shrugged haplessly. "I need everything you can find on George Henderson; newspaper reports, magazines, anything that bares his name, no matter how insignificant you consider it to be."

"You're taking the case on?" she gasped.

"Just looking at present, Sylvia. Can you do that without bombarding me with a million questions?"

"Wouldn't Penny be a better choice? I'm busy."

"Penny is secretary to Andrew and Tom, and the Driscoll case shows all the signs of falling apart; she's needed," I sighed heavily. "You, however, are my secretary, which in layman terms means I tell you what to do. Added to which is the fact that I actually own this company, making me the employer and you the employee. For reasons that escape me at this moment, I pay you a weekly wage. So, to summarize, Sylvia, I am not asking you—I'm telling you. Find everything on Henderson and find it quick."

-5-

The concourse at London Bridge Station bustled with people. Men both in army and navy uniforms crowded by the turnstiles, saying their goodbyes to loved ones, to tearful young ladies and inconsolable mothers, to proud fathers and grieving sisters. How dashing they looked clad in their standard-issue regimentals and their kaki knapsacks bearing their names, the adventure ahead akin to a ripping yarn straight out of a Boy's Adventure magazine; a fantasy played out in every mind that could never become reality. Yet here they were—hundreds of young men destined for Europe, uncertain of the future or the consequences of war. But the women knew it, and while the fathers swelled with parental pride for their son or sons bravery and loyalty to our great nation, the mothers' eyes filled with pain and regret in knowing that this time was probably the last they would behold them. Coastal-bound steel locomotives sat anxiously between platforms hissing out jets of white steam from their wheels, while the black, sooty smoke bellowing from their stacks swirled and rolled between the overhead gantries and beneath the confines of the station canopy. It was a sight to be seen daily—as the government's recruitment regime gathered momentum and any young man capable of shouldering arms was either willingly or unwillingly enlisted. Ear-piercing whistles shrilled out a fanfare to herald the exodus and mothers hugged their babies for one last time; fathers turned away to hide their grief, but all watched with a mutual sadness as their brave boys were herded through the turnstiles and consumed by the iron monsters that would spirit them away to an unknown destiny. It was surreal. In the shortest of time the concourse and platforms were empty save for a handful of doleful families unsure of what they should do, but still the trains rolled in.

These expressions of loss and hope had become a source of boredom for the enterprising man seated with his female companion on the bench by the ticket office. He had witnessed it at Charing Cross and King's Cross Station, at St. Pancras and Victoria, and no matter how poignant or woebegone the situation was, nothing moved him; his was a different agenda. His colleague, a raven haired beauty of a friendly disposition was, in fact his accomplice—a confederate who excelled in the art of befriending and gaining the trust of anyone she came in contact with. She was thirty-two but blessed with a Chameleon-like character, capable of appearing younger depending on the application of make-up, proficient in adapting to those around her, suited to all environments; a nocturnal creature and so-called club hostess—or what the Yanks belittlingly referred to as a dime-a-dance broad. Her purpose was clear—to ensnare the innocent. She had all the appropriate credentials—a fully-fledged member of the Red Cross Organisation, as well as the addresses and personnel appertaining to the YMCA's across the city. Tonight her name would be Veronica, tomorrow something different entirely, but in reality she was a 'Taker', one of many who worked throughout the metropolis specifically targeting young women. Runaways were a prime choice; those who had forsaken their families, their guardians, or orphanages in search of a new life. The outbreak of war had created new opportunities for the Takers as girls, who had been evacuated back in thirty-nine, escaped their mundane lives and returned to the city in search of their true families and their real friends. Some, of course, had no one; simply the lure of the city brought them here. The Blitz of last year created the ultimate opening for the Takers, for after weeks of relentless bombings the morgues were filled with nameless victims, and in the great scheme of things a handful of missing girls were of little significance.

A young girl of fifteen, slightly awkward in her stance and appearing somewhat bewildered, stood quite alone on platform six after alighting the train from Southampton. Her face was nondescript and her features not yet fully developed into the promising beauty that lie beneath, her body stubbornly refusing to enter the realms of womanhood. She had potential. The man on the bench, suave in appearance with playful eyes and a Cockney banter stretched himself and fixed his stare to the bemused waiflike creature and at once nudged his companion. His associate turned, following his gaze to the lone figure on platform six. She nodded approvingly. "Looks promising," she said. He agreed as he wrung his hands, searching out the immediate vicinity of the concourse. "She could be waiting for somebody," he murmured to himself. The raven haired companion shook her head and began rummaging through her handbag, glancing up at the young girl occasionally. "A runaway if ever I saw one. YMCA ought to do it," she commented, drawing a card from the inside pocket. They watched as eventually the girl raised a small holdall and began to walk to the ticket barrier with uncertainty. "Well? Yes or no?" the accomplice asked her partner. He watched the girl for a moment, taking in everyone gathered about the expanse of the concourse and weighing up the disadvantages of the opportunity. Finally he nodded. "She'll do," he said. Veronica left him and walked directly to the turnstile of platform six, bobbing and stretching her head as if she were expecting someone to appear from the confines of the stationary train, looking through the approaching target rather than directly at her. At the barrier the girl passed over her ticket to a youthful porter and Veronica sighed heavily to attract her attention.

"Would you happen to have seen a young lady on the train; well, no more than a child really, small, blonde and slightly portly—goes by the name of Linda?" she asked, feigning anxiousness.

The girl shook her head as she silently passed her by.

"Oh, dear! This is the Southampton train, isn't it?"

The girl slowed and confirmed with a nod that it was indeed the Southampton train.

"I wouldn't wonder if the poor child has fallen asleep;" proposed the Taker, "a long and arduous journey for one so young."

She then approached the porter idling at the barrier.

"Would you be kind enough to let me through?" she said to him. "I should be meeting a girl and I fear she may have fallen asleep."

It was difficult to refuse such a beguiling beauty and at once the accommodating young man swung open the gate within the barrier.

"Best be quick, sweetheart," he said with a smile and a wink, "that train's off in ten minutes."

Immediately Veronica turned back to the girl.

"Would you do me a kindness and help me?" she asked. "I swear it won't take but a couple of minutes."

The girl hesitated and looked about the station as if searching for an excuse. The Taker turned her gaze to the adolescent railway employee leaning against the turnstile who instinctively anticipated her next question.

"Don't look at me, gorgeous," he said. "I got enough to do—what with the timetable all messed up. The station master will have my guts for garters if I go wandering about."

Again she turned back to her target and expressed a look of despair. "Please."

Her partner-in-crime observed from the bench, occasionally shifting or standing whenever his view was obscured by passing or static pedestrians, cursing their presence under his breath and frustrated at his associate's long-winded approach on the situation, but he also knew Veronica excelled in her role as a Taker and must be given a little latitude.

Together Veronica and her new-found companion began to walk the empty corridors of the eight carriage train, peering into the compartments through their glazed and wooden panelled frontages. "I do appreciate your help. Are you visiting London or do you live here?" she asked as they continued the search. The teenager shrugged haplessly, as though she did not possess an answer or chose not to divulge it. "It's not that I'm nosey," explained the experienced beauty as she walked on, "it's my job—to ensure the safety of young women, much like yourself. But you obviously have family hereabouts. Am I right? I didn't catch your name." The juvenile made no comment and at the corridor's end Veronica turned to face her with a disarming smile. The girl answered coyly, "Emily. Emily Shaw."

Veronica swirled about, heading towards the rear of the train. "Well, Emily, London is not the same as it was. You know, I'll go so far as to say it's a damn dangerous place. It must be the war that entices men to do the things they do."

"Things? What things?" asked Emily nervously.

"Rape for one thing," returned Veronica over her shoulder. "Don't tell me you haven't heard about the recent spate of murders; killed eight women—probably more . . . who knows? Okay, he's behind bars now, but how many more like him are out there—just waiting for the chance to pounce? I try to instil into all the girls that come into my care the dangers of the city. There are opportunists on every street corner these days; seedy little reptiles willing to take advantage of some poor innocent child. Not that the police are much help. God knows they have enough to do."

Reaching the final carriage and with no sign of the fictitious girl that influenced the search, Veronica sighed with disappointment and sat down in the last compartment. The young Emily stood in the doorway staring down at the dejected woman, and as was her caring nature she timidly entered and sat opposite.

"Perhaps she changed her mind," she suggested.

Veronica nodded and smiled bitterly. Oh, it isn't the first time," she exclaimed. "It is the third to my recollection. Unfortunately Linda can be decidedly mercurial. I wouldn't mind so much but there are other girls who genuinely need help, and I would be better put to use helping those who need it rather than waste time on station platforms. Her dilemma is whether to live with her mother in Southampton or return to her father in London. I thought that this time she had made her mind up once and for all; we made all the arrangements—even sent the money for her fare; still, no matter. I'll just contact the 'Y' and let them know she's failed to turn up again."

"The 'Y'?" questioned Emily.

"The YMCA, dear—for women in need of help," explained Veronica passing over an official looking card. "For my sins I am attached to the Welfare Department, recently promoted from administration. It's my vocation, I think, to help people like Linda—I enjoy it."

For one so young Emily appeared brutally neglected. Her clothes, a blouse, beige cardigan and turquoise skirt were certainly hand-me-downs, obviously from someone taller and larger proportioned. Veronica discretely took in her overall appearance in a passing glance and rose from the seat.

"Best we disembark before we find ourselves bound for the French coast," the beauty quipped.

As they walked back down the platform Veronica put a comforting arm around Emily's shoulder and initiated her subtle act of extracting information. For her part the young girl was not so forthcoming with answers and instead shrugged her shoulders or evaded the enquiry completely. The young ticket collector was still leaning on the barrier as if he had been frozen in time throughout the duration of the search, but straightened and smiled brightly as they approached.

"I take it she wasn't on board," he said.

Veronica smiled and shook her head and thanked him for his help, and on the concourse she extended her hand to the teenage girl who now had taken on a distracted air, looking around for a familiar face that would never appear and daunted at the prospect ahead of her. Having been evacuated on the declaration of war, young Emily was put on a train by her father to stay with his sister, fearing London would be the only city to be attacked by the German Air Force, but she had not seen or heard from him in fourteen months and took the decision to return to the city to find him—without consulting her aunt. She remembers vividly the morning she was to be taken to the station. That morning she came down stairs and walked into the kitchen where her father stood motionless, looking out at the laden gutters overflowing on the outhouse in the back yard. Her mother had absconded with a younger man when Emily was nine-years old, and her older brother was last heard of fighting in Belgium, and although she looked upon her father as the bravest and kindest man who had ever lived, she sometimes heard him crying late at night. Preoccupied with his own personal thoughts on what was and what could have been, her father turned on hearing Emily enter the kitchen and forced a smile; his eyes were red and glazed—he had been crying again. He immediately moved to the stove where a saucepan of porridge bubbled over a low flame. "I packed your bag—your usual clothes and a few personal items. Oh, and that favourite dress you wore to your cousin's birthday party; the one with the frilly sleeves," he said. Emily sat silently watching him move between the stove and the two bowls already waiting on the counter. His voice ached and every spoken word was designed to instil encouragement into an otherwise heart breaking moment. He placed down a bowl of steaming porridge before his daughter and turned back to the cooker.

"Now, remember what I told you, Emmy," he said in a cracking voice. "You be a good girl while you're up there with your Aunty Irene, and give a hand whenever she asks you. And don't be asking your Uncle Alf loads of questions. I know you only do it because he stutters and it makes you laugh." Emily began to giggle to herself at the thought of how she would intimidate her uncle with a barrage of miscellaneous questions just so he could stumble his way through the appropriate answers with accompanying excruciating facial contortions and spasmodic head-jerking motions. "He's funny," cackled Emily and clapping her hands. "I like Uncle Alf."

That was the highlight of that particular day. As much as her father tried to make conversation it was a lost cause. He only had to look at his little girl and he broke. So he would busy himself washing up and making ready for her departure. They caught a bus at Bermondsey and her Father held her hand all the way to the station, and after purchasing a one-way ticket to Southampton he ushered her to the wall of caption boards. He prayed the train would be cancelled. He hoped that Southampton as a whole had been seized by the British Army and was now one immense headquarters in which the warlords would conduct the war effort and ban all citizens. Was it too much to ask that anyone under the age of sixteen should be excommunicated from that particular area, or better still that Adolf make an announcement declaring that his threat of war was just his little joke? The train was on time, ready and waiting at platform five. He drew a deep breath, gently squeezed her hand and led her to the platform. "Now, don't forget your Auntie Irene will be waiting at the other end to collect you at the usual place—by the newspaper kiosk just by the entrance—remember?" Emily nodded assertively as she walked by her father's side. "Now then, I will call her as soon as your train leaves this station so she'll be waiting. If for some reason she isn't there then find the station master and wait with him till she arrives. Her address is in your bag, just in case. Do you understand, Emmy? It's important you understand." Emily sighed exhaustively and shook her head. "I'm thirteen, dad, not five!" she huffed. Her father stopped on the platform and turned her towards him, gazing at her through tear filled eyes. "Yes, you are," he smiled. "You're a young woman now. You have your mother's grace, but you have my heart." They hugged for a while—until the porter raised his green flag to hurry the commuters along and the engine of the train began to animate into a hissing and thunderous demon, occasionally obscured by clouds of white steam that evaporated like a ghostly apparition. Her father embraced her and kissed her cheek repeatedly. She felt his tears as much as she felt her own, and at that moment she wanted to say all the things she meant to say that somehow never seemed important at the time. She wanted to ask questions about her mother, about her brother, about the future and about a conflict of war she had yet to understand. But the cry went up—even above the sound of the throbbing noise. "All aboard!"

It all seemed long ago and far away now, as though it were a story told by someone else and appertaining to someone else, and she struggled to remember her father's last words to her as the train pulled away. Even staring at the very spot where they hugged on the platform she could not recall their exchange of words if, of course, any were exchanged; emotion clouded her recollection. But she remembers sitting on the bus and her father holding her hand until her fingers ached and the accumulated sweat made her feel uncomfortable. Peering down on the pedestrians from the top floor, the grimy streets of London seemed somehow charming to a young girl embarking on her first journey away from home, and as the bus buffeted its way through the afternoon traffic her father pointed out places of interest along the London skyline. The city then was in one piece; not yet decimated by the Luftwaffe and wounded by their incendiaries. She heard on the radio of the Blitz, a no-holds barred commentary of the incredible destruction and the victims it claimed. What would it look like now? And how would she tell her father that her sweet, childless aunt who adored the company of children, had little time or patience for a homesick pubescent girl, or that the passing of so much time had turned her funny Uncle Alf into a cantankerous old man who regarded her presence as an invasion of privacy and ignored her at every opportunity. In her mind she had little choice but to leave and return to the city where she was born, and so taking money from her aunt's purse Emily gently closed the back door on the house at the first rays of light and walked the empty streets towards Southampton Station. She never even told her best friend Jenny she was leaving, a girl she had befriended the first day she arrived and who had also been evacuated to the next street. The erratic train timetable created cancellation after cancellation, and she sat out the accumulating hours in the waiting room, forever looking out the window and expecting to see her aunt and uncle marching towards her down the platform; they never came. On the journey back Emily held the pendant between her fingers that once belonged to her mother and now adorned her slim neck; a worthless St. Christopher, and the only item of jewellery her mother left behind in her bedside drawer. Her mother's whereabouts and wellbeing occupied her every waking hour, and in a strange way comforted her in believing that one day they would be reunited. But for the time being all she had was her father, and standing on the concourse shaking Veronica's hand, she suddenly blurted, "Bermondsey!"

Veronica tilted her head to one side and smiled politely.

"Bermondsey?" she echoed.

"My father lives there. I was born there. It is still there?"

The raven haired beauty laughed and patted the girl's arm assuredly.

"Of course it is! But I should tell you that it was hit pretty hard. What street in particular?"

"Catherine Street—by the school. I haven't heard from dad in over a year and . . . well I need to know if he's all right."

Veronica took in every golden word, and at the mention of the street name she adopted a look of suppressed horror. Emily glared at her with wide, tearing eyes. "What? What is it?"

"I remember the name," said the bogus official warily. "A girl in my care came from that very street—perhaps you know her."

Emily shook her head and pursued her original question. "What happened?"

"The street was hit—a lot of casualties."

Again Veronica placed her hand on the distraught girl's arm as if to console her.

"That doesn't mean to say your father was harmed," she assured her sympathetically.

"Then why haven't I heard from him?" Emily began to sob.

Veronica put a comforting arm about her shoulder and glanced over at the empty bench where she had been sitting with her associate.

"I'm sure he's fine and that there's a rational explanation for not contacting you. You must understand, Emily, that although Southampton goes about its business without a care in the world, London is very different and in a constant state of chaos. Time passes quicker here. We never get round to doing the things we promised."

"But my father . . ."

"First we must set your mind at rest," Veronica interrupted. "I'll make a few phone calls and see what I can find out. I'm sure he won't be hard to find. Do you have somewhere to sleep tonight?"

Emily had not given the subject a thought, never having considered the possibility that the street where she lived might be obliterated and she would be left homeless. And the official looking beauty with her kind smile and sympathetic air had never heard of Catherine Street, let alone know of its fate, but the lies were all part of the game; the requirements needed to entrap and ensnare prey.

"I'll phone the 'Y' and let them know that Linda has failed to arrive, and then we'll set about the task of finding you somewhere to sleep. By morning you'll be back with your father—promise," said the official as she led the teenager across the concourse.

Outside the station, close to Borough Market, Emily waited on the pavement while Veronica pushed pennies into a phone box on the pretext of contacting the YMCA. In reality she was phoning her confederate, who seeing that his partner was in complete control of the situation had taken his leave.

"Well?" he said, predicting her phone call. "Is she a runaway?"

Veronica smiled reassuringly through the glass at the anxious girl.

"As good as," she returned. "Evacuated two years ago and back in the city to find her old man, but he hasn't contacted her in over a year and she's worried about him. I think we should cut this one loose."

After a short pause her friend spoke up. "And why would I want to do that? You have her. Take her the rest of the way. You know the score. You know the schedule."

"Listen. This girl is a good girl—a nice girl, and what I know about her is that she's been through a lot—more than most. There'll be other girls."

"But you have her in your grasp and now you want to let her go. Why? Do what I pay you to do."

Veronica expressed another confident smile through the misting windows and turned her back.

"Now you listen to me," she growled. "You pay me to do a job—a job I do well, even if I do say so myself. So as a favour to me, let this one go. We can make up the numbers. We'll get two tomorrow."

She heard her associate sigh impatiently.

"I won't tell you again," he snapped. "Bring her to the house—NOW!"

The phone went dead, and with the receiver still held to her ear, Veronica stared at the kiosk wall before her emblazoned with cards and phone numbers—some written in lipstick—all advertising personal services, massages and even unrestrained debauchery. Her part in this girl's abduction would assist in the same fate. She held the same pose for a minute or so, to give the illusion she was still talking; time to gather her thoughts and suppress her indignation. In her three years as a Taker she could not calculate just how many girls she had deceived in order to make extra money, but it was certainly hundreds. And till now she had never felt guilt or remorse for playing her part. Out of sight is out of mind. It was an adage she adopted and retained whenever her conscience haunted her. Besides, many of the girls were destined for a life of prostitution; sex and glamour went hand in hand, and most were obsessed by the prospect of appearing in a glossy magazine or on film. They were pretty, and most had been blessed with all the necessary attributes, but they were uneducated and certainly not bound for an administrative career. Nor was Veronica come to that. She too had aspirations of becoming an actress, even enrolling at her local drama school, and for a while she prospered with a repertory company staging plays by the likes of Noel Coward, travelling as far as Woking, Guildford and even Plymouth. But such dreams whither and fade with time, and what once appeared glamorous becomes an ordeal. She was always cast as the gangster's moll, the dumb blonde or the frustrated and sexually precocious lover, and more often than not she awoke with the leading man in some seedy hotel or anyone who could help stave off the loneliness—if only temporarily. She came to realise that her looks and her body was all she had. She even considered prostitution for a while but selling herself entirely repelled her and the possibility of being beaten or perhaps even killed scared her more than words could say. Now she was a part-time hostess—a seductress trained in the art of extracting money from the men who came to ogle and maul her as she served drinks, or danced with her for a fee, or slept with her if the mood took her. Either way she controlled her own destiny, and like it or not the young runaways she delivered to her advocate.

Emily Shaw stood shivering on the pavement as the night began to fold in around her. She watched the commuters spilling out of the station and making their way home and at the static lines of cars caught up at the traffic lights, and at the strange faces filling the windows of the buses. She hoped that Veronica was making some headway in locating her father and that the street where she lived had not been destroyed. Indeed, through the striped glass of the phone-box the artificial welfare officer appeared deep in conversation with the receiver pressed to her ear. It had to be good news. Veronica drew a deep breath and placed down the phone, and adapting an air of hope stepped outside.

"They're looking into it as we speak," she said, lacing her arm through Emily's and steering her towards the viaduct in the market. "They'll call as soon as they hear anything."

The young girl pulled back a little and Veronica turned towards her.

"Anything wrong?" she asked.

"Well—what shall I do till then?"

Veronica half shrugged her shoulders and smiled. "Well, you could stand here in the cold and dark but I wouldn't advise it. Otherwise we can go back to my house and wait for the call, and while we're waiting I'll make you something to eat—you look famished."

Emily walked a few more steps and stopped again.

"But they will definitely phone, won't they?" she questioned.

"One way or the other they will. Now look lively—the streets 'round here can get awfully sinister come nightfall."

In a backstreet not far from the medieval Clink Prison and with the River Thames idling close by, they approached a dismal looking three-storey house that even at dusk and cast in shadow appeared dilapidated and in dire need of care and attention. A tall, thin house with a rather sad façade, it stood detached with a van in the driveway parked in front of a rusty corrugated iron garage bereft of doors. "It's quite cosy inside," said the treacherous official as she registered the young girl's trepidation. And to Emily's surprise it was. The hallway was quaint—carpeted throughout with a small table supporting a large, leafy plant and a telephone, and off the hallway the front parlour looked homely with soft, easy-chairs facing a tiled fireplace; the kitchen sparse but exceedingly clean and everything in its place. But that was where the illusion ended; beyond the rise of the stairs the landing and rooms were bare boards and empty. Veronica sighed as she took off her coat and laid it over the back of one of the hardback chairs surrounding a round table. "You look like you could do with a cup of tea," she said. Emily smiled gratefully and took up a seat at the table. Always a quiet girl, she sat and watched Veronica place the kettle on the stove and prepare the teapot, the way she always watched her father before she was sent away, and every now and then Veronica would pass her a glance and a friendly smile. "Are you married?" Emily enquired as she surveyed the kitchen. "You look like you're married—or at least that you ought to be. I mean, you're far too beautiful not to be married. Any man would be proud to have you on his arm." There are some words or phrases that touch a nerve within us all; the way a smell, a song or even the sound of laughter can evoke a long forgotten memory. For Veronica it was of missed opportunities, of a man who once loved her and would have done anything if she would be his; a man she shunned because she believed her beauty would elevate her to a higher plain and to a life she vehemently believed she deserved. In time she wore him down and his advances were few and far between until finally they ceased altogether. At that moment in time it was what she wanted—to continue her quest for a superior partner, her knight in shining armour, her soul-mate. A never ending stream of misbegotten suitors was all she received—some so vague in her memory she cannot recall their names, others not even their faces. But never a day passes when she does not regret her vanity thwarting her future and the man who declared his undying love for her. Preoccupied with a dream she played in her mind time and time again she was oblivious to the clouds of steam jetting from the spout of the kettle until Emily called her name. "Sorry. I was miles away—must be overtired, I guess. Why don't you go into the parlour; you'll be more comfortable in there." The young girl disappeared along the hallway but Veronica remained at the sink with her hands resting on the draining board, staring at her reflection in the window and sickened by the image before her. How had she allowed herself to be reduced to this? And when had she lost sight of her values?

The comfort of the parlour was a pleasant distraction for a young girl who had spent the day either loitering around on station platforms or travelling in cramped and musky compartments, and in the shortest of time she was joined by the counterfeit official with two mugs of tea. She pulled to the curtains and turned on a small lamp atop of a sideboard and sat down next to Emily on the settee. "So, Emily, tell me more about your dad. What does he do?"

The young girl smiled with uncertainty and thought for a moment, for she wasn't sure exactly what her father did do.

"I know he works in a factory . . . very high up . . . organises everything."

"He's a director?"

Emily looked affronted at the trivialisation. "Good grief, no! He's a foreman; says if it wasn't for him the place would have gone to the dogs years ago."

Veronica smiled with an agreeing nod. "He sounds very powerful," she said.

The innocent victim sipped her tea and immediately adopted a look of dissatisfaction at its acetic flavour.

"Not to your liking?" Veronica laughed. "Tea is hard to come by these days. I have to take what I can get. It can be a bit sharp but you'll get used to it—an acquired taste."

Emily took another sip and fought to keep a straight face.

"It's fine—really," she winced. "My aunt always drinks Chinese tea and that's much worse—like drinking a bottle of perfume," she added with a shudder.

The two girls laughed, and as Emily reluctantly drank her tea she spoke of her days at home before the war rudely interrupted her comfortable life. And the more she explained away her mundane existence the worse Veronica felt. It reminded her of her own upbringing but under the rule of an uncaring mother and without the guidance of a loving father, where too many nights were spent alone with her younger sister while her mother was out romancing a catalogue of misbegotten admirers whose interest extended no further than knowing they were onto a sure thing. Veronica had inherited her mother's beauty and curvaceous body as well as her callous disregard for others and precocious lifestyle. She had been cursed with a name she despised—Elizabeth—Elizabeth McCauley, and had been the brunt of schoolboy jibes ever since the metamorphosis of puberty changed her into an overdeveloped adolescent. Thereafter she constantly changed her name to a denomination she believed befitted her stunning looks and perhaps, swayed others to conclude she was of wealthy standing and not borne from a life of poverty and a defective family. Indeed, she nurtured the notion of others that she was well-bred and privately educated and could—when called upon—regale them with stories of banquets and private functions gleaned from overheard conversations of the opulent. In essence her existence was a lie but one she willingly conserved to keep the bad memories at bay. She regarded her mother as needy and damaged—who courted sexual experiences to reassure herself she was still admired and wanted but who was destined to wake up very much alone and unloved, and as much as Veronica fought the comparison there were moments she felt very much like her.

Emily was talking fluently about her stay at her aunt's and uncle's and how she had made a new friend in Jenny, and the conversation moved steadily onward until she suddenly fell silent and looked disorientated. She felt overwhelmed by exhaustion and desperately needed to lay her head down and sleep. Veronica's smiling face moved in and out of focus and Emily shook her head as if to shake off the lethargy. "Let me take this off you. We don't want you staining your nice clothes," said Veronica as she took the cup from the girl's limp hand. Emily tossed her head and slouched back on the settee, her eyes rolling backward before closing. "What is happening?" she mumbled. The charlatan patiently put the cup on the table and stood up. "To my eternal shame I've drugged you—a mild and harmless tranquilliser. Tomorrow you'll wake up somewhere else and in time you'll be transported to another country. I'm truly sorry, Emily." She heard the creek of floorboards above her and the intermittent squeak of the treads as someone moved down the staircase. She felt the presence of someone standing behind her. "That's the last one. I can't do this anymore," she said. The man who had shared the bench with her at the station moved past her and stood over the unconscious girl slumped on the settee.

"Don't give me the tart with a heart routine, Liz," he said, addressing Veronica by her real name. "And don't ever tell me how to run my business."

"Your business!" she retaliated. "You're a pimp with a stable of girls who earn your money for you. You deal in prostitution, not abducting innocent young girls and turning them into slaves."

He laughed as he walked to the window and pushed the curtains slightly to one side.

"You've always known what we're doing," he said. "It's dark enough now. Give me a hand to get her into the van."

She shook her head. "I told you: I'm finished. Do whatever you have to do but leave me out of it."

"You're here to do a job. Don't forget that," he growled.

"I've done my job; delivered to you in one piece and unconscious."

"Don't play games with me, Liz, I'm warning you. Now, grab her feet."

She stubbornly shook her head again and he walked towards her, an anger burning in his eyes.

"Listen, there are people within the organisation I work for that won't take kindly to a rebellious bitch like you upsetting their schedule. I'm already behind on the quota and will have to work twice as hard to meet it. Now stop fucking about and help me."

"You're worried about a shortfall?" she sneered. "Then why not make up the numbers with a few of the whores that work for you? God knows you could do with some new ones—prettier ones."

"Are you volunteering? Sorry, sweetheart, the requirements are for young and untouched—you're neither. Your looks are fading, Liz, and as time goes by you'll find it harder to make a living. I mean, who wants to dance with a decrepit slag like you?"

She drew her hand back to slap him but he held her arm fast and laughed again.

"I haven't got time for your tantrums," he growled. "I have people to answer to."

The distraught woman snatched her arm away from his strong grip and took steps backwards.

"And what would the authorities have to say about that?" she snarled, "a London pimp in business with a German for the purpose of human trafficking! They'll lock you up and throw away the key."

He walked to the comatose waif and pressed a thumb gently against her eyelid.

"That sounds awfully like a threat, Liz, and you know how I react to threats," he said as he peered into the victim's lifeless eyes. "I pay you good money—twenty pounds a girl. Do you think you can make that dancing with rich drunks? You couldn't make half that on your back. Now I won't tell you again—help me get her into the van."

When he turned she had disappeared, and he stepped out into the hall to see her pacing towards the kitchen to retrieve her coat.

"Come back here now!" he demanded. "Come back here and give me a hand or I won't pay you a penny. Do you hear me?"

Elizabeth knew him well—knew his business, his girls and his associates, including the man he had to answer to—German entrepreneur Phillip Heidegger, the man in charge of human trafficking in London. She knew, also, that her colleague was a man of a violent disposition, especially when disciplining women under his jurisdiction, and she awaited his wrath with a foreboding expectancy while attempting to make a hasty retreat. Reaching for her coat she turned to see him racing towards her, and turning again to the back door he was suddenly upon her. He struck her on the side of the face, grasped her by the shoulders and hurled her across the kitchen, and no sooner as she hit the ground he was standing over her and kicking her frenziedly. Her natural defence instincts deflected several contacts, but too many made it through her flaying legs and thrashing arms to prevent severe injury. After what seemed an eternity all motion stopped and he stood staring down at her panting and exhausted. She could hear him but daren't open her eyes, and she was thankful the spasmodic exertion of rage had left him spent. She remained curled up in a foetal position—as she had in her mother's womb before she was spat out into the terrifying reality we call life. With eyes shut tight she felt pain searing through her legs and torso, and she could feel her ribs beneath the burning pain clicking as she exhaled—cracked or broken. Her face would be unscathed, of that she was certain; he would not steal her livelihood, for when he administered his punishment on the women in his charge, on those he believed had wronged him or on those he reasoned deserved it, he would not mark the face; why jeopardize ones earning capacity? And this was not a new experience. It had happened twice before when she rebelled, and always her disapproval of his methods or her refusal to participate met with the same consequences. But wounds heal and bruises fade, and tender loving care or walking the righteous path is no match for cold hard cash. He knew she would return—she always did. She felt his presence evaporate but she never heard his footsteps, and cautiously she opened her eyes. Scattered before her were a number of crisp, white banknotes, that when counted some time later, amounted to thirty pounds; twenty for the successful apprehension and delivery of the targeted female, and an additional ten for the pain and suffering.

Perhaps Elizabeth could have forgiven herself had she unwittingly played her part, or been coerced into abducting young females and delivering them into the hands of white slavers, or been ignorant of the facts regarding that deplorable trade, but in truth she was an accessory—before and after the fact. She willingly participated for gain, and she could quote chapter and verse the true meaning of her part-time activity, that according to the Rome Statute—article 7 (2)(c) *Sexual Enslavement means the exercise of any or all powers attached to the 'right of ownership' over a person.* Nor, that despite the abolition of slavery in 1807, white slavery or, moreover white sex slavery, had not gone entirely underground. Indeed as recently as 1937, Japan flagrantly resurrected the abominable act with *Jugan ianfu,* or *comfort women* used for the purpose of military sex slaves before and during World War II. Far from clandestine an estimated one hundred to four hundred thousand females were forced to deliver sexual services to Japanese soldiers on the behest of the emperor, representatives of the armed forces and cabinet members. It was the biggest mass rape in recorded history—ten million—involving mostly Korean and Chinese women. And closer to home it was all around her, blatantly thriving in the city streets, in the best known haunts of pubs and clubs, hostels and rooms booked by the hour, in alleyways and bombed out warehouses. Despite the threat of German bombardment the girls plied their trade during the hours of darkness, provocatively dressed and enticing, and behind each and every one was a powerful man, a ruthless gang, or consortium. Supply and demand, the promise of wealth and independence swelled the streets with more, and to satisfy the insatiable obsession of man demanding a higher degree of salaciousness and vile activity, so the temptresses grew younger—some barely children. Far from being covert transactions the deals were executed openly, in front of judges and policemen, politicians and lawyers, of the upper echelon and before royalty; the enterprise flourished to unfathomable heights unchallenged.

Her associate reappeared at the kitchen door from the hallway, with the stupefied young girl slung over his shoulder like a life-size ragdoll, her limbs swaying in unison like the branches of a tree pushed by the wind. She weighed no more than a shadow, barely seven stone. Elizabeth was doubled up on the kitchen chair, her arms curled about her stomach clutching her ribs either side, the blemishes and abrasions threatening to destroy and disfigure her perfectly shaped legs; the short distance from floor to the seat an excruciating journey and a display of endurance. "You know the rules, Liz," he said as he passed her. He disappeared through the back door to the rear of the corroded garage, where he would load the merchandise into the back of the van under the veil of darkness. 'The rules' as he said, concerned protocol—that being an operative such as Liz, and one who wanted to quit her position as a Taker, leave any keys or any forged papers used for the purpose of abduction and never breathe a word of their role to a living soul; the repercussions could be catastrophic. The house had served its purpose and was close to the end of its short-term lease. It was, after all, a mere prop—a means to an end to dupe the innocent who entered it, and soon another house would be rented close to the station and destined to serve the same purpose. With trembling hands Elizabeth removed all bogus identification from her handbag, and dipping into her pocket retrieved the front door key, leaving the assorted items on the table. This time would be her last. The money strewn about the cold tiled floor represented something entirely different now and she felt tempted to leave it there—as a stand against the hypocrisy that she herself was guilty of, that in light of her defiance symbolized blood-money, ten pieces of silver, payment for imposing a lifetime of misery on some undeserving soul. But she earned it, with literally blood, sweat and tears, and painfully she stooped to gather it up and cram it into her coat pocket. Pressing the palm of her hand against her damaged ribs she took one last look around, straightened a chair that had been knocked askew at the kitchen table and turned off the light.

I can't recall ever moving up Fleet Street so fast, nor can I recall the journey itself; the people I must have bumped into, the faces I had become familiar with over the passing years or, for that matter, old Sid who worked from the newspaper stand on the corner of Aldwych where I stopped every morning and purchased a copy of The Times; on this morning I remembered nothing. My mind throughout the walk to the station, the train journey and the jaunt up Fleet Street was occupied only by Jonathan Sandpiper, the old gentleman who appeared at my father's funeral. To the best of my recollection he said he knew my father well but appeared to hardly know him at all, which through my sleepless night made the statement and, indeed, his presence that more difficult to unravel, but either way he knew my father and he was a living, breathing person and certainly he would be able to shed some light on those early days at the London Hospital. My dilemma was finding him without drawing attention to myself and an incident that happened half a century ago, but if such a search was carried out on a professional level then why should it attract any unwanted attention? My trust in Sylvia would now be tested to the limits.

As usual she moved out of her office the moment I descended the stairs with her usual welcoming smile and a clipboard under her arm, but I motioned her into the office with a nod of my head and once inside I immediately closed the door. "I need you to find me a man," I said as I walked to my desk. When I turned she was grinning broadly at me. "Michael, surely things can't be that bad," she quipped. She registered my scowl and slowly her amused expression dissipated without any sign of resurfacing. "Who?" she asked, taking a pen from the top of her clipboard.

"His name is Jonathan Sandpiper; mid-seventies," I replied. She transferred the name to paper and then looked back at me. "Anything else?" she asked. I shook my head and began to shuffle through the indecipherable notes on my desk. "No. Let me know when you have an address," I said without looking at her. A minute passed and she was still standing by the door, the clipboard cradled in her arm like a newborn. "I meant have you any other information about Jonathan Sandpiper other than a hit-and-miss estimate of his age?" she asked with an air of sarcasm. I was reluctant to impart any more information than absolutely necessary—not that I had much—but I knew if I wanted this man found I had little choice. "He was a medical student with my father at the London Hospital, Whitechapel in 1888," I said nonchalantly. She scribbled the information down on her paper. "So, I'm looking for a doctor, retired," she mumbled, and then flicking her dark eyes back up she asked. "And do we know if he's still alive?" I nodded patiently and looked hard back at her. "He's alive, Sylvia, and I can't emphasize enough how important this is. It must be treated with the utmost discretion and never mentioned to anyone inside or outside this office; it is just between you and me. Understand." She narrowed her eyes slightly and for a moment they expressed concern, but she smiled faintly. "Fine," she said. "I'll see to it right away."

The various newspapers in Fleet Street were more than accommodating, furnishing us with every written article on George Henderson and a lot more. In their entirety they amounted to no less than 572 separate pieces, compiled by various reporters, and Badger—against his better judgment—set about cutting them out and pinning them to his office wall while I sat in his chair engrossed in a crime magazine with a four page spread on The Blackout Butcher that Sylvia had come by. The object of this exercise was to compile our own dossier on Henderson, to separate fact from fiction and eliminate the lies from the truth. Badger slowly walked the office wall studying each and every report, sometimes tearing one off and screwing it up—an indication that it reiterated a previous report and therefore only served to take up precious wall-space. He would sigh exhaustively every now and then, as if the task ahead was a formidable one, and whenever I looked up from my magazine he would be staring at the mass of reports, shaking his head hopelessly and scratching his chin, and once he reached the end of the wall, he would return to the beginning and start again. Within the hour he concluded that in all every report told the same story, and the condemning factor was that five weeks after the last killing, George Henderson entered a police station and gave himself up. Notwithstanding a few spelling mistakes of the names of the victims, the times and dates were correct and corresponded with Carlisle's report as well as Henderson's statement. Some of the reports appeared more informed than the others, actually monitoring his movements prior to a murder and interviewing work colleagues such as Edward Foster, a fireman who described his associate as extremely eccentric who, when the day was over, would walk back through the empty carriages of the train, gathering up everything the commuters had purposefully or unknowingly left behind. "It was an obsession with him," Edward reportedly told the Daily Mirror. "He would find all sorts of things; wallets, purses and sometimes diamond rings, but more often than not he would just end up with a handful of discarded newspapers."

The eight murders attributed to Henderson took place in what the newspapers dramatically referred to as the 'Death Diamond' between the Elephant and Castle, Camberwell Green and Kennington. The first murder took place on October 7th 1940, midway down Walworth Road, a main route out of London heading south. Her name was Angela Deacon, a twenty-four year old shop assistant. She was found two days later by her landlady, lying naked in an empty bath—her wrists and throat cut open. The second murder occurred in Kennington on the very day Angela Deacon's body was discovered. She was a thirty-three year old secretary working in Cannon Street, married with two children whose husband was fighting the war. Her name was Judy Moore, and her mutilated remains were discovered within two hours of her death by her ten year old son who had slept soundly while his mother had been raped and her throat cut; she had been sodomized; the consensus being after death occurred. Marion Price was barely nineteen and discovered in an alleyway behind a tenement at the Elephant and Castle on October 18th. Her clothing had been removed from the waist down and the obvious wounds—which by now were the killer's calling card—inflicted in a most brutal manner. When she was found the next morning she was discovered in an upright position, her forearms tied to railings with string, and experts opined that sexual intercourse took place in a standing position. Despite heavy police presence in that area, the fourth killing took place again at the Elephant and Castle on October 25th, in a small terraced house off the main road. Susan MacDonald, a fifty-two year old widow was discovered naked on the kitchen floor, and it was clear that the murders were becoming more ferocious. As well as her throat and wrists being slashed, her head had been crushed by continuous and forceful contact with the stone floor, and her abdomen had been laid open. It was seven days before neighbours, infuriated by her pet Alsatian's incessant howling, broke in to be confronted by the gruesome sight. Her dog, starving with hunger by this time, had feasted itself on its master's intestines. The following murders happened in quick succession, within days of one another. On November 3rd, Betty Weller, a sixty-two year old spinster was found in her bedroom on the outskirts of Kennington, and ironically had not been sexually assaulted, though she bore the killer's traditional execution wounds. Leslie Cross, just sixteen, was found in Kennington Park on the morning of November 6th, naked, raped and murdered, her clothes strewn along the grass. Christine Charmaine was a twenty-two year old prostitute working in and around Walworth, exceptionally pretty with dark hair and a fine figure. She was discovered three days after the last murder, in a public toilet off Camberwell road. She was naked to the waist, her throat severed and her head in the toilet bowl to contain the blood-flow. Her slashed wrists had been bound by wire behind the toilet, between the toilet outlet and flush pipe and she had been sodomized, probably after death or while she bled to death. The seventh victim was a thirty-one year old seamstress, Jean Smith, found dead on November 12th, at her home between Kennington and Camberwell. She had been stripped naked, tied to a dining room table and a knife plunged into her neck and drawn down to her vagina. The last murder victim, found two days later, was by far the most horrific. Stella Clark was a model, who as well as being an exotic dancer also posed in provocative positions for men's magazines. She was a buxom twenty-seven year old with peroxide hair and was discovered in a disused garage in a side-road in Walworth. Her naked torso was found in a mechanics pit, her throat and wrists cut and her breasts removed. Her face and body had been savagely mutilated with a cut-throat razor and her stomach opened up back to the spinal column; she lay in her own intestines.

Badger and I pored over the newspaper clippings for the best part of the day, having tea and sandwiches brought in, and Sylvia, with her indecipherable writing which may well have been written in sandstone, took notes in an attempt to compile the series of events appertaining to Henderson. Badger was obviously disgruntled that I was willing to waste time researching a hopeless case, and he stood at the far end of his office, his jacket off and shirtsleeves rolled up, frustration etched on his thin face.

"The man is guilty, Michael," he grumbled. "Why are you doing this?"

My intentions were obvious but only to me. This was my opportunity to find out how a serial killer becomes a serial killer, and in doing so, may discover what fuelled my father and Pip to create one if, of course, it was true.

"What have we?" I said, turning to Sylvia and ignoring Badger's anger.

"Probably the sickest bastard to walk this planet," she replied.

I gave her a withered look.

"Sorry," she said. "Well, they all say the same thing; eight women dead and Henderson did it. Police investigators, including Carlisle, agree that all the murders were random and unconnected—simply opportunities. George Henderson lives in Camberwell and that is the route he would take home from the city. Alternatively he could walk towards Kennington and then left towards Camberwell. Either way that has him encircling the 'Death Diamond.' Between the second and fifth murder Henderson was stopped and questioned no less than three times, twice in Walworth and once in Kennington; the dates and locations matching exactly with the killings. That put Carlisle on his trail."

"It doesn't make him the killer," I said.

"No, it doesn't," Badger intervened, "but his confession does."

"Which is inadmissible as evidence," I argued. "There is no evidence to connect Henderson with these murders!"

"The newspapers—every one of them—say different."

"So the media are responsible for handing out the death penalty now, are they?"

"Listen, Michael, he gave himself up, and whether you like it or not his statement is probably true despite Carlisle's shady past."

I flipped open the magazine I had been reading and found the name of the person who wrote it, Peter Egan. His interpretation differed vastly from the newspapers. It was exceptionally well written and was approached from a different angle. He had a nameless source that shed a different light on the story; who confirmed that Carlisle's statement was indeed a fabrication, and by now I was tiring of Badger's incessant scepticism.

"Find this man," I said to Sylvia, pointing to the name at the foot of the page, and then turning to Badger I added, "If you don't want to do this, get back to your swindles or whatever it is your working on."

I moved directly from his office, up the stairs and out into the street.

I sat in the Cheshire Cheese, at Dickens's table, staring into a double scotch and mulling over everything in my mind; Henderson, my father, and Mr Sandpiper and my infidelity with Penny and the possibility of my own wife's infidelity. The evening after my sexual encounter with Penny, I returned home to an empty house, and though it was an unusual occurrence, I welcomed the solitary time to acclimatize to my surroundings and rehearse my story. I was riddled with guilt regarding my own stupidity and weakness, but I took comfort in the knowledge that men—all men—are weak and any one of them would have done what I did. In my defence, it isn't easy lying in a strange bed, in a strange place next to a beautiful, naked secretary; I mean, what is a red-blooded man supposed to do? Nevertheless, my own shame induced me to avoid Penny at all costs, but there were times when such confrontations were unavoidable. If we passed one another she would simply smile, the way she always did before she seduced me with her candlelit conversation and casserole, and when we spoke there wasn't a hint of flirtation in her voice and no glint of passion in her eyes. I wondered then if I had dreamt the whole thing; that we hadn't performed like a couple of sex-starved Baboons for two and half hours, but then it occurred to me that this is what women do, seduce and sod off.

In my eyes, at least, I was an innocent man who had been seduced by a nymph masquerading as my secretary, to which if presented before any judge and jury I would surely be acquitted and forgiven my moment of weakness. There were, however, our ancestors to consider who, I'm sure, may not be as forgiving. Adultery was, and still is, a crime detested by the wise and good, as scandalous in its nature, pernicious to society and destructive to religion. The opinion of the ancient heathens considered the act as an abomination, tantamount to sacrilege or the robbing of temples. The old Ethiopians likened it to treason; the Egyptians punished the man with a thousand stripes of the whip, and decreed the woman should have her nose cut off as a mark of perpetual infamy; the ancient Athenians committed an adulterer to death; the Persians threw an offender down a deep well; and Greece punished the crime with death—without mercy or pardon. Crete was more lenient, and a certain city would place a woollen crown on the head of the adulterer as a derision of his soft and effeminate nature, imposing a heavy fine and forbidding he hold any office in government; the King of Tenideans beheaded adulterers with an axe, and condemned his own son found guilty of the same crime to be put to death in the same manner; the Lepreans ordered that the man should be led around the city for three days and then branded in the face with an iron, while the woman should stand in the market-place for eleven days—so all could see her—wearing little else but a loose-fitting transparent grown. King Hippomines of Athens caught an adulterer with his daughter Limona, and had him tied to the wheel of a chariot and dragged around until he was dead; Dio, the first king of the Romans passed law that an adulteress should be put to death in whatever way her husband and relatives thought fit; Tacitus, the chief officer of Rome, found in the public records the names of 3000 who were put to death for adultery; the Hungarians punished adulterers by death; the Old Saxons strangled the woman and burnt her to ashes, and the man would be hung over her grave or scourged with whips and rods by the womenfolk and chased from village to village; the Levitcal law adopted by the Turks decreed that offenders should be stoned to death, and traditional punishment demanded that women should be drown and the men castrated; the Spanish and Italians preferred the stabbing of the heart with daggers, and five-hundred years ago in France two brothers found guilty of adultery were flayed alive and their carcasses hung on gibbets; while Belgians and Hollanders opted for the civilised punishment of banishment. In all I think I got off lightly.

It was gone 10 o'clock before Sarah returned home. I was sitting in my usual chair reading the paper when I heard her come in softly singing to herself the way she used to when we were younger, but she suddenly fell quiet, and after a few moments she entered the lounge and walked straight up to me and gave me a kiss. She was always impeccably dressed, and her make-up and hair was no less than flawless, but tonight she had a glow about her; genuinely happy to see me.

"I didn't expect you home," she said. "The radio said that there was a possibility the trains wouldn't be running again."

"The blackboard at Farringdon Station said the same thing, but a few were still running; I got lucky."

"I'm sorry. What do you want for dinner?"

She headed off to the kitchen and as usual we carried out our conversation through the serving-hatch.

"A sandwich will be fine," I replied. "I'm not hungry."

"Have you eaten?"

I hadn't but replied I had.

Guilt and worry had stolen any appetite for food, and I simply waited out the inevitable question to be asked.

"So you stayed at the office last night," Sarah said. "I thought you'd be there tonight, that's why I went round to Mrs. Driver."

I slowly looked up from the newspaper, wondering how she could have possibly reached that conclusion. Suddenly she appeared at the serving-hatch.

"I phoned the office today; Joyce told me. Didn't she tell you?"

For once I was indebted to the power of office-gossip.

"She never mentioned it," I said, dropping my eyes back to the sports section. "It's been a busy day."

"Me, too. Mr. Fletcher sends his regards. What do you want in your sandwich?"

"Anything will be fine."

It's strange the things we notice when there not there anymore and it isn't like me to pay attention to minute detail. I have walked through London and never noticed that entire buildings are missing, courtesy of a German bomb, but when Sarah entered the lounge and handed me my sandwich, it struck me straight away.

"Why aren't you wearing your wedding ring?" I asked.

She looked at her hand, suddenly rushed from the room and padded upstairs. When she appeared again she flashed her left hand at me and the band of gold was obvious.

"I left it in the bathroom when I was cleaning," she said.

Another double-scotch appeared next to my half-empty glass and Badger sat himself at the table brandishing one of his schoolboy grins; the one he always used when he wanted to call a truce.

"Still mad at me?" he asked cautiously.

I shook my head and sighed wearily.

"It isn't you, Badger, it's me."

There and then I needed to offload some of my problems or, at least, share them with a friend.

"I think Sarah is having an affair," I explained.

"That's terrible."

"And I'm fucking Penny."

"That's great!"

I turned my eyes to the ceiling.

"It isn't 'Great' Badger, it's a catastrophe." I hissed. "This isn't me; I don't jump in and out of bed with my secretary."

"Evidently you do, Michael," he said, haughtily. "Look, is that what is worrying you?"

"Isn't it enough?"

"Excuse the pun, but every man slips up once in awhile, Michael. Don't worry about it; pretend it never happened. And what's all this nonsense about Sarah?"

"I'm not sure," I sighed. "I'm not sure of anything anymore. When I went home last night she wasn't there, and when she finally came home she told me she had been to a neighbour's. She looked nice—you know, the way she used to—but I don't think she expected me to be there. She wasn't wearing her wedding ring. She said she left it in the bathroom."

"Perhaps she did, and perhaps she was visiting a neighbour. Remember, Michael, she's on her own."

"Apparently she phoned the office. She never phones."

"Women are like that," Badger shrugged. "They don't give you a second thought, and the next minute you pop into their heads and they have to see you or hear your voice; women do that. So how was Penny?"

"Not a word, Badger!" I scowled.

With a wolfish grin Badger let the matter drop.

"Sylvia found your intrepid reporter—Peter Egan," he said. "She explained we represent Henderson and he's agreed to meet with us in the week. I read the article and it made me have second thoughts."

"So you're with me on this?"

"You have my undivided attention," he smiled.

It had been two days since I set Sylvia her task and in that time I hardly saw her at all in the office, but on that third morning she placed a piece of paper down and stood nervously before me. My hopes in finding Jonathan Sandpiper were dashed when I dropped my eyes to the typed page. For here was a man of the same name, born in 1869, in Forest Hill, South-London, who joined the Metropolitan Police Force in 1888 and within three years was promoted to sergeant. In 1895 he was an inspector and by 1901 transferred to Scotland Yard where after ten years as a local inspector in and around Forest Hill was promoted to Inspector First Class. For the last three years of his career he was Assistant Commissioner of the Metropolitan Police. I cast my eyes up at Sylvia in disbelief and waited for an explanation but she simply stood in silence like a naughty schoolgirl awaiting the wrath of a staunch teacher. "Two days. Two days and you come back to me with this!" I said, attempting to control my anger and disappointment. Her head dropped and she emitted a short sigh. "Did you not hear what I said? Damn it, Sylvia, we're looking for a doctor and you bring me a policeman. How difficult can it be? You should have started looking at the London Hospital Archives; it would have given you the appropriate information," In temper I screwed the paper into a ball and threw it in the bin and fell back into my chair frowning at my desk. I just wanted her to leave then. If I never saw her again it would have been too soon, but she remained stock still as if waiting for my anger to subside. "Have you finished sulking now?" she asked. I swear if looks could kill she would have been dead in front of my desk, for I shot her a look that should have at least induced a coronary, but she returned a shallow smile. "Jonathan Sandpiper was never a student at the London Hospital, nor was he a student at any other London hospital; there is no mention of his name in any hospital archives, but I did manage to find your father's. I checked the records back to 1886 and up to 1900; there is no Jonathan Sandpiper!"

My mouth fell open and my anger manifested into one of utter confusion, and I looked to the bin, running Jonathan Sandpiper's words through my head and then looked back to Sylvia. "There is only one man of that name alive in this country and you have just thrown him in the wastepaper bin," she said. I rose from my chair, sat back down and stood up again. "But he told me his name. He said he was a student with my father," I explained as I tried to make sense of it all. "Then he's a liar!" Sylvia returned confidently. "There's only one way to find out." She left the office, closing the door behind her with a tad more force than usual and I just stood there unsure of what to do next. Perhaps if I continued reading my father's book I may glean more, it may become clearer, and I opened the desk drawer and stared at it, not daring to touch it in case it contaminated me in some way. I could only stare at the faded leather binding and imagine what those unread pages held in store for me and my father's good name. My mind filled with so many analogies, so many alternatives that I found it impossible to unravel one from the other. Why would Jonathan Sandpiper lie about his name and his occupation and why, in God's name, would he choose to do it at such a delicate moment as a funeral? I took the screwed paper from the wastepaper bin and ironed it out on the desk with the palm of my hand. There was an address.

-6-

A taxi spirited me out of the city, across the Thames, through Clapham and Norwood and eventually into the quaint surroundings of Dulwich Village, and I found myself before a modest house unworthy of the proprietor's credentials; a bland-looking terrace sandwiched amongst a long line of identical facades, their thresholds boasting an abundance of greenery and multi-coloured flowers separated by a straight gravel path leading to the front door. The wrought-iron gate squealed painfully as I opened it and the gravel beneath my feet forewarned of my impending arrival, and before I reached the door it slightly teased open and an elderly woman with a polite smile suddenly appeared. "May I help you?" she asked. I was barely midway down the path but realized my noisy advance must have alerted her. "Does Mr. Sandpiper live here; Jonathan Sandpiper?" I enquired. Her look was gentle but her stare demanded more information. "He was a friend of my father's," I explained. "I believe he came to the funeral. I came to thank him and we really never got the chance to . . ." Her smile brightened and she pointed to the left of her. "He'll be in the park, by the pond," she interrupted. "Or you're welcome to come in and wait. He won't be long." I looked in the direction she was pointing. "It's barely a minute walk; just across the road," she added.

I entered the small park through two stone pillars that opened out onto a wide tarmac path where, on either side, tall trees bowed towards each other, their branches entwined as if holding hands forming a natural arch, and at its end I saw the pond leading from the road, down a slow, grassy incline, and a lone figure sat on a bench; Jonathan Sandpiper; the same Jonathan Sandpiper I had met. He was tossing bread into the water from a paper bag for the benefit of the ducks and geese congregated in front him at the waters edge. He hadn't appeared to have seen me approaching and neither did he look at me when I stopped in front of him, but he continued his task and said, "Michael! I expected you before now." He rose from the bench, tipped the last of the crumbs into the water and smiled at me before resuming his seat. "Mr. Sandpiper," I said. "Or do I call you Pip?" His eyes closed and he nodded his head slowly, and after a moment they opened and he smiled bitterly.

"So he did write it," he said, quietly.

"Don't tell me you didn't know about the book," I said, accusingly.

"Oh, I knew, Michael," he replied solemnly. "It's something I have lived with for nearly thirty years, but I was never quite sure, you see. I was never quite certain if it wasn't just an empty threat. You being here confirm it wasn't. So, now you know."

"Tell me it's a lie. Tell me that my father wrote this as a prank."

Mr. Sandpiper's eyes remained fixed on the wildlife before him and he shook his head.

"I wish I could, Michael, I truly wish I could, but whatever is in those pages you can be assured every word is true; your father, after all, was an honest man."

"Honest! Honest!" I spat. "You're casually sitting there and telling me that you and my father slaughtered six women because you wanted to create a myth!"

For the first time he turned and acknowledged my anger.

"Six?" he questioned, calmly. "How much of the book have you read, Michael?"

"I've read about the first murder," I said. "I couldn't bring myself to read another word; I felt physically sick."

"Then how did you come to the number of six?"

I hurriedly moved to the bench and sat beside him.

"I know about history. I needed proof; something to substantiate what my father had written."

"And does it?" he asked patiently. "Does your vast knowledge confirm his words as true?"

I sat with every emotion incarcerated inside me, but reluctantly I nodded.

"As much as I know, yes—everything," I replied.

He expressed little emotion and I mused whether it was life itself that hardened you to death; that as you aged it was easier to come to terms with.

"I would imagine that as assistant commissioner it was relatively easy to have your name erased from the hospital registers; that you never existed," I said.

He straightened and stared at me indignantly then dropped back into his slouched frame.

"You really do over-estimate me, Michael," he said with a wry grin. "I never erased my name from the hospital archives; I neither had the authority nor the access, but your father did. It was an exceptionally clever move on his part. He knew a deeper search would reveal my existence. Erasing my name implies I had something to hide. I buy books on the subject, and every one of them takes you further from the truth; and for that I must be grateful. God! Even our own people couldn't get it right.

I read the 'MacNaghten Memoranda,' penned by Melville MacNaghten, a so-called, self-opinionated expert on the case, who knows as much about Jack the Ripper as I know about constructing suspension bridges. They're all there, all the madmen. Fortunately for me, and for your father, all files appertaining to the case are closed and will remain so for another fifty years, so any author willing to tackle the subject will have to make do with unreliable memoirs, exaggerated press releases and hearsay cobbled together by fishwives and over-zealous reporters. Your father was correct: the written word bolsters the myth, blowing it all out of proportion. You see, Michael, we lived in a world occupied solely by death; it was everywhere, and we inherited a cavalier attitude towards it. Outside the hospital it was much the same. We would see the whores on the streets, the same whores who had come to the hospital the previous day seeking medication for their venereal disease, knowingly passing it on to some innocent man whose only crime was a form of sexual gratification. They were an unspeakable species; the lowest form of life."

"Diseased or not, they were not responsible. They had a living to earn."

He leaned back and slowly shook his head, appraising me with disbelief.

"Michael, I truly don't wish to sound condescending, but you have seriously been misinformed. There were an estimated 80, 000 prostitutes in London at that time, perhaps as many as a 100,000; they were so difficult to monitor and practically impossible to police. They didn't just sell sex. Notwithstanding their habitual disease spreading, they stole more money than they earned. They would lure drunken sailors and the like down alleyways where their criminal friends would wait to roll them for their pay; some were kicked to death. They would roam the East End in packs, threatening any lone prostitute who dares trespass on their patch. They were thieving, deceitful liars devoid of respect or compassion. Despite your beliefs, these women were not driven into prostitution out of necessity. They did it out of choice. How many men do you think they condemned by passing on their diseases, Michael?"

I felt I was losing grip on the situation, for although he expressed that he did not wish to sound condescending, it was difficult to believe he wasn't.

"You can't justify murder," I said in attempt to retrieve my authority.

"It is not my intention to, Michael," he replied. "I merely wish to familiarize you with the way life was for us and, of course, our attitude towards those we murdered. I use the word 'Murdered' by way of definition—a label for our actions. In my six months as an intern, do you know how many deaths I witnessed?" He looked at me coldly. "Seventy-three, Michael. As students we would often watch operations undertaken by a renowned physician, usually for the benefit of fellow doctors, governors, the leading minds of the medical profession, and all would applaud politely once he had finished. But how do you think such operations became successful? Perseverance and understanding. The operating theatre was exactly that—a theatre, a form of expression; a chance for a physician or surgeon to gain recognition and get that little bit closer to a knighthood, but with every successful operation, there were a dozen that failed. What fellow doctors, governors and the leading minds of the medical profession didn't see were those we experimented on; the East End cemeteries are filled with them. And for those who displayed the slightest trace of madness, we had a new adversary—electricity. Those charlatans truly believed that madness could be brought under control by electric shocks to the brain. And then there were the botched operations undertaken by inexperienced medical students such as your father and me. Of course, we weren't allowed to perform on anyone of breeding. Our guinea pigs were the unfortunates, the homeless, the ones who had nothing to look forward to but degradation. I took part in many of those operations; our betters regarded it as a form of initiation, a way of learning and, of course, their hands and their consciences remained clean. Many were healthy . . . or as healthy as they could be given their way of life, and their lives were brutally terminated by a medical student who didn't know the difference between a scalpel and a crowbar. The dead were taken away in covered wagons at the rear of the hospital and disposed of in the usual manner. Enquiries concerning loved ones were few and far between as most were loners, but those who made the effort were fobbed off with blatant lies. Put a man in a white coat and he'll convince you of anything; a position of authority can fool you every time."

The ducks and geese had devoured the last of the breadcrumbs and sailed off to the far side of the pond in search of a new benefactor, and Jonathan Sandpiper watched the glinting ripples left in their wake.

"I still find it difficult to define 'Murder,'" he continued, solemnly. "I hold myself accountable for the slaying of those women and that being the case then surely I must be held accountable for a dozen more human lives I lost on an operating table. As for the others I would be an accessory, as would my fellow students and attending doctors."

"What you did was deliberate!" I barked. "You purposefully hunted down prostitutes and killed them."

"Michael, Michael, Michael," he sighed wearily. "It was all deliberate. Do you honestly think a student with barely three months training should be let loose with a scalpel? I understand your repulsion, but you're asking me to put value on lives that didn't have any. They were not the women you see in magazines today; blue eyes, blond hair and sparkling teeth. These were broken down, drunken toothless hags whose agenda was to extract money from men by whatever means possible, and in return the men they serviced were left syphilitic. Have you seen what that disease can do to a healthy body, Michael? Untreated, the bodily organs degenerate, as do the tissues and, eventually it attacks the brain; it is a slow and excruciating death. Don't you regard that as cold-blooded murder, involving yourself in a sexual act in the knowledge that you have a congenital venereal disease? True, not all of them were cursed with the condition but given time they would be. That's why the younger ones were more expensive; less chance of contagion, you see."

"So you think that by killing a handful of whores, you actually made a difference?" I argued passionately. "Did the other nine-hundred and ninety four suddenly take a vow of chastity? Your argument is sound, Mr. Sandpiper, but the definition of 'Murder' is the unlawful killing of a human being with malice aforethought."

My spontaneous reply was ridiculous. Jonathan Sandpiper had been a high-ranking police officer and who had made it to the dizzy heights of assistant commissioner, and I was spouting the law at him. He never retaliated but instead cast eyes over to the far side of the pond, to a mother and child feeding the ducks, and a nostalgic smile formed on his lips.

"I used to bring Spike here, every morning without fail, no matter what the weather, and you would have thought it would have been a natural instinct for him to attack the ducks, but he never did; he liked them." He paused and registered my confused expression. "He was my dog, by the way; a golden Labrador with an insatiable appetite for sticky buns and rice pudding. I would bring him here for two hours every day. He lived to a ripe old age, nearly fifteen, and when he died I cried for days and I still miss him. Strange, but I have never been able to break the habit. I still come here for two hours every day and sit on this same bench; I would find myself talking to him. Do you know, I told him everything? He was the only one who ever knew what your father and I had done. It's a burden I've carried all my life."

His words trailed into a silence and he continued to look out over the water.

"So, what do you plan to do, Michael?" he asked without looking at me. "I understand your passion to have me punished, even hanged, for you've inherited your father's ambition and greed for recognition, and in the process it will make you a very rich man; every publisher in the western world will be clamoring for this story; the identity of the notorious Jack the Ripper."

"It's about justice!" I snapped. "You murdered six women!"

"There's that number again," Mr. Sandpiper smiled. "And since when did a lawyer know anything about justice? You're familiar with the word 'Vivisection', are you, Michael?"

"What?"

"Vivisection. Post-mortem." He rose from the bench and stared down at me. "Don't judge me, Michael, until you've read the book completely, until you have all the details, because when you have the complete story, the truth, you'll come to realize I never killed anyone; they were already dead."

He walked away then, the way he had at my father's funeral, and whether I liked it or not, I knew I had to read the book in its entirety.

-7-

Peter Egan was everything I thought he would be. When Badger and I entered the Cheshire Cheese that evening and saw him sitting at Dickens's table, I knew instinctively who he was. He was a broad man, mid-forties, with a strong jaw and swept back greying hair. He stood out from the other pinstripe-suited gentlemen who frequented the pub, dressed casually in grey trousers; dark blue jacket and a pale blue shirt open at the collar. I knew only what Sylvia had told me; that he was freelance and took up any cause he thought worth fighting for. He loathed corruption of any kind but especially police corruption and exposed it—warts and all—at every opportunity. He, perhaps, looked on it as a quest, as if it were a fiery dragon he had to slay and he was the knight in shining armour who could achieve it. He was fearless in his reporting and looked upon the Fleet Street hacks as nothing but Neanderthals who were barely capable of writing a shopping list, and his own unique style, his tenacity and brutal endeavours to expose the truth—no matter what the consequences—more often than not had his pieces rejected by cowardly publishers. As much as many considered him to be dangerous, he was honest in his reporting, and the countless liable cases he had faced in the past by disgruntled policemen, lawyers and even barristers, Peter Egan faced head on.

After collecting our drinks from the bar we approached him at the table, and he looked pleasantly surprised to see me, especially once I introduced Badger and myself.

"I wasn't expecting someone so young," he said with a smile. "So, you are representing George Henderson. Have you spoken with him yet?"

"The Home Office are aware of our situation," explained Badger.

"Takes time," he nodded. "And in this case it could take a lot longer. Those bastards will bury you in paper for a while; forms, application, licences, governor's approval, you name it and they'll find it. It's their way, you see. They don't take it lightly when one of their pupils goes awry. They'll sit on it for as long as they can and hope the problem goes away. By away I mean forgotten. One thing you can guarantee, you won't get to see Henderson until Carlisle's trial is over. They'll make it as difficult as they can for you."

"Why would they do that?" I asked as I took a seat opposite him.

He smiled wryly and raised his eyebrows.

"Because they can," he returned with a slight shrug. "Listen, Mr. James . . ."

"Michael," I broke in.

"Yes, Michael. They like to hedge their bets. They want to know the outcome of Carlisle's trial before they commit themselves; much like the Vassarri case. If Carlisle goes down, and he probably will, then all the lost paperwork concerning Henderson will be conveniently found and you'll be granted a visit to see him; pure and simple."

Exactly who and what Vassarri was I had no idea and dismissed the remark.

"And if Carlisle walks free?" questioned Badger.

"Then it's back to the beginning. The statement taken by Carlisle will be deemed honest and Henderson will have to take his chances on the stand, but that's never going to happen. Neither the police nor the government like a policeman who thinks he can run riot, least of all someone like Carlisle. Henderson is just the tip of the iceberg! When war broke out it opened up a whole new perspective of villainy, and Carlisle was into everything; racketeering, prostitution, the moneylenders, even the cargo ships. He wanted his cut. Mark me, he'll go down for a least thirty years. Put him out of your mind. Carlisle is gone."

I watched him as he sipped his glass of red wine, purposefully allowing a lengthy pause before speaking.

"I read your piece on Henderson in 'Fallow's Crime Magazine,'" I said. "I was very impressed. You say you have proof that Carlisle fabricated Henderson's statement."

He thought for a moment as if searching for an answer and then he nodded his head.

"Ah, yes! I wrote that when the story first broke. There wasn't a newspaper who would touch it, but Earnest Fallow, who to be frank doesn't give a fuck about anyone, took it. I've done a lot of work for him in the past but he can be frugal when it comes to paying for a story. But you're correct, Michael, I did have a reliable source."

"Which, of course, you can't divulge," said Badger.

"I can tell you! You, after all, are defending Henderson, the very reason I let the story go at half price. Stephen Rawlings was the source."

Badger and I exchanged wary glances at one another, that Peter Egan had been so forthright and divulged a source without the slightest coercion; taboo in the world of journalism.

"And Stephen Rawlings is who?" Badger enquired.

"Sergeant Stephen Rawlings—to give him his full and past title. He was in the interview room when the statement was taken from Henderson. According to him, Carlisle already had it written out; nine pages of it; times, dates, places. Rawlings was very much led by Carlisle and up to the same tricks, but when they were put under surveillance by their own people, he was found to be accepting bribes that amounted to no more than a few hundred pounds. I'm sure he took a lot more, but that's immaterial because their prize was Inspector Carlisle who was literally receiving thousands, either in cash or in goods. Pressure was put on those who handed over the money but no one would speak; all of their so-called businesses were iffy to say the least, and they could ill-afford any backlash from Carlisle's bent associates. So pressure was put on Rawlings; talk or face a long spell in prison. He chose to talk, of course. Well, why wouldn't he? Prison can be daunting enough for anyone, let alone a corrupt copper. So he informed them of every scam Carlisle was involved in, and for his sins he was dismissed from the force without any charges brought against him. The Met. hoped to keep the whole thing quiet, but Rawlings saw it as an opportunity to make money to fund his getaway and suddenly every newspaper was on the story. It opened up a whole new can of worms. Every villain to be nicked by Carlisle was screaming 'Injustice'; the Home Office were besieged by every bent solicitor for a retrial for their innocent clients who had wrongfully been incarcerated. At present there are 29 individual cases concerning Carlisle under consideration; thieves, rapist and murderers could walk free because of his greed."

"Whatever Carlisle is guilty of, it doesn't stray from the fact that Henderson gave himself up and admitted to all the murders," said Badger.

Peter Egan's face fell quite still and he appraised Badger as if he were an imbecile.

"And who told you that?" he returned indignantly. "Listen, my friend, Carlisle was on Henderson from the early stages. At around about the third murder, Henderson was stopped and questioned, and then a further two times after that, and every time he gave his real name and address. Carlisle's investigation was going nowhere so he did what all good coppers do; he went back to the beginning and came up with several possibilities, all of which proved to be completely innocent. The Home Office were putting pressure on the Met. and the Met. gave Carlisle an ultimatum; catch the killer or get off the case. With no suspects and no evidence Carlisle started to look at Henderson; a man who had been stopped and questioned three times, all of which corresponded with the times, dates and vicinities of the murders. George Henderson was a prime candidate, illiterate, slow-minded with strange habits. He was something of a miser. Every night he would fill a carrier-bag full of coal and take it home, and neighbours reported seeing him several times rummaging through dustbins. Carlisle went to Henderson's house and left a message with his wife that they were eager to speak with him and he should go to Camberwell police station at his earliest convenience; and that is exactly what he did. Before he knew it he was in a cell with eight counts of murder hanging over his head."

"So he never gave himself up?"

"Not willingly," Peter Egan shrugged. "He just did what he was told to do. Of course, he pleaded he was innocent and the confession was false, but that's what they all say. Besides, Rawlings witnessed the statement being taken, and being the corrupt bastard he is, verified that every word of the statement came from Henderson's mouth."

"But in court Rawlings will have to tell the truth."

"If they can get him to court. Shortly after I interviewed him he took off somewhere abroad; I paid him a lot of money for his information, written and verbal. He isn't about to return to face the courts when there's every chance of being found as guilty as Carlisle and spend half his life in prison."

He gulped down the last of his red wine and Badger instinctively took it and headed for the bar, and as if he were waiting for the opportunity, he looked directly at me.

"Michael, it's my policy never to talk to anyone without knowing who they are first, and there are some questions you must ask yourself before you continue. Who brought you this case?"

"Mr. Randall of the D.P.P." I replied.

"Ah, yes, good ol' Mr. Randall of the D.P.P." he grinned. "And why do you think he brought it to you?"

"We've represented Henderson in the past."

"So you might have, Michael, but this isn't paper law; it's criminal law, and neither you nor your associate is a criminal lawyer. I don't wish to sound disrespectful, but why would the D.P.P. hand over a case of this magnitude to a novice?"

I must have unconsciously frowned at the insult because he smiled again.

"They know you'll make a meal of it," he continued, "and they also know that you'll fuck it up. Henderson will go to the gallows leaving his wife and five children behind, Carlisle won't look as black as the media has painted him, and justice has been seen to have been done; everyone's happy. Listen to me, Michael, no respectable lawyer in this city would touch this case. Do you want to know why?"

I nodded grudgingly, still frowning from the first insult and the barrage that followed.

"It is believed that Carlisle perjured himself no less than 32 times at separate trials. Notwithstanding the blatant false statement of Henderson, corroborated by Sergeant Rawlings, they have no evidence and no witnesses. All they have is a corrupt copper. If you swing into action the D.P.P. will wring their hands with glee, and as much as you're tempted to play David against Goliath, you'll never win. Rawlings will never resurface again to discredit Carlisle and neither will the pimps and money-lenders he leaned on. Then you have the weight of the government and the Metropolitan Police Force to contend with. Sure, they want Carlisle punished, but how much other shit are you going to drag up? You may expose a hundred more like him. The Met. will look like a bunch of gangsters, and the government will be held responsible for employing them. The D.P.P. has nothing and they know it. In my view they'll have no alternative but to let it drop, providing you walk away from it. Henderson will be released with a small token for his trouble, and Carlisle's trial will be short, swift and probably undertaken behind closed doors. And never forget that Randall's sole purpose is to protect the government from any embarrassment. He's their watchdog, their protector. To pursue this case is to relieve the government of all responsibility. They want you to pick up the ball and run with it. Take my advice, Michael, and call their bluff. Let them know they have nothing to prosecute with."

"Despite Carlisle's alleged conduct, Randall believes that Henderson actually made the statement and admitted to all the crimes."

Peter Egan looked back in bewilderment, his eyebrows high on his head and an uncertain smile dashed across his lips.

"Well he would, wouldn't he? He has a job to do."

Badger returned then and set a glass of red wine down before Peter Egan. He smiled by way of appreciation and raised it to his lips.

"I guess it's a shame that Carlisle's antics were discovered," he said, thoughtfully. "The Henderson case would have made a great trial; a show-trial; the trial that should have happened fifty years ago had Jack the Ripper ever been caught."

My blood suddenly ran cold and I was consumed by absolute paranoia.

"Because he was the first serial killer?" I said, desperately trying to appear unaffected.

"The first we know of but there have obviously been others."

"Why are you so sure Henderson is innocent?" asked Badger.

The paranoia dissipated with the change of subject, much to my relief, and Peter Egan gulped down half the contents of his glass before grinning back at us.

"You have the alleged statement of Henderson?" he asked.

Badger and I nodded in unison.

"And have you read the newspaper articles on the murders?"

"I have every one of them pinned to my wall," explained Badger.

Peter Egan swallowed the last of the wine hurriedly and rose from the table.

"Paper law is black and white. Criminal law is grey. Sometimes the proof is right in front of you but you can't see it for looking. Bear in mind that Henderson is illiterate and you'll find the answer."

He shook our hands alternately and handed me his business card.

"It's been a pleasure, gentleman. I hope I've been of help."

Chapter Two

Knowledge

-8-

A dead East-End whore barely warrants a full-page spread in the national newspapers, and Mary Ann Nichols, or Polly as she was fondly referred to, was no exception, though the evening papers reported on it with much more gusto. The radical press turned it to their advantage, highlighting the plight of the poor and the depressed social conditions in which they lived. It was interesting how reports on the murder were clouded by presumption and blatant guesswork from so-called experts whose opinions bore no more resemblance to either Pip or me than the tooth fairy. For example, Dr. Ralph Llewellyn, the doctor called from his bed to examine the body of Nichols, concluded that the murderer was left-handed; neither Pip nor I are left-handed, and one can only wonder how these so-called men of learning ever found their way out of their mother's womb without a light. To be fare, Llewellyn believed that the bruising was the result of a hand being placed over the face, as a thumb mark was clearly evident, and that much is correct, but his interpretation as to the Modus Operandi was too preposterous for words. And to put salt on an already open wound, when he examined the body in situ he assumed that only the throat had been cut, when in reality Pip had cut into her abdomen; a wound that wasn't discovered until the body was taken to Old Montague Street Workhouse Infirmary. The press, seizing the opportunity to bump up the sales of their newspapers, willingly took our creation and made it their own, connecting Nichols' murder with Martha Tabram's Martha Tabram's a month earlier, but they can't be held solely responsible for the deception that occurred during the investigation. When the police took the body to the morgue they gave instructions that it wasn't to be touched, but to their surprise, two mortuary attendants stripped and washed the corpse prior to the second examination by Dr. Llewellyn, thus erasing any evidence either Pip or I had left behind. The police were therefore handed a profile on the killer, a left-handed or maybe right-handed assailant who left not one single trace of evidence and who had neither been seen nor heard by anyone. Our creation was born.

Pip and I sat on our beds scouring the daily papers for any new reports on the subject and read them to one another, consumed by an insatiable appetite for more information concerning our monster, and sometimes we would howl with laughter when the subject was so badly misreported that it could not have been further from the truth. As for us, the creators, we were unaffected and detached of all responsibility, taking only comfort from the fact that one less whore was walking the streets. "It's strange to read a story we're responsible for," said Pip. I was off the bed and standing before the mirror, appraising my appearance and new suit of clothes with an approving nod. "Indeed it is, Pip, and there'll be a lot more written about 'Jack' to come. Now look lively. Remember today we are having our photograph taken; the students of 1888." Pip collected the newspapers and hid them under his bed. "Do you mean we are to kill more?" he asked as he looked into the wardrobe for the appropriate clothes to wear. "But of course, Pip. Our creation will have no impact otherwise." He took a shirt from the shelf and shook it from its folds, and as he held it up in front of him, I frowned disapprovingly. "Please tell me you do not intend to wear that for the photograph," I said. Pip stared back innocently. "Look at the cuffs, Pip, look at the collar!" I growled. Despite his endeavours to soak and wash it to the best of his ability the shirt—the one he wore the night of the first murder—was blood-spattered and stained a pale pink. "That is very remiss of you, Pip. Soak it in salt; scrub it if you have to. I won't be ending my days in Newgate because of your irresponsibility and failure to pay attention to detail."

It was a week later, September 7th, to be precise, and Pip and I had walked into the city for no other purpose but to see it in all its nighttime glory and rub shoulders with the West-End rich instead of the East-End poor. We visited many public houses in Bloomsbury, and in Holborn we befriended three young lawyers who insisted on taking us to a brothel in St. Giles. Our companions were George, Henry and Steven, all of which obviously came from good stock and were articulate when conversing despite their overall drunkenness. It would appear that on the first weekend of every month these three young men would partake in imbibing as much alcohol as humanly possible without rupturing their bladders and sampling women brought in from all four corners of the planet. It was a chance for Pip and me to make comparisons with the whores we despised so much, and it has to be said that there were many to be drawn. The difference was stark. Steven, a fresh-faced graduate with a shock of ginger hair, theatrically referred to the whorehouse as a Bordello, whereas his companions opted for the Americanism of Cathouse, nevertheless we arrived around midnight or the early hours, at a backstreet house that bore no sign either boasting whorehouse, cathouse or bordello; a nondescript house of little character on the edge of Old Oxford Street and in the shadows of St. Giles's Church itself. "This area is renowned for its prostitute population," explained Pip as we walked. "In Medieval times, their rising numbers were such a threat that they were cast out beyond the city walls, mainly here at St. Giles, and here they remained until the walls decayed."

Obviously our new-found friends were regulars to this house of ill-repute, for they were greeted by a voluptuous woman garbed in mauve satin and long blond hair who showered them with kisses and snapped her fingers at a nearby beauty to attend to their every whim. Henry, a self-elected leader of the trio, introduced us as friends whereby we were instantly showered with kisses and ushered through to the vast lounge. It was dully lighted, the gaslights turned down to barely a flicker, but large candles were strategically placed on tables and stands and twinkled upon the staircase that coiled around the room to the floor above. Men of breeding, of high-standing consorted with the scantily-clad girls who entwined themselves around them like serpents and purred like adoring felines, as the lady in mauve led us to a long, leather settee and spoke in a foreign dialect, and in moments we were sipping Champagne. Our three companions looked anxiously around the room and then sat still and breathless as a half-dozen beautiful figures moved fluidly down the staircase, bathed in shadow and feeble mantles of light, and there they stood before us. Pip looked decidedly nervous and after absorbing their obvious attributes whispered in my ear. "We should leave. We should leave right now! They're just whores." It was decided back in Holborn that we would take up the invitation in order to view and not sample, but my needs as a man were consuming me, aided by the exquisite beauty standing before me. "Not so hasty, my young friend," I whispered back. "Do you not consider this wonderful specimen of womanhood to be nothing less than ravishing?" Pip slowly appraised her from the ground upwards, to her long slender legs, to her body incarcerated within a black Basque that exaggerated her breasts with every breath she inhaled, and her face; her face belonged to a goddess, framed within a heavy halo of light brown tresses resembling a lion's mane. Henry was already walking up the stairs with his choice and the lady in mauve was introducing George to his. I had to seize the opportunity and turned to Pip. "Call it research," I said. But as I rose to accept my prize, Steven had already claimed her. He could see the disappointment in my eyes, and as I was about to resume both my seat and my dignity, he suddenly released his grip on the girl's hand and said, "Where are my manners? As my guest I give her to you." As I walked to the foot of the staircase, with Pip's eyes burning into the back of my head, the lady in mauve approached and said in a French accent and an accompanying smile, "She's new. Can you speak Spanish?" I informed her that I could not and had never set foot off the British Isles in my whole life, to which she smiled brighter and nodded. "She comes from a small island off the coast of mainland Spain; daughter of a horse-breeder whose expertise is in the training and the exporting of breeds used specifically at Vienna's Lipizzaner. Her name is Maria and she speaks no English." I thanked her for the summary but was moved to add that my presence in such an establishment had little or no bearing on conversation whatsoever, let alone conversations on dancing horses.

When I came back down some two hours later, the atmosphere that had robbed me of all reason and influenced me to cast caution to the wind had all but evaporated, but for a few painted ladies looking withered and used slumped in chairs and Pip coiled up on the settee sleeping like a newborn. I paid the lady in mauve the catastrophic sum of three guineas and roused my companion from his slumber, manhandling him down the passage and into crisp early morning air. "You will call on us again, I hope," smiled the lady as she waved from the doorstep. "Most certainly we will, ma'am," I returned. I looked up at the house as the front door closed and saw Maria standing at the window. She held her hand up as if to wave but was distracted by someone entering the room and I saw her speaking with the lady in mauve who gently touched her face and kissed her on the head. "Well, I hope it was worth it," snarled Pip sulkily. I put my arm around his shoulder and we headed off in the direction of Holborn. "It was an extremely pleasant experience. It would do you no harm to indulge every now and then," I replied. He brushed my arm away and scowled back at me as if he wished me dead. "You are a hypocrite! You can dress them up as you like but they're still whores!" he barked. I smiled and returned my arm about his shoulder. "You are indeed correct, my friend, and I can only apologise for my moment of weakness, but there is a difference between the whores about this place and the whores who walk our streets. The whores we have seen tonight are handpicked for their beauty, servility and their sensuality; they are nought but employees, Pip, governed by the lady in mauve with her false French accent . . ." Pip suddenly stopped and stared back at me. "She's not French?" he questioned. "About as French as spaghetti," I continued. "You see, Pip, girls like Maria are scouted for all the attributes I have mentioned, looks, a fine figure, and their heads are filled with promises of a better life, money and even marriage to a wealthy man, but alas it is all a ruse, and many are shipped abroad to a life of slavery or as a concubine to some fat industrialist. Maria and her friends are ruled with an iron rod. They are never allowed to walk the streets and they get little of the money paid for their services. They are monitored regularly for their hygiene and venereal disease, and should they contract that unfortunate ailment, then they are discarded with no more compassion than the slaying of a lame horse. These women do not steal or rob, Pip, and neither do they spread contagion like the strumpets we have come to know. They are respectable whores who have been ensnared by opportunists, who have invested considerable amounts of money in a young woman and seek only profit. They are not the wild, unspeakable creatures we have come to know." Pip agreed with a nod and appeared willing to put the episode behind us, but I knew I would return to see Maria again.

Our walk took us through Clerkenwell and the length of Old Street to Shoreditch, into Great Eastern Street and Commercial Street, Spitalfields. The night was surrendering to the day and the sun rose low above the city skyline, shooting shafts of light through the gaps in the buildings, radiating a modicum of warmth between the shadows, spotlighting the market-traders on their way to the workplace, the horses being led from their stables and being harnessed to their wagons. Curtains twitched and opened and their occupants appeared at their doors with sandwich-boxes tucked under their arms and marched off to the factories, and the solace Pip and I experienced throughout our long walk, was suddenly and rudely interrupted by the city coming to life. We would walk our usual route, through Hanbury Street and into Baker's Row, directly opposite New Street; the road which housed our digs and was occupied by our contemptible, nymphomaniac landlady. "Whatever will we tell Mrs. Steere? She will most certainly inform the hospital that we've been out all night," said Pip, nervously. I slapped him on the back and gave him a wink as I strolled onward. "The woman need never know," I said. "If she isn't asleep or under some Polish sailor, I guarantee she'll be oblivious to our absence."

As we turned into Hanbury Street, a small, stout woman was walking before us somewhat unsteadily and at once I grabbed Pip's arm and slowed him down. "Have you the knife?" I asked, looking surreptitiously around me. Pip patted his chest pocket and then gasped, "Now—In broad daylight?" I peered down the street over his shoulder and saw the woman talking to a man, and further a way up the street was another woman who paid them a cursory glance and walked on leaving the road empty except for them. We watched for a moment as she and the man engaged in a short conversation and then the man broke away, heading in the opposite direction. "Follow my lead, Pip. As we were before," I said. I hurried up the street, passing an endless line of grimy four-storey terraces and shop-fronts with blistering paint and cracked windows, eventually stopping her outside number 29. She was barely five feet tall, with brown hair, broad nose and a double chin, and I used the same tantalizing lines as I used on the previous victim, but she looked me up and down suspiciously and folded her arms. "And why would a young man like you, wearing those fine clothes be interested in a woman like me?" she asked with a curious tilt of her head. I was momentarily lost for a witty retort and leaned myself against the wall. "Truth be told, I am a medical student, and students being what they are I have been set several challenges as part of my initiation. I may add at this point that there are rewards for every challenge undertaken, so I am willing to double my generous donation of sixpence to a shilling." She looked greedily at the coin nipped between my thumb and forefinger and looked back at me with doubt. "And who's to say if you have carried out this initiation?" she asked. I thumbed in the direction of Pip still loitering on the corner behind me. "My companion is witness to the challenge. I assure you he doesn't have to see the actual event, only that it has been achieved successfully," I explained with a smile. She backed up to three doors, the two either side serving the shops and the centre door leading into the back yards of the premises, and opening it she nodded her head and walked inside.

We were in the gloom of a hallway, with a straight staircase leading up to the floor above and all manner of discarded litter about our feet, and I could barely make out the squat frame of the woman as she walked on in front of me, but suddenly there was light and air and we were in the back yard, the door banging against a six-feet paling fence to the left. I stood on the first of three shallow steps leading down into the yard observing, the best I could, over the fences for any signs of activity. She was standing with her back against the fence with a simpering smile devoid of any sincerity, and as I descended the steps I briefly glanced up at the windows and specifically the window looking out directly into the yard; all curtains were closed and no signs of life visible. I appraised her as I approached, a white handkerchief tied about her neck with a red borderline along its edges, and as she opened her arms to embrace me, I threw out my hands and grasped her neck, my thumbs pushing into her windpipe, my whole strength channelled into my grip. I expected a harder fight than I received, for her heavy frame presented the illusion that she was blessed with considerable strength, but her eyes bulged and her tongue protruded slightly and she slowly slid down the palings and laid slumped at my feet. Again I looked up at the surrounding windows but saw no one and suddenly Pip emerged from the passage. Obviously he had not forgot my reprimand earlier in the day, as his jacket was in one hand, a knife in the other and his shirtsleeves were rolled up to the elbows. Within just a short time we were walking back down Hanbury Street, Pip's blood-spattered shirt hidden beneath his jacket.

I sat in silence, pushing the palms of my hands against my eyes as I digested the contents of what my father had written and the magnitude of his crime, but as I wallowed in self-pity and suppressed anger, a new imbroglio was standing before me—Penny. I had intentionally avoided her over the past few days and was relieved that she had neither confronted me nor, as far as I knew, told the other staff-members of our liaison, but as much as my initial reaction concerning her silence eased my feelings of betrayal, I found myself consumed by jealousy. Obviously I had passed her in reception or in Tom or Andy's office and her acknowledgement of me was unchanged, and on three occasions I overheard her talking to Sylvia about a man she had met two nights ago and the seduction that had taken place. She spoke as if he was special, mentally, physically and sexually, leaving me feeling nondescript and sexually inadequate; that my endeavors in the field of love-making were so bad that her silence was designed to protect her from ridicule and embarrassment from anyone she told and may well have induced my own wife to seek out the advances of the local grocer's son.

"Can we talk, Michael?" she asked, glancing nervously back through the open door to reception.

I made the best of it, forcing a smile in an attempt to appear cavalier.

"Certainly," I replied in my best employers tone. "How can I help?"

She gently closed the door and faced me. Her doxy veneer had all but disappeared and there was a moment she reminded me of how she looked in her apartment, when she was devoid of make-up and office garb; she appeared a frightened child.

"It's about the other night . . ." she began.

"Oh, that," I returned callously. "Those things happen; forget it."

She was momentarily stunned.

"You've done this before?"

"Done what before, Penny?" I retaliated patiently. "You see—I'm not sure if anything happened at all. Did I dream it? Were you and I actually entangled in those bed sheets for half the night and gasping for breath? Because from where I'm sitting I think it was just a fantasy."

"You've been avoiding me."

"No more than usual. I'm running a business, Penny. Besides, from what I've heard you haven't wasted any time in finding a replacement. Were your expectations of me so high at the beginning that I was destined to be a total failure in the end?"

"No, but . . ."

Something stopped her and she bowed her head. All I could do was look at her and curse myself under my breath for being so spiteful and childish.

"Do you want me to leave the firm?" she asked quietly.

"No, Penny, I don't want you to leave the firm," I sighed.

"Will you give me the chance to explain something to you, tonight at my place?"

"Penny, I don't think . . ."

"It has nothing to do with sex," she interrupted. "I just need to explain and then you can go; everything will just go back to normal."

Just then the door knocked and Badger entered. He had locked himself away in his office, and taking Peter Egan's advice, began to trawl through the newspaper reports on Henderson and comparing them with his alleged statement.

"Sorry," he said, noting Penny's obvious alarm. "Michael, Egan was right. I think you should come and see this."

Badger returned to his office and I rose from my desk.

"Okay, Penny, if you think it will help. I'll see you after work."

She nodded and smiled sadly.

Badger was sat on the edge of his desk, grinning wolfishly when I entered.

"Love still blooming?" he asked.

I was still reeling from what I had read in my father's book but continued the masquerade of appearing normal, or as normal as I could appear given the fact that my whole world was in turmoil.

"So what is it I need to see?" I asked, ignoring his smart enquiry.

He passed me a newspaper clipping on Susan MacDonald, the fourth victim found at the Elephant and Castle on October 25th.

A fifty-two year old woman was found brutally murdered on the kitchen floor. The murderer had obviously entered through the rear of the house, where an adjacent alleyway gives access to the line of terraces. Henderson may have waited out his time to strike in the outside toilet . . .

Badger stopped me there, pointing to the statement allegedly given by Henderson to Carlisle.

I entered the house from the back, down the alley and waited in the outside toilet until the time was right to attack, until she was in the kitchen . . .

"That statement was supposedly given five weeks after the Daily Mirror surmised the movements of Henderson, yet no police report suggests that he entered the house through the backdoor. On the contrary, they imply that Susan MacDonald willingly allowed the murderer in through the front door, that she either knew him or he was working under the guise of a maintenance man or some type of council official. All the other newspapers play the same game, supposing and guessing at the killer's movements prior to the murders, and all are reiterated in Henderson's so-called statement; some practically word for word. The upshot, Michael, is that every word of that statement has been cribbed from a dozen or more newspapers."

My eyes darted back and forth from the clipping to the statement, and then I looked back at Badger curiously.

"But Carlisle would have known the contents of the police reports," I stated.

"With all the things he was up to, I doubt it!" he replied. "Remember he was given an ultimatum to find the murderer or get off the case; he just made the best of what was available. George Henderson being illiterate proves that Carlisle framed him."

"But why didn't Peter Egan mention that in his magazine article?"

Badger smiled.

"Because as brave as he may be, he knows the difference between what can and can't be proved. When Carlisle's antics were exposed, the Met. closed ranks and refused to make any comment. Egan has simply handed the glory to us."

I grinned victoriously and patted Badger on the arm.

"Then we shall contact the D.P.P. and tell them of our findings," I chirped.

As enthralled as I was about discovering Henderson's innocence, it did not detract from the fact that my father and his friend had murdered their second victim, and as much as I thought I knew about history, I was obviously ill-informed when it came to the most notorious murderer of the Victorian age—Jack the Ripper.

That evening Penny and I walked silently over Blackfriars Bridge amid a thin straggle of pedestrians, and a light September breeze with the hint of a chill moved gently up the Thames but became lost amongst the buildings on the south side, and throughout the walk of the expanse we never uttered a single word but I could feel her looking at me every now and then. She continued her usual route and turned into Southwark Street where I stopped, waiting to cross the junction and continue down Blackfriars Road. Realizing my absence she turned about and walked slowly back to me. "Is everything all right, Michael?" she asked timidly. I had taken Rachel's card from my pocket and was searching it for a street number. I nodded and smiled, saying. "Everything is fine," placing the card back in my pocket. And then came that awkward moment when there was nothing to say or, at least, if there was, it could easily be misconstrued. "Aren't you coming back tonight?" she asked, raising her voice over the noise of the passing traffic. She appeared overwhelmed by sadness, and as she waited for a reply her head lowered. "Nothing can come of this, Penny," I said, impulsively. She nodded as her eyes rose to meet mine. "I know that, Michael," she said. "Look, if you're worried that I'm going to turn into a bitch and tell your wife, I'm not. If you think I'm going to tell Sylvia or Badger, I won't. I'm not the brazen hussy you think I am. If you never want to see me again then it's over; you won't hear another word from me. You have my word that I won't fall in love with you, Michael." There was no trace of emotion in her voice and no tears welling in her eyes, and her explanation was delivered with no more sentiment than if it were a verbal contract of mutual agreement, despite her sad refrain. "I have something to do first," I said, my eyes fixed on the outstretched road before me. She nodded and half turned. "I'll make you some dinner and leave the front door on the latch. If you come back then I'd like that. If you don't, I'll see you at work tomorrow." She smiled and I watched her figure turn into a silhouette as she walked beneath the railway bridge.

I continued with my quest, taking the card from my pocket once again, and I reached the conclusion that Fishers Bookshop must be a vast concern if it could dispense with its precise location on its business cards, and when I had almost walked the length of Blackfriars Road and considered turning about, I saw a small shop nuzzled within a row of terraces; a greengrocers to its left and a hardware shop to its right, and the weather-beaten sign above the door, barely legible even in broad daylight, boasted the name 'Fishers Book Shop.' I gingerly entered, a tiny bell on a spring sounding above my head, and what surprised me was the depth of the shop, where every available space was lined with books and the aisles between the racks appeared to disappear into infinity. "Best be quick, we're about to close," said a familiar voice. "Rachel?" I called. She emerged then from an opening half way down an aisle, carrying a pile of books, and she smiled brightly as soon as she recognised me. "Michael, this is a pleasant surprise. What brings you here?" she said, placing the books on the desk by the door. "No, let me guess. You're at a loose end and want to take me to the Ritz." I smiled back at her. "Actually, no," I said, still surveying the bookshop. "A restaurant, then?" she continued. My smile remained. "Okay, I'm not fussy, but I warn you, I can't be late back." I shook my head. "I'm after a book," I explained. She feigned disappointment and cursed. "Damn it! That's what everyone says when they come in here. Why should I think that your reasons would be different? What book—exactly?" I moved a little closer in until I was facing the thousands of books lined on sagging shelves. "Jack the Ripper."

I was expecting the response to be one of alarm, but she calmly circled her desk and began to thumb through a thin tray of index cards, and removing two she walked directly to the far aisle, saying as she passed, "That'll be in 'Crime', follow me." The narrow aisle, which two people could only pass through if both were seriously emaciated, stretched on forever, but eventually we stopped and she scanned her eyes over the spines of the books, pulling one out and handing it to me; '*The mystery of Jack the Ripper*' by *Leonard Matters*. "That was released in 1929," she said, still studying the shelves. She stooped slightly and pulled out a larger book from the collection. "Or there's this. Sorry but there isn't much on the subject," she said, resting her shoulder against the shelves and folding her arms. "I may be able to help you here, to save you wasting valuable time. Nobody knows who he is," she added with a nod. I was looking at the face of the book with an obvious confused expression; *'How I caught Crippen,'* by *Walter Dew* and stared back at her. "According to the index card, two thirds of the book is dedicated to the Ripper case. That was first published in 1939." I turned to the first page, to the 'Introduction' and much to my surprise, read that Walter Dew was a serving police officer in H Division and was active in the Whitechapel Investigation. "He must still be alive," I mumbled as I read. "Probably," said Rachel. "It's only two years old so there's a good chance he is. Sorry, but they're all I have." She waved her arms, ushering me down the narrow corridor of books until we were back at the desk where she proceeded to organise her pile of books, the largest at the bottom and smallest on top.

"Damn it! I'm going to be late for the pub and I have to deliver these books to Stamford Street," she said as she looked at a large, black clock on the wall. "I'm sorry, Michael, but I really am in a rush."

"I understand. How much do I owe you for the books?"

"That's all right, have them on me. Call it my half of the taxi fare. If anyone asks I'll just say they were stolen."

With the half dozen books in a neat pile she disappeared into a back room and emerged threading her arms into the sleeves of her coat.

"Would it help if I delivered the books for you? I have to walk back that way," I suggested.

"Oh, Michael, would you?" she sighed with relief. "It would save me a thirty minute round trip."

She scribbled down the address and handed it to me and all her urgency disappeared.

"So what is your interest in a Victorian murderer?" she asked, taking a small mirror from her handbag and assessing her image.

"Just a case I'm working on. I thought the books might help me. How is your job?"

"Boring," she replied, taking a lipstick and applying it. "And yours?"

"Enlightening and getting worse."

She smiled with uncertainty, and pulling the mirror away from her, began to pick and prod at her hair.

"So how is your beautiful wife?"

"Very well, thank you," I replied in a hopeless attempt to look and sound convincing.

She paused from her task and passed me a suspicious sideways glance.

"Michael, a man never gives a reply like that when answering to an enquiry about his wife. You make her sound like a traction engine."

It occurred to me then that if I was to return to Penny's she might ask questions about the books I had purchased.

"Could you wrap these for me?" I asked.

She continued to busy herself in the small mirror.

"There's a bag in the desk drawer, will that do?"

I agreed to accompany her to Southwark, carrying the books for her like a love-struck schoolboy. She was different, happier, with a spring in her step and a bright mood, and whenever the conversation petered out she would hum gently to herself.

"You seem full of the joys of spring," I said.

She turned to me and beamed a smile.

"I've heard from David," she replied. "I don't know exactly where he is, but I can't tell you how relieved I was to know he is all right."

For a moment I was hoping that David was her own creation; an excuse to stave off any unwanted admirers, but as she rummaged through her handbag to find the communication, I realised he was very real and found myself resenting his existence.

"Ah, here it is," she said, handing me the letter. "Read it."

I declined the offer with a shake of my head and her response was one of disappointment, but with a shrug of her shoulders she placed the letter back in her handbag.

"He wants to have children when he gets back," she said as she continued walking. "He says we'll move out of London and to the country; just like you suggested, Michael, eh?"

"That's great news, Rachel, it really is. Hopefully this wretched war will be over soon and you'll be together. I'm happy for you."

She stopped and faced me, her brown eyes searching mine.

"Are you, Michael? Are you really happy for me?" she asked.

"Of course," I replied, turning away to disguise my own disappointment.

She nodded thoughtfully and looked to a public house across the street.

"Well, here I am," she sighed. "No rest for the wicked.

"Yes, no rest for the wicked."

She leaned closer to me and kissed me on the lips. It wasn't a passionate kiss. It was a clumsy attempt, like a boy and girl in the throes of puberty, hell-bent on experimentation, made worse by my stubborn reaction to turn my face away at the last second. Her happiness for her war-hero turned Rachel into just another acquaintance, and any intentions I had to make her more seemed to dissipate in the warm summer evening.

"I hope the books will be of use," she said.

I watched her walk across the street and disappear into the pub without turning back and I set off towards Stamford Street to deliver her books.

When I arrived back at Penny's flat the front door was, as promised, left on the latch, and when I reached her door it was partly open and not a sound coming from inside. I hesitated for a moment and pushed the door open wider until I could view the hallway entirely, and when nobody came into view I slowly entered and walked to the lounge. Penny was sitting on the settee with an upright posture, her hands placed on her knees and wearing her red, satin robe, her face motionless. "I need to show you something, Michael. Will you sit down?" Her behaviour was cold and strange and as I sat she rose, standing before me, where she untied her belt and let the robe fall to her feet. My eyes roamed her perfectly proportioned naked body, and as I was about to ask the obvious question, she turned around. A scar ran from the right of her neck, across her shoulder blade and down the entire length of her spine, sporadically punctuated with short, horizontal scars and trailing off above her right buttock. "An operation of some kind?" I asked. She stooped, picked up her robe and placed it on and resumed her seat next to me.

"I was nineteen and working for an insurance company," she began quietly. "A young man had been transferred from our Portsmouth office to be our new supervisor. He wasn't regimented like the others we'd had in the past; he was funny and friendly and he knew his job. Then I loved to flirt and he was handsome and showed me a lot of attention, and one evening he asked me out. And once, perhaps twice a week, we would go back to his or my flat and have sex even though he knew I had someone else. He didn't mind, it suited him; there were never any questions, no signs of jealousy, and this continued for about six months. I was a lot like Sylvia, precocious and gullible; I'd sleep with anyone as long as they said the right things. Anyway, one night I came home and I found him sitting in my kitchen, a half drank bottle of whiskey on the table in front of him. He called me all the names a girl like me would expect and I told him to get out. Suddenly I was on the floor and he was sitting astride me, punching me in the face and head; he wouldn't stop. He just kept punching, and then he was on his feet and kicking me. I'll never forget the look on his face. He turned away and started rummaging through the kitchen drawers and somehow—I can't remember how—I crawled to the front door and opened it, screaming for someone to help me. I was on my knees in the doorway, and suddenly I felt the knife in the base of my neck and as I fell forward the blade dragged down my back. I heard a noise, people running up the stairs, scuffles all around me. Anyway, I spent three months in hospital, and they fixed me up as good as new; to look at me you'd never know."

I gently touched the small scar on her forehead.

"So this wasn't a childhood accident? Is that why you touch it every time a man looks at you?

"Is it that obvious?" she asked.

A single tear wove its way down her cheek but she never broke.

"Can you keep a secret, Michael?" she said.

I put my arm around her shoulder and pulled her closer to me.

"There are no men in my life," she continued. "I sometimes lay awake and invent them. Some are perfect and some not so perfect, but for one night they're mine. Competing with Sylvia can be difficult but I try hard."

We all live two lives and we all posses a dark side. It may come in the form of a fetish or a perversion, a suppressed anger that surfaces from time to time, but usually they are secrets; some long-ago misdemeanour that we hide from the rest of the world, whether you be the aggressor or the victim. Rape victims rarely speak about their ordeals and less than half are reported. The act of rape or sexual assault is not the act itself but the aftermath; what the victim has to carry with them for the rest of their lives; the demons we live with every day. Until recently I was unaware I had any demons but now I know they will haunt me for the rest of my days. Why Penny felt the need to confide in me I'll never know. I can only assume she trusted me. Without thought for Sarah or my own treachery, I sat cradling Penny in my arms until she fell asleep, and covering her with a blanket I took my books and headed into the kitchen.

According to Rachel *'The Mystery of Jack the Ripper'* was the first hardback to tackle the subject on the Whitechapel Murders though various short stories and articles have appeared ever since the murders began. Leonard Matters, the author, had an impeccable record and was an outstanding journalist. There remained an element of doubt within me; that what my father had written was a complete hoax, even though the names, times and dates corresponded exactly with the facts and Pip, or Jonathan Sandpiper, had admitted to taking part in the crimes. I was in an honoured position. To give his own slant on the story and, of course, to furnish motive, Matters created his own myth and names the perpetrator of the crimes as Dr. Stanley, a brilliant London doctor whose son Herbert contracted syphilis from Mary Jane Kelly in 1886 and died. Thereafter he set out to avenge his son by murdering the whore and her friends. I knew the victims were not associated with one another and that a motive did not exist. I read the book in its entirety, whereas I had only read to the murder of Annie Chapman in my father's words, shuddering on its closure as I realised the worst was yet to come.

It was the early hours and I was consumed in Walter Dew's book *'I Caught Crippen'* which concerned itself more with politics of the murders than the murders themselves. Suddenly a hand touched my shoulder and I jumped to my feet, certain I was about to have a heart attack.

"Michael, are you all right?" asked Penny drowsily. "I thought you had gone."

"So did I," I replied, still clasping my chest.

I slowly sunk down into my chair and Penny sat opposite at the kitchen table.

"What are you reading?" she asked, registering the books.

I unconsciously closed the book.

"Nothing. Nothing much."

"Jack the Ripper!" she said with an uncertain grin. "Are you thinking of ways to kill me?"

"No, Penny, not yet. Just a little research," I smiled.

"Henderson?"

I nodded but she stared back with a puzzled expression.

"But don't you and Badger believe he's innocent?" she questioned.

"We know he's innocent, Penny!"

"Then why the need to research a multiple murderer? Are you having doubts?"

I was stumped for an answer.

"Have you any tea?" I asked.

"No milk."

"No matter."

-9-

The weekend was upon us. Friday, as usual, was always a short day for me and I would leave at lunchtime to ensure I arrived home. That morning Penny and I left her flat together after I had spent the night on the settee while she returned to her bed. By no means did this make me a saint or a reformed gigolo; it simply made me a weakling who, like so many men, allowed himself to be seduced with a smile and a stark naked beautiful woman lying next to him. Penny made no mention of why I didn't return to her bed but I felt she knew I was drowning in guilt, despite my reservations about my own wife's infidelity. Badger had left a note on my desk, saying he was out tracking down Henderson's past, and could I meet with Edward Foster, Henderson's friend and work companion, at the railway goods depot in Aldgate, at 10.30. I was relieved to be out of the office for a few hours, away from Penny, away from Sylvia and her incessant questions and away from Tom and Andy and their wretched Driscoll case. Although my destination was coincidental, I could not help but feel that fate played a hand, for I found myself in the back of a cab moving through the same streets my father and Pip had walked through. "You realise you're in Ripper territory, don't you?" said the cab driver over his shoulder. I was in no mood for a guided tour and feigned ignorance. "Really," I replied. "Oh, yeah!" the cabby continued with immense authority. "That bastard killed twenty women. Tore them to pieces and hung their body parts all over the place. They never caught him." I was moved to say that he killed five and five only, you ignoramus, but instead simply sat nodding my head and turning my nose up as he detailed the bloody massacre. I must admit to turning my head and looking up Commercial Street as we passed before driving into Mansell Street and the entrance to the goods depot.

The noise was deafening on entering the yard. Trains shunted back and forth bellowing out plumes of steam that swirled about the rafters of the vast wooden shed seeking escape; tractors ferried fuel from mountains of coal stored in bunkers around the perimeter and above me men walked gantries, feeding hoses into the iron horses and filling their tanks with water. All around me there was activity and noise, and if my initial concern was how I would recognise Edward Foster, I realised he would have little trouble in recognising me as I stood in my dark grey suit and pristine white shirt while everyone else was attired in sooty boiler suits and caps. Eventually I was approached by a young man barely twenty years of age, wearing a brace-and-bib overall and covered in soot from his head to his hobnail boots; his teeth and eyes his only recognisable features. He dispensed with talk, realising its futility over the din, and instead beckoned me to follow him into the yard. We walked to the far corner, until the noise faded and a conversation was possible.

"Edward. Edward Foster?" I said.

He nodded and extended his hand but abandoned the gesture on acknowledging my horror at the prospect.

"Eddy," he said. "Your man phoned the yard and told them you'd be here. You're lucky, I'm on a turn-around; back on the plate in half-hour."

"The plate?" I asked.

"That's what we stand on when we shovel the coal. They've put me with Henry Stubbs at the moment, a right miserable bastard; not the same without George. How is he?"

"I haven't met him as yet," I said, handing him my card. "It's complicated; different channels to go through. Tell me, Eddy, how long have you known George?"

"Three years we've worked together. I left school at fourteen and worked for a while in the stores, but I used to see George in the canteen and we became friends. George got me the job."

"Can you tell me a little bit about him; his habits. What is he like?"

Eddy smiled warmly and slowly began to nod his head.

"He's a good man, a funny man; always has a story to tell; loves his family. He must really miss them being banged up twenty-four hours a day."

"Yes, he must," I agreed. "You told the Daily Mirror that he could be eccentric sometimes."

"Sure I did, but can't we all be—at times?" said Eddy defensively. "A lot of what the press said is shit; he never carried bags of coal home or searched through dustbins but he would walk back through the trains to see what people had left behind. He found some good stuff. He used to take the old newspapers home for his fire, that's all; don't make him a murderer."

He took a small, square tin from his pocket and popped the lid, then delving his fingers inside took out a small heap of tobacco that resembled shredded tar and a crisp, white paper and thereafter began to fashion a cigarette between his filthy fingers.

"It's all that Carlisle's fault," he mumbled, preoccupied with his creation. "George is a good man; one of the best. How long before they let him out, do you think?"

"Not long, Edward," I replied. "First we have to prove that George is a good man and not capable of such terrible crimes. Has he ever done anything out of the ordinary?"

Edward ran his slender tongue along the edge of the cigarette paper and sealed it, and with a flash of a lighter was engulfed for a moment in a smoky haze.

"How's that?" he croaked as the fumes attacked his eyes and throat.

"Well, did he do anything unbecoming his usual self; anything out of the ordinary?"

"Nothing I can think of," Edward returned, finding his voice. "He could be a bit offish sometimes, though. If he didn't like someone he wouldn't talk to them. Many a time I've seen him turn his back on someone he didn't like."

"But that was the full extent of it? It never resulted in violence?"

"What George! Leave off, he wouldn't hurt a fly."

Once again Edward disappeared behind a veil of smoke only to remerge looking doubtful.

"I am saying all the right things, aren't I? I mean—I don't want to ruin his chances of getting out."

"On the contrary, Edward, you're saying all the right things. If you had to describe George Henderson in a court of law what would you say?"

Edward thought for a moment, staring at his soot-sodden cigarette that was beginning to lose the fight for life.

"I'd say he was a good'un, one of the best; a good friend and a good father. Do you think I'll have to say those things?"

"I don't think it will come to that."

Extracting information from a witness was never my forte and I had hoped that Edward Foster would blurt out every decent trait George Henderson possessed without any coercion from me. Instead he sat silent, studying the extinguished cigarette between his fingers with great interest and debating whether the short, thin stump was worth igniting again. Eventually he opted for its rebirth and craning his head to one side miraculously avoided catching his face on fire.

"So, George won't have to stand trial?" he asked, picking a rogue strand of tobacco from his bottom lip.

"He was simply at the wrong place at the wrong time," I explained. "Simply Carlisle set him up. Neither the government nor the D.P.P. want to launder this in public."

I picked at Edward like a bird pecking at breadcrumbs, but all to no avail. He said nothing derogatory about his friend but, instead, reiterated what he had already mentioned, annoyingly adding, 'George is a good man,' as a tag line at the end of every recollection. The short interview reached one indisputable conclusion; George Henderson was indeed a good man, a good friend and a respectable human-being who wouldn't hurt a fly, and as the adoration poured fluidly from his mouth, I could not help but think that until recently I harboured the same opinion of my father.

"Did you know his wife?" I asked.

"May? Sure I know her," Edward returned. "Haven't seen her for a long time, though. It's terrible what they did to her; smashed her windows, bullied the children—forced her into hiding. The public can be bastards, can't they?" His mood darkened in a moment and he began to shake his head. "Do you know what those fuckers did?" he continued. "They pushed dog's shit through her letter-box and threatened to kill the kids, saying they would all grow up like her ol' man—a butcher. She had to take them out of school and then . . . well, and then she just vanished. Bastards!"

"Does nobody know where she can be found?" I asked.

Just then a whistle distracted Eddy and he looked to the entrance of the vast wooden shed, to a plump man waving his arms.

"That's me," he said, tossing his withered roll-up to the floor and screwing it into the ground with his hobnail boot. "Someone must know where she is. George is bound to know! Listen, I have to go, but when you see George give him my best."

I watched him walk away and disappear into the shed, leaving me no more informed than I was before meeting him.

-10-

Sunday dinnertime was a ritual; a masquerade Sarah and I constantly went through. At 12.30 we would stroll up the pathway to the Dog and Duck, an aged country pub of low ceilings, black beams and gleaming brass coalscuttles, patronised by bankers, shopkeepers and farmers who proudly announced themselves to strangers as 'locals' or 'town folk'. I never considered myself as one of them but Sarah, however, tried desperately to be part of it and part of them. And so promptly at the same time every Sunday, no matter what the weather, we would enter with forced smiles and seemingly without a care in the world, imbibe and engage in meaningless conversations with people who were musts to avoid any other day of the week. To them we presented the illusion of the perfect couple; the successful lawyer and the doting housewife, and once even I believed it. Today was different. We were greeted in the usual fashion, a half-dozen or so voices crying "Here they are," by way of a fanfare, and thereafter Henry, the pot-bellied landlord who always sported a white shirt and bright red bowtie would serve us, always commenting on Sarah's beauty and on my good fortune to be her husband. Secretly, I'm sure, he was something of a pervert, for his eyes would constantly roam the bodies of any woman remotely good looking even while he was talking to their husbands. And then there were the rounds that followed, moving from couple to couple, to talk about work, the price of eggs and, obviously, the war. They were the same crowd, the same clique, the same conversations that I would endure under enormous duress, and when such signs of fatigue became obvious, Sarah would shoot me a disapproving scowl and attempt to lift the conversation to new heights.

It was during such a debate about the church fete or raising funds for the church roof and I was seriously losing the will to live, that I noticed Judge Newland seated at his usual table. Although retired, he was still fondly referred to by the locals as Judge, a man who rarely engaged in conversation and demanded privacy, especially on a Sunday when he would simply sit and study several newspapers and clean off a whole bottle of port. Amiable enough he would acknowledge each and every one of us with a nod and then return to his reading matter, but today he was looking directly at me, even though I was partly obscured by a small, nattering crowd. I can't recall ever speaking with him in great depth and looked upon him as something of an eccentric who lived on the outskirts of town with his wife and several cats. He was eighty if he was a day, but sharp and sprightly, and the few times I had heard him talk he spoke eloquently and intelligently. Had I not known his past occupation I would have thought him to be an actor, as his gestures and banter were somewhat theatrical. His eyes bore into me and I gladly broke away from my fellow patrons and moved in front of his table.

"Michael isn't it?" he said, resting on his elbows and looking up at me. "A little bird tells me you're defending George Henderson, The Blackout Butcher."

"Merely considering it, nothing more," I replied.

He smiled knowingly and looked to the empty chair before me.

"You'll join me, of course; get you away from the village idiots."

I looked briefly behind me to see Sarah talking with the usual fishwives, none of which had registered my absence.

"An interesting case," he said as I took up the chair. "I've been following it most closely. Senility has yet to reach my door and I fight it off at every opportunity. Reading keeps the rusty wheels turning, albeit slowly. Will you join me in a glass of port, Michael?"

The offer was tantamount to sharing a cigar with Winston, as Judge Newland was considered something of royalty in our sleepy little town, and already the ones who were unaware I had left their company, were now staring in our direction.

"Pay them no mind," said the judge as he fleetingly cast his eyes over the watchful crowd. "So, what made you take this case on?"

"As I said: I'm only considering it at present."

"It obviously intrigues you. Why else would you take it under consideration?"

"George Henderson was my client several years ago. Ostensibly he still is. The case was brought to me but I can refer it if I so wish."

"That wasn't my question. You could—if you so wished—have referred it immediately, yet you chose not to. Why would someone such as yourself take on a case he can't possibly win?"

I was taken aback by his bluntness and somewhat confused by his hard line of questioning, and in a moment concluded that Newland considered himself to be royalty and resented the idea of a fellow local defending a murderer. I looked behind me at the staring faces and then scowled directly back at him.

"Are you some kind of self-elected spokesman? Is that why you're taking this tone with me?"

He registered my anger and suddenly roared with laughter, leaning forward and patting me on the hand.

"Is that what you think?" he cackled. "You think I represent these small-minded yokels? Pay me no mind, Michael. I was once a judge and still think like one, and I know at times I still act like one. I'm not criticising you, Michael, I revere you. I admire you taking on such a case. Do you know I play a game where I think of myself as the judge presiding over a forthcoming trial I have read about in the newspapers and I predict the outcome? If the outcome is different from my own, I write a strongly worded letter to the real judge and reprimand him for his stupidity. I have been reported on several occasions to the police. It's all I have left; a suffering wife, my cats, and a legal brain that refuses to retire. So forgive my overbearing manner and indulge me . . . please."

A glass suddenly appeared, courtesy of Henry, and the judge poured out his precious port into it, passing me a smile as he did so.

"Henderson is innocent," I said.

The judge leaned back and folded his arms, composed and serious now.

"Is that just your opinion or have you proof?" he asked. "I ask because the reports are vague; they're reluctant to give the full story and that usually means the government are playing some part in it. Am I correct?"

"It appears that way, yes. Carlisle's trial is looming which means Fleet Street have probably been put under wraps."

"It's usually the way. So why are you so convinced your client is innocent?"

I was reluctant to answer, suspicious of his questions, thinking that as a judge, albeit a retired one, he may have connections with the government, the D.P.P. or worse Jonathan Sandpiper.

He saw it in my eyes immediately and grinned.

"Michael, I am not your Nemesis. I'm just a silly old duffer who craves intelligent conversation once in a while. Do you think the numbskulls that patronise this establishment can fulfil my needs?"

He shook his head, rolled his eyes and laughed and I was at once put at ease. He despised these people almost as much as I did.

"Henderson is illiterate," I said.

"And why does illiteracy make him incapable of murder?" he shrugged.

"It doesn't. Inspector Carlisle took his statement and read it back to him, and thereafter Henderson signed it . . ."

I paused as the judge shook his head in total bewilderment, and I realised at once the reason for his reaction.

"Henderson had learned to sign his name, and this he did only because his wages had to be signed for. When it comes to reading and writing it was all he was capable of. Learning how to write his name was a means to an end and only served one purpose," I explained.

The judge appeared satisfied and nodded.

"At present Carlisle is under investigation; fabricating evidence, perjury. Henderson claims he never made such a statement and that Carlisle made it all up . . ."

"Michael, you can't just fabricate a statement. Somewhere in those pages there has to be facts; facts to corroborate his testimony; times, dates, places and, of course, the victims."

"They're all there; everything to send Henderson to the gallows. And who better to know all the facts than Carlisle; the man who had been on the case from the very beginning. He had witnessed the victims in all their glory, bled to death with a cutthroat razor and raped before and after death. But he had no evidence. No sign of breaking and entering, no witnesses, no fingerprints or footprints, nothing to indicate how the victims were chosen or why. When the story first broke every sleuth in England was on the case, surmising how Henderson carried out the atrocities. Carlisle used fragments of those stories when fabricating Henderson's statement. He cribbed them almost word for word."

Judge Newland fell back in his seat, gazing at me with an element of admiration sparkling in his aged eyes.

"I see," he murmured. "You've done a man's job, Michael, but there are other avenues to go down before you allow yourself to be totally convinced. Perhaps Henderson did give the statement."

"Not according to Sergeant Rawlings. He claims that Carlisle had the statement already written out before he interviewed Henderson. A sleight of hand, a little misdirection and Henderson signed Carlisle's version instead of his own. Rawlings witnessed the statement being taken but like Carlisle was found to be corrupt; at present he's in hiding. You see, Carlisle was ambitious, greedy, and he was told in no uncertain terms to find the killer or else. He wasn't about to let this one slip through his fingers. Henderson was as close as he could get; stopped no less than three times in the vicinity of the murders."

It was in a moment, when Judge Newland raised his glass and I raised mine that the door opened and in walked Billy Fletcher; a chance to have my suspicions verified. He entered with a smile, greeting everyone as a local greengrocer might, a peck on the cheek here and there, a casual handshake, but never once did he acknowledge Sarah, and she was looking anywhere but at him; suspicion confirmed. I turned back to the judge who was calmly appraising me with a sympathetic smile.

"Something wrong, Michael?" he asked, leaning slightly to get a view of my rival at the bar.

Perhaps he registered the red mist in my eyes, the tightening grip on my glass that was nearing breaking point or maybe he could hear the grinding of my molars; either way he could sense my discomfort. He sat for a moment, absorbing my agitation, as if to give me time to acclimatize to the present company.

"Have you asked her?" he said.

The question slipped by me, lost amongst the babblings and chinking of glasses, and as I stared back at his curious stare, the enquiry manifested once again, 'Have you asked her?' For years this man had sat at his usual table, saying little and rarely engaging in conversation; simply observing. Through the years he had sat in judgement over the entire population of the town, or at least those who frequented the Dog and Duck, never making comment; he knew infidelity at a glance.

"There are few reasons for your present condition," he continued; "betrayal, jealousy; few stay the course. The pure of heart politely romanticise such treachery as 'Affairs' but here in the real world we look on it as something far darker; the violation of someone who belongs to you; an indiscretion they willingly undertake, be it for love, gain, even revenge on their wayward spouse."

Something about my misdemeanour must have changed, for he stared at me intensely, gazing into my eyes as if searching for my very soul.

"Have you ever been indiscrete, Michael?" he asked, almost in a whisper.

The night with Penny returned with vivid clarity and he read my hesitation as a declaration of guilt, and thereafter he smiled and nodded as if I had imparted every seedy detail.

"As I said: few stay the course. Let them know you are wise to their little game. Her own shame will drive her back to you. At present she is no guiltier than you."

"I am not the one continuing an affair," I suddenly hissed, confirming my moment of weakness.

"But just as guilty, nonetheless," smiled the judge. "Of course, you could fight for her honour but why engage in the art of fisticuffs over something she gave away willingly? Besides, a man who spends sixteen hours a day humping heavy sacks of potatoes is bound to make mincemeat of you. If you confront her there is every chance you will have to admit your own indiscretions; leave it be, Michael."

I was calmed by him and affected by his authority, and turning slightly I registered Sarah who smiled back at me though it was devoid of warmth especially when I cast my stare towards Billy Fletcher. The judge nodded as if to express his satisfaction.

"So, tell me, Michael, how did you come about your information regarding Henderson?" asked the judge, coaxing me out of my paranoia.

I sat silent for a moment with the image of my wife and Billy Fletcher making love on a bed of cabbages, carrots and King Edward's, him squashing ripe tomatoes into her soft skin, and her fondling his prize marrow.

"Michael!"

I stared back at him until the vision dissipated and the question at last registered.

"Peter Egan," I replied. "He's a freelance writer . . ."

"I've heard the name," the judge nodded thoughtfully. "Wrote a piece on prison reform and generally condemned the present-day penal system and those who pass down the sentences; an anarchist of the highest order—a radical."

"I found him to be intuitive and level-headed," I rebuffed.

Judge Newland tilted his head slightly, the corners of his mouth turned down, suppressing his wont to condemn someone I regarded as a friend.

"I've never met the man, of course," he said with a shrug. "Needless to say, you shouldn't be influenced by an unrelated source. You need to talk to those involved direct; face to face."

"Weren't you an unrelated source, judge? Haven't you passed the death penalty simply on hearsay; influenced by the testimonies of others, people you've never met in your life?"

He grinned broadly and shook his head.

"We live in a democracy that is governed by laws, laws we decent human-beings are expected to abide by. At the end of the day it is the jury who has the final say, not the judge."

"And you have never coerced a jury into making a decision?"

"I don't think you quite grasp how the system works, Michael."

"I think I can. Lawyers, litigators, solicitors—call them what you will—are considered to be corrupt, and by association so is the system in which they work. The D.P.P. believed they had a case worth prosecuting, but Carlisle's antics have thrown everything into turmoil. They won't commit until they know the outcome of his trial."

The judge nodded his head as he held up his glass of port against the window, searching it out for any imperfections.

"This brings me back to my first question. Why would you want this case? You believe Henderson is innocent and the D.P.P. believes there's an element of doubt despite the corrupt police officer. Either way there isn't any gain unless, of course you're relying on hand-out's from Fleet Street, and you must also take into consideration that Henderson may be a murderer, and the public don't look favourably on a small-time brief looking for recognition on the back of a famous case. It could destroy you, Michael."

"I haven't yet made a decision."

Judge Newland smiled back at me knowingly.

"Yes, you have, Michael. If I can be of any service to you don't hesitate to call on me; you know where I live."

-11-

I had managed to read Leonard Matters book '*The Mystery of Jack the Ripper*' in its entirety and notwithstanding embellishments and deliberately purveying fiction, the fact remained that Jack the Ripper murdered five victims, so I was surprised to read my father's account and discover that Matters, the Metropolitan Police Force and, indeed, history itself had got it very wrong. My father described it as *'A diabolical liberty; an unashamed travesty.'* He was referring to the third victim, Elizabeth Stride who had been found just within the entrance of the International Workingman's Educational Club in Berner Street, and the days leading up to her death.

It had been a pleasant day; what I would call a constructive day, a day of recognition and of praise. It was also a day when the creators of Jack the Ripper would face their own demons while the myth lived on forever. In the morning our class was tutored by Dr. Thorpe, a charismatic physician with an eye for the nurses, who was a tad less regimented than his counterparts and who had a unique way of teaching. Unlike his fellow teachers he would expect his students to know the answer to any question he fired at them, and should the recipient fail to answer correctly, they would be bombarded with insults and forced to write a twenty-page essay on the subject. He reminded me of a music-hall act engaging in audience participation, pacing up and down a raised platform, pointing randomly at an individual and demanding the correct diagnoses. Today he stood before a large blackboard on which was chalked the outline of the human body; one representing the front, the other the back, and today he spoke on a subject that Pip and I were experts in. "You will obviously be aware of the recent murders that have taken place in Whitechapel," he said, "and on September 10th and throughout this month I attended the inquest of Annie Chapman, the second victim. Now, why should that be of interest to either me or this class?"

Pip slowly sunk down in the seat next to me, hoping to disappear forever, but I retained my composure and like the other students shook my head.

"According to Police Surgeon Bagster Phillips, the murderer showed definite signs of anatomical knowledge, having removed certain organs," he continued. Pip shrunk even lower and I sat in a totally bewildered state knowing that neither Pip nor I had removed any organs whatsoever. Dr. Thorpe registered my bemused state and pointed directly at me. "And you are?" he asked. With a look of embarrassment and a brief turn of my head from side to side, I rose up, grabbing my lapels and feigning confidence. "Charles James, sir," I said. Dr. Thorpe nodded and smiled slightly. As a student I was exceptional and he had always awarded me the highest marks on written tests. He appeared pleasantly surprised to at last see me in the flesh and put a face to a name. "You look troubled, Mr. James," he said. "Have you not heard of the recent killings?" I returned a broad grin by way of undermining his patronizing remark. "Indeed I have; the work of Jack the Ripper, no less," I returned confidently. An exasperated sigh came from my left and Pip slunk down almost to the floor. Dr. Thorpe expressed a bright smile as though the name had evoked a spectral image of a cloaked assailant melting into the London smog. "An interesting title and one I confess to have never have heard . . ." Before our tutor could finish his sentence, I interrupted. "Oh, yes, it's a well known fact." Unconvinced Dr. Thorpe cast his stare over my fellow students, and in typical music-hall fashion engaged in participation. "So who else has heard this name before?" he asked. Every hand was suddenly raised, for all were familiar with it, for either Pip or I had told them. For weeks we had been whispering it in public houses, in shops, around the corridors of the hospital and even to patients. Recently, whilst running an errand for Mrs. Steere, we were in butchers' in Whitechapel and two women were talking about the terrible murder of the last victim while Pip and I were waiting to be served. "They say it's a wolf with razor-sharp claws who feasts on their insides," said one. "No more than they deserve. Women with no dignity should be punished," said the other. I gave Pip a nudge and sprang into action. "You are indeed correct, madam. Women without morals should be punished, and that is why Jack the Ripper has been sent to this earth. Yes, ladies, you heard me correctly: sent to this earth; for he is neither man nor beast." The two women exchanged puzzled glances and almost in unison asked, "Who?" I shook my head in response to their ignorance and sidled gently up to the portly lady who had just purchased

a string of sausages and enough steak and kidney to last her husband a year. "Jack the Ripper!" I said, confidently. "He has been sent to avenge mankind, to stop immoral women from spreading their vile and deadly diseases. He is here to clean our streets of such vermin." The thinner lady of the two pushed a side of ham into her basket and grumbled. "Then he should come to my street—it's filthy," she groaned. By degrees the name became known, became part of the East End vocabulary, to be forever associated with anything evil, and as it spread so its origins became unknown; like a lie that manifests into fact with every telling; what we refer to as folklore.

Dr. Thorpe had not finished with me yet and pointed to the spot next to him, the place I was expected to and, indeed, would take up, and as I made my way towards the raised platform he addressed the rest of the class. "A portion of small intestines and the abdomen were found over the right shoulder and parts of the wall of the stomach were found over the left shoulder. The pelvis, the uterus and appendages, a portion of the vagina and posterior and two-thirds of the bladder had been entirely removed. The skill the killer conveyed is in the incisions being cleanly cut, avoiding the rectum and dividing the vagina low enough to avoid injury to the cervix uteri." He took a piece of chalk from his pocket and handed it to me. "Mr. James, be kind enough to show the class where you would make the incision to give access to the particular organs I have mentioned." I caught Pip's stare, his eyes slowly closing, believing this was nothing more than entrapment and half the London Police Force were waiting outside with warrants to arrest us. I, however, was not about to jeopardize my future as a doctor or my spotless record, especially in the eyes of Dr. Thorpe, and thereafter walked to the blackboard and made the correct incisions on the diagram.

"Very good, Mr. James," he said. "And how long do you suppose such an experiment would take had it been performed under the appropriate conditions? How long would it take you, Mr. James?"

Again I caught Pip's boggle-eyed stare that screamed at me to give the wrong answer.

"In a theatre, under surgical conditions, I would estimate anything up to an hour," I replied.

"Then would it interest you to know that the murderer performed it in half that time?"

I looked to Pip and winked, knowing he achieved it in just fifteen minutes.

While my associate and partner in crime was busy dissecting Annie Chapman, I was observing from the shallow steps within the yard, and with the exception of blood, gristle and organs, certain other artefacts were strewn about her, to wit personal items; two small combs and a piece of coarse muslin which when Pip was done, I placed at her feet in a neat and deliberate arrangement. I also removed two brass rings from her finger; worthless brass but essential nonetheless to strengthening the very myth Pip and I had created. Indeed it worked. Newspapers on the case were asking why a killer would go to such trouble and the police were searching the local pawn shops in the hope the killer had pawned them—or at least attempted to—believing them to be gold. Reporters added to the combs and muslin brightly polished farthings and gold rings, and would-be sleuths all over the country searched for some hidden meaning in the hope it was a cryptic message. Fact turned to fiction almost immediately. Pip had cut the woman's throat right down to the vertebrae and it was supposed that the neckerchief she was wearing was intentionally tied on after to stop the head rolling away.

Classes finished early and I remember being in a bright mood. Being incarcerated in the cell Mrs. Steere had the audacity to call a guest room held no charm for me, and I walked straight up Whitechapel Road towards Aldgate with Pip scampering behind. "Where are we going?" he asked. I strolled briskly onward, nodding and smiling at the passing ladies and bidding them 'Good day,' and turning to Pip I replied, "Today let us forget about studies. Let us forget about our duties as residents and for once be young men and do what young men do. What say you, my friend?" Pip was hesitant but reluctantly shrugged, succumbed to my will. We spent an hour or two meandering around the shops and cloth market in Goulston Street but eventually ended up in a grimy public house off Aldgate High Street where a mixture of sordid characters and well attired gentlemen consorted with one another over a glass of warm beer. Pip and I sat talking, but more often than not whispering over the day's events and the consequences—if any—we may have to face.

"Why did you play up to Dr. Thorpe that way?" groaned Pip. "He may have been testing you."

"Testing me for what?" I returned wearily, tiring of his incessant suspicions.

"You know," he hissed.

"No, I don't know, Pip. And were that the case then I dealt with the situation as I would under any other circumstances. To change my character now would only attract suspicion. Have you not learnt anything, Pip? One has to be assertive if one is to be taken seriously."

My companion nodded in agreement and then stared aimlessly into his half empty glass.

"It hasn't made much of a difference, has it?" he said. "I mean, what we created hasn't made a ha'penth of difference. The whores are still on the streets."

I sat for a moment, mulling over his opinion.

"Of course it isn't going to be immediate. Women of these parts are not easily frightened; they're defiant and fiery. They believe it's their right to be on the streets, but they'll change . . . in time."

"You mean there'll be more?"

"There has to be more, Pip, or it will all be meaningless. Obviously these reptiles are accustomed to such violence and, probably, look at it as part of life. They believe it will never happen to them. They have to be convinced it will. They have to be convinced they're not exempt from the will of Jack the Ripper. That is why the next one has to be worse than the previous."

"Worse!" cried Pip. "How much worse can it be? I nearly cut the last ones head off," he added, dropping his tone to an irritating hiss.

"Would it appease you if we swapped roles?"

Pip considered the prospect for some considerable time. "Perhaps," he said.

Time passed and gradually the pub began to fill with market traders and vendors; their day over and all gathered for a well deserved drink. A man with one leg played an accordion in the corner and a few sang along as the bar-staff tried desperately to fulfil their demands. It was while I had set my gaze on two young women sitting at a table that my eyes raised slightly to see a woman peering through the window from outside, her hands cupped around her eyes like makeshift blinkers pressed against the glass, channelling her vision inward, and suddenly she appeared at the door and walked straight to us. Perhaps it was because I had seen her twice before—once at night and once in daylight—that I recognised her. Pip appraised her with a curious uncertainty.

"Found ya," she said. "Been lookin' all over the place but I found ya."

"And who may I ask do you think you have found, dear lady?" I replied nonchalantly.

"You. You an' him. Ya don't remember me, do ya?"

"How could I when I haven't laid eyes on you in my life?"

Pip suddenly realised who was standing before us for he straightened at once and stared intently at her.

"You really do not look like the kind of woman I would consort with, madam. Now I seriously recommend you leave before I am forced to step outside and fetch the nearest policeman," I said.

"I wish you would," she returned stubbornly. "Then I could tell him who I saw that night Mary Nichols was murdered walkin' away from Buck's Row."

"You're mistaken, madam," Pip broke in.

She stared at Pip with an indignant leer; the fiery look of defiance that only the East End breathes into you on a daily basis; she wasn't about to leave. Her clothes were threadbare and baggy on her emaciated frame and her hair greasy. She wore an apron, the white of which had long ago disappeared beneath a surface of dirt and stains. Her gaunt face belonged to a harridan and reminded me of a gargoyle, thin and skeletal.

"That night I saw you I went back to Buck's Row and saw her in front of those stable gates. She was dead all right and you killed her. You done for her good an' proper. Tell me it's a lie," she said.

It was inevitable that sooner or later this wretched woman would attract unwanted attention and leaving was not an option, for undoubtedly she would cause havoc and may tell her story to any policeman summoned to the premises.

"One would not be rude enough to call it a lie, madam, but more a case of a mistake on your part," I said. "Where was it you said you had seen us?"

"Coming out of Buck's Row into Whitechapel High Street in the early hours," she replied.

"Well, why wouldn't you? We are doctors at The London Hospital; we had a right to be there, but I assure you we were never in Buck's Row. We frequent many public houses in Spitalfields and our journey back would take us into Baker's Row. You must have seen us on our way home."

"P'rhaps I did. But I know this; I walked up Buck's Row not ten minutes before and there was no dead woman there then. Besides I saw you the next day, returnin' to the scene of the crime. What do ya say to that, doctor whoever you are?"

"I can only suppose that you are indeed correct and that you did see us returning home. As for seeing me the next day at that location, it was because I saw the crowds and went to offer my assistance. Now with that misunderstanding clarified I believe we should have a drink. What will you be having, Miss . . . ?"

It appeared that whatever preconceived ideas she had in accusing Pip and I of murder were considerably weakened once I offered my explanation, for uncertainty reflected in her eyes and off her furrowed brow.

"Eddowes. Kate," she said. "An' I'll join you in a gin an' splash of water, if I may."

I pulled out a vacant bar stool next to me, patting the seat gently and motioned her towards it. She consumed gin as if her very life depended on it, and as is its effects she soon fell into a state of melancholy, dispensing with her accusations and highlighting her own miserable existence. Inevitably she spoke of her spouse, a man called John Kelly, a name she could hardly mention without appearing as if she were sucking on a lemon. He was a brute, of course. He ill-treated her, of course. He was a womaniser and used her to his advantage, of course, and would fly into fits of rage for no apparent reason, of course. Never once did she confess or deny her own inadequacies or give reason for his womanising or what brought about his fits of rage, nor why he ill-treated her or why she allowed him to take advantage of her. Like all women she was blameless, nothing less than perfect, and if she was drunk—which she so often was—and if she was whoring—which she so often was—and if she was the shadow of her former self, an innocent woman who had fallen on hard times, then surely he, and only he was responsible. Within two hours and nine gins later Kate had difficulty sitting on the stool without sliding off, and though Pip and I played along an element of doubt regarding our innocence still existed in her pickled brain.

"There's a reward, you know," she burbled drunkenly. "A substan, a substan, a sub . . ."

"Substantial?" Pip intervened exhaustively.

"Yep. They'd pay a lot for you two."

"And you would be deserving of every penny, Kate, if, indeed, your assertions had any foundation to begin with, but we are respectable doctors and our job is to save lives not take them. Now enough of this foolishness and let us have another drink," I said.

Her eyes slowly wandered to the clock on the wall, and with a gasp of horror she cried, "God, he'll do for me this time. I have to go. I have to go now!" She slid from the stool and for a moment stood unsteadily appraising Pip and myself through one beady eye. She was mid forties, perhaps older, perhaps younger; it was difficult to tell, and she swayed almost rhythmically to the sound of the accordion. "I must go to my sister's house" she slurred. "You can walk me there, to Southwark."

"I would deem it a pleasure, ma'am, but we have a prior and an important engagement elsewhere."

She looked disappointed as she steadied herself at the bar.

"Then you come back here after. We 'ave things to talk about."

She wagged a spindly, filthy finger at us as a warning and staggered out into the street. Both Pip and I exhaled a sigh of relief as if the Grim Reaper himself had just taken his leave.

"God! What are we to do, Charles? She knows!" said Pip, nervously.

"Be calm, my friend. Do you think the police will take the word of a broken down whore over respectable medical students? Still, I'll not leave to chance the possibility that she may tell her story to the wrong person. She's poor, greedy and conniving and may look for easy money by going to the newspapers. She has not been responsible for anything in her life but her death. She has chosen her own fate. This time, Pip, we have not chosen the victim. She has chosen us. She must be silenced."

Pip's face turned pale and he looked to the door, fearing that at any moment the police would enter.

"Charles, listen to me," he implored. "What if she has already told someone else? If we kill her then the police will certainly be looking for us. You

heard Dr. Thorpe; definite signs of anatomical knowledge were prevalent. Her accusations will be justified by our very positions at the hospital; medical students. Trust me when I tell you I know what I'm talking about. I know the justice system and how it works."

I smiled warmly back at my companion and patted him on the shoulder.

"Indeed you do, young Pip. You have missed your vocation, but we must consider the possibility that she hasn't yet told someone else. We must act before she does. Or would you prefer to end your prosperous career at the end of a rope? It's irrelevant whether the police believe her or not; it's the stigma that will destroy us."

I was interrupted by Badger standing at my office door, noisily clearing his throat.

"Still reading that damn book?" he said as he entered.

I adhered to the usual procedure, closing the book and dropping it into the bottom drawer of my desk.

"So, what's it all about; the book, I mean?" he asked as he took up a seat in front of me.

"It's boring; early days as a medical student, that's all," I replied, casually.

"Can't be that boring, Michael, you're always reading it. Maybe I can look at it after you."

"I doubt it."

"Why ever not?"

"It's personal, for my eyes only."

Badger shrugged his shoulders.

"How was your weekend?" he asked.

"How was yours?"

He acknowledged my evasiveness and smiled slightly.

"I was going through the medical reports. Did you know that the autopsies on all eight victims were carried out by the same pathologist; a professor, no less; impeccable record, especially assigned to The Met. but freelance? He's used as a second opinion. If anything was found either incriminating or exonerating Henderson then he's the man to see."

"I'll have Sylvia arrange a meeting. Anything else?"

He was glowering back at me, tiring of my incessant bluntness.

"Sorry; things on my mind," I said.

"Sarah? You still think she's having an affair?"

"I know she is. I haven't confronted her about it yet. I guess I'm hoping it will all go away."

He nodded and expressed a brief but caring smile.

"I met with Edward Foster on Friday," I said, changing the subject.

"And?"

"And nothing. In his opinion George Henderson is a good man, but I met someone yesterday who may be of help to us; a retired judge."

"A what?" Badger gasped.

"Judge Newland. It may help to have someone on the inside; someone with the know-how."

"But we're supposed to have the know-how, Michael. We shouldn't be relying on outside sources."

He registered my cold stare and his shoulders sank.

"Fine, you're the boss," he grumbled.

My mind felt like a small room or a dark cellar, crammed from wall to wall, floor to ceiling with thoughts of my father; compacted so tightly that I couldn't squeeze another thought in, and I had visions of my head exploding under the pressure. Yet it was like a novel I couldn't put down; a story I was eager to know its ending. Ironically I knew the ending and had read enough to know my father and Pip evolved unscathed, to become a revered surgeon and an assistant police commissioner. What troubled me was the lengths they went to in order to accomplish their seemingly unblemished pasts, to convince the likes of Catharine Eddowes they were not the murderers she was suspicious of. It was difficult to make comparisons with my father and the young medical student, who wreaked havoc in Victorian London, and there was a need in me to share this secret with the first person willing to listen, to offload the burden on to someone else, but I knew in my heart that this burden belonged only to me.

Badger was patiently appraising me across the desk, as if searching out my problems without asking. He instinctively and naturally attributed my troubles to Sarah where, in reality, she was the last of my worries.

"We lost the Driscoll case," he said, suddenly.

Badger's statement obliterated my father's memory in an instant and I stared at him coldly, as though he were personally responsible and not Tom Grieves and Andrew Pitt.

"Friday afternoon," he continued. "The judge gave it to the prosecution."

"Appeal," I mumbled.

"We can try, but I wouldn't hold out much hope."

The Driscoll case had been ongoing for the best part of two years in one shape or form. It began with innuendo, rumour, and his undoing appeared more the work of Fleet Street reporters than it did legitimate witnesses. Adam Driscoll was a theatrical agent, enigmatic and a celebrity in his own right, often seen in the company of music hall stars like Bud Flannigan and the outrageous Max Miller; he had the Midas touch and if there were ten people on the bill at any given time then you could be sure that six of them came from the Driscoll stable. He was—for his sins—a Champagne Charlie, constantly throwing expensive bashes at London nightclubs and even owning one of his own in London's Piccadilly. A strong willed man of considerable stature, Adam was a no-nonsense character who fought bravely on behalf of his stars, securing unspeakable amounts for their talents. His weakness was women, young women, little more than teenagers who came to the city in search of fame and fortune. The only recognition most received was a notch on his bedpost, though some made it to the dizzy heights of the chorus line, while others willingly posed naked for a seedy magazine he owned under one of his many aliases. Film was to be his downfall, for he moved into the shady world of pornography as a lucrative sideline, and they could be viewed in his club in the early hours of the morning by special invitation only and, of course, for a substantial fee.

Driscoll was arrested by a policeman who simply wandered in off the streets after seeing lights shining from windows at the rear of the club; a breach of blackout regulations, and so on entering saw with his own eyes the flickering images of a young servant girl being ravished by her master, the gardener and a wired-haired terrier affectionately known as Norman. Now, these, shaky fifteen minute black and white films were nothing like the great epics that can be viewed at the local picture-house. There were no end credits informing the viewers of the actors, the cameraman or the director. Importantly there was nothing to connect Driscoll with the hundred or so other pornographic films found in the store-room of the club or the girls who performed so arduously in them. The girls, who were promptly rounded up by the City Police and brought to various London police stations, were all of consenting age, and there was nothing whatsoever to connect Driscoll with the enterprise—except Norman . . . his dog. Norman was not an overnight success in the world of pornography. Like the other participants he appeared in many still photographs first to gain a modicum of recognition. In fact he could be seen in numerous photographs; at the grand opening of Driscoll's nightclub, attending music-halls and banquets, even being cuddled by Gracie Fields. Any one of the photographs could be retrieved from the Fleet Street archives, pulled out whenever Driscoll hit the headlines. Norman was the condemning factor because everyone knew that he never went anywhere without his master and vice-versa, thus placing Driscoll at the very location of filming.

"What persuaded the judge to see in the prosecution's favour?" I asked.

Badger grimaced a little.

"Dog food."

"What?" I blurted.

"Norman was spoilt, and would eat only a certain kind of dog food; a recipe Adam Driscoll had the pet-shop specifically make up—just for him." shrugged Badger. "Fussy, little bastard."

"So one of the rebuttal witnesses was the pet-shop owner!"

Badger nodded. "The other was the girl who delivered it."

A stony silence hung in the air as we looked at one another; a void borne out of coming to terms with unbelievable circumstances and banal evidence. And for no apparent reason I started to laugh, and so did Badger, until two grown men were cackling like a pair of old witches, laughing so loud and so hard that I nearly slid of my chair and Badger was doubled up and holding his ribs. Tears of joy welled up inside us and the more we looked at one another, the more we lost control.

Normality was restored by early afternoon when Badger came to my office with all he had learned about George Henderson.

"I thought the best place to start was at the beginning," he said as he started pulling files from his briefcase. "I went to Stewart Road School at Mile End. I wanted verification of Henderson's illiteracy."

"Good idea. And?" I replied, enthusiastically.

"Stewart Road School wasn't there. Neither was Stewart Road; bombed last September. The surviving residents had been re-housed at Rotherhithe. I managed to speak with Mr. and Mrs. Duffy; they lived next door to the Henderson's. By all accounts Brian Henderson, George's father, absconded leaving his wife to look after three boys—Graham, George and Mark. All three boys went to the same school and joined the army at the outbreak of war. As far as we know only George returned."

"And the mother?"

Badger shrugged his shoulders. "Uncertain. According to the Duffy's she was always a sickly woman. She may be living with her sister in Blackpool or she may be dead. Either way George lost contact with her when he married. The Duffy's remembered that George was rarely at school. He helped delivering milk for the local dairy and coal with a Fred Knocks; Mr. Knocks was killed in the September raids and the dairy closed down business in 1927. I did manage to track down a Mr. Weatherby in South Bermondsey who worked in Stewart Road School as an English teacher when George and his brothers were there."

"He remembered George?"

"Well—he said he did or, at least he thought he did; he's very old now. All three boys were very dim-witted; his words not mine, and rarely at school. Lastly I obtained the medical reports on all the victims."

I was hoping for better news and stared at the array of folders before me that were leading us nowhere.

"Edward Foster said Henderson's wife has gone into hiding," I said. "She has five kids that need to be educated; they must be registered at their individual schools."

"You want me to look into it?" asked Badger as he rose from his seat and gathered up his folders.

"Couldn't hurt—we've got nothing else. But if we can't find anything neither can the prosecution."

"Meaning?"

"The only witness presiding when the statement was taken was Sergeant Rawlings—who is now also missing and is not likely to show his face. At present we can't prove Henderson is illiterate so we have to focus on Carlisle and look into Persuasion and Inducement of the statement; that he fabricated the statement to his own ends."

"What about the pathologist?"

"Sylvia's already arranged a meeting for tomorrow."

-12-

Pathology is a specialized craft, a precise art; it cannot be undertaken by a general practitioner. A cadaver will undergo a post-mortem in an attempt to establish cause of death, and in questionable circumstances such as murder an examination can reveal clues as to who the murderer may be. How, exactly, this is achieved I had no idea, but every post-mortem report regarding the Blackout Butcher was signed by a certain Professor Graves—an unfortunate name given his profession—but someone worthy of an interview nonetheless, if only to satisfy my own curiosity and learn how my father and Pip evaded its science and successfully avoided capture. Sylvia had made the arrangements by telephone, opting for an appointment at his office in Clapham, South London, and so on the assigned day and time I arrived having digested a modicum of knowledge on the subject from a book I had purchased, all of which may as well have been written in hieroglyphics.

His office was the ground floor of a large, nondescript house on the busy main road that cut through the common and forked off in different directions to Balham and Streatham and, so it appeared, was forever a constant stream of noisy traffic twenty-four hours a day. After announcing myself to an elderly lady with a kind smile, I was pointed to a chair in a waiting-area and so took up the next twenty five minutes familiarizing myself with Pathology that went under the heading of 'Familiarizing Yourself with Pathology.' By the time a tall, slender man with jet black hair and a dark grey suit entered, I was sipping tea and engrossed in how the wounds of a victim can yield the identity of the person who had administered them. To my relief he was too far away to identify my book or the subject I was reading, and as it lay on my lap neither was he able to read its title. I snapped it shut and buried it in my briefcase, placing down my cup and saucer on a small coffee table and following him in the direction in which he beckoned. Within a few steps we were in his clinically tidy office and after shaking my hand warmly he took up his place behind a vast mahogany desk.

"You'll forgive me I hope, but aren't you the son of Charles James?" he asked.

I sat motionless for what seemed a lifetime but mustered a shallow smile and replied,

"Yes. Yes, I am."

To say I was a little curious as to how he made the connection is no exaggeration, and probably to save me further embarrassment he stood up and began to walk his fingers along a bookshelf, where eventually he stopped and pulled out a hardback entitled 'The Talking Dead by Charles James.' I couldn't recall ever seeing the book but nodded as if I had always known of its existence. Professor Graves sat back down and opened the book to the first page on which was a printed dedication that simply read, 'To my son Michael.'

"I've met him on several occasions, the last time shortly before he died," he explained nostalgically. "There's not a pathologist in the country that doesn't possess a copy of this book; we regard it as our bible. You've read it, of course?"

With the possibility that he may ask questions later, I decided honesty was the best policy and shook my head. I was more preoccupied as to how Professor Graves established a father and son relationship on the strength of a one line dedication. Michael is a common enough name and so is James. He saw it in my face and smiled.

"Your secretary was very forthcoming when it came to arranging this meeting. She told me your father was a famous surgeon."

Sylvia had a quality of using whatever means were available to get what she wanted, be it her beauty, her body or information that may coerce an unwilling party to take part, and in Professor Graves' case it worked.

"I know nothing about pathology, professor," I admitted. "It's the reason I'm here."

"Because you're defending George Henderson?"

"Yes, sir. I see that you carried out the post-mortems on all eight victims. Wouldn't that be considered unethical?"

"Not at all. It was established as far back as the second victim that the murders were associated with one killer. There were various doctors called out to the scene of the crimes but they aren't pathologists. By using the same pathologist nothing will be missed; not that there was a great deal to miss."

"By that you mean you found something?"

"Only by association; that all the victims were murdered in a similar way. All eight victims were exceptionally clean; no hair fibres, no pubic hairs, no finger prints and no semen, even though sexual intercourse took place. We did find woollen and cotton fibres but nothing that matched Henderson's wardrobe. Even the fingernails of the victims revealed little, or at least nothing to incriminate Henderson with the crimes."

"Fingernails?" I asked.

"The fingernails of each victim were scraped for traces of skin and hair. Sometimes defence wounds are prevalent, but we found nothing."

I had been harbouring a question ever since meeting Edward Foster; a question I hoped that would make me look intelligent in the eyes of any pathologist worth his salt; a question so groundbreaking that it would shake the very foundations of pathology and leave criminologists throughout the western world utterly dumbstruck.

"Soot," I said.

The professor slowly closed his eyes, and I'm sure it was only out of kindness or sympathy that he never actually yawned.

"Did we find traces of soot? Is that what you're asking?" he smiled.

I nodded assertively; slightly miffed that he wasn't dancing around his office and screaming 'Eureka!'

"Certainly we did . . ." he began.

"Well, there you are," I interrupted, taking up a confident posture and adopting a tone designed only to gloat.

"Where's what, Mr. James?" he asked with a shake of his head.

"The soot. George Henderson is a train driver and trains run on coal and they emit soot."

He paused for a moment, probably to gather both his thoughts and his patience.

"Traces of soot, small particles of coal were found on some of the victims but not all, especially not Marion Price or Leslie Cross of whom, you are no doubt aware were murdered outside."

I nodded as though I knew each and every victim intimately.

"Those traces were confined to the victims found in their homes; all of which had coal fires and an adequate store of coal in their backyards," he continued. "Given that we live in the age of coal, that every home and industry relies on it, that our cities are consumed by smog of which coal is responsible, that every street and surface is layered in coal dust, that every railway station and factory pumps out literally millions of gallons of coal-dust a day, and both emit tons into the atmosphere that falls back to earth as rain, I could hardly hold George Henderson solely responsible."

I sat quiet. I thought it best given my stupidity.

Perhaps being the son of a revered surgeon afforded me a little latitude, for the professor stared patiently back awaiting my next remarkable deduction. I smiled back at him like a baby with wind.

"Mr. James," he sighed, "are you familiar with the work of Alexandre Lacassagne and Edmond Locard?"

The first, I thought must be something to do with food; the second was bound to be an inventor of ironmongery or something of that nature. I shook my head.

"Edmond Locard was an assistant to the famed physician Lacassagne . . ." he explained.

So close, I thought.

". . . and in 1910 he established the first forensic laboratory in Lyon, France. Locard's motto was 'Every contact leaves a trace.' Similar laboratories have since been set up all over the world; the Los Angeles Police Department in 1923, the FBI's Technical Laboratory in Washington DC in 1932, our own Police College at Hendon in 1935, and The Royal Canadian Mounted Police laboratory in Regina in 1936—all of which abide by Locard's theory . . ."

"Every contact leaves a trace," I intercepted.

"Quite so, Mr. James," he returned politely. "Although still in its infancy forensic science has taught us a great deal and improved the efforts of the police tenfold. Not so long ago we had little to associate the criminal with the crime—unless of course he was captured red-handed, but today we can glean information from a crime-scene that will lead us directly to the perpetrator. Take for instance fingerprinting. True, England was slow on the uptake, believing it was just another crackpot science, but it has proved to be invaluable in crime-detection. The first suspect to be convicted by fingerprinting was in Argentina in 1892; England was ten years later; America one year after." He held his finger in front of my face. "Each fingerprint has three distinctive characters—arches, loops and whorls; arches or ridges as they are sometimes referred to, make up five percent of the overall area. Loops make up sixty percent of the pattern, and whorls thirty-five percent. What makes every print unique is in the pattern, usually definable by ten or twelve points where arches, loops and whorls merge; no two people have the same fingerprint. A crime-scene can yield two kinds of prints—patent and latent. A patent print is visible, the result of blood, paint, grease. A latent print is invisible but can be enhanced by bright light or a magnifying glass. Both can be lifted with clear adhesive tape or print cards and reproduced on glass for the purpose of classification. Neither on any of the victims or at any of the crime-scenes were Henderson's prints located."

A little long-winded I mused but I forced the best refrain of perplexity I could muster.

"The victims' clothes were examined for trace evidence," he continued. "Trace evidence refers to fibres, hairs and fluids. The bloodier the crime-scene the more trace evidence will be found; fibres from the attacker or airborne fibres will stick to the blood—like insects to flypaper. We found cotton and woollen fibres; some were matched to household furnishings—carpets, blankets etcetera, but nothing unusual; no skin or hair fibres other than that of the victims. Likewise no seminal fluids were found, yet most had been raped. The killer wore more than a balaclava and gloves, Mr. James."

It began to slowly dawn on me that pathologists have lots of time to talk. They live by detail and therefore speak in detail—minute, laborious detail that, in my case, droned on for the best part of two hours. Just when I thought I knew all there was to know about forensic pathology he outlined the importance of forensic anthropology, followed by forensic odontology, forensic toxicology, forensic serology and forensic entomology. He explained how forensic entomologists use a technique dating back to thirteenth century China in which insects are used to gauge time of death. He spoke of contaminated crime-scenes and how forensic science can prevent contaminating crime-scenes. Locating and collecting evidence was of prime importance, and recording evidence was tantamount to treason if conducted haphazardly. I did the best I could given the circumstances, but there are only so many ways one can nod or shake one's head or grunt, 'That's fascinating,' or 'You don't say?' Abrasions, concussion, contusions, fractures, lacerations and trauma are obvious signs of the cause of death, but the absence of such wounds can be just as telling. "Did you know that King Harold's body was identified after the Battle of Hastings by a tattoo on his chest?" asked Professor Graves. I didn't, and by this stage I couldn't have cared if he was found with a Bengal Tiger on his chest. "Oh, yes. And what do you think it said?" he pursued eagerly. I managed a faint shake of my head. "Edith and England," he replied with wide eyes. "No! Really?" Admittedly the professor had kept me captivated for the first five minutes—it was the following one hour and fifty minutes that was somewhat of a blur. When we moved into the realms of rectal thermometers I had little choice but to bring the lecture to a close.

"Professor, at how many crime-scenes was you present—I mean, actually there?" I asked.

He paused to give the question consideration.

"Three; the last three," he said.

"Christine Charmaine, Jean Smith and Stella Clark."

He looked genuinely surprised at my power of recall.

"I don't have the files at hand but I'll take your word," he smiled.

Christine Charmaine found in a public toilet; Jean Smith tied to a dining room table; Stella Clark found in a disused garage."

"I remember—very messy."

"Why didn't you attend the previous five murders?"

Professor Graves inclined his head curiously and hesitated.

"Availability, I would say," he replied.

"But were you called to attend?"

"Certainly the last three; it isn't compulsory for a pathologist to attend every crime-scene; a local doctor will always be present and his findings will be passed on."

"But a local doctor isn't a pathologist is he, professor? And at best he can only establish the time and cause of death."

The professor appraised me with a suspicious leer, his eyes slightly narrowed.

"Are you working on behalf of the defence or the prosecution, Mr. James?" he asked.

"I'm merely trying to establish the facts. Can't something be missed, say, from an M.D. at the crime-scene and the pathologist at the lab; human error, corruption of trace evidence?"

"Not enough to change the outcome—whatever it may be. The F.O.A. will secure the scene and separate any bystanders from the immediate scene to minimise trace-evidence contamination. Transference of trace-evidence is always a possibility but not common."

"And moving the body from the scene to the hospital or morgue?"

The professor shook his head. "Transportation of the corpse is via a shell; the shell being a coffin for the want of a better name—a sealed unit. It is common practice for a pathologist to assess the crime-scene with the aid of photographs and the notes of the doctor who initially attended the scene; there is nothing lax or unethical about the procedure."

I nodded. "Then why were you called only to the last three?"

"A good question," he replied, "and my answer is, I don't know. Multiple murderers are a rare breed and this particular murderer was wise to the system; the system of detection and the system of pathology. Usually it is only a matter of time before the killer makes a mistake and unwittingly leaves clues, but this one was different and never let his guard down. As the murders increased the police needed every scrap of information they could get—no matter how insignificant it appeared; perhaps that is why they felt the need to call me to the later crime-scenes."

"So the murderer was intelligent?"

"Inasmuch as knowing what we would be looking for. We lifted fibres from every victim and matched them to a handful of fabrics; a crombi overcoat, Tweed, a Blazer, even an army tunic—no two were the same, and nothing similar was hanging in George Henderson's wardrobe. I compiled a profile of the killer—what I imagined him to be; sharp, cunning, between thirty-five and forty-five, probably affluent considering his extensive wardrobe; I considered Henderson to be an unlikely suspect. I've never met him and nor would I wish to, but he doesn't strike me as a man who would possess the requisite intelligence to be a multiple-murderer; a lot of attention was paid to detail."

"In the way the crimes were committed?"

The professor looked unsure and slowly shook his head. "We found no pubic-hairs other than those belonging to the victims and that led me to the obvious conclusion—he shaved his nether-regions. Not only that, he took time to put on protection even though he was in the midst of a sexual frenzy; unless, of course, I am evaluating him in the wrong light. Maybe the murders were executed calmly."

Of all the reports I had read, police, medical or otherwise, there was not one that made reference to pubic-hair or, for that matter the absence of pubic-hair.

"So had Henderson shaved his nether-regions?" I asked. "The prison doctor would have given him a thorough examination on his arrival; you must have seen his report."

"I have, and it's scant to say the least; a typical evaluation on a new prisoner. When asked if he had any allergies or phobias Henderson replied 'Claustrophobia.' There was no mention of pubic-hair in the Medical Officer's report."

"But wouldn't that have been a vital piece of information?"

"Certainly."

"Yet you didn't feel the need to follow up it up?"

"And why would I?" the professor smiled back almost smugly.

"Because it would have confirmed Henderson as a likely suspect as opposed to an unlikely one."

I was irritated by his smile and he appeared offended by my tone. He leaned forward, resting on his elbows and his grey eyes stabbing into mine.

"I am aware of my responsibilities and my duty," he said, pointedly, "and under any other circumstances I would have pursued that particular piece of information for verification—but for one reason."

"Which was?"

"Henderson had already confessed."

The next morning I rose up from the bowels of Farringdon Street Station with the thousands of other tired and weary commuters, compacted on a rickety, wooden escalator that slowly and steadily climbed to ground-level, spewing them out onto the pavement where they made their way to the workplace, and as I emerged in the grey morning to face the rampart of heavy traffic and heavier rain, I was distracted by a news-board before the newspaper kiosk boasting 'Corrupt Met. Officer's Trial starts tomorrow.' It occurred to me then that the ten short days I had been given to prepare Henderson's defence had now expired and without a doubt the D.P.P. would want to know of my progress. So with a heavy sigh I turned up the collar of my raincoat and made ready to brave the storm that awaited me, but just as I was about to leave the dryness of the overhanging canopy for the torrential downpour, an arm entwined about mine.

"Rachel!" I said with surprise.

"Buy me coffee," she demanded.

It was my intention to launch into a catalogue of excuses and set off straight to the office, but she stared back at me with her penetrating brown eyes that demanded nothing else but a little of my time, and without a word I nodded and led the short distance through the bustling crowd to the coffee shop.

"I've waited for you for the last two mornings but you never showed," she said as she settled at a table.

"Sorry. My schedule has been a little erratic lately, you know, work. Speaking of which, shouldn't you be at your new job?"

She unbuttoned her coat, slipping her arms through the sleeves and leaving it flayed on the back of her chair while she was still actually sitting on it, which brought a smile to my face. It was a manoeuvre that any magician would be proud of, an exhibition that only women can execute and remains a source of fascination to all men; how they can make the simplest of tasks appear so complicated yet achieve it with relative ease; like removing a bra under their blouse without unfastening a single button and whipping it out of their sleeve.

"The supervisor wasn't just interested in my legs. He was more interested in what was between them, so I left. Are all men like that?"

"Not all, Rachel," I replied, taking my coat and folding it over the back of a chair next to me.

I instinctively concluded that she had fallen on hard times and took my wallet from my inside pocket and opened it, to which she looked at me in horror.

"Michael, what are you doing?" she gasped.

"I can give you twenty pounds for now and some more when I get to the bank," I said as I fingered through the few notes there were.

The silence brought my eyes up to hers, which were narrowed and filled with disappointment.

"Shame on you. I didn't come here for a handout. I'm more than capable of looking after my own finances, thank you very much" she said, huffily.

Despite my declaration that 'All men weren't like that,' I was beginning to feel like they were; me included, and quickly buried my wallet back into my inside pocket.

"Again, I'm sorry. Only I thought . . ."

"Then you thought wrong, didn't you?" she said, cutting my heartfelt apology short.

I was looking to the counter, hoping the waitress would bring the coffee over we ordered on our way in, and seeing she was preoccupied I foolishly started looking at my watch.

"Go if you have to," Rachel snapped as she stared intently at the wall. "I'll pay the bill."

I was in no mood for tantrums or being given the silent treatment by someone I hardly knew, so I decided that retreat was probably the best action, given the circumstances.

"Probably best," I said, taking my coat and rising from my chair.

She sat in a stubborn posture, head down and arms tightly folded like a spoilt brat, and before leaving I placed the money for two coffees on the counter and made my way out. Suddenly she was there, standing in the pouring rain, her coat still on the back of the chair in the shop.

"Would it make it easier if I took the money?" she shouted. "Do you want to take me to some seedy motel and tear me inside out? That's okay, I can do it. I can be your bit on the side and your wife need never know. Twenty pounds is fine! For twenty pounds I'll do anything you ask."

She was trembling as she raged at me, her hands clenched into fists and every muscle in her body rigid.

"Have you quite finished?" I retaliated. "You sought me out, Rachel. I neither have the time nor the inclination to speak with someone who treats every act of kindness with utter contempt. Get your coat and go home."

I turned away from her, across the pavement to the curb, angry and eager for the lights to change so I could cross the road and leave her behind forever.

"I have no home," I heard her say.

She was sobbing into her hands, her shoulders rising and falling like waves on the sea, her hair and clothes glistening with raindrops. I slowly returned and put my hand on her shoulder.

"What do you mean, you have no home?"

She was incapable of giving a reply. Her anger at me inside the shop had manifested into total despair outside and, as is human nature, those closest will be on the receiving end. Time appeared to stop in that moment, no movement, no sound, and I simply watched her until she raised her head where her tears had become lost in rain. In time, whatever time had passed, we were back in the shop, where two cups of coffee had been placed at the table in our absence and I waited patiently until she had regained composure, her sad, bedraggled figure shaking.

"Do you want to explain why you're so angry at me?" I asked.

"I'm not, I'm not," she said in a shuddering voice. "I didn't know who to talk to."

"What about the pub where you work? You must know people."

"They're not people like you. They're Dockers, factory workers. No respectable man would be seen dead in there."

"And you think that because I wear a suit it makes me a better person? It doesn't, Rachel. A lot of people I know are amongst the most twisted and perverted kind you'd ever have the displeasure of meeting."

"But you're not one of them!"

"I've had my moments," I smiled. "Any one of them would have taken you up on your offer and whisked you away to some seedy hotel and had their wicked way."

"But not you?"

I shook my head. "No, not me."

If there was any sign of disappointment in her face I never saw it, if of course, I was looking for it in the first place. She sat staring into her lap, ashamed at her outburst and almost too frightened to talk in case her words were misconstrued.

"So why have you no home?" I asked, gently leading her out of her guilt.

She shrugged like a little girl.

"I have four days to get out," she explained meekly. "I needed the extra work to pay my rent but now, losing my job, well . . . And to make matters worse I haven't heard from David. I'm worried, Michael."

"I'm sure David is fine. What I need to understand is why I'm here. You obviously need money."

"Yes. No. Oh, I don't know," she said, tossing her head back and searching for the words. "I owe a substantial amount, fifty-five pounds, and I've owed it for over a year. When David was called up we just went crazy, out every night, buying this and buying that; living the good life, you know? I thought I'd never see him again. Three days ago my landlord—fat pig that he is—devised a way for me to repay the debt."

"Which was?"

Rachel looked at me for a moment and somewhere in her brown eyes the explanation for her outburst was answered.

"Oh," I winced.

"Anyway, I declined his kind offer of turning me into a whore and told him to leave."

"So . . ." I began cautiously, "would I be correct in assuming that if I loaned you fifty-five pounds—and I emphasize 'Loaned'—that everything will be hunky dory?"

"No," she replied. "I can't stay there, Michael, knowing what he really wants. He lives downstairs, right beneath me. I have to leave."

"Then leave; find somewhere else to live."

She sighed heavily and shook her head.

"I have considered it, you know," she muttered after a long pause. "They come into the pub; good looking, nice clothes. Some I grew up with. Men will give a week's wages just for a couple of hours with them."

I stared into my muddy coffee and sighed.

"You don't mean that."

She looked sharply back at me, as though she were personally affronted.

"If you meant it you would have accepted your landlord's offer," I said.

"But he's fat and smelly!"

"Would it have made a difference if he were tall, dark and handsome? Don't confuse necessity with desire."

She smiled for the first time and nodded.

"You're right, of course. You're lucky, Michael. People like you don't have to face that kind of indignity. You live in big, rambling houses and have more money than you know what to do with, buying your wife nice things and taking her to fancy restaurants. People like you wouldn't want to be people like me."

Strange how we see ourselves differently from others, that we all believe that somewhere the grass is greener; we spend our lives in a constant state of jealousy, idolising others, wanting so much to be like them, to be anything other than we are.

"Let me tell you something about people like me, Rachel," I said. "People like me live with the legacy of a dead father; a greatness I can't even begin to fathom or ever aspire to. People like me are scared to father children because they believe they are failures; they walk in shadows because they're afraid of the light. People like me live in modest houses and have adulteress wives because their husbands are boring and have allowed their professions to consume them completely. People like me are clockwork toys, devoid of spirit and emotion, lacking the endearing qualities of people like you."

Rachel sat motionless, her mouth partly open and her eyes barely blinking. For a brief moment in her mind she traded her life with mine. She was wealthy and lived in a big, rambling house, had a handsome and doting husband who would give her the world if it were his to give; no bills, no demanding landlords, no unsociable working hours, no desire for anything more; no dreams, no hopes.

"Stop it," she began to laugh nervously. "You're a good man, Michael; a kind and gentle man. You have everything."

I nodded and smiled away the moment until it had completely evaporated into the humidity of the coffee shop.

"Let's get to the point, Rachel. Why did you want to see me?" I asked.

Her composure failed her once again and she shook her head, staring skyward, tears glistening on her perfect eyes, the suppressed hopelessness of her situation beginning to surface once again.

"I don't know. I guess I just needed someone to tell me what to do. I don't know what to do."

Her voice quivered and sometimes the words tailed off to almost a squeak, her face flushed with embarrassment as she looked nervously around at the staring faces.

My wallet put in a second appearance and I gave her a business card.

"Do you know Mansall's? They're estate agents at the Elephant and Castle. Bernard Mansall is a friend of mine. See him, find what you want and tell him to send me the bill."

She sat staring at the card until tears blurred her vision and trickled freely down her cheeks.

"You can't do this, Michael. You don't know me."

"But you know me. Why else would you be here?"

My eyes averted from Rachel's tear-stained face to an attractive, blonde bombshell standing at the counter who expressed a brilliant smile and performed a delicate wave.

"Shit!" I blurted, unconsciously.

Rachel turned in her chair and looked back at me in horror.

"Who is it, your wife?" she asked as she hurriedly began to thread her arms into the sleeves of her coat.

"No, no. That is Sylvia, my secretary; Miss Busybody, 1941," I sighed.

Realising that the peroxide blonde in the tight pencil skirt had no claim or jurisdiction over me, Rachel smiled with relief and took a second look.

"God, how does she breathe in that? Attractive, though."

"A real peach," I agreed. "And God help me, she's coming over."

Suddenly Rachel rose from her chair and buried her hands in her pockets.

"I don't know what to say, Michael. Thank you. I'm so sorry for what I said."

"Don't be. Get yourself to the Elephant and call me when you find something."

"But . . ."

That one word was every doubt she had about men. How would she repay me? What would I expect in return? Would I be no better than her lustful landlord?

"Call me, okay?" I said.

I was grateful to the fat gentleman at the next table who was acting as a temporary blockade and slowing Sylvia's advance on us. Rachel leaned down and kissed me on the cheek.

"I'll call you."

The timing was perfect. As Sylvia arrived, Rachel left, and it was with a look of total dissatisfaction that Sylvia took up the seat Rachel had just vacated.

"Tell me that wasn't Miss Bookmark," she asked inquisitively.

"Yes, that was Rachel," I surrendered.

"Well? What does she want?"

"Sylvia, it really has nothing to . . ."

"Oh, my god, she's pregnant! I bet he's a soldier; Canadian probably or American . . ."

"Sylvia, she's married!"

"Oh, please," she sighed wearily. "She's pregnant and has come to you to pay for some backstreet abortionist to get rid of it."

"Do I look like I consort with backstreet abortionists?"

"You're well connected and you have money. Any Spiv will put you in the right direction. So she has to get rid of the baby, right, before her father finds out and cuts her off without a penny. I mean, she's relatively good looking but perhaps a little frumpish, but she knows that she'll never find Mr. Right with a baby hanging off her tit. Only one thing to do—get shot of the kid. That's the problem, see; a fumbled grope, a quick bang and your life turns to shit just because you let your guard down; or in her case her knickers."

My eyes were fixed to the ceiling and I felt life draining away from me. After completing her fanciful rendition and total character assassination of Rachel, Sylvia smiled and looked at me for approval.

"I'm right, aren't I?" she said, raising her eyebrows high on her forehead.

"This may come as some surprise to you but you're not. Furthermore, why are you swearing so much these days?"

"Am I? I can't say I've noticed."

"Well I have, and my advice to you is to stop it."

Sylvia took a sip of her coffee and wiped the froth from her top lip.

"Shit! I hate this stuff. Sorry. So why was Miss Bookmark really here?"

I shook my head.

"So why is she going to call you? She said she was going to call you. And that kiss. Well that said it all."

"It was a peck, Sylvia, just a peck. Now drink your coffee, we have to go. Any appointments this morning?"

"Only Mr. Randall."

"Randall? When?"

She took my wrist, craning her neck to look at my watch.

"About fifteen minutes . . ."

"We must hurry," I said, jumping up and grabbing my coat.

". . . ago."

"What?"

"About fifteen minutes ago. I made the appointment early because you've been getting in early recently."

"For god sake, Sylvia," I cursed as I hurried to the door.

"It isn't my fault. How was I to know you had a secret liaison with what's-her-face?"

"Rachel."

"Yes, her."

The journey from the coffee-shop to the office, at break-neck speed in the driving rain and under the veil of Sylvia's chintzy umbrella, took about 12 minutes, in which time I was forced to endure a bombardment of questions, the most significant being, "How come you and Miss Bookmark only meet when it's pissing down with rain?" It was a fare question and one that would have gained Sylvia an accolade for observation had she known about the second meeting with Rachel when I met her at a bookshop—which she didn't—and I wasn't about to mention it, so instead I reprimanded her about her language to which she apologised again and again and again. In fact every time she spoke she had to apologise afterwards.

Descending the staircase of the office was like descending into Dante's Hell, for suddenly distorted and twisted creatures appeared to stare and hiss at me, outraged by my lateness and audacity at keeping Mr. Randall—who in their eyes was nothing short of royalty—waiting. "Morning," I smiled at my disciples as I passed my rain-sodden overcoat to Penny. "Bring coffee, Sylvia," I added as I moved towards my office.

"But I'm wet," she protested.

"Prepared as always, Sylvia; just do it."

The D.P.P. official was seated in front of my desk, and Badger was conserving his energy by leaning on the filing cabinet, and both shot me indignant stares as I breezed in.

"I'm not used to being kept waiting," said Mr. Randall, half rising from his chair.

"I'm sure you're not, sir, and I have no excuse apart from being waylaid at the station, the atrocious weather and a secretary who is numb from the waist up."

I took my seat at my desk, passed Badger a worthless smile and looked directly to Mr. Randall for an explanation.

"Have you made a decision?" he asked.

"Decision—decision concerning what?"

"Henderson!" he snapped impatiently.

"Ah, yes, Henderson, of course, of course. I was going to ask you the same question."

Mr. Randall was not a man to be trifled with and expressed as much in his unflinching eyes. His eyebrows lifted slightly and he cast a weary stare towards Badger, who by this time was wishing he was anywhere but here.

"Are you taking the case?" he enquired without making eye contact.

"Is there a case to answer?"

The official stood up and shook his head.

"Of course there's a case to answer! Eight women have been slain and at present the suspect is your client. Do you intend to proceed or opt for a referral?"

Mr. Randall was on the verge of walking out and Badger suddenly sprung out of his comatose state to rescue the situation.

"To date we haven't had a chance to discuss a referral, Mr. Randall, but it would probably be in our client's best interest," he said as he ushered the official back into his seat.

I was reclined in my chair and absolutely oozing calm and composure.

"There will be no referral, Mr. Randall, because there is nothing to refer," I said.

"This is absurd! You have a sworn statement from a multiple-murderer; an admission that he killed eight women."

"Not according to him. True, I haven't yet interviewed him face to face, but he denies ever making such a statement and we can prove that Carlisle fabricated it all from various newspaper articles. Professor Graves, the pathologist who undertook the post-mortems on every victim, has no evidence to associate Henderson with one murder let alone eight. There is not one single witness who can place him at the scene of any of the crimes, and we can give you twenty character witnesses who will testify that Henderson is a good man and incapable of murder."

A long silence ensued in which Mr. Randall pursed his lips staring alternately at Badger and myself, and only when Sylvia entered with a tray did he break out of his pensive refrain. He remained silent until the coffee was poured and she made her exit.

"You see, Mr. Randall, we have not been given a fair crack of the whip. Despite endless contact with the Home Office, we have not been granted permission to interview our client nor Carlisle, come to that. Why is that, sir?"

"Carlisle is not your concern."

"If he is responsible for falsifying evidence that may send my client to the gallows, I think he is."

The phone rang at that moment and I picked up the receiver.

"How far do you want to take this?" a voice asked.

I looked to Badger and then Mr. Randall.

"Who is this?"

"Peter Egan. I know you're with Randall. Get rid of him and meet me outside in ten minutes."

The call ended abruptly and returned to its acoustic purr.

"Sorry about that," I said, placing down the receiver. "As I was saying . . ."

"I'll arrange for you to see Henderson," he interrupted; "after which I need a guaranteed decision; take the case or give it away."

"And Carlisle?" asked Badger.

"I expect an answer as soon as possible," said the official, ignoring Badger's question and rising from his chair.

"Preferably before Carlisle's trial reaches a conclusion," I said.

"Preferably," he returned tersely. "Consider this a final warning. Your inexperience was once tolerable, but now you are coming dangerously close to retarding the motion of British justice. You may wish to consider speaking with someone familiar with all the facts regarding this case; an independent adjudicator whose allegiance is neither for the government nor the Metropolitan Police Force. Inspector Foggerty can be found at Lambeth police station. My apologies for not sampling the coffee but I'm running late as I was kept waiting."

Mr. Randall moved hurriedly from the office, neither saying goodbye nor offering a deadline; he simply left, leaving Badger and I looking blankly at one another.

"What the hell was that about?" said Badger, shaking his head.

"I'm not sure, but it would seem we've been given a second chance," I said, sipping at my coffee.

"Or enough rope to hang ourselves with. Why give us more time? And why give us Henderson?"

"And why mention the government? No one said anything about the government."

Badger shrugged his shoulders. "Then why mention it?"

I shook my head and put my cup down.

"Not sure, but maybe I can find out."

A racing green Jaguar was waiting on the edge of the pavement directly outside the office door, its windows slightly misted and droplets of rain pulsating on the gleaming bonnet synchronised by the swell of the engine beneath. Inside I could barely make out a figure of a man at the steering wheel but suddenly the passenger door swung open. "Get in," said Peter Egan. We moved into the traffic, down Fleet Street and into New Bridge Street. "How did you know I was with Randall?" I asked. He cursed as he nudged his way out of the junction, seemingly oblivious to my question, until the car was gliding effortlessly towards London Bridge, the River Thames speeding past on our right. "I saw him arrive. You were late," he said. I gave no reply and remained silent until we passed London Bridge and slowed in heavy traffic at Tower Hill. "Well? What did he have to say?" he asked as we picked up speed. "Not much," I shrugged. "He's arranging for me to meet Henderson." Peter Egan nodded and chuckled to himself as we crossed Tower Bridge Road and moved towards Shadwell. "Well, he would, wouldn't he? He doesn't want to let you go now. Giving you Henderson will take your mind off the real problem—them," he said. I sat there inhaling the smell of new leather upholstery, wincing slightly as we overtook several cars that were foolishly and recklessly adhering to the speed limit. "Where are we going?" I asked at last. We stopped behind a string of cars at Shadwell; bombed houses deemed unsafe were being pulled down and policemen were diverting us around the town. "Ever heard of Harry Griffin?" Peter asked as he manoeuvred out of the line and into a side street. I shook my head. "If you want to know what's going on in the London underworld then he's your man," he explained as we sped down a succession of side roads. We braked suddenly as a woman pushing a pram stepped out in front of us. She gave us a hard stare and mumbled angrily; Peter simply nodded and smiled.

By all accounts Harry Griffin was somewhat of a gangster, a natural born criminal who, apart from a few spells in prison as a teenager, had evaded the long arm of the law ever since and built an empire in the process. "I phoned him while I was waiting for you," explained Peter as we returned to our intended route. "I wanted to make sure I could bring you along." I was unsure as to what interest I should have in an aged gangster and must admit to feeling quite daunted at the prospect of meeting him, but Peter Egan appeared relaxed which assured me I wasn't going to end up in concrete boots somewhere at the bottom of the Thames. We followed the line of the river into Limehouse and continued down East India Dock Road towards Poplar. Here was where the devastation of the bombings highlighted the success of the Luftwaffe and would have made any German bomber pilot proud; they hadn't missed a thing. Entire streets had been obliterated, factories and schools levelled and once proud houses simply burnt-out shells, and the roads were much the same—a mass of destruction, pock-marked with craters, making our intended destination that more difficult to achieve. But soon we were on the Isle of Dogs, weaving through rubble filled streets, reversing up dead-end roads and taking in the total devastation around us. "They hit this pretty hard," said Peter, easing two wheels of his car onto the pavement to circumnavigate a 'No Entry' barricade spread across the road. "Here we are."

We were before a large public house on the edge of Millwall Dock, pristine despite its age, and as I climbed out of the car I looked down both adjoining streets, the ends of which abruptly ended, the line of terraces gradually depleting to nothing but brick rubble. Peter expressed a nervous smile and knocked on the pub door and then looked at me. "It isn't too late to turn back, Michael," he whispered. As I hadn't the slightest clue as to why I was there in the first place, I simply shrugged my shoulders. "After you," I replied at the sound of a key turning in the lock. The door was opened by a small lady I immediately took as a cleaner who, with a jerk of her head, beckoned us in and locked the door after. The smell of brass cleaner and new paint attacked my osmatic senses and the bottles and glasses upon the shelves glistened and sparkled under the lights behind the bar. "Wait here," said the woman as she disappeared into the next bar. We stood silently, as if to break into conversation was forbidden, and as Peter took up a seat at a table I wandered aimlessly around looking at the framed photographs on the walls, most of which were of the docks, group photographs of Dockers, and soldiers marching through the nearby streets setting off to war in 1915. I wondered how many of them had returned. The sound of voices broke my train of thought, brought my head turning and brought Peter to his feet. "Good morning, Peter."

Peter was shaking hands with a small man attired in casual clothes; beige slacks, V necked jumper and open collar shirt beneath. He was perhaps five feet five inches tall, mid-sixties, bespectacled and slightly balding with brown hair, but he vanished behind a thick wall of cigar smoke, the source of which appeared the same size and weight as him. He suddenly emerged, pacing towards me with an outstretched hand, shaking mine warmly with a grip unbecoming his wiry frame.

"And you'll be Michael," he said in a gruff voice, accompanied by a sincere smile.

"Yes, sir," I said, looking to Peter for guidance.

"No need to call me sir. Harry will do. Now, what will you be drinking? A red wine for you, Peter?"

I was looking at my watch, barely 10.30, but Peter gave me a hard stare and nodded, as if to refuse a drink would insult our host. Harry poured a glass of red wine and then looked to me. "A small scotch would be fine," I said. He nodded approvingly and turned with a current of smoke swirling around him. "A mans drink. None of this grapes and vinegar shit," he said. His duties performed, Harry took a seat at the end of the bar, on a high leather chair with one elbow resting on the counter and the other on the arm of the seat.

"Peter tells me you're involved in the Henderson case," he said, exhaling a cloud of the finest Havana cancer.

"Yes, sir . . . Harry," I stumbled.

"So you know all about Carlisle?"

"A corrupt policeman," I said confidently and leaning on the bar.

Harry looked at Peter and grinned.

"One of many, Michael," he replied with a shake of his head. "His case starts tomorrow and they'll bury him; it's a foregone conclusion. He's a hard man and they won't break him, but then they don't want to. They'll take him in exchange for the others, probably give him ten years to appease the public; in a few weeks it will all be forgotten about."

Harry spoke as if he knew Carlisle but I failed to grasp the connection between them.

"Peter tells me you're a history fanatic. Do you know why they call this place the Isle of Dogs?" he asked. "I was born here and I've never known."

"As I understand it, it was because Henry VIII kept his hunting dogs here."

"Fuck me! You learn something new every day. Who'd have thought it—hunting dogs, eh?" He paused to suck on his diminishing cigar, to momentarily vanish behind a screen of smoke like a magician. "I own this island, Michael, or should I say I inherited from King Henry. From Limehouse Stairs down to Silvertown is mine; every pub, restaurant, warehouse and factory; even the boats moored along the Thames are answerable to me. I know every Stevedore, crane driver, waterman and landlord in this manor. It's a result of a lifetimes work. I personally own thirty four pubs and drinking dens along the river, and though the Germans have deprived me of most, I endeavour to make an honest bob or two. You must be wondering why I'm telling you this."

It had crossed my mind. I didn't expect to get his life story just because I told him the origins of the Isle of Dogs.

"My old dad worked these docks, you know, and I worked them for a while. Ships moored here from all over the world; they would queue to get in, sometimes for days. I spent my childhood on the river and me and my mates would walk the embankment looking for anything that had been washed up; you know, like Mudlarks." Harry began to chuckle nostalgically and screwed the butt of his cigar into the ashtray. "Dad would work all the hours going, seven days a week for a poxy wage, and every night he would come in this pub and sit in this very chair, and every night me and my brothers would have to carry the old sod home. Mum would give him what for. You know, I don't think I can remember him without a cut or a bruise on his face. We were a big family, four brothers, two sisters, and of course he would have to work his cods off to pay for us. He was like everyone else, a bit of pilfering here and there, selling it to the highest bidder to make ends meet; it was not a life I wanted. So my brothers and me took to crime, specifically the boats. It was all very lax back then, and such was the backlog that many of the boats were tied up for a week because there was no one to unload them. Night watchmen could be bought as could the seamen left aboard while the crew went ashore. We weren't pilfering. We were taking it away in lorry-loads." Harry paused and looked at my untouched scotch. "Another?" I declined with a shake of my head, immediately lifting the glass and holding it like some kind of prop. "It was easy back then," he continued. "But sooner or later someone else wants a piece of the pie. We had a good five years before the muscle started to move in on us. By that time I had everyone in my pocket and I wasn't about to lose it to a load of thugs, so we went to war. It was a hard ten years."

Harry suddenly fell silent and lowered his head, staring at his hands for no apparent reason. Then he held them up to face me. I could distinguish small circles in the palm of each hand; puncture marks. "We had a running battle with MacKinney, an Irish firm running Silvertown; guns, knives, you name it," he explained. "It was the winter of 1900; we were outmanned. I lost two of my brothers in that and three dear friends. My younger brother was shot in the face at point blank range and Freddie, my older brother was found floating in Victoria Docks the next morning with a gun shot hole through the back of the head. I was shot in the leg. I was caught and three big Micks dragged me down the steps of Poplar Docks at low tied. They said if I wanted to play God then I must suffer in the same way. They nailed me to the side of a small, wooden cargo boat called 'Sabrina;' I'll never forget that name. There I was, knee deep in mud, waist deep in freezing cold water with one bullet hole and three six inch nails through my hands and feet. I was bleeding to death and fell in and out of consciousness, and every time I looked up, there was that bloody name 'Sabrina' and all around me the tide was rising. There wasn't a moment I didn't think I was going to die. The last time I woke up it was just getting light but there was no one around to help me, and by this time the water was up under my chin. I had a choice, die or die trying to live.

The thought of revenge on those bastards gave me strength, the thought of my two dead brothers and that everything I had worked for was about to be taken. I pushed my back against the side of the boat, pushing myself from side to side, screaming as the holes in my hands grew bigger, enough to pull the nail through. My right hand broke free first, and then I prized off my left hand. I fell forward and the freezing cold water attacked me like a million pins piercing my head. I pulled myself back, so my arse was against the side of the boat and then pushed forward with what strength I had left. I felt the nails tearing through my feet, snapping the small bones, but that first breath I took when I reached the surface made it all worth while."

My hands were shaking slightly and a cold sweat engulfed me completely and I sank the scotch with one gulp. "Same again?" asked Harry. I nodded furiously.

"I was found barely alive on the West Quay by a waterman who was good friends with my dad," he explained as he topped up my glass. "A Portuguese vessel was in the inner dock and the ship's doctor took care of my wounds. After that I was moved from one ship to another, being tended to by anyone who had the remotest idea about medicine. Technically I was dead; I couldn't be found. My father got me out of London and into the country, staying with an aunt who looked after me for five months, until I had recovered; I didn't even attend my own brothers' funerals. They say what doesn't kill you only makes you stronger, Michael, and I came back stronger. I got them all. In no time they were all gone, never to be seen again. We live in a world covered by water; unexplored territory, and that's where I sent them all. No body, no crime, just missing people."

To say I was petrified would be understatement. I stood looking at this little man who, by his own admission, had wiped out half of the Irish population and spoke as if murder on a daily basis was no more important than putting his socks on in the morning. I mused whether I was the only one in my life that hadn't actually killed anybody.

"Which brings me to your friend Carlisle," said Harry. "My telling you about my history is not a form of bragging. It is simply a way of informing you of the ordeals I have been through in order to retain my status. Am I criminal? Most certainly I am. Am I proud of it? Not especially. As a young man I used to see my father sitting in this very chair, mentally and physically exhausted from a hard day's work; within ten years I bought this pub for him and my mum. As I explained, when people see how easy it is—or how easy it appears—everyone wants a piece of it, call them opportunists, thugs, whatever; their goal is the same. I fought the muscle and won, but a different muscle moved in."

He arched his eyebrows and grinned as if I were supposed to understand, and then passing Peter a smile and a wink, he turned back to me.

"Carlisle is part of a syndicate; a group of corrupt police officers numbering 247 at last count. I have their names, addresses and ranks," he clarified. "As criminals, successful criminals, we have always been leaned on by the police and till now it has never been a problem; we pay for their silence, their blind-eye, and occasionally their help. Their percentages are nonnegotiable and forever rising. Now, if these people were chancers out for easy money, then I would deal with them in the appropriate manner; as I have explained; I'm not afraid to fight for what is mine. But these aren't your every day thickheads. These people are the law, Michael, and they use it as leverage. The money they have accumulated is a pension fund. It pays for holidays, their wives desires, their children's schooling, and once it was acceptable, but I'm too old and too tired to fight it anymore. Peter will write a story exposing them, exposing all of them. We shall put an end to them and fight the law with the law. Of course, Peter will never mention his source. He knows I am an honourable man and as an honourable man I can't abide treachery in any shape or form; he's aware of the consequences."

Peter nodded in agreement, albeit nervously, and I stretched myself to my full height and tried to find my voice.

"Isn't this all a little late? Carlisle stands trial tomorrow. Why mention it now?"

"It's the precise time, Michael. It will ensure Carlisle is sent down for a long time along with his friends. The trial could run on for months, giving you time to work on Henderson's defence; nothing short of perfect for everyone."

"But Peter can't print any names, not without proof, not unless he wants to face a major liable suit."

“He doesn’t have to print the names,” said Harry with a shake of his head. “He merely has to imply, their rank, the area.” Harry lifted two large brown envelopes from the bar. “The names are yours for safekeeping. What better than a writer who exposes them and a lawyer to protect the writer?”

I was beginning to feel like a pawn in a very dangerous chess game, and my eyes moved back and forth between Harry and Peter, searching for my part in all this.

“This is your leverage, Michael,” continued Harry. “Apart from the names, there are photographs and film, images of these bastards taking money—it can’t fail, Michael.”

Peter was quiet and distant on the way back, his face pale and his driving skills affected. The journey there was executed at breakneck speed, but the trip back was performed with all the urgency of a Sunday afternoon outing. I attributed his reserved manner to the amount of alcohol he had consumed during our short stay—6 large glasses of wine—but as we continued I recognised fear in his eyes and in his movements. I sat staring at the two envelopes on my lap, and not until we moved past the Tower of London did I break the irritating silence.

“What am I supposed to do with these, Peter?” I asked as I stared out at the slow-passing scenery.

“Keep them safe for the time being,” replied Peter, his eyes staring straight ahead.

“For how long?”

“I’ll write the story—get it out in time for this months edition of Fallow’s, that’ll coincide with Carlisle’s trial; wait for the shit to hit the fan.”

“The trial starts tomorrow and is expected to run a week—there’s no time.”

Seeing the traffic backing up in front of us, Peter jerked the wheel and moved off the Embankment towards Monument.

“There’s plenty of time, Michael. I’ve already written the body of the story, just need to add a few details. I won’t release the list of names until next month’s edition; keep these bastards guessing. It’ll give you time to gather your evidence for Henderson’s defence.”

As the city began to close in around us, I hoped he may have a change of heart and take the envelopes with him, and when the offer was not forthcoming I began to feel uncomfortably nervous.

"I still don't see why I should have these. It's your story, Peter."

"And yours, Michael. Do you want to see Henderson hang because he was fitted up? This will put the cat amongst the pigeons—give you time. Once the story breaks there will be 247 irate coppers out there who will kill their own mothers for the contents of those envelopes. And the first place they'll look will be at the man who wrote the story—me. You and I are not associated, or at least not known to be associated. Besides, they'd think twice about leaning on you, given your profession."

As we sat in an endless stream of cars, lorries and buses in Cannon Street I was contemplating a thousand different scenarios to get out of the situation, even considering hiding the envelopes under the car seat and leaving them.

"You heard Harry mention murder, didn't you?" said Peter, giving me a sideways glance.

"It's branded on my brain. I'll have sleepless nights for weeks."

Peter smiled for the first time. "Well that was Willie Watts, colloquially known as the Snark. Willie was a double-sided sword, a collector of information which he would use for profit or as leverage to retain his liberty. He worked for Harry Griffin, running some of the seedier drinking dens, collecting money, doing all the things nobody else wanted to do. He and Harry grew up together—like brothers, they were. One day the Snark was pulled in, accused of murdering an ex-girlfriend, which in itself was laughable as Willie was as frail as autumn leaf and didn't have a good fuck in him; the so-called ex—girlfriend was barely in her thirties. But according to reliable sources the police had him banged to rights, everything to lock him up for life or send him to the gallows. So Willie, in exchange for his freedom told the police the story of the corrupt officers regularly collecting money down at docklands. Suddenly he was gone—vanished."

"The police killed him?" I gasped.

Peter shrugged. "Or had him killed; no one is really sure. I looked into the case and the police furnished me with all the appropriate documents—including his release papers, released without charge. Some say it frightened Willie enough to just disappear. Others say that the 247 were responsible, or it could just as well have been the government who erased him. Either way he was never seen again. Harry's convinced the police murdered him."

The hairs on the back of my neck were standing up on end and my stomach felt like a abyss, and as we circumnavigated St. Paul's and met the incline of Ludgate Hill I felt decidedly sick.

"Maybe you should drop me here," I suggested. "I can walk—get some air."

The truth of the matter was I didn't want to leave to chance that someone, anyone, may see Peter's car outside my office. He read my doubts immediately and grinned.

"Michael, nothing is going to happen yet—the story isn't out yet," he said.

"Yet! This may come as a surprise to you, Peter, but I don't want anything to happen at all—ever—never. I'm not even sure I want to fight the Henderson case."

He sighed wearily. "For God sake, you're not fighting anything; you don't have to. You just have to let the D.P.P. know they have nothing and that you want Henderson, your client, released immediately. After my story breaks they'll have little choice but to concede."

As the Jaguar revved angrily at the junction of Ludgate Circus, I was struck with a brilliant plan to solve my problem. I suddenly swung the car door open, burying the envelopes under my jacket.

"What are you doing, Michael?" Peter growled.

"I'll tell you what I'm doing," I said. "I'm going to the bank to put these in a safety deposit box—when you want them, call me."

I could hear him calling me, but in seconds I had melted into the crowd and his voice was consumed by the noise of the city.

Elation filled me as I left the bank and made my way up Fleet Street, as if I had freed myself of some great burden. Never before had I requested my bank manager for a safety deposit box and I was surprised at how easy it was; that nobody asked questions or looked at their fellow tellers with a nod and a wink. Simply I was taken to a room by an accommodating employee who opened one of many small doors that lined a wall, drew out a silver box and placed it on a table and quietly slipped away, leaving me to my own devices. I placed the envelopes inside the box, returned it from whence it came, locked the small door and left the room where the accommodating clerk was waiting. I passed him the key and he smiled and thanked me—a piece of cake, so to speak.

I hurried straight to Badger's office. He was hunched over a document at his desk, his half-moon bifocals perched on the end of his nose and a half-burned cigarette smouldering in the ashtray.

"You'll never guess what I've found out," I said, breathlessly as I breezed in and took up a seat opposite him.

"The Pope isn't a Catholic?" he replied without looking up.

"No."

"Adolf Hitler has seen the error of his ways and has become a missionary in Outer Mongolia where he plans to spread peace and good will to the natives."

"You're getting warmer, but no. What are you reading?"

"Henderson's military records. They arrived during your long, long absence. Where have you been, Michael?"

"Do they mention if he can read and write?"

Badger looked up and slowly removed his spectacles.

"They're military records, Michael. You don't have to be Wordsworth or Shakespeare to blow someone's head off. But in answer to your enquiry, no they don't mention whether he can read or write. In fact they say very little. Henderson enlisted in 1915, was wounded somewhere in France and was invalided home a year later. It would appear he was bringing up the rear when his unit was overwhelmed by shell fire."

"Bringing up the rear?"

"I believe it's a military term for hanging back, detached from the main body of men, to ensure the enemy aren't following. Where have you been?"

I pulled the folder towards me, turning it right way up. It appeared to have been written on an ancient typewriter where most of the letters were blotches and the words barely legible. The contents of the information were bespattered with spelling errors, and the ink on the ribbon must have dried up probably before the war began.

"So, George Henderson wasn't a war hero?" I said.

Badger looked at me suspiciously and slowly raised himself off his seat, leaning forward and sniffing at me like a Bloodhound.

"Have you been drinking?" he said, slowly settling back into his chair.

"Two; I just had two small scotches. Anyway . . ."

"You've been out drinking while I've been going blind reading Henderson's failed military career!" he growled. "Well, I'm glad you think this case is going to be so easy that you can take off to the pub whenever you feel like it."

Disgruntled he snatched back the folder and placed it amongst the pile specifically set aside for the Henderson case.

"Aren't you interested to know what I know?" I asked timidly.

"If I must," he snorted.

"Carlisle wasn't working alone; there were others—extorting money, racketeering, prostitution, laundering; and by association there will be perjury, falsification of legal documents, falsification of statements, payouts from unscrupulous solicitors, even murder."

Badger smiled as he shuffled his folders into a neat block. "I think you've had one too many. It's plausible that Carlisle wasn't working alone—they seldom do; there will always be a few that will follow him."

I shook my head. "Not a few, Badger; two hundred and forty seven. Two hundred and forty seven serving police officers involved in every seedy operation you can think of."

The tidy block of files suddenly collapsed from his hands like a house of cards and he fell back in his seat. He stared at me for a long time, not speaking and hardly blinking and suddenly, regaining his composure, he rested on his elbows and grinned mockingly at me.

"Of course, you have their names," he asked.

"Every one," I replied.

"And you can prove they're involved?"

"I have film, photographs, transactions; dates when money was paid, and to whom."

His face fell still again and he slowly slumped back in his chair, his eyes never leaving mine. After a while he slowly began to shake his head, pinching the bridge of his nose with his thumb and forefinger, and when finally all movement ceased and his hand fell away, he resumed staring at me again.

"Where? How?" he burbled.

I told him the story, omitting the name of the source or the Isle of Dogs location, saying only it was a public house in the East End. Why I felt the need to protect Harry Griffin I cannot say, unless of course, it wasn't Harry I was protecting but Badger.

"And why would this man choose to do this now?" said Badger. "Why didn't he do it a long time ago? If, as you say, he has photographs and all the paraphernalia to put a stop to it, why leave it so long?"

"I think he believes his friend was killed by the police—it's a form of revenge. I wasn't with him long, but the opinion I got was that it wasn't about money, it wasn't about giving the police payouts for turning a blind eye; he'd been doing that for years. What I gleaned was this man despised losing what he regarded as his—his friend."

It wasn't the reaction I expected. He gathered up his scattered files and stacked them in a presentable pile, muttering angrily under his breath throughout, and finally settling back in his chair and appraising me as if I were an imbecile.

"What?" I said, defensively.

He shook his head and sighed. His subdued manner was an indication of a forthcoming lecture.

"Michael, when we started off back in thirty-three, I hoped . . ."

"Thirty-two," I interrupted. "July, actually—you were working for . . ."

"The year and month is immaterial. The point I'm trying to make is that I joined you because it was fun . . ."

"And still is. Or can be."

"It isn't! I said I would look at this case, but if I ever felt uncomfortable I would be out."

"But can't you see? We can win this."

Badger grinned, opened the top drawer of his desk, and tossed me a large white envelope.

"We have a fly in the ointment," he said. "Randall left that at reception on his way out."

I drew out a single document from the envelope; heavily stamped in rings of mauve, recording the date it was received at the Department of Public Prosecutions offices and the Approval of the director. It was scant, giving the name of a woman as Wendy Marshall, aged 27, who was attacked in Newington on October 1st 1940. At the bottom of the page was an abridged version of her statement taken at her bedside at St. Thomas's Hospital, October 3rd. The D.P.P. implicates Henderson as her attacker.

"She's a key witness, Michael; a survivor for the prosecution," said Badger.

I lifted my eyes to his but never said anything, and he shook his head.

"Not so cut-and-dried now, is it?" he continued, taking his stack of files and walking to the filing cabinet. "Did you honestly think it was going to be that easy?"

"She's alive? There's no mention of her—anywhere. The first victim is recorded as Angela Deacon, October 7th in Walworth Road," I said.

"Look at the dates," said Badger, wearily.

The bluish official stamp was smeared but legible; 'RECEIVED SEP 16. 1941.'

"Three days ago!"

Badger was patiently placing his files in the appropriate drawers and passed me a withered look.

"We must find her—talk to her—find out what she knows," I said.

"And that's exactly the kind of behaviour that is going to get us both disbarred. She's a witness for the prosecution, Michael."

It was barely midday when I walked into the Cheshire-Cheese. The musky fragrance of antique furniture and aged floorboards somehow complimented the bouquet of beer and assorted spirits that, in such a unique environment, belonged nowhere else. Peter had phoned me that morning, and sounding brighter than his usual self, and I asked if I could meet him sometime during the day. The pub was empty save for a barman busying himself with slop-trays and replenishing the shelves, and Peter sat quite alone in the corner. He smiled and rose the moment he saw me, and

I couldn't help but notice that he was already working on his second large wine. He took the empty glass and placed it on the bar, and shaking my hand, gained the barman's attention. I opted for a Coke-Cola and we went to the table. "I got here early," he said. I glanced at the half drunk second glass and smiled courteously. "So I see. How's the big story?" I replied. He smiled enthusiastically and nodded. "On the press as we speak; better than I could have imagined. By Friday it will be on every newsstand in England. I hope you're ready, Michael." I observed him curiously from the opposite side of the table. "Ready? In what way?" I asked. Peter took a large gulp of wine and leaned forward. "Have you been keeping up with the Carlisle trial? It's a complete mess. The prosecution is laying it on thick and fast, and the defence doesn't know whether they're coming or going. Carlisle keeps contradicting himself. One day he's admitting it, the next he's denying it, and nobody's coming forward to corroborate either. The whole thing stinks. I'm telling you, Michael, those bastards are going to strike a deal." I was still staring at him with the same curious leer. "Once the story breaks, and if things go the way I think they're going to, all hell is going to break loose. And I mean serious, Michael. Once my story hits the streets, Carlisle is dead and buried—so to speak. And if the prosecution cut him a deal, then how's that going to make the great British judicial system look? I tell you, the rest of the world will look at this so-called great nation in a different light—corrupt from the highest judge right down to the lowest paid constable." He swallowed the remains of his drink and hurried back to the bar.

There was something a little unnerving about his ranting, not dissimilar to that of the small-minded reptile with a tiny moustache pounding furiously on his podium back in Berlin. Nevertheless the contents of his prologue left me uneasy.

"Peter, I'm unfamiliar with the seedy world of journalism, so help me out here," I said as he returned with yet a third glass of red wine, "but could anything in your report be considered . . . you know, libelous?"

He stared back at me with an unconcerned grin.

"What I'm asking is: has your story been written without due cause—to bring the subject into disrepute? Is it false or insulting? Is it undeserving, intentionally setting out to discredit the subject?"

He raised the fresh glass to his lips and began to laugh.

"Of course! It's all of the things you've mentioned," he chortled. "But it can't be deemed libelous or malicious if it's true or unless it can be proved false. I know the rules of war, Michael."

"I'm not suggesting for one moment that you don't, but aren't there guide lines, certain protocols that should be adhered to before a story can be published?"

"Certainly, but that authority begins and ends with the editor, which in this case is Earnest Fallow; it's the reason I use him."

"To air your grievances on society?"

He nodded and smiled shamelessly.

"I work for other newspapers, but they've pretty much read me the riot act. So I'm consigned to write pieces on cats up trees or the new one-way system under construction at Tottenham, and they never allow me to spread my wings. I'm rebellious but not stupid; I have bills to pay. Fallow allows me a lot of latitude. You see, Michael, the newspaper industry is ostensibly one big parasite, and a cowardly parasite at that. Their survival relies on the gamble, that being to publish a story that could possibly be open to a libelous action being pursued through the courts yet benefiting from the rewards of being an exclusive, or shelving the story and letting another newspaper either take all the glory or all the blame—it's a fine line. Once Fallow releases my story, every other tabloid will be sucking on it because they don't own the exclusive rights."

"And are therefore blameless because they're just regurgitating the original story?" I anticipated.

"Exactly right, Michael," said Peter with a firm nod.

"And this never gets you into trouble?"

"Oh, shit, yeah. About a year ago I wanted to publish a piece on Government Intelligence . . ."

"Wanted to?" I intercepted.

"Fallow refused to touch it. Too dangerous, he said. I even offered to edit it down to the bone, but still he refused. It was the first time he turned me down, so the story got shelved."

"So, how did you get into trouble?"

He took another large swallow of his wine and sat back in his chair.

"Ever seen a newsreel, Michael; you know, at your local cinema?"

"Pathe News, you mean?"

He nodded.

"Have you noticed how all those newsreels are designed to raise your spirits? You can be watching images of entire East End streets wiped out, but they always end with the inhabitants giving you the thumbs-up and raising their cups of tea to the camera; Britain the defiant. Never once do they show you footage of the mother pulling her dead children from the debris."

"Have you no respect for British pride, Peter?" I smiled.

"As much as the next man. What interested me was the source of those newsreels. Who made them? Who funded them? And why?"

"I would imagine they're government funded and designed to raise public morale."

"Government Intelligence," he replied, bluntly. "An S.O. Department was set up during the first war, specializing in the recruitment and training of government agents. In 1920 the department was closed down; lack of funding, lack of interest because we weren't at war any longer. Agents were still recruited, but their jobs entailed little else but monitoring potential uprisings and filling in reports. In 1938, on the brink of the Second World War, the S.O. Department was reestablished but to a greater degree. Immigration, emigration and tourism were monitored on an unprecedented scale; every passport on anyone entering or leaving the country came through that department to eliminate terrorism or infiltration of those we consider our enemies. Banks were subject to checks and obligated to inform the department of anyone making a deposit of over one thousand pounds, or the sudden shift in any particular company's income, or any large transaction of money from foreign shores, including bullion, diamonds; all would be thoroughly investigated in fear that our enemies were flooding the market with forged currency. Copies of autopsy and coroner reports, even hospital records came under close scrutiny, especially if they involved some high-profile minister or army personnel. Visiting heads of state, including their entourage were checked for their pedigree. And the media, we fared worse under the regime; constantly scrutinized by government officials; every story spoken on radio or printed on paper, analyzed by some pinhead searching for a coded message that wasn't there. Their role was, and still is to placate the British public—by wrapping them in cotton wool and suppressing information that both the Home Office and War Office should have made available; a form of brainwashing, much like the newsreels you can see at your local flee-pit. We call it propaganda, but the reality of the tale is their blatant disregard for our civil rights; that we have a right to know what is going on. And me? I was the one they scrutinized the most; the radical, the anarchist. Any story remotely linked with government was immediately blocked, so I found myself moving from one newspaper to another. Life was becoming uncomfortable. So I took a form of revenge—I investigated them. I had everything; names, addresses, their roles within the S.O. Department. Like I said, Fallow wouldn't publish. It wasn't that he was scared—Jesus, he thrived on scandal; this was different, as if he had a personal interest. Anyway, one day I came home and the house was in pieces. They had searched everywhere for the story, even ripping up the floorboards. When I entered the lounge, she was sitting there."

"Who?" I asked, so intrigued that I was leaning forward and staring boggle-eyed at him.

"She introduced herself as Eleanor Cole, Section Head of the S.O. Department. She sat cross-legged on my settee, thumbing through my manuscript; not bad looking for a government, pen-pushing lapdog."

"They found your story?" I gasped.

Peter nodded and slightly winced.

"She just continued reading as if I wasn't there or she hadn't heard me come in. After a while she looked up at me. "Compelling reading, Mr. Egan. You are an intuitive and creative writer, but you understand this can never be published," she said. She had one of those patient but deadly smiles that slipped away the moment I told her I had every intention of publishing it. "With whom, may I enquire?" she asked. I snatched the manuscript from her hands and that same patient but deadly smile returned. "The public has a right to know," I told her. She stood up and walked to the window, pulling the curtains back so I got a clear view outside. There were three or four suited heavies loitering around, who certainly weren't there when I walked in. "It isn't conducive to the survival of this country, Mr. Egan. We are aware of your persuasions; your radical leanings. Tell me, is there something we've missed? Are you a communist?" I laughed at her but she didn't break. She plucked the manuscript from my hand and walked to the door. "I have a good memory. I can easily write another," I said to her. She turned and looked at me with that same patient but deadly smirk. "Why do you insist on being conspicuous, forever searching out conspiratorial issues that benefits nobody else but you? Don't test me, Mr. Egan. We have places for people like you; cold, grey buildings where the public are reluctant to go—asylums housing those who believe they are superior beings or have a calling beyond the reach of the common man. Please believe me when I tell you how easily it can be arranged. You are an exceptional journalist, Mr. Egan; don't jeopardize your liberty and your craft on a hopeless quest." I followed her to the front door where she stopped with my manuscript tucked under her arm. "What of your reference notes; the information appertaining to this story?" I have to admit that the sight of those government paid thugs standing outside my house, and her threat of incarcerating me in some far away dungeon, sent chills down my spine; she meant every word she said. So I told her I had destroyed all my notes. She didn't believe me, I could see it in her eyes, but she left without saying another word."

"And you rewrote the story?"

Peter shook his head and raised his glass of wine.

"Are you mad, Michael," he grinned. "These people are capable of absolutely anything. Besides, there wasn't a paper in the country that would have touched it. I still have the notes if I ever change my mind."

"So you never destroyed them?"

"Let's just say I keep them about my person."

He emitted a gust of raucous laughter, undoubtedly induced by his alcohol consumption. He was an extremely likable character who had little or no respect for the laws that governed his own profession and, perhaps, even less for those who imposed them on society. I purchased another two drinks and returned to the table. A thin line of patrons began to fill the bar and occupy the surrounding tables, and Peter eyed every one of them with suspicion.

"Doesn't it ever worry you?" I asked. "Doesn't the consequences of writing a story frighten you" It would me, I'm sure."

"It comes with the job," he replied with a careless shrug. "You could be writing about someone's wife, someone's dog or someone's garden; sooner or later you're bound to piss someone off."

I smiled at his comparisons.

"But the government . . . Well . . . they're the government," I said.

"Michael, you deal with the government every day; every time you walk into a courtroom. Are you intimidated by them?"

"No, of course I'm not. But I don't intentionally set out to annoy them either."

Peter smiled broadly and raised his glass by way of a toast.

"I enjoy it. I like to see how far I can push. If I write a story that manages to slip past the editor and the government and makes the reader sit up and listen, then I've done my job. This country still retains the freedom of speech, Michael, and no chinless bureaucrat is going to tell me otherwise. Rules, legislations, whatever you want to call them, are merely guide lines. I never write anything unless I'm one hundred percent certain of all the facts. I'm governed only by injunctions; what we call gagging orders—I never run out of lavatory paper."

I admired his blatant disregard for authority but turned to the real purpose for meeting him.

"Wendy Marshall. What can you tell me about her?"

Peter looked vague and shook his head.

"I can't recall ever hearing the name. Who is she?"

"According to the D.P.P. she is a key witness; a surviving victim of George Henderson, apparently attacked by him five days before Angela Deacon."

"That's news to me, Michael—I've never heard of her. Let me see what I can find out; I'll have a dig through the archives and get back to you."

-13-

Elizabeth McCauley sat in a greasy café in Deptford High Street, staring out at the wet streets and the miserable facades of the dreary shops. After a week she regarded the table by the window as her own, as if it had been specifically reserved in her name and was her sole property. Far from refined and bordering on grotesque the establishment was thin but deep, clad out in white brick tiles that were now crazed and discoloured cream, with a wooden counter at its end and a small kitchen beyond that catered for the working class, or offered cheap food for the unemployed, and on Thursday's 'two for the price of one' for old age pensioners. But more often than not it was frequented by the patrons of the local dosshouse, who were neither working class or unemployed but unemployable—a lost strand in the human chain who suffered ailments far beyond the understanding of medical science, their condition having been induced by drugs or alcohol or trauma or good old fashioned hardship. They sat in solitude at lonely tables, muttering to themselves or to friends who had long ago shed this mortal coil. Some stared into empty tea cups with perplexed expressions and on the verge of tears, while others grumbled aloud and were occasionally prone to abusive outbursts and spasmodic leg and arm tremors; unsettling to any bystander, but in general they were inoffensive—imprisoned in a world they were reluctant to escape. In seven days Elizabeth had grown accustomed to them, and a few she even acknowledged and enquired after their wellbeing even though their response was vague and quite often disassociated from the subject. On the night of her beating at the hands of her counterpart Elizabeth returned home to Islington and immediately crammed her belongings into two leather suitcases and made her way across the city to the south side of the river, and the next morning she phoned her employee with a lie of a sick sister and the urgency to nurse her back to health. Her new abode, a rundown, scantily furnished flat in an early Victorian block that appeared uninhabitable from the outside, was courtesy of a friend who had vacated the premises on impulse and the promise of a happier life with her lover. Notwithstanding the garish décor and the wooden furniture that appeared to be infested by woodworm, the apartment was dull and gloomy, and the only window in the living room was obscured by a hefty iron fire escape that zigzagged upward on the outside flank wall. It also had many uninvited visitors—bailiffs in the main, attempting to collect the many unpaid debts her friend had accumulated and failed to mention. When Elizabeth arrived in the early hours of the morning the place was a shambles, with a kitchenette leading off the living room concealed behind a curtain as a door, the sink filled with pots, pans and plates soaking in a stagnant bowl of congealed fat, the bedroom a jumble of dirty and discarded clothes. That night she slept in her coat on top of the bed, and at first light she was awakened by a heavy but unmistakable knock. A bailiff garbed in sombre clothes and traditional bowler hat demanded the sum of thirty-six shillings, and less than two hours later a money-lender threatened violence for failing to pay fifteen pounds; both took convincing of her true identity. The intrusions, the steady flow of officials laden with summonses and demands was relentless and Elizabeth sought out the isolation of strangers in the nearby eatery.

She looked different now. Her first task was to cut and bleach her long black tresses and choose a wardrobe befitting the downtrodden area in which she lived. Once again she changed her name—to Linda Knox, and even adopted a south London accent, telling the proprietor of the café she had fled a violent husband in Clapham and was now living with her sister. It was ironic that as a Taker she had spent three years abducting runaways, and now she herself was the runaway, abandoning her job as a hostess, her home and her identity in exchange for a clear conscience and, perhaps, redemption. She knew enough about her colleague and his employer Phillip Heidegger to appreciate fear, but she considered it a small price to pay in light of her monstrous past. Her agenda now was to take stock of her life, and if at all possible, undo all the wrongdoings she held herself accountable for, and this could only be achieved by recording each and every deplorable act on paper. As a hostess it was imperative to remember the names and faces of all the regular and not so regular clients, and this she had augmented to a fine art, so calling to mind all the girls she had deliberately deceived was a relatively easy operation, beginning with Emily Shaw and backtracking through the years. She carried a small notebook and pencil with her at all times and whenever a name came to mind she immediately wrote it down, even if it wasn't in sequence of events, and that she could achieve with a calendar and occurrences of her own personal life. For example, she recalled a name of one girl from Durham, seventeen years old and extremely pretty. That particular seizure took place before the Blitz at St. Pancras on a warm summer evening, so she reasoned it was between July and September 1940, and she remembered introducing herself under the alias of Judith Parker, a name she used only on four occasions during July. On her walk back to Islington she saw young men and women dressed in their best, congregating in their locals and at bus stops and taxi ranks, on their way to parties and dance halls—Saturday—the last Saturday of the month; Saturday 27th 1940. Within seven days she had listed 85 names and locations and dates as near as damn it.

Between 7.30 and 8. am she would arrive and take up her usual seat in the unsavoury café, and after purchasing a cup of tea and sometimes a round of toast, she would scan the local newspaper for job opportunities, of which there were few, and there she would remain until midday, knowing that debt collectors were in the habit of calling in the mornings, during which time she would compile her list. Initially the names came easily but inevitably gaps began to form representing weeks between one abduction and another, but she had retained her diaries that served no other purpose but to remind her of when and when she was not working—either at the dance hall or as a Taker. Suffice to say not all commissions were successful, and she could recall numerous occasions when missed or bungled opportunities resulted in her and her companion leaving the station empty handed. To her calculations she had assisted her colleague some 215 times in the last two years and nine months, of which at least 25 were unsuccessful and 12 were aborted because of unforeseen circumstances. The thought she was responsible for a possible 180 missing girls made her feel physically sick. The reality of her transition was simple—revenge; on those who had wronged her and for those she had wronged. She would be lost in time to reminiscences of the young women she had misled and gave up to a life of degradation for a mere twenty pounds, which in turn funded her own extravagances. Sometimes her shame was such that she dropped her head into her hands and wept. And it was at such a moment that she heard the friendly voice of the proprietor, colloquially known as Sniffer, owing to his constant endeavours to clear his nasal passages without the aid of a handkerchief. "Cheer up, lovely—can't be all bad," he said, chirpily. Elizabeth looked up, sliding her notebook surreptitiously beneath the newspaper. The owner stood before her; garbed in an apron stained with every juice and concoction known to man and brandishing a cup of tea. "'Ere you go, 'ave this on the 'ouse." He placed down the tea and pulled up a chair opposite. "I've been watchin' you, and I 'ave to say it's no good you frettin' over fings long gone; you 'ave to look forward to the future. Now you take me. Ol' lady left me years ago . . . mind, not such a bad fing when all is said and done. And then there's this bleedin' war deprivin' me of my livelihood. Eggs is like gold dust. And bacon . . . well that makes you fink, dunnit? Why's it so bloody 'ard to get bacon these days? It's not like we trained 'em to fight and they've all sodded off to France, is it? And it ain't like they've stopped breedin' neither. Pigs is pigs and they do what pigs do! So why's it so 'ard to get bacon? What do they expect me to serve up with no eggs and no bacon? My point is . . ."

"Do you have a point, Sniffer?" Elizabeth smiled as she wiped her eyes.

"Bloody right I do! My point is we get over it—or go round it, and get on with it the best way we can. All I'm sayin' is we can't give up our hearts to the past. There's not a cause great enough."

Sniffer was older and wiser and, most probably, had experienced most of what life could throw at a living soul, and by the grace of God had emerged on the other side halfway sane; his personal hygiene, however, was questionable but somehow complimented his overall rancid appearance. "And tell me this," he continued, prodding his finger on the table top. "Why would a firecracker like you spend her days in a dump like this?"

"It's only the mornings. My sister's husband works nights."

Sniffer nodded as if he approved of her consideration for her sister's privacy, and he sat for a moment appraising her with a curiosity. He dropped his stare to the newspapers and registered the circled job availabilities.

"So what is it you're lookin' for?" he asked.

Elizabeth evaded the question with a smile and picked up her newspaper and notebook.

"Is there a library close by?" she asked.

Sniffer thought for a moment and nodded.

"Not much cause for one 'round here; most 'round 'ere can't read," he replied. "But there is one; loneliest place in south London; down to the main road and turn left."

Elizabeth found the cold, grey building exactly where he said it was, and moving straight through the doors she approached a young man busying himself with index cards at a raised counter. He wore small, round spectacles, had a youthful complexion and a spray of red hair that appeared to have lost all sense of direction, and he looked to Elizabeth and transmitted a transparent smile. "I would like to become a member," she said. Again he smiled, pulled a drawer out before him and placed down a form in front of her. "If you would care to fill this out, ma'am; membership is two shillings and sixpence." Immediately Elizabeth filled out the form as Linda Knox and gave her present address. "How long does this form take to process? How long before I can take a book out?" she asked as she completed the form. The librarian checked the document and filed it in the appropriate drawer and assured her she could take a book out whenever she liked—and as many as she liked. "Are you looking for anything specific?" he asked her as she counted the fee into his hand. "Trafficking," she answered. The young man looked slightly mystified and struggled to retain his position of authority. "You mean cars and such?" he enquired meekly. Elizabeth snapped her purse closed and raised herself on tiptoes to meet his eye-line. "No, young man, I don't mean cars and such. I'm referring to human beings; those abducted and sold into slavery." Totally perplexed by her request, he stood motionless like a cardboard cut-out with his eyes searching the ceiling as if it held the answer. "You're new to this, aren't you?" said Elizabeth with an air of sarcasm. He nodded with humility. "A bit, but I know all the classics," he said, optimistically. "Perhaps what you're looking for is in the history section." Huffily she walked towards the corridors of books, saying as she went, "I'll start in the 'Current Events' section."

It was all to no avail, though Robert, the young and misplaced librarian, tried desperately to assist and continually disappeared and reappeared at different aisles with piles of books that in the main reverted back to history and not present day. Nevertheless Elizabeth glanced through every one, jotting down references of interest in an attempt to truly understand what she had been a part of. After five long hours Robert placed down a large mug of tea on the table and pulled up a chair opposite her. Elizabeth smiled at his thoughtfulness and closed her notebook.

"Thank you," she said. "Sorry I was a bit short with you earlier; it was unkind of me."

Robert shrugged his shoulders haplessly and rested on his elbows, holding a small book he had found.

"What have you got there?" she asked as she raised her mug of tea to her mouth.

The young man appeared uncertain and held the book between his hands.

"Well . . . it's about . . . it's to do with . . . You know!" he stammered.

"No, I don't know, Robert," Elizabeth grinned. "What is it about?"

The young man looked embarrassed and squeezed his eyes closed.

"Them! Women who . . . whats-name . . . that go with men. But you might think bad of me for showing it to you. It's just that there are some books we're not allowed to put on the shelves, and we keep them round the back and . . . well, I've read this one."

"It's about prostitution."

Robert nodded shamefully.

"It isn't rude, as in really rude, but there's something in there about trafficking."

"Then why didn't you say earlier?"

"I told you," he said, lowering his voice to a whisper. "We're not allowed to put them on the shelves. And I didn't know what trafficking was till you walked in; I'm still not certain. Anyway, if you want to read it?"

He stood up, his face flushed and wiping his sweaty palms on his thighs.

"We close in an hour," he said.

'Jessica Bennett.' A victim of trafficking:

The first I remember was awakening on the concrete floor of a barren room consumed with such intense heat and humidity my clothes were soaked in sweat, but more frighteningly was the sudden realisation that I could not move—not a solitary muscle from the neck down. My whole body felt weighed down by some incredible force but I could see enough to know I was not constricted in any way. I was lying on my side, in what would be medically termed as the 'recovery position' as though I had been purposefully positioned that way and left. It was to my estimation an hour before I could wiggle the fingers of my left hand on display in front of me, and perhaps a further hour before I could straighten my leg. For all my efforts I could not raise my head from the stone floor and my torso was so bereft of feeling it was as if it had been detached. Breathing was extremely difficult and I likened the sensation to drowning, gasping for deep breaths that never came and only left me exasperated and scared. How much time passed I cannot recall, but I had managed to roll onto my back and was staring up at a discoloured and cracked ceiling that bore only charred patches of soot caused by candles, and behind me a barred window partly obscured a blue sky with a burning sun. The sound of crickets broke the silence and for a while kept me company during my confused and incapable state, but feeling slowly returned—first in my toes and feet and then in my legs and body, and after some considerable exertion was exercised I managed to drag myself and support my back against the wall. The small room was desolate except for a tin bucket standing in the corner, and the whitewashed walls were marked in abstract patterns of graffiti and doodles breaking the bland monotony; a heavy wooden door secured me from the outside world. Where was I? Crickets and intense sunshine were never evident in my hometown of Chatham—not even on the hottest of days. On the contrary, it was cold and miserable the last I remember. I was walking along Pier Road, a short distance from the dockyard gates and on my way to see Adele, my best friend from school. I can't remember actually completing my journey or seeing her. I could not recall anything.

My whole body ached and I remained slumped against the wall, my breathing shallow and erratic. I was like the many drunks I had seen rolling out of the pubs of Medway, pivoting and staggering in no certain direction, only to collapse in a heap in a shop doorway or alley, incapacitated by alcohol with a brain devoid of reason. Certainly my symptoms were similar but at only fifteen years old I had never consumed drink and certainly had not experienced its effects. As feeling slowly returned I began to rub and scratch an irritation on my forearm and my head began to pound. My throat was dry but I endeavoured to call out. Perhaps, I thought, I had not been heard but I felt too exhausted to try again. I sat there watching the sun slide across the window until it disappeared from sight, and as the heat of the room slowly began to evaporate and the sky began to dull I made an attempt to stand up. After several failed attempts I remained on all fours and edged myself towards the window, and grasping the rusty iron bars managed to pull myself up. The view was alien to me; a dusty and desolate landscape that had no place on God's green earth, bathed in rusty coloured sand with areas of lifeless clumps of grass. Nothing moved except the shadows beneath the skeletal trees, slowly lengthening as the sun dropped over the horizon. Where was I? Still clasping the bars I pushed my legs out behind me alternately, trying to restore feeling and the capacity to move. Guiding myself along the wall I reached the door and called out again, and had there been a handle or knob I would have undoubtedly attempted to open it. "Hello! Is anybody there?" There was no response and I shuffled back to the open window. "Can anybody hear me? Can anyone help?" My voice was lost in the void of the darkening panorama and I realised all my attempts were futile. I was, as far as I could establish, in the middle of nowhere—in an arid desert where people seldom came. And then I did what all frightened little girls do—I cried. The day was almost gone and soon I would be swallowed up by the night.

That night was the longest I had ever experienced, broken only by bouts of dozing, sporadic episodes of weeping, relentless screams of help, and the overwhelming feeling that all was lost. I suffered the indignity of relieving myself in a bucket and had to use my cardigan to clean myself, of which I discarded through the bars of the window. I believed I had suffered an insect bite, as I unconsciously and frantically clawed at my arm to alleviate the constant annoyance, and still my head retained an excruciating pain. I saw faces in the darkness, images that were lost to fear and panic but now, in a state of alertness and sharpened anger, I recalled vividly. Adele's house was in a narrow thoroughfare that stood in the shadow of Chatham arches, accessible by way of the high street or roads leading to Rochester and Sittingbourne. I would always opt for the high street and take the opportunity to look in the shop windows. It was 1908, a leap year, and the air was charged with an excitement because Wilbur Wright had flown to France to demonstrate controlled powered flight, and we all looked to technology to at last pull us away from Victorian life and its staid values. A fine coach drawn by two proud horses and glistening with brass drew alongside me as I approached my friend's street beyond the arches. The door opened and a lady dressed in fine clothes smiled back at me. She enquired after a local street and before I could answer I was pulled inside by a brutish looking man who, by his dress and manner, appeared completely disassociated from both the woman and the grand carriage they traversed in. Thereafter everything is fragmented and vague, and what I thought may be dreams or the result of a young and overactive imagination, were actual incidents. I recalled motion, undulation and extreme sickness, of girls sobbing uncontrollably, and of being physically restrained by powerful hands. A horizontal jagged shape began to manifest beyond the window, like an image emerging from a bleak fog, growing bolder with every passing minute as a feeble light behind enhanced its shape—the horizon.

I met the new day a stronger person, enraged and embittered at my unjust imprisonment by miscreants unknown. It was not open to question whether my father would find me and take me home; undoubtedly he would. He would rescue me and take me back to the wet and cluttered streets I grew up in but had never appreciated—till now. But then how could he when even I had no idea where I was? I sat on the floor assessing my pathetic condition. My clothes were wrinkled and stained, and my white blouse bore embarrassing yellow marks under my arms and across my back. It was then I discovered the source of irritation on my forearm; a track extending an inch or so visible beneath a bluish bruise—minute puncture marks caused by a syringe. Fear consumed me again and I went to the window and began to scream at the top of my voice—but to no avail; the world beyond my window shimmered under the growing heat and remained utterly silent. And I sat cross legged on the floor and began to cry again. But then hope! Beyond the opening came the familiar noise of hoofs scuffing on gravel and wheels clattering over craggy rocks, growing louder and closer. Instinctively I rushed back to the window and began to scream, and to my relief all sound stopped; I had been heard. But as I waited for my saviours to free me from the confines of my hot and stinking cell I was overwhelmed by a terror I had never experienced before or since. What I misconstrued as graffiti and doodles were, on closer inspection, messages from those who had come before me; those who had been drugged and kidnapped and brought to this Godforsaken hell. One read, '*To my mother, my father and brothers. I do not know what will become of me. I have been here for three days and I am hungry and without water. Mother, I fear the worst and truly believe I will not live to see another day if help does not come soon, but I have come to realise I was put here for a purpose—surely it cannot be to die. If I am to be saved of what purpose can I be; what cause can I serve? If I am to die then I beg your forgiveness for leaving you under such circumstances. Your loving daughter Clara Pinter. Bexhill, 1906.*'

I stood breathless and trembling with fear for what seemed an eternity, knowing that the noise of the horses was not bringing my saviours but my captors. A bolt was drawn with a heavy thud that made me jump back, and the door gently swung open and buffeted against the wall, and there in the square void stood a man with a dark complexion and jet black hair. His shirt was open to the navel and his sleeves were rolled up revealing bodily hair matted by glistening sweat, and over his shoulder hung a rifle. His fearsome presence was enough to strike me dumb, and if I reacted in any way I cannot remember; we simply stared at one another until he stood to one side of the doorway. It was then a woman entered, tall with auburn hair, handsome and smartly dressed in jodhpurs and loose fitting white blouse; a riding crop looped round her wrist hung loosely from her hand. She slowly closed and circled me two or three times before staring at me directly with an uncertain expression. When she reached out to touch my face I instinctively backed away, but she raised her riding crop and I froze with my arms crossed over my breasts, and thereafter she circled me several more times, pushing, prodding and clutching me as if I was a slab of meat. At last she stopped to appraise me with the corners of her ruby lips turned downward. After a long deliberation of assessing my form she looked to the man and jerked her up, and hesitantly he raised four fingers to which she laughed mockingly and shook her head, and without undue care she pushed her thumbs into my mouth and spread my lips apart to examine my teeth. Still staring into my mouth with great interest she said "Two," and the man shook his head angrily and began to shout at her in a foreign tongue, but she smiled and faced him with a barrage of counterattacks in his own native language that appeared to grudgingly placate him. "Two fifty—no more, and you arrange transport to the border," she demanded. He stared at her sceptically and she sighed and began to walk to the door. "Stop wasting my time!" she hissed. "Show me something befitting your exorbitant prices or sell the child to someone who hasn't got so much to lose." The man suddenly but reluctantly nodded his head in agreement and she paused and expressed the grin of a conqueror. "Good. We have an agreement. Have her at the border-town by midday tomorrow. And for God sake give her some food and water; she's of no value to me dead."

I was to find out much later that after my abduction I was placed aboard a cargo-ship, and by way of the Bay of Biscay and then Spanish territorial waters, transferred to a fishing vessel that landed me in an isolated bay between Bilbao and San Sebastian and thereafter transferred me by road to the outskirts of Pamplona, close to the French border; an overall journey of eight days. After my life had been negotiated away I was awaken the following morning by my captor, who at the point of his rifle directed me to a boxed wagon tethered to an emaciated horse that appeared barely capable of sustaining its own weight but nevertheless set off on a long and tedious journey across a rocky and unstable terrain.

Fear no longer consumed me the way it had when I was alone, for like Clara Pinter who was oblivious to her purpose, I at least suspected and realised that with every breath I drew there was a chance of survival. From that moment on I would be accommodating, submissive and as affable as I could be within my spectrum of tolerance. When at last the door opened and I was pulled out into dazzling sunlight, I found myself standing in a dusty street of dilapidated wooden houses knitted together by a stretch of sagging balconies and absent balustrades at first floor level, where beneath shops with broken windows or covered with boarding conveyed the story that this place was all but abandoned. But there was life spattered here and there, of curious faces staring from windows and two or three buxom women observing from the balcony, a gaggle of old men sat in the shade of a tree and playing dominoes; their initial interest waned and their eyes searched out other subjects; I was a sight they saw every day. My gaoler held my arm and led me towards a deteriorated frontage of peeled and blistered paint and broken shutters and where a collection of woebegone furniture decorated a bare-boarded raised platform. The woman who bartered for my soul sat in the cooling shade of the overhead balconies with a long-stem glass of red wine cradled between her slender fingers. On a table before her were the remnants of a light snack and a bulging white envelope. "Has she eaten?" she asked curtly, looking directly at my keeper. He nodded, to which she picked up the envelope and passed it over, but he clasped my arm tighter as if to enforce ownership. "You may go," said the woman with a wave of her hand. "I am more than capable of administering discipline on this wretch should the need arise," and looking at me through narrowed eyes, she added, "But the need won't arise, will it?" I shook my head and muttered, "No, ma'am."

The woman, dressed in a green skirt and matching bolero jacket, watched the peasant as he walked back to the wagon without uttering a single syllable, and not until he had disappeared in clouds of swirling dust did she set her gaze back to me. "I've no doubt you've eaten but I'll wager it wasn't much. Sit down." I obeyed, and she raised her hand and clicked her fingers. A small, elderly woman appeared through a beaded curtain and listened intently as my hostess babbled an order and then promptly retreated back into the decaying house. “I would imagine you have some burning questions to ask,” she said as she sat back in her chair, composed herself and arched her eyebrows. “I urge you to seize this opportunity—you may not have another.” I was looking at the boards beneath my feet and the blown sand that had formed patterns into images only I could see. She spoke perfect English but possessed the hint of an accent I could not define. “Then perhaps I should begin,” she suggested. “What is your name?” I pushed the sandy images around with my foot until they lost their original identity, and then she placed her finger under my chin and raised my head. “You must have a name.” I backed away from her touch until I was totally reclined in my seat. “Jessica. Jessica Bennett,” I replied, meekly. She nodded approvingly and smiled. “Well, Jessica, you must want to know what my intentions are now you're here. You are in my custody, so to speak, but it is only a temporary arrangement; they have plans for you.” At the mention of ‘they’, and the daunting prospect that my ordeal was far from over, I eased forward in my chair. “My part in all this is to negotiate your value and deliver you in one piece. My advice to you is to obey in every way possible. Do not provoke them; it is not beneficial to your predicament.” The old woman remerged with a plate on which sat an assortment of food; cheese, ham, tomatoes and bread, and placed it on the table with a tall glass of water. “I would eat If I were you, Jessica. A long journey awaits us,” said my hostess advisedly as she lifted the bottle of wine and topped up her glass. I pulled the plate closer to me and stared hopelessly at the arrangement of food. “Why me? And what will be done with me? When can I go home?” I asked. She sipped her wine slowly as she considered my questions and then placed the glass on the table. “First you mustn't take it personally . . .” she began.

“There were other girls—I remember, aboard the ship,” I interrupted.

“Yes, there were, Jessica, you are quite right but they have already been distributed. I can't say with any certainty as to where, but I would imagine Constantine in Algeria or Monastir, Kaitouan or perhaps Tripoli in Tunisia; it's hard to say.”

"So why am I not with them? Why have I been left behind?"

She assessed me with a patient smile and then shook her head. "The truth of the matter is you were surplus to the buyer's requirements; he took what he wanted and left what he didn't—you. And at present you should think yourself a very lucky girl. I've had the displeasure of visiting the dens of Tunisia and Algeria and I would not consider either as being wholesome. Far from it; the buyers are ruthless and demand more than most. You, however, will be taken across the border to France, where you will live like a princess, with beautiful clothes and have many friends. As for your third question I believe it has been answered. Now eat up."

I had no appetite. I put the plate on the table and dropped my head into my hands. "Have I been kidnapped?" I sobbed.

She raised her glass to her lips and took another sip. "Kidnap is a harsh word, Jessica, and one where the act is associated with a ransom, if I'm not mistaken. You can rest assured that nobody will be sending your family any demands."

We travelled through the remaining day and most of the night, finally arriving in a narrow street of tall houses in Lyon, close to the basilica of Saint-Martin d'Ainay church. I slept randomly throughout the long journey, and stepping out of her splendid carriage and onto the pavement the sun was just rising to chase away the shadows and bathe the rooftops in a magnificent yellow glow. I shuddered in the chilly morning air and my escort placed a blanket about my shoulders. Her name was Maggie, and what I gleaned from her character during our occasional night time conversations was that she was not selfish or spiteful but blessed with a kindness most would admire, and her display of assertiveness back in my cell was designed only to dupe my captor that she had control. "Head up, Jessica, and don't slouch. Speak only when spoken to, and try not to burst into tears; they thrive on weakness." We moved through an unlocked green door that immediately led to a steep staircase of plush red carpet with golden ropes either side set in ornamental brass hooks that guided us upwards, only to emerge in a vast room decorated in the Renaissance period, with gold framed paintings of erotica, pornographic lithographs and alabaster statuettes of nymphs.

Empty glasses adorned every table and wine and Champagne bottles protruded from silver buckets of ice that had melted back to water, and all around the air was poisoned with the stench of cigarette and cigar smoke. A slim but shapely woman wearing stockings and little else entered the room and gathered up her discarded clothes strewn about the floor and passed us a polite smile on the way back, and I gasped at such at a sight. Maggie smiled as she guided me into the adjacent corridor, and remarked, "Ooh la-la! It must have been quite a night last night." I knew about such places, or at least I had heard about them, but never could I imagine ever setting foot in one; I hoped our visit would not take long. A woman dressed in a flowing red evening gown and glistening in Jewellery rounded the corner and at once threw her arms open and cried with joy, "Maggie, I've been expecting you." She hugged my escort and kissed her on both cheeks. Certainly overdressed for that time in the morning, I silently observed as the dark haired lady conversed with Maggie in her native tongue, tactile and theatrical in her manner, with perpetually moving hands and a laugh as excruciating as fingernails being dragged down a blackboard. I was momentarily distracted by the comings and goings of half-naked unkempt, beautiful women moving from one room to another, but then I was ushered into a nearby office.

Whatever words had been exchanged between the two women I could not say, but in the confines of the elegant room, both women were appraising me with an air of hopelessness, though Maggie tried desperately to arouse a modicum of optimism into the dire situation. Claudette, the ageing French proprietor winced with every glance in my direction, and finally sunk into a chair behind her desk and shook her head. "Maggie, Maggie, Maggie, what am I supposed to do with her? Look at her! Could you not at least have made her presentable? She looks like a refugee," she moaned.

It was a fair appraisal given the circumstances. After nearly twelve days of travelling and incarceration, I resembled a street-urchin, in raggedy, filthy clothes and faint with hunger. Maggie stood beside me with her arm around my shoulder.

"A little soap and water, a good meal and some rest and she will be transformed into a butterfly," she returned encouragingly.

"Cockroach, more like!"

"You're being unkind, Claudette . . ."

"No, Maggie, I'm being honest! What do you propose I do with a pale and shapeless, flat-chested child like her? She's not suitable and I don't want her."

"She's a late developer," Maggie proffered.

"Late!" laughed the lady. "I'm in my mid-fifties. I doubt I'll live that long to see it."

Undeterred my negotiator walked to the desk and looked down at the French vixen, who appeared agitated by my presence and immovable as regards to taking me under her wing. I, too, was hoping against hope that arbitration would collapse and I would be taken to the nearest railway station with a one-way ticket home.

"Is that your final word, Claudette?" Maggie asked her in an icy tone. "Or do I tell them she is not to your liking? Do I say you no longer require their business . . . or their funding?"

At first the lady's eyes ignited with terror, but then she feigned composure and behaved as if there had been some dreadful misunderstanding.

"I never said I couldn't use her," she said, forcing a smile in my direction. "Of course I can. Of course I can. My sister Edith will have no trouble placing her. I shall take the girl to her this afternoon. Yes, this afternoon. Be assured, Maggie, she'll be in good hands."

"No, Claudette! Your sister's association with sweat-shops and factories is not what they intend for this girl. She stays with you."

"But, Maggie . . ."

"With you, Claudette, and no arguments!"

The face of the proprietor flushed with resignation and she slowly shook her head.

"But look at her," she petitioned with a heavy groan. "She is . . ."

"She is going to be just fine under your care and guidance," Maggie intercepted.

Claudette agreed submissively as she looked me up and down.

"Perhaps with a little paint and a little powder she may earn her keep," she suggested. "We have clients who enjoy the company of little girls."

"But not this one. Not yet. I was thinking you could use her—to clean and wash, until such time she's ready."

"Ah, Maggie, we all have to learn sometime, and who is to say when we're really ready, eh?"

Claudette was making light of the situation but Maggie was not to be broken, and she returned to my side and put her hand on my shoulder.

"I will be calling in from time to time. You know I'm based in Paris now, don't you? So I would imagine you'll be seeing quite a lot of me."

"It's always a pleasure," smiled the lady bitterly.

Maggie run a gentle hand down my mousy tresses and smiled warmly into my eyes, and suddenly, as if by impulse she broke away and walked to the door.

"She'll need papers, identification, a name," she said over her shoulder.

The deflated lady nodded her head. "I shall see to it," she murmured, dolefully.

In a moment she was gone, and despite her threats of returning on a regular basis, I never laid eyes on Maggie again. And that year—that month—that day, my life dramatically altered to a path I would never have considered taking of my own free will. Outside looking in is to be in no position to know, or to slander with any great authority or, for that matter, to be judgemental with regards to the occupation one is scrutinising. One has to be in it, so to speak, up to their necks to gain even an inkling of understanding. I was thrown into a world that on the face of it appeared glamorous and beautiful, where everything sparkled behind veils of chiffon and satin, and riches could be achieved with a simple smile, but they say that 'all that glitters is not gold', and soon cold reality comes into play. From that moment on my world was artificial, an illusion contrived of cheap reproductions, spurious beauties and false promises, where love bordered on treachery and pretence was accepted as a way of life. With Maggie's warning still ringing in her ears, Claudette put me to work preparing food in the kitchen, making beds, washing and ironing, and making the chimera a spotless reality. Of a night I was confined to the annex, a three floor building of cramped dormitories that housed forty or so girls from all over the world; each with a story to tell similar to my own and only spoken in whispers. Located behind the main house I would sit at my window and watch silhouettes slide across the drapes, imagining the incompatible liaisons and listening to the submissive whimpers carried on a light breeze, forever curious and preoccupied with a destiny I had no part in. Freedom ate away at me every minute of every hour of every day; I lived and dreamt it, but like pain and grief, time rounds off the edges until the execution of the word pales into insignificance. Housebound for four months I was finally allowed out into civilisation, to walk the cobbled streets and shop in the marketplace or visit the basilica of Notre Dame de Fourviere, the ancient theatre or the magnificence of St. John, but only in the company of Yvette my chaperon, followed by Andre, a square faced hulk who was not averse to administering punishment on unruly clients, though he walked several paces behind us and observed in silence. Nevertheless, I enjoyed the independence and the trust Madam Claudette believed me worthy of.

At three months from my sixteenth birthday Madam Claudette summoned me to her office for what she called an 'introduction', and what Yvette enlightened me to as meaning 'a sudden change in direction'. Yvette was a native of France from outside Reims at Varennes-en-Argonne; a woman of breath-taking beauty who was looked upon as a kind of mother superior or authority amongst the other girls; a freeborn who was allowed to come and go of her own free will. "Time to earn your keep, Jesse. Your childhood is over—fin!" she laughed. I was distraught, for I knew exactly what she meant, and I knew what 'introduction' represented, and the more I panicked, the harder Yvette laughed. "Don't take on so, Jesse, you knew this time would come. It is why you are here; the only reason," she said. I was sat before her dressing-table, staring at myself in the mirror in disbelief at the role I was about to play, and Yvette stood behind me, giggling unkindly as she picked and teased at my hair. "I'm not ready, Yvette. I can't do it!" I stated emphatically. She laughed and waved away my resignations. "But you have to! Did you think you were going to clean pots and pans, and play chamber maid for the rest of your life? Sooner or later the piper has to be paid. Madam Claudette believes you are ready. I believe you are ready. So . . ." I jumped to my feet and scurried to the far side of the room, as if I were a child escaping from the hands of a brutal father. At once I was overcome by grief and humiliation and started to cry. Yvette approached, and for a brief moment took me in her arms and held me. "So what do you think will happen, eh? What unbelievable experience do you think will transform you? What life-changing phenomenon will corrupt you? I can tell you—nothing; no fireworks, no hallucinations of angels and demons, no ridicule or finger-pointing the next day—nothing. You see, Jesse, the world isn't waiting just for you—it doesn't care, and nor should you. If you have been yearning for this moment all your life—that you're about to experience the most wonderful and tender act between a man and a woman, then you're going to be sorely disappointed. For All the years and all the men I have encountered, there is nothing more gratifying than when a man puts his hand inside his trousers and takes out his wallet; it puts everything into perspective." I was inconsolable, and so beside myself and grief-stricken that I was incapable of uttering a single word without bursting into tears. Yvette casually opened her wardrobe and surveyed its contents while humming a tune in perfect pitch; seemingly oblivious to my forthcoming dilemma. "Ah, here we are!" she cried, holding up a transparent black negligee. "This will make you beautiful." And there it began—the end of the innocence.

I was systematically ingratiated into the world of whoredom, to sleep by day and entertain by night without abatement or choice, to be at the beck and call of strangers, and to always be ready; refusal was not an option. In two years I had been subjected to all manner of unimaginable perverseness and sordidness that went far beyond the realms of decency and challenged the integrity and, indeed, the sexual aspirations of everything human. I was part of the system now, continually watched over by Andre, who was not as I first believed—simply an employee of the brothel, but an essential part of the organisation responsible for my abduction. At least once every month a small crowd of businessmen would arrive—to examine the books and accounts, record costs of food and overall expenditure, and to interview the girls with a view of moving them to different locations. In the days preceding their arrival Madam Claudette would run around like a headless chicken, ensuring the dormitories were spotless and the girls impeccably presented. Though most of the girls had gone and been replaced, I was spared being transported for five years, by which time I could speak fluent French and a smattering of other European languages, but the thought of home was never far away. I had earned a modicum of liberty, and one afternoon of every week I was allowed into the city to meander around the galleries and shops, but always in the company of Andre. It was a delight to sit by the Rhone and Saone rivers that ran through the Romanesque city and talk with Yvette, who by now had become my best friend, and as always when we walked the hilly terrain of Lyon, I was taking in more than just the attractions; I was secretly planning my escape.

On a chilly October afternoon Yvette and I sat on the steps of the ancient amphitheatre atop of the city, sharing bread and cheese and watching the tourists crowding the narrow thoroughfares and alleyways, taking in the splendour of the decaying and crumbling buildings and the wondrous architecture of the theatre itself; and as ever Andre surveyed from a distance.

"We've been friends a long time, Yvette, and I've never had the opportunity to thank you for all you have done for me," I said, surreptitiously glancing in Andre's direction.

She shrugged coyly. "You talk as if you're leaving," she giggled.

"I am, Yvette, I am. The next afternoon we are away from the brothel I shall leave."

Yvette observed me—at first with an air of disbelief, and then with one of horror.

"Have you gone mad, Jesse!" she shouted.

I grabbed her hand and squeezed it and at once she fell silent and forced a smile in our escort's direction.

"Have you gone mad?" she hissed. "They will find you and they will hurt you. Do not under estimate them, Jesse; you know what they're capable of. They will kill you."

"In comparison with the life I'm leading, one can be no worse than the other. I cannot and will not do this any longer. I will take my chances."

Yvette sat moodily contemplating my intentions, and after a moment or two she held her hands out face upwards.

"How?" she asked. "You are under continuous scrutiny, so how do you plan to make your escape?"

I nodded faintly towards the tourists gathered on the steps.

"With them! You think you can just stroll out of Lyon unnoticed! What about Andre, eh?"

"He isn't with me every minute. I can use a public toilet . . ."

"Where he shall be watching from outside," Yvette interrupted.

"A café, perhaps; an inn or restaurant—somewhere where I can leave through the backdoor while he waits at the front; prearranged where I can change my clothes."

My friend shook her head, stubbornly refusing to accept the method of my plan.

"And where will you go?" She pursued vehemently. "Have you any money? No! And where will the change of clothes come from, eh? You think they will be hanging on the back of the door waiting for you to put them on? You're crazy!"

I smiled as I observed the activity all around us, nibbling at my wedge of cheese and noting the swathes of people ascending the hill towards the biggest tourist attraction in Lyon. At least I was convinced my plan would work—but I could not achieve it alone. Since my transition from housemaid to hussy, I had witnessed the consequences of headstrong girls within the house that subsequently resulted in punishment in one form or another. There was girl from Algeria, a dusky maiden with black hair and large brown eyes, who was found to be receiving gifts in the form of money from an admirer who called at the house twice a week. Madam Claudette found the cash rolled up in a pair of stockings and at once alerted the watchdog—Andre; thereafter he would awaken her from her slumber and subject her to freezing cold baths. By design the brothel appeared to be confined to the upper floors of the house but the ground floor was also a part of it, accessible from the street by an independent front door and used mainly for storage. During my tenure I have known of several young girls and women who were taken there and repeatedly assaulted for what Madam Claudette considered a violation of privileges, and what I discovered was a large cellar where, I would imagine with such devices of torture, such brutal punishments were administered. If caught in the act of escape I would undoubtedly be taken there.

"I will, of course, need your help, Yvette," I said.

She looked horrified at the prospect. "Me! Jesse, have you any idea what they will do to me?"

I nodded and took a glimpse in Andre's direction; he was conversing with a young lady and speaking with great authority about the ancient theatre as if he were personally responsible for its construction.

"Indirectly, I meant," I said, turning back to her. "You could hide the clothes for me—along with a little cash, enough to get me back to England. You have my word I'll send you back every penny once I'm home. You know my predicament—they keep me poor—without a franc to my name. As a freeborn you can help me; you have money and come and go whenever you please. You're my only hope, Yvette."

Fearless pigeons began to gather at our feet, seemingly unafraid of the heavy pedestrian traffic up and down the stone stairs, pecking up the crumbs of our snack as soon as they hit the floor. Yvette was pensive, giving my scheme consideration as she cast her eyes across the rooftops of the city below.

"The bakery," she said suddenly. "That has a public toilet, and Andre always waits outside while we get our food. There's a cupboard under the sink; I could hide clothes in there along with some money."

"You'll do it! You'll help me!" I cried with delight.

She nodded and smiled, but then she frowned as our bodyguard looked over in our direction.

"Yes, I'll help you, but I won't suffer for you. I'll do what you ask, Jesse, but I swear by the Saints that if I am in any way held responsible, I will tell them everything. I will say I was infatuated with you and I did it for love."

She started to giggle, which became a source of annoyance for our overseer.

We reverted to silence for a while, until he looked away.

"But you will do it?" I asked.

"Oui!"

For the next five days life continued as usual, with an endless stream of cold hearted men and warm admirers all with money to burn, and as always I applied myself completely and met all their wishes. Knowing I was just days away from freedom time appeared to slow considerably, but once Madam Claudette informed me that my next afternoon off would be on Thursday, the hours and minutes resumed their normal pace. Yvette agreed to place a change of clothes under the sink of the bakery and hide the money behind the cistern, and once out the backdoor I knew I could make my getaway through the labyrinth of alleyways. But in the early hours of Thursday morning—in a brief but welcome break between clients, Madam Claudette entered my room in the company of a suited gentleman, aggressive both in appearance and in nature. He shouted at me in an alien language, fast, furious and repetitive, and the more I displayed gestures of ignorance the louder and faster he ranted. Even the iron-willed Madam Claudette appeared frightened, flinching with every wave of his hand and wincing at the severity of his tone, until she placed a bundle of casual clothes on the bed and told me to get dressed. To this day I believe Yvette betrayed me, for I was marched out of the house like a convict before a line of girls and Madam Claudette, who murmured, shook their heads disapprovingly and even crossed themselves as if I were being led to my execution. Thereafter I was placed in a stage wagon where several young women sat either side looking pale and tired, while a man wearing a peak cap and cradling a rifle sat between. I took my place at the end of the bench—never once attempting to converse or even enquire as to where I was being taken. I was so indescribably grief-stricken at having had the chance of freedom snatched away from me that I could not even cry; anger and bitterness kept that particular emotion at bay, and I vowed revenge on those who had wronged and betrayed me.

It took almost two days to reach Milan, and my hopes ran high at the possibility of being placed into one of the many brothels within the city, but the stay was only temporary; a mere overnight stopover where all the girls were confined to a single room with only bare floorboards to sleep on. Early the next morning we were put back into the stage wagon, but this time the number in transit had risen to twelve. By the afternoon we reached Verona, but again it was only to pick up more women, and by nightfall we were on the outskirts of Venice. For the first time since leaving Lyon I felt optimistic, and even more so when eight of the girls were removed to an awaiting carriage that was surely the property of a Marquis or somebody of considerable standing, for it was tethered to four white horses and exuded opulence even when set against the backdrop of night. The remaining women and I were not as fortunate. We journeyed on for at least another two hours and arrived at what I can only describe as a farm; a large sinister looking house set in a desolate hollow deep in the countryside. While the driver led the horses to a nearby barn, we were herded towards the house at the end of a rifle, and inside there were three elderly women who appeared to be standing on ceremony at the end of a large stone room consisting of little else but a rectangle wooden table with two benches either side. One woman stepped forward and motioned us to the table, while the second began to place bowls and spoons before us, and once we were settled the third woman set a large pot of steaming stew down and began to ladle the contents into the individual receptacles. It was while we were eating that an argument evolved from what began as a confidential conversation between the driver and the man with the rifle. They barked viciously at one another in their native tongue, and at one time I thought one would certainly kill the other if their disagreement was not resolved. The girl opposite me, pale skinned with blue eyes and light hair, was listening intently to the dispute and muttering angrily under her breath. "Do you understand them?" I whispered to her. She nodded and leaned forward. "Serbs," she hissed disapprovingly. "They're arguing whether to take us over the water or across land. For sure, we won't be staying in Italy. If they take us overland they may be taking us to Hungary, Austria, or possibly Germany. If they take us across the water . . . well, you don't want to know."

The night, or at least most of it, was spent in whispered conversation concerning our undisclosed destiny, but at least they afforded us the luxury of a dormitory with mattresses, blankets and pillows. Greta was Hungarian and seemed familiar with the ways of our keepers and was most certainly the only one amongst us who could understand what they were saying. "I think Slovenia or Croatia," she said. "They are the most likely of places. If they're arguing as to whether they should go by land or sea then it can only mean that no arrangements have been made, and they would not chance long distances in these waters without knowing for sure; definitely Slovenia or Croatia." Early the next morning we were back in the stage wagon and with the passing of time all of us realised that travel by water was not an option, and when we eventually passed through a town called Udine Greta looked knowingly in my direction. In the late afternoon we were allowed a short break, and once the driver manoeuvred the wagon off the main road we came to a stop by the side of a shallow river surrounded by fields bordered by thick forest. We were never allowed to stray far—at least no further than the rifleman could hit a moving target with absolute accuracy. It was the duty of Hannah, a beguiling Belgian girl, to take advantage of her position in the wagon and occasionally snatch a glimpse through the flap for any landmarks that may assist us in establishing as to what direction we were heading in, and she informed us that she had seen a sign for Gorizia facing south. "What did I tell you?" Greta sighed sourly. "Slovenia! The bastards have taken us to Slovenia!" She walked around in a small circle, her hands clenched into fists and cursing under her breath. "Is that bad?" I asked timidly. She stopped revolving and stared at me in disbelief. "You think

Lyon was bad? Compared with here you were treated like royalty. If you want my advice you'll make a run for it and let that pig shoot you. It would probably be best for all of us."

We arrived in a vast city in the early hours of the morning—all of us exhausted and hungry, and from the wagon we were led into the rear entrance of a six storey house. I could barely keep my head up or lift my feet, but the incessant snapping of our escort kept tiredness from taken us completely, and we were ushered into a scantily furnished room and told to wait, and thereafter our armed guard made his exit. "Where are we?" I asked, looking directly to Greta. She inclined her head with uncertainty and replied, "Zagreb, I think. My grandfather lived here. A city this big can only be Zagreb. And don't ask me if I'm certain because I'm not. But it might be. I'm sure it is." Immediately two men entered, both smartly dressed and in their mid-thirties; one, handsome and the other slightly balding and serious—as a man in authority might be. The first stood before us, while the second sat in the corner and laid out a sheath of papers on his lap. As personable as the man on the floor appeared, he had a malevolence about him—a disquieting air and soulless eyes. He appraised us momentarily before turning to his counterpart; "Anton?" The aide turned the pages of the loose-leaf dossier and looked up. "Two French, one Hungarian, one Algerian, one British, one Tunisian and one Italian." The man walked the line scrutinizing each of us individually, until finally he ordered the Tunisian girl to step forward. "Your name?" he asked. She replied her name was 'Shada', and for a while he appeared to draw great pleasure by just staring at her until he she was so consumed by fear that she began to shake and sob. He grinned and returned to the centre of the room. "My name is Danilo," he announced, "and you are now my property. For those of you who don't already know, you are in Zagreb, Slovenia. Your stay can be as easy or as difficult as you choose to make it, but be assured that those of you who betray me will be dealt with in an extremely severe manner. Disobey and you will be punished. Which of you is the Hungarian?" Greta gingerly stepped forward and he approached, staring at her with his cold, menacing eyes. He asked her where she lived in Hungary and she replied, 'Szeged', to which he began to shake his head and adapt an anxious refrain. "Close—very close—just four or five hundred kilometres. You might be thinking that being so near to home it would be worth the risk. Is it what you're thinking?" Greta shook her head bravely. He stared her down the same way he had Shada, and then he looked over us all. "You'll be taken to your rooms now, and tomorrow you will be made aware of your duties. You will learn that you are not here just to satisfy the sexual desires of men."

Accommodation was on the top floor and the rooms exceedingly small, with a bed, a table and a narrow chest of drawers, but at least every individual had an element of privacy. My first priority was to look out of the window to ascertain how dire my predicament was, and to my surprise I was looking over a beautiful city of Georgian and Regency architecture and quaint houses, and not as I had anticipated—a living hell. A knock on the door stole me from my thoughts and Ursanne, one of the French girls, beckoned anxiously from the hallway where she stood freshly scrubbed and adorned in a bath-towel. I joined the line for the bathroom—each of us allocated a towel and a warning of five minutes only from a shapeless, hard-faced woman with brown cropped hair named Neza. From that moment on she would be our guardian, our supervisor and our magistrate, but Greta was highly amused and discretely told me that Neza meant 'Chaste', and hooted, "As if the ugly bitch has a choice!" But the wretched woman was not a laughing matter and immediately set us to work. I was given a mop and bucket and shown the staircase that rose up through the six storey building, of which the floor was constructed of red terracotta tiles, and at its base an immense veranda of the same materials. Greta was confined to the laundry, Ursanne and Hannah to cleaning windows and Shada to playing chamber-maid, and constantly we were overseen by Neza and ordered to go faster. If I believed that once my duties were performed I could return to my room I was seriously mistaken, for by mid-morning I too was placed in the laundry and ordered to iron enough garments that could clothe the occupants of a small country. I set to work under duress and continued without complaint until Narcissistic Neza, as I was inclined to refer to her, left in search of potential workshy damsels to victimize. I crumpled in a heap on the nearest chair and Greta, who was slaving over a steaming sink of submerged bed sheets, wiped the sweat from her brow and leaned her back against the draining-board. "How long, Greta? How long can we do this before we fall down dead?" I sighed. "You can make it home from here. You can leave all this behind you. I'll help you if I can." Greta looked regretful and shook her head, and wandering over to a wooden clothes-stand removed a dry towel and neatly began to fold it. "I was thirteen when they took me," she began quietly. "By the time I was eighteen I had been to fifteen different countries and lived in countless different brothels; some you wouldn't believe. I've been beaten and raped so many times it doesn't hurt anymore; it's just a pain I've learned to live with. They told me that if I ever tried to escape they would kill my family. I can never go home."

We were living in the heart of Zagreb, in a narrow thoroughfare known as Miskek Passage; a charming walkway of colourful terraces with ornate balconies, where shops beneath catered for the locals, their language a mismatch of Slovene, Hungarian, Italian, Bosnian, Croatian, Serbian and English. It was to the everyday sightseer a captivating city, strategically laid out in squares of flowerbeds, monuments and fountains, and the cleanliness of the streets and the houses inferred the inhabitants and the authorities possessed an unsettling fixation with presentation. But for the four walls we had been interned behind, the overall spectacle appeared convincing and in-keeping with the adjacent properties; it was for all intents and purposes just another inoffensive looking house and, perhaps, few knew of its true purpose, and if they did they preferred to remain ignorant. Unlike Lyon, where my only purpose was to entertain clients from ten o'clock to five the following morning, my new location and its administration dictated I sell myself between the same hours, but in addition perform cleaning duties from eight in the morning till five and sleep until eight o'clock in the evening, when I would prepare for the next onslaught of customers. The first three weeks were the most difficult; duties were strenuous and the clientele demanding, but hard labour is a state of mind and can be tolerable once the participant discovers the advantages of abbreviation and pain-numbing stimulants.

For instance, Greta introduced me to the art of short-cutting ironing by simply folding the item in half or sometimes quarters, and Abrial, friend of Ursanne, was familiar with the ways of domestic cleaning and the ploys administered to achieve the illusion of completion seemingly without the advantages of chicanery. And then there was Frantiska, an exquisite Czech lady in her mid-forties who called once a week at the back door of the house, selling pills, concoctions and ointments that no self-respecting prostitute could do without. The first time I met her she was sitting in the basement at a great wooden table with an assortment of various coloured bottles in front of her, and all around were the girls, enquiring to the contents of each bottle and its advantages. Frantiska looked like a midwife and even wore a starched, grey uniform and heavy brogues, but her demeanour suggested a different vocation. The purchases were made via the house and deducted from the meagre allowance we were given; at least Danilo understood that relentless sexual activity was not without a certain amount of endurance and extreme discomfort. After signing a receipt slip, Greta hurried away from the gathering with an assortment of items concealed in her apron pocket. I followed and silently observed as she began to hang washing on the line straddled from one side of the kitchen to the other.

"Who is that woman?" I asked. "And what is she selling?"

Greta continued along the line, pinning up pillowcases and bedspreads until she removed the last peg from her mouth.

"A calm state of mind," she grinned wickedly. "Do you think I could do this without help? It wouldn't do you any harm to get a few things."

"What kind of things?"

Greta dipped her hand into her pocket and drew out a transparent bottle of clear fluid.

"This helps. It numbs the pain," she said.

I shrugged my shoulders and replied innocently, "The pain of what?"

"Sex, of course!"

I never realised there were options left open to me and I took the bottle from her and examined it closely.

"How many times a day do I have to drink it?"

The Hungarian beauty suddenly buckled with laughter—to such an extent she nearly collapsed on the floor.

"You don't drink it!" she giggled. "You rub it on."

"Where?"

"On your fanny, you stupid girl! It's surgical alcohol!"

It was an awakening. From that day on I lived on a steady diet of Absinthe, a herbal green liquid the French called 'le fee verte' (the green fairy) that was 90/148 proof, and what sceptics claimed induced madness but realists insisted only influenced a mellow condition. For me it was the latter, but moderation was most certainly the key. Other girls, like Greta, Abrial and Ursanne preferred something a little more potent in the form of opium—or Tincture of Opium, better known as Laudanum which contains 10% powdered opium and 1% morphine, and can be used for a variety of ailments. In small amounts it made the whole process of seven hour sex marathons bearable and, to some degrees, erased many of the sordid acts from mind. In the irresponsible hands of a depressed person it can be lethal. Abrial was a redhead, whose fiery temperament and mercurial behaviour compounded the canard that all girls cursed with such colouring were unstable. To combat loneliness and low self-esteem she began to abuse the required dosage—administered with drops or a syringe—and appeared unconcerned with the side effects, and culminated with a catalogue of uppers and downers her character dramatically altered; but she cannot be held totally responsible. On the Christmas Eve of 1913 the ordinary looking house in Miskek Passage was positively buzzing with merriment, and a special effort had been made to entertain several foreign dignitaries from the Ukraine en-route to Croatia. After some considerable amount of alcohol had been consumed and the honoured guests had been suitably titillated, they paired off and retired to their designated rooms. In the early hours a loud commotion brought everyone crowding into the hallway as screams emanated from Abrial's room, but not the cries of a female but a male. It would appear that after having sex with the girl of their choice, three of the VIP's thought it appropriate to creep about the silent house where they came upon Abrial asleep in her room and thereafter set about raping her. It was while in the throes of this violation that the distraught girl partially severed one of their members with a single bite. By the time I reached the room the suffering man was being wrapped in blood-stained sheets, while Danilo and his aide Anton were trying desperately to placate the irate guests; Abrial was led away by Neza.

The following morning was much like any other; nothing mentioned about what had occurred the night before, and the room in which this catastrophe took place was magically restored to its former, spotless glory. And throughout the day nothing was said, and all the girls who were fraught with worry for our colleague, were beginning to question whether the event actually happened at all. "It doesn't look good," asserted Greta with some considerable authority. "A similar thing happened when I was in Cordova, Spain; Carmela was her name—she stabbed a client in self-defence because he tried to force his perversions on her. Sadly he lived, but Carmela was beaten almost to death by the brothel-keepers. I dread to think what they will do to poor Abrial." We had all gathered in the basement in the absence of Neza and Danilo, and of course Abrial who was nowhere to be found on the premises. "Perhaps she ran away," suggested Shada optimistically. Brunela, a quiet and demure Italian creature stood at the window looking up to ground-level and passing pedestrians. "The world is too small," she muttered. We all stared in her direction and she turned with a sad smile. "To run away, I mean. It isn't big enough to hide in any longer," she added. It was a surreal moment, when we all realised that what Brunela said was true and we could never escape; we simply stared at one another without saying a word. When Danilo entered we froze, but there was relief when Abrial and Neza followed in behind him. Suave and handsome he greeted us with the smile of a reptile, making no comment about our gathering or the fact that we were not working. Abrial looked contented but slightly ill-at-ease, and stood amongst us like a detached young woman who had had done wrong but had been duly reprimanded for her tempestuous retaliation. Danilo idly circled us in silence and on his meanderings picked a carving-knife from the wall display and leaned against the large oak table. "Why so scared?" he sniggered. "You have no reason to fear me. I am here to help you in any way I can; to ensure we have a good working relationship. Abrial was violated and she retaliated in the only way she could—as would any woman. Men such as the one who abused this poor girl believe in only one thing—and that is power; to do whatever they choose because they feel they have the right . . . They haven't! The only rights available to them are those laid down before any business is undertaken. We have a moral obligation to uphold." He began to walk amongst us, transmitting a sense of true concern and outrage at the hideous conduct of the so-called dignitaries who behaved like farm animals. "Sad to say, men are cursed with primitive instincts and such molestations can never be totally eliminated, but it is my duty to ensure your safety and that you remain safe from harm. You will be pleased to know that the honoured guests have now left our city with, I might add, a substantial amount of money as payment for their discretion; we can ill-afford the likes of the authorities embroiling us in an investigation." He stopped next to Abrial and put a comforting arm about her shoulder. "The lesson learned from last night is a simple one," he continued. "When you cease to be a viable commodity—you cease to be of any value." And in one fluid motion he drew the blade of the knife across Abrial's throat and she crumpled to the floor. To my recollection there were no screams, no gasps of horror or any outward sign of emotion. Such was the consternation of the act—executed without the slightest trace of rage or malice, our brains could not conceive what we had witnessed, and not until some moments had passed and a crimson pool of blood began to slowly expand around Abrial's head lying on the cold tiled floor, did someone actually shriek with terror. Danilo calmly handed the knife to Neza who immediately walked to the sink and ran it under the tap. "You would be well-advised to remember what you have learned today," he said.

After that event I hoped—prayed—to be moved to a different location; somewhere where the opportunity may arise to negotiate an escape from the living hell I found myself in, but any aspirations I had in that particular direction were dashed, for on 28th June 1914, Archduke Franz Ferdinand of Austria was assassinated, thus sparking a war that was to begin one month later and continue until 11th November 1918. They called it the Great War, the War to end all Wars, blissfully ignorant that another was to follow in less than twenty years. Ostensibly the conflict involved the German Empire, the Austro-Hungarian Empire, the Ottoman Empire, the Russian Empire, the British Empire, France and Italy, but inevitably spread worldwide; by its end all but the British Empire had been erased. For countries like Slovenia the transport of girls, or any other commodity come to that, was hindered by the war and here we were forced to remain. Without the liberty to import and export girls, the likes of Danilo and all his other fellow brothel-keepers had little opportunity but to keep the ones they had, and with the exception of recruiting the odd freeborn, we remained relatively unchanged. I had noticed Greta talking to the bakery delivery man on numerous occasions, usually on the steps outside the basement window or sometimes outside in the passage, and whenever I enquired as to their conversation she would purposefully evade the questions and busy herself with whatever duty she was given. “Have you found yourself an admirer, Greta, or are you the admirer? He’s a little old for you, isn’t he?” I said to her with a suggestive grin. Greta as always occupied the moment by way of avoiding me, but I relentlessly pursued her until I confronted her in the back yard as she hung out washing. “Will you stop with your questions,” she sighed impatiently. “We just talk, that’s all. Can’t a girl talk to a man without everyone thinking there’s something going on? Why is it so strange for me to want to engage in conversation with a man?” Clearly she was hiding something and I grinned at her. “You can talk to your clients,” I suggested. Greta shrugged her shoulders and shook her head. “My mother always taught me not to speak with my mouth full,” she laughed. It was no secret that Danilo was not just running a brothel; he was supplying a laundry service for the locals, and twice a week Greta was allowed to deliver ironing to a nearby hostel a few streets away. She was allowed just fifteen minutes to complete the round trip, and always Neza would be waiting on the front step to ensure she was not one minute later.

I was now nearing my eighth year in captivity—I was twenty-three. The war being fought in Northern France was of little concern to us or any of the population of the city; it was simply a subject people pored over in the cafes and restaurants, in the bars and on street corners. On rare occasions soldiers would pass through the city and seek recreation, and now and then they would visit us—for the purpose of getting drunk and engaging in a night of passion before disappearing completely. But the preoccupation with war cast a dark shadow over all red-blooded males and sex was considered almost a sacrilege when set against the suffering of the brave men who were fighting for our liberty. Inevitably the clients diminished, and we the girls would sit around in the plush interior of the brothel with little else to do but talk amongst ourselves. "What will become of us after the war?" said Ursanne as she lounged on a settee clad in her sultry best. Shada sat by the fireside, positioned sideways with her legs hanging over the arm of an easy-chair. "Do you think anything will change? It will just be the same as it always was. It depends who wins the war, I suppose," she said. I spontaneously intervened. "We'll win!" Brunela looked sceptical and appraised me through slightly narrowed eyes. "By 'we' you mean who?" For the first time in many years I suddenly realised I was amongst a multi-cultured assemblage, and everyone gathered was looking in my direction and awaiting my response. I felt myself shrink in my seat. "I think what Jesse means is them—the enemy will lose," Greta stepped in to save me further embarrassment. Hannah leaned on the back of Shada's chair and argued huffily, "But who are the enemy? As a Belgian wouldn't I be considered of German origin?" Greta sighed impatiently and stood up. "Not unless you're the sister of Archduke Ferdinand! The war is being fought out there—not here. Now there'll be no more talk of enemies, do you hear!" She angrily paced out of the room and slammed the door behind her. "Well, what's the matter with her?" grunted Hannah with a shake of her head. I had noticed a change in Greta over the past few months. She appeared anxious and short tempered, but I attributed her manner to the predicament she was in—what we were all in. Within a year all would become clear.

In Zagreb, at least, the end of the war went almost unnoticed. There were celebrations of course, which was only to be expected, but being constantly incarcerated in the house in Miskek Passage I never witnessed the elation of the conquerors or had the chance to be part of it; life just drifted aimlessly on. Until one day Greta appeared more neurotic than her usual self, preparing her washing and ironing and continually looking at the clock. On that day she was obviously agitated but refused to comment on what was troubling her. She had made up two large baskets for delivery and waited for Neza to give her consent to take them to the hostel. I was washing when Neza came down into the basement, and Greta broke out of her perturbed state and feigned a composed air. Neza observed the two large baskets sitting on the large table and shook her head. "And how do you propose to deliver both baskets? You can't carry two," she said. Greta shrugged her shoulders childishly and replied, "I could make two trips." Neza shook her head. "And waste more time!" Greta gingerly turned her head in my direction. "Then cannot Jesse help me?" she suggested meekly. The brutish women considered the prospect for a moment and began to walk up the stairs. "Fifteen minutes, and no gossiping on the way." I immediately dried my hands, ecstatic at the thought of being allowed out for fifteen minutes, to see streets I had never seen. Greta looked at the clock again. "Hurry, Jesse! Hurry!" Rising up from the steps of the basement, I followed Greta along the passage and crossed the street into an alleyway cut between a line of terraces. She turned suddenly and hissed at me. "Drop the washing, Jesse, and run." I smiled at her with uncertainty, but she knocked the basket from my hands and grabbed my arm. "Run!" We ran the length of the alley to the next streets that steadily inclined down to a large stone square, and people actually stopped to see two grown women rushing frantically through the streets. By the side of the square stood a black lorry with gold lettering on the sides; I had seen it before parked at the end of Miskek Passage. As we hurried towards the vehicle a man grabbed my arm and hurled me in the back. Greta climbed in behind and at once we were moving. Breathless, Greta clapped her hands, laughed aloud and hugged me. "What is happening?" I asked. "We're going home, Jesse. Can you believe that? We're going home!"

The cause of Greta's constant state of anxiety was the result of a painstaking search for her family or, moreover, those still remaining in the city of Zagreb. Through the bakery delivery man she was able to trace two cousins still living in the city, and with her weekly jaunts to the hostel she arranged to meet with one of them and so organise an escape. She had learned that prior to the outbreak of war her direct family had moved to none other than England—and by a course of correspondence via the delivery driver, funded our transport home. We were given a change of clothes and driven to Zurich, and by train went to Reims and then to the French coast and Calais. It was meticulously planned, right down to her brother who was waiting at the port with papers and tickets for our passage across the channel. Their reunion was emotional and contagious, and I found myself sobbing and hugging him as if he were my own flesh and blood, but all to soon we were bound for England and Greta and I stood on the deck looking back at France as is slowly diminished. As much as freedom filled me with a boundless elation, I could not help feel sad for those we had left behind. Greta squeezed my hand encouragingly. "Do not worry, Jesse, as soon as we get to England it will be reported. I have it all written down; their names, and what they did to poor Abrial. Those pigs will be made to suffer." I wasn't convinced and hoped the remaining girls would not be held responsible for our escape. "We have to get them out, Greta," I said. She nodded her head assertively. "Oh, we will, Jesse. We will."

Since stepping from the gangplank I was completely befuddled. I was but fifty miles from home and the thought of meeting my family left me completely flustered and infused with excitement. On the train I was fidgety, standing up and sitting down, walking up and down the corridors and mumbling to myself like a woman possessed by demons. Greta observed me and concealed her amusement behind a masking hand until she pulled me back into my seat. "Will you calm down, Jesse, for God sake, you're making me jittery," she exclaimed. "Me? I am calm," I returned. "I just need time to get used to the idea. If you had let me in to your little secret I'd be more prepared . . . Do you think they'll recognise me? Suppose they don't live there anymore. Suppose they're dead! What will I do if they're dead? Or worse—they disown me because of the life I've lived for the past ten years. Ten years! Christ! I was fifteen when they last saw me. What will I say if they ask me what I've been doing all this time? What will I say? Oh, you know, nothing much—just fucking fifteen men a night while out of my head on drugs . . . They'll pretend they never had a daughter. They'll say I'm an imposter. Well, who wouldn't? I would! Who wants a daughter whose been doing those kind of things for the whole of her adult life?"

"Jesse! Will you just shut up! Please!" Greta shrieked.

And here I was—in the very spot where I was taken as a young girl. Everything looked the same as I had left it—as though no time had passed at all. There were subtle changes, of course, but with the exception of noisy automobiles that had replaced the horse, it was all very much the same. Greta laced her arm through mine and we walked towards my house free women, and when it began to rain I stood with my face towards the sky; it felt good. I hadn't felt the rain or the sun for so many years. I hadn't seen people who simply looked at me as just another person. For the first in such a long time I felt like me—and I knew I would survive. "What will you do now, Jesse," Greta asked as she rested her head on my shoulder. "All of it. Everything I've ever wanted to do. Tomorrow I'll come to London and meet your family, and then . . . and then whatever the hell I want to," I said. Greta agreed with a wistful smile. "You plan to settle down and have children?" she asked. "Oh, God, yes," I declared. "Hundreds . . . of children, I meant, not husbands. And you'll be doing the same?" Greta said she would, but not until she had learned to live life her way. Which was poignant in many ways, for we had all lived without free will, without choice, without rights; it would take some getting used to. We reached my insignificant house in my nondescript street and I stood outside physically shaking. Greta smiled back at me tearfully and nodded towards the front door. "Best let them know you're back from the dead," she said. I took a deep breath and gingerly walked up the short garden path and hesitantly knocked on the front door. A woman, small and frail answered and observed me as one stranger would another, and after an extended pause she mouthed

"Jessica." I stood sobbing uncontrollably and suddenly she cried. "My God, Jesse!" and threw her arms around me. She took my face and held it gently in her trembling hands. "Hello mum," I said.

Elizabeth stared at the written page with tears filling her eyes; the hurt she had ignorantly and selfishly bestowed on the innocent suddenly tearing her conscience to shreds and stabbing at her heart a thousand times. She gazed around the vacant library in the hope that nobody had entered while she had been reading and were now gazing at her with obvious concern. She had—as emotion commands—taken leave of her demeanour and surrendered to a spontaneous an unrestrained reaction that like joy and laughter cannot and should never be suppressed just to appease those who may stand in judgement; tears for happy endings, tears of pity, tears of shame and tears of remorse. Like Judas she had sacrificed the soul of another—of many—for a pittance, which made her the greater offender, the more treacherous, the most despicable. How many had she inadvertently sent to their deaths? How many had suffered at the hands of their keepers and all for the price of a satin dress, or a pair of shoes, or a handbag; of £25 that was easily squandered on any Saturday night in the knowledge it could be reimburse tenfold with just a few kind words to unsuspecting young girls. The undertow of grief pulled her down into the depths of despair to face the consequences of her actions; to at last accept herself no less guilty than those who inflicted the punishment or sanctioned their deaths. Robert, in his kindness and aspiration to assist and, probably, to win favour with the beautiful woman, locked the doors of the library on time and pulled the blinds in order that she could continue perusing the many books at her leisure. He noted her distraught disposition but continued regardless, filing index cards and returning books from whence they came. He hoped she may stay for a while. He thought, or maybe assumed, that such a woman, whose inward beauty must surely be as pure as her outward beauty, may find in him a kindred spirit—someone she could trust and converse with. He disappeared into the backroom and put the kettle on the small stove, and after preparing two more mugs and warming the teapot, he opened a pack of biscuits and arranged several on a small plate. Maybe he could walk her home, he thought to himself. Or better still, perhaps they could stop in the pub on the corner, and she could explain why such an exquisite specimen of womanhood was living alone and friendless. But he heard her call and he emerged from the kitchenette to see her standing at the counter.

"May I keep this book for a few days?" she asked.

The disappointment on Robert's face was evident, but he smiled and nodded.

The book was entitled 'Women of Woe'; a compilation of true events as told by those who had experienced cruel injustice administered by men; of those sold into slavery, forced marriages, prostitution, sweat-shops, pornography and everything we regard as exploitation. It was published by Fallow's Publishing House, and compiled by a young journalist named Peter Egan.

"It's hardly light reading," said Robert. "Keep it as long as you like; it won't be missed."

She smiled warmly, and for the first time since she had walked in, he felt the knot in his stomach begin to unravel, and as he attempted to summon up the courage to ask her out—to put his intentions into words, she suddenly walked to the door.

"Ah, it's locked," he said as he rounded the counter. "I guess I'll see you again quite soon."

She forced a smile as he stretched to release the top bolt of the door, and dropping to his heels he looked directly at her.

"I was wondering . . ."

Elizabeth instinctively shook her head, for she knew the beginnings of a line when she heard one.

"Robert, you're very nice," she said, lowering her head, "and I'm sure you're very sweet, but I need to be alone right now. Can you understand that?"

The young man gave no response, which made Elizabeth feel more the worse.

"Do you know, there are times when I crave the company of someone like you; someone caring—without a malicious bone in your body, but I have things I must do before I consider myself . . . without distractions."

Robert opened the door and smiled as though he understood.

"In the meantime . . ." she said, pausing within the doorway and smiling back at him, "perhaps you could find me everything you can on slavery."

And there, for the next two weeks, began a routine, in which Elizabeth would awaken in the morning and go straight to the café, and after writing down her thoughts and experiences, would then set off to the library in an attempt to discover the origins of what she was embroiled in. She knew enough. And she had seen enough to realise she was part of a vast organisation that specialised in slavery and, no doubt, every other act of exploitation. In the days when trust knew no bounds and Elizabeth was considered to be amongst one of the best Taker's in London, she and her associate met with Phillip Heidegger in a small bistro on the edge of Trafalgar Square. Prior to the declaration of war Heidegger claimed to be German, but once the prime minister announced that war was unavoidable, he changed his nationality to French. Notwithstanding her natural beauty and ability to coerce even the strongest willed client to part with his money, Elizabeth was a considerably talented listener; a trait she had learned as an escort. Heidegger was a smart man, in dress and in conversation, but he was a man of considerable power and used it to his advantage at every opportunity. Elizabeth remembered the day she entered the small restaurant with her colleague. Phillip Heidegger was sitting alone at a table and, as a true gentleman would, rose immediately on seeing her approaching. His interest appeared to be only in Elizabeth, for although her associate attempted to make the appropriate introductions, he was dismissive and concerned himself only with furnishing her a chair next to him. "You have been very successful of late, my dear," he said as he poured her a glass of wine. "You obviously have talent—in all directions I would hope," he added. Now, Elizabeth would say that his presence repelled her, but the truth was she was enamoured by his success, his charm, and the way in which he ignored her counterpart as if he wasn't there. She played along for a while, smiling provocatively and toying with her glass. He leaned into her and whispered in her ear, "Perhaps we could go somewhere more private after our meeting?" She smiled, out of courtesy and not as a form of concurring. Her opinion of him changed in the blink of an eye;

his power had dwarfed his charm and she regarded him as presumptuous and arrogant. At once Elizabeth abandoned her flirtatious game and Heidegger turned his attention to the nature of the meeting, taking out an envelope from his inside breast pocket and surreptitiously passing it to her colleague. "Payment for this month," said the foreigner. "I have instructions direct from BLANCA to recruit more Takers. "Can I leave that with you?" That was the first time Elizabeth had ever heard the name BLANCA, the organisation responsible for abducting teenage girls. Over the passing months she had learned more about Heidegger and the conglomerate he represented. He did not work alone. He had a partner in Matthew Pilinger; an obvious alias for someone born and bred in Hamburg, Germany; a man of an oafish and brutish disposition who administered his own special kind of punishment on those who could not and would not conform. Elizabeth wrote down every detail that came to mind.

On one evening, after many weeks of transferring memory to transcript, Elizabeth had compiled a dossier not only on herself but on those she worked for, and had listed the names of 173 young girls that she was partly responsible for abducting. She sat alone in the library staring at a completed twenty-page manuscript with an element of pride, while Robert pushed a broom around the aisles. She observed him with an affectionate smile; he had been kind, considerate and helpful and now, in her present state of mind, she wanted to show her appreciation. He had, after all, behaved as a gentleman might in spite of constant rejection, and had been more than accommodating in helping her. Now she had completed her task and she placed the document in a large envelope; the address: *Peter Egan. C/O Fallow's Publishing House, Whitechapel, London.*

"So, how about that drink, Robert?" she called.

"Now!" he gasped. "You mean with you? Us? Together?"

Elizabeth nodded and laughed. "But if you don't want to."

Robert dropped the broom at once, hurried behind the desk and grabbed his coat.

"Ready," he said.

Peter Egan lived at Seven Dials, London, an area that had retained its name since medieval times and would, had it not been for its geographical mystery, have lost its identity to the adjoining Covent Garden many years ago. Standing on the very edge of St. Giles, Seven Dials was so named because seven roads meet at its centre to form a seven sided star; a folly of Sir Thomas Neale's, dating back to 1694. Today it is a respectable area and many of the eighteenth century houses still exist, and even Dickens made reference to it in Bleak House. But once it was a formidable place, a rookery in which prostitutes, thieves and murderers took refuge and the police dare not enter, filled with gin shops and drinking dens and inhabited wholly by vicious criminals. The plague started here in 1665, in St. Giles, whose namesake was the patron saint of lepers who were hospitalised within the shadow of the church, away from the city and amid the surrounding fields and marshes. Next to the church was The Resurrection Gate, a public house that was rebuilt in the nineteenth century and renamed The Angel, and church officials would pay for the last drink of any condemned man or woman being traversed from Newgate to the public hanging at Tyburn. It is an historical fact that this area is deemed unlucky; businesses fail at a higher rate than anywhere else in London, and though vagrants and prostitutes were constantly moved on, they always returned to take up residents in doorways and integral alleyways. Theorists believe the area is cursed, for back in 1417 Sir John Oldcastle—the model for Shakespeare's Falstaff—was burned here on the orders of King Henry V. Before the flames consumed him completely he was heard to curse the place where he was executed, the executioner, the king and all his descendents.

It was the day of publication and I had waited impatiently in my office, mostly pacing up and down but occasionally re-reading Peter Egan's piece in Fallow's Crime Magazine, searching intensely for references or anything that may implicate me. Sylvia, forever caring, had decided to remain with me until Peter showed and busied herself making coffee or catching up on the new fashions in one of the many magazines she had stored in her desk. As I read she was sitting on the chair in front of me, her feet up on the desk and her tight skirt hoisted up around her thighs.

"You're not in there, Michael," she sighed as she casually filed her perfectly shaped red fingernails. "Trust me."

Peter had phoned me in the late afternoon, sounding decidedly nervous and less than enthusiastic about his long-awaited story. More importantly, he had called to tell me about his findings regarding Wendy Marshall.

"She's nothing to worry about, Michael," he assured me. "She earned herself a small piece in the locals for allegedly being attacked; admitted to hospital with several lacerations caused by a blade or cutthroat razor, and gave a statement that she never knew her attacker; failed to identify anyone in three separate identity parades and the investigation just fizzled out. Wendy Marshall is something of a good-time girl, and she's not choosy when it comes to clients—anyone will do as long as they pay. Her known associates read like a rogues' gallery; pimps, money-lenders; a real motley crew. I believe the police came to the conclusion that Wendy had run into trouble, and her new scars were courtesy of someone she had stolen money from. It's a common form of revenge—slicing up dishonest prostitutes, especially if they're pretty. When Henderson was arrested she was pulled back in and identified him as her attacker. Personally I think she's a headline hunter; a way to make a few quid. Either way she'll be easy to discredit."

"You honestly think so?"

"Undoubtedly. Listen, Michael, I need to see you."

"About what?"

"Fallow's crumbling. The story only broke this morning and already he's had every newspaper in England wanting to know the details. He's never going to stay the pace, and I'm not sure if I can trust him anymore. Wait for me till I get there."

Peter hung up and I sat in my office waiting his arrival. As the minutes moved into hours, I busied myself with reading his piece in Fallow's Crime Magazine again. It was a condemning article; no less than eight pages in which he attacks both the police and government for failing to monitor and, indeed, acknowledge the crimes of their own people, thereby creating their own utopia far and out of reach of the laws they themselves created. It was a scathing broadside on the authority that governs us; a castigation that would not go unpunished.

"Something is obviously wrong, Sylvia!" I said, anxiously; "He said he was coming to see me, and he's late. What time is it?"

"Nearly ten. Another coffee?"

"It's been three hours," I said, returning to my incessant pacing. "Why call me and arrange a meeting if he had no intentions of coming?"

"He's probably been waylaid," rationalised Sylvia with a stifled yawn. "You have his number, give him a call."

"Good idea," I said, snatching the receiver from the phone. "Listen, why don't you go home?"

"In this! In a blackout!" she shrilled. "No bloody fear. I'll wait for you."

I let the phone ring for almost two minutes and then hung up. "Shit!"

"Michael, don't worry. He's probably got a tip for a new story; he'll catch up with you tomorrow."

"And Fallow? He said he couldn't trust him." I questioned.

She shrugged her shoulders.

"Who knows? Either way I don't intend sitting here all night."

Peter's home was but a short walk away and within moments Sylvia and I were out on the streets, me armed with a torch and her with her chintzy umbrella, walking down Long Acre towards Covent Garden. A full moon had rendered the blackout regulations useless and the streets were bathed in a smoky blue light beneath a clear and starry sky. We saw only a few people, mostly milling around Covent Garden, some flashing beams of torch light in our direction and then returning to their own intended route. Sylvia hung to my arm as if I were her newly appointed boyfriend, and she shuddered and sniffed with cold as the warmth of the office finally gave up to the cold, crisp night air. We reached the epicentre of Seven Dials, staring up at the street signs, but then I saw the green Jaguar parked on the roadside that inclined down towards Charing Cross. The car was parked before two iron gates set within the terrace of houses that opened into a courtyard; a convenient plaque just within arrowed the direction of the house numbers; Sylvia led the way, stopping outside the address on Peter Egan's card. After knocking several times I peered through the letter box and saw light in the hallway and felt the warmth on my face as it tried to escape its confines.

"Obviously gone out," said Sylvia.

I rose from my squat and shook my head.

"I don't think so; the car, the lights. Something is seriously wrong."

"Call the police," she suggested.

"And alert the 247 corrupt police officers that I'm working with Peter Egan, the very man who has just exposed them to the western world?"

Sylvia would let almost anything penetrate her body except the cold, and as I stood wondering what to do next and listening to her chattering teeth, she must have been eager to bring this episode to an end.

"Do you want to get in?" she said.

"Have you a key?" I replied sarcastically.

She rolled up the sleeve of her coat and pushed her chintzy umbrella through the letter box, and gently easing her hand inside I could hear the knocking and tapping around the lock from the inside.

"I'm always forgetting my keys. I don't like to wake mum up," she explained as she worked.

With a click she pushed her weight against the door that gently opened, and retrieving her makeshift burglary kit she stepped to one side.

"You had better wait here," I said to her as if to dupe her into believing I wasn't in the least bit scared.

"Not a chance. Inside before someone sees us."

We moved gingerly through the gloom of a lobby and into a hallway, sparse with a Persian rug on a varnished wooden floor and a lamp set beside a phone on a small table. Four doors led into the hall, one of which was partly open, and a straight staircase ascended up to the darkness of the floor above. I gently pushed the partly open door to its full, until it butted against the wall, squinting into the bleakness and groping for a light-switch. Sylvia was standing right behind me, so close I swear I could feel the wires of her bra digging into my back, and suddenly she reached over my shoulder and flicked the switch I had hopelessly been searching for. The light revealed a cosy room of pastel blue with heavy drapes, a comfortable three-piece suite set around a coffee-table in its centre on which sat an empty bottle of brandy and a half-empty bottle of scotch, and a desk with a type-writer and several filing boxes. "Not here," I whispered, referring to Peter. We slowly backed out, like a machine in perfect unison and then broke away to investigate the other rooms. One was used as a store room, one wall racked out with shelves and holding perhaps a hundred or so filing boxes all marked with initials, and a few boxes lay open on a table beneath the window. The kitchen, immaculately clean save for a cup and plate in the sink and some empty wine bottles by a bin, was quiet and appeared hardly used. Sylvia cautiously placed her hand on the kettle and shook her head. We crept up stairs, like children on Christmas morning, and on the landing, engulfed in shadow I stopped. "Come on, Sherlock, move your arse," hissed Sylvia. I moved forward, further from the light illuminating the stairwell and deeper into the darkness of the landing, feeling my way over the panel-doors for a handle of some kind. Once again a light ignited and I turned to see Sylvia taking her finger off the switch.

"What would we do without it?" she said, quietly. "What?" I asked impatiently. "Electricity," she returned simply. "Marvellous stuff," she added with a wink.

The first door I opened was to end our search for Peter, for it opened into his bedroom, and the shaft of light from the landing outlined his form lying fully clothed above the blankets. "Peter." I said. "Peter, it's me Michael." He never stirred and I called his name again and again, louder with every mention until I was standing over him; Sylvia remained within the light of the doorway. "Is he . . . ? Is he . . . ?" she burbled. "Dead?" I said, looking down on him. "I was going to say 'Drunk' but either will do," she returned sharply. Peter Egan was not drunk. I felt his hands and face, barely warm, and pressed my ear to his chest. "Turn on the light," I said. Peter was lying in a perfect straight line with his arms by his side, wearing black trousers and a beige shirt; as if he had purposefully been laid out; his shoes were neatly placed beside the bed.

"What could have happened?" asked Sylvia through her fingers.

All I could do was look down at him; shock held me rigid for what seemed an eternity.

"Michael!"

My mind began to slowly start turning again and my eyes moved across the dead body and around the room.

"No idea," I murmured.

As far as I could tell nothing appeared to be out of place; it simply looked as if Peter had laid down and died; even his hair was neatly combed.

"Are you sure he's dead?" asked Sylvia timidly.

"I'm no doctor, but he's definitely lacking all the attributes of a living human-being; you know, breathing, heartbeat, those kind of things."

"No need to be facetious, Michael," she snapped.

"Well, Sylvia, I'll stop being facetious if you stop being stupid. How's that?"

Sylvia and I were like a couple who had come to the chapel of rest to pay our respects for one last time, gazing down on a corpse with a mutual sadness.

"We'll have to call the police," said Sylvia, taking hold of the situation and whatever implications it may have.

I stared blankly back at her.

"Michael, we have to!"

There is an invisible barrier that encircles the city, definable only by the sudden change in the architecture of the buildings, the businesses and of the people. Once there was a wall, 20 feet high and 10 feet wide, created to separate us from them, and within this structure were openings, manned entrances with heavy barred gates from which vagrants and miscreants were expelled, banished to the marshes and fields beyond its vast structure, to the small cluster of houses dotted here and there, the churches and the farms; the beginnings of villages. In time the Hamlets swelled into towns, built with shoddy and substandard materials, devoid of foresight design or engineering expertise, made up of higgledy-piggledy lanes where raw sewage flowed freely through its streets, inhabited by the poor, weighed heavy by hopelessness. In time the wall disappeared, deconstructed or decayed, and some of it remains to remind us of how fanatical the city dwellers were in those long ago medieval times. Few realise that the underground stations in the city are the exact level of medieval London. The ghost of the wall is still there and the facades of the grand West-End houses look out to the slum tenements of the East.

Fate, destiny—call it what you will—took me there the very next morning, on the invisible line where the wall once stood, where the city ends and the East-End begins. I walked from Liverpool Street along Bishopsgate and turned into Middlesex Street, a conglomeration of warehouses and private dwellings, some dating back to the seventeenth century and a road synonymous with Jack the Ripper, and next to Sandy's Row and Frying Pan Alley was the humble Fallow's Publishing House, a dilapidated looking building even when it was first built. It was set back slightly from the line of terraces on one side, detached with an alleyway and access to the rear, barely wide enough for a human to pass through without scuffing shoulders on the brickwork. Its frontage was simple and bland; three stories with two windows per floor and a front door in its centre. To any passer-by it appeared that its owners had long ago forsaken it and taken up residence elsewhere; the windows obscured with heavy city grime, the woodwork riddled with woodworm penetrating the blistered paint. The front door was slightly ajar and a small ring of keys hung from the lock, forgotten or left there in a moment of urgency. I entered, and for a moment stood in a damp hallway, taking in the faded and peeling wallpaper and cracked plaster, the ceiling above me sagging in places and water-stained. I could have been forgiven for thinking the place had been abandoned had I not heard a noise above me; a muttering voice and the scuffing of furniture on bare floorboards.

I set my hand on the banister and gingerly ascended to the upper floor until I reached a doorway directly above, and inside stood an unkempt man, perhaps in his early sixties and dressed in a threadbare cardigan and trousers that appeared two sizes too big. He was standing in a sea of papers of which were obviously the contents of the open filing cabinets and desk drawers. He stood scratching his head and growling angrily to himself as he surveyed the chaos, and suddenly he looked at me.

"I haven't finished yet," he snapped. "How am I expected to know what's missing when I don't know what I had in the first place? Do you know how many manuscripts are filed in these cabinets? And I have all the other offices to go through yet. Give me a day. I need at least a day. Where in God's name is Mrs. Crowley?"

"Who?"

"Mrs. Crowley," he hissed. "My so-called secretary; stupid old bat; probably woke up this morning and thought it was Sunday and gone back to sleep; never here when I need her, never, never, never."

"Are you Earnest Fallow?" I asked politely.

"No. I am the Messiah, the second coming; sent back to this shit hole as punishment for my indiscretions in the past life. Of course I'm Earnest Fallow! Who else would you expect to see in Fallow's Publishing House? How long have you been a policeman, son?"

He stooped to retrieve more papers from the floor.

"I'm not—a policeman, I mean."

"You're not?" he said as he rose. "Who are you then?"

"Michael James."

He dropped the papers he had already gathered and walked towards me, stopping short and studying my face like a doctor appraising a patient with a skin complaint.

"You say it as if the name should mean something," he said. "Be specific."

"Michael James the litigator."

He backed up and leaned against a desk, arms folded and looking perplexed.

"No, still nothing," he murmured. "What business have you with me? I don't wish to rush you but you can see I'm a little preoccupied."

He dropped to one knee and continued to collect the papers and manuscripts.

"Did they take anything?" I asked edging a little closer into the office.

"Did who take anything?" he returned warily. "How do you know this office doesn't always look like this? I might like it like this. Did that ever occur to you, Mr. Litigator?"

"It's James. I thought you should know about Peter. He called me last night."

He sighed exhaustively and rose again, grasping a sheath of documents in his arms and dropping them onto the nearest desk.

"Little shit!" he huffed. "Mark me; this is a result of his story. I knew there would be repercussions. I shouldn't have taken it. How do you know Peter, anyway?"

"The Henderson case," I replied.

"Ah, yes. The Blackout Butcher; he wrote a good piece on that. Well, he's overstepped the mark on this one. All hell has broken loose." He paused from his task and appraised me suspiciously. "Has he sent you to collect his fee? Has he actually sent you to collect his money?" he smirked.

He shook his head and resumed crawling around on the floor.

"Peter's dead."

He froze in mid-stretch and slowly turned to face me.

"I was supposed to meet with him last night but he never arrived," I explained. "I went to his house and found him dead."

"How?"

"Natural causes, I would assume. It was like he went to bed and died."

He unfurled from his contortion and stood up, and though he looked genuinely upset he didn't appear surprised.

"So it finally got him in the end," he sighed.

"What got him?"

"The drinking, of course!"

"I knew him only to drink wine."

"That's why he only drank wine. When I first knew him he was a typical hack; always drunk, seldom home, out searching for that one story that would make him a fortune. He was a whisky man back then, and I don't mean the odd glass. It wasn't unusual for him to go through a couple of bottles a day, especially if he was writing a story. It began to get the better of him; liver full to overflowing, kidneys giving out, pissing blood, you know the story. A few years ago the doctors read him the riot act, told him to pack up alcohol or die. They said if he had to drink then wine was the only option. Of course, they meant the occasional glass now and then; not a few bottles a day; strange though."

"Strange?"

He stopped to appraise me once again, sitting down at his cluttered desk and scrutinising me curiously.

"Who are you?" he asked.

"My name is . . ."

"I got your name, sonny, and the fact you're a litigator," he interrupted. "What I want to know is who you are. What was Peter to you?"

I waded in through the discarded documents until I was in front of him.

"My company is defending George Henderson, and I read an article Peter had written in your magazine. I managed to contact him and . . ."

He suddenly held his hand up to silence me.

"You're the lawyer!" he shrilled; "the very lawyer who went with him when he got the information for this story?"

"Yes. Peter picked me up and we went to . . ."

"Good God, don't tell me! I don't want to know who, where or why. My ignorance of the facts is probably the only attribute that will keep me alive. When he came to me with the story I asked him if anyone else was with him, someone to substantiate what the source had said. He mentioned you; simply calling you a lawyer. Tell me, was his house ransacked. Did it look like this?"

"No. Everything was neat and tidy. Apart from a few boxes open in his store-room nothing was touched."

"And what was in those boxes? What was the subject matter? Was it the draught of his recent story; the result of which is this mayhem?"

I shrugged.

The publisher averted his stare behind me and forced a bright smile.

"Ah, Mrs. Crowley, how good of you to come. Have you come to work or is this just a social visit?"

A small, round woman stood in the doorway wearing, what I can only describe as a cleaner's overall and a scarf around her head, and I took it that the lumps and bumps beneath were either curlers or some kind of shocking abnormality of her scull. Her skin, her cheeks especially, resembled the texture of corned beef, and a cigarette hung loosely from her crinkled lips.

"God love us, what's happened here," she said.

"A slight mishap, Mrs. Crowley, of which I would appreciate your full attention. First we require two cups of coffee."

She mumbled an incoherent reply and waddled off to wherever coffee was prepared.

"Exquisite, isn't she?" said Mr. Fallow.

"Yes, breathtaking." I replied.

He purposefully paused, staring at the open door and the landing beyond, until Mrs. Crowley's footsteps on the stairs had evaporated into silence.

"Peter informed me that you hold the names of the corrupt officers," he said.

I nodded.

"They obviously don't know about you," he murmured, thoughtfully.

"Who doesn't know about me?" I asked with more than a hint of panic in my voice.

"Whoever did this, whoever killed Peter."

He registered my confused expression and leaned forward.

"In the article Peter inferred that he held all the names of the corrupt policemen, to be published at a later date. It's those names they're after," he continued in a low voice.

"Who? Who are after? He died of natural causes! You said yourself he had a problem."

He held both hands up as if to subdue me, like a charmer willing a snake into a basket; motioning me into a nearby seat which I failed to take up.

"You have been duped, Mr. Lawyer. Peter was walking on egg-shells with this story and he knew it. Giving you the names was his protection; that should anything happen to him the story would still get out. You should be flattered he entrusted you with the list; he must have liked you. Carlisle was a scapegoat, and the Met. and the government must have breathed a sigh of relief when he told the court he was working alone. Not that he had a choice. After all Carlisle had family, a wife and children. Had he even hinted at the possibility that he was working along side 246 other corrupt police officers then he would have endangered their lives. He knows this way they will be well provided for; the best our money can buy."

"So, you're saying drink didn't kill Peter."

"Before I knew who you were I would have said so, but this is more than a coincidence, wouldn't you agree?"

He leaned back in his chair, waiting for me to collate the information.

"Granted, your publishing house broken into and Peter's death the same night is food for thought. But I saw Peter; there wasn't a mark on him."

"None obvious to the human eye; the condemning factor here is the subject."

He stared at me with his eyebrows arched and a knowing grin, and when I failed to respond in any way he sighed exhaustively and pointed to the chair in front of his desk.

"Sit down, Mr. Lawyer," he said. "This is not the first time this has happened to me. Not so long ago a man came to me with a manuscript he wished to be published. I jumped at the chance because it was such a good piece of work. It was a piece any publishing house would have died for."

"With respect, Mr. Fallow, why did he bring it to you and not . . ."

"A well-established and respectable publishing house?" he intercepted.

I nodded and smiled from embarrassment.

"Because I take chances. Peter and I take chances. This devastation you see around you now isn't new to me. It happened with the Vassarri papers. It happened when Peter got inside government intelligence. Jesus Christ, they nearly locked us up in the Tower. I've learned now how far I can go. Peter never knew when to stop. That's why he was marked by British Intelligence, and that's why he's dead."

"You're saying he was murdered?"

He shrugged. "This has Government written right through it. They have agents, people trained in the art of murder—who can make it appear natural, or an accident, or an act of God."

As he spoke he was looking at a velvet-backed picture-frame face down on his desk. He lifted and shook off the broken glass. It was a photograph of him in his younger days, aboard a fishing boat off the coast of somewhere exotic, and posing with a monstrosity of a fish. He was in the company of an olive-skinned man with a gleaming smile who had his arm about his shoulder. He was quick to hide it from me, placing at his feet behind the desk.

Certainly what Mr. Fallow told me was informative, but if he was suggesting a conspiracy—which he obviously was—I failed to make the connection.

"Good grief!" he grumbled as he stared at my vacant expression. "Have you any concept of how big Peter's story is? He has accused 247 police officers of corruption and possibly murder, all serving policemen with the Metropolitan

Police Force who is, as you know, accountable to the government. What could we discover if forces all over the country were investigated? How much more corruption could we find? And will it end there? Will we start looking at the politicians? If the government fails then the realm has failed. At present I have published a story; an unsubstantiated story of which its source will never come forward. Only the names of those 247 corrupt officers can corroborate the story once, of course, they are investigated and the allegations against them found to be true. Peter was silenced by government assassins—pure and simple. They were looking for the names, Mr. Lawyer."

"His house was clean and tidy," I said.

"It would be. These people are clever. They don't want the two incidents associated; one appears normal, the other the work of amateurs. But the devastation they have left me to clear up is a reminder, a warning to me that if I hold the names I should give them up."

I gazed around the office at the open filing cabinet drawers, the carpet of loose papers and folders.

"Aren't you scared?" I asked him.

"Scared? No. I am but the messenger not the instigator. I can only know what Peter has told me and a good reporter will never reveal a source. Killing me would serve no purpose."

Mrs. Crowley reappeared and placed down a tray on the table which slid slightly on top of the mound of papers and slopped coffee over the sides of the cups.

"How kind, Mrs. Crowley," said Earnest Fallow with a hint of sarcasm. "Would you be a dear and start tidying up the back offices?"

In her absence she had inserted another cigarette into her thin lips which had burned down almost to the end and was now just a thin tube of ash that threatened to break off at any moment.

"So what's happened?" she asked, the tremors of which severed whatever bound the thin line of ash together.

"I think it's referred to as being 'Turned over' Mrs. Crowley. Nothing appears to have been taken which leaves us only to reinstate everything back into its rightful place," he replied, brushing the specs of ash from the sleeve of his cardigan.

"Mrs. Crowley's eyes roamed over the carnage and she looked back to him.

"How on earth do you know nothing has been taken?" she said.

"Because I don't possess what they want."

The woman shook her head and walked off.

He passed me a coffee which, despite its appearance, tasted quite reasonable.

"Poor Peter," said Mr. Fallow with a shake of his head. "Is he still at the house?"

"The police were called—anonymously."

"I hope you didn't use a private phone; they can trace you."

"From a public call-box in Shaftsbury Avenue."

He nodded approvingly.

"Very good. At present, Mr. Lawyer, they don't know who you are, but given time they will. Are the names in a safe place?"

I nodded.

"Well, they won't come back. Come tomorrow the news of Peter's death will break and the world and his wife will want an explanation. What do you intend to do with the list of names?"

"I don't know; destroy them, perhaps," I returned nervously.

"And let 247 corrupt policemen walk free! Peter will have died for nothing. No, I suggest you keep them safe and discard everything that may connect you to Peter, including his front door key."

"But I don't have his front door key."

The publisher gazed back at me.

"Peter lives alone. If, as you say, you found him dead, however did you get in?"

"An umbrella through the letter box," I explained, omitting that it was Sylvia's initiative that gained us entry and not mine.

He grinned and nodded.

"He has a brother who lives in Ireland," he said. "I shall contact him as soon as the story breaks or if the police inform me of Peter's death; whatever comes first. As for you Mr. Lawyer, you are quite safe as long as you hold the names. The story will receive a modicum of interest, especially on the back of Carlisle's trial, but people will see it for what it is—just a story."

The next morning I stood in a crowded underground carriage, swaying and jerking around along with the thousands of other strap-hangers en-route to their required stations, far beneath the streets of London, zigzagging over and under the sewage systems and plague pits with nothing to see through the windows but blackness and the occasional lonesome light speeding past. I was tired, mentally exhausted from the events of the last two days, and the smoke expelled from cigarettes, cigars and pipes hung like a white cloud in the claustrophobic confines awaiting the opening of the doors in preparation of its great escape. My mind was poisoned by everything associated with George Henderson and Jack the Ripper, to such an extreme I could think of little else and was unable to function neither as a human-being nor as a litigator. Paranoia had set in like a disease, robbing me of all reason and I found myself appraising every male in the carriage with suspicion; that any one of them could be a government assassin out to stick me with a knife the moment I made any attempt to disembark from the oversized coffin I was travelling in. With my head resting on my raised arm I cast my eyes over every individual seated and standing, wondering which one of them possessed the requisite skills of an assassin and which of them would terminate my life on Farringdon Street platform. I whittled the possibilities down to nine; the others being too old, too young and inexperienced, or women. And suddenly there he was, standing by the doors and wearing a gabardine raincoat, with one hand buried in his pocket—obviously concealing the murder weapon—and the other holding a newspaper which was nothing more than a prop. He was staring directly at me, and then he nodded and smiled as if to say, "You're a dead man." I had seen him before. He had probably been following me for days, waiting for his chance to pounce, or awaiting orders to terminate me. I was consumed by a cold sweat and began tugging at my collar; I needed air. To my horror he began to push his way through the commuters towards me; my life was over.

"Morning, old chap," he said, brightly. "How's life treating you?"

I stared back vacantly, numbed by his presence, waiting for him to pull his hand from his pocket.

"Are you feeling okay?" he asked with concern. "We work in the same building. I'm the manager in the store above you—Reginald Thorndyke."

I gasped a shuddering breath of relief. I had seen him before though I never knew his name; he was simply a nodding acquaintance; someone I unconsciously acknowledged once in awhile but had never spoken to.

"Morning," I said. "Sorry, I didn't recognise you. How are you?"

Everything about Reginald Thorndyke oozed the soldiery. He had a small, upturned moustache and sharp, green eyes and an upright posture. If I had to take a guess at his history, I would say he was once a major or a high-ranking army officer who had taken early retirement. The headlines of his newspaper caught my eye and with a brief, "May I?" I snatched it from his hand. 'CORRUPTION RIFE IN POLICE FORCE.' I had been too preoccupied with spies and assassins to see what was in front of me. Every newspaper in the compartment, no matter what their persuasion, boasted the same headline in one form or another. The Daily Telegraph reported:

It has been revealed that 247 police officers in the Metropolitan Police Force have allegedly been pressurising businesses in and around the docklands in an extortion racket that involves hundreds of thousands of pounds. The story appeared in Fallow's Crime Magazine earlier this week and claims to hold the names and ranks of all the corrupt officers, along with photographs and film-footage of the policemen receiving payouts, which are to be published in next month's edition. Reporter Peter Egan, who was responsible for the story, was found dead at his London home in the early hours of yesterday morning, but police believe his death is coincidental and do not suspect foul play. The story, however, has raised questions regarding the lenient eight year prison sentence Inspector Carlisle received yesterday at the Old Bailey. Egan names Carlisle as being one of the 247 and proposes that both the Metropolitan Police Force and the government instigated the outcome of the trial in order to avoid a scandal, and journalists following up the story opine that he received just a third of his estimated sentence in return for his silence and cooperation.

Badger was predictably irate. He paced up and down in front of Sylvia and I like a headmaster debating what punishment to hand out to a couple of schoolchildren who had scrawled obscene remarks about his wife on the blackboard. After purchasing several newspapers from old Sid, I went to the office and confessed everything to Badger—well as much as I could remember.

"You actually broke into Peter Egan's house?" he asked for the third time, and every time as bitter as the last.

I nodded for the third time, and like the two times before nodded in Sylvia's direction.

"This is unbelievable," he growled; "un-fucking-believable!"

"Now, now, Badger, there's no need for profanities," I objected.

"No? You and Calamity Jane here broke into a dead man's house and then tiptoed into the night without telling anyone."

"We notified the police!" Sylvia snapped defensively.

"Anonymously!" Badger barked back. "And at present we have the names of 247 policemen who may or may not be corrupt, along with photographs and a reel of film, and according to Earnest Fallow, Peter Egan was murdered for it. You didn't want to mention this before now?"

I shrugged like a scolded child. "It happened so fast," I replied sheepishly.

He continued pacing but eventually came to rest on the edge of his desk, shaking his head and pinching the bridge of his nose.

"Don't worry about Fallow," I said, reassuringly. "He reads too many books. I don't believe any of it."

"That is not the issue," Badger growled through gritted teeth. "I agreed to look at Carlisle. Now we've got half the British police force. What do you plan to do with the wealth of information you've inherited? And please don't tell me you intend to pursue it."

"No. I'll get rid of it."

"When?"

"Soon."

"How soon, Michael?"

"After the autopsy; a few days, I suppose."

"Jesus Christ!" Badger cursed. "So there is an element of Fallow's story you believe?"

"Well . . . no, but maybe if . . ."

"Listen carefully, Michael, I will not be part of this. I for one do not intend to be assassinated."

"You're not comfortable with this, are you?"

He stared at me through narrowed eyes.

"What would you have done in our position, Badger?" asked Sylvia.

"I wouldn't have got myself in this mess in the first place," he retaliated.

"But I didn't know what I was walking into," I said, defensively. "I got a phone call, and the next minute I was in a car. Would you have gone to the police if you had found Peter Egan dead, knowing what you know now?"

I welcomed the calm and tried to resume business as usual, sitting at my desk and looking through the new cases brought to us for consideration. Before reading a word I knew I would take at least half, especially as Andy and Tom had allowed the Driscoll case to slip through their fingers and were now sitting in their office twiddling their thumbs. There were the usual deferrals—nothing special—but they paid the bills and kept the wolf from the door. Most of the cases were brought to us by firms who had literally been bombed out of business or who had lost a substantial amount of their staff to conscription; a stop-gap until business returned to normal. We would work on their behalf, adopting their name, reaping the monitory benefits whilst retaining the good name of the company who deferred it. A gentle tap on the door brought my eyes up to see Penny standing there.

"Someone to see you, Michael."

A man moved in, square faced with a stocky build and short hair. He was around the same age as me and possessed rugged features, and he took a moment to absorb Penny's form as she left, leaving the door slightly open. Before he uttered a single word I knew something was wrong; I could see Sylvia, Penny and Badger standing anxiously outside.

"Mr. James?" he asked. "Mr. Michael James?"

I nodded and smiled. "Yes."

"Sergeant Forbes," he said, reaching inside his jacket pocket and producing a notepad.

My eyes moved to the door, to the peering faces staring intently through the gap, and although I was consumed by an overwhelming desire to jump up and offer my wrists for restraint and surrender, I feigned composure and another warm smile.

"What may I do for you, sergeant?" I enquired.

"Just routine, sir," he said, drawing a pen from his top pocket. "You're aware Peter Egan is dead?"

I paused for what seemed an eternity, devoid of any sensible reply; paranoia seized every nerve within me, but I managed a faint nod. Sylvia was nodding furiously and pointing to a document in her hand.

"I read it in the paper," I said.

As thuggish as the sergeant appeared he was also astute, for his eyes settled on the pile of newspapers I had purchased on the way here.

"May I offer you tea, coffee?" I asked.

"Thank you, no. Can you tell me a little about your relationship with him?"

'Relationship' is such an obscure word, especially when set in context with two men; the imagination can run wild. I took my cue from Sylvia who shrugged her shoulders.

"There wasn't one," I replied. "Not one to speak of."

"But you do know him?"

Sylvia nodded firmly.

"He was interested in George Henderson. At present we are engaged with his defence. Mr. Egan wrote an article exonerating Henderson; that was the extent of our relationship."

Sergeant Forbes scribbled vigorously in his notepad.

"Have you seen him recently?" he asked.

Sylvia shook her head and then held a clenched fist to her cheek.

"No, but we have spoken on the telephone—occasionally. Is there a purpose to these questions, sergeant, only I read that foul play wasn't suspected?"

"Foul play isn't suspected, but I have a job to do."

His look and his voice hardened.

"Have you read his recent story on police corruption?" he asked, his eyes settling on the stack of newspapers again.

"In Fallow's Crime Magazine, yes," I replied.

"You read that?" he said, his serious exterior threatening to break into a smirk of disbelief.

"Avidly."

"He's my next port of call. Do you know Earnest Fallow?"

I looked to Sylvia for guidance; she shook her head.

"No."

His question regarding Fallow appeared to be nothing more than small-talk; idle chit-chat contrived to lighten the mood.

"What did you think about the story?" he asked.

I shrugged my shoulders. "Ludicrous; nothing more than sensationalism."

His eyes locked to mine, assessing whether I was sincere or simply appeasing him. After a moment he smiled coldly and closed his notebook.

"Would it interest you to know that you were one of the last people to talk to Peter Egan," he said.

Sylvia had frozen rigid as she peered through the gap in the door. I looked back to the sergeant and opened my mouth to speak but with no words to accompany my actions. Suddenly Sylvia breezed in holding a document. "Here's the file you asked for, Michael." She stopped on seeing the sergeant and feigned surprise. "I'm sorry. I didn't know you were in a meeting." Hussy that she is, she had unbuttoned her blouse to reveal most, if not all, her ample cleavage and expressed her best man-eating smile. "You must be here about Mr. Egan," she said. "Such a terrible shame. And so young. It's no age to die, is it?"

"No, miss," the sergeant replied, his stare fixed firmly to her breasts.

"And to think I spoke to him the very night he died," she said, thoughtfully.

"You? You spoke to him?"

"I was working late. He phoned about eight o'clock . . ."

"7.46," said the sergeant, flipping open his notepad. "Why did he call?"

"He wanted to know if there was any progress with the Henderson case. He would call every now and then; looking for another story, I would imagine. I told him there wasn't any progress but if he cared to call back at a later date then . . ."

"And that was the extent of the conversation?"

Sylvia adopted her seductive posture, hand on hip, weight resting on one leg, and bosoms thrown out so far I could almost hear her back click.

"That was it, sergeant," she simpered. "Should I have reported it?"

The sergeant, it would appear, had set out on a fishing expedition and landed a rusty bicycle wheel. With his face flushed with embarrassment he put his notepad back into his pocket.

"Through no fault of his own Peter Egan has become somewhat of a celebrity," he explained.

"And you have to be seen to be doing your utmost concerning his death?" I said.

His eyes roamed over Sylvia's curves and he nodded.

"Pretty much," he agreed. "The autopsy is ongoing as we speak and we have no reason to suspect anything suspicious, but . . ."

"You have a job to do?"

He nodded.

"Like it or not we answer to the press. They ask questions and we give them answers. We have to reassure them that we have done everything in our power to examine the evidence; that every avenue has been checked—thoroughly. We were hoping you may have seen him; given a little insight into his condition—did he look ill, you know?"

"I understand, sergeant; no harm done. I'm only sorry I couldn't have been of more help."

Sylvia instinctively moved into her 'Gagging for it' mode, pouting like a Guppy fish and fluttering her eyelids like a shop-awning caught in a wind-trap. I moved from my desk, grabbing the waistband of her skirt. "Easy, girl."

"I'll be on my way, then," he smiled, taking in Sylvia's attributes for the last time.

"I'll show you out," she said hurriedly as she took his arm and whisked him out the office.

No sooner had the sergeant ascended the staircase, Badger appeared with a fraught expression. I sensed he was about to launch into another reprimand and glared back angrily.

"I'm not saying a word," he said, holding his hands up in surrender.

"Good," I returned sharply.

Sylvia reappeared, easing the office door closed behind her.

"I appreciate you pulling me out of a hole, Sylvia, but it doesn't have to be plugged by Sergeant Forbes. Please don't tell me you've arranged to meet him," I moaned.

"No, I haven't," she snapped back. "He was rather dishy though, wasn't he?" she added wistfully.

"Makes Gary Cooper look positively repugnant," Badger chirped up.

Chapter Three

The Kiss of an Angel

-14-

In just four weeks my life had changed dramatically—nothing short of a Greek tragedy. I had discovered that my revered father was a notorious killer of women, and I had taken the Henderson case in the hope of finding out why. I had been unfaithful, and my own wife had sought both the affections and passions of another man during my constant absence. I had befriended and lost someone very dear to me in Peter Egan, and may have made an enemy in Earnest Fallow. I had corrupted the minds of those who trusted me, and most probably lost the respect of my partner. I had questioned and ridiculed the beliefs of my best friend Bernie Mansall, who had extended me every courtesy and privilege a friend could bestow. I trusted no one, and failed to see how they could trust me. And still I held Jonathan Sandpiper's future in my hands. I felt I was clinging desperately to the few threads there were left of my mundane life, and secretly hoped to restore it to some kind of normality. But I knew, also, that life could never be the same, now that I had been entrusted with so many secrets, which in turn, had enhanced so many failings within me that had always been present but had lain dormant throughout adulthood. The bad things were beginning to easily outbalance the good things, the joyous occasions

I would remember for always; already they were beyond recall and slipping into the realms of worthlessness. My brain was reorganizing itself, undergoing a spring-clean, mercilessly discarding the memories I once valued, and replacing them with brand new events that induced only fear.

I had not been home for three days, and slowly came to realize that of all the threads I was still hopelessly hanging onto, that was the one I willingly allowed to slip from my grasp. I was surplus to requirements, a stranger who moved intermittently in and out of someone else's life and expected all the benefits appertaining to the contract Sarah and I had signed when we married. At sometime since the war began I had breached that contract and now all conditions were null-and-void. At night I would return to the small hotel on the Embankment, where I would always stay in the same room on the second floor, with an immediate view of flank, brick walls, black, slated roofs and clusters of tall buildings separated by a labyrinth of thin alleyways, which in the hours of darkness were occupied by prostitutes and cats. It was solely a place to sleep, and occasionally eat a light meal or sandwich. After leaving the office of an evening, I would go to The Cheese, and after, once whomever I was with had departed, I would disappear down the narrow streets in and around Fleet Street, stopping in at any pub that took my fancy. I would sit at the bar and merely observe, and from my pedestal I assessed the lives of those around me, of the lines of lonely men who turned to alcohol to escape their own demons, and at the solitary women who kept focused on the door hoping beyond hope that Mr. Right would come in and sweep them off their feet. Most went home with a consolation prize, knowing they would wake up in the morning alone.

I tried to remain aloof and retain the illusion of normality; that nothing had changed, nor was ever likely to. I bought suits, shirts, underwear and socks and paid for my room on the Embankment one month in advance, even taking my father's book from my desk and storing it on top of the wardrobe, and in the morning I would go to the same coffee shop in New Bridge Road, the way I always had before the terms and conditions of my marriage contract were revoked. In the eyes of those who knew me life had not changed, and if somebody asked how Sarah was, I would regale them with tit-bits of information regarding a conversation or an event that took place the night before. I hadn't seen her and didn't want to, nor did I surmise that I'd ever hear from her again, unless it was via a solicitor. Still, the betrayal, of both of us, ate away at me like a cancer. I would, of course, return home in my own time, perhaps when my head was clearer and not so cluttered with the secrets of others; when the thoughts, opinions and decisions were mine, free from the contamination and influences of somebody else. My life was gradually turning in a different direction; slow but sure, like the shadow cast by a sundial, only to fade and die when shadows engulfed it entirely.

As soon as I opened the office door and set my foot on the top tread of the staircase, I knew another change awaited me. I gradually descended down into the office, looking over the banisters to the reception area where Penny and Sylvia were comforting Joyce Turner who was seated and weeping into her handkerchief. When I reached the bottom Sylvia looked at me and expressed a hopeless shrug, her eyes glistening with tears; a contagious reaction induced by Joyce. "Bad news, Michael," she said. She handed me a brown envelope, stamped 'War Office' in the left hand corner. I realised at once what it was but, nevertheless, took out the letter and ran my eyes over the page that resembled a court summons. Joyce had been conscripted to a munitions factory in Fulham. She looked up at me and burst into tears. "Why are you crying, Joyce?" I asked. Both Sylvia and Penny shot me scornful looks. I knelt in front of her and took her trembling hand. "Listen, you should be proud to be doing your part. It may be one of your shells that win us the war. What are we going to tell our grandchildren when they ask us what we contributed? What will I say? What will Sylvia or Penny say, eh? We'll say we sat out the whole conflict in a dungeon of an office in the Strand. You, however, can boast that you were an integral part of Britain's victory." I glanced at the letter. "Now it says here you are to start Monday, so I suggest you take yourself home; today is your last day at this office." She erupted again, in a flood of tears more ferocious than the last, shaking her head and sobbing uncontrollably. "There will always be a job here for you, Joyce," I assured her with a smile. "Stay till lunchtime, if you wish, and then take yourself home." She nodded, her face still buried in her handkerchief. I looked to Penny and jerked my head in the direction of my office, and then placing a comforting hand on Joyce's shoulder I signalled with my eyes for Sylvia to console the poor woman, and then followed Penny.

"Give her a month's severance pay," I instructed her as I closed the office door.

Penny nodded. "Very generous, Michael, but you only owe her one week," she reminded me.

I rounded my desk and sat down.

"I'm aware of that. She's distraught; she can buy herself something nice—cheer herself up. Tell her to come and see me before she leaves."

"I will."

Penny seemed anxious and remained fixed to the spot.

"Can I talk to you, Michael?" she asked, quietly.

Thinking that she was about to launch into recollections of our night of passion I began to shake my head.

"Not that!" she said, anticipating my reaction. "I need to know where I stand," she added.

"About what?" I sighed exhaustively, convinced her line of questioning undoubtedly had something to do with that one night.

She took a seat in front of me and paused before speaking.

"What will happen to me now Tom and Andy are leaving the firm?"

I stared back at her in stunned silence.

She acknowledged my reaction, tossed up her head, and gasped.

"Oh, God, you didn't know. They were supposed to tell you."

"They didn't."

"I'm sorry."

"When? When are they leaving?"

She shook her head. "I'm not sure—soon, I think."

Once again I felt betrayed.

"Are they here?" I asked, abruptly.

Penny shook her head.

"Send them in as soon as they arrive."

Penny stood up, gazing down at me sympathetically. "Sorry."

I dismissed her with a wave of my hand, like a master excusing a servant girl.

I sat scowling at my desk for what seemed an eternity, enraged at their treachery and their disregard for everything I had done for them. Admittedly they came to me as a pair, and I had no doubt in my mind that they would leave the same way. They were extremely close and possessed the same legal minds, went on outings and holidays together with their wives, and even had the same sense of humour. Inevitably they would leave my firm, but now, after losing Joyce, I felt this was the beginning of my own end. It was at moments like this I wished I had a window to stare out of instead of four red brick walls; a form of distraction or a calming view. As I had neither I simply sat, trying to break out of my gloom and suppress the rage inside me; searching for composure. I thought of the exploits of my father and Pip, knowing they were the cause of my obsession regarding Henderson. It was ironic that I should use the bloody escapades of my father as a form of escapism, to bring my own trivialities into perspective and the realities of my life that much easier to deal with. My thoughts repulsed me, but for a few moments I was lost to myth and legend and my anger evaporated into the images conjured up by my unsettled mind.

Tom and Andy gingerly entered, both smiling nervously. I had regained a modicum of composure, but I never smiled or greeted them in my usual fashion.

"I understand you have something to tell me," I said.

Andy, with his sandy hair and boyish features fixed a smile, the kind he reserved for clients with money to spend.

"We weren't keeping anything from you, Michael," he assured me, pulling out a chair.

"I'd prefer you stand."

Tom looked decidedly worried and remained by the door, and for a while nobody spoke.

"We weren't sure," said Tom.

I inclined my head curiously.

"About our new venture," he added.

"And we have no intention of leaving you at present," Andy intercepted.

I looked at them both alternately and mustered a shallow smile.

"At present?" I questioned. "So you are leaving?"

"Only when all present cases are finalised," smiled Andy. "First you'll want to find replacements—for us."

"I may have done so already. What cases are outstanding—*at present?*" I emphasised.

Andy looked to Tom for guidance.

"The Fortuna Shipping Company versus . . ." Tom began.

"Paperwork! They'll settle out of court. What else?"

"And the Collins v Collins case."

"Which Badger is more than capable of handling. Anything else?"

Tom shook his head with a mystified stare.

They both stood before me exchanging worried glances.

"So," I said, breaking the silence and still retaining my self-assured smile, "may I ask which of my rivals has poached you?"

"No company, Michael," replied Tom. "We intend to set up our own firm."

"Commendable, Tom, but pickings are slim out there. In case you haven't noticed we're at war."

"And it's the war we shall benefit from," interrupted Andy enthusiastically. "We have been approached to set up our own company, the purpose being to locate relatives of those killed in the bombings; the settlement of estates in the absence of Wills; tracing benefactors; money and property bequeathed in a Will . . ."

"Approached?" I broke in. "Approached by whom?"

"The government are overwhelmed, Michael; thousands have been killed and injured, entire streets erased, families scattered to all four corners of the earth. We have been assured of more work than we can handle—it's very lucrative."

"The government are contracting you to do their work?" I seethed with a narrow look.

Tom intervened and stepped forward.

"So many city firms are doing it, Michael; it's merely a way of farming out the workload the government have accumulated since the war began . . ."

"But nevertheless it still makes you little more than a hearse chaser."

Tom's gentle demeanour forbade him to retaliate with any venom, but Andy's eyes were beginning to mist over. I defused the situation there and then and stood up.

"I wish you the best with your new venture," I said, extending my hand. "You'll keep in touch, I hope."

Tom's mouth began to sag.

"Now! You want us to leave now!" he gasped.

"No time like the present, Tom," I smiled. "Who knows, the war might end soon and what will happen to you then? Strike while the iron's hot."

Tom managed a limp handshake, but Andy gave me a hard stare before making an exit.

"I'll clear my desk," said Tom.

"I'd appreciate it," I said, sitting down and lifting any old file that came to hand. "Penny will forward any payments due to you; retainers and such."

He stood there for a moment, as if he wanted to speak, but then left.

The sound of silence was deafening. I could see Sylvia and Penny looking in the direction of Tom and Andy's office and occasionally turning to look at me through my half open door. I ignored them and pretended to read through correspondence and files until I saw them all in reception saying their goodbyes. I felt as though the walls were closing in on me, and the ceiling slowly descending to meet the floor, until inevitably I would be crushed; flattened like an irritating bug underfoot and freed of all my thoughts of betrayal. I sat—staring at the wall in front of me, barely blinking, until the silence was broken by the familiar drone of my junior partner. He was leaning against the doorframe with look of righteousness burning in his eyes.

"Are you leaving me, too?" I asked.

He sauntered in slowly and took up a seat in front of me, studying my features with a hopeless air; an attitude he adopted whenever he felt the need to drill some sense into me. His eyes lifted above my head—to the cross-swords he had bought for me when we first joined forces.

"You never have been able to shed that childish temper of yours, have you? Tom and Andy are not your toys to do with as you please, so I suggest you pull that silver spoon out of your rectum and face the realities of life," he said.

"Isn't that what I'm doing? Perhaps you'd rather go with them."

"I could do worse," he replied with a smile. "But my problem is that unlike you I wasn't born into a wealthy family. My father was an accountant—one of hundreds employed by a vast company in the city. He was just a number, who sat out his life in a small cubicle trying to balance the figures of conglomerates who believed they should be exempt from paying tax and, indeed, demanded it. He would work every hour available to put me through law school, and at weekends he would do the accounts for local businessmen in our area. He didn't want me to end up in some, small grey box making the rich richer. He wanted the best for me—the best he could afford, and although my small input will never change the world, I've tried to be worthy of the blood, sweat and tears he put into me. You, however, are a different specimen of mankind—a spoilt brat who rebelled against the world his father made for him. Friends are few and far between, and your family are either dead or living on the other side of the world. Even your own wife can't put up with your overbearing ways any longer. And now, to add to your catalogue of disastrous business and personal decisions, you have fired half the employees of this prestigious enterprise."

"They were leaving anyway!" I snapped.

"But not yet. They weren't leaving yet, were they, Michael? So, as like always, when things don't go your way, you start stamping your feet like a little girl and screaming injustice. You need to grow up, Michael—seriously. As for me, I have no intention of going anywhere; God, knows someone has to save you from self-destruction and this morbid curiosity you have in murderers. May I make a suggestion?"

"Why stop now?"

"The best decision you've made all day," he said. "Abiding by the adage that you can't turn a bad day into a good one, I suggest that come midday we abandon this prehistoric pit and take Joyce to the Cheshire Cheese for an appropriate send off."

He looked at me with a broadening smile, and conceding to my better judgement, if I actually possessed one at this present time, I agreed with a nod.

It was two days later and I left the noisy street behind me and descended the staircase into the depths of the building. As I moved down I looked over the banister to Tom and Andy's office, and then to Badger's, both of which were dark beyond their glazed frontages. Nobody was in the reception area but I could hear the unmistakable sound of tap-tapping coming from the office Sylvia and Penny shared. I slowed at the door. "Morning, Sylvia." She was perched over her typewriter, the index fingers of each hand fully extended, adorned with perfectly shaped red nails.

"Morning, Michael," she replied as she continued with her two-finger composition.

"Where's Badger?"

She suddenly stopped. "Shit! I've chipped a nail."

I waited for an answer to my question but she was already delving into her handbag for a repair-kit.

"Sylvia."

She drew a nail-file and set about repairing the devastation caused by the jammed typewriter key. "What?" she returned abruptly.

"Badger?" I asked again.

"With a client—one of the new cases," she explained.

"And Penny?"

She sawed away with the file with such vigour I expected her to catch on fire.

"With Badger." She held her hand up in front of her, appraised it for a moment and then displayed it in front of me. "Does it notice?"

I slowly walked away towards my office. "Any messages?" I flicked the light-switch and the room illuminated.

"On your desk," I heard her say.

Another day—another exercise in futility. Like most mornings I felt an utter failure because I was unable to decipher Sylvia's notes; today was no different. Today there were two messages, and there was a brief moment when I actually believed I could break the code of the first. On the top page of my notepad she had scrawled, '*funforalat ioactionceremony.*' I studied it for a moment, rewriting it out beneath, incorporating spaces where I believed they should be placed and omitting unnecessary letters. Today I was actually getting somewhere. '*Fun for all at Location. Ceremony.*' Clearly, this was an invitation, probably a black tie bash, dinner or luncheon with fine wine and afterward an address by a prominent city lawyer. Thrilled at the prospect of making sense out of the gobbledegook at long last, I marched to Sylvia's office armed with the notepad.

"So—where exactly is the location?" I smiled around the door confidently.

She had completed her letter, almost at the cost of severing her right hand, and was now peering into a filing cabinet drawer.

"What was that?"

"The location," I purged; "Where is it? Furthermore, when is it? God help me, I could do with a break."

"What location?" She straightened and perched her hands on her hips. "Have you been drinking?"

"Your note," I said, "I've cracked it. *Fun for all at location—ceremony.*"

Sighing exhaustively she stomped towards me and snatched the notepad from my hand.

"Funeral at 10, Acton Cemetery," she read. "Have you gone mad?"

Failure consumed me once again, like it had every day since employing her.

"Peter's?" I said, looking at my watch. "How am I supposed to get to Acton in forty-five minutes?"

"You can't—obviously," said Sylvia, walking away. "Earnest Fallow called last thing yesterday and left the message. They're having the wake at Peter's house from 3 o'clock this afternoon. Have you forgotten where he lives or do you want me to draw you a map?"

I was reluctant to ask about the second message, but nevertheless made the enquiry.

"Wendy Marshall," said Sylvia, tapping a delicate finger on the notepad. "Called first thing this morning and wants to meet you."

I stared at the scrawl looking perturbed.

"Sylvia, Wendy Marshall is a witness for the prosecution, as you are well aware. Do you know the consequences if she's seen in these offices?"

"She's not coming here. She wants to meet you tonight on Tower Bridge—midnight; sounds all very cloak and dagger to me."

I felt duty-bound to put in some kind of appearance at Peter's funeral. Secretly, perhaps, I was hoping for a little insight into his death and, indeed, the whole absurd predicament I had unconsciously walked into. Peter had unselfishly given me his time, his knowledge and, for a very short while, his friendship—I owed him my respect. So, in the late afternoon I walked towards Seven Dials, stopping briefly at Covent Garden to purchase some flowers, and once there I entered through the iron gates and into the courtyard. I was unsure of what to expect; I would be a total stranger but I resigned myself to the fact that as a friend I had a right to be there. I knocked on the door, waiting with the flowers cradled in my arm, and I could hear the sound of many voices coming from inside. The door opened and a familiar face looked back at me. The last time I saw him he was standing knee-deep in discarded manuscripts, in a threadbare cardigan and a week's stubble decorating his chin. Now he looked immaculate, dressed in a black suit, his face clean and hair neatly combed. I went to speak but he held a single finger to his lips, stepping outside and easing the door closed behind him.

"Good of you to come, Mr. Lawyer," he whispered, taking my arm and walking me across the courtyard.

"I'm sorry I couldn't make the funeral but . . ." I began to explain.

"You're here and that's all that matters," he said. "Nice flowers."

"Mr. Fallow, why are you frog-marching me away from the house?"

He released his grip at once and stopped.

"Some advice before you go in—say nothing to anyone about the publication. Don't mention how you and Peter came by the story. At present the house is infested with every journalist in London, sniffing for the source, the list of names. You're just a friend. Okay?"

"I'm not about to talk to anyone regarding that, am I?"

"That may be your intention, Mr. Lawyer, but the people in there are experts in extracting information. They make the Spanish Inquisition look like a bunch of social workers. Don't even hint at it. Better still, don't engage in any conversation with them; safer that way. Give your condolences to Helen, have a drink and then slip away."

"Helen?"

"Peter's wife."

"He was married? I never knew."

"You didn't?" he questioned with a look of surprise. "Well he is . . . or was . . . He was up until about six years ago. They kept in contact because of the children. She adored him but couldn't put up with his ways; a good girl."

"If you'd prefer I won't go in at all," I said, about turning and looking back at the house.

"Please don't be offended, Mr. Lawyer, but Peter's story is bigger than I could ever have anticipated—everyone wants to know. At present you hold what they want. It's best that while in that house we are not associated in any way. We are strangers."

"As you wish," I agreed with a nod. "I'll say a few words and be on my way."

Earnest Fallow patted me on the shoulder and we walked back towards the house.

"You must have read the post-mortem results," I said. "Peter died of a heart attack."

Mr. Fallow stopped short of the door. "You just don't get it, do you, Mr. Lawyer? They could have found him chopped to pieces with an axe, and they would have still come up with a heart attack. Now, remember what I said."

Inside the ambience was sombre, as to be expected. The lobby, hallway and the staircase was taken up with small groups of people conversing in whispered conversations; smiling taboo; laughter outlawed. I followed Earnest Fallow into the lounge where the crowd was denser, gingerly pushing my way through the dark suits and black ties to the far end of the room where a beautiful woman sat on the settee talking quietly to a young gentleman who was speaking with great authority about journalism.

"Excuse me, Helen," said Fallow quietly and placing a subtle hand on the young man's shoulder to shut him up. "This is Michael James, a friend of Peter's."

Her hair was long and black, her eyes the bluest I had ever seen, her complexion flawless and her smile disarming. She rose at once as if I had saved her from a fate worse than death and shook my hand. "A reporter?" she enquired, lifting a glass of sherry from a nearby tray and handing it to me. I glanced briefly around at the staring faces and shook my head while Mr. Fallow relieved me of the flowers and disappeared. "A litigator," I replied. At once she took my arm and began to steer me back through the route I had just taken. "Would you be kind enough to escort me outside? I need some fresh air." Outside she disengaged her arm from mine, walked directly into the courtyard and sat down on the low wall encircling an ornate garden area.

"Thank you, Michael," she sighed. "I swear if I talk to another reporter I'll go mad. Don't they ever switch off?"

She popped the clasp on her handbag and took out a silver cigarette case and matching lighter.

"You would know—being married to a journalist," I smiled as I took up a place next to her.

She lit a slender cigarette and tossed her head back, the layers of hair falling back into place as if they had never been disturbed. "I know only too well," she replied, inhaling deeply and exhaling a tube of white smoke through her pursed lips. "I'm being rude. So, how did you know Peter?"

"He helped me on a case I'm working on." I replied, staring aimlessly into my glass of sherry.

"Well it was good of you to come. It's a relief to actually speak to someone who isn't connected to a newspaper. Have you noticed that reporters are incapable of holding a conversation? They don't partake—they just ask questions. Did you know Peter Well?" She suddenly rolled her eyes and started to laugh. "It must be contagious; now I'm doing it," she said.

I laughed along briefly.

"I can't say I knew him that well," I explained, "but I liked him as a person and I thought his work was outstanding."

She smiled back at me through a haze of smoke.

"Did you rehearse that line on the way here?"

I shrugged with embarrassment. "It sounded better in my head," I grimaced.

She tilted her head back, staring through narrowed eyes into the afternoon sun.

"Did Peter ever mention me?" she asked, delicately placing the cigarette to her lips.

"Well—it's as I said: I didn't know him well."

"Typical," she mumbled. "Well, why should he? We haven't been man and wife for so long."

Her words were loaded with disappointment rather than bitterness and she brushed her cheek on her shoulder as if it comforted her.

"Still—life must go on," she said, almost in a whisper.

She let the sunlight play on her face for a while before sitting upright and focusing on my glass.

"Are you drinking that?"

I shook my head with uncertainty before she picked it out of my hand and consumed it almost in one.

"Why is it customary to drink sherry at such occasions?" she shuddered as if she had swallowed a dose of bad medicine. "I'd sooner have a gin and tonic."

She took a final draw on her cigarette and tossed it into the shrubbery behind us.

There was no doubting that Helen was beautiful; the kind of woman that could wear a potato sack and still look stunning, but I had my reservations as to her character. Her clothes, jewellery and overall appearance exuded wealth and her sometimes offhanded remarks suggested she had little patience for trivial conversations, but her tolerance was tested only by her own failings and there was a look of regret in her eyes every time she allowed her own frustrations get the better of her. And for that she hid in long, silent pauses as though she were carefully constructing a question or remark without it sounding disrespectful.

Her cheek was on her shoulder again, her blue eyes sad and staring aimlessly out over the courtyard, her composure devoid of expression. Suddenly she came to life, stretching herself and smiling at me.

"So, Michael, how did you know about the funeral?" she asked.

"Through Mr. Fallow; he called my office yesterday but I never got the message until this morning—hence the reason I never made it to Acton."

"Peter was born in Acton," she said, wistfully. "Working in a factory held no charm for him so he educated himself; he done very well. You know Earnest Fallow?"

His warning rang in my head like an alarm clock.

"Not at all," I replied emphatically. "Peter must have given him my number."

"They go back a long way," she said, "but Fallow can be arrogant, publishing anything without thought for the consequences or the damage it can do to the innocent. Peter helped him out on more than one occasion—especially after the Vassarri case; he was lucky he stayed in business."

Peter had mentioned Vassarri when I first met him and so had Earnest Fallow, but as neither had elaborated I knew nothing more.

"What is Vassarri?" I asked.

She smiled almost sympathetically at my ignorance.

"Vassarri isn't a 'what', Michael, Vassarri is a person; Nicolia Vassarri. He was an assassin, a mercenary who wrote his memoirs and took them to Fallow for publishing. This was the big one—the story that would break Fallow out of that miserable publishing house and put him up there with the big boys in Fleet Street. He put everything he had into that—cost him his house and his marriage, and no sooner were the books on the shelves the government intervened. The publishing house was raided, the original manuscript seized, even the printing presses taken away. Fallow was left destitute but Peter helped him back on his feet."

"But why would the government get involved?" I asked, intrigued by the subject.

"O.S.A." she said, pronouncing it as a word—Osah.

"Official Secrets Act!"

She nodded. "Vassarri worked as an assassin for various governments—including the British; they buried the story and threatened Fallow with imprisonment. It was about that time he and Peter met. Peter wrote a story about it but changed the names just in case there were any comebacks."

"And were there?"

"She nodded again. "About a week after the story was published Peter got a visit from three very official looking gentlemen asking why he felt compelled to write such a story. Peter told them it was purely fictional, but anyone who knew Peter also knew that he didn't write fiction. The story was out—that was enough. I met Vassarri once when I was with Peter, or at least Fallow introduced him as Vassarri; a good looking man; you know, steel grey hair, sun-tan, expensive clothes. And shortly after Peter and I decided to go separate ways."

"I'm sorry."

She rested her cheek on her shoulder again. "Me, too," she murmured.

It occurred to me then that Helen was considerably younger than Peter; he being in his mid-forties and her somewhere in her early thirties. Even the penetrating sunlight could not enhance any trace of aging on her face, and her hands were like that of young girl's.

"A silly question, but were you surprised by his death?" I asked.

Her eyes slightly widened and for a moment I expected to be reprimanded for being so familiar, but she appraised me momentarily before turning her face to the sun again and closing her eyes.

"Peter was an alcoholic. He needed drink to function—personally and sexually . . ." Her eyes opened slightly as if she were gauging my reaction but then gently closed. "And I'd like to say it was the reason why we broke up, but I can't. He was always reliant on booze. I can't recall ever seeing him drunk; I think he had gone beyond that. Give him a bottle of whiskey and he was funny, witty, extremely intelligent and someone I loved to be around. Without drink he was cold and miserable—a recluse. So, probably due to my own selfishness I did nothing to stop it. When he finally realised his problem and the doctors warned him of the consequences I stepped in, but he wouldn't listen; he just carried on—chasing stories, drinking, missing for weeks on end, and I found someone else."

I must have looked shocked when she opened her eyes for she smiled regretfully, as she probably had to everyone she had ever confessed to.

"A lonely heart will go anywhere, Michael, and to anyone," she said, as if to give reason for her conduct. "I was weak in every sense of the word. Had I been stronger I wouldn't be sitting here talking to you now. So the affair continued for six or maybe nine months, and one night I sat Peter down and told him. I thought he'd explode; you know, force my lover's name from me and hunt him down and kill him—he didn't. He just listened, nodded his head and quietly went upstairs and packed his bags. He kissed the children goodbye and left; the bastard didn't even give me an argument. God, he could be so insensitive."

Her eyes were filled with nostalgic tears and her voice faltered from time to time, but she smiled warmly as she reminisced.

"Where did you two meet?" I asked.

Her face flushed with embarrassment and she looked away.

"I'm sorry. I had no right to be so personal," I said.

She looked back and smiled regretfully. "Do you remember the Underwood Scandal?"

Most did. About eighteen years ago Sir Henry Underwood was a prestigious member of parliament as well as a cabinet member of the Conservative Party. Handsome, debonair and charming, Underwood was a sprightly sixty-three year old who vigorously campaigned for social reform, lobbying the House for better schools, improvement of living conditions for the poor and benefits for parents. He was often seen around his constituency in the company of his wife and two teenage daughters. His world collapsed back in the mid-twenties when he was accused of molesting a girl of fifteen. Underwood shrugged off the allegations, attributing the rumour as nothing more than a smear campaign, but the girl in question, who by law could not be named, made a full statement and verified that the rumours were indeed true. Sir Henry died in prison while on remand.

"You!" I said. "You were the girl?"

Helen nodded. "That's how I met Peter. I was the news; the story everyone wanted to know. Henry was a relative of my friend, her uncle. He would visit with his daughters and we would all sit in the garden while he regaled us with his stories of politics and how a change was needed, especially for the poor and needy. I found him fascinating, funny and vibrant; a breath of fresh air in my suffocating world."

"So," I began cautiously, "you weren't molested?"

"In the eyes of the law I was; just fifteen. When the story broke my father marched me down to the police station to give a statement. This was my only chance at redemption, he said. If I admitted that I willingly slept with Henry then I would carry that burden for the rest of my life. People would spit at me in the streets and call me a whore. No man would ever take me as a wife. So with his guidance I said I was sexually assaulted. They made mincemeat of Henry, dragging up every sordid detail they could either find or manufacture. He was in no position to protect himself, confined twenty-four hours a day to a cell. And he died; of shame, probably; of how he had betrayed himself, his wife and his daughters. And I lived to fight another day, but the damage I caused that poor man haunts me still."

"It was only going to end one way. You were a minor," I reasoned.

"A willing minor; a young woman, hormones going ten to the dozen, engaging in sticky fumblings in the backseats of parked cars with spotty young men who thought that a clitoris was a Roman amphitheatre. I craved intelligence, consideration, respect."

A man appeared at the door of the house, staring anxiously in our direction.

"Oh, God;" she grimaced, "seems I'm needed to do my duty."

"Who is he?"

"Graham, Peter's brother from Ireland—the poorer side of the family. Probably only here to see what he can get his hands on."

She stood up and shook my hand.

"Nice to meet you, Michael," she said. "Thank you for coming."

"My pleasure."

She walked a few steps away and turned.

"Do you drive, Michael?" she asked, still looking in the direction of the greedy relative.

"I do, but I haven't got a car—sorry."

She opened her handbag and tossed me a key tethered to a fob with an emblem of a Jaguar's head.

"Peter would want you to have it. Safe driving, Michael."

She smiled over her shoulder and I watched her disappear back into the house.

-15-

At midnight I was standing on Tower Bridge and staring down into a black void; the flowing waters beneath me audible but invisible. Small, glimmering lights glided aimlessly about in St. Katharine's Dock as boats shuffled into their moorings, and the occasional pair of dipped headlights approached from the city and passed over the monumental expanse to the south, their red tail-lights disappearing into the darkness. Even in the grey of night The Tower of London stood black and stark beside me—the medieval architecture and associated horrors imaginable even in silhouette, and beyond its dark walls the city spread out like an abstract water-colour in shades of grey and black. A light breeze flowed in from the sea tinted with a bitter chill, making me shudder and inducing me to turn up the collar of my jacket. In the distance I could hear the faint sound of foghorns; a warning to oncoming vessels as they passed under bridges in the inky blackness. The lights that once decorated these bridges were extinguished now, until the war was over and the bombardments ceased, when they would be restored to all their nighttime glory. I stood in silence with my hands on the cold, iron rail, staring out at a view that had been stolen by the night and wishing I was cuddled up in a cozy bed. Minutes passed like hours, and with every passing the chill of the night began to seep into me and speckled my hair and clothes with tiny droplets of moisture, until the occasional shudder manifested into a constant shiver. In the distance I heard Big Ben strike twelve-thirty and decided there and then to wait fifteen more minutes and not a second longer.

Sooner or later even the strongest willed mind will succumb to the darkness and allow the brain to take revenge on its owner. The few hopeless lights dotted around the black canvas of night were of little comfort and I was beginning to feel vulnerable, hearing strange, ghostly whispers rising up from the water as it hurriedly made its way back to the river-mouth; rolling along the embankments and rushing through the bridge supports. The sound brought back memories of my short time in the Spider's Web, when Sylvia and I were at the mercy of the water's rage. I would stay no longer than absolutely necessary. At the sound of the famous clock chiming quarter to the hour, I pushed myself off the rail in readiness to make my way home, and when I turned I jumped back in surprise. I couldn't see her clearly, barely the outline of her face, but I could smell cheap perfume and could see her eyes smiling back at me with amusement. "You're, Michael?" she asked. I was hoping she couldn't see me, for I was clutching my heart, fearing that at any moment it was about to stop. "Yes, I am Michael James. You surprised me. Wendy?" She laughed quietly and began to walk away. "Follow me, Michael James."

We crossed the bridge to the south-side without saying a word, and only when we reached the main road did I see her clearly, caught in the dull lights of the odd passing car. She was slim to the point of being emaciated and her hair was short and mousy. Her clothes were designed and, indeed, chosen to leave no one in any doubt as to exactly what she was—a prostitute, and as she walked before me I mused whether there was a school or academy that trained such women to walk in that particular way. Off the main road we walked down a succession of thin, cobbled streets that led back to the waterfront, and passing a line of dormant warehouses she stopped before an iron, studded door that resembled the entrance to a meat locker. She slapped her hand against it three times and it was immediately opened by a muscular man with a bald head and grizzly beard. His arms were heavily tattooed that crept up his neck like decorative ivy. He eyed me with doubt, but she nodded as if I was her guest and he stood to one side. I could hear people talking and laughing, and once down a short corridor we slipped through a beaded curtain that opened into a crowded bar, where all around men gambled at the surrounding tables and women, much like Wendy, blatantly plied their trade with enormous success. The inhabitance of this room were river people; Watermen, Dockers, Lightermen, sewage-workers, steamboat and barge personnel, Stevedores and crane drivers. No one turned a head when we walked in. Wendy stood at the bar and snapped her fingers at a gangly barman in his fifties with worn features, who headed straight towards her with an elated grin.

"Not seen you around lately, Wen," he said. "What'll it be?"

She stared at me with arched eyebrows.

"Scotch," I shrugged. "Scotch will be fine."

"You heard him. One bottle, two glasses."

He fulfilled the order in seconds.

"So what's new?" he asked her as he looked me up and down. "Going up market, ain't we?"

"You know what these suits are like. They like a bit of rough; makes 'em feel human. Anyone in the snug?"

The barman shook his head. "Don't think so—best check, though."

She took the bottle and glasses and jerked her head towards a closed door at the end of the bar.

The whole place was basic, spit and sawdust with a clutter of chipped and damaged furniture, and the bare floorboards were sticky underfoot as a result of spilled drinks. The snug obviously had the same interior designer, though it did boast seat-covers on the hardwood chairs. Wendy sat at a table, pushed a few empty bottles and glasses to one side and removed the cork from the whiskey bottle.

"A pleasant establishment," I said, as I gazed about disapprovingly.

She expressed an impish grin as she passed me a glass.

Wendy was nondescript, a plain looking girl with lifeless green eyes who even at her tender age had been ravished by life. Her teeth were small and white, like those of a child and her nose, although petite, was slightly crooked—a result of being broken once or perhaps numerous times. She wore several small studs as earrings, one of which was missing and was now substituted by a fierce scar that ran from the pierce and off the lobe. She was the kind of girl who was destined to destruction, either by her own doing or by someone else, and when that day arrived she would not be missed.

"Is everything free here? I noticed you never paid," I said as I took up a chair.

She leaned forward and filled up my glass.

"It's deductible," she replied. "I pay for it—in the long run."

"You work here?"

"When needs must. Nobody owns this place—the bar owns it. The booze is off the merchant ships—cheap. The men pay for the girls at the bar, and the girls get a percentage; the rest stays behind the bar. The girls work here because it's safe. Anyone out of line goes in the river—that's the law . . . our law."

She swallowed her drink in two large swallows, cringed slightly and topped up her glass again.

"I know a man who professes to own most of the bars along the river," I said.

She looked at me curiously and smiled slightly.

"Harry? You know Harry Griffin?"

"We've done business," I nodded. "So you know him?" I added, enthralled that someone else on this planet knew of his existence.

"He's a good man," she returned. "Comes in here from time to time, but would never dream of muscling in. He pays for everything he owns, and he doesn't expect anything in return. He could have easily taken this place from us, but it's not his way. I wouldn't have thought Harry was your type of person. Maybe you're not as straight as you look."

She smiled like a pirate and took another gulp of her whiskey.

"I charge by the hour," she said, and then looking at the bottle of scotch, added "So I'm thinking two hours to hold this conversation. Call it an even forty. If you want to fuck me it'll be extra."

"Forty's fine," I agreed. "Why did you contact me?"

"Because you want to know what I know; the evidence that might send your client to the gallows, and will probably make you look like a fuckin' idiot."

"I know what you are, Wendy."

"Oh," she said with dull surprise.

"Born Hackney 1914; in and out of an assortment of reformed and industrial schools for most of your childhood, claims of being raped by your father and uncle; underwent psychiatric analysis as a child and up until recently on the orders of the court; spent three lengthy terms in Holloway Prison for violence, one term for stabbing your probation officer; admitted to hospital no less than twenty-seven times, four of which were the result of failed suicide attempts; known to consort with a catalogue of miscreants; recent psychiatric assessment reports that for the past several years you have been harming yourself with sharp instruments—notably razor blades; according to your arrest sheet you took up prostitution at the age of twenty but have probably been soliciting since puberty. You can see where I'm going with this, can't you?"

Her face was unchanging; calm and bereft of humiliation.

"You're saying I'm worthless."

"I'm saying that a retard would have no problem in discrediting you. Imagine what a highly trained barrister could achieve once you're on the stand. You claim you were attacked October 1st 1940, and thereafter gave a statement from your hospital bed three days later. You failed to pick out your attacker on three separate occasions but you did, however, identify George Henderson on Christmas Eve in a line-up at Lambeth Police

Station. The D.P.P. has put you forward as a witness for the prosecution as of September 16th 1941. Nine months, Wendy; nine long months from the identification of Henderson till now. That's what I am having difficulty with. Without sounding insulting you're hardly a model citizen, are you? You've spent your adult life willingly being abused, and now you want justice because you were raped!"

She took another gulp of whiskey and replenished her glass, and still she remained unruffled, as if she were used to being downtrodden and insulted.

"I was more than raped," she argued. "The night it happened I'd been at The Borough, going round the pubs—the usual dives. Business was slow and by 1 o'clock I was cold and tired, so I made my way home. When I got to Newington I saw him on the other side of the road, and me being me I thought I might be able to earn my rent before going home. I crossed the road and talked to him. He was okay, the kind I thought I could trust, and he asked me how much and I told him. I was surprised he agreed to go with someone like me. He was smart, expensive suit—hand made; Savile Row, I wouldn't wonder . . ."

"Wendy. The man you identified is a train driver with five children who lives in a Peabody Trust home—he certainly would not have been wearing a Savile Row suit, and the inventory of his clothing confirms that he never possessed one. Isn't it possible you picked out the wrong man—someone similar?"

"No! It was him. It was George Henderson."

I held up my hands. "As you wish. Go on."

She raised her drink and I detected a faint trembling of her hands as she recalled the night in question.

"He said he had to collect his car," she continued. "He said it was parked in a garage a few roads away, and from there we would go to a hotel. Sure enough, a few roads away we came to some arches beneath the main railway track, and he took out some keys and opened the padlock. Then he put his arm around my throat and pulled me inside; I can't remember what happened then. I woke up on the floor, staring up at a single light bulb. I was naked, and I could see him taking things out of a bag in the corner. There were lots of shelves; bits of engine, cogs, rods—things like that all around. When he saw I was awake he came over and punched me. I've been hit before but this man was strong. I don't think I was unconscious, just dazed; I've had worse. The next thing I remember was he was naked and knelt beside me, and I felt pains down my arms and legs . . . but they were warm. I tried to scream but he had pushed a rag in my mouth. I couldn't move. I was spread out on the floor, my wrists and ankles tied to iron pegs, but I managed to lift my head. The warm sensation I was feeling was the blood pouring from my arms and legs; he had sliced me from shoulder to elbow—from pelvis to knee, and now the cutthroat was slicing in my chest and dragging downward. Any street-girl will tell you that sex is in the eyes; they say 'Yes' they say 'No;' they say 'Take me' or they say 'Fuck off and leave me alone.' No words are needed. The eyes say it all. The pegs . . . the things the ropes were tied to, were just dropped into holes in the concrete; I could feel they were loose. I pushed the pain away and just stared at him. I never flinched. And he just stopped doing what he was doing and got on top of me, rubbing himself in the blood that was running out of me, panting like a mad dog and aroused to the extent that he was detached from what was happening—from what he was doing to me. His rhythm and motion helped me free the peg from the ground, and once it was out, I smashed it down on the back of his skull. I pulled at the ropes, gathered up my clothes and just ran."

She emptied her glass and filled it again.

"You went straight to the police?" I asked.

She shook her head.

"I just kept running," she explained. "I didn't even scream. I thought if I screamed and he was looking for me, he would know where I was. I hid in an alleyway behind the gas works and then collapsed. Two workmen found me next morning; I'd lost so much blood."

Her story chilled me and I shook my head.

"You're lucky. You survived," I said.

For the first time she looked offended, and standing up she removed her jacket to reveal long, wavering lines down her arms. Once I registered the atrocious scars she raised her skirt. "Lucky! Are you fuckin' subnormal?" she barked. "Do you think men find this attractive? Do you think I deserved this?"

"I never meant it in that way," I retaliated defensively. "I simply meant . . ."

"I know what you meant! You think of all his victims, how come a whore like me survived? It's the reason I survived—because I'm a whore; because I'm used to the beatings and the pain; because I'm worthless."

Her lifeless eyes ignited with rage, her face red with anger, and the veins in her neck and face prominent. I remained silent, lifting my glass of scotch and quietly sipping at it as though I were at the Thames Regatta. She held her irate posture for a moment, before her head dropped and her tense body lost all rigidity.

"Sorry. I know what you meant," she sighed.

The police inquiry into Wendy's alleged attack amounted to nothing. The garage, one of several arches that had been converted into commercial premises along Newington Causeway, were owned by a company named Meredith-Hall who went into receivership in July 1940, and they had remained vacant until all were destroyed by fire on October 2nd—the day prior to Wendy giving her statement to the police. As London was in the midst of the worse bombardments in its history, the destruction of several dilapidated arches was of little concern. It was assumed, not least of all by the already overwhelmed fire department, that the blaze was probably the result of a stray incendiary which, therefore, rendered Wendy's fanciful tale as inadmissible, as any evidence had been totally obliterated. The extent of her wounds influenced the police to keep the case open, and she was called to no less than three identity parades in which she failed to identify her attacker. When George Henderson was arrested she made a positive identification.

"He made no attempt to disguise his appearance—no balaclava?" I asked.

She shook her head, staring intently at the table as though she could see his face somewhere in the spilled beer and empty glasses.

"I know people, some real hard bastards, and for a while we went looking for him. I wanted to see that fucker burn for what he did to me. But what was I looking for? I was looking for a man with an expensive suit who obviously had a good job—not a poxy train driver. When I saw him in that line up I wanted to tear his heart out—fuckin' animal! It was him who burned the garages down—not a bomb."

As the weight of her hard stare began to lighten, so she began to grin.

"Still, what would somebody like you know about someone like me?" she said. "And I don't just mean what's on paper. What they say. What they think is best for me. I know that when I go to court there won't be a soul there who believes me. Why should they? I know what I am, Michael James, and I'd change if they'd let me, but nothing will ever change. As sure as time nothing's ever gonna be different."

"At hospital—did they check for sample evidence; blood, semen, anything of that nature?" I asked.

"They cleaned me up pretty good. I don't think they found much, though."

"No semen? He used protection?"

She shook her head solemnly. "I don't think so."

I inclined my head to one side.

"But intercourse took place. You said . . ."

"I know what I said! He didn't fuck me if that's what you're askin'. He just rubbed himself all over me. Bastard! I'm sure it was his intention—before he killed me, or maybe even after. They did the usual things; swabbed my mouth, scraped my nails—all the things they do to rape victims. But when they got my medical records they sort of just gave up. I wasn't important then—till now. I'm the only one who can identify him."

"You noticed distinguishing marks on his body?"

Wendy shook her head.

"If I did I don't remember, but I'll never forget his face. Never," she replied. "All I can do is go into court and say my piece, and you—as you said—can do your hardest to make me look what I am. But at least I'd have tried."

Memorabilia, artefacts and aging photographs decorated the walls of the small, decaying room, in the form of ropes, compasses, and several pictures of Tower Bridge under construction back at the turn of the century. There were a selection of various sized barrels, either used as seats or tables, and above a black stricken fireplace hung a boat's anchor at an oblique slant. There was one window that would have looked out over the river had it not been encased with heavy shutters, streaked a rusty brown from its latch and hinges. The depleting level on the scotch bottle had slowed considerably, as Wendy now seemed content to sip rather than gulp. She offered to top up my glass but I declined. In a silent moment I observed her. She was so inexpressibly sad and forlorn that I could not imagine the life she had experienced, but I could see that once her face was expressive of beauty, and her lifeless eyes were filled with lustre and laughter. Before me now, she was a pathetic picture of extreme misery rather than sadness.

"Who are 'they', Wendy?" I asked. "You said earlier that you would change if they would let you—so, who are *they?*"

Her eyes dropped and she crooked her head slightly.

"Are you going to lecture me? Or worse, try to convert me and lead me to the straight and narrow path? It'll never happen. They won't allow it."

Admittedly my knowledge of prostitution was scant, but I knew enough to know that few worked alone and most were controlled, either by one person or several.

"You have a pimp?" I asked.

She glanced at me with distrust.

"What's it to you?" she snarled.

I responded with a faint shake of my head and began to look around the room as if there were nothing more to say on the subject, and Wendy gazed thoughtfully into her half empty glass. After a long silence I heard her grumble, "Fuck it!" and she stood up and walked towards the entrance, dragging her chair behind her. After opening the door of the snug and taking a brief look outside, she closed it again and jammed the chair under the handle and returned to the table.

"You don't have a fuckin' clue what you're getting into, do you?" she hissed. "You think this is about Henderson—Carlisle? I can read, Michael James, and that story is too close to home to be ignored. This isn't about a bunch of criminals paying off the odd copper to turn a blind eye. It's so organised it'll make your head swim once you know the truth."

She patted the pockets of her jacket, and dipping her hand inside pulled out a pack of cigarettes and a box of matches. Her anger, either being the fault of myself, those who controlled her or perhaps the world in general, had yet to dissipate completely, and I watched her fumble and ignite her cigarette with trembling hands. She pulled over a small barrel and sat down. As she stared at me, considering whether to disclose the knowledge I was oblivious to, a thunderous and repetitive knocking shook the door in its frame. A muffled and slurred voice sounded from the other side, brutish and full of malice, accompanied by a woman's incessant giggling. "Open up! I got a woman here who's trying to earn a living." Wendy drew on her cigarette and looked at the door. "What the fuck do you think I'm tryin' to do? Fuck off!" she blasted back. The intruder mumbled a few incoherent words and we heard him walk away, obviously in search of a quieter place in which to spend his hard-earned wages with his female companion.

"What do you know about the story of police corruption?" she asked, almost in a whisper with her eyes still focused on the door.

"I shrugged as if the subject was of little importance.

"Only what I've read;" I lied, "a number of policemen receiving bribes from criminals."

"A lot of policeman—three hundred or more; a lot more," she said. "Just how close are you to Harry Griffin?"

She spoke so quietly that I had to watch her lips to confirm her words. She rose slightly and shuffled her seat from the opposite side of the table to the side, until she was next to me.

"It was a property; a lessee Mr. Griffin wanted to evict. He wanted to know the legalities of the situation," I explained confidently.

Her eyes narrowed at once and her eyebrows slightly furrowed.

"Harry came to you 'cos he wanted to kick someone out of his house?" she questioned.

"That was it, yes. Why?"

She sat upright and scrutinised my face, as if searching for honesty, but I refused to turn away from her or let her stare me down. She drew on her cigarette, filling her mouth with smoke and then blew it in my face, forcing me away from the poisonous cloud that stung my eyes and instinctively compelled me to search for cleaner air. She emitted a short gust of cruel laughter and shook her head.

"Harry would rather die than pay someone like you. But I'll take your word for it."

"Glad to hear it," I returned as I wiped my tearing eyes. "What has Harry Griffin got do with what you have to tell me?"

"Absolutely nothing! And if he ever found out what's been goin' on under his nose, the Thames would run red. Stealing is one thing, but this . . . ? He'd kill 'em all."

Without appearing too interested my eyes began to wander the dimly lit room, but my curiosity regarding Harry Griffin, but moreover his decision to entrust someone he had never met with the list of corrupt police officers, was fast manifesting into an obsession. Nevertheless I purposefully looked at my watch as if to influence my host to a hasty conclusion. She glanced at me, and leaving her drink on the table, walked to the far side of the dingy room and sat amongst the shadows, as though what she had to say could be communicated without eye contact. She sat in silence for a while before speaking.

"It was 1927. I was thirteen when my father and his brother walked out of court and went straight to the nearest pub to celebrate. Well, why wouldn't they? They had just been cleared of rape, sexual assault, incest, and despite the objections of the social services, they walked free; I never laid eyes on either of them again. My mother had died two years before—of a disease I could never pronounce or understand. It was at that moment when I watched my father leave the courtroom that I knew I was alone, and for all the things he done to me, for all the pain I suffered at his and his brother's hands, I was scared of being left—with no one. My father's defence was simple; I was precocious, a slut—cursed with an hereditary obsession with sex—just like my mother; they even put my friend's fourteen year old brother on the stand to say he paid me two-shillings to see me naked when I was twelve. The judge called me a 'hysterical and spiteful girl of unsound mind' and the doctors labelled me as 'morally degenerate.' After a few weeks I was sent to a workhouse in Poplar, run mainly by nuns but who were answerable to the Master—a so-called God fearing Christian named Chives, Alistair Henry Chives. I had long, yellow hair then, just like my mother's before the disease took it from her. On my arrival I was taken straight to Chives' office, where I was assessed by Mother Superior and two other nuns. Chives' wife, the Mistress, was sitting next to him looking through the court report and medical assessments. He gave me a lecture about the evils of sex, of lying, and of my wickedness for attempting to destroy those who cared about me. From there I was taken to the dormitory where I was made to strip and sit on a chair in front of all the other women. A nun shaved my head and then put me a tin bath filled with cold water. After, I was given a uniform, still stained and marked by whoever had it before. I was to spend the next two years there . . ."

"You don't have to tell me this, Wendy," I interrupted in a sympathetic voice.

"Yes, I do," she returned patiently. "The next day I was set to work, scrubbing endless stone corridors and stairs. The day after I was put in the laundry, but if they took a dislike to you, they would make you pick oakum, and that's what they made me do—week after week, month after month. Do you know what oakum is, Michael James?"

"Rope?"

"Yes, rope impregnated with tar and sea-salt. When picked the fibres would be used to stop up the gaps in the planks of wooden boats, but what it does to the hands is indescribable. The fingers crack and bleed and the fingernails are torn out; it's a form of punishment, you see. And these duties were given to me on the instructions of Mrs. Chives, the Mistress. She had a sexual appetite worse than any street-walker I've ever known. Her and her husband had living accommodation on the top floor of the workhouse, and three nights a week Mr. Chives went home to their country house. It was on those nights that she would order a girl to be taken from the dormitory and brought to her apartment. She would sit in a fine armchair by the fireside and watch the girl performing sexual acts with maybe one or two young lads; sometimes grown men—old men. The first time I was taken there I refused. I kicked and screamed until eventually they took me back to the dormitory. The next day I received twenty lashes. I've never felt such pain. I think I fell unconscious after the first five. A week or so later the same thing happened. They came and got me in the dead of night, and the next day I received twenty strokes of the cat. And so it went on for six months or more—until I changed—until I did what they wanted me to. They gave me a job sowing sails after that and life was so much easier. What I never realised, was that I wasn't just being used as a form of entertainment. I was being assessed. When I was fifteen I was brought before the Master and Mistress, and they introduced me to a Mr. Frykberg, an old man from Hamburg, Germany who smelled of stale food and had long, bony fingers. He pushed and prodded at me as if I was a slab of meat, and after a long time of circling and touching me, he looked at the Mistress and shook his head. She was quite put out at his decision, and I was taken to another room while they talked. In the room there were four other girls all of my age, girls I'd known since the day I arrived, and it occurred to me they were all pretty, all well shaped. I knew then who Frykberg was; he was a buyer."

I listened intently, staring over to where she was sitting, her silhouette barely definable in the shrouding shadows that engulfed her almost completely. There was intelligence in her narrative that had been missing, or purposefully suppressed, during casual conversation. Gone were the profanities, her constant and obsessive compulsion to be seen as anything more than she was.

Contrary to belief workhouses, or poorhouses as they were originally known, did not expire with the death of Queen Victoria; in fact they outlived her by almost a century. In general, our knowledge of such places is confined only to fragments of what can be read in novels, such as the work of Dickens and his creation of Oliver Twist who, burning with hunger dared to step forward on the behest of the starving workhouse children and ask for more. It is probably the only image the majority posses, as few of the actual inmates ever wrote of their workhouse days. The stigma of being associated with such an establishment was just too painful and humiliating to recollect. In medieval England, the monasteries and convents felt it their Christian duty to offer help to the poor and needy, and despite Henry VIII's Dissolution of the Monasteries during the 1530s period, Queen Elizabeth I passed the Act for the Relief of the Poor in 1601, in which a small shelter in each individual parish should be put aside for the destitute—poorhouses. The Act continued for over two centuries, until the Industrial Revolution came to prominence in the late eighteenth century.

The philanthropic Act of Queen Elizabeth was ideal at the time it was passed through Parliament and probably for the following two hundred years, but what wasn't foreseen was the population explosion during the nineteenth century. Excluding Ireland there were only 10.5 million souls living in the British Isles in 1801, but fifty years later the number had doubled to 20 million, and by 1901 it had climbed to 45 million. With the Revolution came the influx of England's poor as well as foreigners to the city in search of work, and when work could not be found, they demanded succour the 1601 Act promised to provide. The fourfold explosion rendered the Act inadequate and the allocated shelters were subject to overcrowding and hunger. The overspill was inevitable, and soon London's streets were choked with homeless families and beggars whose only refuge was shop doorways and cellars. Under the old regime the government could not cope, and in 1834 the 1601 Act was amended to the Poor Law Amendment Act in which responsibility was removed from the individual parishes and given to the Union of Parishes who would have to provide larger houses, each to accommodate up to several hundred people. The object of the union controlling larger houses was to generate money by setting the homeless to work to meet the running costs subsidised by the local poor law rates, which therefore became known as working houses.

The working houses soon became synonymous with pain and suffering and were colloquially known as workhouses, where even the poorest of society would rather die than be part of. Certainly the intentions of the government were good, creating the foundations of a welfare state by feeding, clothing and housing the destitute, but their running were usually at the hands of tyrannical Masters and Mistresses, man and wife who, as well as enforcing the laws laid down by the Board of Guardians, also administered their own form of cruel punishment. The early poor houses were mixed, where men, women and children were allowed to cohabit, but the bigger workhouses were segregated and the inmates, or paupers, categorised according to their age and gender. The old were put with the old, the sick with the sick; men were taken from their wives to separate dormitories. All were given an ugly coarse uniform, usually made of hemp, and able bodied inmates were set to work. Children over the age of seven were removed from their mothers, and the buildings were designed to make it impossible for men, women or children to consort with one another. Food was meagre and punishment regarding the breaking of the rules was dealt with by birching, flogging, starving, and solitary confinement.

The workhouse was known as a place of last resort, an inflexible system infested with disease, insanity and death, and always ruled with an iron fist, whose employees were considered to be of the lowest order. Complaint and defiance was dealt with in the most brutal manner, and if someone died during or as a result of punishment being administered, few if any questions were asked; the Master and Mistress had the final word. Fallen women, especially those without family or the means to support her and her child, would inevitably end up in the workhouse. Once the child was born in the infirmary, the woman would be encouraged to leave and look for employment to help pay for the child's education and welfare, and if she could not find work outside she would have to return to the workhouse to pay back her debt to the Poor Rates. The child would be put up for adoption. As much as the workhouse is depicted as a hell on earth, anyone was free to leave proving they were not restrained by the courts or the guardians, but as few, if any, had little outside the workhouse walls but death to look forward to, they remained. Once outside the doors you were no longer the responsibility of the Board of Guardians, though boys were often apprenticed out to builders, chimney-sweeps, or like Oliver Twist, to funeral directors. Girls, however, were considered to be troublesome, incapable of generating money or even the necessary funds to look after themselves.

"So I walked out of the workhouse and straight into the thirties depression," Wendy explained, emerging from the gloom of the shadows. "There was only one direction to go in. For two years I tried to make my own way, but it could be dangerous. I've lost count of how many times I was beaten up, robbed, and left unconscious in some alleyway. And then I met Vinnie . . ."

"Vinnie?"

"Vincent Pierce; he's a pimp—my pimp, though few would say it to his face." she explained as she sat down by the shuttered window. "He was twenty-six then and had about a dozen girls. He found me somewhere to live, set up the clients, and sort of watched over me; it was a safer way to live—I've been with him ever since. He's a no-nonsense character and expects his pound of flesh; you don't fuck him about—not if you want to stay healthy, and if he ever found out I was talking to the likes of you I'd be in big trouble."

Her wary stare remained fixed on the door, as it probably had all the time she had been sitting in the shadows, but despite her occupation there was an innocence she clung onto as if it were the last remnant of her true self; the values the nuns had instilled into her at the workhouse—that she still believed in.

"Before he had his own girls, Vinnie was a scout; runaways, and girls coming to the city attracted by the bright lights and potential riches," she continued. "Some ended up in the clubs, others in the pornographic industry, and some as escorts. But his real job was to search out girls without family, or at least without family who were concerned for their welfare. They could be found most places—railway and coach stations, off the boats, workhouses, or from small villages all over England; either way, if they came to London Vinnie would find them. They were the ones they wanted; no family connections, less risk. They would be promised a new life abroad, their own houses, the possibility of marrying a rich, handsome man. When they found out their true purpose, it was too late."

I realised then why she was so insistent to explain her early life to me. Frykberg was a buyer of young girls and Vincent Pierce a scout, which could only add up to one thing, had I the capacity to believe that such shocking crimes were still being committed.

"Are we talking about slavery, here?" I asked.

She gave no reply and made no negative or positive gesture. She simply stared at me with lifeless eyes.

"Sex sells," she shrugged. "It also generates a lot of money for those in control. Your average pimp expects his girl to turn fifteen tricks a day. Say the going rate is twenty pounds a trick. That's three hundred pounds a day; nine thousand, three hundred a month; one hundred and eleven thousand, six hundred a year. Accumulate that by thirty girls and you've got three million, three hundred and forty eight thousand pounds. And that's just for your everyday, average girl like me. Think what the real pretty ones can command. Once abroad a girl will be sold for ten to twelve thousand, and if she's young the buyer will get a good fifteen years out of her."

"And then?" I dared to ask.

"Depends. Some are given their life back, but when that time comes they're usually too set in their ways to do anything else if, of course, they survive that long—many don't. Some try to escape the system but few make it. They're hunted down, returned to their masters or they conveniently vanish. Few are missed because technically they never existed. Little and often, that's the takers' motto. Nobody misses a few girls."

"No family, no connection."

Wendy nodded and smiled sadly.

"And Vinnie, your pimp is involved in this?" I asked.

She began to laugh, which in itself was refreshing because it was far removed from her image or, at least, the image she tried desperately to convey; that of a tough, streetwise girl totally devoid of emotion. The sound was contagious, like that of a child's; boundless and unrestricted by self awareness. However, I was still unsure why Wendy chose to familiarise me with the intricacies of the slave-trade, which as far as I was concerned had been consigned to the history books long ago and would never again raise its ugly head. Yet she spoke as if this disgusting enterprise was still alive and well. Suddenly there was a soft knock, and her sound of laughter suddenly fell silent. She moved stealthily to the door and pulled away the chair, and I heard her talking to the barman. After she closed the door she stared at me in horror, consumed by blind panic.

"Give me the money," she said. "Hurry!"

No sooner had I the chance to absorb her command, she was standing over me, pulling me out of my seat. "Give me the forty pounds!" As I reached in my pocket for my wallet, she undone my tie and unbuttoned four or five buttons of my shirt. "Take off your jacket." She snatched the money from my hand. "Jacket! Jacket!" she ordered. I did as she asked but without the slightest idea why. At the door she appraised me with frightened eyes and nodded her head. "Give me a few seconds and leave. Don't look left or right. Just go. Understand?" She disappeared leaving the door partly open. After a few moments I followed and headed straight for the entrance, but throughout the short duration, I felt eyes following me. The bald, tattooed man swung the door open and I stepped outside into the crisp, morning air, and once round the corner I ran as fast as I could.

It was barely 6 o'clock in the morning, and I found myself standing in front of old Sid's kiosk surveying the hundreds of photographs pinned to the outside of the folding doors. It had taken me a little under two hours to walk back along the Embankment, and I found myself constantly stopping to look across the river to unravel the events of last night. Clearly Wendy was frightened by the arrival of someone I never saw, but my guess was that it was her protector, Vincent Pierce. In an attempt to protect me, but moreover herself, she removed my necktie and unbuttoned my shirt. When I left, the observing eyes saw only one thing—a man who had just had sex with a prostitute in the snug bar, and she had the money to prove it which, no doubt, she handed straight over to her pimp. Her talk of slavery had me clutching at straws, backtracking through history to establish a time when the slave trade was terminated, and the conclusion I reached was that it never really was terminated. The plight of the Negro slaves is well documented in our history books, but little is mentioned about the white slave trade, and is practically non-existent regarding the sex trade. It is a subject without authority, a hinterland most authors shy away from because it lacks both substance and proof. In Africa parents who considered their child to be possessed by the devil, may decide to have it killed, and in the Islamic world, a girl speaking with anyone outside the family may also face death. These are acts that fall into the category of 'Honour Killings' and go unchallenged by the authorities and are free from prosecution. Barbaric, some might say, but Britain was not without its own form of cruel retribution. Even as late as the nineteenth century, parents regularly sold their children for sex or into domestic service. The great writer Dostoevsky came to London in 1863 and was horrified by what he witnessed at Haymarket. "*—I saw mothers who had brought their young daughters, girls who were still in their early teens, to be sold to me. Little girls of about twelve seize you by the hand and ask you to go home with them.*"

Blocks of tightly wrapped newspapers were stacked between the decorative archway and the side panelling of the kiosk, delivered prior to my arrival and awaiting the attention of the vendor, and at such an early hour few people were meandering around Aldwych. I studied the display of photographs intently. So dense were they that many overlapped the ones beneath. Some were old and faded, weather-beaten and dating back to the Blitz and the handwritten notes beneath were barely legible, the words bleeding into one another like a watercolour. But others had been placed there recently, the pictures crisp and clear, the notes beneath not yet decimated by the elements. "What brings you here so bright and early, Mr. James?" Old Sid had shuffled quietly up behind me and was inserting a key into the padlock that secured the doors of the kiosk. "I was early. Thought I'd wait for you to open up," I replied. I helped him peel back the doors and he pulled out his fishing chair from inside. "Early, you say? Can you distinguish between late and early? You look to me as if you've been up all night." The old man was withered with age, slightly stooped, and looked barely capable of lifting a lightweight pencil, but he heaved the bundles of newspapers from the side of the kiosk and dropped them in front of his chair with the stamina of a man half his age, and then taking a penknife from his pocket, proceeded to cut the string that bound them. "The Times, as usual, Mr. James?" he asked without looking up from his task.

"Sid, how long have these photographs been appearing on your kiosk?" I enquired, tapping the side of the structure with my hand.

He straightened and expressed a tired look.

"For as long as I can remember," he replied. "There were always a few photos dotted here and there, usually of kids, but never so many since war broke out, and during the Blitz the whole kiosk was plastered with them. I've never had the heart to take them down. They belong there—till they're found or someone can account for them. They're everywhere in the city; railway stations, hospitals, town halls, all over the place. I look at them whenever business is slow. I wonder what's happened to them and where they are now. Most are dead, I'd imagine."

He sat down on his fishing chair and began to assemble the newspapers into individual piles on the pavement. I half closed one of the doors and began to study the pictures once again.

"Have you ever noticed that so many of the photos are girls; specifically young girls?" I said.

Sid looked up at me and smiled sadly.

"You saw that too, eh? Sure, I've noticed."

"Does that not bother you? Doesn't it make you wonder?"

He got up and lifted a stack of papers onto the counter.

"Have you any kids, Mr. James?"

I shook my head. "No. No, I haven't."

"Well, I have six—three of each, and the boys come visit me every week. Come rain or shine, they're always there. They bring me tobacco or occasionally a half bottle of rum. Sometimes they give me money, usually on my birthday, but the girls . . . I'd think myself lucky if just one of them turned up at their old man's funeral. They're headstrong creatures, you see. They see something and they have to have it now. They're unconcerned with how much it costs, or the pain and suffering we have to go through to get it. It's not that they're spiteful—it's just the way they are—headstrong. That's why runaway girls outnumber runaway boys. They're not contented in the way the boys are. Boys don't go searching for a better life. They accept what they're given and make the best of it, but the girls always want more. Does it surprise me that there are more photographs of girls than boys on those doors? No, Mr. James, it doesn't."

He sat back down and set about organising his next stack of newspapers.

I stood next to the kiosk, the collar turned up on my jacket and my hands buried in my trouser pockets. I was tired and therefore susceptible to the morning chill and shivered in delayed spasms. Sid opened a small leather bag he was carrying when he arrived and pulled out a flask. "Soup?" he said. "It's hot." I thanked him and he poured the steaming broth into a tin cup and passed it to me, to which my stomach and I were eternally grateful. I watched him as he organised his newspapers into neat slabs on the counter and then empty a small bag of loose change onto a round tin tray. Until now I had never given the old man any consideration as to his past occupation. I knew him only to pass me a copy of The Times every morning and, on occasions, spend a few moments with idle chit-chat. What struck me about him was the intelligence that shone through his East End dialect and his powers of observation. The image he conveyed was that of a rickety old man clad in a brown duffle coat and wearing fingerless mittens, whose face resembled that of washed leather that somehow complimented his tobacco stained teeth, but I couldn't help but think there was a lot more to him.

"Have you always done this—selling newspapers?" I asked him.

"Not always," he smiled without looking at me. "I've done many things and been many things. I've not much to show for it, though. After the war selling newspapers was all I could get."

A gentleman sporting a dark overcoat and black bowler approached, utilizing his umbrella as a walking stick but in a sprightly fashion. Old Sid whipped out a copy of the Telegraph and held it out. "Good morning to you, Mr. Jefferies. How is everything at the bank?" he asked, handing over the newspaper and receiving a few coppers in one fluid motion. "Your millions are quite safe, Sidney," quipped the gentleman as he strolled onward towards the Strand with a spring in his step. The old man tossed the few pennies on the tin tray and took a brief look up and down the street for any approaching customers. Seeing nobody he leaned his back on the counter.

"I bought this kiosk from old Albert Clapp for seventy-five quid back in 1922, and he'd had this plot since 1897, so I've been here for twenty odd years. Mind you, if those Bosch bastards unload on us again, who knows how long I'll be here for?" he grinned slyly.

I smiled along with him and sipped at my hot soup.

"Tell me something, Sid. In the time you've been here, have you noticed an increase in missing people, specifically missing girls? I noticed that many of those photographs are recent."

A man wearing overalls and a donkey-jacket stopped in front of the newspaper stand and Sid flew into action. "The Daily Mirror, my old mate—tuppence. Gord bless ya." I smiled at the old man's congenial approach. His address purposefully differed from one class to another; even his annunciation changed from West to East End in the blink of an eye.

"Whatever are you working on, Mr. James?" he asked, throwing two pennies on the tray. "You seem to have got yourself an unhealthy appetite for young runaways."

"Just curious," I replied with a shrug.

He sat on his chair, his elbows resting on his knees, giving my question consideration and nodding every now and then whenever his conscience agreed with his thoughts.

"I suppose I've seen an increase since war broke out," he said. "Come to think of it, quite an increase. But that don't surprise me in the slightest.

A lot of these kids were sent to the country when the war began, not just by the authorities but by their own parents, to friends and relatives who were lucky enough to live out in the sticks. After London was bombed many returned to find their families dead, and they just drifted off—who knows to where?"

"But if their families are dead, who puts the photographs on your kiosk?"

"Grandparents, friends, distant relatives trying to pick up the pieces of their own lives; those who have lost their direct families. A girl came here the other day—Jenny I think her name was—all the way from Southampton and pinned a photo up there of a friend she had been evacuated with back in thirty-nine. Her friend came to London and was never seen again." The old man stood up with a groan and folded back one of the doors and studied the pictures. "Her!" he declared, pointing to a photograph of a young waiflike girl. "Emily Shaw," he added, reading the attached details. "Look at her—fifteen if she's a day. Do you know her friend has reported her missing at twenty-three local police stations? Why anyone would want to come to this Godforsaken city is beyond me. And you, Mr. James, should have stayed in the countryside after they blew your office to pieces. How are your new offices, by the way?"

I dropped the money for the newspaper onto the tray and handed back his tin cup.

"The offices are just fine, Sid. Thanks for the soup."

I was shaken awake by inconsiderate hands; rattling my body with such vigour there was a distinct possibility of my teeth and eyeballs shooting out of my face. Returning to my office I had fell asleep facedown on my desk, with a brain consumed by doubt and a liver saturated in whiskey. My eyelids weighed heavy from sleep-deprivation and my mouth tasted like rancid cheese, and my whole body ached as a result of the contorted positions my unconsciousness forced me to take up. My bleary vision focussed on Badger, the demon who had abruptly awakened me from my slumber with all the subtlety of a Gestapo interrogation. "Well?" he asked impatiently. I sat there for a while, watching his frame drift in and out of focus, until my eyes cleared and the aches and pains alerted me to the fact I was back in the real world. "Coffee?" I managed to mutter. Badger pointed to a cup in front of me and I immediately lifted it to my lips, feeling the caffeine jump-starting my senses and chasing away the fatigue.

"Did you meet her?" asked Badger.

I nodded slowly, the cup attached to my lips as if it were part of my anatomy.

"Well? What was she like?" he pursued.

"You mean, apart from being a mathematical genius?" I replied, lowering the beverage.

"What do you mean: a mathematical genius?"

"It doesn't matter. Our meeting was rudely interrupted sometime in the early hours. All in all it was a very expensive meeting—forty pounds."

Badger slumped back looking astonished.

"You paid her?"

"Had to—to make it appear convincing."

I gave a brief account for my hasty retreat from the waterfront drinking-den, from which I ran as fast as my legs could carry me and never slowed until I was halfway across Tower Bridge. The conditions during my retreat were much the same as my arrival; executed in pitch darkness and alone. When I reached Billingsgate Market by London Bridge, an insipid blue light began to highlight the buildings in shadows, and songbirds heralded a brand new day, and by the time I got to Mansion House the whole of the city was bathed in bright sunlight. There was something exhilarating about walking the streets of London at dawn, a feeling quite unique and rarely experienced by the stiff, shirted brigade, for they had only seen it choked with traffic and people, or blanketed with acres of umbrellas. I took the time to take in the architecture, the higgledy-piggledy lanes that had remained untouched since they were constructed hundreds of years ago, even the bombed out buildings of which little was left but the twisted and shattered infrastructures. With every step I tried to piece together what Wendy had told me or, at least, what she tried to tell me before she was interrupted by the arrival of her pimp. I sat on a bench in St. Paul's churchyard observing the street-cleaners and the labourers' armed with shovels and wheelbarrows en-route to the surrounding streets that even a year after the last spate of bombings were still scenes of total devastation. I attempted to anticipate Wendy's conclusion, and it wasn't until I reached old Sid's kiosk, that I believed I had achieved it.

-16-

The brain is a complex piece of machinery. It can evoke an image from a smell or a sound; it can make grotesque and sinister shapes form from shadows and darkness, and play reasoning false when intoxicated or in a fevered condition. Sobriety and good health brings clarity, and the ghouls recede back into their own dark world. My own paranoia was not a result of any of the aforementioned conditions, nor were they coincidental. Three days ago I passed a man standing opposite Temple Bar. There was nothing to set him out from the crowd or give me cause for concern; he was just a grey, suited man standing on the pavement outside the Royal Courts of Justice who happened to glance my way the moment I glanced at him. He looked away and moved to the curb and held out his arm as if he were hailing a cab. I continued my walk to the office, and when I reached the door I turned to see the very same man standing at the end of the street looking in my direction. What occurred to me, although not immediately, was the fact that he was seemingly hailing a cab going in the opposite direction. I saw him again later, passing through the crowd of patrons in the Cheshire Cheese, and disappear out the door. The next morning I thought I saw him standing at a newspaper kiosk at Farringdon Street Station, though he was in casual clothes and seemingly oblivious to my presence. On another occasion I was followed by a man from my office, his stature and walk far removed from the first man. He stayed close behind me as far as Chancery Lane where a third man took up the chase.

We were living in an age of hats; an American fashion-accessory that England felt compelled to follow. The three classes adopted their own choice of headwear befitting their status. The civil-servants opted for the bowler or Derby, as the Yanks called it, while the middle-classes sported Homburgs, Trilbys or Fedoras, and the lower-classes adorned their heads with flat caps, Wideawakes, Billycocks and Tam-O-Shanters. Not only were they a way to enhance ones overall appearance, but they were also a source of disguise, and my three covert companions continually exchanged them in the hope of remaining incognito. Knowing I was being followed left me feeling violated, but as the days passed I accepted their presence as much as my own shadow, yet there was a need to lose them at every opportunity. Sometimes whenever I left the office I would hop a passing bus, leaving my surreptitious stalkers scrambling for taxis, and once they secured their ride I would simply step off the bus and hop another going in the opposite direction. Sometimes whenever I walked into a shop, I would see one of them standing outside and I would make my getaway out the back, leaving him, hopefully during a downpour, waiting for my re-emergence. On one rainy afternoon I allowed two of them to pursue me as far as Trafalgar Square, but easily lost them through the labyrinth of alleyways I had come to know so well.

-17-

The threats of that wretched woman Eddowes hung over us like a curse, and Pip was decidedly nervous about the possible consequences of our past deeds. I, too, was at my wits end, but had resigned myself to silencing the interfering witch once and for all, but my friend was yet to be convinced. "We have no choice, Pip," I said as I raised my drink to my lips. "That greedy whore will lead us straight to the gallows otherwise," I added. Pip turned his face away as if I were personally responsible for the whole untidy affair, and I knew now my powers of persuasion were desperately needed if we were to remain at liberty. "Ever seen a man hanged, Pip? It's not a sight for the faint hearted. My father saw one outside Newgate once; he said he was nearly sick. Contrary to belief it is not a quick death. It is slow and excruciating, and once that trap drops you are left suspended in mid air, kicking like a man possessed for solid ground, until every drop of life is squeezed from your body. The tongue protrudes from the mouth and the lips turn blue. It is not way for a man to die. My father said that the hangman swings on the legs to accelerate death and after, the crowds surge forward and rip the clothing from the corpse and drag it away." Pip gave me one of his knowing looks. "That's all stuff-and-nonsense," he declared. "That may have been the case a long time ago, but since the abolition of public hangings, they are conducted in a civilised manner, and the length of rope is gauged by the weight, size and physical stature of the condemned prisoner, ensuring instant death." I smiled as he enthralled me with his vast knowledge. "You're nobodies fool, Pip; least of all mine. I should know better than try and dupe you, especially in light of your unfathomable wisdom concerning crime and punishment. But consider this: painless or not, we will face the executioner if something isn't done about that conniving woman."

It was 8 o'clock, or thereabouts, when Pip and I left the public house, but as we struck off in the direction of Whitechapel, we heard a commotion, and seemingly the noise, and indeed the activity, emanated from a crowd gathered on the pavement in Aldgate High Street. We closed nearer on the gathering who were hooting with laughter and applauding some unseen form of entertainment, and as two burly policemen waded in through the mob only to emerge moments later with the blackmailing Gorgon we had encountered earlier, my friend and I gasped in unison. Eddowes, it appeared, was so drunk she could hardly stand, and prior to the arrival of the two constables, she was laying on the pavement behaving like only drunken women can. "She'll do for us this time," said Pip, backing into a shadowy doorway. "She'll tell the police everything," he added. I observed the scene with an air of undue concern as the vamp was marched away. "You're being paranoid, my friend," I returned. "At present the women is drunk and incapable of talking, let alone capable of telling tales of murderers; besides who would believe her in her present condition? It's her inevitable state of sobriety we have to fear, when her words are fluent and her brain is no longer pickled. The arresting officers are City policemen and the closest police station is Bishopsgate. Therefore I suggest we give chase and await the release of our Nemesis, and once she is free of her shackles we shall strike." We both knew that arrested drunkards were usually allowed three to four hours before being released; they were rarely kept till morning, as the cell space was required for the increasing influx of drunks at throwing out time.

Pip and I took up position in Catherine Wheel Alley, a straight and narrow passage running from Bishopsgate and into Middlesex Street, and a mere twenty feet away from the police station. My friend was agitated, pacing up and down the alleyway while I kept watch on the police station entrance, and when his incessant striding back and forth began to press on my last nerve, I snapped my head about. "Could you please refrain from your continuous meanderings! Now is the time to be impassive, dispassionate, not behaving like a deserter about to face a firing squad." There was no response; not even a glance in my direction. I simply watched him move up and down, up and down, disappearing into darkness and then emerging into the meagre light of the streetlamp that barely touched the entrance of the alley. Finally he came to a stop. "And how do you plan to dispatch her?" he asked. "We," I emphasised, "will dispatch her the way we have the others; in the manner the public have come to expect of Jack the Ripper." Pip lacked any enthusiasm for our quest, sighed and walked back down the dark passage. I took another peek into the quiet street and receded back into the shadows. My friend was on his return cycle. "Admittedly this woman is cause for concern, but couldn't we dispense with the disembowelment process and just kill her?" he said, thoughtfully. I glowered at him in dismay. "And make it look like a common murder?" I said. "We have spent the late afternoon and early evening in her company, with witnesses and people who know for certain we are medical students. No, my friend, her death must appear to be the act of a madman. You above all people should recognise that. You are the expert on crime, not I." Again Pip anxiously resumed his pacing while I watched for any activity at the police station doors, and on his return he tapped me on the shoulder. "And how do you propose to kill her?" he asked. I was fast running out of patience for my infuriating associate and scowled hard at him. "Don't test me, Pip," I spat angrily. "My tolerance is at a low ebb at present, and you, my friend, are hindering rather than helping our dire predicament. You can be insufferable at times!" Pip smiled, shook his head and retaliated. "And you may wish to revise your strategy the next time you consider expediting your next crime. There is major flaw in your plan," he said. I sighed impatiently and turned to face him. "Which is?" He leaned his back against the wall and calmly surveyed the few pedestrians milling up and down the dark street. "The weapon; we don't have one," he replied.

Under normal circumstances I would have taken full responsibility for the oversight, but as Pip and I were a duo, and in a predicament neither of us could have foreseen, I was willing only to accept half. Therefore, in order to free ourselves from the spell of the old crone, Pip set off back to our lodgings to collect the weapon while I waited out the time in the chilly, dark passage.

It was arranged I would meet with him at the Aldgate memorial, and under no circumstances should he leave without seeing me. And so, in the cold and gloom, and the constant pounding of my beating heart, and the cold sweat forming on my brow, I idled in the dank and smelly passage for what seemed an age. At 1 o'clock in the morning, almost to the dot, I heard a woman's voice say, "Goodnight, old cock," and gingerly pushed my head out to see the blackmailing whore tottering away from the station doors. She paused at the curb unsure of which direction to take. I gathered my composure and nonchalantly stepped out onto the pavement. "Well—upon my word, if it isn't . . .?" I feigned absentmindedness. "Kate," she said, observing me through one beady eye and swaying like a fern in a light breeze. "Of course, of course!" I cried. "And how is your sister? In good spirits, I hope." She stumbled slightly and held my arm to steady herself, and then she took a step back and appraised me curiously. "You speak funny," she said. I threw out my hands and expressed the suggestion of a bow. "That is because I speak from the heart, madam. That is because I regard you as a friend—someone I would be proud to be seen with in any drinking establishment." She eyed me suspiciously and then bobbed her head left and right to see behind me. "Talking of which, where is your friend?" she slurred. "My colleague is setting the drinks on the bar as we speak, so I must bid you a goodnight and be on my way back to Aldgate. You may, if you wish, care to accompany me." I replied, stepping off the curb as if it were my intention of leaving her stranded. Once across to the other side she called after me. "Then I will."

She was still befuddled with alcohol, still lacking coordination, still speaking with great authority on subjects she knew nothing of, but still suspicious of my presence. She told me about her earlier apprehension and of her unjust confinement by the City police, bitterly spitting their colloquial name with colourful parlance, "Fuckin' Runners!" and damning the day such an organisation was put together. "So—it was just by chance you happened by the moment I was released?" she said. "Seems unlikely," she added sceptically. I laced my arm through hers and inhaled her perfume of filth and cheap gin. "My dear woman, my occupation does not afford me the luxury of uninterrupted recreation. I was called to attend a woman whose child was as close to death as it could be, but as are the wonders of modern medicine I was able to revive her and put her back on the path of the living," I returned confidently. She took in everything I said and interpreted every spoken lie as fact, until she believed me to be everything I claimed to be, and by the time we reached Camomile Street, all doubt as to my dubious character had gone. As we closed on Aldgate my beating heart returned with a vengeance, but then almost ground to a halt when Pip was nowhere in sight. It was now 1.18, and I purposefully slowed at the corner of Leadenhall Street, gazing over at St. Botolph's Church. As usual there was a thin trail of prostitutes, all circling the church in a clockwise direction. This continuous movement prevented the police from arresting them for soliciting. Either way Pip was absent, and his earlier reluctance to take part was giving me cause for concern. "And what pub is your friend in? Everywhere will be closing now," said the evil Harridan. I was preoccupied, looking towards Mansell Street, the Minories and back up Houndsditch, but he was nowhere to be seen. "Take heart, my dear lady. We are members of a private club specifically attached to the London Hospital; an establishment where we can imbibe as much alcohol as we please until we have had our fill—and for free."

It was with a great sense of relief that I saw my gangly associate approach from the direction of Aldgate High Street, but he stopped at the curb-side and beckoned me over with a surreptitious motion of his hand. I left the deceitful witch on the corner of Duke's Place, assuring I would return momentarily, and thereafter crossed the road to my alarmed friend. "Did you get the knife?" I hissed at him. Pip looked exceedingly troubled, took my arm and led me beneath the shadow of a dark awning. "A woman has been killed in Berner Street," he stated. "There were people running everywhere, up and down the street and calling for the police. Her throat was cut." I glared at him in dismay. Women being murdered in the Whitechapel district, or men come to that, was a common occurrence, and I conveyed a look of surprise rather than empathy. "So—a woman has been killed in Berner Street. Will you concentrate on the job at hand?" Pip shook his head. "They say it's the work of Jack the Ripper," he said. I looked at him astounded. "But how, Pip?" I questioned. "We have neither been near or by Berner Street." My friend agreed with a nod and reiterated the accusation. "We? Are they saying that Jack the Ripper is responsible?" I said. Pip nodded again. I looked back across the street, to the greedy whore engaging in conversation with a stranger, and then looked back to my companion. "Just a cut throat?" I said as if I were personally affronted. "That is what I heard; outside the International Workingmen's Educational Club," he replied. I considered the probability that Jack the Ripper, the diabolical monster Pip and I created, would resort to dispatching a victim with nothing more than a cut throat, and the more I considered the possibility, the more I was enraged by the association of such a feeble act. "How on earth could they reach such a conclusion, Pip? Why, it's outrageous! It is nothing less than a slap in the face of the creators, a travesty! I'll not hear of it. How dare they say such things? Have they no vision? Have they no imagination? Jack the Ripper ascends from the very bowels of hell to take revenge on these diseased parasites, and he leaves them completely decimated. That is his mark, Pip. That is how we distinguish him from your garden variety murderer. Cut throat indeed! It's preposterous!" I was incensed and paced away a few steps. What occurred to me then was the opportunity to turn this demeaning character assassination to our advantage. "If the police are busying themselves in and about Berner Street with a wound that amounts to little more than a shaving nick, then we shall show the world his true wrath. We'll leave these benighted imbeciles in no doubt of Jack's true potential. We'll kill two in one night."

As apprehensive as Pip was, he realised as well as I that the woman Eddowes had to die and she had to die tonight. "I'll lead her into Mitre Square. Be waiting, Pip, in the southern corner," I ordered. We parted, and I crossed back over the road the moment the stranger disengaged himself from the hag and strolled off. "My apologies for the delay;" I said, "someone you know?" I added, looking towards the stranger who was heading towards Houndsditch. She shook her head. "Just someone asking for directions," she replied. "I see," I said, knowing she was lying and that the stranger took her for exactly what she really was. "Then let us be off to Lime Street, to the drinking club." We moved straight into Church Passage, a long, arched thoroughfare that led into Mitre Square. Greed induced her to walk by my side like an obedient dog and not question the short-cut through the dark and secluded square. There was but one pathetic light, a wall-lamp above the archway of the passage, which at best threw out a feeble, yellow mantle below the immediate area. Another streetlamp was located in Mitre Street, on the corner to the entrance into the square, which because of the obstructing three-storey houses facing the street, plunged the south-side into absolute blackness. Ostensibly Mitre Square was nothing more than a loading depot, serving the warehouses that took up the remaining three sides, with an alternative route out into James Square and King Street. Once through Church Passage we were enveloped by almost complete darkness, heading towards the light that marked the opening into Mitre Street. "So what's it like being a doctor?" she asked. I took a brief look around me, and before she could utter another word, I clamped my left hand across her mouth and my right arm across her neck, dragging her towards the blackest corner of the yard.

Pip emerged from the inky darkness, and as I lay our new victim on the pavement behind the terrace of houses, I took the knife from his hand. "You must hurry," he warned. "This is a well known haunt for prostitutes, and beat constables enter the square every ten minutes." I tore open her black jacket and plunged the weapon into her chest, dragging it down her torso and down to the vagina, splitting her clothes and apron in half. In moments my eyes adjusted to the meagre light, and I worked vigorously and without abatement, inflicting cuts and stab wounds to her stomach and thighs, opening her abdomen and removing the womb. To hasten the process, Pip knelt by my side, plunging his white hands into the bloody cavity of her stomach. And my masterpiece was to remove her kidney through the stomach. "Enough! We're out of time!" Pip snapped. I continued, too preoccupied to hear the warning cries of my lookout. In just four minutes I had disassembled the treacherous whore, her body parts scattered all about her, and now I started to disfigure her face. Pip gaped in absolute horror as I placed the blade beneath her nose and pushed the knife upwards. "What in God's name are you doing?" he shrilled. I whittled at her face like an artist. "The curiosity of this fishwife has been her undoing, so I'm cutting her nose off . . . to spite her face." A light started to bob and weave towards us in Church Passage; a light that could only belong to a beat constable. I took half her filthy apron and wrapped it around the knife. Pip seized my shoulder and pulled me to my feet, dragging me across the square to the entrance into James Square, and in a moment we were crossing the main street of Bevis Marks and dissolving into the bleak East End backstreets.

We moved stealthily down Stoney Lane and into Harrow Alley, on the edge of Middlesex Street and in the heart of Spitalfields. Beneath the gaslight on the corner of Cobb Street, Pip looked me up and down for the first time, his eyes wide and unblinking; his mouth agape. "You're drenched in blood!" he stated. It was an inevitable outcome, and we decided to make our way home through the quieter and unlit streets running parallel with Whitechapel High Street, but we did however overlook the power of our own creation. In the silence of the early hours the sound of police whistles carried on the breeze from all directions, as if armies of police personnel were advancing into the East End from every point on the compass, and in Goulston Street, at junction of Wentworth Street, officers on foot with torches flashing moved towards the city boundary. Obviously our victim had been found, and now Pip and I appeared hemmed in by the authority searching out Jack the Ripper. We took refuge in a Goulston Street block of apartments, specifically occupied by Jews. We looked on as the police, five, six, sometimes a dozen handed, pass the junction and head towards Mitre Square. On the first floor landing we waited out the time until it was safe to leave. My companion, as usual, was stressed, but I sat cross-legged on the landing floor, as calm as I could be given the circumstances. "Where did you say that woman was killed in Berner Street?" I asked. Pip was at the entrance, feverishly staring out at the activity. "What? Where was what?" he returned. "Berner Street? Where was the victim found?" I asked again. "The club . . ." he stammered, ". . . the International Workingmen's Educational Club. Why?" I smiled and took the stick of chalk from my pocket given to me earlier by my tutor. "A Jewish concern, if I'm not mistaken," Pip was still on the lookout, like a faithful dog. "Jewish. Yes, probably. I think so . . . most likely Jewish," he mumbled. I began to write on the black tiled wall in small writing: 'The juwes are the men that will not be blamed for nothing', removed the knife from its covering, and tossed the remnants of the apron beneath my scrawl. I then accompanied my friend at the entrance—to look out at a vacant, dark street devoid of people. "Seize the moment, Pip. The situation can only get worse if we dawdle," I urged.

Reading of the total obliteration of Catharine Eddowes was, to say the least, the straw that broke the camel's back. On the closing of that particular chapter I wanted nothing more but to swear out a warrant for

Jonathan Sandpiper's arrest, but first I had to consider the consequences. I needed the advice of a wiser man; someone I knew I could trust without question.

There is a smallholding on the outskirts of my town—a farm by definition, situated down in a hollow and shielded by trees, with a barn and outhouses and squared enclosures surrounded by rickety fences that once contained livestock. It rose from the ground hundreds of years ago along with the church, when it was just a landscape of fields and little else. The main-house or cottage as it would now be categorised, was simple by design, made beautiful by its slow decay, weather-beaten on the south-side and characterised by blistered paint and loose roof-slates that had lost their purchase and had collected in the gutters. It was accessible from the north-end of the town, down a winding, narrow lane leading off the main road flanked by heavy forest, where several narrower lanes spurred off to other farms. I parked my car in a lay-by on the main road and approached on foot, along the bridle path, clamouring over the stile before the stone bridge that spanned the weir, across the hill that looked down on my local The Dog and Duck, and down a stony path. The morning was crisp and fresh, and the blue sky was corrupted only by a few inoffensive white clouds. In the distance the local church bells tolled to ten and then fell silent. At the perimeter I was greeted by an inquisitive Border collie who barked several times before consigning itself to being my friend for life, walking obediently by my side and nudging my hand with his nose. As I closed on the house with a small parcel tucked under my arm, the familiar figure of Judge Newland appeared, clad in Wellington boots and a heavy tweed coat. He stopped on recognising me, standing on the muddy path with his hands on his hips and smiling broadly. "We have visitors, Daisy," he said as he fussed over the dog that circled him rapidly and then sat beside him.

"Sorry to call unannounced . . ." I began.

"You're apologising to an old man who never sees anyone?" he said. "I won't hear of it. Come inside and I'll have Martha make tea."

A lopped porch with a broken window centred the house and the judge removed his boots, motioning me with a smile to do the same.

"Very house-proud is Martha," he whispered. Entering the house was like stepping back in time, to an age when Queen Victoria ruled the Empire. An old woman with silver hair and a walking-stick appeared unsteadily at the end of the hallway, her head bobbing up and down to see who was standing behind her husband. "Who is it? Who is with you?" The judge hurried towards her, putting his arm around her shoulder and then pointed towards me. "That is Michael James, a friend of mine. He lives in the village," he explained softly. "Would you make us some tea, Martha? Could you do that for me?" She stared at me but her eyes were vacant, and as I was about to speak the judge shook his head. Clearly there was something wrong with her apart from the need to use a walking stick, for her husband spoke to her as if she were a child; slow and deliberate. She appraised me intently but then her eyes began to wander the gloomy hall as if she didn't know where she was. "Martha, Michael and I will go to the study. Can you bring the tea there?" After a long pause she nodded and looked back at me; the traces of a smile forming on her lips. "I'm very pleased to meet you, Mrs. Newland." She shuffled away through an adjacent doorway.

The judge watched her with a sad smile and then turned to me. "To the study."

He led the way, slightly unsteady on his feet and trailing his hand along the wall in front of him, guiding me down a passage towards the rear of the house. "Martha is unwell," he said, over his shoulder. "The cells of her brain are deteriorating, and every year at a faster rate. She has reverted almost back to a child. Strangers scare her, but she means no harm."

I realised then why such a distinguished person, and one who above everyone else in the town had an image to convey, had allowed his home to fall into such a sad state of disrepair; builders would be considered strangers.

"I noticed that you referred to the town as a village," I said, not wishing to delve deeper into his wife's mental condition.

At the end of the passage we reached a door that he swung open.

"Michael, the last time my wife went out, this town *was* a village."

We were now standing in a room that spanned the entire width of the house and was flooded with natural light—unlike the main-house which was grey and dull, and contained the remnants of a bygone age; gas-lights for example that, no doubt were still in perfect working order. I raised my eyes to the pitched ceiling in which were cut two large squares of wired glass, tainted by moss but nevertheless just as effective as when they were new. The surrounding walls were a mass of books on sagging shelves, and on the top of the vertical books were horizontal books crammed between the shelves above. On the floor and around the skirting were more books, stacked in flat piles so high they were in danger of toppling over. A desk sat beneath a window, again cluttered with mounds of books, and an easy chair stood off-centre of the room on a large rug. Judge Newland edged his way around the room, his hand gently gliding along a shelf, leading him like a guide rope toward his desk. "Please, Michael, take a seat," he said. I sunk into the easy chair and the old man, with an aching moan, eased himself into his seat behind the desk. My head was swirling around, eyes squinting at the spines of the books, the titles of which were prominent or faded, or damaged making the words ineligible; Science, Newton, Einstein, Dickens, Tolstoy, The Bible—every conceivable subject known to man.

"My God, have you read all these? There are thousands."

The judge raised his eyebrows and smiled.

"I had this room built on about twenty years ago—before I retired, before I lost Martha to the shadows. A man needs a haven, doesn't he? It keeps me sane."

I agreed with a nod.

"So," he said, resting forward on his elbows, "what brings you to see me? Is it the Henderson case—your wayward spouse? Your absence has not gone unnoticed."

I found myself staring at the patterns in the rug, wringing my hands nervously and debating whether to speak or leave. I heard the creak of the old man's chair, and when I lifted my eyes he had reclined, arms folded and staring down his nose at me.

"Michael. You once asked me if you could trust me and my answer was 'yes.' Whatever you say will go no further than these four walls. You have my word."

I nodded again and straightened myself, placing my hands on the arms of the chair to contain my fidgeting. Judge Newland smiled, sighing gently under his breath, waiting with the patience of a saint. My stare wandered to the window, to the grassy inclines layered in a gossamer mist being slowly evaporated by the sun's rays, the blades of grass and delicate flowers twinkling with droplets of morning dew.

"Jack the Ripper," I said, suddenly.

The old man looked unprepared, batting his eyes at me as if his hearing had played him false. "Jack the Ripper?" he echoed. "The same Jack the Ripper who terrorised the East End in the autumn of 1888?"

I nodded.

"Well, I remember the event. Can't say I have any books on the subject," he said as he surveyed the shelves around him.

"You remember it?"

He nodded thoughtfully. "Why, yes. Let me see, I'm seventy-three next birthday, God willing, so I would have been somewhere about . . . nineteen. I was on the circuit then; a young whippersnapper learning his trade, presiding in a dingy annex near Holborn Viaduct, studying for all I was worth; a strange topic, Michael."

I wanted to elaborate but I simply stared back in silence.

"I know only that he, or they, murdered between five and ten women and the killings suddenly stopped," he continued.

"They?" I said.

"Expert opinion differs from one author to another, and some believe it unlikely that the killer worked alone. The M.O. or modus operandi, method of operation, call it what you will, varies from one victim to another; then, of course, there were the witnesses of whom it must be said were extremely unreliable. The whole episode was and still is shrouded in mystery. I wouldn't imagine for one minute he's still alive so the likelihood that he requires your services is out of the question. Therefore there must be another purpose for your visit."

I slowly shook my head. "What if I were to say I knew the identity of the killer?"

"What if you were?" the judge shrugged. "The world and his wife have investigated that story to death. Is this really the reason you came here?"

I hesitated while his aged eyes studied my face intently.

"My father recently died . . ." I began.

"A brilliant mind. I have his books," intercepted the judge as he rose, running his eyes down the sagging shelves.

"On his death he bequeathed to me a book he had written . . ."

"He wrote many books, Michael, to which I am proud to say I purchased," he intercepted again.

"Not a publication, Judge Newland, a handwritten confession—a declaration of guilt; a no-holds barred account of how he murdered four East End prostitutes when he was a student at the London Hospital in 1888."

The old man's eyes widened and he pushed himself back in his seat as if to pull me into sharper focus.

"Your father was Jack the Ripper—is that what you're saying?" he said warily.

I nodded assertively.

He smiled.

"Have the mindless patrons of The Dog and Duck put you up to this, Michael, as a form of ridicule for my desire to remain detached from them?"

"No, sir."

He surveyed me curiously, slowly shaking his head from side to side.

"Good God, man, you're serious!" he gasped.

"Absolutely."

His look of surprise never faltered, and his searching wide eyes stared back at me.

"If what you say is true, why tell me?" he asked.

I hesitated, folding my arms and gazing down at the rug.

"He didn't work alone. He had an accomplice."

Judge Newland observed me in silence, so as not to distract me from the subject I was so reluctant to admit.

"The accomplice; he's still alive," I said, keeping my eyes downcast.

"And you know this for certain?"

"He was at my father's funeral, but I'd never met him before. Neither had my father ever mentioned his name."

"And you're not about to tell me his name, are you?"

I raised my eyes. "No."

I imagined that as a judge he must have presided over some extraordinary cases in his time and been confronted with a catalogue of peculiar people, because my admission did not seem to phase him. If anything it was the association of such an infamous murderer that appeared to take the wind out of his sails.

"Then the accomplice is a man of standing, much like your father, something of an icon amongst his own kind. Am I correct, Michael? Is that why you insist he should remain anonymous?"

I gestured with a faint nod.

For a while the judge sat there without saying a word and hardly moving a muscle, as if he needed time to collate all I had said before sharing his words of wisdom.

"And what of you, Michael? How has this knowledge affected you?" he said. "Or need I ask? It's on the lips of all these country bumpkins that you have flown the nest, and your wife has since been seen on the arm of Billy Fletcher. Their secret is out, and now they parade around the town as a happy couple in the hope of being accepted as you once were—when you were the happy couple. Such treachery can do little for a man's dignity. And this mind-boggling confession gives reason why you are so far out of your depth, doesn't it? As a child may disassemble his favourite mechanical toy, you're eager to find out how it works—what makes a killer a killer; how a distinguished man such as your father evolved from a monster. It's eating away at you, and will continue to do so until it destroys you completely. This is the price we pay for shouldering the burden of others. Secrets cease to be secrets once they are divulged. How did it make you feel when you read his words, Michael?"

"Sick. Ashamed."

He agreed with a slow nod, but his eyes now were focused on the parcel sat on my lap.

"Is that it? Is that your father's confession?" he asked, holding his hand out. "May I?"

I passed it over and he placed it on his desk, squaring it before him.

"Having this with you leads me to believe it is for my benefit; that you want me to read it. You're quite certain are you, Michael? Reading this could I not discover the identity of the surviving assassin?"

The book, as much as I had read, only referred to Jonathan Sandpiper as Pip. I believed his identity would remain undiscovered. I said nothing and the judge slowly began to unfurl the brown paper, pausing occasionally to register my approval. Eventually he gazed at the leather-bound ledger before him as if it was of the greatest importance, gently gliding his fingertips over the embossed cover. But there he paused, to recline in his chair and observe me cautiously.

"I will read this, Michael, if that is what you want," he said. "But please don't ask me to stand judge and jury over your father's accomplice. These are your father's words—not his. The best I can do is guide you."

"I understand," I agreed.

He smiled sympathetically and leaned forward.

"You curse the day you saw this book, don't you?" he said. "But I cannot and will not proffer an opinion on such a revered man as your father. Some actions just cannot be explained. I remember the case of Ricardo Kaminski; the strangest event I have ever encountered."

Ricardo Kaminski was born in Gdansk, Poland in 1878. His father was a cabinet-maker of some repute who also furnished the local funeral director with coffins as a sideline, and as Ricardo was the youngest of six children his mother had a fulltime occupation. However, she also had a sideline, and three nights a week she held séances. She was said to possess special powers and over the years, like her husband, she too gained a reputation. People traveled as far away as Warsaw and Kaliningrad to attend the meetings, hoping to make contact with loved ones who had passed away years before; few left disappointed. Those who knew her referred to her as The Witch of Gdansk; a woman blessed with exquisite beauty that possessed the gift to speak with those on the other side. It wasn't a quality she spoke of lightly, and especially not in front of strangers. By day she was simply a mother who took her children to school and prepared her husband's evening meal, and everyone she met would talk to her and enquire as to the condition of her problematic son. Ricardo was a sickly child, weak and constantly in a state of melancholy, who was prone to bursting into tears for no apparent reason and was sometimes found in the most peculiar of places in the dead of night. He would sleepwalk, not just in the house or even around the immediate neighbourhood, but occasionally almost two miles away at his father's workshop where he would be found sleeping in a newly made coffin. Most blamed his condition on his upbringing and would remark that it was an unhealthy environment to raise children by day when their mother was trying to raise the dead by night.

In an attempt to rid her son of his demons, Ricardo's mother taught him everything she knew about the afterlife. "The world in which we live is full of openings that lead us to another world beyond," she told him. "And these openings may not present themselves in the way we might expect. There are no doors, no gateways, no pits or pathways that can take you there. They may reveal themselves in the most strangest of guises, in a treasure, in an artefact that's been buried for a thousand years, or maybe in the eyes of a complete stranger. Yes, Ricardo, in the form of a human being. We call them windows. And I am a window. The strongest are always women. We are born with the capacity and the faith to see and converse with those who have gone before us; who have forged a life to which we will continue until we die, making way for the next generation—a perpetual cycle." By degrees Ricardo grew stronger, and on leaving school joined his father in his workshop to learn the trades of a carpenter. In his spare time he made small, deteriorative boxes with seamless wooden inlay from the surplus remnants, of which he gave away as gifts to the locals and were used as jewellery-boxes or containers for precious heirlooms, but as he honed his craft he began to incorporate secret drawers and false bottoms into the tiny boxes. He applied the same idea to larger objects, and a perfectly ordinary looking cabinet or wardrobe was fashioned with a multitude of pop-out boxes, hidden compartments and detachable back panels. It was the beginning of Ricardo's obsession with magic, but moreover, of all that was instilled into him by his mother—the afterlife.

He learned the fundamentals of magic, of presenting himself on stage with a cabinet of his own design, in which he would choose a member of the audience and after placing them inside the wooden structure, would make them disappear. But it was in the year of 1900 that he made his greatest discovery. Ricardo had joined a travelling circus that took him across Europe and to the tip of Algeria, and it was while he was in Marrakech, searching the shops for new exotic props to use in his act, that he came across The Magic Mirror. It stood nearly seven feet high and three feet wide, and was supported on a stand hinged either side and could be turned to various degrees or fully up and over.

The mirror frame, he was told, was made from smelted down gold artefacts looted from the Valley of the Kings by grave robbers, and the mirror emitted a powerful blue light when called upon. Ricardo was given a demonstration. The shopkeeper, a decrepit old man who could barely walk unaided, read from an aged book in Arabic phrases, and the glass misted over with a gossamer film of fog almost tangible. He watched a young shop-boy walk into the mirror and vanish in a swirl of mist—a mere uneducated child unable to speak any language but his own native tongue. When the smog evaporated and the dazzling blue light began to fade, Ricardo could see him on the other side. The old shopkeeper smiled at Ricardo's astonishment. Sceptically the magician approached the mirror and began to circle it, stopping behind and searching out velvet cloaks, screens or trap doors in which the boy may have disappeared. The ground beneath him was solid brick and the area behind the mirror was empty. He looked to the ceiling, to the walls, even behind the old shopkeeper in case he was concealing the source of the blue light; he found nothing. He stood before the mirror, tapping its face gently with the knuckle of his index finger, and then he ran his hands all around the golden frame for a mechanism that may cause the mirror to retract into its frame; enough to allow a small child to pass through. This was no trick.

From behind the glass the boy looked patently back, but it wasn't the child so much that fascinated Ricardo, but what was behind him. Lush, green fields and mountain waterfalls occupied the backdrop and not the brick interior of the storeroom it should have reflected. The old shopkeeper touched his mouth and gestured to the magician to speak to the child. Ricardo stood before the mirror, his own image absent, and searched for something to say. "Where-are-you?" he asked slowly and precisely, emphasising every word as if the boy were able to lip-read. "I am where I belong. I am in the world I created; the world I've never seen," replied the child. The boy, if he were genuine, was little more than eleven years old; too young and too poor to have escaped the arid landscape in which he lived, yet he spoke in perfect English without accent. Ricardo turned to the shopkeeper for an explanation, but the old man smiled and gestured towards the mirror once again. When the magician looked the boy was now a young man in his mid-twenties, wearing a fine suit of clothes and standing before a grand building. The scenery around him had changed to a bustling city commercial centre that Ricardo recognised at once—Casablanca. "What are you now?" the magician enquired nervously. The young man smiled. "I am employed by a prestigious shipping company engaged in the export of phosphates and manganese. My future is secure." The magician took in the landscape with a frightened wonder. He could see horseless carriages passing back and forth, noisy and clattering, erratic in their manoeuvres and seemingly uncontrollable. Ricardo had seen an automobile once, but now the sight of so many unnerved him. "What year is it?" he asked. "1917," returned the young man.

The shopkeeper bowed his head and read an Islamic verse from the sacred book, and the surface of the mirror began to frost over as if it had been transported into the fiercest of winters. The magician observed as the glass crystallised into a misty ice, and again he turned to the shopkeeper. His words echoed around the room like an incantation as the blinding blue light seeped out between the mirror and the frame, shooting out beams of concentrated energy, until the inanimate object began to shake ferociously and the floor beneath trembled, and suddenly the light stopped and a heavy sheet of ice slid from the mirror and exploded on the floor. Ricardo thought he would die and backed away as far as the small room would allow, but the ancient shopkeeper simply smiled and pointed a bony finger at the dormant object. An old man sat outside a stately home where behind, the bluest sea met the descending cliffs that stretched out to miles of white sand while the waters roamed in and retracted back into their depths. "I am at one with life and those who surround me; my family and friends. I have done my level best to be what God permits me to be; what he expects me to be. I have not failed my friends. I have not failed those who accept me as a power or as an equal. I am I. I am all I hoped I would be." Ricardo recognised the old man as the young boy; a successful man, a wealthy man, a devoted husband and a generous father." He looked to the shopkeeper. "These are not visions of what will be," he shouted. "These are the dreams and the hopes and the aspirations of a mere child, all of which proves nothing. It isn't real!"

The shopkeeper silently approached the mirror and began to recite a passage from the book, and then he held out his hand. Ricardo watched in awe as the boy emerged back through the mirror and rush straight into the comforting arms of the old man. The magician hurried to the mirror, his hands groping blindly at the back panel and the stone floor beneath, searching in vein to the key of the deception, clawing at the ground like an animal until his fingers began to bleed. The old man observed him with a wistful smile, his eyes glistening and brimming with a knowledge the magician could not begin to fathom. "It's here!" said Ricardo. "It has to be a trick! There's never been magic without it." The old man sat down and placed the small boy on his lap, gently stroking his black hair as if to comfort him after his ordeal. Ricardo scrambled to his feet and was suddenly upon the child, shaking him ferociously until he screamed with fear and sought refuge in the shopkeeper's arms. "He knows! He's part of the illusion," cried the magician angrily. "Make him speak to me. Make him speak in English, the way he did in the mirror." The old man guarded the boy with an outstretched hand and frowned at the behaviour of the conjurer. "You've drugged me! It's the only possible answer. My mind saw what it wanted to see. That's how you did it," the magician snapped accusingly. The shopkeeper cuddled the boy and shook his head, and after a few moments he ushered the child into the shop and walked to the mirror, covering it with a multicoloured blanket. He turned then to Ricardo and pointed him towards the entrance, his stern features demanding he leave immediately.

Ricardo returned the next day, bringing with him an armful of gifts for the boy he had upset and a heartfelt apology for the shopkeeper, and after a short deliberation the old man agreed to a second demonstration, taking the magician by the arm and leading him outside and suggesting he make the choice of the participant. Ricardo chose a young Portuguese girl of eighteen who was visiting her family just for the week. A payment was agreed between them for her trouble, and while her mother waited in the shop, she was shown into the storeroom. The mirror was prepared, and on the instructions of the old man, she slipped effortlessly through to the other side; her role was far removed from that of the young boy's. Hers were recollections of past lives. She claimed to be a servant girl of Aristotle, the Greek philosopher and pupil of Plato in 335 BC. She claimed to be the seductress Morgan le Fay, the half-sister of King Arthur, who was present at Camelot when he married Guinevere. She knew Sir Galahad, Sir Gawain, Merlin and Sir Percival, and expounded in minute detail the search for the Holy Grail. She also claimed to have had an intimate relationship with the American author Edgar Allan Poe in 1832; that she was a nurse in the Napoleonic wars in Austerlitz in 1805; an acquaintance of Daniel Defoe and the inspiration for his Moll Flanders in 1722. And as she elaborated on each subject, the scenery behind her changed. Athens melted into

Avalon and then morphed into Baltimore; melting into the mountain ranges of Austria and finally ending with the streets of eighteenth century London.

When she emerged through both the glass and the blue light, she looked to the magician and the shopkeeper seemingly for instructions as what she should do to warrant the arranged payment. Ricardo observed her curiously from the back of the storeroom. "You have fulfilled the arrangement. Can you not remember?" The Portuguese beauty shook her head. "I have done nothing," she replied. The magician stepped forward and stood next to the mirror. "You can't remember stepping through the glass?" She stood before the mirror gazing at her reflection. "Is this what you want me to do?" she asked with uncertainty. Ricardo shook his head and handed over the arranged fee to her. "You have done everything required of you," he smiled. The girl looked at the money and then back to Ricardo with a bewildered expression. "I may go?" she said. The magician escorted her into the shop and her waiting mother. "May I ask if you're familiar with Celtic literature?" he asked. The young girl and her mother exchanged puzzled glances. "Gottfried von Strassburg? The lady of the lake? The Knights of the Round Table? Camelot?" he asked. Both women nodded frantically. "The Knights of the Round Table, yes! The sword in the stone!" Ricardo smiled, and thanking both women showed them out of the shop. Certainly they knew the legend of King Arthur, or at least they were aware of the existence of the myth, but beyond that they knew little else.

Despite the fact that the mirror preceded the discovery of the Valley of the Kings by Howard Carter and Lord Carnarvon by twenty-two years and the invention of the mirror as we know it was barely fifty years old, Ricardo Kaminski gave everything he had to purchase the mirror, even borrowing a considerable amount of money from the owner of the travelling circus, assuring him it was the greatest discovery of all time and people from all over the world would come just to behold its amazing powers. In no time he became known as Ricardo and the Magic Window, and for five years travelled all over the world with his incredible spectacle. As he predicted, people came from all four corners of the earth just to witness the spectacular find, and on the very day he paid back the last penny he owed to the circus owner, he went on his own. He was billed as the Great Ricardo and the Magic Mirror, and performed before kings, presidents, tsars—the world's elite. It took six strong men to move the mirror from one place to another. It was packed in a crate that Ricardo designed and made himself, lined with horsehair mattresses to prevent breakage, and it would be transported on a flat wagon, reinforced with steel bars. The mirror was guarded day and night by three armed guards; it was untouchable by any other hand but that of the Great Ricardo.

In four years he become one of the wealthiest men in the world and took up residence in a mansion in Somerset, England. In the summer of 1909, Ricardo was summoned to perform before no other than King George V. On the night in question 135 guests arrived at Buckingham Palace to see the great magician and marvel at his window into other worlds. The procedure of the performance was simple. The mirror would face the audience, and after Ricardo introduced himself and gave a little insight into his wonderful discovery, he would pick someone to participate, usually a woman as, like his mother had told him, were more susceptible and blessed with a sixth sense. The mirror now had wheels, making it easier to manoeuvre both on stage and off, and once a participant was chosen, the mirror would be turned sideways on to assure the audience that anything passing through the glass was not simply passing through to the other side. Ricardo chose the prettiest girl he could see, a vision of loveliness with long brown hair and beguiling features whose name was Christina; it was her twentieth birthday. Holding her hand, The Great Ricardo looked over the faces of the gathering. "Ladies and gentlemen, over the years I have witnessed a phenomenon that few have been privileged to see, and most cannot understand. We are familiar with the term reincarnation; that we have all lived other lives and have been different people, yet there exists no evidence—no tangible proof. The mirror is the key to prove beyond any doubt that reincarnation is very real—that after death we live again. Once through the mirror the subject, or in this case the beautiful Christina, will recall her past lives with crystal clear clarity and regale us with stories of days long forgotten. But when she remerges, she will not remember one single detail."

For the sake of entertainment, that in the annuls of theatre was regarded as claptrap, the mirror would be tumbled over three times before the chosen one could enter the doorway to the other world, and turned another three times before they stepped back into reality. It was, as Ricardo said, a mere form of distraction, the hocus-pocus the audience had come to expect at any magical show. He positioned the mirror into its sideways position and motioned the girl to stand before it, and softly mumbling the incantation he had come to know by heart, the glass began to glow with an incandescent blue light. King George and his guests looked aghast as the light grew stronger—until everyone was shielding their sensitive eyes from the powerful rays. "Please step into the mirror," commanded The Great Ricardo. When the light dulled the beautiful girl was gone, but when the magician turned the mirror face on to the audience she was there, framed in heavy gold with the cathedral of Notre Dame de Paris behind her reflecting on the River Seine. Ricardo circled the mirror and leaned his weight casually on the golden frame. "We know where you are, Christina, but not who you are," he said with a wink to the audience. "Please tell me what year it is." The girl now was dressed in a pastel blue silk gown with layered flounces, her make-up heavy with rouge coloured cheeks and blood red lips. "The year is 1660," she calmly replied in a French accent. The 135 gathering gasped in amazement and applauded politely, but King George, who observed the illusion with an air of scepticism, stepped forward and addressed the magician. "One moment, young sir," he said. "May I be permitted to approach the mirror?" Ricardo humbly bowed and took two steps away. The King was in a joyful mood, playing to his privileged guests as if it were he they had come to see and not The Great Ricardo. He rounded the mirror twice, eying the sorcerer with a doubtful smile. "I have seen such trickery before, but I must say I am impressed. May I speak with Christina?" he asked while he grinned at the sea of spectators. The magician bowed again. "You may, sir, but she won't hear you. I am the only one she can converse with." Not to be upstaged the king scoffed. "Bah! I have known this girl since she was a child; she'll know my voice." Ricardo nodded, "As the King wishes." King George abruptly rapped the glass with his knuckles. "Now hear me, Christina. Tell me when it was the . . . Great Ricardo prepared you for this moment. You are, are you not, part of his game?" Christina stared blindly back through the glass, neither seeing nor hearing the voice of the king. The guests were highly amused and began to laugh, but just as the king was about to embark on a second attempt at making contact, Ricardo intervened. "I am not a charlatan, sir, and I have never met the subject before. If the king would be so gracious and allow me to continue with my presentation?" King George reluctantly agreed and slapped the magician on the shoulder.

Ricardo allowed the king his moment of approval from family and friends and then resumed his place before the mirror. The quiet murmur died down and all eyes focused on the display and the magician. "Who are you, Christina?"

asked Ricardo. "My name is Yvette Casselle, and I am mistress to King Louis XIV. I am the King's whore." There were gasps of disapproval from the audience, and mothers covered the ears of their young daughters while their husbands cursed angrily at the magician. Ricardo stepped forward, his hands akimbo. "I offer my apologies to His Majesty and his distinguished guests, but I have no control over the subject once they pass beyond the glass." King George, who at first could understand the reaction of the majority, was now not so eager to bring the performance to a stop, for he knew Christina and knew also she would never speak in such a way unless, of course, this was not a music hall trick. "Anyone who feels the need to leave should do so now," he said. "We shall continue." A handful of women took their children away, and only three men left. The Great Ricardo awaited the authority of the King to commence. The gathering settled, and King George who considered himself to be somewhat of an authority on anything royal, said, "Ask her what Louis XIV was known as." The magician nodded, and turning to the mirror posed the question. Yvette smiled and replied "The Sun King." The king applauded enthusiastically knowing the reference to be correct, and one by one the audience joined in. The Great Ricardo, enthused and reassured by the praise, began to fire a succession of questions at Yvette to which she replied earnestly. She said that at present Louis XIV was a minority and France was ruled by Mazerin, which indeed was correct, but in her time and place of 1660, she had the capacity to see into the future, marking the evolution of her lover with wars waged against England Spain and Holland. Time after time the throng burst into rapturous applause, none more so than King George himself.

Ricardo had won the hearts of the crowd and one by one stray voices suggested questions for the great magician to ask. He obliged, infusing his own brand of comical anecdotes into the dialogue and challenging the audience to be more daring with their enquiries. Near the close of the performance Ricardo placed his ear close to the glass as Christina or Yvette asked him a question. He nodded and looked directly to Mary of Teck, the king's wife, surrounded by her five sons and daughter. "Ma'am, have you ever considered changing your name?" he asked. The woman laughed and shook her head at the absurdity of the question. "Why would you say such things, sir?" the king intercepted spontaneously. The Great Ricardo bowed his head. "Begging His Majesty's pardon, but a greater power than I assures me that in the very near future you will change your name," he replied. The king put a comforting arm around his wife's shoulder and smiled. "And why would we consider such an option?" he laughed. Ricardo raised a finger and smiled towards the crowd. "I shall ask," he said. And he posed the question but Yvette simply shook her head, reluctant to give the reason as to why King George V would abandon the name of Saxe-Coburg-Gotha for Windsor because of the approaching Great War. "Unfortunately she will not give a reason," Ricardo told the audience. "I believe it is time to bring back Christina." The gathering clapped as the magician returned to the mirror.

It was then that the Great Ricardo's world literally fell to pieces. Prior to reciting the incantation to release the subject, and for the benefit of the audience who believed they were witnessing a magical act rather than an inexplicable phenomenon, the magician began to turn the mirror over. It was on the third and last cycle that one of the two hinges secured to the robust ebony frame loosened. The mirror spun uncontrollably, wavering like a buckled wheel, and despite the efforts to stop the weighty frame from turning, Ricardo was thrown on his back to the floor. The audience shrieked in horror as the hinge sheared off, its weight tearing the fixings on which the whole mass pivoted, lopped to one side like a wounded galleon but still driven by the momentum of the cycle. The mirror twisted in on itself, yanking the frame round and severing the remaining hinge. As Ricardo scrambled to his feet the mirror spun on its corner one and a half turns before crashing to the ground. The result wasn't just the sound of shattering glass. It was a massive explosion. The mirror fell on its back, and from within a power erupted like the awakening of a dormant volcano, with such a thunder and such ferocity, with beams of red, green and blue lights shooting skyward, enough to blow a hole through the ceiling and into the room above. Women screamed and everyone there tried to make their escape; most made it outside into the hallway.

When all was silent the men slowly entered. The room was dense with acrid smoke, and the few who had not made it to safety could be heard coughing and gasping for breath. King George ordered the servants to throw open all the windows, and slowly the smoke began to clear. Ricardo was on his knees beside the frame, lifting slithers of glass in his bleeding hands and frantically trying to piece them together. Like a man possessed he crawled around the floor gathering up pieces of the mirror and placing them inside the frame, as if they would miraculously arrange themselves into order and become whole again. He wept uncontrollably as he continued to execute his task, muttering over and over the name 'Christina'. King George immediately ordered that Ricardo be taken to the bathroom and cleaned of his wounds, but the magician refused to leave, shunning off the reaching hands and searching for the smallest particles of glass. Seeing enough of the pathetic figure the king insisted Ricardo be physically removed from the room, and all around the palace Christina's name was screamed in pain and remorse.

"Ricardo never fully recovered from the events of that summer evening and drove him to the brink of insanity," explained the judge sadly. "He devoted the rest of his short life and the whole of his vast fortune in the search for Christina Elsmore."

"She was never found?"

Judge Newland shook his head. "The window was broken, Michael—the doorway was closed. Ricardo travelled the world three times over in the meagre hope of finding a similar artefact, all to no avail. He attended séances in every major European city in an attempt to make contact with the lost girl and consulted with every known spiritualist; it was all very sad. Two years after the event he returned to Marrakech, but the shop where he purchased the mirror had gone, and he was informed by the locals that the old man had died just one week after their last meeting. However, three days into his stay he was confronted by a young man who sought him out at his hotel. Ricardo recognised him, not by who he was but by what he aspired to be in the mirror—the young shop-boy. Now in his twenties he had come from Casablanca for the weekend to visit his mother and heard of the magician's enquiries. "The mirror was cursed," said the young man. "It was the old man's fate for selling something that never rightfully belonged to him, and he was punished. The mirror was never intended to be a cheap, second-rate magician's folly, Mr. Kaminski."

Ricardo lowered his head in shame and his hands shook, as they had ever since he lost Christina to the afterlife. "I know," he murmured. "Truly, I know."

"It may be immaterial to you now, but the mirror was a form of learning—from the past and from the future. It is what made the Pharaohs such an advanced race."

Ricardo thought for a moment and looked at the young man with anticipation.

"Are you suggesting there may be more mirrors?" he asked.

"Leave it be," smiled the young man. "Undoubtedly there are more, but they would be buried with their kings, and thousands of years have since erased their hiding place."

"The Great Ricardo never practiced magic again; he was a lost soul. He spent the rest of his life pining for a girl he hardly knew yet loved as if she were his own daughter. He felt responsible. It was as if he had killed her with his own hands. Sadly it destroyed him in the end. I remember the preliminary. I was second-chair for the prosecution, and The Great Ricardo stood in the box, a grey and distant figure, looking twice his age and oblivious to his surroundings. The prosecution were given a case—but what case? Somebody had to be held responsible for the absence of poor Christina Elsmore, and it was up to us to assign blame. I'll never forget the look of that man; he was busted and broken beyond repair. And us, the prosecutors, what did we have? Kidnapping? Assault? Abducting someone against their will? They were none of these things. 135 people, guests of King George, witnessed a young woman willingly enter a mirror—unharmed and without coercion—and yet, with the breaking of the glass she was gone—forever. How do you explain that? How does a rational human being explain that we have lost a beautiful young woman to a conjuring trick? Truth is we couldn't. There are no laws that entertain the notion of magic being the protagonist; that the guests of King George had witnessed the total evaporation of a loved one, or that Ricardo Kaminski was solely responsible for her abduction. We, the great thinkers, place everything into neat and tidy piles, believing we have the wherewithal to offer a rational explanation for every deed committed, where in reality we haven't got a clue. We are governed by laws, but we cannot impose laws on things we do not understand. Ricardo's mirror was not magical. It was far beyond the understanding of any rational thinker. It was what he always believed it to be—a window into another world, yet he had found the closest thing to God and turned it into a sideshow act—for fame and money. And with all these selfish deeds there are consequences. Ricardo died a young man, utterly destroyed by the memory of Christina, and the court had no option but to acquit him; Christina remains to this day just another missing person. Needless to say, the decision was not without its influences. On the request, nay orders of King George, the hearing was held behind closed doors, and the location and indeed the identities of the guests were a closely guarded secret; even the 'Elsmore' name was an alias."

Judge Newland turned his face towards the window, his eyes glistening with tears. The tale of Ricardo Kaminski influenced him greatly, and his voice cracked from time to time as he recalled the sorry life of the magician.

"I would imagine it was the wish of the king to play down the royals' obsession with death," continued the judge, "Queen Victoria had an unhealthy appetite with the afterlife ever since her beloved Albert died. So much so that those close to her believed her to be quite mad. But the Victorian period was infested with Mediums and spiritualists. R.J. Lees was a Medium, who enjoyed a brief moment of fame by claiming to be the Queen's very own spiritualist. And wasn't it he who assisted the police in the search for Jack the Ripper."

As he spoke he slowly turned the pages of my father's book, half of which were blank, and on turning the last page he looked intently at the inside cover. In its centre was a dome of red wax, like that used for sealing documents, and with great interest the judge began to pick at it with his fingernail and then with a sharp letter-opener. After a few moments he discovered whatever lay beneath and rubbed away the remnants of wax between his fingers. He held up a key, small enough to put in a matchbox with plenty of room to spare.

"I believe this must belong to you," he said.

I stared at it curiously.

"Whatever can it be for?" I murmured.

"Your father put it there for a reason. Whatever it unlocks must still be in your possession—or maybe his."

-18-

With the exception of Penny, we decided to work late and catch up on the backlog of work regarding Henderson, but Badger had to leave at 8.30. I parted company with him in reception, and as I reached my office door I turned to see him at the foot of the stairs, his hand raised in my direction. Suddenly the life I knew was gone. I was laying face down, heavy weight pressing down on my back and legs, my lungs bereft of air and wheezing violently. Pain soared through my head and abdomen, an excruciating, searing pain that held me paralysed and incapable of movement; and all around me the ground trembled and shook, accompanied by the sounds of falling debris and creaking timbers, of running water and buzzing electrics. My eyes, whether open or closed, could define nothing but black—no shades, no shadows, no outline of anything familiar—only black. Above me I could hear layer upon layer of weight crashing down and stone dropping from above and smashing to the office floor, the tinkling of glass and the metallic chink of steel. I lay hopeless until the ground stopped shuddering, until all sound above me ceased, until everything was still in my dark world. Now I could only hear the sound of gushing water—a heavy volume plunging from above and hitting the ground. Then a popping sound. Hope returned as flashes of intermittent white light ignited my eyes—streaking across the floor and office walls; electrical arcing, severed cables. Those split seconds of light gave up the devastation. I raised my head slightly to look around and behind me. The entire ceiling was down, crashing around the partitioned offices from a height of thirty feet and into the reception area, smashing to the floor and pinning me down, filling every molecule of space with heavy concrete and plaster dust. The Luftwaffe had found us.

I felt myself slipping into unconsciousness, my thoughts sporadic and senseless, and I lay my head back down and slowly closed my eyes. My pain-level evened out, confined only to my head and legs and not my whole body, but breathing was harder, my lungs constricted by the heavy weight crushing down on me. Yet I was peaceful. Suffocation, they say, is a serene death as long as the participant remains calm. The brain, when starved of oxygen, falls into a dreamlike state, and the survival instinct gives way to surrender. This was my time. A strange sensation began to rise through me, a cold chill starting in my legs, absorbing my torso, my arms, hands, and finally my face. Water! I could hear gentle moaning from nearby, barely definable above the sound of rushing water, but nevertheless there. "Sylvia?" I groaned. "Badger?" The arcing flashes shot overhead, bouncing off the remaining glass in the partitions, slicing through the veils of dense dust. "Michael? Michael, can you hear me?" I slowly opened my eyes and raised my head. "Sylvia, are you okay? Are you hurt?" I could hear movement—of furniture being pushed around, of drawers opening and slamming, but above all else I could hear a grinding coming from above; concrete crunching on concrete and more debris tumbling down. A beam of light crossed back and forth and then spotlighted me, growing brighter as it moved nearer, until it was inches in front of my face. "Oh, God, Michael, can you move?" I shook my head weakly but managed a smile. "You are an angel after all," I muttered. Sylvia was knelt before me, in the expanding water, amongst the glass and timber splinters.

Sylvia looked as if she had just been shot out of cannon, her peroxide hair falling lank in front of her face, the left sleeve of her blouse completely torn off, and her knees protruding through her holed silk stockings. Blood spots speckled her face and cleavage, and a deep wound in her arm oozed blood. "What's holding me down, Sylvia?" I wheezed, breathlessly. "She shone the torch down my body and then stood up to shine the beam over me, and while she undertook this task I was raising my head higher. "Where's this water coming from?" I groaned. I felt the weight of Sylvia's body scramble over whatever was pinning me to the floor. A beam of light shone up from my feet to my squinting eyes. "Can you pull yourself forward?" she asked. My right arm was under me, and the accumulated weight of my body and whatever was above me, made any hope of freeing it almost impossible. However, I tried, rocking from side to side, trying to arch my back and push the mass upward. "Wait, wait, wait, I see it." There was a rummaging above and behind me, and I could hear timber being thrown to the floor. I felt the weight ease across my legs, and I heard Sylvia's straining voice. "Forward. Slide forward!" I attempted again but failed, and the heaviness returned. Sylvia appeared in front of me again, armed with the torch and what appeared to be one side of a doorframe.

She was panting for breath and tossed her hair from her eyes. "Listen to me. There nothing in front of you. You're half in and half out of your office. It's the ceiling that is on top of you. Another two steps and it would have missed you. The office ceilings took the impact of the main ceiling falling down." She jammed the doorframe inches from my body and positioned her shoulder beneath. "Now free your arm," she groaned as she pushed upward. The weight lifted across my back and shoulders, and I rolled to my side and pulled my arm out. The weight eased back down, pinning me once again. Sylvia was climbing over and was now behind me, preparing to execute the same manoeuvre. The water was deepening, climbing up my neck. "One last chance," said Sylvia's voice. "Now stop fucking about and pull forward." The mass rose, and digging my fingers into the carpet's surface, I inched forward, dragging myself out from under the weight. The mass splashed down at the moment I freed my legs.

I was spent from the exertion and opened my eyes to see Sylvia looking down on me, cradling my head in her arms; the both of us submerged in at least six inches of water.

"Is anything broken, Michael? Can you move your legs?" she asked.

Laying flat on my back I managed to pull one leg up, and then slowly the other, though I winced and groaned with pain at the attempt.

She was gently stroking my hair, which in itself soothed me, like a mother nursing a child, and when she pulled her hand away her fingers were crimson with wet blood. She saw the alarm in my eyes.

"It's not serious, Michael," she said, softly. "Give yourself a moment and then try to stand up.

I was on my feet, supporting my weight palms down on my dust-laden office desk with Sylvia behind me, examining my head wounds by torchlight. I trembled as I stared at the shadows sliding across the wall in front of me—drawing in deep breaths, filling my lungs with life, and with every inhalation strength returned, coordination restored, and the dire predicament we were in slowly manifested. The roar of water turned my head in the direction of the office door, to the bleakness beyond, illuminated intermittently by the sparking lights. "Sylvia, did you hear anything—an explosion, the air raid siren—anything?" She was gently teasing at my hair, layering it to one side to assess the damage. "I don't know. Perhaps. Maybe I heard something. I think I heard an explosion of some kind, but I'm not certain," she replied. Trapped under the dead weight of lath and plaster, timbers and steel girders, my body had been numbed, as if I had been injected with a large dose of anaesthetic. Now all feeling restored itself, and any wounds I received were highlighted by concentrated pain. Disorientation slipped gently away to be replaced by recall; broken images of a few moments ago. "Badger!" I fumbled with the top-drawer of my desk and pulled out a torch—retained for the purposes of blackout—and began to scale the debris piled outside the office door, but as the torchlight broke through the pitch dark and falling dust, I stopped dead. "God help us."

The entire staircase was down, its skeletal frame barely definable beneath tons of splintered concrete, smashed masonry and plaster; the wrought iron banisters buckled and twisted and protruding out of the pile of debris. The stairwell above was compacted by concrete and bricks, and smaller fragments trickled through the spaces between, falling like a dry waterfall—expelling more acrid dust into the confines below. The ceiling mass—the slab—what I had been assured was three feet thick, had dropped perhaps a distance of ten feet, and wedged only between the four walls, had settled at an oblique rake, split into four quarters and threatening to fold in; the cracking and crunching clearly audible even above the roar of water. Its short descent had severed the cast iron drainage and galvanised pipes, and now raw-sewage spewed from the twelve inch splintered pipe and mains water jetted from the contorted galvanised pipes, cascading off the walls and running down like a waterfall. All devastation appeared confined to the reception, and with the exception of Tom and Andy's office that was crushed by the falling cast-iron drainage, the ceilings of the other offices had withstood the impact of the collapsed false ceiling. My light searched out the wreckage beneath the stairwell, between the twisted steel, oak stair-treads and rubble, for any trace of Badger.

"Nobody could have survived that, Michael," said Sylvia, shining her torch in the same direction.

I agreed with a solemn shake of my head.

"Was I unconscious?" I asked. "Were you?"

Sylvia put her hand on my shoulder as if to allay my doubts.

"I mean, maybe Badger made it out before the explosion," I reasoned. "There may have been enough time, right?"

I can't remember if I had stopped to speak with Sylvia prior to the ceiling *literally* falling in, and if I had there was every chance Badger had safely left the building. Perhaps I hadn't fallen unconscious. Perhaps I had remained awake throughout. But shock is a form of unconsciousness; wide-awake you can still be unconscious—simply the nervous system fails to react—to anything. I slowly began to resign myself to the fact that he couldn't have possibly made it out. I began to move closer but it was difficult to manoeuvre. We were standing on the infrastructure of the ceiling—joists, steel, lath and plaster—and worse, it was submerged under . . . I stopped and stared down. The murky water now was above my knees and rising. As I began to move again, Sylvia held my arm and pulled me back. She stared at me and shook her head grimly. "Get us out of here, Michael," she said, firmly. I submitted, spun my torch one last time in the direction of where I last saw Badger, and then turned the light to the ceiling.

"They'll come for us, won't they?" Sylvia said, hopefully. "They'll dig us out. The fire brigade are probably on their way. And the A.R.P. will notify the army. How long do you think before they get us out—two, three hours?"

I was wading deeper into the devastated area, unsteady and stumbling over objects beneath the brown fluid, the torchlight scanning the cracked and splintered concrete overhead. The breaks were widening, and where they converged sagging was evident. My initial thought was that it was a trick of the light; the shifting of shadows, light glinting off the soaked walls, but the beam picked up thin streams of what appeared to be dust; concrete particles streaming down like sand through an hourglass, falling freely as the faults widened. The ceiling wasn't sagging—it was slipping down. Above us was once a five-storey building that had been reduced to thousands of tons of rubble resting on a three feet slab cracked into quarters. "Can this get any worse?" I mumbled to myself.

"Can you smell something?" Sylvia shouted, her torch flashing across the ceiling.

Sewage poured down from the damaged drain, plunging into the expanse of rising water, pushing shallow waves outward; its stench effluvium.

"Gas!" shrieked Sylvia. "I can smell gas!"

So could I. It *was* getting worse.

One of the mangled pipes appeared dormant, and though broken no substance was being expelled from its jagged opening—no visible substance, that is. The invisible poison began to filter down into the confines of the office; the arcing sparks spitting from a twisted length of conduit was but a few feet away. The department store had been constructed on what was referred to as a ring-beam—its entire weight resting on independent foundations outside the walls of this chamber. Wren applied the same idea when building St. Paul's, to house crypts far beneath ground level. Whole or dismantled, the weight of the department store remained the same, and its mass threatened to breach the slab separating us. I began to scale the rubble piled up against the walls of the unscathed offices, until my feet were out of the mucky water, and using the door and windows as footholds, I pulled myself up on top of the roof. Sylvia was looking up from below, her hands clasped to her face, to staunch the fowl smell of sewage and seeping gas. The slab, having dislodged and dropped down, was almost in touching distance, just ten feet above the office roofs, but from this angle the extent of the fracture was clear. Either way it made no difference; there was no escape.

As I clamoured back down, there was only one thought on my mind. How was I going to explain to Sylvia that we were about to die? It was late evening—the department store would be closed—no people, no deaths. Why search for casualties that weren't there? And why would anyone be working in the offices below—blatantly ignoring the blackout regulations? Why indulge in excavation at this time of night when it could wait till daylight? By that time the building above would be occupying my office space, and not withstanding its inevitable collapse and the leaking gas-main that threatened to ignite at any moment, there was the rising level of water to contend with—now foaming around my thighs as I waded toward my secretary.

Sylvia examined my eyes intently, searching for an answer I didn't have. "They will find us, Michael?" I flashed my torch across the ceiling for no other purpose but to avoid her gaze. "Undoubtedly; I'm sure I heard workmen above us," I lied. "Not long now, Sylvia."

Just then there was a thunderous groaning noise, of grinding stone and snapping steel—of sheer weight surrendering to the laws of gravity. Sylvia seized my arm. One quarter of the slab began to fall, and loose debris began to rain down from the stairwell. I closed my eyes. This is it! Suddenly there was silence—only the sound of running water prevailed. My eyes slowly opened and I shone a trembling light above. A section had slipped down sixteen inches and lodged itself at an acute angle; a remaining fourteen inches held it—for the time being. Through cold, the darkness, the rising waters, but probably through unadulterated fear, Sylvia shook uncontrollably; the bravery she had fought to maintain finally giving up to reality. "It won't hold for long. According to Bernie the slab is three feet thick," I said, being of little or no help to either of us. "Bernie?" she replied in a tremulous voice.

Bernie!—He of the Masons, a devout member of the brotherhood, the friend who had convinced me to set up a business in a hole in the ground nine years ago; an underground torture chamber attached by a network of tunnels!

I found myself hurrying toward my office, dragging Sylvia behind me, explosions of contaminated water showering upward, crashing against our bodies and thrusting knees as we surged onward. Inside I tried to close the office door, sinking in the mire to clear any obstructions and, eventually securing it within the doorframe. "Help me, Sylvia," I demanded as I lifted one side of my desk. We heaved it up, pushing it hard against the door, and on top we piled on anything that came to hand, chairs, filing cabinets, file boxes, and while Sylvia searched for anything weighty to add to the obstruction, I sank again, groping beneath the surface and grasping the edge of the large rug. With a surging wave I rose, peeling the carpet back, dragging it and flapping it on top of the desk. "Michael, what are you doing? Michael! Michael!" The flooring beneath was wood—staggered eight by four sheets of ply laid loosely on kilned sand—a form of insulation, a flat surface as opposed to uneven bricks; what builders ironically call a 'floating floor.' "Top drawer, Sylvia—letter-opener," I shouted. Her torch flashed away from me and back to the desk; my fingertips ran the surface to one sheet abutted against another. Handing me the letter-opener, I plunged it beneath the surface, digging it into the joint, pushing down and levering up. "Something else! Give me something else." The weight of water and suction secured it to its bedding of sand. "Hurry!" Sylvia was in a state of blind panic, yanking the drawers' open and delving her hands inside. "What kind of thing? What in God's name are you doing?" she screamed back at me. As she turned the light to me, it glinted across an arc of steel; Badger's gift of crossed daggers above my desk—his little joke. I seized them and sunk back into the depths, locating the seam, digging in and levering up with one, sliding the other between; the water would flood beneath, evening out the weight of fluid—undermining the suction. It slowly began to lift, until my fingers gripped the edges, and my body rose, pulling it up until it was vertical. The dark waters around me turned a milky white as the kilned sand was absorbed by the penetrating water. I dropped again, peeling another sheet up.

Sylvia observed dumbstruck, the torch shaking in her hand. The closed office door temporarily dammed up the rising waters, but my primary concern was the ceiling. How much time before it gave way altogether? My hand groped blindly in the sand, searching out a steel ring, praying I was searching in the right place. "Please, please, please. It's here. I know it's here." And in a moment there it was, resting in the palm of my hand and clutched tightly between my fingers. I grabbed the length of timber Sylvia had freed me with, feeding it through the large, iron ring, and now I was bent over, grasping the timber in my hands, preparing to lever the door open. It was difficult enough nine years ago when Bernie and I raised it. Now, with water and suction, it would be practically impossible to achieve. I looked to Sylvia and nodded towards the chair atop of the desk, just visible beneath the carpet. "Bring the chair over here, Sylvia," I ordered. "When I lift the trap, jam it in; I won't be able to do this more than once." Even in the bleak light I could see her bewildered expression. "Michael, what trap?" she asked. "There's nothing there." Every muscle in my body ached; blood from my head had stained my shirt red, and I could still feel its warmness soaking my back; I was shivering from the freezing cold water and dripping in foul sewage. And then there was the prospect of the ceiling falling in at any moment, or the gas main exploding reducing us to little more than ash. And by some divine intervention we should happen to survive both events; we still had drowning to look forward to. "Fuck it, Sylvia, will you do as I ask?!" I screamed.

I began to pull up with what remaining strength I had left, until all the muscles in my shoulders and back were rigid and the wood began to cut into my hands; my whole body shaking under the strain. Sylvia watched me for a signal, crouched low in the putrid water, her hands clasping the back of the chair, preparing to push it forward. No movement but for the bending wood. No hope. Suddenly Sylvia released her grip on the chair, sank lower in the water and shuffled backward until she was underneath the timber lever. She pushed upward; her knees and palms emerged in the kilned sand and jagged red brick floor, her face barely above the surface of the water. Tiny bubbles began to emerge, filtering up from the seal of the trap door in perfect straight lines, growing larger and dense as the trap began to yield. A noise, like a loud gulp sounded beneath, followed by an enormous dome of air—the wooden lever straightening and slowly moving. The expanse of water suddenly surged toward us, floating debris pulled toward the opening, sucked under the dark surface. I changed position, turning myself from over the lever to under, pushing my shoulder into the timber, straightening from my squat and rising up. The trap opened, like the mouth of a great beast, swallowing water and debris, sucking it into its dark stomach, consuming everything floatable in the room. As it opened wider, the chair was pushed forward to prevent it slamming shut should strength escape us, but we continued until the trap was almost upright, Sylvia pushing up with her feet on the edge of the opening, and me still pushing forward. The door splashed down, sending a wave crashing against the walls. Gallons of water cascaded down the steps leading underground, almost emptying the office. The desk was beginning to slide away from the door, dragged by the suction of the tunnel and pushed by the accumulating weight on the other side.

There was no time to spare. Soon the passageway below would be obstructed with debris making it impassable. I grabbed Sylvia's hand, buried my torch under my jacket and submerged into the dark void, the water pouring around and down on us. We emerged in the long, narrow tunnel, out of the waterfall and into the acrid stench of a thousand years. Fishing out my torch from under my jacket, I shone it ahead. The waters rushed forward in a long, straight line, picking up speed as the passage floor inclined steadily down; rushing like a rapid, foaming and bubbling, washing up the walls in rocking motions, the debris churning and tumbling on its erratic surface. Sylvia's torch began to flicker and fade, and she shook it desperately to give it life. "Leave it!" I ordered. The level of water was relatively shallow at our feet—reaching to just below our knees, but it would deepen as the passage plunged deeper towards the Royal Courts. Bernie said the passage entrance was still there, concealed behind panelling in an anti-room; it was our only chance. We moved as quickly as we could, splashing onward, the beam of light flashing before us, gleaming off the saturated walls and dancing off the roaring surface of the thin torrent. Pain rose through me, my legs heavy and aching, barely incapable of taking another step. Sylvia slowed, her weight pulling backward, until she stopped and rested her back against the wall, doubled over with her hands on her knees, breathing heavy and erratic. I shone the torch back in the direction of the office, at the water running down through the hatch opening and steadily rising. We were now waist-deep, due to the slope of the floor, and with every step forward it would grow deeper still. If and when the ceiling finally gave way, it would send a volume of water down the tunnel so dense that we would drown, or be speared to death by the broken timbers and shards of glass; it would travel with the velocity of a bullet being fired from a gun. We had passed several opening within the passage wall, presumably entrances into other chambers; some as Bernie had said, had been bricked up. We were half way. "Sylvia, we have to move on," I said, holding her arm gently. I expected her then to recite a line from one of the many movies she had seen at her local picture-house; where the heroin, weak from exhaustion falls to the ground while being pursued by a ruthless gangster, hell bent on revenge for her daring to fall in love with another man; laying on the ground she would look up weakly at the hero and utter, 'Go on without me. I'm only slowing you down.' Instead her breathing steadied and she looked up at me, a curl on her lips and a look in her eyes that wished me dead; she nodded. "You got me down here—now get me out, or God help me, Michael, it won't be this shit that kills you—I will!" It was a fare comment given the circumstances.

We trudged on, the waters climbing higher to chest-level, the stinking effluence rushing around our bodies towards the tunnel's end, but the strong current began to slow, and a little further on it ceased altogether; still, like a millpond. The torch-light illuminated the shallow area ahead, between the surface of the water and the arched passage ceiling, between which was a dense volume of floating obstacles, wood, paper and even the chair Sylvia had used as an obstruction. We passed an entrance to our right, to which I shone my torch down, but there was little to see except the light reflecting off the concaved ceiling and the rippling surface. We were there—below the Royal Courts. We gently inched forward, teasing the driftwood out of our path, until my feet touched against a solid object—steps? The water descended away from me as I climbed upward—the light shimmering on a stone staircase leading straight up. Soon we would be out. On the top step I faced my worse nightmare; concrete blocks incorporated within the red brick that was once a doorway—heavy stone secured with strong mortar. All hope evaporated, and as I stood staring at the only obstacle separating life from death, it happened.

It sounded like a distant explosion, of weight falling, of cracking and rumbling. The passageway shook and the surface of the water trembled. Think! I jumped down into the water and grabbed Sylvia's arm, pulling her back the way we had came. Ahead I saw it—a foaming mass filling the entire volume of the tunnel roaring towards us—a tidal wave created by the total collapse of the ceiling and the mass above it. I surged forward, yanking my secretary behind me, toward the raging torrent that would inevitably terminate our lives. It sped closer, moving like a freight train, pushing splintered timber before it, dragging a vast mass of water and fragmented concrete behind. It was almost upon us. "Michael! Michael!" Sylvia's screams were barely audible above the thunder. It was upon us, looming above us and roaring like a monster, threatening to consume us entirely, to push us back and crush us against the wall, crashing its weight against us, pummelling us with its cargo of jagged debris. Left! Left! Left! Into the side passage the mass raged past, exploding at the end of the tunnel. "Swim, Sylvia! Swim!" The aftermath followed behind us, pushing us forward into the blackness on a wave, and though I was beneath the surface, pushed on a current channelled by the narrow walls, I made every effort to keep the torch above the surface.

The power of the wash depleted as the passage floor rose towards higher ground, until the wave was no more than a ripple, until Sylvia and I were standing in shallow waters again. The fading torchlight encircled her, and she stood bedraggled and trembling with fear. It was a moment for appreciation. "Are you all right?" I asked, putting a comforting hand on her shoulder. She broke then—like a little girl, squeezing me tightly and gently sobbing. "Are we going to die, Michael?" she cried. I held her for a few moments and then broke away, forcing a smile. "Not today, Sylvia. Come on, let's get out of here." We moved onward, the waters receding below us as the incline of the floor grew steeper, until we were at a concrete slab beyond the arched passage, and above was a concaved ceiling; Gothic by design and constructed of white stone. Ahead I could see the bottom treads of a spiral-staircase entwined round a fluted column, cast also in white stone. I helped Sylvia up onto the slab and shone the fading light around. A large doorway nearby had been bricked up, sealing in whatever was behind it for all eternity.

"Where are we?" Sylvia asked, her head turning from side to side.

I moved in a little closer.

"If my theory is correct, we should be directly under St. Mary's Le Strand," I explained thoughtfully. I directed the light to the brick façade. "That would have been a crypt of some kind. The authorities had all the bodies removed and the vaults sealed back in the late 1840s. The architect James Gibbs was a secret Catholic who had trained for the priesthood before taking up his true vocation. The church was built for Anglican worship, but it had the style of a Roman Catholic Church. In order to get the commission, Gibbs concealed his true persuasion."

Sylvia was glowering at me indignantly.

"You're waffling again, Michael."

I agreed with a slight crook of my head, shone the faltering beam on the spiral staircase, and slowly began to climb. I counted each and every step under my breath, for no other purpose but to retain it for posterity;

so that with every telling of my miraculous escape from the bowels of hell—and there would be so many—I would remember every fine detail. A heavy oak door faced us set in a Lancet Arch, and for the first time since our ordeal began, I turned off the torch. "Michael, what the hell . . . ?" I breathed a sigh of relief on seeing a dull but thin strip of light seeping through the foot of the door. I handed the torch to Sylvia and began to pound relentlessly; banging with my fists, kicking with my feet, and from her position on the top step, Sylvia screamed with what strength she had left. Three, four, perhaps five minutes passed before the weak strip of light below illuminated brighter. "Hello. Can you let us out?" I shouted. I pressed my ear against the door. I could hear movement and a muffled voice of a man.

"Ah . . . Who's there? How did . . . ? Who are you?" asked the voice timidly.

"My name is . . ." I began to shout back.

"Please. Please, one moment. There are things in the way," returned the voice. "Verger! Verger, come quickly, there is someone in the Undercroft."

Something was in the way of the door. I could hear small obstacles being moved, chinking glasses, metallic vessels, heavy thuds, and then the dragging of a heavy piece of furniture juddering across a smooth floor. "Mr. Simms, what are you doing?" Another voice came into play.

"Verger, thank heavens," sighed the voice of Mr. Simms. "There are voices—coming from behind the cabinet—from behind the door leading to the crypt."

"Utter twaddle, Mr. Simms," laughed the verger, nervously. "No one has passed through that doorway for—must be a hundred years or more . . ."

I slapped my hand repeatedly against the oak. "Please open up! Hurry! Please!"

There was a long, silent pause, and the dragging of the substantially sized cabinet resumed.

"Can—can you hear me, whoever you are?" asked the distinguishable voice of the verger, low and articulate, clearer and closer now. "How did you . . . ?"

"Sir, my name is Michael James. I own a small law firm a few hundred yards away. There was an explosion and . . ."

"I heard the explosion! The fire Brigade are there now. The building has totally vanished. However did you . . . ?"

"Sir, can we talk about this when you open the door? I have my secretary with me, and we're in pretty bad shape."

There was a lot of clunking and clattering which, from my side of the door, made no sense at all, but then I could hear hammering; metal on metal, intermittent squeaking of moving iron—rusty bolts being knocked through the tight clasps of a swollen, oak door that had been closed for over ninety years. In the fading light of the dying torch I turned to Sylvia and smiled. Her eyes were laden with tears and she nodded her head. We had made it out.

We were enveloped by a dazzling light and breathing clean air, both as pure as if it were sent from the heavens itself, and if the verger and Mr. Simms had never witnessed a miracle—they had now. Comforting arms folded around us and kind words of reassurance were whispered in our ears. We were led directly into a small room, a cluttered vestry and placed down in chairs at a small table. "Put the kettle on, Mr. Simms—I'll fetch some blankets." The verger vanished momentarily and returned, placing a blanket around my shoulders, and then Sylvia who was fighting hard to contain her tears of happiness. My eyes slowly rounded out of their squint as the pain of bright light began to fade. Mr. Simms was a small man in his early forties with shiny black hair and parted down its centre. Together, with the verger, a tall, thin man with grey receding hair, they stared down on us with utter disbelief. What a sight we must have looked; cut and bleeding, attired in torn and shredded clothing, dripping in putrid and foul stinking sewage water, and grinning like a couple of imbeciles. However, for the benefit of both gentlemen I gave an abridged version of the sequence of events that had led us here—to their vestry—in their church.

"Passages, you say? Tunnels? Under my church?" questioned the verger with genuine surprise. "But for why, Mr. James? What possible purpose would they serve?"

"They're very old tunnels," I proffered, not wishing to elaborate further.

"And unsafe, I wouldn't wonder," he frowned. "No doubt disused sewage tunnels; remnants of a bygone age—perhaps?" he added thoughtfully.

"Perhaps," I agreed.

Mr. Simms had located a first-aid kit from a cleaning cupboard and opened it on the table, holding up a small bottle in front of him and shaking it vigorously before splashing some of the contents of a clean, lint cloth. "This may sting a little," he said as he circled behind me. I stared at the small window cut into the vestry wall that looked out at the rear of the church, toward Aldwych, and what was evident was the silence beyond; no commotion or chaos, no air-raid sirens, no devastation and no fires burning.

"Has London been bombed tonight?" I asked the verger, who was knelt before Sylvia and holding her hand.

"Not to my knowledge," he replied, "and certainly not this part of London."

"But I heard an explosion," said Sylvia.

"And you said, you heard an explosion," I reminded him.

"Ah, yes! There was indeed an explosion but not the result of German bombers," he clarified, turning his eyes to mine. "Mr. Turpington spoke to the fire brigade chief, and he believes it was probably an unexploded bomb that had lain dormant since last year."

Suddenly pain shot through my brain as Mr. Simms applied the ointment to my head-wounds, and I realised that what he thought was an inoffensive bottle of iodine, was in fact nitric acid. My bottom lip folded in under my top teeth, and before I could scream out, 'Fucking Jesus Christ!' Sylvia barked my name to make me aware of my surroundings and the present company we were in.

"I did say it might sting a bit," Mr. Simms nodded assuredly.

"Yes, Mr. Simms, you did." Trying to muster a kind smile when your eyes are filled with tears and your head feels like it's ablaze, isn't easy, but as the pain eased some form of appreciation must have registered, for Mr. Simms bent to administer another lethal dose.

"Mr. Turpington?" I questioned to the verger while trying to hold Mr. Simms at bay.

"The A.R.P. Warden; he keeps us updated at all times. We still conduct morning, afternoon and evening services. Mr. Hitler will never prevent us from doing God's work, but it would be remiss of me to ignore the advice of an authority such as Mr. Turpington."

I felt my body beginning to seize up, and so began to stand, motioning Sylvia to do the same.

"But whatever are you doing, Mr. James?" cried the verger with concern. "You are in considerable discomfort. I shall have Mr. Simms fetch Dr. Goodwin from New Bridge Road and bring him back directly."

"Thank you, verger, but no."

"Then hospital. Your wounds must be attended to, and the authorities must be notified at once. Someone must be informed of your survival. Now sit yourself down and have some more tea while Mr. Simms . . ."

"Sir," I interrupted, "does your church still afford the right of protection and refuge if so claimed?"

The slender gentleman appeared confused and clasped his hands together.

"Sanctuary? You're claiming sanctuary?"

I nodded. "I give you my word that I will return and explain everything within a few days."

The verger looked to Mr. Simms, the Sexton, for, perhaps approval, a comforting word, or maybe an argument, and when all he received was a blank gaze he turned back.

"You have that right," he said to me.

"Thank you, sir."

I pulled the blanket off my shoulders and offered it to him.

"Bring them when you come back to see me," he smiled. "If the excitement is over I shall return to preparing my vespers. May God go with you, Mr. James."

Sylvia and I shook the verger's hand, and Mr. Simms led us the short distance to the entrance. "Vespers?" whispered Sylvia as we walked. "Aren't they something to do with spaghetti?"

"No, sweetheart. Vespers are late afternoon or evening services."

"Really? No kidding!"

The streets were dark and silent, and dispensing with the opportunity of viewing the devastation of the department store that had fallen through into my office, Sylvia and I headed straight down Fleet Street. The few pedestrians that were around never gave us a second glance, and the darkness concealed our grotesque appearance as we limped towards the south side of the river. I heard the chime of Big Ben strike midnight as we ambled over Blackfriars Bridge, carried on a chilly breeze following the line of the Thames; the moon fought for supremacy behind the low clouds far off in the distance. Wrapped in our blankets, Sylvia was hobbling by my side, her arm round my waist and her head resting on my shoulder, eyes closed, wincing every now and then as shocks of pain bit her. And I was no better—dragging my feet like a hundred year old man, the muscles in my legs and back tightening with every feeble movement, threatening to seize my limbs completely. "We'll have a few bruises tomorrow," I said.

"Why did you do that, Michael?" she asked, wearily. "Why did you claim what's-it-called with the vicar?"

"Sanctuary?"

"Yeah, sanctuary! I mean, shouldn't we be curled up in a nice, clean hospital bed by now—instead of walking across London in the pitch black? And what about Badger? The police should be told he's still in there."

She was right, of course. When I had come to my senses under the weight of the collapsed ceiling, I was absolutely certain we were in the midst of a Luftwaffe bombing and we had taken a direct hit. Then it was the only possible explanation, but once the verger had informed me that it was a suspected unexploded bomb, I was sceptical. Had I been assassinated tonight? Had someone deliberately blown up the department store to stop me from divulging my knowledge of police corruption? And if they believed I was dead—then let them believe it. I needed time to think before showing my face again.

"We'll inform the fire brigade and police tomorrow," I said, grimly. "It will take days before they dig down to the office."

"And that's another thing," she said, stopping to gaze at me. "The hatch, the tunnels—how did you know?"

I put my arm around her shoulder and resumed walking.

"Once upon a time there was a myth—a myth that history refers to as the 'Spider's Web', yet there was no proof of its existence, and those who did know of its whereabouts were saying nothing, lest they themselves ended their days there. The Web, as it was called, was a series of vaults and chambers interlinked by a network of tunnels, allegedly under the streets of London and used exclusively for the purpose of torture and death. Nobody would have ever known of this secret torture chamber had it not been for the writings of Cedric Falkirk, published in the sixteenth century. Falkirk was something of an eccentric, but highly intelligent. He claimed to be the illegitimate son of Henry VIII and Jane Seymour, brother to Edward VI and step-brother to Queen Elizabeth I; heir to the throne of England. Cedric it would appear, was one child too many, and spirited out of the royal household. He dedicated his life to fighting for his right to be king, continuously lobbying his alleged family and demanding recognition. When all else failed he took to writing his memoirs and claiming his birthright—nobody would publish. So he took to writing penny-dreadfuls, and handing them out around the city. Passion soon turned to resentment, and soon his writings were designed to entice the poor into an uprising against the royals—to bring them down and expose them for what they really were—fascists. Soon he found himself in a dungeon, somewhere beneath the London streets; so deep that nobody could hear the screams of the government's victims. He spent six days there—six days, suffering unspeakable punishment; tortured close to death, yet he still professed to be the rightful heir to the throne. The dead were piled onto large barrows and wheeled down a passage to the river; and under a veil of darkness were loaded onto a barge, to be weighted and dumped in the deeper area of the Thames. Falkirk managed to hide underneath the pile of corpses, and once on the barge, managed to slip over the side. He survived long enough to tell his tale of the Spider's Web; he vanished suddenly, supposedly killed by government assassins."

"And that's a true story?" asked Sylvia, drowsily.

"There were other tales—vague stories dating back to medieval times and beyond, but none as vivid and as detailed as Falkirk's; he even drew sketches of the interior. He was killed simply because he knew the whereabouts of the Web."

"Wait!" said Sylvia, slowing to a stop. "Are you saying that our office—my office—the place where I have worked for years—was once a torture chamber—a Spider's Web?"

I grimaced. "Till the late 1840s, yes. It was the very reason I wanted it; you know, history."

She stomped onward. "Jesus! That place almost got us killed tonight, Michael," she said over her shoulder.

"It also saved our lives," I argued. "Would you have preferred an office on the fifth floor of the department-store?"

She stopped rigid, considering the alternative, waiting for me to catch up.

"So what happened? Did they find out about the Web?" she asked, resuming her previous position; arm around my waist and head on my shoulder.

"Around the time of its closure they found a substantial amount of corpses under St. Mary's—bodies that may have come from the chamber. The discovery put the government in a very precarious position and the Web was suddenly closed."

"But you said the dead were taken to the Thames and disposed of."

I nodded in agreement. "Obviously over the centuries that passageway was sealed up, flooded by the river, or maybe it collapsed. Either way a new place had to be found to house the dead."

"St. Mary's?"

"My initial thought was that it was with the permission of the church, but now I'm not so sure; the powers that be may have been far greater," I explained. "The original church on that site was built in the twelfth century, and maybe it was then that the Web was constructed. In 1548, Lord Protector Somerset was in the midst of having a new house built; a palatial edifice on the grounds of what we now know as Somerset House. The lord practically had the church dismantled stone by stone, needing the materials for his new home, and likewise he demolished a chapel in St. Paul's and part of the priory at St. John's in Clerkenwell—the church were powerless to stop him. Four years later they had their revenge and executed him on Tower Hill."

"Michael, you're waffling again."

"Masonic intervention is the point I'm trying to make," I said. "Masonry is deeply entrenched in religion, and I'm wondering now which came first. Who, while Somerset was helping himself to London's landmarks—had the power to overrule the government and the church? The office was brought to me by a Mason. And did you count the steps leading up from the crypt? Thirty-three, Sylvia; the key number of masonry and religion."

We stopped in front of a tall Victorian house silhouetted against the dark sky, and I looked up.

"Penny's?" Sylvia said with surprise.

"I was going to book us in at the Savoy, but my tuxedo is at the cleaners. Any better ideas?"

"Smartarse!"

When the door opened Penny stood in a bathrobe, gawping at us in complete horror, her face motionless, her eyes flashing back and forth between us. Clearly she had been crying and now, at this moment, she could not comprehend what was standing in front of her. Suddenly she burst into tears and lurched toward us, hugging us both as she wept uncontrollably. "Thank God. Thank God." She led Sylvia down the hall and into the lounge, sitting her down on the long, leather settee. "I'll make tea. No, hot soup; you need something hot. I'll run a bath and fetch you a robe, Sylvia," she said, excitedly.

"Penny, there's something you should know," I intervened.

She was grinning brightly through her tears as she passed, turning her nose up as she surveyed my dreadful appearance and the acrid vapours I was giving off.

"Tell me everything later. Let's get you fed and cleaned up," she smiled.

"Badger's dead, Penny."

Her smile dropped away in an instant to be replaced by utter confusion. She looked to Sylvia who confirmed with a grim nod.

"Tonight—in the explosion," I said.

A smile of uncertainty returned to her lips.

"Badger left not an hour ago," she said. "He's been with the police and fire brigade all night outside the office. They told him there was nothing more he could do and sent him home. He came by to tell me what had happened; he's devastated."

"Badger made it out? He's alive?"

Penny nodded and her smile expanded.

"He's fine, Michael."

In the early hours, after Sylvia and I had bathed—although not together, I hasten to add—and our clothes had been bagged and thrown away, we all sat eating soup, talking about the night's events. Badger had exited the office moments before the explosion, and the force of the blast threw him into the road. According to the fire chief, the blast originated in the side alleyway of the department store; apparently an incendiary dropped during the blitz of last year, and the confinement of the narrow passage concentrated the explosion upward, tearing out the side of the aged and unstable five-storey structure, collapsing it like a house of cards. It was difficult to believe that a bomb had been dropped from hundreds of feet and buried itself in an alley barely three feet wide and not caused damage to the adjacent properties; nevertheless, I was willing to accept it; after tonight I was willing to accept anything. Penny had found Sylvia a fluffy white, candlewick robe, and I had to make do with a towel to hide my modesty. "Tomorrow I'll call Badger and have him bring me some new clothes," I said as I bathed the cuts to my legs with antiseptic."

"Already done," said Penny. "I called him while you were in the bath. He was ecstatic when I told him you were alive. He'll be here in the morning."

I smiled and nodded.

Penny moved toward me and took the bottle of antiseptic. "Lean forward, let's take a look at your back."

Sylvia was curled up in the corner of the settee, her eyes heavy and barely able to stay open.

"Go in my bed, Sylvia, and get some sleep. I'll be in shortly," said Penny.

"All right, but no funny business, you know what happened last time."

Both girls laughed as my head filled with lewd fantasies.

"Sylvia," I said as she reached the bedroom door. "Thank you."

She smiled warmly back at me, and for a moment I thought she was going to break again, but instead she grinned and struck a provocative pose. "Why, however will you repay me, Michael?" she pouted. Both girls roared with laughter again and Sylvia disappeared.

"You're a mess;" Penny said as she dabbed my wounds, "lots of grazes and cuts and some pretty serious bruising taking place. How do feel in yourself?"

"Lucky," I replied, "but I've got nothing; no business, no case-files, no cases."

"You have money, Michael. I know because I do your accounts—you'll start again, get a new office. In a week everything will be back to normal—you'll see."

She continued examining the cuts to my back.

"They're clean; no glass fragments or dirt. The cuts on your head look pretty bad, though." She gingerly teased my hair away from the wounds and proceeded to dab them with antiseptic. "Have you phoned Sarah yet?"

"I'll phone her in the morning. She won't have heard about the bombing so why worry her?"

She continued her task in silence, gently patting the ointment on the back of my head, and finally she straightened, sealing the lid on the small bottle. "There, all done, though I think you should see a doctor."

"I'll be fine, Penny, thank you."

"Then I'll let you get some sleep." She bent and kissed me on the cheek. "I'm glad you're alive, Michael," she said.

I laid my head down and gently slipped away into the arms of Morpheus—away from the pain and anxiety.

I heard a voice say, "Are you trying to mimic our Lord by rising from the dead?"

I stirred and opened my bleary eyes to see Badger standing in front of me, smiling brightly.

"Well—I have to model myself on someone, so it might as well be him," I replied.

He laughed and sat on the edge of the settee, gripping my shoulder firmly and then snatching his hand away as I emitted a pathetic groan.

During the night the fairies had come and adorned my body with gifts—aches, muscle seizures, and bruises as black as Newgate's knocker.

"I thought you were dead."

"Me too," I moaned as I attempted to sit up. "We had a rough time of it."

"How's Sylvia?"

"Still sleeping," said Penny as she breezed in carrying two mugs of tea. "Toast?"

"Toast would be fine."

I swung my legs around and eased my aching body upright; pulling the blanket around my shoulders, sitting hunched and huddled like a shipwreck survivor. At some time during the night someone had dismantled my spine and reassembled it at random, tossing away the squishy bits that separate the vertebrae and replacing them with sharp, metal objects.

"Penny says you escaped through a series of tunnels," said Badger as he passed me a mug of tea, "something called—the Spider's Web?"

I nodded. "Something that *may* have been the Spider's Web," I clarified, though a little embarrassed.

"And this Spider's Web was used for the purpose of torture?"

It was going to be difficult to explain, especially to someone as cynical as Badger. He observed me with a suspicious leer and a grin on the verge of eruption.

"It may have been part of the vaults that made up the Web, but just as easily it may have been a disused slaughter-house; hundreds still exist under the city. Either way I knew of its existence—the geometry of the tunnels—and used them as a means of escape."

"And at no time did you feel the need to impart this information with any of us?"

I evaded the question by burying my face in the mug of tea, but when I resurfaced he was staring intently back at me.

"Does it matter?" I shrugged. "Shouldn't you just be happy we're alive? Or—if you want a history lesson on the Spider's Web, starting from the medieval period to present day, I'm more than willing to . . ."

"No, spare me," he winced, shrinking at the prospect. "Explain it to me one day when my nerves are capable of handling the boredom and I can control the urge to vomit."

Penny was buzzing around, making tea, burning toast, flitting to and fro between the kitchen, bathroom and bedroom, and continuously asking if I was okay whenever she flashed across the hallway.

"I bought you what you needed," Badger said, nodding to a heap of shopping bags in the hallway; "shoes, shirt, trousers, underwear; everything. You like pink?"

Sylvia emerged from the greyness of the bedroom, attired in the fluffy, white robe and looking remarkably like someone I had never laid eyes on in my life; devoid of ruby red lipstick, black eye-shadow, and hair that had lost its gravitational force-field and now framed her face like a pair of cheap curtains. Badger rose at once and gave her a soft hug. She hobbled to the settee and collapsed into it.

"I feel like I've just spent the night with ten of the biggest men in . . ." She paused, realising her private analogies were actually being heard. "Doesn't matter," she said.

A taxi collected us at the door, crossed the river and swung left into Fleet Street. My head turned toward The Royal Courts of Justice as we passed, and I fixed my stare to St. Mary's as it approached from its strange location in the centre of the roadway at the top of the Strand. Everything appeared to be normal until the cab rounded Aldwych and turned right into the road where I had worked for nine years. "Stop!" The five-storey building above my office was now just a mountain of bricks and rubble sandwiched between the surviving buildings either side. The road before it was clear, as was the pavement, neatly swept, and with the exception of a lone policeman stationed outside, there was no other activity whatsoever. "A bomb went off here last night," the cabby informed us. "Bleedin' lucky no one was killed." I gazed at the scene in utter disbelief, and when the driver turned, he acknowledged it. "Somethin' up, governor?" he asked. I shook my head. "Change of plan—Elephant and Castle, please." The taxi pulled a large circle back around Aldwych and crossed over London Bridge. Badger had seen exactly what I had—nothing.

"You did tell the police that there were two people buried under that rubble, didn't you?" I hissed.

"Of course I did. I was three hours with the police and the fire-chief. I talked to every official there."

"Then why is nobody digging us out? Why isn't there anything that remotely resembles a shovel at that bomb-sight?"

Badger could only shake his head in bewilderment. "I honestly don't know."

The cab slowed on the south side of the bridge, and I suddenly turned my head to Badger. "Officials—what officials? You said you talked to officials!"

Badger took on a pensive refrain, frowning into nothingness and muttering quietly.

"Badger?" I coaxed.

"Wait!" he snapped. "You're not the only one who suffered a traumatic experience last night, you know. I thought I was dead. I thought you and Sylvia were dead."

At this moment in time I was only person on this planet with problems. No one else had gone through what I went through. No one had suffered in the way I had suffered. My friend's brief reprimand reminded me how lucky I was. I nodded silently and turned my face to the window, to the stagnant traffic all around us.

"I was out the office but a few steps," Badger recalled thoughtfully, "maybe I was crossing the road—half-way—and suddenly BOOM! I was on the floor, bricks flying everywhere and this noise that sounded like thunder; and then there was yellow. I just ran as fast as I could, until I was out of this dust-cloud. As the haze cleared I walked back. Jesus, Michael, I was scared. I thought another one was going to explode, but I couldn't hear any planes or sirens. Slowly I saw it; the whole building was down, and as far as I knew, you and Sylvia were dead. I can't remember how long it was before I heard the clanging of bells and saw the fire engines. The police arrived and threw up barriers across the road, and then army personnel, and local authorities searching for the gas and water supplies. But then this black car pulled up right in front of me; you know, one of those big, shiny limousines, and three suited men got out and began asking me questions. I told them what I had told the police—that you and Sylvia were down in the office—trapped. The man asking all the questions had a skin complaint, like dermatitis, you know, his face blotchy and flaky. Come to think of it, they stood quite alone from everyone else, just looking. I thought they were police, plain-clothes. He told me that there I was nothing I could do and should go home . . ."

"The man with dermatitis?"

"Yes, he said the area had to be cleared and there was the possibility of a second incendiary, or even a third detonating. I just did as I was told."

The Elephant and Castle is a well-established landmark on the south side of the river and a borough in its own right, but it could easily be Southwark, Walworth or Kennington. In itself it is an insignificant place, made significant only by its curious title and the importance of its location. Like Rome, all roads seem to lead there, yet there is no great monument, no obelisk, no pantheon or cenotaph; not even an informative plaque to explain away its vainglorious name. Traffic heading to and from the city merge at this point, spiralling out to Clapham, Camberwell, Peckham, Southwark, New Cross and Blackheath, to the suburbs and home-counties beyond. Like arteries serving a beating heart, the ventricles and veins spread outward, across the river and into the city, pumping life into the offices and industries. But for the clothes and the power-driven vehicles the Elephant and Castle is unchanged, a remnant of the Victorian period, its long, grimy terraces of tall houses still intact, the narrow side streets unchanged, the East Lane market in Walworth Road flourishing and filled with shoppers, as it has for hundreds of years. The pages of the history books pay scant attention to it, if any. There are no wonders to be seen here, no famed inventors, architects or leading authority who ever resided in any of the sorry houses occupying the many rundown streets; it can lay claim to absolutely nothing. For me, it is significant only because a certain broken down prostitute once lived here—in the workhouse in Renfrew Street, before she ventured to the East End and my father found her—his first victim.

The taxi drew to a stop outside the offices of Mansall's, and stepping onto the pavement I leaned in through the window and paid the driver, who fingered the pound notes with a troubled expressed. "These are wet, mate," he grumbled. "Just off the press," I informed him with a wink. "Keep the change." The offices were plush to anyone peering in from the outside; thick piled carpet, shiny desks, and a dozen or so beautiful girls drumming away on typewriters behind the Mansall name emblazoned in gold lettering across the glazed façade. “Give me a few minutes, will you?” I said to Badger. He looked around and fixed his stare to the nearest public house. “Take your time,” he smiled. I ventured inside to be greeted by a young lady, who immediately rose from her seat, pushed her mousy coloured hair behind her ears, and expressed a smile that any red-blooded male would interpret as an invitation to deflower her. “Mr. Mansall?” I said. She crooked her head to one side, flipped open a ledger on the edge of her desk, and then looked back at me. “Mr. Mansall is indisposed at present. Have you an appointment?” she asked, her sensual smile enhancing her possible sexual proclivities. “But he is here?” I pursued. She cast her eyes back down, placing her index finger to her bottom lips. “Ah, he is, but he won’t be seeing anyone.” I looked to the end of the office, at the solitary closed door centring the wall. “Wanna bet?” I replied. I marched down the aisle between the line of desks and the beautiful, staring faces; their flashing eyes anticipating trouble ahead. Bernie was engrossed in deep conversation, phone pressed to ear and elbows on the desk, muttering and nodding, and after a few moments his eyes looked up to wander the room, but instead settled on me. “I’ll call you back,” he blurted into the receiver. I stood in the open doorway with the concerned receptionist standing behind me.

“The prodigal son,” said Bernie, standing up and throwing his arms open.

I was in no mood for humour, especially from someone who had furnished me a tomb as an office.

“It’s okay, Susan, I can handle this. Go back to whatever it is you do,” Bernie said as he rounded his desk and ushered the girl away.

“You’re a lucky man, Michael,” he said as he took my arm.

“Do I look lucky?” I replied tersely.

He studied my face; the small cuts on my forehead and cheeks, the larger cuts above my right eye and across the bridge of my nose, the abrasions to the left side of my neck, the variations of lacerations embellishing my hands. And that was what was visible.

“You’re alive,” he shrugged callously, “and that’s all that matters.”

"You don't appear surprised to see me, Bernie—alive, I mean. Only, I was wondering why nobody is digging out the broken and crushed remains of my secretary and me. Everyone is going about their business as if nothing has happened."

He was hesitant, the words trying to form on lips, but his capacity for lying—especially to a good friend—escaped him and his robust frame deflated.

"Truth is, Michael, I knew you were alive three hours after the explosion. I was contacted."

"Contacted?"

He allowed the question to deliberately slip by him, and busied his hands with an empty coffee cup on his desk, turning it slowly on its saucer.

"We sent people in as soon as we heard," he explained sheepishly. "They found the hatch open; they knew you had made it out."

"You sent people in? Bernie, those tunnels were flooded!"

"Michael, there is a drainage system down there as well as a ventilation system. At no time were you ever going to drown."

"Well—that's a relief. I honestly don't know what I was worried about."

"It's been an ordeal, I know," he sighed, "but you're safe now. True, you look the worse for ware, but what have you lost?"

"Everything, Bernie—I've lost everything."

"Oh, you've lost nothing; nothing that can't be retrieved from medical reports, police reports, the national archives—your memory," he said, tapping his finger on the side of his head. "You just need a new office."

"And you have the very thing?" I grinned.

He pulled a file from his top drawer and opened it.

"What people, Bernie?" I asked. "You said you sent people in. Who were they?"

He studied the file before him as if it were of the greatest interest in an attempt to sidestep my question.

"Bernie!"

"They were just people—people we use in matters like this," he retorted defensively.

"Masons?"

He took up the position—staring blankly ahead, eyelids barely moving—but he realised I wasn't about to let the matter rest, and reluctantly he nodded.

"Yes, Michael, they were Masons; army personnel in one form or another," he explained wearily. "I received a phone call that the department store had collapsed, and immediately went there. One didn't have to be a genius to see that the heap of rubble had not yet fallen into the thirty-foot void beneath. The police and fire brigade were talking of two people trapped in the office below; I contacted certain people, but shortly before their arrival the inevitable happened. Nevertheless, we ordered our people in to find you—in the remote hope you had survived."

"You went in through St. Mary's?"

My friend shook his head and looked surprised.

"There's a passage that leads to the church?" he asked.

"That's how we got out. Don't tell me you didn't know."

"I didn't, I swear."

"Then how did you get in?"

His face fell still and serious, and he leaned forward, resting on his elbows.

"I have no idea how they got in, Michael," he said, patiently. "I only know that I called on every resource available to me to get you out of there, and they will never let me forget the debt I owe them. I cannot and will not give out any more information regarding the people or the organisation that endeavoured to save your life. I only know that once the hatch was discovered open, word was given to call off the search of the collapsed building above. That said, I have office space to let in Blackfriars Road; recently vacated by an accountancy firm who have moved their business to the suburbs—less chance of bombings, you see. Interested?"

I had been abrupt and sometimes down-right rude towards my good friend, never once taking into consideration to what depths he went to in order to pull me from the wreckage, and although I made no apologies, I felt consumed by a true sense of regret for my behaviour.

"How many square feet?" I asked, turning the dossier slightly toward me.

"Approximately the same as you had—one entire floor with all modern amenities. It's not the Strand and it's not the city, but needs must, eh? On the up side, it has nothing whatsoever to with me apart from the fact that I am acting as the agent. On the down side, you are responsible for all the bills; rent, rates—the whole deal—still interested?"

I nodded and smiled. "Can we meet tomorrow? I'll give it the once over."

"No problem, Mike. We can have a beer after."

I shook his hand. "I look forward to it."

-19-

Like most people I am a creature of habit, and despite the obliteration of my office, my journey into the city remained the same. Now, instead of leaving the station and heading up Fleet Street, I would turn left and walk over Blackfriars Bridge. On this morning I was early and walked directly to the nearby coffee shop. Notwithstanding the crisscross tape the glass was misted, save for a small circle close the entrance. No sooner was I through the door than arms embraced me and a head nuzzled into my neck. Having used the same shop for many years I cannot recall ever being greeted with such affection and quickly concluded that this wasn't the manager ecstatic about my impending purchase of a coffee with one sugar but something of a completely different nature. Rachel stared up at me through blinding tears.

"God, Michael, I thought you were dead," she said in a trembling voice as her soft fingertips gently touched my scars. "I've been here most mornings, but when I never saw you I went to your friend Mr. Mansall; he said you have new offices."

"The old offices are a little cluttered; mostly with department store," I said.

"Thank God you're okay," she said as she hugged me again.

Having blocked the entrance entirely I stood in the thin queue of grey-suited gentlemen and made my order of two coffees and then took up the nearest vacant table. I told my story, dispensing with the history of the Spiders Web, its Masonic connections or how my best friend had persuaded me to set up business in a chasm not far from the centre of the earth. I mused whether Bernie had set Rachel up in a tree house.

"And how is Celia?" asked Rachel as she held my hand across the table.

"Sylvia," I emphasized, "is doing fine; cut and bruised but recovering."

"She must mean a lot to you."

I shrugged and smiled. "She saved my life; what more can I say?"

"Well," she said, patting me on the hand, "I'm glad you're both safe. Have you spoken with Mr. Mansall yet? He was very helpful; found me a beautiful flat in Southwark—big windows and bright; very roomy, and it has a garden."

As Rachel described her Shangri-La her eyes were wide and her voice full of enthusiasm, and she went into minute detail of her intentions concerning furnishings and colours for each individual room. On completion she smiled warmly back at me.

"I don't know how to thank you, Michael," she said, and then as if struck by an epiphany she began to delve into her handbag. She placed down on the table a small pile of creased and twisted paper that at one time must have resembled currency; one-pound notes and a scattering of pennies, halfpennies and silver. "First month's rent," she beamed.

It was difficult to look at the assemblage of beer-sodden notes without bursting into uncontrollable laughter. The pathetic heap looked as if it had been picked out of slop-trays or found in gutters or down the back and sides of an old settee. I registered Rachel's elated smile. What was initially a source of amusement for me was now a source of embarrassment; she must have scrimped and scraped up every penny she could find.

"I can't accept that," I said with an incline of my head. "Illegal."

"Illegal?" she rebuffed. "Why? Just take it."

"Misappropriation of funds," I winced as I tried to spout anything that sounded remotely lawfully correct. "As a lawyer it would be unethical to take money in the absence of a contract the said money appertains to . . . eh, that being the contract between the first part, that's me, and the second part, the tenant—that's you. The contract, as you know, is a legally binding . . . thingy . . . founded on mutual agreement between the first part and the second part—you and me."

Rachel gawped at me in total disbelief.

"Receive any head injuries in that explosion, Michael?" she asked.

"Until Bernie—Mr. Mansall gives me the contract I cannot legally accept that money."

"Then accept it illegally!" she growled through gritted teeth.

"Sorry," I replied, dismissing her remark. "Best thing you can do is put it back in your handbag; buy some paint for the new flat, or curtains. Once I have the contract some arrangement can be made between us."

I concluded with a polite smile.

"You people are certifiable you know that, don't you," she said, scooping the cash back into her handbag. "And when do you think you'll have the contract?"

"Weeks—months; who knows?" I raised my coffee-cup. "Chin-chin."

She knew what I was doing. She smiled warmly and squeezed my hand again.

"You're a good man, Michael James," she said.

She started to laugh as my face emerged over my cup. Frothy coffees are all very romantic but they're not for the faint hearted—or those who wish to keep their top lip free of white moustaches. She took a napkin and began to dab it away.

"Heard from David?" I asked, taking the napkin from her and completing the task.

She shook her head grimly but forced a shallow smile.

"Not for a while. Do you think the war is over, Michael; it's all gone very quiet?"

"For the time being; England, perhaps, but the rest of Europe is still under siege. Don't you listen to the radio?"

She shook her head. "I try not to," she said, and then inhaling deeper asked, "How's your lovely wife?"

"Fine; Sarah's fine," I returned, looking towards the window.

She appraised me curiously.

"Something's wrong, Michael. What's the matter?"

Last night my house was dark and quiet save for the gentle moans of my wife coming from the bedroom. It began in the early hours and terminated some two hours later in a noisy crescendo. Soon she and Billy Fletcher appeared at the bottom of the stairs and kissed passionately by the door. "See you tomorrow?" she whispered, softly rubbing her cheek against his. He nodded and smiled. "In a few hours," he said. Trains to the surrounding counties had all been cancelled though a sporadic service was laid on for the London boroughs. I managed to cadge a lift from Andy who was visiting his sick mother in Maidstone and arrived home about 10 o'clock. Sarah was nowhere to be seen and I took my place in my easy chair in the darkness of the lounge. At around about 2 o'clock I awakened from my bout of dozing to see Sarah and Billy Fletcher walk in through the front door and head straight up stairs. I did nothing but listen as they made love in my bed. Why I did not defend my castle and its contents I cannot say; some things are inevitable and not worth fighting for. As they engaged in their farewell kiss I leaned against the doorframe looking into the hallway. As Billy pulled his face away from hers he saw me and a look of horror washed over him. He suddenly pushed her away.

"Too late for that now, Billy," I said.

Sarah appeared mortified but her face still glowed as a result of her two hours of passion.

"Michael, what are you doing home?" she gasped as she fastened her robe and fingered her hair.

"I live here;" I said, "not much I'll grant you but I pay the mortgage." I averted my stare to her lover. "And you, Billy—delivering a little more than groceries, aren't you? Here you are in my house, in my bedroom, in my wife."

As big and as muscular as Billy Fletcher was he dropped his stare to the floor. "I'm sorry, Michael," he said, quietly.

Throughout the exchange Sarah was looking at the marks on my face and edging closer. She put her hand out as if to touch me, but thinking better of it backed away to her original place.

"Are you hurt, Michael?" she asked with concern.

"You'll never know," I returned, bitterly.

"I should go," said Billy.

Sarah went on the defensive almost immediately.

"What did you expect?" she snarled. "You haven't come near me for months—you're never home . . . You think I don't know what you're up to?"

"Save it for your solicitor, Sarah. Are you still here, Billy?"

Billy opened the door and stepped out into the early morning air.

"Again, Michael, I'm sorry," he said.

"You stay there, Billy!" demanded Sarah as if he were an unruly dog.

"Yes, you stay there, Billy," I echoed as I stepped outside to join him.

I was remarkably composed given the situation, stopping before him and looking up at his face half concealed by shadow. He sighed nervously and looked away.

"You know, Billy, I don't blame you for what's happened," I said. "But you might want to consider that if she can do it to me she can just as easily do it to you. Good luck."

Thereafter I headed for the station, huddled myself on the platform bench and awaited the arrival of the first train.

"We've decided to have a trial separation," I said.

Rachel's stare fixed rigid and then animated itself into one of shock.

"But—but . . . Separation—for how long?"

I shrugged. "Death would be about the time-span I have in mind."

"So it's serious?"

"About as serious as it gets. So now you have somewhere to live and I don't."

She began to stir her coffee slowly, glancing at me sporadically as if she were considering an alternative to my dilemma.

"Michael, if you like you could . . ."

"No-no-no! I have enough problems," I said, spontaneously.

"But you don't know what I was going to say."

"Yes, I do, Rachel, and it's the worse idea in the history of worse ideas. Besides, I'm seeing Bernie this morning and I'll have somewhere in no time. Thank you, anyway."

She began to grin flirtatiously. "Scared I'll try and have my wicked way with you?" she teased.

"Petrified. Do you know that after copulation the Black Widow spider devours her lover, consuming him completely?"

"I'm not a Black Widow," she grinned.

"No, you're not. You are a happily married woman awaiting her husband's return, so behave yourself."

She giggled like a teenage girl but then patted me on the hand again.

"Thing's will work out, Michael," she said, optimistically. "You'll see. I'd like you to see the new flat; after all it's yours. What do you say you pick me up from the bookshop one evening and come back—I can make dinner?"

The only word I heard was 'bookshop' and pushing my coffee cup to one side, leaned forward.

"Could you do me a favour, Rachel?" I asked.

She nodded, staring back as if what I had to say was of the greatest importance.

"Have you ever heard of a book called The Vassarri Memoirs? It was published about six or seven years ago by Fallow's Publishing House."

Rachel shook her head, picked a paper napkin from a chrome dispenser on the table and then started to rummage around in her handbag.

"What was it called?" she asked, eventually finding a pen.

"The Vassarri Memoirs—I think."

She wrote down the title. "Published by Fallow's?"

"Yes."

"I can't say I've heard of it but I'll look through the indexes. Failing that I can ask; we have a lot of contacts. If it's around I'll find it; Reedy's bound to know."

"Reedy?"

"Charlie Reed; he's in charge of the warehouse at Wapping Wharf. Any books that aren't sold, unwanted or are too damaged to be restored usually end up there. Some are shipped abroad but most are burned or sent to the pulp mills. What's the book about?"

I shrugged my shoulders. "I'm not sure, but as you deal in books I'd thought I'd ask."

"Well, I can only try. Now, what about my invitation?"

"Can you give me a few days to sort myself out?"

She smiled, took another napkin and scribbled down her address and contact phone number.

"If I'm not there I'll be in the shop or working in the pub; I'm not hard to find."

-20-

Badger and I entered a large room; half glossed in bottle green and white paint with cast-iron radiators around its perimeter, and save for a table in its centre and a few chairs, contained little else. The governor of Wandsworth Prison, no doubt heavily influenced by both the government and the D.P.P, had afforded us and the prisoner complete confidentiality; no wardens, except stationed outside the door, no bars between us and no time limit on the interview. On leaving the room we would all be searched for any passed contraband, and they were the conditions we had to agree to in order to speak with Henderson. And there he was, seated at the table, watching our every nervous move; a large man with receding black hair, square jawed and forearms straining to burst out of their confinement. He was wearing a grey prison uniform, the number 90716 emblazoned across the left pocket of his jacket, and his posture appeared contrived and lacking confidence. As we approached he smiled slightly and drew back in his chair, and I'm certain I detected a slight tremble in his hands resting before him. It was agreed that Badger would take the lead as he was more experienced, but in my own thoughtless fashion, I placed my business card on the table as a form of introduction, to which Badger sighed exhaustively and immediately took the reins.

"We meet at last, Mr. Henderson. My name is Mr. Banner and this is Mr. James, and our company is to represent your defence. Obviously you know the purpose of our visit?"

George Henderson's eyes were focussed on the card but he raised his green eyes to mine and then looked to Badger.

"I was told," he replied.

On our arrival the chief warden informed us that prisoner 90716 could be decidedly slow when it came to understanding or answering questions, and that he had a curious habit of tilting his head to the left whenever he was confused. It would therefore be beneficial to us to rephrase and simplify the question should this affliction ever become apparent, as he was prone to get muddled and thereafter would fall silent. "Speak to him as if he were a child," the chief warden explained.

I took a pen and notepad from my briefcase and set it on the table to which George Henderson stared at it momentarily and then smiled at me.

"I have a brain like a sieve," I explained. "They're just for reference."

"I understand," he nodded.

Badger half reclined in his chair, crossing his legs and tucking his thumb into his waistcoat pocket; a posture that exuded authority and one that appeared to unnerve Henderson. I caught Badger's eye and shook my head, to which he fell back into his previous position, his fingers laced together on the tabletop.

"George. May I call you George?" said Badger with a friendly smile.

"No one has called me George for a year now. I've been here so long with nobody to talk to. Is the war over yet?"

"Not yet, George, but if Churchill has his way it soon will be."

"He's a good man. He'll save us I know he will. Do you know they bombed my house; the house I was born and raised in? The whole street was wiped out in a moment; the school I used to go to, Mr. Crabtree's Grocers and the laundry where my mum used to work. Why would the Germans want to do that?"

"It's war, George," I intervened. "There's no rhyme or reason for it."

He agreed with a nod but sighed huffily.

"George, do you know why you're here?" asked Badger.

"Murder," he replied, simply. "But I never killed anyone. I swear, Mr. Banner, I never killed anyone. They said I confessed but I never did. My family have had to move away. My wife can't visit me because she's too scared."

"We know you're innocent, George. Unfortunately you were in the wrong place at the wrong time. We know Carlisle framed you."

"But why would he do that? Why frame an innocent man for all those horrible murders?"

"It's complicated. The purpose of our visit is to compile a profile on you," I said.

George Henderson tilted his head slightly.

"We need you to tell us about your life, George;" I continued, "to prove you're a good man and that Carlisle used you to his own ends. That established the D.P.P. will drop the case."

Again the prisoner tilted his head.

"The D.P.P. is the Director of Public Prosecution, George. They decide what goes to trial and what doesn't," Badger intervened promptly. "They know Carlisle is the guilty one. It is our view that this case won't go to trial and you will be released. After which we shall seek compensation for wrongful arrest and damages."

"I'm to be released?" the prisoner cried brightly.

"Certainly, George, but first we need to establish your history, leaving them in no doubt that you are completely innocent. Can you do that, George? Can you tell us about your life?"

George Henderson appeared elated at the prospect of freedom.

"How much do you want to know?" he asked.

"All of it, George. Start at the beginning," I said.

He thought for a moment, muttering to himself as if he were trying to collate his past into order.

"When were you born?" asked Badger.

"April. April 6th 1896," he replied spontaneously.

"Where?"

"Mile End, London, in the house the Germans blew up; Stewart Road. It was a good street, filled with good people. I had a lot of friends in that street. There was Billy, he was my best friend, and Stephen, Peter, Arty, Bobby, and in the next street there was Johnny. P, Johnny. T, Keith and the Moffet twins; we all went to the same school."

"What about girls, George? Were there no girls in your life?"

He nodded and smiled warmly and then began to laugh.

"Suzie West, Billy's sister. He found us in the shed when we were twelve, half naked. He broke my nose. God, he beat the shit out of me. But I would have taken a thousand beatings just to be with her; we were childhood sweethearts, and it didn't matter what Billy did to me or her, we never left each others side. Everyone in the street thought we would marry one day. I thought we would marry one day, but we never did."

"What happened to her?" I asked.

He shrugged his shoulders.

"I left school at fifteen and became a fireman. My dad was a train driver and the best way to become a train driver was to be a fireman first."

Badger and I exchanged puzzled glances and Henderson, registering our confusion, smiled and leaned forward.

"A fireman is the man who keeps the boilers stocked with coal," he said proudly. "But in 1914 war broke out, and me and Billy wanted to do our bit for King and Country. We rallied everyone to join us, and so shortly after my eighteenth birthday we were all marching off to war and Stewart Road was filled with people. Men cheered and the women cried; we felt like heroes before we'd even left the East-End; we were so proud."

"But you were back in England before you were twenty," said Badger.

The reverie that Henderson was caught up in dissipated and the reminiscent smile fell away.

"Invalided out—back to Blighty," explained Henderson morosely. "I had to go straight into hospital for a while. I was in pretty bad shape."

"But you never came back alone?" said Badger.

George shook his head. "Me and Brian came back. We were the only two left; whole unit gone—all gone."

"And Brian? What happened to him?"

"We lost contact. He was deeply affected by the war. It changed him."

"And Suzy? Did you rekindle your relationship with her?"

The prisoner tilted his head.

"Did you see her again?" I emphasised.

He slowly shook his head and his eyes began to wonder the room, as though his train of thoughts were distracted. I wrote the name 'Suzy West' and circled it with a question mark.

"Did you see her again, George?" I asked again.

"She was gone, like all the others; no idea where she went—just gone," he replied.

He shook his head disapprovingly at an event that happened twenty-five years ago as if it were yesterday.

"But I met May," he said, his dull eyes brightening slightly.

"Your wife?"

"She was pretty then; a good looking woman."

"And you had a family," Badger intervened.

He nodded. "Five children. Who'd have thought it, eh? Five kids."

George Henderson spent the next thirty-five minutes talking about his children, exuding great pride in their school efforts and their social activities. He took great pride, also, in being responsible for their good upbringing and for their wellbeing. He smiled nostalgically as if it were some long forgotten dream that had come to mind—a contrived invention of an overactive imagination that belonged to someone else other than George Henderson. Badger and I exchanged weary glances as he continued, seemingly without abatement. His heart swelled near to bursting as he recalled his youngest child's first day at school, and his expression and tone fell dismally morose when he spoke of his five-day vigil at his daughter's bedside when she contracted meningitis. His hands were constantly in motion to demonstrate visually as well as verbally, his true meaning, enhancing the vocabulary and certain words he was bereft of. Now and then either Badger or myself would insert a missing word into his narrative whenever he struggled for the correct description, and with an assertive nod of his head, he would resume the theme of his subject.

"That's very nice, George," said Badger with a feigned smile, "but can you tell us a little about your work?"

"As a train driver, you mean?" he asked, a little fraught at being coerced away from his favourite reminiscences. "Didn't I tell you that?"

"You did, George," Badger replied, exuding patience but tapping his pencil on the tabletop frustratingly. "My question has more to do with your journey home from the workplace. Am I correct in assuming that ostensibly you worked out of London Bridge Station?"

I groaned at the words 'Assuming' and 'Ostensibly', for George narrowed his eyes in confusion and looked to me for help.

"What Mr. Banner is asking, George is that London Bridge Station is where you went to work and the place you left every evening when work was finished. You were stopped three times by the police at different places; not your direct route to Camberwell and home," I elaborated.

"Not always," said George with a shake of his head. "I'd end up in all different kind of places," he added.

Now I was confused. According to George Henderson's employment records, on the three occasions he was stopped, he left London Bridge Station and no other.

"That's not strictly true, is it?" I said.

Badger began to nod as if he knew the answer and leaned closer to me.

"George's overtime entailed running munitions to the coast," he whispered, "which would be considered a government operation, and therefore protected by government restrictions; secret."

And that basically meant that the Great Eastern Railway was obliged by government regulations to keep the activities of their employees a secret when working on assignments specifically for and on behalf of the government. In other words, if they say Henderson was at London Bridge Station on any of the given nights in question, then he was.

"I'll contact the War Office," Badger added.

I nodded and smiled across the table at the prisoner.

"Have I said something wrong?" asked George.

"No. Everything is fine. Tell us some more about your children."

For one full hour George spoke about his family, and no matter how much either Badger or I tried to lead him to his whereabouts regarding the nights of the murders, he somehow led us back to the same excruciating subject. It was a lost cause, and with a signal from me Badger closed his notepad and stood up.

"Looks like we're all out of time, George," he said as he looked at his watch.

"Really," replied the prisoner with disappointment. "I really miss talking to people. Hey, how's Eddie?"

"He's fine, George," I said as I gathered up my belongings. "He sends his best to you."

He smiled. "Do you think I'll get to see him soon?"

"Very soon," Badger said, assuredly. "One more thing, George. Can you remember what you told Inspector Carlisle the day you went to the police station?"

George reclined in his chair and folded his arms.

"There were quite a few things I couldn't tell him," he began. "When I was doing the night-time runs we were told not to say anything."

"Because it was for the war effort?"

"The bosses said it was secret—that we weren't allowed to tell. He got angry, really angry. He called me a liar and started making all these things up, saying I was at places where I wasn't and threatening me with hanging. I never told him where I was because I wasn't allowed to. I was just doing what I was told. Was I wrong?"

"No, George, you weren't wrong," I said. "We'll have you out of here and back with your wife and children in no time."

Badger was already knocking on the door, signalling the warden that we had completed deposing the prisoner. I gave George a comforting pat on the shoulder and walked away.

"Thank you, Michael," he said.

I raised my hand and disappeared into the corridor.

It happened on the A3212, in Grosvenor Road as we headed down the side of the Thames towards Westminster. A light rain was falling when we left the prison, but it developed into a torrential thunderstorm by the time we crossed the river. Never having experienced the sensation before, I felt like the car was sliding on ice, as if it wanted to go anywhere other than in the direction I was pointing it. Being the excellent driver I considered myself to be, I gave Badger a reassuring smile as I grappled with the steering wheel. "Just the weather; tyres lose grip in the rain," I explained with considerable authority. "Feels like there's something broken," he replied, as he looked through the notes he had taken at the interview. "Nothing at all to worry about," I added. The car suddenly began to bump and shake with such ferocity Badger's notes became an inky blur. "Are you sure nothing is broken?" he asked with alarm. I conceded and pulled over to the roadside, and winding my window down squinted through the rain, expected to see a ship's anchor dragging behind. Badger at once deduced that my trusty automobile had suffered a stroke, owing to the fact that it had dropped on one side. I braved the stormy conditions to investigate, circled the car once and spotted the problem and then climbed back in. "We have a puncture," I informed him. He glanced up from his notes. "I'm not mechanically minded, but that would account for your tyres losing grip." I ignored his remark and gazed out at the haze the passing cars kicked up through the incessant motion of the windscreen wipers. "Can you fix it?" I asked him. He calmly observed me and slowly shook his head. "I once had a puncture on my bicycle when I was eleven years old. But my father, who was a mechanical marvel, undertook the challenge and had me back on my paper-round within the hour. He exploited me every chance he got." I fell short of grinding my teeth, staring back at him questionably. "Not a chance in hell," he said. "And certainly not in this monsoon."

We sat there for a while, in the dry confines of the car as traffic sped by and tooted occasionally, the drivers of which were oblivious to my dilemma and concerned only with reaching their own destination. The mist on the windows began to thicken, and I wiped a circle to peek outside to monitor the downpour and consider the possibility of it ever easing.

"So what did you think?" asked Badger as he continued to study the notes.

"Think—about what?" I replied, preoccupied with the world outside my stranded magic carpet.

"Henderson—who else?"

"He didn't tell us anything we didn't know. And in all fairness he was limited to what he could tell Carlisle because he was sworn to secrecy by the war department, which only makes the matter more problematic. Suzy West knew him better than anybody. We should contact her and see what she has to say."

"I'll try and track her down," he said, jotting it down in his notepad as a reminder. "So, what conclusions did you reach?"

I thought for a moment. "It is what it is. Carlisle falsified his statement. He's innocent."

A few minutes melted away into history, and with a look at my watch I opened the car door.

"Whatever are you doing, Michael?"

"Changing the wheel; how hard can it be?"

"You'll drown, you idiot. Leave the wretched thing and we'll get a taxi."

I half stepped out of the vehicle and glared back at him disapprovingly.

"You want me to abandon an expensive car on the side of road? What if Peter's wife happens to pass by, what would she think? It was a gift, Badger. And may I remind you that we have a 3 o'clock appointment."

"It belonged to a dead man. It's cursed, I tell you, cursed," cried Badger with an unconvincing ghostly quiver in his voice.

The rain hit me from all directions, caught on a chilly, erratic wind that pushed down the river in cloudy sheets and turned the bridges and adjacent roads into a delta of fluid motion, and notwithstanding the waves expelled by the passing traffic and the black clouds overhead that appeared to be dropping lower owing to their weight in water, I was subject to all manner of abuse by the drivers trapped behind me on the inside lane. I opened the boot and surveyed its emptiness with a hopeless curiosity, searching out the necessary tools required for the job at hand. On the left a pristine car-jack was secured to the bulkhead of the wheel-arch, along with a disjointed handle and a misshaped bar with a hexagon shaped end that could have only been designed for loosening nuts. The spare wheel was in an upright position, one third sunk into the floor and covered with a purposefully made cover complete with poppers that secured it to the interior body. Drenched to the bone I set about approaching the chore with optimism, setting the tools out on the pavement and removing the cover from the spare wheel. It was then I discovered it. Inside the hub of the wheel was a leather-bound book; an expensive covering for your every day notepad. Given its location, I initially thought it was a car manual, and I looked forward to finding the section on 'Changing wheels for cretins and the mechanically challenged' but it couldn't have been further from it. Inside there were pages of hand-written notes in Peter's handwriting, and in the sleeve pockets, back and front, were a half-dozen business cards. The contents of his notes referred to the Government Intelligence story he had been forced to shelve, and the business cards were a variation of contacts or were in reference to the subject of his story. One was scant, giving a Whitehall address and a business phone number; the name—Eleanor Cole; the government lady Peter had mentioned last time we met.

Within the hour we were circling Westminster Square. Badger had surrendered to his selfishness and accompanied me, along with the car manual from the glove compartment. I placed Eleanor Cole's card in my top pocket and tossed the leather-bound note pad in the tyre-well to save me any unnecessary questions, and together we managed to replace the wheel. Wetter than Venice we headed towards Trafalgar Square, the heater blowing to full capacity, and the windows steamed to the density of a pea-soup fog.

"You have yet to fill me in on your sexual escapades," Badger grinned slyly. "Were you going to tell me?"

"It wasn't my intention, no," I replied.

"Why ever not? If I were in your position, or to be grammatically correct 'Positions' with a young nubile mystery, I wouldn't hesitate to fill you in on the details."

"Nothing has happened."

He stared at me with suspicion, tears of rain sliding slowly down his face until they became trapped within the crevices of his smile.

"Your reluctance to brag about such an auspicious occasion leads me to several possibilities. The first is that you were unable to function to your full capacity because Sarah came to mind whenever you looked at Rachel. The second is that you did function to your full capacity but she lapsed into a deep sleep induced by boredom. The third . . ."

"Will you be serious?"

"My dear chap, I am being nothing less. Now please have the common decency to regale me with your good fortune, and spare no detail no matter how gory."

"Nothing has happened, Badger," I sighed wearily.

Lord Horatio Nelson stared out across the city skyline, oblivious to our presence as we circled around his feet and headed off up the Strand and immediately slowed to a stop in the dense volume of traffic. Badger took in the female pedestrians as they hurried past and nodded approvingly even though they were garbed in heavy raincoats and often obscured by umbrellas, and when he began to lose interest in that pastime, he acknowledged our location and looked confused.

"Where are we going?" he asked.

"Back to the office," I replied.

"But the office is . . ."

"I know where the office is."

There was a large space where the departmental-store had once stood, before the bomb exploded and collapsed in on the world I had built for myself. The void between the lines of tall buildings had been replaced by a wall of wood panelling with big signs that read, 'DANGER. SITE CONSTRUCTION.' The makeshift timber surrounds had been painted a battleship grey, incarcerating the ground like the London Wall had once incarcerated the city. I stepped out of the car, looking for an entrance that wasn't there, and after walking back and forth, I pressed my eye to the gap between the heavy shuttering. The ceiling of my office, which was once the plateau the store had sat on, had been completely replaced by a new slab of white concrete, where all around the perimeter thick, steel rods protruded out to all points on the compass. There were no gaps, no entrance into the Spiders Web beneath; it had been consigned to history, reminiscent of the sealed tombs of the Pharaohs; a gift to future archaeologists.

"Feeling nostalgic, Michael?" asked Badger as he stood in a light drizzle beside me.

I pulled away and leaned back on the coarsely constructed facade

"Doesn't this make you wonder?" I asked. "Up until now, up until the Henderson case, life had been pretty normal, and suddenly everything changed."

"You're referring to the bomb?" he replied, staring up as if the department store was still there."

"Amongst other things," I nodded.

Badger looked uncertain, walked a few steps away and then turned back to face me.

"You read the report from the M.O.D. it was clear enough," he said.

"I know, I know. But don't you think it could all be a cover-up."

"A conspiracy," he began to smile, "by whom, Michael?"

It was my intention to choose my words carefully, especially in light of Badger's scepticism, but I casually exclaimed, "The government."

His eyes rolled skyward and he shook his head.

"Listen to me," I continued. "We lost Joyce to the government. We lost Tom and Andy to the government. Henderson was working on . . ."

"No. We lost Tom and Andy due to your incessant fixation with the very subject you're spouting now. You know what you need? You need a holiday. Take a break, Michael. Do something. But please, please, please drop this ridiculous obsession you have with conspiracies."

-21-

Tuesday evening was my arranged meeting with Rachel. Yesterday she phoned the office and left a message with Sylvia, saying it was important she had to see me. "And who shall I say is calling?" responded Sylvia as she surveyed her perfectly shaped nails and knowing full well who was speaking. Rachel gave her name in full. "Miss Bookmark! Ah, yes, I remember you from the coffee shop; a dowdy looking girl—no dress sense. How are you?" Rachel managed to utter, "Fine," before Sylvia interrupted. "I'll tell Michael you called. Doubt if he'll phone you, though; busy, busy, busy. Cheery-bye." I sighed exhaustively when Sylvia sheepishly explained the contents of the conversation to me. "Why do you have this insatiable desire to protect me, Sylvia? You're not my mother," I growled. She smiled callously and began to swing her hips from side to side, like a little girl stumped for an answer. "I can see who I like and when I like without your permission," I continued, searching through the drawers of my desk for the napkin on which Rachel had written her phone number. "God, Michael, you and Sarah have only recently parted and already you're acting like a gigolo." I stared back at her dumbfounded as she hitched her dress up a little and sat on the side of the desk. "She's all wrong for you; a ten-a-penny dream," she went on. "Well, not so much a dream really as a nightmare. Have you seen the clothes she wears? She looks like a clotheshorse . . ." At last she acknowledged my scowl and her words trailed into silence. "You can be such a bitch," I said, handing her the napkin. "Now phone her back and tell her I'll meet her in the Cheshire Cheese tomorrow at six. Do you think you can do that without being insulting?" Sylvia swung on her buttocks and headed for the door. "I'll try but it won't be easy. You know what we bitches are like."

The Cheese, as we called it, had its usual early evening atmosphere, thick with cigarette and heavy cigar smoke, of nameless people I knew only as nodding-acquaintances, the occasional women who may or may not pass you a wink or discretely give you the once over. I was leaning on the bar and staring thoughtfully into my glass of scotch when there was a light tap on my shoulder. When I turned Rachel was standing before me, looking like I had never seen her—absolutely breathtaking. She wore a light grey high-banded, crossover blouse, a dark blue pencil skirt with buttons up the side and blue high-heeled shoes. Her make-up had been applied as if by an artist, liberally but enhancing the finer points of her face but not overdone. I had purposely chosen a public house as our meeting place for the sole reason that it was public—as opposed to an intimate place, such as her flat. My stomach turned at the thought that she had misinterpreted the location as a date.

"Going somewhere?" I asked.

I regretted my choice of words immediately but thank God she laughed.

"You invited me to a pub. The least I can do is not be an embarrassment to you," she smiled. "Were you going to buy me a drink?"

Her beauty had momentarily stunned me, but I nodded and smiled back at her.

"Where are my manners? What will you have?"

Ordering a port and lemon we found a vacant table. I remained standing until she was seated and then sat opposite. Her eyebrows lifted slightly, acknowledging the fact that I had gone to great lengths to put as much distance between us without actually leaving the building.

"You said you wanted to see me," I said.

She paused for a moment, looking towards the door as if she were wondering why she bothered coming at all.

"Sorry," I said, reading her disappointment. "I've been losing myself in work so much lately I sometimes forget when to switch off. How's everything with you?"

"Pretty much the same. I take it you're still apart from Sarah."

"Best for the both of us; I have my own place now."

"If I don't ask—you won't have to tell me," she said.

I laughed, though I wasn't quite sure why.

It's not far—walking distance."

She grinned at my evasiveness.

For several weeks I had been carrying around a still picture in my head of Billy Fletcher and my wife canoodling at the bottom of the stairs after a night of passion, and my defence mechanism was to consume myself entirely in work. Looking now at Rachel, and considering the effort she had gone to, I considered the possibility as to whether I could function as a human-being again.

"Have—Have you eaten?" I asked nervously.

She shook her head as if the question was unworthy of a verbal reply.

"Only I was thinking we could go to a restaurant . . . if you wanted . . . if you're hungry. Are you hungry?"

Women can turn on a sixpence—from tantrum to elation in the blink of an eye.

"You must have forgotten there's a war on, Michael," she smiled, finding her warmth again. "Restaurants are few and far between these days."

"I know a few," I replied, a trifle too smugly than I intended.

She raised her glass to her lips, staring playfully at me over the rim.

"Do you think of yourself as a free spirit now you're no longer with Sarah? Has the institution of marriage disappointed you to such a degree that you would purposefully corrupt another who still believes in its values? I will never give myself to you or let you destroy my view on the sanctity of marriage."

I sat staring at her with my mouth agape. Was my invitation worthy of such a venomous retort?

She started to laugh wickedly. "I read that in one of those old fashioned books; Mills & Boon, or something like that," she giggled. "I've never had the chance to use it—till now."

"Very good," I nodded.

"I'm sorry, Michael, it was cruel of me. Yes, I'd love to go to a restaurant with you."

And so we made our way to Covent Garden, to an English restaurant I frequently used to entertain clients, my staff, and once even my own wife. It wasn't ostentatious by any stretch of the imagination; bare floorboards, low ceilings and a scattering of tables, but the food was excellent.

"Michael, why is your secretary such a cow?" asked Rachel in the middle of the main course.

"Who—Sylvia?" I smirked.

"She was mean to me. I don't even know her. Are you and her . . . you know?"

"Good grief, no! Sylvia is a little possessive. She thinks of every woman as a potential threat."

"A threat? Then who is she trying to protect?"

"I don't know," I said as I pushed my food around on my plate; "all the other Sylvia's in the world, I expect; that and the fact that she was once very good friends with my wife."

"Did they have an argument?"

"Not as far as I know," I shrugged. "I think Sarah got it in her mind that something was going on—but there wasn't."

Rachel placed her knife and fork together and lifted her glass of white wine.

"Do you miss her? Aren't you curious as to what she's doing?" she asked.

"You know, you'd think I would miss her. Truth is I don't. And as for being curious, what's there to be curious about? I had a front row seat; little was left to the imagination. It's a closed book as far as I'm concerned."

"Book!" shrilled Rachel, staring wide-eyed.

She ducked down to retrieve her handbag from the floor and delving inside pulled out a tattered thin, yellow book that looked at least a thousand years old.

"Your wish is my command," she said proudly as she handed it to me.

The flimsy paper cover was torn in several places, held together by tape, the edges of the pages, that amounted to no more than two hundred, were discoloured brown but the title along its spine was clear enough, 'The Vassarri Papers, published by Fallow's.'

"Jesus, Rachel, how did you find this?"

"Told you I would," she gloated. "Well, to be honest it wasn't me. Reedy found it in the warehouse, bundled up and destined for the pulp mills. What's so special about it?"

I thumbed through the pages. "Nothing special," I replied, "but it angered the government enough to have every available copy destroyed, and I'm intrigued to know why."

"Pornographic literature, I bet," said Rachel with a firm nod.

"No, not pornographic, Rachel," I smiled. "Please thank your friend for finding it."

Less than an hour ago she was on the verge of walking out, now I seemed to have Rachel's full attention. With dinner complete, save for coffee, she rested on her elbows, her fingers laced beneath her chin and her eyes shining in my direction. Women in general seem to have an agenda, a time they believe is right for them—to move the relationship along. Her whole appearance wasn't thrown together at a moments notice, but instead strategically worked out with no less precision than a military invasion of the French coast. I imagined her earlier, standing before a full-length mirror in her flat and trying on an assortment of garments from her wardrobe; the blouse with the plunging neckline—too provocative; the skirt slit up the thigh—too sluttish; the dress buttoned up to the neck—too matronly. Then voila; the image she wished to purvey is created—sensual without appearing desperate and a little dab of perfume as a form of distraction. But as I ran my fingers through the tattered copy of 'The Vassarri Papers' I wasn't prepared for her next utterance.

"Sex."

I lifted my eyes to hers and slowly shook my head.

"Sorry. What was that?" I enquired with uncertainty.

"Sex," she repeated without blinking. "It's been on my mind for a while; quite a while, actually. And I was thinking on the bus on the way here that if you tried to seduce me I wouldn't put up a fight. Obviously I'd have to go through the motions of defending my honour; it's expected of decent girls, but you can rest assured that I will succumb to your persistence eventually. I mean, you don't have to if you don't want to, but if the mood takes you then I'm just letting you know that it won't all be for nothing. Of course we could pussyfoot around for the rest of the evening—you wondering if I will, me wondering if you'll try, but what's the point in that? So, Michael, I just want to put your mind at rest. And I don't want you feeling bad about yourself in the morning. It won't be so much a seduction as a mutual agreement. Truth is I'll probably rip you to pieces." She motioned then to a passing waiter. "Two coffees, please."

My uncertain smile was close to breaking.

"Mills & Boon, again?"

She shook her head. "Doubtful that Mills & Boon would depict the heroin as such a brazen hussy," she said. "You didn't mind me mentioning it, did you? I thought you ought to know—what with the dinner and everything."

"Ah . . . Rachel," I managed to blurt. "I hate to bring this to your attention at such a passionate moment in our relationship, but since I met you you've been pining away the days waiting for a communication from David. Don't you think you're being a little . . . er, over-zealous."

"Over—what?"

"You know—promiscuous, given your married status."

"It's been a year, Michael," she sighed. "Do you know what a year without sex can do to a woman's mind? I swear to God I've never strayed before, but then I've never felt the need. And who knows when David will be home or if he'll ever come home?"

I felt flattered and intimidated at the same time—the hunter being hunted.

"Oh, I see," I said after briefly analysing my situation. "I'm the outsider, completely detached from your everyday life; the bookshop, the pub. So when David returns I'll be discarded and no one else will know of our illicit relationship, no one except us."

She paused for consideration for a moment and slowly nodded her head.

"You paint a cold and selfish picture, Michael, but that's pretty much the crux of it. What do you say?"

Numbed by her honesty I could only stare back, but as her straight face turned to a grin, and then a smile, and then to laughter, I concluded it was all a joke and began to laugh along with her.

"So you're teasing me?" I said.

She shook her head, still giggling. "Not for a second. I can't wait to get you between the sheets. It's just that you think that everything is a conspiracy—that you don't possess one endearing quality; the fact is you do. You're sweet, charming, generous and not bad looking in a dull light. For God sake, Michael, I like you!"

My facial muscles were teetering under the weight of my fixed smile but I managed to regain and sustain a modicum of composure.

"But what about David?" I asked.

"David isn't your type. Besides, he's miles away. Am I so repulsive that you won't even consider it?"

"Good God, no, you look beautiful, but . . ."

"Listen, Michael," she interrupted. "I don't mind admitting that I am having trouble getting through this war, and there isn't one single minute of the day I don't feel lonely; then, of course, there's the whole sex thing going on. I don't think I can get through this on my own so I've devised a plan. As long as I know I have someone or even believe I have someone, I can make it. True you were way down on the list of candidates but beggars can't be choosers."

My fixed grin and my confidence suddenly dropped but Rachel started to smile.

"Just joking—you were the only candidate," she said. "You're sensible, level-headed and not a man to go blabbing to your mates down the local. Above all, I know you can walk away with no regrets when and if David comes home; it's simply an arrangement between you and me—no strings."

She concluded with a smile, as if it was a business meeting and she had completed laying down her terms and conditions.

I dropped my eyes back into The Vassarri Papers as the waiter approached with two coffees. Rachel thanked him and he moved off to serve another table.

"So—has that got something to do with one of the cases you're working on?" she asked, dropping the subject of sex as quickly as she had raised it.

I shrugged. "Inadvertently, it has connections. It pays to know who you can trust."

"You know him—Vassarri?"

"No, and I don't think I'd like to," I replied. "He was a government assassin who wrote his memoirs. The British took exception to it; well, at least the British Government did."

"He killed people?"

I grinned. "That's what assassins do. They're like machines; get up, eat breakfast, kill a few heads of state, pick the kids up from school—you know, mundane stuff."

"And that interests you, does it?"

I closed the book and slipped it in my inside pocket.

"What interests me is why a murderer would want to give up a secret he's spent his whole life safeguarding. Why not just take it to the grave?"

The streets were dark and silent when we left the restaurant, cutting across the piazza of Covent Garden and heading towards the Strand. My new abode, courtesy of Bernie, was a plush, three-bedroom apartment that faced south, overlooking the Thames from its third floor position. The building, set in ornate gardens behind the grand Savoy Hotel, housed just six palatial apartments; an extravagance for the rich whose owner was, ironically, an eminent physician who was now residing in Austria for the next twelve months. After passing through the security doors and climbing the stairs, we entered the apartment where I took Rachel's hand and led her down the dark corridor and into the lounge. "Take a look," I said. We stood before a large window and looked out at the skyline. The Thames glistened and twinkled below us and the expanse of Waterloo Bridge stretched like a black ribbon to the south bank. The panorama was intermittently speckled with small and lonely lights, as if the heavens above had fallen to decorate the landscape with stars. "It's beautiful. So peaceful," murmured Rachel, her eyes glistening with wonder in the soft shadows. I allowed her a few moments to indulge the vista before closing the blinds. When I turned the lights on she surveyed the room with absolute amazement; the leather settees and chairs, the long mahogany dining table, the glass cabinets, the lush, deep-pile carpets and marble lamp-standards. "Wow! This must cost a fortune," she gasped.

"Not really. Bernie thought he owed it to me. I got it cheap. Wine?" I said.

Rachel nodded, her eyes still roaming the vast lounge.

She headed off to explore the rest of the apartment while I busied myself at the drinks cabinet. I heard her shriek in disbelief with every door she opened, and then scream with excitement when she entered the bathroom. I heard the sound of gushing water as she tried every appliance. She came rushing back into the lounge, bubbling with enthusiasm.

"Can I take a bath, Michael? Can I, please, please, please?"

"Of course; there's a robe hanging on the back of the door."

She raced off again, pulling at her clothing as she disappeared down the corridor. I poured two glasses of wine and placed them on the glass coffee table, and removing my jacket took out the Vassarri book and sat on the settee.

The Introduction of the flimsy book opened with a heart-warming but hypocritical dedication, *'For my daughter'* and promptly moved on to give insight into the man himself. *'My name is Nicolia Vassarri and I am an assassin. In my fifteen year career I have dispatched 786 human beings; 52 a year; one every week . . .'* Rachel whooped with delight as the bath filled, and looking down the hall a shaft of light cut the bleakness from the half-open door. "What are these pink things in the bottle?" her voice asked, rising over the splashing water. "Bath salts," I replied, turning my eyes back to the book. *'By definition I am a mercenary—a cold blooded killer; a hired gun. My forte, such as it is, is to terminate the lives of those on the behest of the highest bidder, and this I have done without conscience or the desire for redemption . . .'* I sipped at my wine, looking down the corridor at the light splitting the darkness of the hall; the steam escaping from the break in the door and swirling around before evaporating in the black surrounds. Was Sylvia's appraisal of me correct? Was I behaving like a gigolo? "Want to wash my back?" said Rachel, her voice barely audible over the sloshing water. I smiled to myself, debating the prospect but suppressing the urge. She had her needs, as did I, but what of David? Weren't his needs worth consideration? Could I live with the responsibility of discolouring his rose-tinted view of matrimony; the loyalty of a wife he expected and, indeed, demanded? Why would I wish on him the hurt and anguish of knowing your life's partner considered you to be nothing more than an accessory? I made no reply and began to read the exploits of a government assassin.

1927:

Nicolia Vassarri sat outside a little restaurant on the waters-edge perusing the menu and sipping a small coffee. He would look up every now and then, seemingly distracted by a passing car, a noisy child, or feigning interest in a sailboat gliding back and forth across Lake Geneva. The day was warm and the sky clear, and his overall impression of Geneva was little more than 'Quaint', reminiscent of Weymouth or Eastbourne seafront—but with considerably more money. Both the weather and location inspired him to opt for a seat outside rather than inside the restaurant, where a handful of couples sat chatting and sampling the local cuisine as well as the exquisite wines. The city clock optimistically chimed a quarter past the hour, giving Vassarri the excuse to look around once again, to take in the faces of the passers-by, the drivers in stationary vehicles, the people who were simply sight-seeing and meandering outside shops. In reality he was searching out Otto Weilermann, who was now already fifteen minutes late for their appointment. Vassarri was prepared as always, like Laurence Olivier the great British actor; living the part of someone else, entrenched in another identity and a fictional history; possessing answers to any question posed to him.

British Intelligence had given him a dossier three days before—a role; a new name, a different nationality, his purpose and what was expected of him. Like so many occasions he read the script, absorbing every syllable of information until he could recite it word-perfect, until he became the character depicted within the pages of the dossier. Sometimes he would change his appearance, hair-dye, optical lenses for eye-colour, even his posture. His name was now Olav Sabaski, a junior director in a Dutch-based firm STENTHALL AVIONICS, a modest sized company specialising in aeroplane components. For all intents and purposes Vassarri was Olav Sabaski. He had all the necessary papers to prove it, an expensive house in the suburbs of Leiden, Holland, a beautiful wife and two children in private school; he would carry a photograph of the family he had never laid eyes on in his wallet. Intelligence would furnish the props and make the fiction reality; Stenthall Avionics would have a long history as well as an impressive list of clients, and information regarding their directors and even their employees could easily be accessed should anyone feel the need to look into them. Intelligence knew that a country hell-bent on world domination would never take defeat easily and inevitably would try again, and so the

British who had successfully infiltrated German Intelligence during World War One, remained to monitor their movements. Britain was receiving information concerning their uprising as early as 1925, but silently observed from the wings—the stage was almost set.

To ensnare prey, bait must be set. Intelligence filtered information through the appropriate channels that a certain Dutch company had manufactured a component that would improve cargo-drops from aeroplanes one hundred percent, and that the load, despite its size or weight, would be guaranteed to hit a target within thirty feet either way. A French newspaper hardly gave the story a mention, which was precisely how the British Government intended it, and the European press could elaborate no further, but it did receive a modicum of interest from a few aircraft manufacturers. Written enquiries went straight to a PO Box, and phone calls went directly to British agents in Holland under the guise of Stenthall Avionics. When after several weeks the story failed to make an impact on those targeted, it was resurrected, boasting that the British were interested in purchasing the invention. If Germany were about to wage war, they wouldn't want anyone—least of all Britain—to have the upper hand. Within three days the phone rang in an empty office in Leiden, and was immediately intercepted by British Intelligence. A young woman with an impeccable telephone manner answered with a flawless Dutch accent. "Stenthall's." A man gave his name as Otto Weilermann, pronounced 'Veilman,' expressing interest in Stenthall's invention. The telephonist was polite but wary. "Where did you get this information, sir?" she asked. The caller did not respond immediately. "It was not intended to be public knowledge, Mr. Weilermann. The component is no longer for sale," she explained. The caller hung up.

"Got a live one," she said to the three agents crouched over a coffee table playing cards.

"Who?" asked one, anxiously looking up from his losing hand.

"He gave his name as Otto Weilermann."

"I'm on it," said another, tossing in his cards and walking to an attaché case on the far side of the room.

The third agent walked directly to the telephonist, resting his hand on the back of her chair; both staring at the dormant switchboard. "He'll call back. Don't make it easy for him, Lucy."

She laughed, sliding the headphones down around her neck and shaking her head vigorously before shaping her hair into a ponytail and fastening it with an elastic band.

Waiting was always the hardest. Minutes passed like hours, and the monotony was combated with card games or reminisces of past contracts.

"Got him!" said the agent who had been sitting in the corner studying the contents of the attaché case for the past two hours. "Otto Weilermann, a fully paid-up member of the Nazi Party, used by them as a scout to locate anything that may further their cause; ostensibly an arms-dealer—an astute businessman."

"Weilermann is his real name?" asked his counterpart.

"As far as we know," his associate shrugged. "He claims to be Swiss but was born in Bonn, Germany. His father was a high-ranking officer in the first war, loyal to the Nazi regime until his recent death. This association put Weilermann in a trusted position and gave him access to all the key-players; the respect his father earned was passed down to him."

"That's all?"

The agent shrugged again. "What can I say? Sixty years old, wealthy and married to a woman half his age. He was—"

The phone rang and a soft click signalled the interception; everyone in the room stared at the flashing light on the exchange.

The telephonist placed on her headphones and flicked the switch below the light indicator. "Stenthall's," The three agents crowded around her. "This is Otto Weilermann. We spoke earlier," he said. With a jerk of his head the lead agent signalled to his associate to return to the coffee table where a solitary phone sat tethered to the exchange. "I wish to speak to someone of authority—someone who represents your company's marketing."

"Certainly, Mr. Weilermann. May I ask what your enquiry concerns?"

"You may not," he replied tersely. "You may, however, mention that I represent a very powerful body of businessmen."

The telephonist looked up at the remaining two agents and arched her eyebrows, mouthing silently into the receiver, "Nazi Bastard!"

"I'll see who is available, Mr. Weilermann," she said.

She flicked the switch below the lifeless green light which then began to flash slowly—Call waiting.

"Who am I? the agent asked staring intently at the phone on the table.

His associate ran his eyes over the bogus list of company directors for Stenthall Avionics compiled by British Intelligence.

"Ackerman," he said. "Bjorn Ackerman."

"Ignorant Shit!" hissed the telephonist.

"Patch him through."

With a flick of a switch the phone began to ring. The agent allowed a moment before lifting the receiver.

"Ackerman speaking. How may I help you, Mr. Weilermann?" said the agent, adopting a hint of a Dutch accent.

"Ah, good, your girl has formally introduced us." Weilermann's finger had run down the names of Stenthall's board of directors and located Bjorn Ackerman. "I have it on good authority that your company has designed a system appertaining to cargo-drops—I'm interested."

"Oh, I see," the agent returned sheepishly. "Mr. Weilermann, it is common knowledge that we are in the process of selling the patent."

"But not yet. You haven't sold it yet. Or have I been misinformed?"

"We are in the process . . ."

"Process does not mean 'Finalised', does it, Mr. Ackerman? We are both businessmen, and our purpose is to generate money for whatever business we are in. I would like the opportunity to speak with a representative of your company regarding your system. If it is to our requirements we shall go ahead with the purchase. Of course, we are willing to pay substantially more for the system if given that opportunity. And one cannot be certain that your potential clients may want your invention."

The agent passed his companions a wink.

"Perhaps I haven't made myself clear . . ."

"But you have—perfectly;" Weilermann interrupted with a heavy sigh, "your representative's name?"

"We don't have a representative as such. Our junior director is dealing with all matters concerning the sale . . ."

Weilermann's finger lowered down the list and stopped at Olav Sabaski.

". . . and he is meeting with the client at the end of the week," the agent continued.

The caller fell silent but the agent could hear the faint sound of breathing and the rustling of paper.

"I will call again tomorrow to arrange a meeting," said Weilermann.

"I don't think that will be possible . . ."

"All things are possible, Mr. Ackerman. You may wish to discuss it with your fellow board-members. Either way, I will call back and arrange a meeting."

The phone clicked dead momentarily and then returned to its dialling tone.

A thin waiter with slick-backed hair hovered outside the little restaurant, eyeing the young ladies and smiling at the passing tourists, occasionally motioning them inside with a majestic sweep of his hand. A white towel was slung over his right shoulder and he tapped a silver tray rhythmically on his thigh as if it were a tambourine; an act borne out of boredom and frustration. Vassarri observed him with a smile as he whispered sexual innuendo's at the passing girls, and as the waiter casually gazed up and down the waterfront, like any other young man in search of an opportunity, he suddenly resumed the position; towel over his arm and tray balanced on his fingertips. A large man with silver hair and a matching grizzly beard was walking towards the restaurant, his weight bordering on obese, his walk affected and uncomfortable in appearance to any observer. Vassarri paid him only a passing glance and looked out over the glistening water. He had seen him before; studied his photos in the dossier; knew the colour of his eyes and even how heavy he was. The waiter smiled at the man. "Good to see you again, sir." Vassarri felt them pass behind him and enter the restaurant. In the shortest time the waiter was back out with the man standing behind him. "Mr. Sabaski?" Vassarri rose, adjusting the round spectacles on the bridge of his nose. 'A nice touch,' he thought when he was constructing Olav Sabaski's appearance.

"Yes, I am Olav Sabaski," he said, taking in the waiter and the man alternately.

The waiter smiled and pulled out a chair on the other side of the table.

"Mr. Weilermann?" Vassarri asked as he extended his hand.

Vassarri was prepared to converse in any of the sixteen languages he was fluent in and awaited Weilermann's preference.

"My apologies, Mr. Sabaski," replied Weilermann, opting for English and settling clumsily into a chair opposite. "Forgive my rudeness."

Vassarri shrugged and smiled.

"Your usual, Mr. Weilermann?" asked the waiter.

"Cognac, small coffee."

The waiter nodded and looked to Vassarri.

"Just a coffee, would be fine."

"Will you not join me in a Cognac?" Weilermann began to laugh.

Vassarri removed his spectacles and began to polish the lenses on his napkin, squinting back at the German entrepreneur to feign short-sightedness.

"I rarely take alcohol," he replied.

"Corrupts the mind," Weilermann chuckled.

"So they say."

Vassarri knew that Weilermann was an intermediate for the German Government, as a whole and individually, and although he masqueraded as an entrepreneur he was, in reality, an integral part of their war-machine. His vast wealth afforded him the luxury of travelling the world and purchasing commodities—usually arms—and selling them at profit to anyone with a cause to fight; even arranging the cargos and transportation. Over the past six years he had worked specifically for the German Government, buying in anything and everything in preparation for their uprising, storing the merchandise in acres of warehouses. In the great scheme of things Weilermann was considered little more than an opportunist, but as British Intelligence monitored the German Government's campaign, the name Otto Weilermann was mentioned more frequently and he was soon considered to be a threat as well as a major force in Germany's rebirth. His sheer bulk and size induced him to purchase a luxury apartment in the heart of Berlin, from which he conducted his business—usually by phone—and could be transported to nearby Head Quarters should he be summoned. This was the only address and phone number British Intelligence possessed, but they were aware that his real home was somewhere in Switzerland; Weilermann's choice of location for his meeting with Sabaski was verification, and the waiter's familiarity with the man was a sure indication he was local.

"A beautiful day," said Weilermann, casting his stare over the lake. "I would like to thank you and Stenthall Avionics for this opportunity. Will you be staying in Geneva long?"

"Till tonight." Vassarri smiled back.

Weilermann took out a silver case, and removing a cigarette, placed it into a six inch long holder.

"And then to England?" he said, lighting the cigarette.

Vassarri nodded. "We—Stenthall Avionics—are quite certain that they will make the purchase. However, as you have shown considerable interest in the system, I have been instructed to offer you the same terms; they are nonnegotiable."

"You have a figure in mind?" Weilermann calmly blew out a thin tube of white smoke.

Vassarri smiled nervously, and removing a pen from his top pocket, wrote down a figure on the table napkin and turned it to the entrepreneur. Weilermann stared down at it, unflinching and looked back to the Dutchman.

When the waiter returned with a tray, Weilermann took the napkin and placed it in his pocket. "Thank you, Andre. We may be eating later."

The waiter nodded and disappeared back into the restaurant.

"Explain the fundamentals of the system to me, Mr. Sabaski."

Vassarri lifted up a brief-case at his feet and moved his coffee to one side.

"You understand I can't go into depth in fear of jeopardising . . ."

"Just the fundamentals, if you please."

Vassarri fumbled with the straps of the case.

"You're familiar with Sir Isaac Newton? Our system is based on the principal of gravitation and the three laws of motion; everything—no matter how large or small—falls at the same rate." With the buckles undone, Vassarri pulled out the contents of his briefcase; papers, contracts, drawings, all identifiable with STENTHALL AVIONICS' headings. Weilermann appeared impressed, stretching himself slightly to view the inside of the leather briefcase. "Once installed the system receives information from the aircraft's panel; longitude, latitude, altitude. The co-ordinance for the target is programmed into the system, and a sensor attached to the underside of the fuselage registers velocity, wind-speed and turbulence. The system calculates all the information and the payload can be automatically dropped. It has been undergoing test for the past several months by various companies in Australia, Canada and America; extinguishing forest fires, crop-dusting etcetera." Vassarri passed over a half dozen business cards of various aviation companies and smiled again.

Weilermann sorted them before him, in a straight line and studied them as he sipped his Cognac.

"You have the blueprints?" he asked, looking up with a crooked smile.

Vassarri shook his head and began to gather up his papers. "No, sir. They are sent directly to a bank in case of . . ."

"A little joke," Weilermann laughed.

Vassarri laughed along to humour the arms-dealer.

"But if I wish to purchase the system, you can hand over the blueprints?"

Weilermann's eyes studied the business cards as he spoke.

"They are close at hand," replied the Dutchman.

The arms-dealer looked up, his stare demanding elaboration.

"I deposited a full set of blueprints at the bank this morning; they are irretrievable. If we are unable to do business I will not collect them—they will remain in the vaults until Stenthall's issue the bank orders for their destruction."

Weilermann reclined, appraising Sabaski with an air of admiration, and then collecting the cards, placed them in the top pocket of his jacket.

"How big is the component—the system?"

"No bigger than a shoe-box," Vassarri replied.

"And how long to install?"

"In a freight-plane—no more than two hours."

Weilermann nodded and sat pensive for a few moments.

"Once a drop is made, does the system have to be recalibrated for the next drop?"

"That is the beauty of it, Mr. Weilermann," Vassarri grinned. "As I explained; size and weight falls at the same speed; the target, or drop-zone as we call it, remains unaffected even if the payloads are dropped in quick succession."

Again Weilermann looked thoughtful, unconsciously stroking his beard, and looked to his cigarette which had burned down to the holder and immediately reinstated it. Vassarri watched him with a smile as a new cigarette was ignited.

"It's bad for me, I know," said Weilermann blowing out a plume of smoke. "I use the holder to prevent my beard from yellow stains." His eyes dropped to Sabaski's soft, white hands. "Do you smoke, Mr. Sabaski?"

"No, sir!"

Vassarri smoked more than he should—forty a day—give or take a dozen, but to him nicotine stains were the equivalent to tattoos, a form of identification; of which all signs must be erased by scrubbing and soaking the fingers in bleach. Moreover, smoking was a sign of weakness to be likened with alcoholism—an image he could ill-afford to portray.

"Very wise," returned the entrepreneur with an approving nod.

Two tourists, looking very much in love and carrying knapsacks gathered outside the restaurant studying the menu on the framed stand. They debated the prices for a short time and took a table close to Sabaski and Weilermann, who stared hard at them as they spread out a map and considered their next location. They babbled in French, and the fat arms-dealer appeared quite taken by the female whose blouse was far too tight and her breasts far too prominent.

The city clock chimed again which brought him out of his sexual reverie and focusing back to a patient Sabaski. Nice breasts or not, the tourists were an intrusion and Weilermann struggled out of his seat, pushing the table forward and scraping the chair backward. As he passed Vassarri he stopped and bent down, whispering in his ear as his eyes studied the well-shaped form of the female tourist. "What bank, Mr. Sabaski?" Vassarri pulled back and hesitated. "The name of the bank where you deposited the blueprints, or we have no deal. I need verification." Vassarri swallowed hard and blinked repeatedly, appearing decidedly nervous. He looked warily at the couple on the next table and leaned into Weilermann. "Geneva," he said, quietly. "The Bank of Geneva." The obese man nodded and lumbered into the restaurant just as the waiter appeared to serve the young tourists.

Otto Weilermann walked to the far corner of the restaurant, to a phone-booth barely adequate to take his immense frame, but he wriggled inside though the folding doors had to remain open. Vassarri smiled to himself. The German would make one call to Command, giving the names and numbers of the aviation companies he had given him, and also the name of the bank where the blueprints for the system had been deposited that morning. They would call back as soon as they had the information.

"We should eat," said Weilermann when he returned and eased back into his chair.

The thin waiter had followed him out and was now standing by the table.

"Another Cognac—large," Weilermann demanded. "And for you, Mr. Sabaski?"

"Perhaps a small beer," replied Vassarri.

The waiter smiled and handed the men two menus.

Vassarri leaned forward, resting on his elbows, as if to speak confidentially, but Weilermann shook his head and scowled, taking a sideways glance at the tourists who were laughing loudly between nuzzling into one another's necks.

"Well, I think I'm ready to order."

The afternoon sun shone across the shimmering, blue waters of Lake Geneva, and steadily the road along the waterfront busied with locals and tourists, clogging up with traffic. The waiter, who not two hours earlier was standing idle on the pavement touting for business, was now run off his feet, tearing in and out of the restaurant as more tables were taken up. Sabaski picked at a light salad and Weilermann consumed a large plate of Spaghetti Bolognaise and was now swirling his fifth Cognac around in a ballooned glass and exhaling clouds of white smoke. Clearly he was agitated to have not received his phone call, constantly looking through the glass into the restaurant or stealing a glance at the parked limousine a short distance down the road. Vassarri had registered the car pull up shortly after Weilermann arrived, and the driver within had remained almost motionless ever since. Nevertheless, the two gentlemen engaged in polite conversation. Sabaski spoke about the beauty of Holland, and especially his hometown Leiden, as if he knew it intimately. He produced the photograph of his wife and children, waving it in front of Weilermann's face with glowing pride. "Her name is Astrid," said Vassarri, kissing the picture and placing it back in his wallet. "She looks very nice," Weilermann replied as he snapped his fingers at the passing waiter. "Has there been a call for me?"

The waiter stood over the obese man and shook his head solemnly. "No, sir, I don't think so."

"You don't think so? Find out!"

The thin waiter vanished for a few moments and then returned at the door and shook his head again. Weilermann appeared to deflate.

As the city clock chimed, Vassarri checked his watch and leaned forward across the table. "I don't wish to rush you, Mr. Weilermann, but I need an answer. I do have a train to catch."

The German nodded; lips pursed and frowning deeply. Suddenly he was up and waddling back into the restaurant, moving directly to the phone-booth. Inside the female tourist with the prominent breasts was repeatedly dialling a number and then cursing the damn contraption. Weilermann watched her impatiently, taking in her rear form from the ankles up. She slammed down the handset and shook her head with frustration. "No!" she shrilled. Turning and seeing the fat gentleman she smiled and said, "Taxi? Uh, number?" Weilermann almost pulled her out of the booth and lifted the receiver. Dead! He dialled the number and waited for the connection. Nothing. He dialled again. Silence. After three attempts he left the receiver hanging and stomped back through the restaurant, where the French tourist was enquiring after a taxi company at the desk and complaining about the broken phone. When he got outside, Sabaski was standing by the table with his briefcase under his arm; ready to leave. Weilermann looked up and down the street and registered the throngs of people crowding the pavements, and with a sigh of exasperation he turned to the Dutch businessman.

Sabaski stepped forward and extended his hand. "I believe Stenthall's have extended you every courtesy and your opportunity has now expired," he said, politely.

"You're leaving?"

"I have an early train to catch."

Weilermann could see his business venture slipping away. And then there was Command to answer to. His stare fixed to the parked limousine and then back to Sabaski.

"How much would it cost for you to delay or even abandon your journey?" he asked, leading Sabaski onto the pavement.

"You wish to purchase?"

Weilermann was hesitant and Sabaski shrugged his shoulders.

"Perhaps we could do business in the future?" he said. "Good day to you, Mr. Weilermann."

He turned to leave, to vanish into the crowds and be lost forever.

"Wait!" cried the German.

Sabaski turned.

Otto Weilermann's weight and size had got the better of him. He was constantly lethargic and breathless and despised even the shortest of journeys.

His luxury apartment in Berlin was a means to an end; a place for his business transactions and a short trip from Command. His privileged position afforded him an untraceable phone-line from his home, and more frequently he conducted his business from his study rather than travel to Germany. The mute phone in the restaurant now placed him in a precarious position.

"You understand that I don't usually conduct business in such a casual manner, Mr. Sabaski," he said, sliding his arm around his shoulders. "I have nothing but your word that the system exists."

Sabaski stopped, his eyes shining menacingly through his round spectacles. "Sir, the system exists! Secondly, the choice of location for this meeting was yours."

"I understand that," Weilermann said, steering Sabaski onward. "How much for you to reconsider? I ask just a few more hours."

Sabaski was moved to cringe as Weilermann hung all over him; his breath reeking of Cognac and cheap cigarettes, the pores of his skin emitting the stench of stale sweat.

"Two hundred and fifty thousand," Sabaski replied, shuffling out of the German's tactility.

"Francs?" Weilermann smiled, relieved that Sabaski was willing to grant him extra time.

"Dollars."

The eyebrows of the arms-dealer arched high on his forehead and the smile dropped away.

"That would be a down-payment, so to speak," explained the avionics expert.

Both the amount and the choice of currency had astounded Weilermann, and he stared intently back at Sabaski while toying with his beard.

"And what do I get in return?" he asked. "You want me to hand over two hundred and fifty thousand dollars on the strength of a conversation?" he added with a cruel laugh.

"I don't expect you to hand over anything, Mr. Weilermann. Payment will be transferred into Stenthall Avionics' account, and you will be permitted to view the blueprints at the bank—in the presence of their security, of course. I will give you a reference number, and when payment is received in full, that number must be given at the bank on your arrival. The bank will contact

Stenthall's and we will give instructions for the blueprints to be released. You will, of course, have to sign the appropriate contracts which will record you as the owner of the patent. Business complete."

Sabaski made it sound very simple. All Weilermann needed now was verification that the system existed and indeed, as Sabaski had assured him, that it worked. Not that Weilermann, or Command come to that, had any intentions of using the system for crop-spraying or extinguishing fires. Such a component, when fitted to a bomber, would guarantee direct hits every time, whereas to date they were reliant on visual landmarks, and more often than not costly incendiaries failed to hit the intended target and were wasted. For Weilermann, Stenthall's invention would do for bombers what the telescopic sight did for the rifle; accurate targeting.

Weilermann looked across the road to the stationary limousine and raised his hand.

"Let us conduct business," he said, looking to Sabaski with a smile.

The limousine drew up along side of the pavement.

The suspension of the car groaned for mercy as Weilermann climbed in. Vassarri sat in the front, next to a chauffeur who had the appearance of a lorry driver, both in stature and in dress. The car moved slowly away towards the snow peaked mountains. Out of the city and into the countryside the car pulled to the side of the road and stopped, and the chauffeur opened the glove compartment and took out a folded white garment.

"My apologies, Mr. Sabaski, but would you mind?" said Weilermann.

The hulking driver smiled as he unfurled the garment; a hood.

Vassarri stared at it with horror and turned his head to the German.

"No harm will come to you, but I'm protective of my private life. Under any other circumstances we would have completed our business by now, but the broken phone in the restaurant has left me little choice. The journey isn't long. You understand, of course; you have family."

Vassarri reluctantly nodded and the driver placed the hood over his head.

Enveloped by blackness, he could feel the road beneath him. He felt the vehicle slow and speed up, registered every twist and turn along the way, could hear the intermittent rush of wind as they passed trees, smelled the pine of the forests and the grass of the countryside; the cleaner air as the car climbed higher, the sound of clanging bells and the mooing of cows in the adjacent fields; even the clattering wheels of a cart as it passed. Within thirty minutes the smoothness of the tarmac road and the glide of the car gave up to a made-up road, bumping and tossing everyone within to such a degree the driver cursed that inventors of the motor vehicle were selfish bastards who only considered the needs of city dwellers. Vassarri felt the suspension yield as Weilermann climbed out of the backseat and opened the passenger door. The hood was removed and the fat German smiled back. Vassarri's bleared vision pulled into focus to see a large house, half stone and half timber, where from behind two large Alsatians were bounding towards their owner and barking incessantly. Sabaski took steps back, much to the amusement of Weilermann. "They won't hurt you," he laughed. "They look vicious but they're quite friendly."

"Quite! Quite!" cried Sabaski as he climbed back in the car and slammed the door. "I wouldn't consider Quite as a precise description," he shouted through the open window.

Weilermann roared with laughter and shooed the dogs back to the rear of the house.

"Come," he said, motioning Sabaski from the safety of his steel shell. "Come inside and let us conduct our business."

When Vassarri climbed back out of the vehicle the driver confronted him, his arms outstretched.

"A mere precaution," said Weilermann.

Vassarri raised his arms as the chauffeur patted his pockets, sliding his hands down his arms and legs—searching for a concealed weapon of some kind. On completion he seized the briefcase but Weilermann shook his head; he had already seen its contents.

"This way, Mr. Sabaski."

Otto Weilermann led the way, along a stone footpath and up several wide steps where a veranda expanded the full width of the house, decorated with potted plants and wooden chairs surrounding an oval slatted table. Vassarri glanced about, towards the mountains and the acres of fields between, to the desolate, winding road that wound its way down towards civilisation; everything was calm and still.

"Henga," said Weilermann as he entered the house.

A vision appeared from a side door, perfectly formed with long blond hair and searching green eyes. Vassarri knew she was thirty-two but she looked younger. Two children descended the stairs towards their father, mirror images of their parents; an overweight boy of ten years old and his sister, a prepubescent version of her mother.

"Henga, I have to make some calls. Look after Mr. Sabaski."

Weilermann hurried off to the far end of the house while Henga smiled warmly and motioned her husband's guest to join her.

Vassarri followed her into a large room, one wall of which appeared to be completely glazed, staring out over the veranda at the misty Alps. A black grand piano stood at the far end of the room, and a tiger skin rug adorned the marble floor in front of an immense stone fireplace. At the other end of the room was a round pine table set for dinner; a bottle of white wine open and set in an ice-bucket, chilling; the smell of savoury spices hovered from another part of the house. Henga Weilermann sat herself in an easy chair by the hearth, her knees together and to the left, her posture upright. Vassarri smiled gently as he appraised her; a convent girl; finishing school.

"I hope this is not an inconvenience," he said as he sat down opposite her.

She shook her head. "Not at all."

Her eyes were ablaze. So few had entered the house, and never one as masculine as Mr. Sabaski. With his briefcase on his lap he sat like a garden gnome, gazing around the room as if nothing else mattered in the world. For the time being the children had disappeared, back to their bedrooms, and Henga smiled coyly at the visitor.

"Have you eaten?" she asked, looking at the dining table.

"A while ago; a light salad," Vassarri replied. "You have a beautiful house."

Henga smiled out of courtesy. "You have business with Otto?" she asked.

Vassarri continued to gaze around the room.

"A few details to complete," he replied.

She nodded. "May I offer you a drink; tea, coffee, wine . . . Cognac?"

"Nothing, thank you. Did you choose this location? It's quite breathtaking."

"It was my husband's—before I met him; it's lovely."

"You're a privileged lady, Mrs. Weilermann . . ."

"Please, call me Henga. You'll join us of course?"

Vassarri smiled timidly. "Join you?"

"For dinner."

His eyes roamed the beamed ceiling and the surrounding walls, trying to fathom the rooms above and behind, but he felt her eyes boring into him and caught her smiling; a smile reserved for the art of seduction. Henga was barely in her twenties when she married. She was the daughter of a buyer of arms, who Weilermann double-crossed, and when left broken and owing a substantial amount of money, Weilermann took the only thing her father possessed—Henga. Giving herself to save her father's life was a sacrifice; as it was every night to have Weilermann lying beside her; to feel his hands clumsily groping her body, and to feel his grotesque form writhing on top of her. The children eased her burden; a form of distraction to escape his overbearing ways, if only in her mind; an alibi to have a few precious hours away from him. In the early years business constantly took him away; a chance to breath again, to feel like a woman instead of a prize, even if she was constantly overseen by the chauffeur who doubled as a bodyguard. But recently, and owing to his increasing weight, Weilermann had confined himself to the house, to conduct his shady dealings from his study. She resented his presence and despised the occupation he wallowed in. Above all else she loathed the arguments when he constantly reminded her that her father only drew breath because he permitted it. What she desired is what had evaded her, her whole life—warmth and passion.

"Are you staying in Geneva, Mr. Sabaski?" she asked.

"I'm bound for England—tonight."

"Ah, England," she nodded approvingly. "Have you ever seen London? I've always wanted to go there."

"My first time," he smiled.

For the past two years Nicolia Vassarri had been living in an Edwardian house off St. James's Square and frequently jogged around the perimeter of St. James's Park. He knew London as well as any native. In comparison, London was one of his favourite cities, second only to Paris.

Henga eased her shoes off and curled her legs beneath her. Vassarri could hear the dogs barking at the back of the house and the children playing up stairs. He looked at his watch.

"An hour," she said, her eyes shining back at him.

"An hour?"

"He's in his study—always an hour; at least an hour."

"That's a long time to make a call."

"Perhaps we could find something to do."

Vassarri let the proposition pass and walked to the expanse of windows.

"This is certainly a beautiful view," he said.

Suddenly she was there beside him, her breasts brushing against his arm and her breath warm on his cheek.

"We have a summer-house. I can show you—something more beautiful," she whispered.

Vassarri stared into her sparkling green eyes but felt nothing, and then he averted his gaze to the door, to the noise of footsteps growing louder on the marble floor until the large frame of Weilermann appeared. Henga drew back and pointed to the view.

"The mountain tops are often shrouded by cloud, but today is clear," she said. "Ah, Otto, I was just showing Mr. Sabaski . . ."

"Never mind what you were showing him. Prepare dinner," he ordered.

As Henga breezed out of the room, Weilermann smiled and pointed to the dining table.

"We can eat and then I'll sign the necessary papers," he said.

"Everything is to your requirements?" asked Vassarri.

"Your product has had good reviews, Mr. Sabaski. The bank has confirmed your deposit this morning. We are prepared to go ahead with the purchase, but first we should eat."

He was distracted then, by the sound of a car labouring up the steep incline of the mountain road and shuddering to a halt, and walking to the window he looked down on a man grappling with the catch of the bonnet of a Citroen from which smoke bled out of the front radiator grille and wheel arches. He was accompanied by a young girl; the same young girl with prominent breasts who sat at the next table at Lake Geneva; the same young girl in the restaurant phone booth. "Why did she ask for a taxi?" he mumbled to himself. When Weilermann turned Vassarri had a revolver aimed at his head. The briefcase was on the floor, and clearly a false bottom was protruding; the place where the gun had been hidden. Weilermann's eyes widened and he smiled nervously.

"I have money," he said.

"So do I."

Weilermann's head was thrown back by the blast and his body crashed to the hard, marble floor; blood trickled from a small hole above his right eye.

Henga rushed into the room, throwing her hands to her face as she first looked at Vassarri and then the lifeless shape of her husband.

"Where is the study?" said Vassarri.

Henga just stared in shock.

"The study, Henga, where is it?"

She could barely raise her hand to point. "At the end of the corridor."

He could hear the children clattering down the stairs in search of the commotion.

"Take them upstairs. Take them now. Stay there and don't move."

Henga nodded and hurried from the room, gathering up the children in the hall and ushering them upstairs. Vassarri followed and opened the front door to be confronted by the two tourists.

"At the end of the passage; take what we need, destroy the rest."

The chauffeur lay dead in the driveway; the two Alsatians lifeless on the lawn close by. Vassarri lit a cigarette and sat on the wide veranda steps, looking towards the mountains, satisfied with his day's work.

Vassarri referred to Weilermann's assassination as a 'Blatant Kill' as opposed to a 'Discrete Kill', inferring he had honed the art of murder to a fine art. *'A Blatant Kill is obvious, both to the victim, the bystanders, and to whichever government or organisation who employed him. It must be left in no doubt that the target was executed because he was considered a threat.'*

Rachel appeared out of the darkness, like a smiling apparition, garbed in a blue, silk dressing gown that appeared to swim around her petite frame, her face glowing like a freshly boiled lobster and hair glistening with droplets of water. "That was incredible," she sighed as she picked up a glass of wine from the coffee table and sat next to me. "How much would a place like this cost?"

"More than you can afford," I replied. "More than I can afford. As I said: Bernie let me have it cheap."

She sat smiling, her eyes moving all over the room, until finally they settled on me.

"How's the book?" she asked.

"So—so," I answered, flicking to the next chapter. "I'm reading about discrete and blatant killings."

"There's a difference?"

"Apparently. A blatant kill is direct; you know, brains splattered all over the wall, and no attempt made to hide the murderer's identity or his reasons."

Rachel took a sip of her wine.

"Then a discrete kill must be to remain anonymous?" she questioned.

I shrugged and continued to read. "Perhaps. I haven't got to that part yet."

Vassarri does not detail the other 785 killings to the degree of the Weilermann assassination; some barely get a mention. The contract on Weilermann was the last he undertook, for the British Government, or any other government, come to that; he officially retired from the murder business. As the story unfurled it soon became obvious that as a mercenary Nicolia Vassarri was unique.

He was the son of the world famous scientist Antoni Vassarri whose forte was diseases and cures. Antoni Vassarri believed vehemently in botany, that the plants and shrubs of this earth could offer the antidote for any disease, and this theory he proved time and time again. Of course, young Nicolia, being the son of a well-respected and wealthy scientist was privileged to go to some of the finest schools in Europe and by the tender age of fifteen he could speak no less than eleven different languages. In 1910, Germany had a plan and offered Antoni Vassarri vast amounts of money to move from his native home in Barcelona, Spain to Germany, working in their laboratories. So, that same year the Vassarri family took up their palatial residence just outside the city of Berlin. It soon became obvious that the German government had little or no intention of finding cures. On the contrary, they wanted to manufacture a disease there was no known cure for, nor ever likely to be; germ warfare. On the brink of the First World War the German government set up an intelligence department, the operatives of which would be able to infiltrate enemy agencies undetected and transfer information back to the homeland. Nicolia was a prime candidate. By 1912, he was an assassin, moving freely around Europe and terminating the lives of those the German government wanted dead; army personnel, politicians, even heads of state. What was unique about Nicolia was the way in which he administered death; not so much with a gun or knife or explosives, but with a syringe. In his quest for disease and cures his father had inadvertently discovered dozens of plant toxins that were completely undetectable when injected into a living being; the cause of death would appear totally natural; one inducing a heart attack, another a blood clot, another massive trauma. Needles were manufactured, as thin as a human hair, no larger than a single pore of the skin, inserted in the back of the neck just above the hair line, penetrating the underside of the brain and into the spinal cord, or though any orifice on the human anatomy, nipples, ears, mouth, rectum, even the eye of a penis; totally undetectable. Nicolia was able to produce a cause of death, and because it appeared natural or the result of some unfortunate ailment, no one was held accountable, especially those who had signed their death warrant; Discrete Kills. Shortly after the war he escaped Germany and the clutches of the Nazis to Italy where he still lives, and from there he set up his own business, offering his talents to any government willing to pay handsomely for it. By this time every country in the world had an intelligence service and Nicolia trained their recruits in the art of subtle assassination—including Britain.

"Well, this is romantic," said Rachel, huffily. "Is this your subtle art of seduction—reading a book on a murderer?"

I raised my eyes, forgetting she was even in the room.

"Sorry, I was carried away."

"Obviously! Did you find out what you wanted to know; why a killer would confess a secret he spent his whole life safeguarding?"

I closed the book, staring at the tattered cover.

"He says he owed it to us—to the British for winning the war, which inadvertently freed him and his family from the clutches of the German's. That's why he wanted his memoirs printed in England. He doesn't elaborate as to why he chose to confess his sins—as yet."

"As yet?"

"I haven't finished reading it," I said.

Rachel stared at me disapprovingly.

"You mean, I'm sitting here wearing absolutely nothing under this dressing gown, and you're just going to carry on reading that book!"

I nodded cautiously.

"How rude," she said, her face igniting with alarm.

"I won't be long, promise."

She shook her head. "Okay. Do you want to point me to the bedroom or would you rather I slept in the guest room?"

"First on the left," I smiled. "I'll be in shortly."

She rose, kissed me on the head and walked off towards the dark hallway.

"Sounds stupid if you ask me; paying a murderer vast amounts of money for a book that no one will ever read."

Her words hung in the air like an approaching thunderstorm, and I found myself staring into the darkness of the corridor long after she had disappeared from view. The wine on my lips felt tepid after standing untouched for so long, and I opened the book on the page where I had left it.

I awoke the next morning with Rachel lying next to me, her arm across my chest and her face nuzzled into my neck. I could hear the sound of the city coming to life, of milk bottles clinking and the throb of traffic outside my window. I gently removed her hand and slid out of bed, barely disrupting the bedcovers, and headed for the kitchen. I could have taken any one of three options. I could have slept in the spare room, but I considered it an insult to Rachel. I could have told her directly that sleeping with her, or more to the point, having sex with her, would have made me no better than my wayward wife—treacherous. Or I could have abandoned all my morals and gave her exactly what she so delicately asked for. There was a fourth option, cowardly, yes, and certainly an exercise in denial, but the one I chose nonetheless. I stood at the lounge window, looking down at the river and nursing a cup of steaming coffee when Rachel entered, her hair looking as though it had just received a 240 volt charge and a sleepy smile on her face.

"Morning," I said, chirpily.

"Morning," she yawned.

"I've made you a coffee; on the table."

She fell into the settee and lifted the cup, cradling it in her hands, her lips pursed to gauge the temperature, and finally taking a sip she smiled.

"Did you read your book?" she asked matter-of-factly.

"Until 2.30; sorry."

"You could have woken me. I mean, if you wanted you could have woken me."

"It was late. I didn't—sorry."

She took another sip of her coffee and shrugged her shoulders.

"It's okay. I enjoyed last evening. It was fun. I'm not holding you to anything."

I nodded, even though she wasn't looking in my direction.

During the ensuing silence she lifted the battered paperback and turned it in her hand, and placing it back on the coffee table, stared at it curiously.

"What, exactly, are you looking for, Michael?" she asked.

My eyes focused on the people walking along the Embankment, under a veil of heavy greying clouds that threatened to darken deeper and pull a storm in from the coast.

"Happiness, good health . . ." I replied, giving the question brief consideration.

Rachel sighed and rolled her eyes.

"Not your aspirations on life, Michael. This . . ." she said, grabbing the book and waving it at me. "Assassins. Jack the Ripper. Such subjects have no place in the life of a litigator. You're not some kind of twisted sadist, are you? I mean, your wife is still alive and well, isn't she? I bet you have a secret room in your house, decked out with weird contraptions devised to administer sexual torture."

"And if I had?" I smiled, giving her a sideways glance.

She shrugged and grinned. "You could have given me a call. You had my number."

She chuckled to herself and resumed drinking her coffee.

"Call it research," I said.

"Research! Why would you want to know why someone kills?"

I sat on the arm of the settee, still gazing out at the grey morning.

"That doesn't interest me anymore. What interests me now is the legend, the myth that particular person creates, albeit unintentionally. And I've come to the conclusion that we are all myths and legends; some just smaller than others."

Rachel stared at me, her lips still pursed in mid-sip.

"Michael, Jack the Ripper wasn't a fable, and according to you neither is Vassarri. They are cold blooded murderers with massive brain disorders. They are very real."

"You're right, of course, but I disagree with your brain disorder analogy. Nicolia Vassarri is as sane as you or I, and certainly better educated; a highly intelligent human being; not your everyday mindless thug."

"And you regard him as a legend, do you?"

"No, I don't. He just is. Probably, had the government not gone to such great lengths to erase his story, it would have been forgotten. They created his legend by trying to suppress his connection with them. Vassarri is the ultimate bogyman; someone who exists but there's always that element of doubt—like Jesus."

"You're likening an assassin with Jesus Christ?"

"Not as a person—as a myth. Take women for example . . ."

"God, Michael, is there no end to your poisonous evaluations! Now womankind is being brought into question."

"And not for the first time," I said arching my eyebrows. "Cast your mind back to the days before David, when you were a young and pretty teenage girl and sex occupied your mind every waking hour."

"Like now, you mean?"

"Every Saturday you'd hurry home from work, take a nice hot bath and put on the sexiest clothes in your wardrobe. You wanted to be the one the boys all stared at, the one they longed to take home, the one who might."

"I wasn't that kind of girl," she protested.

"But you did go through the ritual of dressing up, the stockings, the make-up?"

"Every girl does. There's nothing wrong with being admired."

"The image you created had nothing to do with admiration. You created a myth; your own myth; the way others perceived you but not the real you. For a few hours every Saturday night you were someone else."

Rachel thought for a while and nodded her head.

"I did have this friend Rita. Now she was a legend, especially down the local."

"That's my point. Women go to great pains to purvey an image detached from their real selves; smooth skin, hair dye, provocative clothes."

"Alright, Michael, if it's hairy women you like I'll stop shaving my legs, but I draw the line at personal hygiene."

"And men are no different. A man wearing a suit or a uniform demands respect, but who really knows what lies beneath; what dark secrets or degraded thoughts occupy his mind?"

"You wear a suit."

"Exactly," I said, returning to the window. "Come and look at this."

She came and stood beside me, threading her arm through mine, looking out at the London skyline.

"What's so interesting?" she asked.

My eyes dropped to the river, to the obelisk on the Embankment.

"Cleopatra's Needle," I said.

Her eyes strayed, but she followed the direction of my pointing finger and nodded.

"It is one of a pair, originally erected at Heliopolis in Egypt around 1475 BC and later moved to Alexandria. One was presented to us back in 1878, the other to the Americans, which now stands in Central Park, New York. Do you know that there are more attempted suicides here than anywhere else along the Thames. It's just an inanimate object, a slab of red granite, but some believe it's cursed; they can hear it whispering to them, willing them to throw themselves into the river and end their miserable lives. Others believe it has healing powers; they touch it, hoping to pass on good health to anyone they have contact with. It is a legend just by its existence."

Rachel nodded with interest, borne more out of appeasement than the desire to listen to the ravings of a lunatic.

"Well—I could listen to you all day had I the capacity to stay awake, but work calls," she said as she headed off to the bathroom.

The sun broke through the clouds then, glinting on the river and turning the windows of buildings into squares of severe light.

"Fancy doing something reckless, Rachel?" I said.

She stopped and turned. "About bloody time," she sighed.

We left the city behind us, to the city-dwellers, the stockbrokers, the shop owners and the war regime with their newly appointed wardens who behave like they have been bestowed a knighthood rather than been given a tin helmet with ARP printed on it. With my newly acquired Jaguar and full tank of petrol, we sped towards Brighton, soaring like an eagle over the mountain ranges, or gazelle racing across the African plains; the windows open and Rachel shaking her hair wildly and laughing as my shiny machine rocketed onward with the velocity of a falling meteor—or so I hoped. The truth of the matter was that I hadn't driven a car for so long it was like conducting needlework while wearing boxing gloves. Rachel sat with her head resting against the window, staring out at the slow passing scenery. Boredom had set in like rigor mortis, and I could almost hear her contemplating that of all the bad judgements she had ever made this had to be the worse. Coordination is an advantage when operating machinery, but a little more is required when operating machinery that moves in any particular direction, and although Rachel appeared to allow me some latitude for my clumsiness, other road-users were not so understanding. I ignored the miles of traffic straddling behind me, and the overtaking lorry whose driver shouted rude things about my mother as he passed, but after thirty-five miles I felt I was beginning to get to grips with the beast.

Probably out of embarrassment Rachel had taken the car manual from the glove compartment and was calmly perusing it, ignoring the snarling faces and the obscenities hurled in our direction.

"What day is it?" she asked.

"Friday," I replied as the car hopped and bounced its way towards the coast.

"Well, we're in luck. It says here that on Friday's you can use all four gears and not just the two you've been using since we left London."

"No need to be facetious, Rachel, I'm doing the best I can."

"I knew I'd hear those words from you sooner or later," she muttered.

"What? What was that?"

"Nothing."

The green machine chugged into the countryside with all the finesse of an epileptic dustbin, and while Rachel stared at me indignantly, I fumbled with the gear stick, debating whether to push, pull or leave it.

"Go on, Michael, slip it in," Rachel said with a playful grin. "You know you want to."

"At present I'd like you to be quiet. I'm getting the hang of it now," I returned.

She put her hand to her mouth to staunch her laughter.

"Do you think you can do any better?" I grunted.

"Couldn't do any worse."

I stamped on the breaks and climbed out, standing in front of the car and pointing at her as if she were the accused standing in the dock.

"Come on then, out you get. You have a go at driving, but I'm warning you it isn't easy."

We swapped places, and after she had adjusted the seat position, rear-view mirror position and window position, the car purred off and was soon gliding down the country lanes of the A23. I sat, sulkily staring out of the window as small villages blurred past.

"Don't you think we should be going a little slower?" I suggested.

"As slow as you were? Michael, I've known continents to move quicker. Glaciers move at a faster rate. Compared with you the ebb and flow of the ice fields are like a white-knuckle ride. Are you that slow at everything you do?"

"Not everything. And do all your replies have to be laced with sexual innuendo?"

"Mostly."

"And why didn't you tell me you could drive?"

"It never came up in conversation. David is a mechanic. I'd like a pound for every car I've had to deliver or pick up. How's my driving?"

"Not bad. But you're still going too fast."

We emerged on the south coast, the sea stretched out before us. We had left the city behind and seemingly the impending storm. The sky was blue speckled with white inoffensive clouds, and the sea foamed as it rumbled up onto the stony beach. A warm breeze and fresh air filtered in through the open windows as we drove along the waterfront, and all along the promenade sightseers stared out at the water as if they were witnessing a miracle. After parking the car Rachel and I headed into the town, gazing into the shop windows and displays purposefully designed to entice any other image but the war. Indeed, in this atmosphere it was difficult to believe we were at war. We moved into the Lanes, a tangle of straight and jagged alleyways with lopped and tilted shops either side selling antiques, jewellery, bric-a-brac and sweets galore. We took refuge from the crowds in a small public house in a side street that led down to the seafront. I wondered at the Victorian décor and ornaments that adorned the interior, the yellow mantle of light given off by the gas lamps even in daylight hours, the scarred and chipped tables and chairs that had been lovingly restored and highly polished. Even the barmaid appeared to be caught up in the Victorian period, garbed in a frumpish dress that I was dubious to comment on just in case she wasn't caught up in the Victorian period. This public house was borne of an age when the south-east of England was the richest and most densely populated area of Britain. Once no more than a fishing village, Brighton owed its fast expansion to the railways that brought thousands of tourists in from the city and surrounding suburbs. The Prince of Wales visited in 1783, and the town flourished.

"I feel like a naughty girl; running away without telling anyone," said Rachel as she gazed about her. "Can we go to the pier later?"

I smiled to myself. She was like a child, barely able to control her excitement.

"Have you never been here before?" I asked, collecting the drinks and moving to the nearest table.

"David and I went to Clacton once. That was nice, but there's something daring about Brighton, isn't there?"

"Is there?"

She nodded assertively. "Men bring their mistresses here, you know, so they can be strangers amongst other strangers. They take them to beautiful hotels to be waited on hand and foot and buy them trinkets as souvenirs, a gift she can stare at and reminisce after love has long gone."

"I'm not buying you any trinkets, Rachel," I said, obstinately.

"Don't want one," she returned with a smile. "This is enough. Imagine, me sitting in Brighton on a work day and drinking alcohol at lunchtime? Beats the bookshop any day."

"And I'm not taking you to any beautiful hotel to be waited on hand and foot."

"You'll reconsider as the day goes on. You're just touchy because you can't drive. I understand."

I welcomed the change as much as her. It was good to be away from the city, away from the office and the Henderson's, the Vassarri's, the Griffin's and the Jack the Ripper's; it was good to escape. I still treated Friday's as my half day, the day I would finish early to ensure I made it home for the weekend to be with my deceitful wife who surreptitiously eyed her lover in the snug of the Dog and Duck; the office could do without me.

"Did you know they call Brighton 'The Queen of Watering Places'?" I said, still looking around at the surroundings. "At least the Victorians did."

"Wouldn't it have been easier just to call it Brighton? It rolls off the tongue easier than 'The Queen of Watering Places.'"

"Have you no romance?"

"Lots; just not for a stack of old houses by the sea."

I shook my head in dismay, and she laughed and clutched my knee.

The problem with Rachel was that she was hard to fathom. You never really knew when she was joking or when she was serious. I guess in my heart I believed that the levity she injected at every opportunity was a ruse, a camouflage and distraction to hide her loneliness. I realised, also, that days such as this were few and far between for her; that she had seldom ventured outside the city, or the borough of Southwark, come to that.

We headed off along the promenade towards the pier, looking down with mutual joy as bathers braved the stony beach under bare feet only to scramble back once the chill of the cold sea numbed their toes. Men with rolled up trousers and women with hoisted skirts paddled and kicked water at one another, laughing uncontrollably at the others saturated state, and children buried their dads up to their necks in stone tombs. Ice cream sellers, toffee apple sellers and candyfloss sellers plied their trade at every twist and turn, and at the entrance of the pier a clown with big feet and a spinning bow tie gave Rachel a blue paper flower; probably to compensate for the shilling each entrance fee. We moved through the clacking turnstiles and onto the boardwalk, staring down at the gaps between and the pebbled beach below, the surf and then the sea. Rachel slipped her hand in mine, like a frightened little girl might hold her father's hand, but she smiled and let the gentle wind brush her face before she turned away and giggled childishly. At the pier's end a brass band played renditions of Glen Miller songs, amid flowing union flags and a throng of people who sang along word perfect. We were lost in the celebration for a while, humming along and applauding at every songs end. Strange how the eyes of so many wandered to the horizon, as if they could see beyond to where our boys were fighting for our liberty, but never once did sadness creep into their faces or their voices; they sang heartily for their fathers and sons—and for England.

We gorged ourselves on toffee-apples and orange juice in paper cups, lost a small fortune on the one-arm bandits in the arcade, and moved in ever decreasing circles around the stalls and kiosks that excelled in selling everything that served no purpose whatsoever. We settled on a bench midway down the pier, staring towards the white cliffs of Peacehaven, where between an endless line of palatial hotels and brightly coloured summer houses rose up atop of a sturdy retaining wall that disappeared into the sea and sky.

Rachel stared out at the heaving waves as they surrendered to the undertow, curling in on themselves and exploding in a crescendo of white foam against the stony beach. Her smile was unrelenting and she sighed with contentment almost with every breath.

"Thank you, Michael," she said as she gazed out across the animating water.

"For what?" I asked.

"For today. For making me feel like somebody. For making me feel special."

Tears glazed her eyes, and her teeth gently bit into her bottom lip. If there was such a place as Shangri-La, today she had found it.

"We could visit the aquarium if you want to," I suggested, pointing towards the clock tower on the main road.

It was clumsy form of distraction, to take her mind off what was and what could be.

"There's an aquarium here?" she said with surprise.

"Just over there. For reasons known only to themselves, the Victorians had a great interest in seashells, seaweed and marine life. It opened in 1872 and holds 41 vast fish tanks; steam engines pumped in sea water from nearby reservoirs."

She began to laugh and shake her head.

"What is it with you and history? Wouldn't you have preferred to be a teacher or professor?"

I considered the possibility and shrugged my shoulders.

"I don't think I'm distinguished enough to be a professor," I grinned.

"Nor old enough. But you're certainly strange enough."

"I am?"

"Oh, God, yes," she said, pushing her hair behind her ears. "I think you spout off historical facts to impress people; because somewhere under that city suit and those gold lettered business cards you throw around, you're incredibly insecure. You shouldn't be. I'm glad I met you, Michael James."

The extravagance of the aquarium with its strange exhibition of marine life and reading saloons occupied the afternoon and early evening, and when we emerged beneath the clock tower the warm breeze had all but gone and the night was chasing the sun over the horizon. The day-trippers had only slightly diminished and were still meandered around the pier front, to clog up the promenade as they debated where to eat or where to go next. Some headed for the station, others to any one of the hundreds of hotels that lined the front, in preparation for dinner and to dress in their finest.

"We best make our way back," I said.

Rachel reluctantly agreed. "Do you think we'll make it back to the city before nightfall? It could take two hours, probably longer the way you drive. Then there's the blackout; headlights are illegal. How's your driving in the dark?"

"You drive. We'll get back quicker."

"Not me. I struggle with dull light; it's a family curse; our eyes don't dilate like other peoples. I have spectacles but they really don't help."

"You wear glasses?"

"Not in front of people, silly, and certainly not in front of you. They make me look like an old spinster. Providing the traffic isn't too bad we should be okay."

"Traffic—at this time of day?"

"Of course. Take a look around you, Michael. Everyone will be making their way home shortly."

True enough, the cars and lorries began to queue up along the coast road. Rachel was giving me a wary sideways glance.

"We could always stay till morning; you know, sleep in the car," she suggested with a troubled sigh.

I stared at her as if I had been personally affronted.

"You want me to sleep in a car!"

"To save paying for a hotel, yes," she shrugged.

"I told you: I'm not taking you to any hotel. I'll get us home even if I have to drive through the bowels of hell."

"Fine."

The hotel foyer was a masterpiece, an architectural splendour that only a heathen could ignore; it oozed elegance and opulence. Everything appeared to be dressed out in wrought iron, the reception desk, the surrounding tables and chairs; even the elevator that centred a wide spiral staircase was of black steel guarded by a young man dressed in a grey uniform. Staff attired in the same garb glided to and from the reception desk, setting off in different directions to attend to the paying guests. A deep-pile red carpet spread out before us and I walked directly to a preoccupied hotelier garbed in black behind the desk. He completed his task and smiled at me. "Yes, sir."

"A room please; a double—for me and my wife . . . my wife and I. Her," I said, pointing to Rachel.

"Very good, sir," the clerk responded with a fixed smile. "A double room—fifteen pounds."

I nodded, took my wallet out and began to leaf through a pile of notes.

"Have you identification, sir?" he asked, politely.

"A business card," I replied, pulling out a card and tossing it in front of him.

"I was referring to a legal document, sir; a marriage certificate, a bill of some kind that bears your name—anything of that nature?"

"No. I don't have anything of that nature, but I do have cash. Will that not suffice?"

He shook his head faintly. "You have a car?"

"I do—a shiny green Jaguar."

"Registration, sir?"

"Not a clue, but it's parked out front if you care to take a look."

He signalled to a nearby bellboy to investigate.

In moments the young man was back, whispering the car registration in his ear.

The clerk smiled again and turned the register in my direction, handing me a pen.

"If you care to sign, sir; room 127."

The servile clerk was talking to me but looking at Rachel suspiciously.

I signed the register and thanked him as he handed over the key and I walked off in search of the nearest bar.

Rachel never followed me. In fact the only way she moved was towards the clerk.

"You do have single rooms, don't you?" she asked quietly.

"But of course, madam. But your husband has already booked a double room. Is something amiss?"

"Not exactly, but my husband can be somewhat of a tyrant. I'd prefer a single room—whatever is available."

"But for why, madam? You two look very much in love."

"Oh, we are. We're at it all the time. But the thing is he picks his feet, usually about two in the morning. Isn't that disgusting? Anyway, it's been such a nice day and it's such a lovely evening, I was thinking why would I want to ruin it—with him picking at his feet."

"I appreciate your honesty, but there's little I can do, madam. Perhaps you could have words with your husband."

I was standing in the corridor that led to the bar, just out of the foyer and wondering what the hell she was talking about.

"It's not just the feet," she explained in a confidential tone. "It's the wind. He has this habit of storing it up through the day and letting it all go as soon as darkness falls. I swear that sometimes I can't breathe. And the stench . . ."

"Yes, yes, yes, I get the gist," said the receptionist, looking nervously about him for any approaching guests. "Of course I can allocate you a single room but your husband has already paid for a double. You must consult with him. Sorry."

Rachel shook her head with disappointment.

"Then whatever is a girl supposed to do?" she said.

The clerk smiled tiredly.

"We have a single room if you care to pay an additional sum," he stipulated from the corner of his mouth.

"But I have no money. He takes all my money. And what with the feet and the wind . . ."

"Madam," he snapped. "There's nothing I can do unless you talk to your husband. I'm very sorry."

Rachel glared at him through narrowed eyes.

"Then you leave me little choice," she said, haughtily. "I shall write a strongly worded letter to your employers, informing them that you lacked compassion for my dilemma, and that you forced me to share a room with a tyrant."

"I think tyrant is an exaggeration, madam. I'm sure he's quite charming."

"I thought so too. That was until I started to wake up covered in bits of dead skin and toenail clippings."

I apologised unreservedly to the desk-clerk as I seized Rachel's arm and marched her out of reception and towards the bar.

"You've never worn glasses in your life, have you?" I growled.

"Are you kidding?" she laughed. "I could read you a pocket edition of the Bible from four hundred yards away with a bucket on my head."

I found myself staring out at the early morning, at the empty beaches and desolate promenades that less than ten hours ago had been packed with day-trippers and bathers. The roads were empty and the pier a sad and ghostly image, reminiscent of the Marie Celeste where all had abandoned her, leaving their presence behind in the form of paper-cups and wrappers, lost or forgotten toys and towels fluttering gently over the perimeter railings. At the pier's end, where a military band played with gusto in the faint hope our boys could hear it, union flags raised and fell on a current of soft wind as if saluting their bravery. The window panes of the hotel were speckled in the spindrift of the sea, and everything before me glowed in a soft, satin sheen. The hotel room was dull and austere, garishly decorated with heavy brass-framed mirrors and photographs of Brighton from some long bygone age. The room, like every other in the hotel, was equipped with a buzzer that when pushed indicated the room number at reception, where after a hotel employee, usually an underpaid teenager, would appear to fulfil your every need. I exercised my right and gave my order of a pot of coffee and two rounds of toast to a young girl who looked as though she had worked two nightshifts and a dayshift back to back without a single break.

I laughed quietly to myself at Rachel's ruse; feigning almost blindness in order to squeeze a few more hours in Shangri-La from me, and I laughed even louder at the thought of how I administered her punishment; by pouring as many port and lemon's down her as she could consume before falling unconscious. The young bellboy smiled politely when we entered the elevator, and was more than accommodating when Rachel slid down the wall and collapsed in a crumpled heap on the floor. He helped me get her back to the room and place her on the bed, to which I gave him a tip for his service and his kindness. In all, I thought, it had been a very pleasant day. What I escaped, once again, was consummating our relationship in any shape or form. Whether I was conscious of that fact while I turned a perfectly articulate woman into an incoherent blubbering imbecile I cannot say, but I thought it an appropriate action given the circumstances. I was, however, gentlemanly and brave enough to relieve her of her blouse and skirt before tucking her into bed, even if it was in a dark room.

I was still staring out of the window when I heard the faint rumblings coming from the bathroom, and when she appeared some minutes later, I swear I must have put the wrong woman to bed. Her face was pale and gaunt, her eyes dark and hollow, and her hair appeared to have been ironed into a wild abstract form where all fibres faced horizontally. A bed sheet was wrapped around her, dragging behind like a bride's train, and her posture seemed devoid of strength or even muscle and bone.

"Morning," I smiled broadly.

"Shut your face, you," she groaned.

I laughed, poured her a coffee and handed it to her.

"Eat some toast, it'll do you good," I proposed.

"Dying—that would do me good," she said, holding her head. "What time is it?"

"A little after seven."

She gawped at me as if I had taken leave of my senses.

"A little after what?

"Seven."

"God, what are you—a machine? Don't you ever sleep?"

With a few sips of coffee she began to come to life and the events of the night before slowly but surely began to dawn on her. She pulled the bed sheet away from her breasts and stared downward, and then curiously began to appraise her stockings.

"Who undressed me?"

"I took the liberty. Needless to say, I never took advantage of the situation."

"Not that I would have known anything about it," she returned. "You did this on purpose, didn't you?" she added, still holding her head as if it were going to fall off at any moment.

I laughed again and she winced with pain.

"You lied to me," I said.

"I never lied," she retaliated calmly. "I was just confused. It was my grandmother who suffered with bad eyes."

A look of total dismay must have washed over my face.

"And I thought it was me;" she added timidly, "simple mistake."

At breakfast, amid the chink of china and the metallic chimes of steel, and the steady stream of guests filtering into the restaurant and taking up tables, Rachel stared at her plate of eggs, bacon, sausages and fried bread with wide eyes.

"Eat it up. It'll soak up some of that alcohol," I commanded.

"I plan to. Jesus, don't they have rationing down here?"

"Evidently not. The rules and regulations of rationing have yet to match the demand for cold, hard cash."

She ate, casting her eyes across the room and proffering her opinion on anyone she laid eyes on. The couple in their mid-fifties: "Definitely not married; or they are, but not to one another. He's probably a banker, a stock-broker, perhaps, and she's a legal secretary of some kind—tells her husband she's at a conference." The younger couple looking so much in love: "He's married, she's probably in the throes of getting married, and he lies to his wife about business. She probably thinks he's working up north somewhere, and her boyfriend is being kept at a distance." The quiet couple in the corner: "Now they're married. He's contented, she isn't. He wants to give her everything, and she doesn't want anything he has to offer. She wants a lot more than him. He tries hard but it's not enough." Few escaped her analysis. Even the waiters and waitresses fell foul to over-active imagination.

"So, what have you planned for today?" she asked as she topped up my coffee cup.

"Home. We should go home; me to mine, you to yours."

She hid her disappointment behind a shallow smile and nodded.

"I've embarrassed you, haven't I?" she said, carefully moving the pot over her cup.

I looked at her with surprise and shook my head.

"No, of course you haven't. I really enjoy your company, but we can't stay here forever."

"Why not? Why can't we stay here forever?"

"Because we can't."

"Then just another day. Just one more. Is it compulsory that we have to be miserable all the time? Will one more day ruin God's great plan?"

Her eyes took on a doleful appearance, like that of a kitten or a puppy; designed to melt even the strongest of hearts. She reached for her handbag and took out her purse.

"I have money," she said, unclipping it and offering it to me as proof. "Granted, it's your rent, but I'll make it up before Bernie gives you the contract."

"Contract?"

She nodded. "The contract—for the flat."

"Oh, yes, the contract; slipped my mind."

She looked at me with the face of an angel. "Please, Michael."

I sighed quietly and shook my head. By degrees she was wearing me down.

"I have issues, Rachel; problems I have to deal with," I explained quietly.

She sipped her coffee and nodded.

"All of which can wait till Monday. Monday's always the best day when dealing with issues. Monday is always an issue day."

I stared at her through narrowed eyes.

"Okay. One more day, but tomorrow we go home. And one word of complaint from you and you will be here for forever, or at least the time it takes you to walk home."

She shrieked with delight, pulling disapproving stares from everyone in the restaurant, and leaning over the table she kissed me on the cheek.

My face glowed with embarrassment at the staring faces and I scowled back at her.

"We're having a baby," she announced to everybody in the room.

I thought I'd die and hid my face in my coffee cup.

In the shortest of time we were consigned to the past and the chinking of steel on porcelain resumed.

"What issues?" she asked, leaning forward, "business issues?"

"Amongst others."

She reclined, looking back at me patiently.

"I'm being followed," I said, reluctantly.

A smile began to expand on her face but evaporated when mine remained unchanged.

"Followed? Followed in what way?" she asked.

"Followed in the way that when I leave the office and walk in any particular direction, someone is following me; usually the same person, or one of three. They work it in shifts—two days at a time, then swap. Sometimes there are two. Some days they wear different clothes and bad disguises, but they're always the same three people."

An uncertain grin returned and lingered before slipping away.

"Why would someone be following you?"

She suddenly froze with her eyes wide and turning to the left and right without her head actually moving.

"Are they here now?" she whispered, nervously.

I smiled as I surveyed the busy restaurant.

"No, at least not any of the three."

She sighed with relief and pulled her chair in a little closer to the table.

"More the reason to stay here—for forever," she said. "Are you sure it isn't all in your imagination? Sometimes, when I walk home from the pub in the dark, I swear someone is behind me; you know, following."

"It's isn't in my imagination, Rachel, though at one point I thought it was. I thought I was going mad."

"Then who? Who is following you? More to the point, why would they be following you?"

"To see who I speak with—friends, associates."

"Michael, you're delirious. Give me one good reason why someone would be keeping you under surveillance."

I arched my eyebrows at her choice of words.

"I read a lot of detective novels," she said with a tilt of her head. "God knows I have to do something in that boring bookshop. So why?"

I looked around the room and then leaned forward on my elbows.

"A while ago I took on the Henderson case . . ."

"The Blackout Butcher—you told me," she broke in.

"And the officer who arrested Henderson was a man called Carlisle . . ."

"The corrupt policeman; his trial has just finished. It's been headline news for weeks. So?"

"Well," I began, taking another brief look around me, "he wasn't working alone. He was just one of many corrupt police officers working for The Metropolitan Police Force . . ."

Rachel turned up her nose, and her eyes examined mine as if she were searching for traces of madness.

"Everyone knows about that! Every newspaper in England has got hold of that story. They say there's a list—the names of all the suspected coppers."

I took yet another surreptitious glance about the restaurant and lowered my head.

"And I have it, Rachel. I have the list."

She paused, and again she examined my face with her eyes.

"So?" she said, eventually.

I sighed at her failure to understand the consequences of the item I possessed.

"So—the people who are following me . . ."

"The people you *think* are following you!"

I paused to draw breath.

"So the people who are following me could easily be three of the corrupt two hundred and forty seven officers named in the list. They could just as easily be working for Harry Griffin, or even Fallow. On the other hand they could be government officials."

"Who? What?" she spluttered with confusion. "Who the hell is Harry Griffin? And isn't Fallow's name on that book—the Vaccarri Papers?"

"The Vassarri Papers," I said, correctly. "Yes, he published the book some years ago."

"And the government destroyed all the copies; you told me that, too. And where does Harry what's-his-name come into all this?"

"Griffin. He furnished the list, the film and photographs. Peter Egan and I met him and . . ."

"Peter being your friend who died of a heart attack," she interrupted, screwing up her eyes and shaking her head as if to absorb all the information.

"Yes," I nodded assertively. "But I never did believe he died of natural causes. And now I believe it even less."

Rachel's body seemed to deflate and she began to rub her fingertips on the sides of her head as if to ease her suffering. "I think my hangover is kicking in. Michael, can we talk about this later—after I've had some fresh air and perhaps grown a few million more brain-cells?"

We left the restaurant and walked straight to the reception desk. The same desk clerk who had signed me in had just begun his shift, and after giving Rachel a wary gaze, he smiled at me in the same condescending way.

"Was everything to sir and madam's liking?" he enquired.

"So much so that we'd like to stay another night," I replied. "But just one more night," I added giving Rachel a warning look.

He opened the register but appeared distracted. Rachel was behind me, repeatedly flicking something I could not see from her blouse. She smiled at us both and continued with her task.

"The room?" I said, removing my wallet and gaining his attention.

"Yes, of course" he mumbled, averting his gaze from Rachel and staring back to the register. "Would sir care to pay in the morning when he vacates, after breakfast?"

His eyes strayed again to Rachel and her incessant flicking.

"That would be appropriate. Thank you," I replied, placing my wallet back in my jacket.

"I hope sir and madam have a pleasant day."

His smile slightly lopped to one side as Rachel continued to brush and flick the fabric of her blouse.

"Damn toenail clippings," she said.

The morning was clear and crisp, and the undulating sea appeared to be flattening out before our eyes as we made our way down the quiet promenade. The few people we saw were obviously locals, unimpressed by the breathtaking vista and unconcerned with the invasion of their pleasant seaside town. They walked their dogs and gossiped on street corners, detached from their surroundings and the impending havoc that was but a few hours away. We made our way back into the town, climbing the steep incline to its very peak, staring into the shop windows and meandering around a small cloth market tucked down a narrow lane eclipsed by lines of tall houses either side. Rachel shooed me away as she made a purchase from an unsavoury looking character selling out of a suitcase straddled across a fold-up picnic table. Making our way back through the cobbled lanes we stopped at a small café and took up a table outside. Perhaps it was the breeze, the sea air, or even the exertion spent on walking about in no particular direction, but the colour was beginning to return to Rachel's cheeks; she no longer looked like a cadaver. A young girl with a bright smile served us two cups of coffee that appeared more froth than actual liquid.

Rachel opened her handbag and discretely eyed her newly acquired purchase and nodded approvingly.

"What did you buy?" I asked.

"Things—women things," she replied, securing her handbag and resting it on her lap.

"What kind of women things?" I pursued.

She sighed exhaustively. "Knickers, okay. Two pair of silk knickers."

"Oh, I see. Well, silk is a rare commodity these days."

"I didn't buy them because they were silk, Michael. I bought them because they're knickers; because the ones I'm wearing are beginning to creak every time I walk."

I bravely returned a smile and set my eyes on the passing pedestrians.

"So what was it you were saying earlier?" she asked, the coffee cup cradled in her left hand and steadied by the handle with her right, "all that nonsense about Fallow?"

I sat pensive for a moment, carefully constructing my words before speaking.

"It was something you said."

"Was it? What did I say?" she replied, confused.

"You said: Why would someone pay vast amounts of money for a book that no one will ever read?"

She shrugged. "I don't remember saying it, but if you say so."

"So that got me thinking. Who would benefit most from Peter's death?

"Go on," she said, trying to follow the plot. "Who would then?"

"Fallow. He would automatically own the copyrights to the story, the exclusive, and like you said, every newspaper in England is writing about it. Not only that, when I saw Fallow at Peter's funeral he looked like a man who had just won a fortune. He's even considering moving premises."

Rachel sipped at her coffee.

"Just bad luck for Peter and good luck for Fallow," she casually remarked. "That's the way life is, good for some, shit for others."

I agreed with a nod and raised my cup, giving the subject further consideration.

"You see, I've always thought that Peter's death was too coincidental, given that his story of police corruption broke the same day as Carlisle's trial ended."

"Certainly a little strange, but I still don't get it."

"Peter wrote the story of police corruption. Inspector Carlisle was one of the 247 named on the list I have, and his sentence was a fragment of what everyone thought he would receive," I emphasised.

She thought for a while, staring into her coffee cup.

"I still don't follow," she said, faintly shaking her head.

I placed down my cup and leaned forward.

"The morning after Peter died I went to Fallow's Publishing House," I explained. "The whole place had been turned upside down—broken into. He didn't know who I was. He thought I was a policeman at first. The thing is, there wasn't one mention of any attempted robbery in the newspapers. I think he staged it."

"But why would he do that?"

"To make himself look like a victim instead of a murderer, and when I walked in and announced who I was, he changed his mind. Once he knew I had the list there was no further need to continue with the charade."

Rachel nearly dropped her cup and her eyes flared open.

"No, no, no, Michael," she said, wagging a finger at me. "Peter Egan died of a heart attack; you said so yourself."

"But Nicolia Vassarri had the requisite skills to make a murder—or an assassination—look as though it was natural; the tools of his trade could induce a heart attack; skills he may have taught Fallow."

"The book I got for you? What has he got to do with all this?" She stopped and stared at me without blinking. "Fallow published his book!" she suddenly gasped.

I nodded and expressed a smug grin. "Now you're getting it. Earnest Fallow went out on a limb when he published his memoirs and they remained close friends. I'm sure I saw him in a photograph in Fallow's office; tanned, steel, grey hair, the way Peter's wife described him. This was the big story Fallow had been chasing all his life, so he killed Peter; inheriting the exclusive rights to the story in the process."

She shook her head, staring above me as she collated all the information.

"I'm not having it," she said, dropping her stare to mine. "When you die they don't just drop you in the ground. There are autopsies, Coroner's reports, police reports, and God knows what else. If your friend was poisoned then somebody would have found it."

"Vassarri worked with plant extracts—completely undetectable."

"Completely?" she echoed, nervously.

"One hundred percent. After killing Peter, Fallow searched for the list, but it wasn't in the house, so he returned to his office and made it appear as if it had been broken into."

Rachel nodded as she drank the remains of her coffee, and then placing the cup and saucer down, stared directly at me.

"Sounds plausible so far, but what I don't understand is once Fallow knew you had the list, why didn't he try to kill you?"

I leaned further forward, pointing to the faint scars that embellished my face.

"Who said he never, Rachel," I said.

The matter rested there for the time being. The labyrinth of higgledy-piggledy lanes that led us anywhere but in the direction we wanted to go, took us at the Royal Pavilion where, with a throng of excited sightseers, we explored the monument created by George IV back in 1817. Rachel appeared disinterested, lacking enthusiasm for the spectacle and instead preoccupied with her own private thoughts, and as we left the tourist attraction and headed back towards the sea, she stared up at me.

"None of this makes sense," she said, her arm threaded through mine. "If Fallow wanted the list, why kill you? Blowing up your offices wouldn't get him the list, would it?"

"No. I think by that stage he just wanted rid of the person who had the list. He knew I was suspicious of him. He realised, also, that the list was unimportant. Every newspaper wanted the story and was willing to pay handsomely for it—with or without it."

Rachel gave my theory some thought and nodded with uncertainty.

"I read a lot of books in the shop," she said, her head resting on my shoulder as we strolled towards the sea. "I have a lot of time to read—too much. Anyway, I was reading this book about a married couple; she was a budding novelist and he was an aspiring alcoholic. And she writes this incredible novel, and he chops her up into small pieces and feeds her to their pet dog, and he makes a fortune by pretending he wrote it. Similar thing, don't you think?"

"Not really, Rachel. Not really."

We walked along the coast road, towards the white cliffs faintly obscured by a thin mist that stole the definition between the sea and sky. Above us a wave of brightly coloured houses spilled down to the beach, intermittently punctuated by squares and crescents where clusters of quaint dwellings stared at one another; their window-boxes a riot of colour beneath square eyes reflecting the blue sky as it slid past. Tiny thoroughfares trickled between them like black rain in search of the sea, eventually bleeding into the main road beneath. Buses gathered before the pier spewing out wide-eyed parents and unruly children, scattering in all directions; filling the shops, filling the beaches and handing over money as if their very lives depended on it. The original geography and beauty of the delicate streets became lost beneath heavy traffic seeping into the town like molten laver until it reached the promenades and lost all momentum. We walked along aimlessly, taking in the Georgian grand hotels that decorated the sea front, and like them I stopped and leaned against the railings, to stare out at the sea. I could see small figures standing close to the edge of the cliffs; the Home Guard scanning the horizon with powerful binoculars for signs of approaching enemy battleships. Britain was prepared, as always. It was comforting to know that should ten thousand marauding blood-thirsty German's ever decide to land on Brighton beach, our ill-equipped defence would consist of two dozen retired gentlemen armed to the teeth with soft brooms and toy rifles.

"Perhaps I am being paranoid," I said as I stared out at the sea.

Rachel came and stood by the side of me, leaning on the railings and taking in the same view.

"About Fallow, you mean?"

I nodded pensively.

"What if you confronted him with it? You know, tell him what you think," she suggested.

I looked at her with disbelief.

"Good strategy, Rachel. And you don't think he might be a little offended by the accusation?"

She shrugged. "Okay—okay. Supposing Fallow never killed Peter. Suppose he got his friend to do it."

"Vassarri officially retired back in the late twenties; he lives somewhere in Italy. What I'm saying is . . ."

"Michael," she said, flapping her hands at me. "Just listen to yourself for one moment. If, as you say the list is unimportant, why kill you for it? It isn't that I disbelieve you, but the motive is too weak. As an avid reader of detective novels, your theory has more holes than a tramp's vest. So if you don't want to confront him, at least try to find out a bit more—if only to satisfy your own curiosity."

She pushed herself off the railings and set off down the incline towards the town.

"How?" I asked as I followed. "I can't call Fallow a murderer to his face, Peter is dead, and I don't know anybody else who knows him."

"What about Peter's wife? She seems well-informed," said Rachel over her shoulder.

I slowed to a stop.

"Good idea," I said with an agreeing nod. "But I don't know where she lives."

"Then get that peroxide, man-eating bitch of a secretary of yours to make some enquiries."

"I gave Sylvia some time off, till she recovers and the new offices are set up properly. And Penny's no good at research."

"Then you're stuck, Michael. What's left? You have a book on an assassin who is either dead or who probably never existed in the first place; a journalist who you insist died under mysterious circumstances despite evidence to the contrary; a claim of men following you who aren't really there; and a publisher with an untidy office. You need a holiday, Michael—a long one. You know what I think? If anyone is guilty it has to be the publisher. Maybe you're right. He would, in the event of your friend's death, own the exclusive rights to the story, and that would make him a rich man, given the attention the story is getting."

"You think so?"

She leaned into me and kissed me long and softly. "It has to be the only reasonable answer."

The conversation resumed over dinner. This time it wasn't me who brought the subject up but Rachel. Throughout the afternoon she had been contemplative and quiet, and often it was difficult to get an answer from her with a simple question. At dinner she was much the same.

"Are you okay?" I asked her.

She had, for the best part of twenty minutes, pushed a salad around on her plate without raising a single morsel of food to her mouth.

"I've been thinking about everything you've been saying," she said as she placed her knife and fork down, "and I have to say you're worrying me. You say you got the list from Harry . . . thingy."

"Griffin. Yes, I did," I replied.

"And these so-called corrupt officers were accepting bribes?"

"That's right."

She picked up her glass of wine and took a short sip.

"Why?"

I looked confused.

"Why what?"

"Why were they accepting bribes? And if they were, what did they represent? These bribes must be payment for something. You've overlooked that point, don't you think?"

I shrugged my shoulders.

"The answer to that would have appeared in the second edition of Fallow's Crime Magazine had Peter lived."

"And now you'll never know because he's dead. Harry must know. He gave you the list in the first place."

"Not really," I said with a shake of my head. "People like Harry Griffin have been paying the police bribes for years; bribes for their silence, even for information; it isn't something new. The only difference now is that it isn't some clandestine transaction; now the world knows."

Rachel looked perturbed and slowly shook her head.

"You actually admire people like Harry Griffin, don't you?" she said.

Her reaction unsettled me, and for a moment I observed her in a different light.

"I admire his honesty, and to a point the integrity of people like him. Their world is different from ours. The circles I move in at work are more cutthroat, more treacherous and more vicious than theirs will ever be. They have a loyalty that your everyday, suited office worker lacks. Don't confuse admiration with trust, Rachel."

She took another short sip of her wine and placed down her glass.

"I'm tired. I think I'll turn in early," she said.

As I watched her walk from the restaurant and into the hotel lobby, I knew I had said something wrong, but for the life of me I didn't know what. Nevertheless I didn't rush after her. Instead I went to the lounge, an after dinner location decked out in leather, studded chairs and settees and an accommodating waiter gliding from guest to guest. I secured a brandy, and for the next hour or so began to trawl through the chain of events that had led me to now. Undoubtedly the list, or more to the point being in possession of the list, was the crux of all my problems, and the conclusion I reached was that I had to get rid of it. The question now was to whom. When eventually I went to our room, Rachel was sound asleep in bed, and for a while I sat by the window in semi-darkness simply observing and listening to every soft breath she exhaled. I despised the existence of her husband and the fact that one day they would be sharing their life together left me feeling empty. I wanted to wake her. At that moment and at that time I wanted to make mad passionate love to her, to embrace her till the morning sun illuminated the horizon. I sat on the edge of the bed and gently ran my fingertips over her smooth shoulders, the hallway light dancing across the sheen of her body, and in her slumber she moved slightly and sighed peacefully. Perhaps, I thought, I could win her for all time, so that when her precious David returned home she would tell him that she had found another—someone who cared for her, loved her and would never leave her. How would he feel then, eh? How would he feel knowing he had lost her to a better man? How spiteful. I would imagine he would feel as I did, when I went home and realised I had lost Sarah to someone else—to a better man. I pulled the blanket over her shoulder, kissed her gently on the cheek and resigned myself to sleeping the night on the easy chair. It was inevitable that one day, and one day very soon I would lose her, and I realised my reluctance to ravish her was purely a defencc mechanism, that when she left me it wouldn't hurt so much. I looked over at her sleeping and smiled warmly. She had placed the worthless blue, paper flower into a fluted glass on the bedside cabinet, as if it were a priceless artefact; a treasure—a souvenir.

-22-

On the south-side of the river, close to Waterloo Bridge and Lambeth North Underground is the main police station controlling the south of London of which the boroughs of Kennington, the Elephant and Castle and Camberwell are but a few. I walked the short distance from the office, entered through the main doors and walked straight to the desk, staring up at a slender police officer who was either standing on staging or else had mastered the art of manoeuvring around on stilts; either way the illusion was unsettling. I waited patiently until he had completed a whispered conversation with two other policemen that was suddenly terminated with whooping laughter. He looked straight at me and jerked his head slightly, the remnant of his smile slowly subsiding. "I have an appointment to see Inspector Foggerty." The desk sergeant nodded as he glanced at my business card, and then from his high position on his raised platform began to scan the reception area, and as if I had the slightest clue as to what Inspector Foggerty looked like I did exactly the same. There were but a few people walking back and forth or standing stationary but none caught the sergeant's eye, but after a few moments he fixed his stare to a fat man crossing the floor with a folder in one hand, a cup of coffee slopping from a mug in the other and a sandwich suspended between his teeth. "Inspector, Mr. Michael James to see you," the sergeant called. The fat man deviated from his intended route and walked directly towards me. His walk had contracted a waddle due to his bulky frame and the overhang of his stomach concealed his belt. His white shirt was tight about his shoulders and obviously around his girth, his sleeves were rolled up and his tie loose. He set the coffee mug down on the high desk and removed the sandwich from his mouth.

"Cheese apparently, but it would never hold up to an autopsy," he said as he stared at the contents with a sickly expression. He took a moment to study the marks on my face.

"The wife?" he quipped.

"Unexploded bomb," I replied.

"Same thing," he shrugged. "Here, take this. I hope you like walking," he added passing me the folder.

The inspector was obviously Scottish, his accent thick and heavy, and the lack of hair on his head was compensated by a Walrus moustache, the original red of which had not been completely erased by the greyness of time. Leaving the reception area we moved into a stairwell where he stopped, daunted at the prospect ahead. "So, you're the brief defending Henderson," he said, setting forth on his ascent with a groan. "You got lucky—Neptune must be in perfect alignment with Mercury or something like that." I followed behind, watching his immense buttocks moving up and down alternately, the faint smell of sweat and tobacco left in his wake, the grunt of effort emitted with every clumsy manoeuvre. "Lucky? How so?" I asked. He paused and took a sip of his coffee. "Henderson would be swinging from the gallows by now had Carlisle not been so ambitious. But it happens—it's written. We're all vulnerable, susceptible to greed, lured by money, sex or both." To my surprise and disgust he tucked the cheese sandwich into his sweaty armpit and began to climb again, grasping the banister rail and pulling his weight up. "We are all blessed—or cursed—with a criminal mind," he continued over his shoulder. "That's how we catch them—by thinking the way they do, and that makes it difficult to separate the good apples from the bad ones. It's acceptable if an underpaid footslogging copper helps himself once in awhile. A thief steals jewellery, fences the goods and turns it into money, and when the police arrest him they take a few quid. Everybody wins. The stolen jewellery is insured and the owner is more than compensated for his loss because he has claimed more than their worth, the perpetrator is brought to justice, and the insurance companies are seen to be Samaritans even though they've been robbing everybody blind with their exuberant premiums. I remember when I was a young copper and was sent to a tenement block in an exceedingly undesirable part of Edinburgh to arrest a local pilferer Jamsie Clinton. He put up a struggle but then I knew he would. Besides I was built like a Greek God back then and never shied away from a tear-up. So after a mild beating I slapped the handcuffs on him and began to search the place. I found a large pile of money in a biscuit tin in the larder—at least two thousand pounds. I took a handful—three hundred pounds when I later counted it out—and marched Jamsie off to the nick. I took Mary MacLaggin away for a dirty weekend on the proceeds, and that was worth the risk."

On the first floor landing he stopped again, drawing a deep breath, a sheen of perspiration forming on his face, and a look of consideration as he debated whether to take a bite from his sandwich or another slurp of his coffee. "Acceptable once in awhile but never incessantly," he said looking up through the stairwell to the next landing. "Was Carlisle a good apple turned bad or was he always rotten to the core? My guess is the latter; probably joined the force to further his criminal activities—better opportunities plus recognition for his efforts, no matter how unscrupulously they were achieved. As a student may cheat on a test, a corrupt police officer is a contradiction. You can't aspire to achieve an honest goal by being dishonourable along the way." He set off on the next epic rise upward. "I was told you may be paying me a visit so I'm expected to extend you every courtesy, but I'm sure there isn't anything I can tell you that you don't already know; one more flight, Mr. James." We rounded the next landing with the second floor in sight. "Did the outcome of Carlisle's trial surprise you?" I asked. "With what's going on? Christ, no!" he returned with a shake of his head. "What's to be surprised about? 247 perverted policemen—probably more—extorting money from the local hoodlums, and Carlisle and God knows who else fabricating evidence, it's bound to be squashed by the authorities. The country doesn't need to know they're being protected by a bunch of thugs and murderers. Didn't you know the journalist who first broke the story?" I never gave a reply; I could only wonder how Foggerty connected me with Peter Egan, and then I thought of the inquisitive Sergeant Forbes who had come to my office shortly after Peter was found dead. Inspector Foggerty paused on the stairway, looking down on me with a knowing grin. "Now, that was suspicious," he resumed, "a journalist writes a story accusing 300 Met. Officers' of corruption, specifically naming Carlisle as one of them, and the very day the story breaks Carlisle's trial is suddenly brought to a conclusion—to wit a few lousy years being doled out instead of what he rightfully deserved—makes you think."

On the second floor he retrieved his sandwich from under his arm and walked to a pair of swing-doors, gently shouldering them open and entering a long corridor filled with noisy activity, and passing countless open office doors on either side he stopped and pushed his head inside one. "Get me the files of every officer that's left the Met. in the past eighteen months in a two mile radius of the Isle of Dogs," he said. The murmurings and clicking of typewriter keys suddenly fell silent, but a meagre voice protested, "That could take ages. There's a war on!" Inspector Foggerty looked back at me with an impatient shake of his head and then glowered back at the protestor screened from my view. "I don't care if we're in the midst of an alien attack," he growled. "Get one of your boys in blue to do the rounds and get what I asked for. Furthermore, I don't have ages. I have a wife waiting for me back in Scotland who is passionate about me and fretting away every lonely minute I'm not in her arms."

"But your wife hates you," the same voice returned.

The inspector agreed with a nod. "Good point. Needless to say, I'm the boss and you are worthless scum whose existence relies solely on keeping me in a contented frame of mind. I want those files by the end of the week."

He returned to the corridor and I walked by his side like an obedient dog. "You're from Scotland?" I asked, trumping up a casual conversation. He slowed and stared at me in disbelief. "Are you for real?" he said. "However did you reach that conclusion? Was it the fact I mentioned it, or did you deduce the slightest trace of an accent?"

"I meant—you live in Scotland and not here in London," I explained.

He laughed. "I know what you meant—I'm just teasing you. No. God forbid I should live in a place like this. I hate this city and I'm not over enthusiastic about the British; I never got over what you bastards did to William Wallace. But I don't get a choice where they send me—I just go. Hopefully I'll have this wrapped up in a couple of weeks and I can go home."

"Inspector Foggerty . . ." I began.

"Past tense, Mr. James," he interrupted. "I was an inspector up until ten or twelve years ago, but now I'm on the other side of the fence—detached from the police and those I investigate, which means in layman's terms that

I investigate the police and any wrongdoings that come to light. I am what they call an independent investigator and if there's a problem with one of them—or 247 of them—then they call me in to sort things out. Thanks to Carlisle I have a lot of work in front of me. What were you about to ask?"

"So you're not specifically working on the Henderson case? You haven't taken over from Inspector Carlisle?"

He continued moving down the corridor, his coffee spilling over the side of the mug and leaving a trail behind him.

"Carlisle did his job but he's left a big question mark," he said as he took in the obvious attributes of a passing female secretary. "And as for Henderson, I've been through it with a fine-tooth comb and come up with nothing. The problem is that the Met. thought they could play the whole Carlisle thing down, believing he was the only rotten apple and not part of a whole barrel load. So what did they do? They grilled Sergeant Stephen Rawlings who thought it in his best interest to sing like a bird, got the information condemning Carlisle who, by the way, was Rawlings' partner, and packed him off with a slap on the wrist. Of course Rawlings would testify come the trial. Like Hell! He sold his story and raked up enough money to get on his toes. He's probably laying on a beach in Australia now. But to answer your question—no I'm not taking Carlisle's role or reinvestigating the Henderson case. As a lawyer you will know that nobody can be tried twice for the same crime and Carlisle is no exception. He got off lightly, and no matter what our grievances or who is responsible for manipulating his trial he has been punished for his crime. Do I agree? It makes my skin crawl, but there are bigger wheels turning."

He ducked into an office at the corridor's end and placed down his mug and sandwich on his desk. "Come in and take a seat," he said, picking up a pack of cigarettes and offering them. "I don't smoke, thank you," I said. The inspector walked to the window that gazed out on the busy street, resting himself against the sill and lighting a cigarette.

"These things will be the death of me," he said, blowing out a thin stream of white smoke towards the ceiling and then scrutinizing the cigarette as if it were pure evil. "My role, such as it is, is to find and bring to trial the 247 corrupt officers your friend Peter Egan wrote about. Had he lived another month it would have made my job easier because he would have released the names in Fallows Crime Magazine; unfortunately it wasn't to be."

I tensed up at the very mention of the 'names' but Foggerty misconstrued my apprehensiveness at not making any comment.

"He was your friend, wasn't he, Mr. James?" he asked as he walked to his desk and picked up the coffee mug. "I mention it only because any man who attends another man's funeral must be considered a friend, don't you agree?"

I smiled like a criminal resigned to his punishment. "Have I done something wrong?"

"Hell, no!" said Inspector Foggerty. "It's just that you've made a point of not mentioning it."

"Should I? Yes, I knew Peter Egan but it was strictly business but he isn't someone I would regard as a close friend. As for being at his funeral I thought I owed it him that."

The inspector took a gulp of his coffee prior to his face screwing up in disgust and almost spat it all over me. "Shit! That's fucking freezing. Excuse my French," he spluttered. Turning his gaze to the sandwich he opened it, sighed exhaustively and tossed it straight into the wastepaper bin and took another drag of his cigarette. "To reiterate, Mr. James, I am not a policeman any longer. The Met. put their own people at the funeral, posing as mourners, associates or some long-forgotten friends—they were eager to validate Egan's threat. I'll let you into a little secret. I liked Peter Egan even though I've never met him. You can't buy Fallow's Crime Magazine in Scotland and I'd have my sister send it to me every month from Bristol; I never missed an edition. He would have made a good Scotsman—determined, fiery, and not afraid of the truth or exposing those pen-pushing bastards in government."

"I know him because he wrote an article on Henderson," I explained.

"I read it—excellent piece of work. And how is the case coming on?"

I shrugged in response.

He nodded as he stared into the wastepaper bin, abandoning what he thought was going to be his lunch.

"That's food for thought, isn't it?" he said, looking directly at the domed Imperial War Museum to the left of him. "I took a couple of hours out the other day to take a look around—a splendid looking building. Makes you wonder what will be stored in there once this war is over or if they'll have enough room."

"Bedlam," I said.

"Indeed it is, Mr. James. The whole situation is chaos."

I sniggered quietly and the inspector swung round.

"I was referring to the Imperial War Museum," I explained. "It was Bedlam. The building was designed by James Lewis and completed in 1815, and thereafter became known as Bedlam, a corruption of the name Bethlehem; a hospital specifically for the mentally ill. The patients were brought in from Moorfields in Hackney cabs under heavy guard. It remained a mental institution until 1930 when the patients were moved to Addington in Surrey. It became the Imperial War Museum in 1936."

The inspector's eyebrows were arched high on his forehead. "I'm impressed. How do you know these things? More to the point why would you want to know these things?"

"I just like history," I replied.

"So—that used to be Bedlam," he said, staring back in the same direction.

"Amongst others. The first was built just outside the city walls at Bishopsgate in 1250, and called St. Mary of Bethlehem. At the time Catholic England had a duty to help the poor and needy. By the fourteenth century the priory as it was expanded and parts of the abbey were used to house the mentally ill."

Foggerty had turned, his oversized buttocks resting on the windowsill, his arms folded and listening intently. "Go on."

"Back then we understood little of madness and looked on such people as demons. We tortured them, chained them to walls, whipped them and ducked them in freezing water. In the late seventeenth century the hospital moved to Moorgate, but in five hundred years we had still learned nothing about their illness. Bethlehem Royal Hospital was probably the first madhouse and funded by visitors who would come to view the patients for their own amusement. They would pay good money to see the insane abused either by the wardens or by other patients; for the right price you could watch them copulating or beating each other to death or tied to a post and whipped into unconsciousness. Death was commonplace so the governors had little to explain."

"And this continued for how long?"

"What brought about change was when George III was declared insane; there was a public outcry of sympathy. Until then nobody, including the royals gave a hoot, but suddenly money and great concern was directed towards the mentally sick—bigger hospitals, cleaner environments and the abolishment of violence against patients. You see, those in power don't care until it happens to one of their own—much like the government today."

His cigarette had burned almost down to his yellow fingers and he opened the window and tossed it out.

"If you're looking for a conspiracy theory you'll not find it here," he said as he walked back to his desk. "This is the way things are done. We're all pieces moving around on a chequered board, and depending on which direction we move, we either win or lose; beyond the perimeter of the board is the domain of a greater power."

"You don't think Peter Egan was silenced because he chose to move in another direction?"

"I could think of nothing else; too much of a coincidence. The day Carlisle's trial ended and the story of police corruption broke I was sent for. The next morning I was on a train and went straight to Scotland Yard. I was briefed and learned Egan had been found dead. Maybe because I admired him as a writer I made it my business to investigate his death. That night I went to the hospital and saw him for the first time, lying on a slab while a post-mortem was underway. He was nothing like I expected—he was younger, virile; not old and wise as I imagined him to be. Those people are thorough—took out every piece of him and examined it under a microscope; bottom line, heart attack induced by liver failure. According to the pathologist both his liver and kidneys were saturated in alcohol, showing distinct signs of acceleration in his drinking habits. This was probably brought on by stress—the result being the magnitude of the story he was writing. No way round it; he died of natural causes."

There comes a time when a none-believer is converted and this was mine. I had seen the light or, at least, accepted that Peter happened to die on the same day his story was published. I was comforted by the fact that Inspector Foggerty initially harboured the same doubts but resigned himself to the fact that no conspiracy, no foreign assassin or no government cover-up existed.

"Thankfully Egan got the story out before he died," said the inspector. "As for the list of names it is unimportant."

"You don't want the list?"

"Not unless you have it on you. You don't have it with you, do you?" he asked as he snuggled into his chair.

I shook my head.

"There's more than one way to skin a cat," he winked. "I don't need to be in possession of the list, Mr. James. The guilty only need to believe I'm in possession of the list and they will come forward."

"You believe that? Why would they?"

"Leniency. We have made it known that those who wish to give themselves up will receive certain privileges. Those who don't will be arrested and shall never see the outside world again."

"But there will be those who won't feel threatened especially set against the meagre sentence Carlisle received."

Foggerty grinned wolfishly.

"Listen, there isn't anyone attached to the Metropolitan Police Force who doesn't recognise that Carlisle's sentence was a farce—never to be repeated again. Undoubtedly, Egan's story stamped all over that trial and they probably had twenty-four hours before it went global. What could they do? They offered Carlisle a deal; admit to some of it for a minimum sentence. This achieved, they separated Carlisle from the story even though he had been named. The rest they could deal with later. Now—what with the media attention the trial received, and notwithstanding his puny sentence, the other 246 know they will never be offered the same deal. To date sixty-eight officers have come forward and confessed—uniformed, plain-clothes and even some high-ranking. And I've no doubt that the number of 247 will double come close of business; there's a lot of it going on. You see, that's the beauty of not having the list—I don't know who they are, and they don't know they haven't been named. Mind you, the film and photographs would be handy come the day of reckoning."

There was a lot about Inspector Foggerty that reminded me of Peter Egan; forthright, opinionated and passionate about his work. He was a modern-day witch-finder, loyal to his cause, tenacious in his research and meticulous to detail. I was despondent, uncertain as to what to do next; running Foggerty's accounts through my mind over and over again and finally reaching the conclusion that everything he said was correct. There was no conspiracy. Certainly some authority—either being the law, the government or both—had intervened and brought Carlisle's trial to an abrupt close, but Peter Egan's death was simply coincidental—a heart-attack waiting to happen and induced by stress. The inspector stared quietly at me from his seat, his elbows resting on the desk and his hands cupped either side of his face.

"Why so sad, Mr. James?" he said. "You're practically holding all the winning cards."

I snapped out of my reverie and looked directly at him.

"Look, the way I see it, you and the prosecution are on even ground," he continued, picking out another cigarette from his pack and lighting it. "They have to prove Henderson made the statement and you have to prove he didn't. I'm not talking out of turn when I say there is little evidence against him. Yes, there are a few sightings of him meandering around the Death Diamond, but it's not as though he shouldn't have been there—it was on his way home. We know the times he left work but not the times he arrived home . . ."

"Because his wife has gone into hiding?"

"Right! And the statements she gave prior to disappearing are vague to say the least; she couldn't be sure because she was always in bed when her husband came home. We know for certain that the dates of the killings correspond with Henderson's duties. He was working lates—sometimes moving cargo to the coast for the war effort; it's all inadmissible. So fight the good fight and get this wretched case out of your system."

"I would if I thought it was fair—that I could try the case without interference."

"From the government?"

I nodded.

"So you think they've got some foolproof plan to win—that they're putting on a show to appease the public?" he grinned. He shook his head and sighed heavily as he struggled out of his seat. "Come with me."

I followed him out of the office and we walked a short way down the corridor where he stopped, fishing around in his pockets and looking surreptitiously about him. "They'll have my balls for this," he said, pulling out a key and opening a door. "Inside before someone sees us."

We were in a large room—three times bigger than Foggerty's office, with a line of tables down its centre, abutted together lengthways and chairs either side. Likewise, there was a line of tables beneath the windows, running the complete length of the room on which were scattered files, loose documents, stacked file-boxes, typewriters and telephones. On the far wall were eight separate collages of photographs, each representing a murder victim; the body found in situ, the room or area in which they were discovered, a living photograph—the victims name, location and date of murder labelled above. A sweet odour hung in the air; musky and stale as if we had broken the seal on an ancient tomb. The tables still bore the rings of tea and coffee cups, several ashtrays were full to overflowing with cigarette butts, and wastepaper bins were filled with shredded documents. Foggerty moved directly to one of the three large windows and flung it open, drawing on his cigarette and blowing out a plume of smoke into the atmosphere. "This is where it all happened;" he said, "the 'Incident Room', the heart of the investigation, where all the information is collated and the suspects are flagged or eliminated. Dozens of police personnel were crammed in here, sifting through police reports, autopsy reports, files of well known criminals and those not so well known; dwindling down the possibilities in the hope of finding the person responsible.

I had wandered to the far end of the room. Before every collage was a folder, an abridged version of events leading up to and cause of death. My eyes roamed over the photographs of the first victim Angela Deacon; lying dead and naked in a bathtub, her wrists and throat slashed open. Another photograph depicted her younger, curled up on a settee with a kitten in her arms. There was a group picture with her family taken not long before she was murdered. She was discovered October 9th, though pathology reports calculate she died two days before. October 7th was a day much like any other except it was to be Angela Deacon's last. She lived in a small terraced house converted into two flats owned by a Mrs. Ashcroft to whom she worked as a shop-assistant in a tobacconist a short distance from Camberwell Green. By all accounts Angela had been blessed with attractive looks and a fine body and though she was frequently propositioned by clients she chose to remain alone. "Does Henderson smoke?" I asked. Inspector Foggerty was leaning against the wall next to the window, and taking a final draw on his cigarette and flicking it outside he stood upright and shook his head. "No. We took a mug-shot in of Henderson, and Mrs. Ashcroft said she had never seen him before. She wasn't over-worried when Angela never turned up for work, but the next day she went to the house and found her." My eyes lifted from the folder and back to the collage of photographs. "Could Angela have been a prostitute?" I enquired. I heard a chair scrape the floor behind me and the groan of the inspector as he settled into it. "A strange question; why ask?" he said.

"Good looking, twenty-four years old, no boyfriend and no desire to have one."

"Could be a lesbian."

When I turned he was seated, his legs outstretched and crossed, his arms folded and resting on his heavy stomach.

"I'm teasing you again," he laughed. "To our knowledge she wasn't a prostitute or a dyke. She was a homely girl, content with her own company."

"Why the bathtub?"

Foggerty shrugged. "Expert in human behaviour believe it's a sign of uncertainty, lack of confidence; he isn't that sure of himself yet, thus confining any mess to the tub. He made her undress in the bedroom and then took her to the bathroom before killing her. If he raped her he did it there and not the bedroom which was neat and tidy."

I placed down the folder and raised the next; Judy Moore, October 9th 1940.

"See, this is where all these so-called expert opinions fall to pieces," said Foggerty with a wag of his finger. "The first murder is almost clinical, but this one is the killer at his most ferocious."

Judy was a thirty-three year old secretary whose husband had been sent to war a few months earlier. She lived in Kennington close to the Oval in a house befitting her husband's status and, come to that, her own. She was found in the early hours by her son, lying face down on the settee in the lounge. "Her husband was a city broker," explained Foggerty, "and Judy took a job probably to occupy herself—she certainly didn't need the money. It's thought that somebody knocked on the door around about 10 o'clock that evening and she answered. As soon as the door was opened the killer restrained her; bruising around the jaw and cheek suggest a hand was clamped across her mouth, and further bruising to the side of the face indicates she received a blow to the side of the head—probably a punch, knocking her unconscious. Dressed in nothing but a bathrobe the killer raped her anally. Blood spatters on the wall beside the settee, the ceiling above and directly in front of her lead us to believe that the throat was cut during the rape; clumps of her hair found around the body confirm that he pulled her head back by the hair before administering the death wound to the throat. Judy was barely nine stone but the killer possessed considerable strength and was probably six feet tall?"

"Blood—wouldn't he be saturated in blood? Before Lizzie Borden killed her parents with an axe, she removed all her clothes and put them on after the deed was done. That's how she escaped detection."

"The arterial spray of the wound was in front—away from him; nothing that wouldn't escape the eye of any copper asking questions. Who the hell is Lizzie Borden?"

I looked to the photograph of the crime-scene where every vertical and horizontal surface appeared to be emblazoned in red.

"No seminal fluids were found in the victim even though it was blatantly clear she had been sodomized; he wore protection." Foggerty went on. "So then you have to take another look at the first victim. Was she raped? Probably. It's at this point we know we're dealing with a multiple-murderer—the cutthroat razor being the common denominator."

"Couldn't somebody have read about the first murder and copied it with the second?"

The corners of Foggerty's mouth turned down. "Plausible but unlikely. Multiple murderers can be a vain bunch; they look at it as a form of art, as if they are entitled to copyright their act; killers such as these seldom copy one another. But we did consider the possibility of a copycat killing until Marion Price."

At just nineteen years old Marion Price was found in a secluded alleyway at the Elephant and Castle on October 18th, tied to railings and raped in a standing position, and thereafter her face and abdomen had been repeatedly slashed. "I never saw it for myself but I've been told it was a terrible sight," the inspector said, grimly. "A young constable was first at the scene and he threw up all over the place—thus desecrating the crime scene. According to her friends Marion or Mari as she was known, was gullible, impressionable, you know, but she could also be a bit of a terror."

"So he tied her up," I interjected.

"Looks that way, tied her up with string that matched that found in a nearby dustbin. Nothing special about the knots, but they found woollen fibres under her nails and between her teeth."

"Why would a nineteen year old girl willingly go with a stranger—especially in the wake of two previous murders in the vicinity? Do you think she knew her killer?"

"You'd be surprised what a nineteen year old girl will do for money. Mari was unemployed and, in all probability unemployable; a bit of a tealeaf. She was living in a hostel, spending her days with dropouts and her nights doing the rounds of pubs in the area."

"A prostitute?"

Foggerty inclined his head with uncertainty. "A potential prostitute let's say, depending on how desperate she was at the time. She had the usual boyfriends but none amounted to much, and sooner or later she found herself back in the same predicament—bumming off friends, scrounging drinks and cigarettes. It's likely she was prepared to perform a sexual act for the right price—she was precocious enough."

"But the fibres under her nails and in her mouth would indicate a struggle. Why not just scream?"

The inspector rolled his eyes. "The fibres were probably accumulated during sex. The marks on her wrists showed little or no signs of any struggle taking place."

"She let him tie her up?"

"Yes, Mr. James, she let him tie her up," he sighed. "Aren't you going to question me about the blood—how when facing her did he evade the blood-flow when slitting her throat?"

The question hadn't crossed my mind but I nodded anyway.

"On completion he pulls his dick out the young lady and buttons himself up, moves to one side as if to undo her restraints and then cuts her throat as he moves behind her, and then for his own amusement he spends the next ten or twenty seconds slashing her face and body; no beating heart, no pumped arterial spray."

The inspector ignited another cigarette as I focused on the photo of the fourth victim Susan MacDonald. She was gentle and frail and smiled brightly for the camera, immaculately dressed and obviously well-educated. Her husband had left her well provided for; the pose of her left hand under her chin displayed an array of expensive jewellery. "Were any of the victims robbed?" I asked.

"Admiring the glassware, Mr. James?"

"They're not real?"

"Oh, God, yes they're real—buy a small country with those. No, nothing was taken from any of the victims or their homes. It may mean nothing but it could be a clue as to the killer's state of mind—his resentment for those who possess the wherewithal to get by in life. You see, Judy Moore had money and so did Susan MacDonald. Her husband died and was older than her, much older, and even her close friends said she married for money. She would do anything he said and tolerated years of his womanising but didn't care as long as he came home. She knew that once he popped his clogs everything would be hers; doesn't make her a bad person. Christ, they're all devious bastards. The point I'm making is that the first and third murders were calmly orchestrated but the second and fourth were performed in a frenzy. Not content to strip her naked and raping her, slashing her throat and wrists and disembowelling her, he smashed in her skull on the kitchen floor. There wasn't much left by the time the police got there, and if there was any evidence her dog had eaten it—along with her intestines. Tell me, Mr. James, do you plan to go through the whole list of victims?"

"Ah, no. I'm so sorry. I've taken up too much of your time and . . ." I spluttered, moving hurriedly towards the door.

Inspector Foggerty laughed wickedly and took another drag of his cigarette. "Get back to where you were," he said, ushering me away with a wave of his hand. "Ask your questions and be done with it."

"But you're obviously busy," I replied, stuck in No Man's Land, half way to the door.

"I'm nothing of the sort. Go back and continue with your examination."

"It isn't an examination."

"A rose by any other name," he smiled. "Besides, I like it; makes me feel like a policeman again instead of a persecutor. Pay me no mind and ask away."

I slowly returned to the flank wall bespattered with photographs.

"Can I ask you a personal question?" he asked.

"Please."

"Is having two Christian names a blessing or a curse? Only calling you Mr. James makes me feel like a Negro on a plantation consulting the big white boss-man."

"If it makes you feel more comfortable you can call me Michael."

"I'd prefer that. You know, Michael, they wanted me to shine my arse in a stuffy office in Scotland Yard but I insisted on coming here—where the crimes were committed—so I could see it for myself and reach my own conclusions."

"Even though you weren't brought in to investigate Henderson?"

"No good buying a novel, reading the first chapter and skipping to the last page; you have to read every single word. You have to know the full story. Before you return to the victims give me your views on George Henderson. You believe he's innocent?"

"Why else would I be here?"

"And you can prove that? 'Cos I'll be fucked if I can—excuse my French."

Foggerty screwed his half-smoked cigarette into the nearest ashtray and reclined in his chair, awaiting the one statement that would exonerate Henderson once and for all.

"Well," I began shakily, "Henderson is illiterate but had learned to write his name because . . ."

"An established fact. Go on."

"Carlisle fabricated Henderson's statement and that was corroborated by Sergeant Rawlings."

"Who was paid a vast amount of money for his story to fund his escape to foreign shores by none other than your friend the journalist. Peter Egan, God rest his soul was many things, but above all else he was an exceptionally talented writer; every paper in Fleet Street used him. Do you know how many pen-names he had? Sixteen, Michael; Graham Sawyer, Gerald Gibbons, Paul Owen, Stephen Grant, Andrew Catchmold, George Ferris, even Major Arthur Penshaw. And the reason for that was the stigma attached to Peter Egan and his name. He was an agitator, an anarchist who condemned the establishment every chance he got."

I remembered then the night Peter died. I saw hundreds of file-boxes in his store room, most with lettering on the spines—G.S.—G.G.—P.O—S.G, initials of Peter Egan's aliases. I felt my heart sink.

"It doesn't deviate from the fact that Carlisle cribbed the stories from the newspapers," I proffered meekly.

Foggerty shook his head and pulled himself out of his chair, and walking to the tables beneath the windows opened a file-box and took out a small, black notepad and tossed it towards me. "Have a look at that," he said as he resumed his seat.

The small book skidded down the centre table and stopped close to the end. It was the property of a Constable William Boardman who was the first officer at the house of Judy Moore. "Read it out loud, will you, Michael," said Foggerty. I cleared my throat nervously. *'On my arrival I was met by Mr. Robert Chandler who resides at number 37 next door who informed me that the boy who discovered the body was being cared for by his wife at that address. I asked Mr. Chandler if he had touched anything and he assured me he had not. After checking all the doors and windows in the house I concluded that there had been no forced entry and therefore concluded that the assailant was allowed entry or forced his way in once the door was opened. I assume the perpetrator of the crime entered the street from Kennington Road and made his escape by the same route . . .'*

"That'll do, Michael," said Foggerty.

He was staring back at me, his hands on his head and fingers laced together.

"Tell me you haven't hinged Henderson's defence on plagiarism. Tell me you have something more," he said.

I looked back blandly and the inspector shook his head again, dragging his hands down his face and sighing. He was apprehensive to speak again, or at least appeared as if he was.

"Michael, every officer, no matter what their rank, carries one of those notebooks in which they are expected to write down every single detail at the crime scene—no matter how trivial; it cannot be left to memory. Egan wasn't just buying information from Sergeant Stephen Rawlings; he needed proof, something to substantiate his claim should Carlisle decide to sue, and in return he would protect Rawlings by never mentioning his name on paper. For a fee Rawlings gave Egan Carlisle's notebook which he stole—a similar notebook to the one you are holding—which is to be handed in to the senior investigating officer for the purpose of collation. There's no easy way to say this so I'll just say it. Carlisle never cribbed from the articles written by Egan. Egan cribbed from Carlisle, using the notebook stolen by Rawlings. When Henderson gave himself up Carlisle wrote the statement down as best as he could remember it—the way he had written it in his notebook." He appraised me with a sympathetic smile. "Sorry, Michael," he said.

"It doesn't change the fact that they were Carlisle's words and not Henderson's," I responded defensively.

Foggerty's shoulders dropped.

"You're looking at suppositions, Michael," he sighed wearily. "When George Henderson gave his statement he didn't know what day it was. The man's an imbecile; no recall for detail—Carlisle just filled in the gaps. Like every policeman at a crime-scene Carlisle took down notes, surmising how the perpetrator gained entry, how he made his getaway, where he hid prior to an attack, his purpose for the crime which Egan repeated in his articles; cribbed from Carlisle's stolen notebook."

"He's been found guilty of perjury!"

"So he might have, but he denied any wrongdoing when it came to Henderson."

"He could do little else."

"Why? He'd already been offered a deal. Why not admit to it? Considering everything he was accused of Henderson's case was of little significance, and he vehemently refuted the accusation at the trial." Inspector Foggerty paused. "Listen, Carlisle was about as corrupt as they come, but no matter what his exploits there isn't one person he put in prison that shouldn't have been there. There is nothing more demeaning than watching a known felon walk free—but it happens; we live with it and hope we'll be luckier next time. No matter how guilty we know them to be we must never be tempted to secure a conviction by fabricating evidence—they're the rules. Sure, Carlisle may have embellished Henderson's statement a little but as for fabrication—no. He was on the case from the beginning. Don't you think he could have conveniently found a cutthroat razor when he searched Henderson's house, or a balaclava or some article of clothing belonging to one of the victims? He had every opportunity. When you take that into consideration you are left with one irrefutable fact—George Henderson made that statement."

Running my eyes over the collages I felt lost, completely out of my depth. Paper law and criminal law are two different animals and I stupidly believed the two were the same. The glimmer of hope was the evidence the police had accumulated against Henderson which by their own admission was very little. By degrees Foggerty had disassembled my confidence but I refused to believe my client was guilty of the shocking crimes.

"In the final analysis, Michael, you were used," said Foggerty as he rose out of his chair and slowly ambled towards me. "Egan knew he had a big story on the horizon. Influencing you kept Carlisle in the headlines till he dropped the bombshell."

"Nevertheless," I snapped, dismissing the obvious. "Henderson willingly went to the police station. He was stopped three times during the murders and every time gave his real name and address. Why would he do that?"

"Arrogance," said the inspector as he closed on me. "Some are so sure of themselves they think they'll never be caught. Some leave messages or taunt the police with phone calls and letters . . ."

I thought of my father; the invention of the name Jack the Ripper, the cryptic message he left in Goulston Street, cutting Catharine Eddowes nose off to spite her face.

" . . . but I think he wanted to be caught—he didn't want any more to die. He said so himself," Foggerty added.

"According to Carlisle," I returned, sharply.

The inspector was in front of me and shrugged. "The possibility still exists that Carlisle prefabricated the statement but I wouldn't stake my life on it."

"Sergeant Rawlings saw it with his own eyes."

"Did he now!" shrilled Foggerty with feigned surprise. "That's brilliant! That's just fucking fine and dandy. Then find the miserable bastard and put him on the stand, but I'll guarantee you one thing, Michael; he'll never admit to it because it never happened. Egan spun you a story because he wanted you to defend Henderson; he tied it up with a pretty bow and you bought it."

"But . . ." I began to protest.

Foggerty slapped both hands on my shoulders.

"Listen to me, Michael," he said. "Never at any time was Henderson a suspect, and never at any time during the investigation did Carlisle apply for a warrant to arrest him. Sure he was being looked at but so were a hundred others. He was never a suspect till he walked into Camberwell Police Station and confessed. And let us suppose that Carlisle had a prefabricated statement ready prior to Henderson giving himself up. How could he have known? Carlisle had never met Henderson in his life so how could he have known he was illiterate?"

I reluctantly nodded as the realisation of Egan's ruse began to sink in. Foggerty removed his hands and took a step back. "Earlier I called Henderson an imbecile and that's exactly what he wants us to think he is—a slow-minded idiot," he said. "In reality he's nothing of the sort; cunning as a fox that one. Let me take you back to 1915, to Northern France. Henderson's unit—The Stewart Road Pals—as they called themselves, were on recognisance a few miles outside Amiens when they came under heavy bombardment from German Artillery. The twenty-three strong Company were reduced to just two—George Henderson and Brian

Moffet; both ended up in a field hospital and both were critical. Moffet had suffered severe shrapnel wounds, severing two fingers on his left hand and loss of his left eye. Henderson's injuries again were the result of shrapnel but confined to his back and head. Apparently he's still carrying a lump of artillery shell around in his head today. We traced Moffet to a primary school in Hammersmith where he's employed as a caretaker. He told a story of when they were recuperating. Apparently there were two enterprising young nurses at the field hospital who had honed their bedside manner to a fine art. At night when the lights were dimmed they would offer certain services that you won't find in your everyday hospital, and night after night Henderson would watch these girls giving our brave boys sexual relief for a small price; a trinket, a watch, a silver cigarette case. According to Moffet Henderson was in no fit state to indulge, if of course he wanted to, but on his release twelve weeks later one of the nurses was found dead; her throat cut from ear to ear. All of which meant nothing at the time and probably doesn't mean a whole lot more now—makes you think though."

"You think he was responsible for killing the nurse?"

Foggerty shrugged his shoulders as his eyes scanned the photographs. "Who knows? There were a lot of soldiers coming and going—some so brain damaged they didn't even know if they were still alive. Who knows what lengths a young man will go to once he's had the soft hand of a nurse rummaging around in his pyjamas?"

I agreed with a faint nod, pulled out the nearest chair and sat down. "Henderson's a Catholic, right?" I spurted, more out of desperation than reason.

There was a lengthy silent pause before the inspector began to laugh.

"Michael, Michael, Michael," he crowed as he yanked out the chair opposite and sat down. "Tell me you don't intend to bring religion into this. I'm sure the Vatican would be seriously pissed off with a member of their flock wearing a rubber to avoid impregnating one of the many Catholic female species around these parts, but when it's worn for the purpose of murder it kind of flies in the face of common decency."

The inspector allowed me a moment to wallow in my self-pity. Utterly defeated I found myself staring at the floor for no other purpose but to avoid eye-contact; unable to stare him in the face without being overwhelmed by total humiliation.

"This room was locked up a long time ago," he said, reclining back in his chair. "And do you want to know why it was locked up?"

I had wondered why the room looked like Miss Haversham's parlour and I nodded but never averted my gaze from the grubby floor.

"Because the investigation is over—simple; there's nothing left to investigate. Henderson worked at night but targeted his victims by day; watching their movements, following them home, surveying the surrounding streets and alleyways to plan his escape. He may have dabbled with the prossies on a regular basis but I think if he did it was limited to the ones he killed—the ones he knew and who knew him. The man's a fucking nutcase, Michael; excuse my French, but facts are facts; he belongs over there in Bedlam," he added, thumbing in the direction behind him.

Thoughts ricochet around in my head blindly arguing against Foggerty's convincing statements.

"Henderson underwent psychological and mental evaluations and neither hinted at insanity," I said.

The inspector took a pack of cigarettes from the top pocket of his shirt, and taking out another placed it between his lips and ignited it. "Does anything anger you, Michael?" he asked.

The question seemed inappropriate given the topic of conversation but I considered it with an air of reservation.

"Well?" he coaxed, rising from his chair and sitting on the edge of the table.

"Bureaucrats, nagging wives . . ."

"No, Michael," he interjected with a shake of his head. "Excuse my French but what really fucks you off? What infuriates you? What enrages you to the point that you want to take out your anger on the world? Back home if I'm served a Jameson's instead of a Red Label I swear to God I'd rip out the landlord's throat, kill all his children and subject the landlady to all manner of sexual deviancy. You met Henderson, what did you think of him? I bet he impressed the shit out of you."

"I wouldn't go that far," I replied, "but I thought he was stable enough; your everyday, hard working man. I didn't consider him to be a threat."

"And why should you? Depending on how you interpret madness, what we, the normal consider to be un-normal, Henderson on the face of it appears to be the salt of the earth—the glue that holds the fabric of society together. In reality he's cursed with his own demons, his own agenda on venting his anger on the rest of the world. Like the friends he left on the battlefields in Northern France, Henderson was gullible, believing that war was a big adventure and he would return a hero. There were no street parties when he returned; no flags or banners, no statues or plaques to commemorate his homecoming. His world was different now, cold, empty and devoid of friends. Like millions of others in the same predicament he had to forge a new life, and this he did by degrees, marrying in his late thirties and banging out a herd of kids in quick succession. What he inherited from the war were bouts of severe depression. Didn't you fight his corner back in thirty-three?"

I nodded thoughtfully. "The Great Eastern Railway wanted to sack him due to his habitual absence at work; it was all settled amicably—I'd all but forgotten about the case," I said.

"That was one incident, Michael, and as the years rolled by so the bouts of depression grew lengthier and more frequent. According to his wife he would lock himself away in his bedroom for weeks at a time."

"Depression is not a form of madness, inspector, and to my knowledge Henderson never harmed his family."

Foggerty smiled back. "Years ago I knew a man—had known him all my life. He was quiet, always polite, always had time for a chat, and I would see him and his wife out at the shops or digging the garden or walking to the nearby pub; always holding hands as if they were frightened to let go of one another—I saw them every day. One day his wife passed away and we didn't see the old man for a while; he hid away in his little house behind closed curtains. After that we just forgot about him. It must have been about a year later when they found two little girls, sisters actually, murdered in woodland outside Edinburgh. I was a young constable then, you know, wet behind the ears, aspirations of changing the world. Anyway, we found what was left of the girls amongst the ashes of a large fire; it was never clearly ascertained how they died—one could only surmise what they went through. So me and fifty other coppers began a search of the area. I was walking through the woods and for some reason I suddenly stopped; I felt there was somebody there, someone looking at me, and I looked up and there he was—the old man, hanging quite still at the end of a rope from the limb of a tree. I called my superior over. He took one look at him and said, 'There's your killer, Constable Foggerty.' I refused to believe the two incidents were linked. We found the old man at least half a mile away from the crime-scene so it was plausible that one day he just decided to do away with himself. It was estimated that he'd been hanging there for about three days; the time of death regarding the girls was never properly established because the fire had consumed most of their bodies. So, the theory was that after murdering the girls the old man took his life."

"When in reality he was innocent?" I anticipated.

Foggerty shook his head grimly. "Guilty as hell; found his footprints all round the fire, a pair of the young girls knickers in his coat pocket, blood splashes all over his clothes. If ever a man was guilty of a crime it was him. My point is—I just couldn't believe it, not him, not this kind old man who waved to me everyday and loved his wife; a more decent man you'd never meet. Like Henderson, the old man and probably everyone walking this planet had a rage lying dormant within him—just waiting for something to trigger it off. The passing of his wife was the old man's."

"And Henderson; what triggered his rage?"

Foggerty stubbed out his cigarette and walked to the windows, surveying the bustling streets below.

"We all have our annoyances, Michael; something that really aggravates us, and more often than not it's the silliest things—the way your wife constantly stirs her tea, the way someone eats, or the way a stranger stares at you; such things can tip us over the edge. Most deal with it as humanely as their character will allow; however some are not as understanding. We seek revenge on those who have wronged us, on the society who have forsaken us, on the establishment who failed to recognise our loyalty—we demand recognition in whatever form it takes. So what was it that awakened Henderson's demons? It's all around you, Michael; over there in Bedlam, in the streets and undergrounds . . ." He turned and smiled at me. "Even you carry the scars."

"Are you saying the war is responsible for Henderson savagely murdering eight women?"

"It isn't written in stone," he shrugged, "but it makes sense to me. What devastated his life in the first war he avenged in the second. You know, Michael, when they returned to England, Brian Moffet and George Henderson never associated themselves with one another again; that's strange, don't you think?"

He was still surveying the scene through the window but turned his head in my direction to gauge my response.

"They were the only two surviving members of The Stewart Road Pals and Moffet disassociated himself from Henderson entirely which makes the tale of the nurse that more plausible," he continued.

"Because he believed Henderson killed the nurse?"

"Exactly," said Foggerty, stabbing a finger in my direction.

"Did he say as much?"

The inspector shook his head. "Not really; not in so many words. No matter what his beliefs there existed a bond between them; you know, kids who grew up together and witnessed their friends blown to pieces. He never gave a reason, which in itself is reason enough."

I gave the subject little consideration; it all seemed immaterial now. I felt empty inside, and as the silence extended I rose from the table.

"Thank you for your time, inspector," I said.

"What? You're going?"

"I think we've just about covered everything, don't you?"

"Aye, perhaps," he agreed, "but what about you?"

I walked to him and shook his hand.

"Me? I'll be fine. I need to make a decision," I replied.

"Maybe then, I hope, you can chase your own demons back into the shadows."

"I don't have any demons," I smiled.

I turned away from him and walked towards the door.

"No?" he said.

I slowed to a stop and turned around. The inspector ignited another cigarette and took a moment to study the changing cloud of smoke above him.

"You know, Michael, I hate this miserable, fucking war—excuse my French, but you have to give those German's credit, they really know how to make a bomb. Did you know that in one night they dropped ten thousand tons of high explosive and incendiaries on this city, and isn't it just my luck to be sent to the very place they're bombing the shit out of." His eyes followed the evaporating cloud of smoke as it moved towards the window. "Now to me a bomb is a bomb; they hit the ground and go bang. But to the German's and the destructive bastards who make them they have a catalogue of different purposes. Some go bang—some don't; like the one buried in the grounds of the departmental-store above your office. According to the MOD it was one of many dropped during the raid on London September 29th, last year. More were found in Coventry, Manchester, and no less than a dozen in Bristol after the December attacks. What makes this particular bomb unique is that it doesn't go bang—or at least not straight away. They're timed; some to go off in a week, some a month, some as much as a year; a kind of belated gift—you know, with love from Adolf."

"You knew about my office?" I gasped.

He looked at me and drew on his cigarette.

"Let's say I've had my eye on you since Peter Egan's funeral. I made it my business to find out."

"But why? What's so interesting about me?"

"You were linked to Egan, and as I've explained there were certain police personnel at his funeral posing as friends and associates, some of which may have been amongst the 247 corrupt officers. I needed to know they weren't out to get you for what you possessed, or what they thought you might possess."

"So you had me followed!"

"Had to, Michael; it was the only way to be sure. You say you don't have the list and I believe you. It was probably a myth; something Egan made up to keep us on our toes."

As Foggerty explained, all pieces of the puzzle slipped effortlessly into place but the picture was not perfect yet.

"If there was no conspiracy, who broke into Fallow's publishing House?" I asked.

He took a final draw on his cigarette and dropped it to the floor.

"Ah, yes, Earnest Fallow," he chuckled. "Broken into, you say; news to me."

"I was there the day after Peter died—the place was in pieces."

"Was it now? Strange, because the police were also there the next day and there was no mention of any break in. He already knew Peter was dead but never said who told him; fucking journalists never reveal a source—excuse my French."

"Inspector, I'm not mistaken; somebody broke in," I pursued.

He dropped his head slightly and folded his arms, taking on a pensive refrain.

"So . . ." he said, slowly. "Why were you there, Michael? Why the urgency to visit a weasel like Earnest Fallow?"

I had, as they say, painted myself into a corner. To admit to the purpose of my visit was to admit that I knew Peter Egan was dead before anyone else which, by any definition, could only mean I witnessed it with my own eyes. I shrugged like a schoolboy who had run out of excuses for failing to complete his homework.

"Michael," began Foggerty patiently, "Peter Egan died of natural causes. Nobody is going to accuse you of his murder. So why did you visit Fallow?"

I pulled the nearest chair under me and sat down.

"Peter and I were supposed to meet the day the story broke," I began. "He called me to say he would come to my office that evening; he sounded worried . . ."

"And who can wonder at it? He had just accused the Metropolitan Police Force and the government of bribery and corruption," he interrupted.

"Anyway, he never showed and I tried to call him . . ."

"No answer."

" . . . and to cut a long story short I went to his house and found him dead. I went to see Earnest Fallow to tell him. So that's how he knew."

The inspector fisted his eyes and emitted an exhaustive sigh.

"Which begs the question: why didn't you inform the police?" He paused, and then looking back at me grinned broadly. "You were the anonymous phone-call to the police!"

I nodded shamefully.

He studied me for a moment and the grin disappeared without a trace.

"Your reticence regarding your friend's death would suggest you have something to hide, Michael; on top of which is the crime of breaking and entering, contaminating a probable crime-scene—shall I go on?"

I shook my head slowly.

"Still, no harm done," he said. "Are you going to tell me why you chose to remain anonymous?"

"Are you blackmailing me, inspector?" I asked.

"Not in the slightest," he returned. "Personally I couldn't give a fuck about Egan, excuse my French—it's all in the past; case closed. I am, however, intrigued to know why you chose to adopt this cloak-and-dagger charade at the risk of being imprisoned for perverting the course of justice."

I unbuckled the straps on my briefcase and took out the two large envelopes.

"It's all there—the names, film, photographs," I said.

Foggerty's eyes ignited brighter than the end of one of his fowl, stinking cigarettes and a victorious smile expanded beneath his walrus moustache.

"So, they're not a myth," he crowed.

"No," I replied with a shake of my head. "I know a myth when I see one. They're the reason I went to see Fallow."

Foggerty ripped open one of the envelopes and peered into it like a child staring into a sweetie bag.

"You called Fallow a weasel—why?" I asked.

"I did what?" he replied, preoccupied with the contents of the envelope.

"Inspector!"

Reluctantly he placed down the envelopes and pushed them to one side, straightening his delighted expression and composing himself.

"All journalists are weasels—figure of speech, but there's nothing more elusive than the obvious," he said almost whimsically. "Earnest Fallow had probably waited his whole life for a story like this and Egan, always the tenacious newshound gave it to him. This was the yardstick—the exclusive that would influence the price Fleet Street were willing to pay. If his offices were ransacked we have to ask 'Who' and 'Why'." He glanced down at the envelopes. "The 'Why' is now unmistakably obvious. The 'Who' however is a different matter. Obviously they were after the contents of these envelopes, and Fallow as the publisher would be the natural candidate to be safeguarding them. I can't recall ever reading any reports of a break-in, though."

"So it could have been any of the 247?"

Foggerty nodded and looked back to the envelopes. "Now I have the names I can ask them."

"You said the police went to his offices the same day but never saw anything."

"I didn't say they never saw anything, Michael," he stressed. "I said they never reported it—which can only mean they didn't want it going on record."

"Because they were responsible?"

He shrugged his shoulders. "Or they were protecting those who were. 'The pen is mightier than the sword', and never a truer word was spoken. Fallow knows the power of the press and what can be achieved by the written word; an innocent man can be destroyed with one small condemning article. Write the prime minister was caught having sex with his pet poodle and the world will believe it—because it's written. Like Egan, Fallow thrives on unsubstantiated gossip—they're two of a kind, sensationalists. And playing God is all very well until you start fucking about with the government—as he did several years ago—excuse my French."

"The Vassarri Memoirs," I interjected.

"You know about them?"

I shook my head faintly. "Not much; a government assassin."

Foggerty wriggled within the tight confines of his chair until he found a position less restricting.

"Michael, what I know about journalism you could write on the back of a postage stamp in big letters. What I do know is that something that has 'Government Secret' written all over it should remain as that—a secret. We all know that corruption is rife; we all know the royals are a bunch of sexually frustrated nutters; we know that Britain's wealth was founded on every sordid deal ever invented, but we don't want the rest of the world to know—it's *our* secret."

"So Vassarri was a real person; not the invention of Fallow's wild imagination?"

"He must be real," Foggerty nodded. "When Fallow published the Vassarri Memoirs all hell broke loose. The police swept through every major bookshop in the British Isles and seized all the copies, though some are still circulating. Even Fallow's' printing presses were dismantled, boxed up and carted away; the government were seriously pissed off about it. But Fallow survived it and was back in business within a year. Now he has a new axe to grind in Egan's story; like I said: he's reckless."

I was apprehensive to impart my next barrage of questions and scenarios but continued nonetheless with feigned confidence.

"Isn't it a possibility that Fallow played some part in Peter Egan's death? He had the motive," I said.

The inspector gazed upon me with bewilderment.

"You're a stubborn bastard, I'll give you that," he returned. "Haven't I gone to great pains to convince you he died of natural causes? Have you not heard a word I've said? I like you, Michael, but there's only so much pain a man can take. You're wearing me down . . ."

"Just listen to what I have to say—that's all I'm asking," I interrupted.

With a heavy sigh, and probably a heavier heart, the inspector composed himself in his tightening chair and nodded his head. "Go on."

"I haven't been entirely honest with you," I began. "I do know about Vassarri; I've read his book, have you?"

Inspector Foggerty shook his head.

"Vassarri's father was a scientist who worked for the Nazis back in the first war. Through botany he discovered that certain plant toxins, when injected into the bloodstream of a human, can induce death yet remain completely undetectable; a form of assassination—what he refers to as a 'subtle kill'. So I was thinking . . ."

"That Fallow murdered Egan . . ." he anticipated. "Why would he, Michael? Furthermore, how could he? Does this book come with a list of recipes in the back! Tell me that killing another human being isn't as easy as making a cake. It takes expertise and knowhow; otherwise we'd all be at it. My wife has a sweet tooth and I'd give my right testicle for a book like that."

"Listen! It's a fact that Fallow and Vassarri are friends, and have been for many years. How difficult could it be for Vassarri to send the toxin through the post and for Fallow to inject it into Peter—thus inducing what appeared to be a heart attack. With Peter dead, Fallow would then own the exclusive rights to the story of the 247 corrupt officers—making him a very wealthy man."

Something in my narrative changed the inspector, for instead of mocking my absurd notion, he sat pensive with a vacant stare.

"Okay, I'm with you so far," he muttered, "but you're forgetting one thing: Peter Egan and Earnest Fallow were also friends." He pondered for a moment and added, "Not that that means fuck all—not to a despicable gutter-rat like Fallow . . ."

"You said you liked his magazine!"

"The magazine, yes—Fallow, no. This sounds all very far-fetched to me, Michael, but I can understand your line of thinking. But why are you so adamant that Peter Egan didn't just drop down dead?"

"Too much of a coincidence—I suppose," I shrugged.

He looked to the envelopes and then back to me, and as if he owed me a favour he sighed.

"I'll tell you what I'll do. I'll give this to Rupert; a fine detective and somewhat at a loose end at present. If there's something there he'll find it."

The inspector wriggled out of his chair and picked up the envelopes.

"You've made my job a lot easier, Michael," he said, shaking my hand. "I'll look into this and keep you informed."

His promise lacked sincerity and I smiled faintly.

"Cross my heart and hope to die," he said, slapping his hand on his chest. "Give me your card. When I have some answers, you'll have them. You have my word."

I took out a business card from my jacket pocket and handed it to him. Turning to leave he said, "Thank you, Michael."

I stopped stock-still, staring straight ahead. I can't recall ever experiencing the feeling of déjà vu before but the feeling that was running through me now was clammy and uncomfortable. They say that déjà vu is the result of a brain lapse; an event recorded in the mind and then rerecorded in a split second that is recalled as a long-forgotten memory; the time between experience and recall is milliseconds.

"Something wrong, Michael?" asked Foggerty.

I shook my head. "No. No, nothing. Goodbye, inspector."

Chapter Four

The Maiden's Whisper

-23-

It is a common misconception, least of all by Londoners themselves, that the Isle of Dogs is an island. It is, in fact, a peninsula, a large horseshoe shaped slab of land jutting out between Rotherhithe and Woolwich that geographically has no God given right being there. Its protrusion creates a severe snake in the river, a natural habitat for jetties, wharfs and warehouses hugging its perimeter, as well as the towns of Deptford and Greenwich on the south side. It is an extremely fragile island, of which one third of its mass is water, in the shape of horizontal, rectangle docks and connecting vertical waterways, yet it is heavily populated, mostly by the people who work there. The streets are Dickensian, a remnant of the Victorian age. Grimy tenement blocks skirt West Ferry road that circumnavigates the island, and squat, crammed terraces clutter up the interior streets. The inhabitants are large families where few have the luxury of hot running water and only half have inside lavatories. Cargo ships from all over the world are piloted into the island through a network of canals and locks, and because the ships have to be unloaded manually, the shipping companies employ thousands of people, not only from the island but also from neighbouring Stepney, Bow, Mile End, Limehouse and Whitechapel.

It is a massive industry in which the West India Docks serve the Imports and Exports as well as Millwall inner and outer docks. Unfortunately the distinctive shape of the island is a landmark for German bombers who dropped thousands of tons of high explosives on an area populated by 50,000 per square mile during the Blitz. Unlike most London areas, whose population would seek refuge in the underground during the raids, the Isle of Dogs was left helpless because there were no underground stations, the nearest being Aldgate, and they had to make do with Anderson Shelters, of which there weren't enough because most houses did not possess a garden in which to construct them. Fortunately most dwelling had cellars where families sat out the bombardments.

The docks, but specifically the Isle of Dogs, was relentlessly targeted by Germany's air force during the bombings in September to December 1940, and the expanse of the Thames from Bermondsey to Woolwich was a raging inferno from which no building or human should have survived. But survive they did, and notwithstanding the devastation and countless deaths and casualties, life resumed as best it could. The docks themselves were hit, as were the ships anchored within them, and every morning the cranes would set to work dredging the waters for debris to clear the way for new foreign vessels to enter. The damaged buildings were simply pushed over and the areas excavated to ensure traffic could flow on and off the island. The roads were patched up almost immediately, and where debris blocked the thoroughfares, it was either cleared by hand or by tractors. There existed doggedness within the islanders, a pride no bomb could break, that nothing short of sinking the whole peninsula would prevent them from doing their work—which was to keep the docks working. The people who lived and worked on this island were not made of stronger stuff, yet they proved they were time and time again.

I drove back to the island, taking the same route as I had with Peter Egan when first I was acquainted with Harry Griffin, crossing the iron bridge that had remained remarkably in tact despite the Luftwaffe's attempt at destroying it entirely. The object of my visit was to confront Harry and ask his advice now that I had handed the list of names and the photographs to Inspector Foggerty, and to explain my dilemma concerning Peter's distrust in his publisher and editor Earnest Fallow. It felt like a lifetime ago since I was last here, appraising the devastation in absolute horror and wondering why the occupants of the island had not fled to the countryside. Defiant they remained, and I could see the lines of towering cranes swinging back and forth around the docks and hear the foghorns of the merchant ships as they shuffled into position at Blackwall Reach, filtering into the basin—the waiting area for the West India Docks. Remembering as best I could the roads Peter had taken, I found Harry's pub at the centre of the island, amid a cluster of sooty looking houses with black slated roofs, the area of which had been dramatically scarred by Hitler's agenda, where entire streets had been levelled to the ground. One could only stand in awe and remember the endless nights when this whole island appeared to be one mass of fire, and smile with great pride at the tenacity of the occupants who continued regardless.

It was early when I arrived, around midday, and the pub was empty save for two old gentlemen sitting in the corner playing dominoes and a young man dressed in full navel uniform whispering sweet nothings into his pretty companion's ear in the opposite corner. A barmaid, looking uncannily like Mae West approached with a welcoming smile and asked me what she could do for me, to which I replied, "I've come to see Harry Griffin." She observed me patiently for a moment and then shrugged her shoulders. "Is he any of those?" she asked, first nodding to the old gentlemen and then to the canoodling couple. I shook my head and smiled; obviously she was new. "He owns this pub," I explained, handing her one of my business cards. She glanced at it, and the courteous smile with which she welcomed me melted away. "You want to see the governor?" she asked. I nodded, and with an impatient sigh she walked off. Within a minute or so I was confronted by a large, stocky man in his early thirties who informed me that he was in fact the owner, and acknowledging my obvious confusion he suggested I must be in the wrong pub. I found myself staring at the same high leather chair Harry had sat on when he explained away his early days.

"You are the owner and not the manager?" I questioned.

"It's my name over the door," he said. "Look, are you sure it was this pub where you met Harry . . . ?"

"Griffin. Harry Griffin. And, yes, I'm absolutely sure."

He shook his head pensively and craned his head in the direction of the Mae West look-alike standing by the sink.

"Shirley, ever heard of a Harry Griffin?" he asked.

She thought for a moment and the corners of her ruby red lips turned downward.

"There was a George Griffin who used to come in here; lived in Billson Street, but I think he got bombed out last year; not seen him since; shame."

"Sorry," said the owner, swinging his head back to me. "Now then, if I can't interest you in a drink, I have work to do."

I stood motionless, numbed by the fact that this wasn't Harry's pub and nobody had ever heard of him. Yet I was certain, beyond certain that this was where Peter and I had talked with him and where he gave me the envelopes containing the names of the corrupt officers and incriminating photographs and films. I even started looking at the pictures on the wall to reassure myself that I had been here before. But as much as the familiar surroundings and the pictures confirmed my previous visit, I couldn't help but feel I was mistaken. "I hope you find your friend," said the owner as he walked away. Mae West expressed a sympathetic smile as I left, and I stood out on the pavement, first staring at the pub, and then looking down the adjacent street in the mere hope of seeing a similar building; there was nothing to see but rows of burnt out and crumbling buildings.

I had no one with whom I could confide unless, of course I found a Medium who could trace Peter Egan through the spiritual world. I can hardly remember the journey back because my addled brain was attempting to negotiate its way through the events of the day I met Harry Griffin and, indeed seriously began to question my sense of recall. I had no reason to doubt that he was the owner of the pub because he clearly stated he was—amongst many others along the river, but it could just as easily have been a scam, of which I had yet to fathom. That day when Peter and I arrived it was early and not yet opens to the public, and the woman who opened the door, who I assumed was a cleaning lady, could have been a paid accomplice. In hindsight, the pub had recently undergone redecoration, and maybe Harry, or whoever he was, assumed the position of ownership in the real owner's absence, and that being the case, was Peter Egan part of the rouse? Was I being used, and if so why?

Within the hour I was zigzagging up and down the backstreets of Southwark, with the napkin on which Rachel had written her address lying on the passenger seat, and eventually pulled into a long straight road of terraced houses that once were homes for the affluent. They were large three-storey constructions with large windows, originally built for the Huguenots whose speciality was in silk weaving, where looms would be set up in south-facing rooms to allow in as much light as possible so any imperfections in the fabric could easily be detected. The downfall of the Huguenots came with the industrial revolution, when their looms were considered antiquated and steam power and factories came into play. Their heritage was sold off, and private landlords had the big houses converted into flats to reap the ultimate in rents. Notwithstanding the large windows decorated with ornate masonry, several steps rose from pavement level to the front door between sturdy iron railings, and as was the protocol back in the seventeenth century, the servants' quarters were always beneath the house, accessible by a side opening in the railings and down a narrow, stone staircase. It was such a place that Rachel now lived.

I hesitated on the pavement for a moment, wondering what influenced me to come here and the possibility that I may not find her alone. There was always the chance that she wouldn't be there at all. Either way I descended down the curved stairs to her front door and knocked gently. I could see someone approaching through the obscured glass in the door and forced a grin. When the door opened Rachel's eyes widened and her smile seemed to brighten the dull interior of the overhanging stairs of which I was standing. "God, Michael, you've actually come to see me," she shrilled as she took me by the arm and pulled me towards her. She planted a big kiss on my cheek, closed the front door and led my by the hand down a narrow hallway. "I was just thinking about you. How is everything? You were acting so strange at Brighton, and I was going to come to the coffeeshop to see if things had improved. Have they?" Two or three doors led off the hallway, and after passing a small kitchen we were standing in a vast lounge, homely decorated with a mismatch of furniture and a pair of French-doors at its end, framing a small garden encased by three high walls, on which one leaned an Anderson Shelter awaiting construction.

"Well, what do you think?" she asked proudly. I nodded approvingly and walked to the expanse of windows. "First, I think you should get that built," I said, nodding towards the sections of corrugated steel pockmarked with rust. She came up behind me and threaded her arm through mine and rested her head on my shoulder. "The bombers won't come back, Michael. Our boys gave them a damn good whipping. We scared them off." True, the RAF had done a wonderful job during the Battle of Britain, but I wasn't convinced it was enough to stop the Germans from trying again. "Sit down and I'll make you some tea," said Rachel as she broke away.

I took a seat by the fireplace, screened with a flowery embroidery set in a dark wood frame to break the blandness of the grey, tiled surrounds and hearth, and on the mantelpiece were two small photographs set in gilded frames of Rachel and her husband in happier times, either side of an old black clock that ticked a little too loudly for my liking. David was an exceedingly handsome man who possessed the body of an athlete and a beguiling smile; it was easy to see why Rachel fell for him. She had made the best of what little she had to decorate the apartment, adorning the stained or threadbare soft furnishings with brightly coloured cushions and pretty head and arm covers, and the cheap, reproductions of various shapes and sizes that hung on every wall were designed to inject colour into the otherwise drab surroundings. Yet with the exception of the overpowering smell of new paint, it was a cosy dwelling, fit for a hero come David's return. When Rachel returned from the kitchen, she set a tray down on a coffee table and sat opposite me, still brandishing an elated grin.

"So, Michael, what brings you to see me?" she asked. "Has Mr. Mansall given you the contract for this flat, because if he has I have the money in a safe place?"

I smiled and lied. "No contract as yet, Rachel. Bernie can be a bit slow."

"Oh, well never mind," she said as she started to pour the tea into the cups. "And how have you been? Better I hope since the last time I saw you. Did you see the journalist's wife?"

I shook my head. "I reconsidered."

She set a cup in front of me. "Let me know if it's too strong. So why did you reconsider? Would you like a biscuit?"

"Thank you, no. I thought it would be rude to be poking around in Peter's affairs so soon after his death. Besides, I don't think she could tell me anything."

She sipped her tea and cringed slightly.

"I hate this powdered milk. Sorry, I've run out of bottled—bloody rationing! So, tell me everything, Michael. Are there still strange men following you?"

I raised my cup to my lips and expressed the same sour look. "Bloody rationing!"

We both laughed and then she stood up.

"I'll go to the shops. I still have some coupons left; they may have some milk," she said.

I motioned her back down.

"Don't worry. The war's not about to end tomorrow and neither is rationing. I have to get used it, and so do you."

"Okay," she returned, resuming her seat. "Then we'll suffer together. Next payday I'm buying a cow."

I agreed with a nod.

"Well, you may be pleased to know that I'm not being followed any longer. It just suddenly stopped," I explained.

Rachel raised her cup and sipped cautiously.

"Maybe they were never there in the first place, Michael."

"Oh, they were there, but counter-intelligence was hardly their forte; they were more like the Marx Brothers. I shall miss them. I was getting used to them following me from place to place."

"So things are on the up and up," she said, chirpily.

"Well I thought so till today, but I really am no wiser than when I last saw you; worse, in fact."

"Worse?" she said as she placed down her cup and saucer. "How much worse?"

I took a moment to survey the room and to pay her a compliment.

"I have to say, Rachel, you've done a very nice job of this place. David will be delighted when he comes home," I said.

She looked at the photographs on the mantelpiece and smiled warmly.

"No thanks to you. You've helped me so much," she said. "All the furniture came from a second-hand shop in the high street, and the rugs were given to me by the landlord of the pub; they cleaned up really well. The only things I took from my old flat were these photos and the clock."

"It's quite an old clock. And noisy, too," I said. "Victorian."

"So you're an expert in clocks as well as history, are you?"

Her sarcastic retort made me smile.

"After Albert died, Queen Victoria ordered that all clocks manufactured thereafter, should be encased in black, to mourn the passing of her beloved husband. That's how I know."

She was pleasantly amused by the fact that—once again—I had managed to slip an historical reference into an otherwise normal conversation.

"I did manage to raise the money for a new bed. I couldn't bear the thought of sleeping in a second-hand bed." She shuddered at the thought. "Would you like to see it?" she added with a flirtatious smile.

Declining or consciously avoiding her advances was obviously an issue that Rachel, or any woman come to that, was having difficulty coming to terms with, but instead of letting the matter rest or allowing the evolution of any relationship to take its own natural course, she was content to victimise me at every opportunity. I glanced at David smiling back at me from the mantelpiece.

"I'll take your word for it, Rachel. I'm sure it's very nice."

She nodded resignedly, that any pursuit in that particular direction was futile. She silently observed me from behind her teacup, disconcerted by my dismissal of her charm and my abstinence regarding the art of lovemaking.

"I went to see Harry Griffin today," I said, breaking the long silence.

"Isn't he the man who gave you the list of names?" she replied, thoughtfully. "Why see him?"

"I'm not sure," I shrugged. "Needless to say, my journey was a waste of time. It would appear Harry never owned the pub."

"He wasn't there?"

I shook my head. "And never was according to the real owner; it was embarrassing."

Rachel put down her cup and saucer and looked perplexed. I knew what was on her mind. My claim of being followed was strange enough but now appeared implausible given its sudden cessation, and Harry Griffin seemed to be nothing more than pure invention; an archetypal underworld figure borne of an overactive imagination. Rachel stared at me without blinking.

"I'm not crazy," I said, perhaps to convince me more than it was her.

"I'm not suggesting you are," she replied.

"But that's what you're thinking."

She slipped off her shoes, folded her legs beneath her and rested her arm along the back of the chair, supporting her head on her hand.

"Can I make a suggestion?" she asked.

Before I had a chance to speak she moved straight on.

"Separation from a spouse can be a considerable strain, and if that separation is the result of infidelity, it can be unbearable. On top of which you have the sexual frustrations to contend with . . ."

"I am not sexually frustrated!"

"Then you ought to be. Frankly, I think you should take advantage of the situation while you can. And then there's the Henderson case, which any fool can see is driving you to distraction because it is criminal law, and criminal law is not what you do. My advice to you, Michael, is to get out of it. Give the case to someone else before it does drive you mad."

I averted my stare from hers and shook my head.

"I can't," I murmured.

"God!" she groaned with exhaustion. "You are going the right way to ending up in a padded room with a nice white jacket that ties up at the back. So what if you give the Henderson case to someone else? He'll still have his day in court. Nothing will change the outcome. What you're doing, Michael, is stupid. Stupid, stupid, stupid!"

"Thank you for your vote of confidence."

She instinctively moved from her chair and knelt in front of me, holding my hand between her delicate fingers and staring compassionately into my eyes.

"I *was* being followed, Rachel, and Harry Griffin is a *real* person. I came here today to be reassured, not to be told I'm certifiable."

"I don't think you're certifiable, Michael," she replied in a calming voice. "I'm just saying you've been through a lot lately. And heaven help me, I haven't made things any easier. You broke up from your wife, took on a case that would make the heads swim of even the greatest legal minds, had your offices blown up and barely escaped with your life, lost half your staff in one day, and still you persist in digging deeper and deeper into something you're incapable of understanding. You need to separate yourself from the problems so you can deal with them one at a time. At present you're not solving anything."

She squeezed my hand gently, still staring at me with those large doleful eyes, awaiting a reply that was never going to materialise.

"I believe everything you've told me, Michael. If you say this man Harry Griffin exists, then he does. If you think you were being followed, then you were. I do not doubt one single word. But don't you agree that you're letting all your problems build up instead of dealing with them? Sarah, for example—have you spoken to her?"

I shook my head slowly.

"Then what are your intentions?" she asked. "Is there any chance of reconciliation?"

"None," I returned bluntly.

"So you intend to divorce her?"

It wasn't a question I had considered, and even now, when Rachel's words were still hanging in the air, the notion of losing everything I had worked for filled me with a bitterness I had never experienced. Rachel observed me and squeezed my hand again.

"Divorce her, Michael, and move on," she said. "She's hurt you and deserves no sympathy. Put her where she belongs—in the past. Maybe then you can deal with your workload."

I reluctantly nodded, but I knew she was correct. Passing on the right of ownership was always the easiest way to simplify ones life; be it a troublesome car, a highly maintainable house, or an unruly dog, spouses were expendable and could easily be replaced by someone less troublesome or costly, and hopefully would refrain from biting the hand that feeds them. The question of love and desire is not worthy of consideration if they are not reciprocated or if they're willingly shared with a third party.

What I did with Penny was a moment of foolishness, and never intended to be anything more than one night. Sarah's agenda was of a completely different nature. She purposefully set out to find a lasting relationship, and thereafter parade around the town and ingratiate her new lover into the entourage we considered our friends; from that moment on to be known as Billy and Sarah rather than Michael and Sarah. In her heart and mind I was dead.

"I shall have the papers drawn up tomorrow," I agreed with a sigh.

Rachel nodded and rested her head on my knee.

"Show no mercy, Michael. Don't give her a thing."

"I won't," I replied. "But aren't you being a little hypocritical?"

She raised her head slowly and stared at me indignantly.

"Why would you say that?"

"Because since I've known you you've been trying your hardest to get me into bed."

She rested her head back on my knee.

"That's different," she said. "I explained all that. It would just be . . . an arrangement. Anyway, a fat lot of good it did me. Have you ever thought that your fear in that particular department may have been the reason why your wife found someone else?"

"No, I haven't, and for one good reason."

"Being?"

"Being that I haven't got a problem in that particular department, and never have had."

Her head popped up immediately.

"Then why won't you have sex with me?"

"Because you're married!" I replied, pointing to the photograph of David smiling like an angel from his gilded frame.

"So are you!" she retaliated.

"Yes, but not to you!!!"

She crumpled into a pile of uncontrollable laughter, her arm across her stomach and the other hand pointing at me.

"You can be so gullible, Michael," she giggled. "I know what you mean. Your problem is you have a conscience. What is it they say? All is fair and love and war. How do I know that David isn't in some French village giving the Jezebels a lesson in good old British stamina? Truth is, I don't, and neither do I care. I won't be asking him any questions when he comes home—if he comes home, and I certainly won't be confessing anything. If you don't want to be part of this . . . arrangement, then that's fine—I respect that, but you really have no reason to feel guilty. David is not what you would call a one woman man. That smile can snap the elastic on any girls' knickers, and has on a few occasions."

"You know he's been unfaithful and yet you stay with him?" I asked.

She dabbed the tears of laughter from the corners of her eyes with her fingertip.

"Ah, well, what's a girl to do?" she shrugged as the source of amusement slowly subsided.

Rachel resumed her place on the chair, taking up the same position; legs curled beneath her and head cradled in her hand.

"Go on," she said. "You said it was getting worse." She lifted her cup of tea from the table and composed herself. "I'm listening."

I thought for a moment, trying to recall what I had already told her and what had happened between.

"Recently I met a young woman named Wendy Marshall," I said. "And I might add that she actually knows Harry Griffin," I added assertively.

"Well, there you are. I never doubted you for a moment. And what does this young woman named Wendy Marshall do?"

"She's a prostitute."

Rachel's eyebrows arched and a look of distain flashed across her face. "Go on."

"That isn't to say that the Harry Griffin I met was the same man Wendy knows. The man I met may have been posing as Harry Griffin . . ."

"And why would he do that? Furthermore, why are you meeting prostitutes?"

Her enquiry was loaded with jealousy, and if I were able to see inside her head, it would have been filled with lewd images of Wendy and I entangled in compromising positions.

"It isn't what you think, Rachel, although I did pay her forty pounds . . ."

"You paid her how much!" she shrieked in disbelief.

I slumped back in my chair impatiently.

"Will you be quiet and stop jumping to conclusions?" I snapped, my voice raising an octave higher.

She composed herself and nodded. "Sorry."

"Wendy Marshall was brought to us by the D.P.P. She has been submitted as prosecution witness. It would appear she was attacked by the Blackout Butcher five days prior to the first victim being murdered. She allegedly survived the attack."

"Allegedly? Did she or didn't she?"

I paused, trying to find the words to describe Wendy and the reasons why she would be so easy to discredit as a witness.

"She has a history of self harming, four attempts at suicide. Peter Egan believed her to be nothing more than a headline seeker, you know for money, recognition."

"Can you do that?" Rachel interrupted. "If she's a witness for the prosecution, and you're working on behalf of the defence, can't you get into trouble? Can't they defrock you or something?"

I grinned broadly at her analysis.

"I'm not a Bishop, Rachel. Besides she called me. That doesn't make our meeting ethically correct, but she said she had something to tell me, so I met her."

"And whatever could she have said that was worth forty pounds? I take it that the money was for information and nothing else. I ask only because, as you've already said, you have no problems in that particular department."

I folded my arms tightly and scowled at her until she began to fidget uncomfortably in her chair, pulling her legs around and crossing them and sitting upright with her hands on her lap. Clearly she had a fixation with me, that if there were a possibility of me resorting to the pleasures of the flesh, she would rather it was with her than an overpaid scarlet woman. I observed her intensely until she stopped shifting, until she looked at me with surprised innocence.

"What? I'm just saying that's all!" she said in a defensive tone.

"I can go, if you'd rather," I suggested.

"No! I'll be a good girl, I promise," she cried.

"Okay then."

Satisfied with her solemn oath that she wouldn't interrupt or make any further outlandish assumptions, I was prepared to move on with my narrative, but heard her mumble, "What you do with your money is up to you. Give it all to some flapper. See if I care."

"Rachel!"

She jolted in her seat and smiled meekly. "I'm listening!"

"Wendy gave me a breakdown of her life," I began. "She had an abysmal childhood and a sadistic bastard for a father. But she started to tell me a story of her adult life, how she drifted into prostitution and the people she was involved with. It appears her pimp was a scout; something in abducting girls, and maybe still is for all I know. She knew all there was to know, how much a girl forced into prostitution could accumulate. She spouted the figures right down to the last penny. Now Wendy isn't what you would regard as being well educated; her sad life is testimony to that fact. So how would she know? How could she reel off six figure numbers without the slightest hesitation? Christ! I know mathematicians, and it would take hours for them to come up with the answer."

"So how did she?" questioned Rachel.

"Obviously she's involved, or she's amongst the people who are. She's seen the paperwork, the transactions, bills of sale, so to speak. She's seen it with her own eyes."

"Then why tell you? If she is involved, which I seriously doubt, then why tell anyone, least of all a lawyer? It's absurd, Michael. This is 1941, not the middle ages; slavery is something that belongs in the past. And what would be the point in telling you anyway? What purpose would it serve?"

My shoulders began to sag and I shook my head.

"I don't know. I had to make a quick exit before she had a chance to tell her story in full."

Rachel had turned her nose up and was shaking her head at my preposterous tale, and though she professed to believe I wasn't crazy, I was beginning to think she was having second thoughts.

"I agree with your friend the journalist—she's a headline seeker, and an unstable one at that," said Rachel after short consideration. "Like I said,

Michael: you're gullible. Can't you just deal with the problems you have instead of finding new ones?"

"But I believed her!"

Rachel stood up and perched her hands on her hips, looking down on me with a fraught expression.

"I've heard enough," she said. "I'm not saying you're crazy but you're certainly losing focus. Slavery, indeed! What will you be saying next, huh? Get a grip, Michael."

As she reprimanded me and questioned my state of mind, I stared back at her without saying a word. Rachel sighed exhaustively, shook her head and sat back down.

"Let us approach this logically," she suggested with all the patience she could muster. "Firstly why would she say such things to you? Secondly what has any of it to do with Henderson? I take it that Henderson was the purpose of your meeting?"

"Initially, yes, and in answer to your first logical approach, the answer is I have no idea. And in answer to your second logical approach, the answer is I have no idea."

"God, help me."

"So my question is the same as yours. Why should Wendy tell me?"

Rachel sighed and shook her head, observing my pensive expression with an element of concern. And in those moments, her frustration at my relentless need for answers began to subside.

"Michael, some girls lie," she said, patiently staring into her lap. "They do it to make themselves more attractive or more interesting to their friends or to someone they desire; it is an indisputable fact."

I smiled and reclined in my chair.

"Sylvia said that about you."

Her head suddenly jerked up.

"Me! Why would she say that? That isn't nice."

She looked personally affronted, and her eyes narrowed to mere slits.

"Sylvia can be very enlightening when it comes to the cunning methods of the female species," I laughed.

"I bet she can!" hissed Rachel.

"Oh, yes," I teased. "If ever there was a metaphor for 'wolves in sheep clothing' it has to be women. They create their own myth. And it works, too. Present company accepted, of course."

Rachel looked scornfully back at me.

"So what did that vicious cow say?"

I began to laugh even harder.

"She just said she thought you weren't what you said you were; woman's intuition. She doesn't mean any harm. She's protective of me . . ."

"So you keep saying. Then if I'm not me, who the hell am I?"

"Take no notice. It was just her initial reaction. She doesn't know you like I do."

-24-

My father's house looked out across the lush greenery of Richmond Park, a suburb of London and haven for the affluent; a mock-Tudor house of pristine white with four large columns quartering its front, bathing in the shadows of tall Elms with two large iron gates guarding the crescent driveway. I had spent my childhood there and some of my adult life, but had never returned since setting up my own home. Whenever I met my father it was always on neutral ground and he had never visited me in Kent, though he did manage a short excursion to Toronto, Canada to see my sister. Even my own wedding took place in neighbouring Wimbledon to rob him of any excuse not to come, and when he did arrive it was for the ceremony only, promptly leaving to attend one of his many functions. I believe I tried to be the son he wanted me to be, but his expectations were destroyed by my decision to follow another profession, and I think he believed Sarah to be an unworthy partner. Prior to my wedding we met outside St. Bartholomew's, and went to a nearby pub for lunch; he had only met Sarah once and had already harboured his doubts. "Marriage is a commitment, Michael, and I just don't think this girl is committed," he said as he cradled a glass of brandy in his hand. "You mustn't be duped by them. As young as you are, you have your mother's inheritance, and when I pass on you will have mine. What I'm trying to say, Michael, is that women are attracted to money, and you must never forget what she is, your secretary." There and then I knew that he thought I was marrying beneath me, that like him I should have found a woman with her own wealth, her own history, instead of allowing it to be forged for her. "I know women, Michael, and if you look deep in their eyes you can see whatever future you have with them. Do you know what I see in Sarah's eyes—nothing."

I arrived at the house on a blustery afternoon, the rain blowing from every direction, and Mr. Lothby was standing on the front doorstep, aptly sheltering beneath a black umbrella, with an expression as dark as the racing clouds overhead. As I approached from the taxi he conveyed little expression, just a forced, shallow smile devised to disguise his true concern.

"There was no need for you to make the journey, Mr. Lothby," I said as I accompanied him beneath the doorway canopy. "I still have a key."

"I felt it my duty to be here," he replied. "When you called me and said you wanted to visit the house I was most concerned."

"I understand your commitment to my father's memory, Mr. Lothby, but I can manage on my own."

"You don't understand, Michael," he said, shaking his head. "The reading of the Will was final; you signed the appropriate papers to make your father's estate the sole property of my company. An inventory has been taken of every item in the house; it's to be auctioned within a week. You have never ventured over this threshold since the day you left, so why now?"

I thought for a moment and looked at Mr. Lothby's worried face.

"Perhaps I'm feeling nostalgic," I replied as I took the door-key from my pocket. "I need to take one last look."

"But I must insist you don't remove anything, Michael. The inventory has been compiled and . . ."

"Then whatever I remove you shall be informed and the said item can be erased from your inventory," I returned abruptly. "And I would appreciate some privacy!"

My harsh words visibly shook the old gentleman and he bowed his head.

"I'm sorry, Mr. Lothby, but you have my word that if I intend to take anything, you will be the first to know."

I patted him gently on the shoulder and he reluctantly nodded.

"As you wish, Michael; I can sometimes be over-protective when it concerns family and friends, especially a close friend such as your father. You have every right to be here."

I watched Mr. Lothby walk the length of the driveway before I opened the front door and was at once attacked by the smell of musk; the deprivation of air and life within. It was as I remembered it. I stood in the large hallway, my eyes following the curvature of the staircase as it wound its way up to the floor above. I took the small, ornate key from my wallet and began to look for whatever it unlocked, moving from the lounge to the dining room and then the kitchen, and if it had a purpose—which it must have—then surely whatever it unlocked was in my father's office, a room he considered out of bounds to everyone in the family. I had ventured there only a few times as a child, whenever he was out, and was mesmerized by the walls of books with various coloured spines; now everything appeared smaller than I remembered. For a while I moved slowly down the shelves searching out anything on Jack the Ripper, but there was nothing on the subject; in general all medical reference books and I sat at his desk, placing the key in every lock of the desk drawers but to no avail. The drawers were all unlocked but the key I held had no effect on their mechanisms, and inside one I found a small cash-box. My hopes ran high but the key was too large.

I found myself standing in the greyness of the landing, the incessant tapping of the rain the only sound to break the silence of the house, and I stared at the closed doors before me considering which one to enter first. My old room was my choice, a place I grew up in, that was my kingdom, where I would act out my fantasies of pirates sailing the seven seas or soldiers fighting the Germans in the trenches of the Somme, and later my confidant that kept all my secrets of a potential lover, screening me from the rest of the world as puberty took hold of me like a killer disease, sparing me the indignity of squeezing blackhead and spots in public; a place that afforded me continuous silence as I read history and studied law, that I entered a babe in arms and left a man. Now it was simply a storage room; a warehouse filled with memories and discarded medical journals and law books. Caroline's room was much the same. Her chest of drawers remained as did her wardrobe but her bed had gone, to be replaced by a small mountain of tea-chests, filled to the brim with discarded documents and lectures written by my father. My father's bedroom was the same room he shared with my mother, unchanged as much as I remember, but there were certain items within that required a key for their locks and I tried every single one.

I began the whole process again, snooping like an ambitious detective, looking under beds, moving cupboards, behind paintings, even searching for hidden compartments in the walls of my father's office, and three hours later I was standing in the exact same spot, looking at the spiralling staircase with a total sense of failure, but as my eyes followed its route, they continued upward and fixed on the square hatch that was the entrance into the attic. With a chair, the aid of the banisters and a candle from the kitchen drawer, I ascended into the gloom of the dusty roof-space and saw my goal immediately; an aging wooden chest. It was in my room for a while, in the days when I was a pirate and fighting the Spanish, when the bed was my ship and the window an imaginary panorama of the Caribbean Islands or the coast of Cuba. I remember my father taking it back as I protested sulkily that its presence was an integral part of my upbringing and its absence would not only destroy my efforts to obliterate the Spanish Navy but could inadvertently jeopardize the outcome of the British Empire. "It has another purpose, Michael; a more important purpose," said my father. "I promise one day it will be yours." Till now I had forgotten about the chest and his promise, but now it was all so clear; he wanted me to find it again; it was part of his plan. As I expected, the key slipped into the lock and turned effortlessly, the lid jarring up as lock turned; a puff of stale air attacking my osmatic senses like the opening of a sealed tomb, and as I stared inside I was consumed by doubt and confusion, for it appeared to be clothes. I pulled out the garments one by one; coats, shirts and trousers, dirty, stained and breathing out fifty year old dust as they dropped from their long-term folds, and then I was staring into the bottom of the chest, the candlelight glinting on what looked to be worthless jewellery and the sheen of a picture, and I studied the clothing closer and then looked back inside the chest. "God help me."

I found myself back at Dulwich Village, before the insignificant house of Jonathan Sandpiper, and a fine rain fell in thin, gossamer layers, caught in the strength of the afternoon sunshine and bleaching the surrounding landscape paler than reality. From the taxi I moved directly down the gravel pathway decidedly quicker than on my first visit, tugging the bell-pull and awaiting either Mr. Sandpiper or his wife to appear, and when neither materialized, I rapped heavily on the black doorknocker, the image of a lion's head. As the moments moved into minutes my initial sense of urgency waned, but on the doorstep were Mr. Sandpiper's shoes, wet and muddied from his morning jaunt to the park, and slowly I walked to the side of the house and through the gate where I looked out upon a large, well-manicured lawn, edged by flower beds of rich, black earth, in which plants boasting a riot of colour stretched skyward. I stood there, the rain falling like a heavy mist, collecting in my hair and on my clothes, sparkling like tiny jewels, and a noise of something breaking turned my eyes in the direction from which it came, at the top of the garden. I walked up the straight, stone pathway, passing various beds of cabbages, carrots and gooseberry bushes until I passed beyond a clutch of apple trees and was confronted by a larger than usual greenhouse. Through the misted glass I could see him toiling away at a bench and, dispensing with common courtesy I entered without knocking.

Mr. Sandpiper was taking plants from a shallow wooden tray and transferring them into clay pots, one of which lay broken at his feet, and he raised his soiled hands either side of him, like a surgeon who had been recently scrubbed, and he looked at me over a pair of small, round spectacles. "Michael," he said, turning back to his chore. "You'll forgive me, but these young ones require my assistance otherwise they will surely die."

I watched him as he plunged his hands into a small sack of soil and distribute it into pots of various shapes and sizes aligned before him.

"You obviously have more respect for plants than people," I said.

His hands momentarily paused from their duty.

"You've read the book? You've read it in its entirety?" he asked, gazing at his thin reflection in the glass pane before him.

"Up until you absconded."

He continued to place the straggly, green roots into the appropriate receptacles, pushing the earth gently around them with his thumbs.

"How many?" he asked.

"According to my father—four."

Mr. Sandpiper nodded his head, as though satisfied with the total number.

"And how many does he claim I took part in?"

"Three."

He nodded his head again. "As I said: an honest man. Whatever books you buy on the subject, they're inevitably wrong. Even the memoirs of the policemen involved are faulted. They attributed Tabram and Stride to us, but we weren't responsible."

As I assessed his profile, it dawned on me that his appearance at my father's funeral, his aged, threadbare clothes, were not designed to dupe me into believing he was something other than he was, but were simply his gardening clothes; clothes he practically lived in.

"Three, four, ten, twenty—it's immaterial! You assisted in the murder of three women, Mr. Sandpiper," I barked.

He paused, resting his dirty hands on the bench and staring directly ahead.

"What will you have me say, Michael? Am I beyond redemption? Certainly. If there's a hell I will stand before its gates and know exactly why I'm there. Do I regret those terrible, terrible acts? I relive them every night, whenever the shadows close in around me, whenever I hear the sound of a police-whistle; I live it every single moment of my life, and there is nothing I wouldn't do to change it. I knew after the killing of Catharine Eddowes that I had to save myself, and I believed if I changed my life I could change the man. The shadows serve to remind me that you can't change your memories. I arrived home the next day and told my parents that the medical profession wasn't for me, much to my father's disappointment, but I joined the police force; my true vocation."

"And you never saw my father again?"

He turned around to face me, leaning his back on the bench and folding his arms.

"I received a telegram in September 1910. It wasn't so much an enquiry as an order, telling me to be on the Serpentine Bridge in Hyde Park on Monday at 12 o'clock. At this time I was an inspector and, foolishly with hindsight, believed I was beyond his influence, but I went, perhaps out a sense of duty or, perhaps, because we were bound by a foolish creation. He was quite alone when I arrived, standing on the bridge and looking down into the water, his arms on the rail and his shoulders slightly hunched. He was no longer the fresh-faced kid I knew at medical school but the boyish features remained. He straightened on seeing me, burying his hands in his raincoat pockets, even though the sun was shining down, and I approached him fearlessly, believing my position as an inspector dwarfed his own as a doctor. I had seriously underestimated him.

"What do you want, William?" I asked, tersely. "I have nothing to discuss with you."

He smiled broadly, the way he used to, and almost started laughing.

"Bravado, I like that," he said. "However, you must be intrigued as to why I asked you here."

"I regarded it as more of a summons."

"Ah, yes!" he cried. "A word you bandy around often I would imagine, given your profession. It's Inspector Sandpiper now, isn't it?"

I admit to being surprised that he knew anything about me at all, especially as we had not met in over twenty years, and already my 'bravado' as he called it, was beginning to falter. I stared directly back at him without giving a reply but he was already searching out the fear in my eyes.

"There's nothing I don't know about you, Pip," he continued. "Married to Gwen, three daughters, Michelle, Lucy and Charlene, a house in Dulwich, a Labrador called Spike, and you still rising through the ranks. Tell me, were your three daughters some form of recompense for the three whores you murdered, before you fled—like a thief in the night?"

I wouldn't rise to the bait and my scowl only fuelled his need to degrade me entirely, but his smirk slowly disappeared and he leaned his elbow on the rail.

"Let me get to the point," he continued. "I regard you as a threat and have since the day you absconded leaving me to face the music . . ."

"What music?" I broke in fiercely. "You could have ended it at Mitre Square. You could have stopped! But, no, six weeks later you tore Mary Kelly to shreds for the fun of it, for the sake of a myth."

His face altered in that moment, the lingering grin fell away and his blue eyes pierced into me.

"You just don't understand do you?" he snarled. "Your vanishing trick placed me in a very precarious and dangerous position. The police were asking questions and they were informed that a certain young medical student had suddenly, and without reason, vanished into thin air which, strangely enough, coincided exactly with the murder of Eddowes; they even interviewed our landlady who had little choice but to verify what I had already told them, that on the night of the murders we were in our room. She had much to lose and her own integrity would have been brought into question had she even hinted at the possibility that we were out on the streets at night. Nevertheless, she wasn't the same after. From that moment on her nightly callers ceased to arrive and I cannot recall ever seeing her drunk again, but she was watchful of me after that; she even had the barrel moved at the side of the water-closet; she was suspicious. Murdering Kelly got you off the hook, and convinced the authorities that the killer had not gone to ground but was very much alive and well and still living in Whitechapel. You should be thanking me."

"Thanking you! Thanking you for destroying my life!" I gasped.

He slowly looked me up and down and his thin smile began to form again.

"You don't look a broken man, Pip; good job, handsome wife, three lovely children. And those whores you grieve for would have inevitably died, either with disease or at the hands of the thugs and criminals they favour, and when they died they would have ended up in a pauper's grave. Kelly's funeral was the biggest the East End had ever witnessed, an event on the scale reserved only for royalty, and with it has come immortality, just like the legend you and I created."

The very mention of 'Myths and Legends' made me cringe and I stretched myself to my full height.

"I didn't come here for explanations, William. Say your piece and let me go about my business."

He pushed himself off the rail and walked closer to me until we stood face to face.

"I have children, too, Pip," he said. "I'll spare you the details but I'm sure that after today you'll make it your business to find out. I want you to know I have confessed my sins. Everything we accomplished is written down and in safe hands."

It was my turn to smile now and his reaction was to shake his head.

"And why would you jeopardize your precious career by confessing to the murder of four women?" I asked with a doubtful stare.

"For the very reason you have just highlighted; for the sake of my precious career. I won't bore you but as a physician I am well respected and only this month my fifth book is to be published. I sit on three independent Boards and have the offer of several more. As I said, Pip, I regard you as a threat, and the more I prosper the greater threat you become, and the confession is my insurance that I'm allowed to prosper without interruption. Had you, as a police officer, any intention of discrediting my good name by announcing you have discovered the identity of Jack the Ripper and, of course making a small fortune in the process, my confession is a guarantee that you pay the consequences as well as I. It isn't a prospect I would expect to happen while I'm alive, but it is something you may consider should I die before you. If I outlive you then what harm can come of it?

"And if I outlive you?"

He pushed his face a little closer, his breath hot on my face, and his eyes ignited once more.

"For your sake, Pip, I pray you don't," he hissed. "The book, the confession, will be passed onto my son. He should know what his father really was; it will be left to his discretion. I will leave this world knowing I'm a good man, that I have saved far more lives than I have taken, that I gave much of my time freely to the poor and donated unspeakable amounts of money to London's charities, that my published journals have advanced medicine and sown the seeds to those who follow in my wake. My indiscretions will be forgiven."

"You say it as if I have no right to live once you die, that I should put a gun to my head and blow my brains out the moment they close the curtains on you."

"You left me, Pip!" he growled, pushing his face even closer. "You left me to face the consequences. My only regret is that if you outlive me, I will never see you face the same consequences as I had to."

"He left then, crossing the bridge and heading towards Victoria Gate, leaving me to wrestle with the possibility as to whether the book was just a threat; just another myth he had created. Even so, from that moment on I monitored his life in the same way he had mine. I knew everything there was to know about him; his wife, his address, you and your sister . . . I even bought the books he had written and read them, searching for references about the Whitechapel Murders. He wrote a book about madness entitled 'Normal and Subnormal.' Have you ever read it, Michael?"

I shook my head. "I made it my business not to," I replied.

He removed his gold-rimmed spectacles and carefully folded them, purposefully drawing the time out and placed them into his top pocket, and then he turned again and began to place the clay pots into an order only he could understand.

"You weren't close to your father were you?"

"Not particularly, but it isn't me who is open to question," I rebuffed.

"You took nothing from him, did you? Fresh out of law school and started your own firm in Aldwych, no less; you set your sights high, Michael, considering you had little or no experience as a litigator."

"I had a very competent and experienced partner; the risks were low."

"Ah, yes!" he cried, turning his head towards me. "Kenneth Banner . . . or Badger as he is fondly referred to. I've followed your career. I've followed it since the day I met your father on the bridge. I even know your sister Caroline's address in Canada, her husband and two children's names. Your mother left you well provided for, didn't she? She came from good stock, a family of industrialists, and her wealth made your father's look like loose change. It must have grieved him when you chose the profession of a lawyer against his own wishes, and more so when you used her inheritance to fund your company and your house in Kent."

A chill ran through me like an Artic gust of wind, knowing I had been spied on my whole adult life, that my every move had been monitored and memorised, to be stored as a form of ammunition either against me or my father. But I knew, with few exceptions, I had done nothing wrong—least of all murder—and as the silence stretched longer Mr. Sandpiper turned to me.

"Uncomfortable isn't it, Michael? You must be feeling the same as I did that day back in 1910, but you must understand that your father was playing a cruel game and I couldn't allow him to have the advantage. I know you don't have children, but one day you will, and you will come to realise that you will do anything to protect them." He turned away from me again and my eyes looked to his reflection in the rain-streaked glass. "I have seven grandchildren, Michael, and none are myths or legends; they are the only true creation I have ever contributed to."

"If that's supposed to induce sympathy, Mr. Sandpiper, it won't work. As a lawyer I have a duty to myself, this country and those poor women you killed . . ."

"WE killed!" he emphasised. "I wasn't a lone assailant; your father played his part and a lot more besides. Over the past thirty years I've relived this confrontation time and time again. How could I ever explain to a rational human being what your father and I set out to achieve? These weren't women, Michael; they were vermin, a source of contagion that demanded no more respect than that of a lame dog . . ."

"They were people, Mr. Sandpiper, and you murdered them."

His head dropped and slowly began to nod.

"With all the confrontations between us I've imagined, that is the one answer I've never been able to defend," he sighed. "What do you intend to do, Michael?"

I purposefully hesitated until he raised his eyes to mine and I could see genuine fear in them.

"I shall pass the book over to the hounds in Fleet Street and my knowledge over to the Director of Public Prosecution," I said, pointedly. "I'm going to see you hang, Pip."

The very mention of the name made him wince and he looked away.

"Please, don't call me that," he said.

His eyes began to wander the greenhouse and settled, eventually, straight ahead.

"Would you take the same action if your father was alive? If by some chance the book fell into your hands, and knowing what you know now, would you see your own father hang?"

"Gladly! We've established my father and I were not close. Call it a moral obligation but murder is murder."

He nodded his head as if in agreement and then he looked at me.

"You believe the book will be enough to send me to the gallows; taking into consideration that everyone involved is probably dead by now and there's not one single shred of evidence in existence? Any jury would take some convincing. Who could you call on to substantiate your fanciful story, Michael? Certainly not Dr. Bond; he died in 1901. Dr. Brown died in 1928 and Dr. Phillips in 1897. The defence would simply claim the book was indeed a prank."

I moved closer towards him, angered that he believed he could call my bluff.

"The condemning factor is what you were, Mr. Sandpiper, and what my father was. True, the story is fanciful, and who in their right mind would believe that an assistant commissioner and one of the greatest physicians this country has ever known would have conceived such a monster as Jack the Ripper? And who would believe that the son of the physician would intentionally besmirch his father's good name and impeccable reputation by making such a claim? The case could run for months, maybe years, during which time you and your family will be subject to all manner of interrogation and humiliation. And do you think a frail old man like you could withstand that kind of torture? They'll ware you down, Mr. Sandpiper, and you'll admit to it because you want to admit to it. Sure, you don't believe in God but there's always that element of doubt, isn't there? You'll confess to save your soul, just in case you were wrong all along and there's half a chance he does exist. And that Mr. Sandpiper will be your day of redemption, because when they reluctantly open those pearly gates, you'll be safe in the knowledge that you'll never bump into my father walking the streets of heaven. And you're wrong—they're not all dead. Despite your infatuation with keeping my life and everyone involved in the Whitechapel Investigation under surveillance, Detective Constable Dew is still alive."

"I'm aware of that," he said, resignedly.

"I bet you scan those obituary columns every morning, and as they die one by one the safer you feel. I'm certain Walter Dew would like to see the book."

He took a rag from his back pocket and sat himself on an upturned wooden crate and proceeded to wipe the dirt from his hands with great care.

"You're right, of course," he said, quietly. "But I was a policeman, Michael, and though I may say so myself, I was an exceedingly good one. Obviously I will do everything I can to dissuade you from taking any such action, but as a policeman I have to advise you that book or no book, you have no evidence; you can't win. All that can come of it is failure. You will be a laughing stock. Why destroy your career on the ravings of a madman?"

I scowled down at him angrily.

"Did you know your father worked at Bedlam? He gave one day a week freely in order to study the insane. He was obsessed by the 'Jekyll and Hyde' syndrome, the splitting of one mind; schizophrenia, or dementia praecox, as he constantly referred to it. In his book 'Normal and Subnormal' a great deal concerns itself with mind manipulation; how one person can belittle and humiliate another just by their appearance, by the way they conduct themselves or in the way they speak. He cites 'Intimidation' as the key reference to it all, that we are intimidated from birth, by mothers and fathers and authority as a body or as an individual. The sight of a uniform is intimidating, for it presents the illusion of authority, and few of us rebel against it. He claims anyone is capable of murder under extreme circumstances; that in moments of rage we can commit the most unconscionable acts without recall for detail; a moment that is completely lost. He admitted to using drugs on many of the patients in Bedlam, believing that if certain chemicals could induce madness, then by the same token other chemicals could restore sanity. It was his contention that both sanity and madness are defined by the natural chemicals within us all, and that those chemicals create our character long before we leave the womb. Those capable of intimidation are superior beings, whose chemical structure is different from the weaker. He defines a new madness; madness he calls 'Middle Madness,' someone with a calm exterior, capable of inflicting pain and torture with impunity, undetectable in the eyes of others—a cold, blooded killer. After I read the book I realised that for all his research and for all those he used as guinea pigs in Bedlam, he hadn't discovered anything but his true self."

"You're saying my father was mad?"

"Geniuses usually are, Michael. He believed vehemently that our lives are preordained and that assertiveness is clarity and weakness is disorder. The assertive, the stronger are biologically different, and their chemical structure is superior. To prove his point he defines 'Middle Madness' by naming witch-finders, executioners, even the Spanish Inquisition; that those who administered torture and death on a daily basis were the sanest people to walk the earth, devoid of guilt or remorse because of their calling. They earnestly believe they are serving some great cause. I think the book was an attempt to understand his own dementia; why he never felt the slightest guilt or shame for what we did in the autumn of 1888. In the final analysis his description of 'Middle Madness' is neither sane nor insane; both are equal and one controls the other; that an insane act is justified by the rationality of sanity; it cannot determine right from wrong. Even as we speak those very acts are happening all over Europe. One man will kill another because someone in authority told him he had to, that he was serving some great cause. And will that soldier run the gauntlet of emotion we would expect from a murderer? No. Simply he has a job to do and he'll sleep soundly in his bed knowing he did it."

"That's different!" I said. "That's war!"

All the time he had been speaking, his eyes had been roaming the concrete floor of the greenhouse, but he looked up at me.

"Is it?" he said, warily. "My younger brother was at the Somme in 1916. I'll never forget the night before he was to leave for Northern France; he shook like a leaf. He didn't know why he had to fight; I don't believe anyone gave him a reason. He knew only that someone of authority deemed it so; that he was expected to kill total strangers, brothers, fathers, husbands, and his reward for that insanity would be his own existence, his own survival. And while thousands upon thousands of soldiers emerged from their muddy dugouts only to be hacked down by machine gun fire, those who had deemed it so remained in the safety of their HQ, far from enemy lines. Apparently my brother was found on the very edge of the trench; he never even made it to his feet and probably never fired a single shot; his murderer was never captured or punished."

It was difficult to feel empathetic in light of his past deeds, and his analogies appeared designed to convince me to abandon my quest, but his character-analysis of my father stirred up long forgotten memories. I cannot recall ever seeing my father enraged. I had, however, seen him doleful, and sometimes I would enter his study at home and find him sitting in his leather chair and staring into the fire, as if that somewhere in the flames was the answer to life's great secret. I would talk to him but he would never answer, consumed entirely by his private thoughts, and it would take physical contact, in the form of a poke or a shake, to snap him from his reverie, and thereafter he would stare around the room to familiarize himself with his surroundings; acclimatizing to reality. I attributed these bouts of oblivion to the pressure of his work, but his condition worsened over the years, especially after my mother died, and if I ever showed the slightest concern for his wellbeing, he would simply put the problem down to tiredness; I had no reason to doubt it. Was Mr. Sandpiper's evaluation of my father correct; that he was, in fact, cursed with an insanity he labelled as 'Middle Madness,' an organised state of mind entirely bereft of conscience?

"Were you from good stock, Mr. Sandpiper?" I asked, eager to let the subject of my father rest and not distract me from the object of my visit.

The old man looked up from his makeshift seat, the dirty rag hanging limply from his hand.

"I believe so," he replied, sceptically. "My mother was a nurse and my father a respectable G.P. Why do you ask?"

"It's a sure sign of motherly love when she labels her son's clothes before she sends him off to medical school."

His eyes opened wider and his mouth opened slightly, and as he rose his face was growing paler by the second.

"The book wasn't the only thing my father left," I said. "Sealed in wax on the back cover was a small key; obviously there for a reason. In my father's attic I found a trunk. It reminded me of one of those pirate chests and the key opened it. What do you think I found inside, Mr. Sandpiper?"

He stared vacantly back without so much as blinking, and his breathing was audible and erratic. It was all he could do to shake his head.

"Clothes—both yours and my father's. The jacket and shirt belonging to you is most interesting, both saturated in blood, probably that of Catharine Eddowes and remarkably well preserved considering they had been there for fifty-three years. I think my father was very concerned about the preservation of the trunk and its contents, and I don't believe he had ever opened it in all that time, and the lock had been lubricated with axle grease to make it easily accessible—awaiting its grand opening. But the clothes weren't the only point of interest. Either you or he stole trinkets from the corpses, didn't you—keepsakes, souvenirs? There all in there, Mr. Sandpiper; a feather from Polly Nichols's bonnet, two brass rings prized from Annie Chapman's lifeless fingers, a pawn ticket belonging to Catharine Eddowes and bearing her real name, and a court summons for a certain Mary Jane Kelley from Thames Magistrates Court for drunken disorderliness to which she was fined two shillings and sixpence. The misspelling of her name is immaterial when set against the rest of the contents inside the trunk. And then, of course, there's the actual murder weapon, the knife you purchased, Mr. Sandpiper. True it isn't bloodstained but I think the jury will get the gist of its purpose. But the prize is the photograph taken on the steps of the London Hospital. How dashing you two looked, dressed in your starched shirts, black waistcoats, black jackets and grey trousers; two friends about to embark on a career in medicine. Do you remember that photograph being taken, Mr. Sandpiper?"

He nodded as if in trance.

"September," he mumbled. "I remember now."

Suddenly he blinked in quick succession and drew a deep breath before resuming his seat back on the wooden box, clearly shaken and unnerved. I treated the exercise much like the examination of a witness in a courtroom, gradually coaxing information before dropping the bombshell. He sat with his elbows on his knees and his head in his hands.

"Perhaps I am much like my father," I persisted. "I am ambitious and to a point greedy, though I hasten to add, I don't regard myself as remotely insane. I will bring this to court and see you punished for your crimes, Mr. Sandpiper; both you and my father."

The old man raised his face, his eyes laden with tears and his hands visibly shook.

"This is what my father wanted, can't you see that?" I continued, undeterred by his emotional state. "He wanted to be found out! He wants the world to know that he was responsible, that he fooled everyone and Jack the Ripper was nothing but pure invention. That's why he kept everything, the trinkets, the photograph, the knife. This was his legacy to me, to expose you both as the creator of a myth. He did have a conscience, Mr. Sandpiper, and it's been packed away in a small trunk for half a century."

Through the misty glass I saw Mrs. Sandpiper making her way up the pathway holding a white umbrella above her head in one hand and a coffee mug in the other.

"Time to take my leave, Mr. Sandpiper," I said. "I suggest you find yourself a good solicitor."

I passed her on the pathway, just outside the greenhouse and we exchanged pleasant smiles, but as I reached the clutch of trees I heard her say, "Jonathan, whatever is the matter?"

-25-

It was dusk when I emerged from the office, and after locking the door I took a moment to observe the quietening streets, the thinning traffic and occasional pedestrians' en-route home. The bright day had slipped surreptitiously into a smoky grey gloom, and the interiors of the half-empty buses were illuminated as they navigated their way up and down Blackfriars Road. The street lights and flashing beacons were dormant, as were the shops and offices, surplus to requirements owing to the blackout regulations; soon the streets would submerge into an inky blackness and the buses would return to their depots. A blue van was straddling the pavement outside the offices next door as if for the purpose of delivering or collecting, and checking my watch and gazing up at the dark windows I approached, stepping off the curb to circumnavigate the obstacle. Suddenly the back doors of the vehicle flew open and I was pulled inside, thrown down on the cold, steel floor with a heavy weight pushing down on my head. "Is it him?" I heard a voice say. The weight of a foot eased off and a large hand hooked beneath my arm, pulling me up and pushing me onto a makeshift bench opposite a hulking figure with shorn hair and an expensive suit. "Are you him? Are you Michael James?" he asked in a guttural tone. I nodded, breathless and shaken as the van moved off. "Yeah, it's him," the Neanderthal confirmed to a small, squared window cut into the panelling at the rear of the cab. I felt the sway of the van as it moved into Southwark Street and then straight ahead towards London Bridge, my eyes locked with my captor in the dull light, who bore an irritating smirk. "Where the hell are you taking me?" I said. The Neanderthal was hunched forward, his elbows on his knees, his face lifted and his eyes piercing into mine. "Here's the deal," he said. "You don't talk and I won't hurt you—how's that?" I went to speak but he put a finger to his lips, and leaning back he opened one side of his jacket to reveal the handle of a revolver protruding from the inside pocket. "You have to pay attention, Michael James. It wouldn't do to deliver you full of holes, would it?" The sound of sniggering bled through the small window and I decided it was in my best interest to comply with his demands.

I considered the prospect of escaping; of running headlong at the doors and battering them open and making my getaway through the labyrinth of streets that make up the city. I also considered the prospect that the Neanderthal would shoot me dead as soon as I lifted a buttock off the bench, and the possibility that should I make it out unscathed and burst out of my steel confinement, I would probably be crushed under the wheels of a following lorry. The Neanderthal became more relaxed as the journey stretched on, one leg along the wooden bench and his back resting against the partition of the cab, but his hand remained concealed under his jacket. He was nattering to the driver and the passenger about some fellow hoodlum who had recently received seven years for robbery, cackling like old witches and debating the poor man's chances behind prison walls. In a quieter moment he turned his attention to me. "Aren't you scared, Michael James? Don't you wonder what waits for you at the end of this journey?" I shook my head defiantly, consigned to my vow of silence that fired him with enthusiasm. "I like that. That's good thinking," he said, dropping his foot to the floor and straightening his bulky frame. "That shows initiative that does. You're talking but not actually talking. I don't get too many of them. They're usually scared shitless and unable to move."

I swallowed hard, my stomach an empty void.

"There was this geezer about six months ago," the thug continued. "Thought he was James Cagney—muscling in on our business, putting the frighteners on our people; cheeky fucker. Anyway he had to go, so we collects him and takes him to . . ." He paused for consideration and looked to the small window. "Oi, Frank! Where did we take that geezer about six months ago?" A voice, barely audible over the rattling engine replied, "Epping." The Neanderthal clicked his fingers. "Yeah, that was it, Epping. So on the way there, he's sitting right where you are now and I've got this stuck in his face." At that point he reached inside his jacket and pulled out a revolver, laying it in his left hand and patting it gently with his right, as if it were some precious artefact. "Now, you can say what you like about the German's but they make exceptionally good guns. This is a Lugar, and I've heard it said that Hitler carries this very model. So now this geezer, James Cagney, don't look so tough after all; cried like a little girl and pissed himself; animal. Anyway, we get to Epping and I give him a shovel and we march into the woods. It's the middle of the night and a full moon, and when we stop I tell him to start digging. He doesn't say a word and starts to dig. I tell him it's his own grave he's digging, but he just goes on, snivelling and grizzling and digging this fuckin' great hole. Now I don't want to kill him—I just want to scare him, so about two feet down I say I'll let him live if he just disappears, you know, go back to wherever he came from. Still nothing. Not a word. Well, that's just fuckin' rude, I thought. I gave the man the opportunity to save himself and he blanks me. So I pop him one—straight between the eyes, and he falls in a heap on the ground. Then I pop him again for being so fuckin' rude."

He returned the Lugar back into his inside pocket. "See, that's the thing, Michael James, he gave me no choice. At least you're trying; you know a nod or a shake of your head here and there. That rude bastard couldn't be bothered to make the effort."

The Neanderthal lit a cigarette, chuckling to himself as he replayed the events of that moonlit night in Epping six months ago when he blew a man's brains out because fear had stricken him dumb. I was consumed by a cold sweat, my breathing shallow, and my heart beating so fast it was close to bursting. The tobacco smoke filling the confines of the van fought for supremacy over the stench of oil, grease and filth, and all I could do was stare at the floor, watching small inanimate objects roll about as the van swayed from side to side. I watched a small light-bulb tumble over the raised ribs in the flooring of which there were nine, and laid bets with myself on which rut the bulb would settle once the motion of the van dislodged it from its prior position. This primitive form of roulette occupied my mind until the vehicle abruptly turned and I could feel gravel beneath the tyres as opposed to tarmac. The van slowed to a stop and the engine was silenced. I heard two doors open and close and felt the chill of the night air as the back doors swung open. The Neanderthal pushed me out, to stand before two unsavoury characters much the same. It was not completely dark yet; a modicum of light struggled on the horizons and over the silhouetted buildings, bathing a car park area of some kind in shadows strewn with rubbish and abandoned vehicles. The Neanderthal took my arm and marched me to a fire escape protruding from a sinister looking building, jerking his head skyward by way of a command.

The climb was short and the clang of the iron treads underfoot tolled like a distant bell of doom. On the first floor I was herded through a door and into a dark corridor; the Neanderthal leading the way, his two associates behind. I believed then that this was where my life would end, that I would end up in a shallow grave in some remote wooded area. A second door was opened and we entered a room flooded with light, with many covered snooker tables and a bar that stretched the entire width of the room. In its centre were several people standing around a table, babbling at one another and pointing in various directions. Through squinted eyes I took in the blistering paint, the dirty floor and the cracked windows, and above the stink of acrid beer, dank and rotting timber I could smell a familiar Havana odour. I was brought to a stop and the gathering at the table broke open, and there stood Harry Griffin with a halo of blue cigar smoke hovering overhead.

"Ah, Michael," he said as he walked towards me. "Good of you to come."

He shook my hand and patted me on the shoulder.

"I had a choice!" I said, giving the Neanderthal a sideways glance.

Harry studied the cuts and fading bruises on my face.

"What the fuck happened to you?" he asked, but before I got the chance to answer he smiled and backed up, his arms outstretched. "Well, what do you think?"

I gave the decaying area a brief glance of disgust.

"It's going to be a snooker hall," he said. "They're all the rage in America. I'm going to knock that wall down and put a restaurant in there," he added, pointing to his right.

A timid man, obviously detached from Harry's entourage, stepped forward and shook his head. "It can't be done, Mr. Griffin," he said, pointing to the table on which sat a blueprint.

Harry emitted an exhausted sigh.

"Don't keep telling me that, Gerry," he seethed. "If it's a load-bearing wall we can put steels in. If necessary we can have pillars built to take the weight above. We can make a feature of them, Gothic or Roman, to give the whole place a theme."

I smiled at the thought of Julius Caesar playing snooker.

"Steels and pillars are not the issue here," the man retaliated. "And I would appreciate it if you referred to me as Gerald and not Gerry. I am an architect, not one of your collectors."

The Neanderthal slipped his hand inside his jacket but Harry, who was puffing his cigar with such anger he had almost disappeared in a blanket of fog, paced forward, snatching up the blueprint from the table and thrusting it in Gerald's face.

"Give me one good reason why I can't knock a hole in that wall and put a restaurant in there," he growled.

The architect smiled sympathetically and took the crumpled blueprint from Harry's shaking hand. "I believe Mr. and Mrs. Singh would oppose the idea of a restaurant," he replied patiently.

"And who the fuck is Mr. and Mrs. Singh when they're at home?" rebuffed Harry, barely able to control his rage.

"That's my point, Mr. Griffin. It *is* their home. They own the property next door. Your restaurant would take up their entire floor space."

Harry's cigar suddenly hung from his mouth at a forty-five degree angle, and after a moment he suddenly started to pace back and forth deliberating the oversight, a blue haze following in his wake as we all looked on in silence. Eventually he came to a standstill, gazing up at the troubled architect through narrowed eyes. "Then buy it," said Harry. The architect sighed and rolled his eyes. "I suppose I could send them a letter and hint at the possibility that we may be interested in their property," he proffered. Harry put his hands on his hips, glaring back at Gerald with utter contempt. "There's a war on, Gerry; properties are cheap and people scared—everyone wants out of London. Get your arse around there and make them an offer. And make it cheap."

Harry shook his head as he walked away from the anarchist architect, and taking my arm led me to a corner of the room.

"Now then, what's this I hear about you looking for me at the pub? That's naughty, Michael, and I have to say I expected a little more decorum from the likes of you. You could have been followed."

"You said it was your pub, and it isn't."

"Of course it's my pub! I don't advertise the fact for obvious reasons. Because I own it, it doesn't mean I have to stand behind the bar pulling pints for idiots. They're investments, Michael, much like this snooker room. Once it's been decorated you won't see me in here again; Malcolm will be running this," he explained, pointing to the Neanderthal.

"Malcolm!" I winced.

"He lacks eloquence, granted, but people will think twice before taking him on. Now, what was so important that you had to come looking for me?"

"Peter died."

"I know—tragic," he muttered. "I sent flowers, of course, but I was otherwise indisposed and unable to go to the funeral. Besides, the police like a good funeral; they clock who turns up. I suppose Peter's death left you in an awkward situation. What have you done with the list?"

"I gave it to Inspector Foggerty."

"You gave it to who? Was that wise, Michael?"

"It's quite safe, I assure you. He's removed from the force; presently investigating the 247."

Harry shook his head. "I don't think it's a good idea."

"Then what am I supposed to do?"

"Give them to that publisher—what's-his-name?"

"Fallow."

"That's him. He'll need them so he can publish them in this month's edition."

I hesitated while Harry appraised me curiously.

"Fallow's publishing house was broken into the same night Peter died; it isn't safe. Besides, my part in all this is over. Carlisle's trial is finished."

Harry nodded slowly, sucking out what little life was left in his cigar.

"Do you know the best pick-pockets always work in threes;" he said, "one pick-pocket, two receivers. After the steal the Dip, he's the man who executes the theft, passes the merchandise directly to his associate, and he then passes it to the third man in the team; all walking in different directions, all seemingly disassociated from one another; impossible for any witness to ascertain with certainty which one has the booty. It doesn't surprise me Fallow was turned over. That's why we chose you, Michael."

Harry walked a few steps away and returned dragging two hard-back chairs behind him. He placed one next to me and nodded towards it, taking up the other himself.

"You don't like me, do you, Michael?" he said with a smile.

"I don't know you," I replied.

"Let me rephrase that. You don't like my kind—criminals, in general? The thought of someone like me being affluent, respected, if only by his own kind, repels you, doesn't it? My empire, such as it is, was built on theft, deceit, even murder. You, however, are a hard working young man who, if you found a pound note in the gutter, would probably hand it in at the nearest police station. You gaze at yourself in the mirror every morning, overwhelmed by how honest and hard working you actually are. You regard me as vermin, a plague on society that must be erased. The truth of the matter, Michael, is you're worse than me or my kind will ever be. You feel duty-bound to uphold laws whose origins were nothing but a fairytale, rules carved in stone that man is expected to abide by; thou shalt not steal, thou shalt not kill . . . These wise men that make our laws are of a different world. Life has never fucked them in the arse. They have never suffered the indignity of watching their fathers die of exhaustion, or watch their children crying of hunger, or see their sweet mothers resort to prostitution in order to feed her family. They have never queued for several hours on the wharfs in the meagre hope of being chosen for a day's work, or taken refuge in a cardboard box or park bench because everything was taken from them. They reside in palatial homes and send their children to private schools while their wives play bridge and shop for the latest fashions. They have no idea how we suffer. A few years back an old woman was beaten and robbed in the East India Dock Road; she was seventy-two; jaw broken, cheek bone smashed, and all for a lousy three pounds. She was able to give a vague description of her attacker. Within a week I had him in a disused boathouse down on the docks. I personally cut off both his thumbs, and he was told, in no uncertain terms, that should I hear of any such conduct again, the next time I would take his head. I keep my streets clean, Michael."

I swallowed hard, uncertain as to whether I was being given a warning. But Harry, seeing the growing fear in my eyes, smiled and patted me on the arm.

"I like you, Michael," he said, "and Peter, God rest his soul, liked you. He trusted you and I trust you. Did you know Peter and I go back a long way? He was young when I first met him, a spotty twenty-year old journalist in search of stories about villains and gangsters. He loved anything that went against the grain or undermined the government. So I fed him the odd story now and then. I shall miss him."

"Would I be correct in assuming that you used Peter as a form of revenge—on those who were dirtying up your streets; perhaps on those you considered a threat?"

Harry smiled knowingly.

"We all have our ways, Michael," he said. "But know this. For what you and Peter have done for me, I am eternally grateful. The police no longer come to collect since the story broke. Whether you like me or not, you should know I consider you a friend; no harm will ever come to you as long as I'm drawing breath. Anything you ask of me I will do providing it's within reason and within in my power."

He smiled and I believed every word he said. I believed it then, and still do, that criminals are blessed with a loyalty to one another as long as they adhere to their own unwritten code—to honour one another. He rose from his chair and patted me on the shoulder.

"Wendy Marshall," I said.

Harry looked at me as if I were beginning a sentence, awaiting more information to accompany a simple name. "Who?"

"She's a prostitute; works for someone called Vincent Pierce . . ."

"I know Pierce; a peddler in pornography and depravity," Harry intercepted with a snarl. "And what's this girl to you?"

"Just someone I know, someone I think deserves a break. As a friend, Harry, as somebody who will do anything as long as it's within reason and within your power, I was hoping you might have a word with this man Pierce and release Wendy Marshall from whatever hold he has over her."

He stared at me as if he were witnessing a miracle unfolding before his very eyes.

"You want me to what!"

"Secure the release of Wendy Marshall—along with five thousand pounds," I smiled.

Harry's mouth had dropped open, like a gaping hole cut into a granite façade with two beady eyes staring back at me in disbelief.

"You want me to free some floozy and give her five grand! Is that what you're saying?"

I shook my head.

"Correct on the first point, wrong on the second. I want Vincent Piece to give her the money. Let's call it back-pay for years of devoted service. Would you do that for me, Harry—as a friend?"

He roared with laughter and shook his head at my audacity.

"You're a cheeky, little fucker, I'll give you that, Michael, but I'll do it."

-26-

I was sitting at my desk, looking down on the obscured pedestrians and vehicles through my rain-streaked window. The skies were black and rolling, sweeping heavy layers of rain down Blackfriars Road, chasing the unprepared into doorways and under shop awnings, while the suitably equipped grappled with fragile umbrellas and fought against the gusting wind that threatened to turn them inside out. Never having windows in the workplace before, I was like a child with a new toy, staring out at an ever-moving panorama that was a constant source of distraction, and at times such as these, a great form of amusement. When the road was swamped, which it always was whenever there was a heavy storm, Badger and I would wait with bated breath for some undeserving soul to disappear under a tidal-wave of water created by a passing lorry and then howl with laughter like a couple of schoolboys. Today I surveyed the scene alone, thinking it was on a day such as this when I met Rachel at Ludgate Circus. I found myself thinking of her more and more and of Sarah less and less. Caught up in my reverie, I never noticed the police car draw up beneath my window, nor did I hear the voices outside my office door. Not until I heard a knock did my eyes and reminisces leave the windowpane to focus on a man with dark hair and moustache and wearing a water speckled raincoat. He smiled at me pleasantly and produced a warrant card. He said my name informally, as if he knew me, until I rose from my seat and said, "Yes, I am Michael James. He opened the office door wider, as if he possessed the authority to do so, where beyond Penny and Badger looked on bewildered. "You need to accompany me, sir, right away," he said with an outstretched hand in the direction of reception. I never asked why; I never thought to. I simply agreed with a nod and began to walk to the door. "You'll be needing a coat, sir," he said. I didn't have an overcoat, but Badger suddenly broke away from the girls and returned with his and handed it to me. I can't recall thanking him. I simply followed the officer down the stairwell and out onto the wet street, where a uniformed policeman sat behind the steering wheel of the car with the backdoor nearest the pavement open. "In you get, Mr. James," said the officer with a sweep of his hand. "This shouldn't take too long."

The police car pulled a tight, half circle in the road, causing the oncoming vehicles to swerve and shudder to a halt, and sped off towards Blackfriars Bridge and the city. But almost on the threshold of the bridge the car turned sharp left into Stamford Street and slowed to a stop behind a dray that had shed its load, where barrels, some split and pouring their brown fluid into the saturated gutters, clogged up the road. Helpful pedestrians assisted the driver in rolling and lifting the damaged merchandise to the pavement, but the spillage of beer and splintered casks made the thoroughfare practically impassable. The uniformed driver cursed impatiently and climbed out of the car to give assistance, directing the heavy volume of traffic up side roads and ordering the driver of the dray to clear the way immediately or face the consequences. I sat in the backseat watching the policeman thunder out his orders, but I had no idea why I was there or what the police wanted of me. The plain clothes officer sat beside me, occasionally wiping a circle in the misted glass to get a clearer view of the activity outside, and this he did with an air of boredom, pulling out a pocket watch from his waistcoat to register the passing time. "Sorry about this, Mr. James. Won't be long now," he said, focussing on the sightseers who sheltered under umbrellas to view the mayhem. I nodded, watching the road ahead being cleared of debris. "May I ask what this concerns?" I asked timidly. The officer was slouched, his head resting on the window, his eyes opening and closing slowly as if the unforeseen delay induced bouts of dozing. "No idea, sir. My orders were just to fetch you. I'm sure we'll be off shortly."

As was his prediction, we moved onwards, straggling through remnants of smashed and broken beer barrels and accelerated up the remaining section of Stamford Street towards Waterloo Road. The car turned right, back in the direction of the city, and it was my instinct that we would cross Waterloo Bridge and move straight into Aldwych, the location of my old office before it entombed me. Obviously their investigation into the explosion had yielded new evidence, new information the police felt duty-bound to impart. At least this would be one mystery I could put behind me. But before we reached the expanse of Waterloo Bridge, the car glided off left and down into a cross section of narrow lanes compacted with warehouses and workshops, where commercial vehicles queued to load their wares and lorries and tractors shuffled back and forth without concern for the Highway Code. It was a dark and dismal area filled with enormous buildings blackened by centuries of filth, forever cast in shadow by the supporting walls of the bridge rising from the south embankment and continuing on the north-bank, where between a fragile band of steel and tarmac connected the two. The horse and cart had not yet been completely consigned to the Victorian age, and amongst these cobbled and narrow thoroughfares, they looked very much at home as workers loaded on the goods, filling every available space on the cart with cut price everything; a haven for the spiv and the black-market racketeers.

The police car buffeted its way through the ever decreasing roads, cluttered with packing boxes, handcarts and recently unloaded blocks of merchandise from all over the world, where all around the gloom and shadows grew denser as the facades of the buildings grew higher, shutting out whatever meagre light the bleak day had to offer. Despite the relentless rain and dark skies, the claustrophobic surrounds began to lighten and widen, which was not the result of its original design, but courtesy of the Luftwaffe who had obliterated the waterfront a year ago and had since been cleared, creating wide open spaces where stubs of capped-off gas and water mains protruding from the mass of concrete slabs where they once stood. The car stopped by the waters edge close to Kings Reach, and I looked out across the Thames to Cleopatra's Needle on the north side, paled by the haze of rain as it engulfed the city like a frightening, magical curse. A hundred yards or so away I could see a group of people congregated in a circle close to the bridge, seemingly unmoving and silently observing something on the ground. Around them were several uniformed police officers garbed in waterproof cloaks, ushering away anyone who dare to approach and pointing back in the direction from where they came. "Ready, Mr. James?" said the officer next to me. I nodded and got out of the car, slipping my arms into the sleeves of Badger's overcoat as the rain engulfed me completely.

The officer and I walked through the driving rain towards the gathering, as tugboats and merchant ships bobbed up and down on the river, where their wash was lost in the turbulence of the angry waters. Before we had reached halfway my clothes were saturated, and Badger's coat weighed heavy by the absorption of so much water, and already I could feel the coldness of damp penetrating my back. As we closed nearer the officer took me by the elbow, holding it as if he had no intentions of ever letting go. "Shouldn't you buy me dinner first?" I said, accompanied by a warning look. He smiled faintly and crooked his head. "They expect it of me," he said, almost apologetically. We continued on until we were but a few feet from several suited gentlemen. "Mr. James," announced the officer as he released his grip on my arm. A heavy set man wearing a beige raincoat and a homburg hat looked directly at me and nodded, and then set his gaze back to the floor. Between the circle of heavily clad officials, I could see a man on his knees and heard him muttering to a young man squatted in front of him, while the others looked grimly down on them. What I noticed then shook me. Two bare legs protruded out from the circle and one foot was without a shoe. I looked to the officer for an explanation but he simply shrugged his shoulders. Eventually the man on his knees rose up through the circle, as did his young associate, and after a brief but quiet conversation with the heavily set man, they both walked off a short distance; the elder of the two jotting down notes while the other held an umbrella overhead.

The official who appeared to be in charge of the proceedings jerked his head in my direction, and with a nudge from the plain clothes officer beside me, I walked towards him. The break in the circle afforded me a full view at what they were observing with great interest—the body of a female. "You know this girl?" he asked. His associate, a chubby man with a balding head and a saturated suit, knelt down and moved the matted hair from the cadaver's face. Her skin was slightly bloated and as white as alabaster, and the pupils of her open eyes had disappeared and were now creamy glazed openings. She wore a black jacket I recognised immediately, and one of her many earrings was missing, substituted by a fierce scar that ran from the pierce and off the lobe. "Wendy," I groaned. I closed my eyes and turned away. During my moment of grief, the officer handed me a soggy business card. Mine.

"We found this in her purse," he said. "She looks like a prostitute."

I nodded. "She is."

"Was," he smiled, callously. "How do you know her?"

I had already resigned myself to the fact that I didn't like this man—not even in the slightest.

"I met her once—two weeks ago, I think."

His hard stare searched my face for possible signs of remorse, guilt and evasiveness.

"Were you working on her behalf? Is that why she had your card?"

"No. I just gave it to her. Habit, I suppose."

I ambled away a few steps, until I was standing on the edge of the jetty and staring down into the choppy waters of the Thames.

"Then why the meeting?" he asked.

His voice was distant and almost buried beneath the noise of the rain. He had obviously remained in the same spot, even though I had walked away from him; away from the dead body.

"I thought she may be able to help me with a case I'm working on."

I heard him move a few steps closer.

"And did she?"

I shook my head.

I had not seen many dead bodies before, and the ones I had seen were usually elderly, who had been attended to by the mortician with paint and powder to make them otherwise more presentable and thereafter dressed in their Sunday best and laid out in a silk lined Elm coffin. Wendy's pale and bloated figure presented a horrifying spectacle that quite took my breath away. True, the sight of her lifeless body chilled me to the bone, but that was nothing compared to the sadness I felt for failing to help her.

The doctor and his young aide approached and stopped to speak with my inquisitor. Whatever was said between them was lost to the rain and the wind, the passing traffic on the overhead bridge and the noise of the Thames. Within a few moments they walked on, and the officer moved a few steps nearer until he was standing next to me.

"It's only a preliminary examination, but Dr. McKenna believes the cause of death to be a broken neck."

I nodded my head as if I wasn't surprised.

His face closed in on mine, until the brim of his hat touched my forehead.

"How well do you know this girl?"

I pulled my head away and took a step back.

"I know she's unstable, and that she's tried to kill herself on no less than four occasions."

"You're suggesting suicide?"

"No. I'm merely hoping it is."

I soon learned that the officer was called Inspector Pritchard, and his balding sidekick was Sergeant Parkhouse, a servile character of some considerable ugliness who desperately wanted to be accepted by his peers. For his part, Pritchard strutted up and down the waterfront barking orders at his fellow officers and demanding immediate action. "Get the river-boys to check every bridge and wharf from Greenwich to Fulham. God help us there may be more in there," he said. I looked across to the south-side at the Egyptian obelisk, where less than fifty yards behind stood the apartment block where I lived. I wondered how long it would be before the tenacious detective associated Wendy's death and the vicinity of my home together. A black, unmarked van pulled up, and two gentlemen with mournful expressions removed a blanket and stretcher from the rear and headed towards the source of the activity. The wind had accumulated a boundless energy that in the open stretch of the river created a wind tunnel, and was now caught up in the area of which I was standing, swirling within the confines of the warehouses like a mini tornado and making the prospect of standing in one place practically impossible. It was a sailor's trick; standing motionless on deck alleviated the discomfort of the cold and wet.

My sadness and guilt soon began to manifest into one of anger, and it was with overwhelming bitterness I watched Wendy Marshall's drenched and mud-sodden carcass loaded onto a stretcher and carried towards the black van. Once again I felt betrayed by those I trusted. Harry Griffin had promised to personally ensure Wendy's safe passage out of the city with a substantial amount of money to begin a new life. He said he would take care of it immediately. He shook my hand and gave me his word, and foolishly I believed him. So much for the word of a criminal. So much for friendship.

Once Inspector Pritchard had stopped snapping his orders, he broke away from his colleagues and walked towards me, nodding at the parked car a hundred yards away. I never thought anything of it at the time, but a small vessel scooted along the waters surface, and the pilot called out the name 'Stephen' from the window of the wheelhouse which was obviously intended to gain the attention of the inspector.

"Your girlfriend was plucked from the river by a Waterman about ten this morning," he said, ignoring the cry and walking to the stationary vehicle. "And it's the doctor's opinion she's been in the river about three days. There are no visible injuries except the broken neck. Of course, she may have sustained that when and if she jumped into the river."

"She is not my girlfriend!" I hissed.

"Not so touchy, Mr. James; just an expression," he returned with a grin. "Still, for someone who has only met her once, you seem to know a lot about her. Can you explain that?"

I could, but there would have to be certain omissions in my explanation if I wanted to retain my position as a litigator.

"She was a witness," I said.

"For the case you're working on?" he anticipated.

I nodded. "That's how I know her history."

"I see. Well that explains everything."

The same car that had brought me here was waiting, with the uniformed policeman behind the wheel and the same, plain clothes officer sitting in the back. Pritchard swung the door open, leaned inside and murmured something and then straightened and smiled at me. "Thank you for your cooperation, Mr. James." I breathed a sigh of relief when I climbed inside, and even managed to smile at the officer seated next to me. The sight of Inspector Pritchard's diminishing figure standing in the pouring rain through the back window freed me of a burden that had briefly been assigned to me, and I slid my hands down my face to expel the rain from my skin and hopefully the image of Wendy's blind eyes staring up at me from my mind. As the car moved out of the industrial quarter and up onto Waterloo Road, I felt the knot in my stomach slowly unravel and my lungs inflate to their full capacity, no longer restricted by fear and terror. I settled back in the dry confines of the vehicle to enjoy the short journey back to my office.

"I'll ask you once again," growled the inspector impatiently. "What, exactly, was your relationship with Wendy Marshall?"

"I told you," I groaned wearily. "She was a witness in the Henderson case. The survivor! The one that got away! How many more times do I have to go through this?"

"As many as it takes," snapped Pritchard with a menacing glower. "I must have read every newspaper article and police report on George Henderson. Jesus! I was even involved in the investigation, and the name of Wendy Marshall has never come up once."

I dropped my head into my hands.

At the wharf, when the inspector bade me farewell with a smile, I foolishly thought that the car that had taken me there was returning me to my office. Instead it dispensed with Blackfriars Road and moved directly into Southwark, where I was manhandled through the backdoors of the police station and thrown into an interview room that was empty save for a solitary table surrounded by four chairs and an additional chair by the door. On Pritchard's arrival, he ordered Sergeant Parkhouse to acquire every available file on the deceased, and for the past three hours proceeded to grill me with impunity. I had purposefully avoided telling him that Wendy was a witness for the prosecution for obvious reasons, but with the arrival of his trusty sergeant who placed a file in front of him with D.P.P. stamped on its face, I knew my impropriety was about to destroy my life.

After a brief appraisal of the contents, Inspector Pritchard looked at me with a broad grin.

"You said she was a witness, but you never said she was a witness for the prosecution. Isn't that a tad remiss of you, Mr. James?" He wore a gloating smile and his eyes were fired with delight. "Isn't that tantamount to witness tampering? Malpractice, I think they call it. I would think it is an absolute certainty that the Law Society will revoke your licence when news gets out. You may even do a little time."

Elated by his discovery, the inspector wrung his hands and turned to the constable seated by the door. "Two coffees, Jenkins. And see if you can rustle up some of those chocolate biscuits from the muster room."

"Now then," said the inspector, turning back to me. "It would appear I owe you an apology for doubting your girlfriend was a victim of Henderson's . . ."

"The Blackout Butcher!" I emphasised. "Henderson has yet to stand trial."

He leaned forward, and the smugness he exuded was beginning to irritate me.

"That's all by the bye. At present, I would like to know why a litigator such as yourself, and one who knows the law inside and out, would jeopardise his career with a clandestine meeting with a witness for the other side. It's a risk most would never contemplate. But the crux of the matter is you did have a meeting, and less than five hours ago we pulled her body out of the river."

"Are you suggesting I'm responsible?"

"You tell me."

He turned his head, to ensure himself that the constable's seat was still vacant, and then looking back to me dropped his voice to almost a whisper.

"You do understand that once this information becomes public you're career is in the toilet, don't you?" he said. "It doesn't have to be that way. You obviously know all about her. Tell me who she consorts with, give me some names, and you're free to go on your way and no one need know of your misdemeanour."

I turned my face away.

"I'll find out anyway," he said.

"Good! Then you don't need me to tell you."

It is amazing how easily information can be acquired on any one person. And as the hours moved on, more and more files and papers accumulated in front of the inspector; and specifically the last snippet breathed new life into him. He had found something of great interest, for his eyes began to ignite and his body appeared to inflate as if it had found its second wind.

"I have your address in front of me; your recent address," he said. "Close to the Savoy Hotel, isn't it?"

I rolled my eyes to the ceiling. Like all detectives, Pritchard was surmising rather than dealing in fact.

"Do you want me to tell you what I think?" he asked with an expression of disdain.

"Why not? You're dying to tell me anyway," I retorted.

He leaned forward on his elbows.

"I believe you saw Wendy Marshall more than once; probably befriended her and took her back to your apartment. Who knows, you were probably fucking her. And once you discovered what she knew you killed her; snapped her neck. The river runs past your door. And strange she was found right opposite where you live."

During the several hours since my incarceration in this bland room with nothing else to look at but an over-confident, sour-faced, detective, I had never considered even smiling. Now I found myself laughing so hard, I thought I would be physically sick.

"Is that the best you can come up with?" I cackled.

"I can't think of a stronger motive. She was the only witness who could identify George Henderson—your client! She was the only thing standing in the way of an acquittal. You killed her and threw her body in the river."

My continuous gusts of laughter were a form of annoyance to the over-zealous detective and he pounded his fist on the table to silence me.

"Let's see how funny you find this once they throw you in prison," he snarled.

"It's you they ought to lock up," I retaliated. "Do you honestly think, even in your wildest dreams, that I could remove a body from a second-floor apartment, cross one of the busiest roads in London and toss a dead woman into the Thames—unobserved? It's absurd! And have you considered the tides? The undertow in that part of the river is ferocious. Three days she had been in the water according to your doctor. The current would have swept her out to sea, which is probably where she was heading when she was found. If you want to know the location of where she entered the river, start looking up river."

He smiled knowingly.

"There's a distinct possibility the body was weighted down; tethered to her foot, hence the missing right shoe."

"And she just popped up three days later? It's ridiculous."

"Perhaps. Perhaps not. I have to rule out murder for gain because her purse was in her pocket and her jewellery was still present. And if she was killed by a pimp or a client, why bother to throw her in the river? Sooner or later she would be discovered. Burial is always the best way to hide a body."

I shook my head in wonder at his deductions.

"You're hardly Sherlock Holmes are you, inspector?" I smirked. "You have no evidence against me."

"I have probable cause. It's enough."

Inspector Pritchard was not about to endure my truculence a moment longer and, most probably, in order to impose his authority on me, had the constable remove me to the cells below the station. At the door I was told to remove my shoes, my belt and tie, after which I stepped inside and the door slammed shut behind me. The cell was small, eight feet in length and six feet wide and whitewashed from head to foot. There was a small high level window with horizontal bars as opposed to vertical, and the bed, for the want of a better word, raised out of the floor as one rectangular block of stone, on which was placed a thin mattress, a wafer thin pillow and a folded blanket at its base. I gazed around at my small but dismal surroundings and sat on the edge of my bunk. I was the creator of my own destruction, enticed by my own greed and an insatiable appetite to discover the truth. My quest, if I could describe it as such, was undoubtedly influenced by a dead man and his past deeds, who sold himself to the world as a brilliant mind and a great physician, created through great works of literature and thought provoking lectures that were debated in every medical school throughout the world. The name of Charles James was synonymous with everything associated with medicine, just as Darwin was synonymous with nature and the evolution of man. He was revered by his peers and worshipped by his students, and the accolades bestowed in his honour took pride and place in display cabinets in every major hospital in Europe. In the world of medicine he had few equals, and none brave enough to challenge his theories. He was considered a pioneer, a philanthropist, a saviour for the poor and an example to the rich. He gave much of his time freely to the poor and needy, had rat infested East End infirmaries fumigated and redecorated, and set up a system in which the sick could be treated by qualified doctors and nurses from nearby hospitals instead of unqualified staff and interns. He contributed a great deal of his own personal wealth on medicines to combat consumption and cholera when the authorities considered it to be too expensive. He was an expert, an author, a leading mind of his own profession, a legend in his own lifetime, a husband and a father. Yet he cold bloodedly murdered four women and created a monster. He was the beginning of my end. As he was responsible for my birth, so he would be a contributor to my destruction.

What brought me to this small enclosure, to be considered a murder suspect, was the search for knowledge of the darker side of life, one far removed from my own privileged existence, and one that had flourished since the first rays of sunlight touched the earth. It was always there—being played out in the illegal drinking dens and Victorian rookeries, fought out in alleyways by gangs striving for supremacy and always under the veil of darkness. They would take what wasn't theirs, they would steal whatever brought riches, they would kill for gain or recognition, they would rape, pillage, and destroy the kingdoms of those they considered their enemies and even their friends. They lived underground amongst their own kind, and only came out at night to steal, rape and kill, and by daylight they were gone, only to re-emerge twenty-four hours later to carry out their violations on society, and in the same way they emerged so they would disappear. But time brought them to the surface, to take advantage of the system we had created, to undermine the laws and make a mockery of the values every decent human being abides by. Once they were easily recognisable, clad in dirty, ill-fitting clothes, loud and arrogant in their manner, devoid of self-restraint and respect, but soon they would look and act like us. And in their new suits of clothes and their new found constitutions, they took their delinquency to pastures new; to Congress and Parliament, to the law society and the banks, to the ministers, the priests, the councillors and the police. They corrupted us all by showing us how easy it was; how wealth could be attained by simply falsifying a document, or turning a blind eye, coercing a jury or assassinating someone who could be a threat to the status quo. Everything had a price. Anyone could be bought.

The silence was broken by the tumbling of a hefty lock and the opening of my cell door. The duty sergeant, a medium sized man who resembled an English teacher rather than a policeman, stood in the doorway and expressed a friendly smile. "This way." After almost close to three hours of being incarcerated in a small room, I made ready for my second exchange with the belligerent Inspector Pritchard who, no doubt, had managed to accumulate the body of evidence required to validate his convoluted theory against me. “Don’t forget your things,” said the sergeant, nodding to my personal items placed neatly outside the door. I followed him down a long, narrow corridor and up the staircase, but instead of being taken to the interview room, he led me to the main desk. “I have a note here for you.” said the sergeant in a broad Cockney accent. He sifted through some ledgers and pulled out a slip of paper sandwiched between them. “Ah, here it is. If you’ll allow me to do the honours,” he said. I was confused but managed a nod. He held the note at arms length, seemingly to compensate for his long sightedness and cleared his throat. “Inspector Pritchard would like to apologise unreservedly for the misunderstanding and the apprehension of yourself during the course of his investigation, and wishes to assure you that any information or written statements taken shall be considered inadmissible. He would like to thank you for your cooperation, and should you wish to seek compensation for time lost at the workplace, you should send your claim in writing to this station.” The sergeant nodded and smiled. “Do you wish to make a claim, sir?” I was absolutely bewildered and stared back at the officer in stunned silence. “Sir?” he said. I shook my head, as if I was awakening from a deep sleep or my worst nightmare. “No, that’s fine, sergeant. Thank you.” The officer nodded and held out the note. “And this? Do you want to keep it?” I shook my head again, slipping my feet into my shoes and placing my belt and tie into my overcoat pocket. The sergeant leaned on his desk, grinning expansively. “You must have some influential friends, sir. The Chief Constable got a phone call and tore Pritchard off a strip,” he laughed. “I thought for a moment the poor sod was going to burst into tears.” The desk sergeant chuckled wickedly, and I realised he hated Pritchard almost as much as I did. “The call? Who made it?” I asked. Still giggling to himself, the sergeant shook his head. “No idea. But it lit a fire under Pritchard’s arse, and no mistake.” I grinned, buttoning up my overcoat. “Can I get one of the boys to give you a lift home, sir?” he asked. I smiled back at the officer and shook my head. “Very well, sir. Goodnight, sir,” he said.

I stepped outside and looked at my watch—7.55. The aftermath of the storm had left the streets clean and shiny, and the images of the tall houses in Southwark Street were reflected in the large puddles spread across the road. The drains along the roadside gurgled and gulped as they tried to swallow the last of the downpour still trickling along the gutters, while the clouds overhead had not dissipated and rolled black and threatening across the city skyline as distant flashes of lightening ignited the approaching night as it began to bleed over the horizon. Despite the conditions I was glad to be standing on the street again and breathing fresh air, believing as I did that my next opportunity to feel the rain on my face would be while I walked in a clockwise direction around a prison exercise yard. I didn't understand why I had been released or who made the phone call, and at this point, I didn't care; I was just happy to be out. What plagued me still, and probably would till the day I died, was the sight of Wendy lying on the jetty spattered with silt and mud from the riverbed, being scrutinized by strangers and handled with no more regard than if she were a cheap piece of furniture. When I got home I hoped whiskey may help me forget—if only temporarily.

As I crossed the road away from the police station, the passenger door of a parked car was thrown open and a familiar voice ordered me to get in. Stooping down I looked inside to see Malcolm the Neanderthal behind the wheel. "Harry wants to see you," he said. I made no attempt to move and shook my head. "It's been a long day. I'm going home," I replied. The Neanderthal emitted an impatient sigh and stared back at me. "This ain't a request, Michael James. Harry just wants to set the record straight, you know, about the prossy." I scowled at his spiteful reference and straightened. "Alright! Wendy Marshall. Happy now?" he yelled. "Now will you get in the fuckin' car? I'm runnin' out of daylight here." I lowered my head again to see this hulking figure of a man staring back at me with a pitiful smile. "Harry won't be happy if I go back without you." After a moment of consideration, I climbed inside and the car set off. The Neanderthal said nothing as we moved outside Southwark and headed towards Tower Bridge, driving with all the expertise of a nun who only drove the third Sunday of every month, adhering to the speed limit with breathtaking accuracy. "Did Harry get me out of there?" I asked.

He hunched his shoulders and shook his head. “He heard they pulled you in for questioning. I was told to pick you up. Six fuckin’ hours I’ve been sitting there. What took so long?” I was thinking who could have secured my release, and who had the kind of power to reduce a hard-nosed bastard like Pritchard to an apologetic, spineless lapdog. A mile or so drifted past almost unnoticed as the darkness slowly swept over the city converting pastel shades to grey, and the windows of the houses and shops momentarily filled with light and fell dark again as blackout screens were drawn. I searched my mind for answers until it hurt, exploring long distant memories even I thought I had forgotten, until my head fell back and I was staring at the ceiling of the car. “Your employer let me down.” I said wearily. “He gave me his word and now Wendy Marshall is dead.”

We turned off Jamaica Road into a narrow road that seemingly went nowhere, that indeed signposted the fact at the beginning of the street; ‘Dead End.’ We were slowly manoeuvring along a line of dilapidated terraces, where every window of every house had been smashed and broken glass covered the ground. Some of the front doors were open, and the likes of chairs and sideboards were abandoned on the pavement, left there by looters who considered their meagre value unworthy of the effort. Even by the bluish light of the descending darkness I could see that this street was no longer inhabitable. The houses were riddled with damp and woodworm, wounded by two hundred years of abuse and neglect, scarred by frost and eaten away from the insides by woodlice and vermin. The cast iron gutters and rainwater pipes that once drew a straight line beneath their sagging roofs were now gone; purloined by thieves or confiscated by the government and smelted down to help the war effort. Two brick columns centred the road at the streets end, where a high, flank wall run off either side to the adjacent terraces. Beyond the opening, and in keeping with the eerie and decaying approaching thoroughfare, a Dickensian looking building sat in its own grounds. The Neanderthal pulled over halfway down the street and silenced the engine. For a while he looked around him thoughtfully, a warm smile barely detectable on his lips.

“They’re tearing this all down in a few weeks,” he began nostalgically. “I was born here—two streets away; I used to play here as a kid. All my mates lived in this road. It was a good place, a wonderful place.” He nodded to the end of the road, at the sinister looking building behind the opening, in which two square chimneys rose from its structure some eighty feet above. "That used to be Catlan Iron Works, and we all worked there; everyone I knew. It was the biggest employer around these parts—over a thousand people; gone now. Every Saturday me and the boys would go to the smoke, to the nightclubs where they played all that black music, and we'd dance till daylight, and if we were lucky, pull a smelly. My mum would scream all day Sunday to get me out of bed, but I'd stay there till Monday. And that was it. That was me for the rest of my life. Old man Catlan had us working all the hours going—six till six, one fuckin' half hour break a day. I worked the foundry for five years; hotter than hell, that place. I drifted out—become a bit of a waster. Never had an education to speak of; was never any great shakes at reading and writing, but I was big enough to scare the shit out of most people. I did all the jobs a bloke like me could do—barman, doorman, money collecting, and I reached one important conclusion. It was easier to take than give; easier to steal than work; easier to hurt than reason. You see, people like me, what you call criminals, are like any other people. There are good ones and bad ones. Where we're different is we don't tolerate the bad ones. We deal with them, and their punishment depends on their crime. Trust me, they learn real quick. I'm telling you this because I don't want you embarrassing yourself when you meet Harry. He never let you down."

The Neanderthal, who was slowly convincing me he was more intelligent than I had given him credit for, explained that the following day after I met Harry Griffin, he and two colleagues went to Vincent Pierce's home in Vauxall and proposed that he release Wendy Marshall from whatever contract he had over her and hand over the sum of five thousand pounds as a form of good will and back payment. By all accounts pierce had done well for himself, living in a large house surrounded by high fences, and with the exception of his love of money, doted on his two prize Great Danes that not only defended his fortress but were treated considerably better than the girls under his control. The pimp sat in a large armchair with his dogs either side of him laughing at the absurdity of the request; even scoffing at the prospect that Harry Griffin would take matters into his own hands should he fail to comply. "Just let him try," snarled Vincent. The Neanderthal's response was simple but affective. He drew his Lugar and fired two shots—one apiece in the heads of his precious dogs. The pimp had a sudden change of heart once he was informed that he would be the benefactor of the third bullet. "First thing," he replied in a trembling voice. "It's a done deal. Tell Harry she's free as a bird."

The car passed between the brick columns of Catlan Iron Works and skirted around the enormous construction to the rear, passing several independent workshops along the way and a line of rusty containers. From the car I followed the Neanderthal into the foundry, a vast building of work benches, overhead gantries and huge smelting pots. A track-crane stood motionless above us as if it had literally ground to a halt, and chains with sinister hooks and contraptions of all shapes and sizes hid amongst the shadows like ghouls waiting for complete darkness. The air was metallic, and every surface was either covered in metal shavings or pools of congealed oil, where all around us everything was being eaten away by rust. A small light illuminated the area where the fires once raged beneath the smelting pots, and as I closed nearer I could see two men standing either side of something suspended by chains from the gantry. The smell of Havana cigars drove away the stench of forged steel, and I followed the heavy cloud of smoke through the labyrinth of benches until I found Harry sitting on a packing case with an evening newspaper on his lap and staring in the direction of his two hired hands.

"I was about to send out for sandwiches. You've been a long time," he said with a sideways glance. "What happened?"

"Their questions turned into allegations."

Harry drew on his cigar and nodded.

"The newspapers' are saying the whore committed suicide. Anyway, I guess you have some questions to ask."

It was then I noticed what was between Harry's two gorillas. A man, mid-forties with black hair, had been stripped of his shirt and was hanging by chains wrapped around his forearms and secured to somewhere in the dark eaves of the roof. He had been hoisted up two feet off the ground and his naked torso was striped with red and raised welts that even in the feeble light of an oil lamp were beginning to yellow and form into bruises.

He hung like the proverbial image of Jesus Christ on the cross, arms outward and head bowed to one side. Harry's man, the fatter of the two, clutched a rubber baton in his hand and grinned back at me. Harry stood up and walked towards his prisoner, standing in the light like a music hall entertainer. "Allow me to introduce to you the pimp," he said, throwing his arms out. "Better known to you and me as Vincent Pierce." I edged a little closer until I was a few feet away. He was breathing, and thin trails of blood seeped from his wounds and wove their way down his body intermingling with the sweat of fear that glistened across his skin.

"I want you to know I did my best by you, Michael. I did as you asked," said Harry.

"I know you did," I replied, unable to pull my eyes away from the hanging carcass. "What has he told you?"

"Lies, lies and more lies!" he growled. "He said he paid her. He said he let her go. But what he really did was murder her and make me look dishonourable. He killed her because he thinks he's a big man. He wasn't taking orders from anyone so he murdered her just to spite me—to challenge me."

I noticed that Vincent Pierce's hands were turning grey due to his forearms being constrained by chains; strangling his arms and cutting off the blood-flow. His head moved slowly from side to side and he began to groan weakly. Enraged, Harry Griffin pointed first to the fat man armed with the rubber truncheon and then to Pierce—a signal to start another beating.

"Harry, stop!" I intervened.

The weapon was raised but slowly lowered to the fat man's side.

"This man will die if he isn't taken down," I said. "Can we take him down? Can we do that?"

Harry's eyes were filled with an unfathomable anger.

"I've already seen one dead person. But two in one day! Come on, Harry, cut him down," I reasoned.

He reluctantly agreed. The fat man lifted the weight of Vincent Pierce while his associate untwined the chains from the suffering man's arms and eased him to the ground. He laid there, his eyes partly open and then screwing up as the excruciating pain shot through him in sporadic pulses.

The sight of a man beaten almost to death repulsed me, but for his sake and perhaps even mine, I played the game. I knelt beside him, taking one arm at a time and rubbing them vigorously to restore feeling, much to Harry's displeasure.

"Let the bastard die," suggested the Neanderthal.

"Good idea," I returned, shooting him an incredulous look. "You brought me here for one purpose—to hear what he's got to say."

"We've heard what he has to say!" barked Harry.

"Well I haven't!"

I could almost hear the sharp intake of breath for daring to argue with the legendary Harry Griffin, the man who had been nailed to the side of a boat and ended up becoming a leading figure in London's criminal world. He puffed on his cigar bitterly but nodded.

"I'll give you five minutes, Michael. Come up with something or else I feed him to the wolves."

Harry and his entourage headed towards the exit, leaving me nursing the wounded pimp.

"Can you hear me?" I asked.

He nodded his head and opened his eyes as wide as he could manage.

"I need you to understand something. I'm probably the only man here that can keep you alive—or even wants to. So I need you to tell me what happened to Wendy."

He rolled his head from side to side and slowly closed his eyes.

"The clock's ticking, Vincent."

I sat him up and put my arm around his shoulder. His head lolled lazily about and fell against my shoulder. The hours he had been suspended had sapped all strength from his muscles, and his neck was no longer able to support the weight of his head.

"What happened, Vincent? Did you kill her?"

He shook his head.

"Three grand; I gave her three grand. It's all I had," he groaned.

His head slid to one side and fell back. I struggled to pull him back into position.

"You gave her cash?"

"Cheque," he replied. "Who has five grand lying around? Griffin's fucking mad. I gave her what I had in my account . . . back pocket."

"What?"

He was reaching behind him, but his arms were incapable of moving in the right direction and his hands flayed about aimlessly on limp wrists. I turned him slightly and pulled a folded chequebook from his back pocket. According to the cheque stubs, the last was written out nine days ago for £3000.00 to W. Marshall.

"I even drove her to Lloyds Bank in Walworth Road so she could put it in her account. I never saw her again. Truth is I was glad to be rid of her. She was a liability. I told her she was losing me money and she couldn't hack it as a hooker anymore; I had better looking girls for the job."

"And that was it?"

He shook his head. "I told her I'd send the rest of the money on. I wasn't about to die for some bitch. She said she was going to live in Lewisham until the cheque cleared and I gave her the rest."

Vincent grimaced with pain as he slowly began to flex his fingers.

"Why Lewisham?" I asked.

He clenched his fists and screamed in pain, tears seeping from his eyes and winding their way down his face.

He pulled a deep breath. "Some girl she knows; a dyke with her own tattoo parlour in New Cross; always kicking around together. Look, I don't know who you are, but I didn't kill anyone."

I turned my head towards the exit, in the direction in which Harry and his heavies walked, to assure myself they weren't on their way back.

"Wendy told me that you used to be a scout—picking up runaways. Why?"

Vincent managed to straighten his head.

"What has that got to do with anything?" he said.

"You don't want to tell me?"

"Haven't I been through enough?" he gasped.

I stood up and let his broken body slide to the floor.

"What the fuck!" he shouted at me.

"Tick-tock, Vincent. Tick-tock."

I gave him a precious moment to reconsider and watched him trying to turn himself on the floor with arms beyond his control and hands that could not feel. He floundered around like a tortoise on its back and screamed with frustration with every failed attempt to turn himself over.

"You should think yourself lucky that your blood hasn't yet regenerated your muscles and restored feeling. It'll make it easier once Harry's boys get their hands on you." I started to walk away.

"Wait-wait-wait!" he cried. "So I was a scout. So what?"

"To what end?" I asked, slowly walking back. "What purpose did it serve?"

"I just found girls, that's all. I did it for a year or so—before I set up on my own. They paid me a hundred pound for each one; easy money."

"Who paid you, Vincent?"

"Different people; they never used the same buyer twice. It was all part of a foreign syndicate; fat cats with money to burn. You never got to know who they were. It changed all the time."

"And what was your part in all this?"

"I told you: I just found them . . ."

"And? What was the procedure?"

"What difference does it make?"

"Tick-tock. Tick-tock."

He swung his leg across him and managed to lie on his side.

"We worked in pairs, always in pairs," he explained. "We'd rent a house in the city, always in a backstreet and always close to a busy railway station. You could spot a runaway from a mile off; eyes everywhere; a little scared but with that look of excitement in their faces. We'd get to talk to them, buy them a few drinks and let them know we had a big house and could put them up. Some took the bait, some didn't. It didn't matter. There were plenty more out there. Once we got them back, we'd load them up with booze spiked with sedative; they were easier to move that way, not unconscious and still able to walk. Then we'd take them to storage."

"Storage?"

"A place they were kept until the buyer came to collect."

"Where?"

"Everywhere! They were all over the city, but they were forever changing."

I watched him writhing around on the dirty floor until he flipped himself on his front and pulled his knees up to his chest.

"Help me up! Fuck it, help me to my feet!" he barked.

"Who paid you for the girls, Vincent? When you delivered them to the storage, someone must have paid you. Who?"

He placed his hands on the floor, and his whole body shuddered as he tried to push himself up.

"I told you."

"Not the buyer! The buyer collects them *after* you deliver them. Tell me, Vincent, or God help me I'll tell Harry a completely different story. You won't see tomorrow."

Doubled up in his foetal position with his head resting on the cold, concrete ground, he gasped for breath. "Phillip Heidegger," he mumbled, "a Frenchman; a so-called entrepreneur—a real fucking charmer He would meet us every Friday outside Charing Cross Station by the monument with an envelope. I never knew what was going on at the time, I didn't want to. When eventually I found out . . ."

I nudged him with my foot to silence him. Harry was returning with his henchmen, their footsteps echoing throughout the vastness of the foundry, and a plume of smoke trailing above the racks of metal shelving and workbenches.

"Well? What did the bastard say?" asked Harry as came into view.

"He's telling the truth. He paid her," I replied, handing him the chequebook.

Harry glanced at it without much interest.

"What does that mean? So he filled in a cheque stub."

I looked at him and smiled wryly.

"Why fake it when we can easily find out? He paid her, Harry. He did everything you asked."

Harry sighed angrily, dropped the chequebook and kicked it in the direction of the pimp.

"You're telling me you trust this piece of worthless shit?" he grumbled.

I smiled back at him innocently. "I have to. If he was going to kill her, he'd have done so before paying her any money. Why go to all that trouble?"

"He could be lying!"

I began to slowly walk away. "Harry, you blew his favourite dogs to bits and threatened to kill him. Do you honestly think he would have disobeyed you knowing how easy he was to find?"

The Neanderthal began to laugh, probably thinking of the moment he splattered the brains of two Great Danes over Pierce's living room wall.

"I heard this girl wasn't the full ticket; liked to play with razors," said Harry. "How do you know she never topped herself? How do you know the thought of being a witness in court never scared her enough to kill herself?

I was still walking but turned around.

"Because for the first time in her life she had a substantial amount of money in the bank—enough to escape if she wanted to. She was killed, Harry, but not by Pierce."

"So this is coincidence!"

I shrugged and continued walking towards the exit.

"It looks that way. Goodnight, Harry, and thank you."

Harry cursed and turned to the prisoner curled up on the floor.

"And what am I supposed to do with him?" he yelled.

I held my hand up and waved.

"Let him go, Harry. Let him go."

-27-

The following morning I arrived late at the office, having awakened face down on my settee with a half-empty bottle of scotch and the remains of fish and chips I had purchased on my way home sitting on the coffee table. I felt groggy, and the events of the previous day did little to clear my mind. After washing and shaving I set off for work, but throughout the journey my brain was besieged with scenarios of how, exactly, Wendy Marshall met her fate and who considered her to be such a threat worthy of murder. Pritchard's words still hung in my head like dusty cobwebs when he suggested that burial presented less risk than disposing a body in a river. He was right, of course, and now I was thinking it was the killer's intention. He wanted Wendy found. I consoled myself in the knowledge that I had made the right decision concerning Vincent Pierce; that he was innocent and had followed Harry Griffin's instructions almost to the letter. Yet I had left him in the hands of the very men who had apprehended him and beat him almost to death, and I couldn't be certain if Harry had taken my advice and released him. With what I knew about his history, I didn't care.

On my arrival Penny informed me that Thomas Gallagher, or Thomas Gallagher Q.C to give him his correct and formal title was waiting in my office. An extremely amiable character Thomas was an exceedingly competent defence counsellor, who retained a good sense of humour, even when examining a witness, and shied away from the pomp and circumstance of it all as much as his restraints of office would allow. He was a small man with a paunch for a stomach, who at sixty years old exuded all the passion and enthusiasm of a younger man. We had worked on several cases together, five of which were seen in our favour, and his presence here today inferred we were about to work on another. "Where's Badger?" I asked Penny discretely. She looked at me with a nervous calm. "Away," she replied. I stared at her in disbelief for a few moments before I managed to talk. "Away! Away, where?" She began to look around reception as if she were searching for the correct thing to say. "He said you knew," she said, finally. "Something to do with taking his wife . . ."

". . . To Dorset for the weekend," I injected. "Shit! I forgot."

Thomas was looking out of the window and turned as soon as I entered.

"Michael, nice to see you, it's been an age," he said, shaking my hand vigorously. "I have to say these offices are considerably better than that previous monstrosity. You've made a good choice, dear boy, a good choice."

"Thank you, Thomas. You're looking well. Please, take a seat. What can I do for you?"

He took a chair and paused before answering until I was seated at my desk.

"It would appear I am to defend Henderson," he explained.

I was surprised to say the least and leaned forward.

"Premature, wouldn't you agree, Thomas? Has the Law Society dispensed with preliminary hearings now? It's customary to have a preliminary to establish whether the case is worthy of a trial and, indeed, if the government deems it necessary to waste the tax-payers hard earned money on a case devoid of evidence."

The barrister acknowledged my smile but was not blind to the anger in my eyes and the harshness of my voice.

"Have I touched a raw nerve, dear boy?" he grinned.

I smiled courteously.

"Enlighten me, Michael," he said with a slight tilt of his head. "By devoid of evidence, you mean . . . ?"

"There isn't any; none to speak of, neither for or against. There was, for the shortest while, a prostitute by the name of Wendy Marshall, but she was submitted as a witness for the prosecution."

"Yes, I received her file only last week," agreed Thomas. "Do you consider her to be a strong witness?"

I looked at him sceptically.

"Well, Thomas, she didn't look a tower of strength when I saw her yesterday. But I suppose she wouldn't, having been in the Thames for three days with a broken neck."

"She's dead?"

"I'm no doctor, but all the signs were evident."

"Thomas shook his head. "The poor woman."

My scepticism was valid. Only two weeks ago Wendy began to tell me a story that defied all belief, and despite my endeavours to ensure her safety, I witnessed her corpse lying on the dockside, and today I was being badgered by Chambers to submit my evidence for trial even though no date had been set for a preliminary hearing.

"Undoubtedly a tragedy, but it can only serve to weaken the case for the prosecution. We must move on," said Thomas.

"Did you not hear what I said? A woman is dead, Thomas; the only woman who could identify Henderson with the Blackout Butcher. Clearly she was murdered but the police are calling it suicide. Given her history who will argue?"

"Either way it is to our advantage, Michael."

"But that's my point," I argued. "Don't you find this all very strange? Peter Egan, who broke the original story on Henderson and Carlisle, was found dead, and the only surviving witness is also now dead. That doesn't give you cause for concern?"

The barrister rested his elbows on the table and laced his fingers together beneath his chin.

"Forget Carlisle, Michael, his trial is over."

"But . . ."

"Allow me to finish, dear boy," he interrupted. "At present, Carlisle is serving time for the crimes he committed, or at least the ones he admitted to, and as much as many, including myself, felt his sentence to be a travesty of justice, it is final. When I heard that my good friend Michael James, the young man I had come to know and respect and who had made good with his small firm, was taking on the case of a multiple murderer, I could not believe my ears. However, you have, and here we are. Do not cloud the issue with issues that don't concern us. I don't wish to sound a Prima-Donna, Michael, but it will be me on that courtroom floor. As for the preliminary, I can only surmise that because this case has been sitting on a shelf for a year, the powers that be want it dispatched with as quickly as possible. Of course there will be a hearing, but the trial date will be close on its heels. There will be no time to prepare. And I for one have no desire to be caught with my trousers down because you are allowing yourself to be sidetracked. So to reiterate, what have we?"

There seemed little point in making further arguments. As Defence Counsellor, Thomas Gallagher Q.C. did not wish to enter court with nothing more than a hatful of ifs and buts. His job was to win at all costs, and not through lack of evidence or bad research would he entertain the possibility of losing. He opened his briefcase and took out a collection of files and set them down in front of him.

"What have we to date, Michael?" he asked firmly.

"You have no information whatsoever?" I enquired.

"Specimen form, some dates, autopsy and pathology reports; not much I'm afraid."

Penny brought in coffee, and I ordered her to bring everything on Henderson from Badger's office.

"Firstly it should be noted that George Henderson was never arrested," I said. "While the investigation was ongoing, Inspector Carlisle went to Henderson's house and informed his wife that they wished to speak with him."

"He went to the police station of his own accord?" questioned Thomas as he took a fountain pen from his inside pocket. "Well, that is a good start, dear boy. In the eyes of the jury he looks like a decent man doing what he's told."

"During the spate of murders Henderson was stopped and questioned three times, to which he gave his real name and address every time. Furthermore, on all three occasions he was in the vicinity of his own home."

"Another gold star for us!" crowed the barrister as he jotted down the information. "He has cooperated fully with the police and has willingly gone to the station to assist them with their inquiries. Go on, Michael."

"He gave a statement to Inspector Carlisle in the presence of Sergeant Rawlings, in which he allegedly admitted to all eight murders. Henderson informed the inspector that he was illiterate but he was capable of signing his name. Thereafter Carlisle penned the statement and, after reading it back, Henderson signed it. He was read his rights and taken directly to the cells."

"So George Henderson admitted to all the murders!"

"Not according to him," I replied as I sipped my coffee. "Both Henderson and Sergeant Rawlings claim the statement was false; that Carlisle fabricated it."

Thomas nodded thoughtfully.

"Then we put Rawlings on the stand and let him tell the jury," he said.

I smiled almost out of pity.

"It was Rawlings' confession that put Carlisle behind bars, and now he's gone into hiding. Rawlings is gone. And what with Carlisle in prison, you're left with George Henderson."

"Ah!" Thomas cringed with a vacant stare.

I reclined in my chair and arched my eyebrows. "Or am I clouding the issue with issues that don't concern us?"

Thomas stared intently into nowhere while tapping his fountain-pen rhythmically and irritatingly on the table top.

"Forget that!" he said. "We cannot deal in suppositions. We must deal in evidence. Evidence will win us the case. We do have evidence, don't we?"

I shook my head and grinned.

"None! Not one single scrap."

"You're saying these things to hurt me, aren't you?" the barrister rebuffed. "I am posing a simple question, Michael, which is—what have we?"

I raised my cup as a toast and smiled.

"We have nothing, Thomas. No witnesses, no fingerprints, no blood samples, no trace evidence, no cause; absolutely nothing to associate Henderson with the killings. In fact, what we have takes us further away from Henderson being the perpetrator."

"Okay. Okay. Which is?"

I thought for a moment.

"Pathology reports suggest . . ."

"Not suggest, Michael! We don't want any suggestions. We deal in facts. Fact! Fact! Fact!" he emphasised, pounding his fist in the palm of his hand.

"Professor Graves, the pathologist, undertook the autopsies on all eight victims, and notwithstanding the obvious lack of conclusions, he discovered various particles of fabric, and these he attributed to the killer's clothing, and all were different."

"Simplify, dear boy, simplify!" Thomas huffed.

"The murderer wore a catalogue of different clothing. No two fabrics were the same, and certainly none matched Henderson's wardrobe."

The barrister looked curious and his eyes suddenly flashed with acknowledgement.

"Oh, I see. So am I to understand that our client lacks the wherewithal to discard expensive items of clothing—specifically bloodstained articles of clothing?"

"He doesn't possess an extensive wardrobe, nor for that matter, the necessary funds to obtain one."

Thomas scribbled down more notes and then began to sift through his block of files until he found the pathology report. He ran his eyes down the page, following his finger until he reached the appropriate paragraph.

"Blazer, overcoat, army tunic or greatcoat, tweed," he read. "Unusual," he added.

I looked at him quizzically.

"Despite the mindless antics of these cavemen, the multiple murderer can be extremely regimented when it comes to planning a kill, and the clothing in which they execute these kills is seldom changing; it is their uniform, the garb that makes the killer whole; rarely do they change. In the same way a woman will wear her most provocative dress with intentions of a night of unbridled lust, so a man such as the Blackout Butcher will don his uniform to satisfy his bloodlust. The provocative dress fulfils the precocious woman and drives her towards her goal, and the clothes of a multiple killer achieves the same ends. I will of course be mentioning that at the trial. In my view George Henderson is home and dry."

Like all barristers Thomas was colour blind. He could only see in black and white and occasionally grey. Once colour is introduced into the frame, the whole issue becomes a dazzling blur. Ifs and buts are words that have no place in a courtroom; they are taboo. With the presence of Thomas poring over what little evidence we had, I realised we were on the verge of one of the biggest criminal trials this country had ever witnessed. Media from all over the world would be present to see just how the British judicial system works, and whether we win or lose, it would be the names of Thomas Gallagher and Michael James that would be held responsible. So at this stage it was difficult to convince someone like Thomas that this whole case was full of ifs and buts, and no headway would ever be achieved if we ignored them.

"Who are we up against, Thomas?" I asked.

He appeared relaxed as he sipped his coffee, but his eyes were full of apprehension.

"You mean the prosecutor, dear boy?"

"That's who I'm referring to, Thomas, yes. You know, don't you?"

The barrister winced slightly as he said his name.

"Humphrey's, dear boy. Or Sir Robert Humphrey as he insists on being addressed these days. I can't believe they knighted that manipulating, pompous ass."

I fell back in my chair with a groan.

"Of all people not him. Not Hump the Bump."

Humphrey's was a sharp, intelligent prosecutor with a natural understanding for the law and the many loopholes within its complex embroidery, which he would often use to his advantage. He was known throughout the legal profession as the 'Master of Circular Logic' which is the creation of evidence where none exists, its purpose being to corrupt the minds of the jury with unsubstantiated theories that may or may not be relevant but nonetheless create or disprove motive. The residing judge will undoubtedly consider the ramblings as little more than inferences as opposed to hard evidence, and nine times out of ten have his remarks stricken from the record. The trick to circular logic is to convince the twelve jury members that there must exist an element of truth in his theories if, of course, there is no other alternative provided. During the case of a missing husband, Humphrey's proposed that because a wet shirt was found hanging out to dry, it must have been washed to erase the traces of blood expelled from his head while his wife administered a deadly blow with a frying pan. So convincing was his argument that the woman received the death penalty which was immediately commuted to life on appeal. She served eighteen months of her sentence before her husband showed up and confessed to having an illicit affair with a woman and absconding to Wales.

"This case has to be watertight, Michael. If there's a way in Humphrey's will find it," he warned. "How do you think George Henderson will hold up in court?"

"Against Humphrey's—who can say? He's decidedly slow . . ."

"Inoffensive in his manner, in his gestures?" Thomas interrupted.

"I would say so," I shrugged.

Thomas jotted down more notes with boundless enthusiasm.

"And what of his wife and children?" he asked without looking up. "Have they been located yet? A sobbing wife could win us a lot of points come the trial."

I watched him scribbling vigorously on his notepad and shook my head.

"Michael. Have they been located?" he asked again.

I made no reply and slowly Thomas raised his head, observing my contemplative expression.

"Is something the matter, dear boy?"

"Perhaps she doesn't want to be found," I suggested. "Perhaps she believes he's guilty."

Thomas agreed with a faint nod.

"The possibility cannot be ruled out. When such allegations are levelled at a spouse there has to be an element of doubt, especially once the newspapers get hold of it. Trial by media, they call it."

I was still preoccupied in thought, my eyes focussing on the busy street outside.

"And you, dear boy? Is there an element of doubt as far as you're concerned?"

Subconsciously I nodded.

"Something happened when I saw Henderson in prison, and when I met Inspector Foggerty it reminded me of it; you know, that déjà vu moment."

Thomas hunched his shoulders.

"What happened?"

I turned my eyes to him, uncertain of how to explain the moment when I doubted the client I represented.

"It doesn't matter," I returned with a shake of my head. "Let's move on."

Later that afternoon, when Thomas had gone, armed to the teeth insubstantial evidence that may or may not absolve George Henderson, Penny waltzed into my office carrying a heavy parcel that I recognised at once as my father's book, even though it was wrapped in white paper and bound with tape. I paid it only a cursory glance as she placed it gently on my desk and smiled coldly up at her. "Thank you, Penny," I said, busying myself with my desk drawer to avoid her stare. Now, there are only a certain amount of items that can hold ones attention for so long; a stapler for example, a box of paperclips, or a silver paperweight in the shape of a 1923 Bentley, can hardly be deemed worthy of occupying the mind for so long, and if like me you have the attention span of a humming bird, soon the only option is to look up. Penny was sitting opposite, looking remarkably patient. She pushed a pile of large envelopes across the desk for my perusal. "More commissions?" I assumed aloud. "We really must start looking at replacing Tom and Andy," I added.

"They're not commissions, Michael," said Penny with a shake of her head. "They're bills."

"Then pay them," I replied with a withered look. "You're in charge of the accounts."

"I'm aware of my position," she retaliated icily, "and I do my job to the best of my ability and per your instructions. However, what I can't do is pay demands when there is no money to pay them with."

Her face was granite-like, her eyes hard and staring, and the delivery of her words came on a freezing gust of wind that made my spine tingle.

"I have money," I stated calmly.

"In the company account a few hundred at best. In your private account ninety three pounds, ten shillings and four pence. Money owed to you—zero. Money owed to debtors—incalculable. Shall I continue?"

"Obviously a mistake; an oversight on your part."

She shook her head firmly.

"Tom and Andy were owed a substantial amount in retainers as well as severance pay, which you instructed me to pay. You also instructed me to pay Joyce one month's wages. Added to which was the deposit and six months rent for these offices, as well as the cost for new furnishings, carpets, typewriters, stationary. There was the settlement of costs regarding the Driscoll case, wages for you, Badger, Sylvia and myself; bank overdraft, mortgage for your house, rent for your luxury apartment . . ."

"The apartment is cheap!"

"No, Michael, it isn't. It's cheap in comparison with Windsor Castle or Kensington Palace, but otherwise it has to be considered extravagant. And why are we paying Bernie Mansall money for a flat in Southwark?"

"That's no concern of yours, Penny. Obviously with the Henderson case I have let a few things slide . . ."

"Slide!" she snapped. "Michael, you're penniless, broke! And Henderson is the reason why you're not receiving any commissions. They all hate you for fighting his corner."

"But I shall fight it nonetheless."

"Then you'll die in some urine drenched shop doorway, probably of hypothermia and alcohol consumption, and you'll die friendless."

I frustratingly began to yank open the drawers of my desk, searching for the few personal items I had managed to salvage before exiting the matrimonial home and my deceitful wife. At last, in the bottom drawer amongst a mound of Sylvia's indecipherable notes that had somehow missed the wastepaper bin, I found a bank statement appertaining to Sarah and myself; a joint account in which I placed twelve thousand pounds for a rainy day when we first married. Now I was in the midst of a torrential downpour it seemed the only option left open to me.

"There," I said, tossing it across my desk. "That should hold us till we win the Henderson trial."

Penny barely teased it out of the envelope before sliding it back in. She shook her head and sighed desperately.

"Michael, did you or did you not read the correspondence from Bradbury, Clarke & Beck? They're a firm of solicitors quite close to where you lived with Sarah."

"Never heard of them," I said, dismissively. "Who are they?"

"And you never read any of Sylvia's reminder notes concerning that company?"

"God knows I've tried. Enlighten me."

"The correspondence was just to inform you . . ."

She hesitated and shook her head, as if she found it difficult to continue.

"Go on," I insisted optimistically.

"Well—it was about you and . . . Oh, God, this is hard."

"Penny!"

She lowered her eyes.

"Sarah's petitioned for divorce."

I sat there in silence, wearing an inane grin borne from intense embarrassment, and Penny, who was probably consumed by so much guilt for telling me something I should have already known, kept her head bowed to spare me further humiliation.

“So, am I to understand that Messrs Bradley, Clarke & Beck wish to inform me that all monies, savings and investments appertaining to the late Mr. and Mrs. James have been frozen until such time they can devour me in court and give it all to her anyway?”

Penny nodded. “Probably,” she muttered.

I took my pile of assorted letters and began to sift through them, stopping at a thick and heavy envelope with the return address of Lothby & Sons.

“God doesn’t close one door with opening a window,” I said.

“What is it?” asked Penny, finding the courage to raise her head again.

“Notification of my forthcoming inheritance; hopefully enough to persuade the bank to take pity on us.”

It was exactly what I thought it was, but it was only a fraction of what I’d expected. Penny saw the disappointment on my face.

“Something wrong?” she asked.

“Nothing a few more zeroes wouldn’t put right. It’s obviously a mistake.”

-28-

I had always been consumed by an unsettling feeling whenever I entered a church, as though I were being watched intently and obligated to be on my best behaviour. Even as a child, when I would have to sit through such sacrifices as christenings and marriages, I squirmed uncontrollably and was constantly reprimanded by my parents for behaving unruly. It was in the vein hope that if I misbehaved enough I would never be dragged to such events again, but time after time I was brought back and time after time I rebelled. My sister, however, was quite fascinated by the whole proceedings, no doubt picturing herself on the alter with a handsome man and betrothing her undying love for him. I failed to see its charm. I was never able to come to terms with celebrating a bright future when all around were the graves of the dead. For me the church represented gloom and doom, a place we would all end up, where a total stranger would speak with great authority on someone he never knew in life and had fleetingly come to know in death. It was the end of the line, a constant reminder of how fragile we all are and how we pass through life practically unnoticed; how we are measured by the amount of people who can be bothered to turn up. Such a building still left me cold, and if I had adopted any kind of fascination with such places, it was only to appreciate the craft of the stonemasons or to meander around outside reading the gravestones.

My footsteps echoed on the black and white tiles with an exaggerated loudness, and before me were lines of empty pews leading to the alter beneath an trefoil arched stained-glass window through which shot beams of reds and greens across the facing walls. A lone figure of a spindly man stood patiently on the pulpit with his slender white hands resting on the lectern, to which he expressed a sincere and saintly smile and nodded to the front row of pews closest to him. I coughed nervously to my regret, for the sound bounced around the enclosure for what seemed an eternity until it evaporated somewhere in the eaves. To the left of the alter stood an organ, partly covered with a white sheet, the reed pipes fanning out like the feathers of a peacock above its large frame, and before it stood a basic pine coffin straddled between a catafalque. Composite columns rose up from the floor to support the clerestory above which appeared to be forever swathed in a cold and impenetrable darkness. The clergyman stretched himself and looked to the entrance where a sexton waited by the door to greet mourners and direct them to the appropriate pews. He shook his head grimly. For all that Wendy Marshall was and, indeed, for all her failings, I was the only person who had come to pay my respects.

Nevertheless he began his address with all the reverence expected of him, paying homage to Wendy and casting his eyes over the lines of vacant pews and aisles as if they were occupied with friends and relatives. Only a few times did his eyes settle on me, and on those few occasions, when his stare lingered a little too long and I began to shift uncomfortably in my seat, did he look away, directing his calm narrative to nobody. The lack of congregation did not dissuade him from exercising his cleric position to its full capacity, and the flattering anecdotes of Wendy could have applied to absolutely anybody. Like a fairground gypsy who claims to be blessed with the instinct to read the future, the reverend gingerly tip-toed through Wendy's troubled life stating the obvious attributes that all of us posses. He dispensed with hymns, for obvious reasons, and to his credit his reading lasted almost twenty minutes and was concluded with a reading of the Lord's Prayer. On completion he stepped down from the pulpit and moved directly to the interior entrance, the way he had a thousand times to whisper words of strength to the bereaved as they filed out. "God bless you," he said to me with a sad smile. "Did you know the deceased well? Was she family?"

I shook my head. "Just someone I knew—for a while," I replied. "When is she to be buried?"

"This afternoon, I believe. Wendy will be interned in the west corner of the cemetery—in the paupers section. I'm afraid it is all the parish will allow. Her grave will be marked with a number should you feel the need to visit."

"A number? Just a number?"

The reverend nodded regretfully.

"Since the war began, thousands of people have applied for subsidence to bury their loved-ones, and the cupboard now is all but empty. We were lucky to find enough for Wendy's coffin. Despite the efforts of the local council and, indeed, the church itself, no relatives have been located. We are left with little choice."

"Of course, of course," I agreed.

I opened my wallet and handed him a business card.

"Sir, would it be possible to have Wendy buried in a respectable grave? If you contact my office they will arrange payment; perhaps a nice headstone?"

The reverend nodded and smiled a little brighter.

"I will personally see to it . . ." he said looking at the card, "Mr. James."

"Thank you," I said shaking his hand and walking away.

"The gates of heaven will be open to you, my son," he said.

I turned and smiled at him.

"It's been a long time since anyone suggest I go in that particular direction, but I'll take your word for it."

As I stepped out of the porch and into daylight I saw the huddled figure of a woman sitting on the steps. Her hands covered her face and her body slowly rocked back and forth. Hearing my steps she took her hands away and hurriedly wiped the tears from her cheeks with the cuffs of her coat. She had a small tattoo of a butterfly on the side of her neck, no bigger than a shilling piece, and her brown hair was cut short, like that of a pageboy. I knew who she was immediately. She was the dyke Vincent Pierce had spoken of, who owned a tattoo parlour in New Cross; Wendy's friend.

"May I?" I asked, pointing to the step next to her.

She shrugged her shoulders, wiping the remnants of grief from her eyes.

"Free country," she grumbled.

"Not according to Adolf Hitler," I proffered as a joke.

She smiled but only faintly.

"And what would a fucker like him know about anything?" she snarled.

I expressed an agreeing nod.

"He sends his best to you. He thinks with more people like you in Britain, he's bound to win."

Thankfully she laughed and nodded.

"You're Michael James, aren't you?" she said. "Wendy said she'd met you. She said she would have fucked you just for the sake of it—because you're a good man—because you're nice."

"First impressions count, don't they?" I quipped.

"Not always," she replied. "But I can see with you why Wendy said it; why she entertained the notion of it. You're here. It's enough. It's everything."

I turned my head, more out of embarrassment than anything else, looking out at the busy main road of Balls Pond Road and Hackney. She began to cry again and shake her head. "She was my friend and I loved her." I put a comforting hand around her shoulder. "I don't know your name," I said. She giggled through her tears. "Fiona. Fin. They just call me Fin." I squeezed her shoulder and she broke again, as if she had spent every waking hour waiting for the moment when someone would react to her tears with compassion instead of anger. Her head fell on my shoulder, and I felt her whole being rise and fall as the current of despair run through her, yanking every ventricle from her heart. Fin could not be described as beautiful, and the absence of make-up left her face naked like a blank canvas awaiting an artist's creative expertise. The potential was certainly there; her perfectly shaped grey eyes and high cheek bones. Her clothes, like her physical appearance, appeared to have been haphazardly thrown together, the nearest things at hand, without forethought for appearance or pride. After a few minutes she sat up and wiped her eyes. "Better now?" I asked. She nodded. "I think so," she sniffed.

"Can I ask you something, Fin? I know Wendy was born in Hackney, but why is she being buried here? Didn't she live near the city?"

Fin nodded and stared out across the field of cluttered tombstones.

"At Newington, yes," she agreed. "But she has a place at Hackney Downs, near the station. She'd turn a few extra Johns a month to pay the rent. In that game you never know when you'll be thrown out on the street. Wendy kept it going—just in case. I'd meet her there weekends."

"So, you and Wendy were . . . ?" I hesitated. "I mean, you two used to meet there and . . ."

"What?"

She began to smile.

"You and Wendy were cohabiting—so to speak?"

Her smile manifested into laughter.

"No! We were very good friends. And where the hell did you get that idea from?"

I shrugged my shoulders and felt my face heating up with embarrassment.

"Sorry. I just jumped to that conclusion. Also Vincent Pierce suggested that . . . well, you know."

"That I was a lesbian! Fucking cheek! How do you know that maggot?"

"I met him a while ago. He mentioned you. He said you were friends with Wendy. We didn't really get a chance to talk much; he was bit tied up—chained up, actually."

Fin pushed herself up and descended the steps, her hands buried deep in her coat pockets.

"I'm cold," she shivered, looking at my car; the only vehicle in the church car park. "Give a girl a lift home?"

We got in the car, but on the threshold of the main road I stopped and looked to Fin. "Do you have a key to Wendy's place?" I asked. She looked puzzled, took her purse from her pocket and peered inside. "Yes. Why?" I turned right onto the A104, towards Hackney Downs. "Can I have a look around?" Fin looked sceptical and observed me from the passenger seat with an air of suspicion. "If you must. Do you want to tell me why?"

"You probably read that Wendy killed herself. I don't think she did."

Fin pulled a deep breath, her face mortified.

"Wendy tried to tell me a story of girls being sold. Did she ever say anything to you?" I asked.

Still numbed by the possibility that her friend was murdered, Fin could barely shake her head.

"There were lots of things going on," she explained quietly. "Sometimes Wendy and I would walk in on conversations or hear things, but we knew when to leave it alone. You never stuck your nose in."

"You worked with Wendy!" I said, swinging my head towards her.

"That's how we met. I was the same as her—a prostitute, under the watchful eye of that lowlife Pierce. I got enough money together and got out and invested in a tattoo parlour. It's not very girly, I know, but I love art. When war broke out, every man wanted a tattoo; something to take with them overseas; it's quite sweet."

She directed me into a road that run alongside of the Downs, before a large whitewashed house bereft of character but exceedingly well maintained. It had not been converted like many of the London houses, but was instead a purposefully built three storey house on which each floor was an apartment. Wendy lived on the ground floor, and I followed Fin through the main entrance to the front door. "What exactly is it you're looking for?" she asked me as she inserted the key into the lock. I looked at her and shook my head. "No idea. I'm hoping I'll know once I find it."

When the door opened, I was expecting to see the apartment completely ransacked, like Fallow's office, but to my surprise it was exceptionally clean and tidy. Fin walked directly into the lounge and sat down, peering around the room with a deep sadness and her eyes twinkling with tears. She sniffed and shook her head wildly, as if to rid herself of the grief that engulfed her. If I had known what I was looking for my job would have been that much easier, but as I didn't I entered one room at a time, opening drawers and searching through cupboards. Every room was organised and everything in its place, and all the furniture appeared new; hardly surprising as Wendy only occasionally used it. While I was looking through Wendy's bedroom wardrobe, Fin came in and opened the bedside cabinet, and sitting on the edge of the bed began to leaf through a diary. "Is this of any help?" she said. The diary was not a written account of daily events but more a reminder notepad, full of cryptic messages that Sylvia would have been proud of and only Wendy was capable of understanding. I paused from my task, took a brief look, and returned to the wardrobe. "None of this makes much sense," said Fin despondently. At the foot of the wardrobe were boxes and boxes of shoes which I turned out mercilessly in an attempt to find whatever it was I was looking for. Fin came across a page written in red ink.

22 girls.
Morgana.
Christabel.
Hanley.
Marley.
2015N—1.3843W
BLANCA

"What about this?" she said. I scrambled to my feet and took a brief look. "Do you know anyone called Morgana?" I asked. Fin shook her head. "How about Christabel or Marley?" Again Fin shook her head. "Though some girls use funny names to make themselves sound more exotic. Some do it because they're married," she explained. I agreed as if I knew the devious minds of a woman intimately. "It's nothing. Keep looking," I said. At the umpteenth shoebox I turned out, I yelped with horror. Fin dropped the diary and turned her head, and slowly she got off the bed and walked over, staring at an innocent shoebox. "Tell me that isn't what I think it is," she gasped. We were gazing at a gleaming American Derringer handgun, seated snugly in its original wooden casing, with four boxes of ammunition.

I furled back the layer of transparent greaseproof paper and gently lifted the firearm from its moulded confine.

"It's never been fired," I said, sniffing at the barrel as if I were a forensic expert. "Why would Wendy have a gun?"

Fin shook her head. "You get to meet some strange people in this line of business. You can't leave it here."

I looked at her in disbelief.

"You think she might get in trouble?" I said, sarcastically.

She sighed huffily. "I mean that sooner or later the landlord, the council, or some other authority will be poking around in here, and the last thing they need to find is that. I don't want bad things said about Wendy. Let her rest now."

I agreed with a solemn nod.

Fin looked around the bedroom and shuddered.

"I want to go now. I need to go now," she said, her eyes beginning to glisten with tears once again.

Reluctantly I nodded, tucking the shoebox containing the revolver under my arm and picking up the diary on the way out.

For the first fifteen minutes of the journey Fin never said a word, she simply sat with her arms folded, staring aimlessly out of the window, preoccupied with her own private thoughts, but as if to escape her reminiscences she turned herself on her seat and began to observe me.

"So what's your story?" she asked. "Wendy said you were quite handsome. And you don't look the type to brawl. What happened?" she added, touching my face in reference to the cuts and bruises.

"An accident, so-called; I didn't look like this last time I saw Wendy. Tell me, have you ever heard of someone called Phillip Heidegger?"

Fin shook her head. "Don't think so. Why do you ask?"

"Wendy said that when Vincent Pierce was a scout Heidegger was the paymaster."

"The frog!" she said with an assertive nod. "You're talking about the frog!"

"Yes. He's French . . ."

"Claims to be French, but he's a German and no mistake," she broke in. "Wendy and me met him at Pierce's house a few years ago. He was on the look-out for girls for West End brothels but he turned us down—not refined enough. I used to see him from time to time on the train whenever I came to visit Wendy."

"He's still in circulation?"

"Must be," she shrugged. "But Wendy never believed all that shit about West End gay houses and being paid bundles of money. A few years back there was a girl, Clair-something-or-the-other. She was young, I mean really young. Pierce put her with us for about a month you know, to learn the game. Wendy and Clair got really close, they became good friends, and suddenly one day she was gone—disappeared. Wendy confronted Pierce, but all he said was that she'd been farmed out to a West End brothel; somewhere in the city. Wendy went there every chance she got but she never found her. And then that Christmas Wendy received a card, *'Happy Christmas, love Clair'*. The postmark was Hamburg, Germany. She got another the following year. That began Wendy's obsession with slavery."

I smiled as I remembered Wendy reeling off six figure numbers to me and the value of a pretty girl.

The Old Kent Road was busy, but after slowly edging our way down to New Cross and on to Lewisham Fin directed me along a series of back-doubles and into a street of grim looking houses. "Just here," she said, pointing to an opening in the parked vehicles. I pulled in and she threw the door open. "Well?" she said. I looked at her with uncertainty. "We've had the funeral, now it's the wake. There's a pub on the corner," she added as she climbed out. Throughout the slow journey back Wendy's diary entry occupied my mind, not least of all the reference of *2015N-1.3843W* and *22 girls,* and the exotic sounding names, come to that. What I remembered was Peter Egan's leather-bound notepad still in the boot of the car, and I thought that maybe his notes may make sense of what Wendy had written. So taking Wendy's diary and Peter's notepad, I followed Fin to the pub. It was small and dismal on the outside, the windows crisscrossed with tape and sandbags piled up against the walls. Inside wasn't much better; dull and gloomy with a fog of cigarette and pipe smoke, occupied mainly by old men staring reminiscently into their half-empty glasses at the bar. But the landlord's demeanour compensated for the bleak atmosphere. He was a heavy set man in his mid-fifties, with a round face and a bright smile, whose bare forearms displayed a montage of ships anchors and naked ladies. "How was the funeral, Fin?" he asked. "Sorry I couldn't be there, but I had no one to look after the pub." Fin smiled sadly and introduced me, to which he shook my hand so tightly I nearly yelped in pain. "What will you be having?" he asked. I ordered two large scotches, and when I offered to pay he shook his head. "They're on the house. For Wendy," he winked. Fin and I took a table by a feeble fire crackling in the fireplace at the far end of the bar.

"I shall miss her," Fin said. "We'd come here most weekends and upset the locals, have drinking competitions with the factory workers—and usually win. Wendy would always a flirt but she never meant anything by it. I think she forgot how to have sex without actually getting paid for it. I think that's why I got out. I lost my identity—what I was."

"Which was?" I asked.

"A woman, of course!"

I smiled and agreed with a nod.

Fin took a sip of her scotch and looked at me.

"You think Wendy was murdered. Why?"

"Do you think she committed suicide?"

She shook her head. "It wasn't her way. She could be extremely brave; brave and stupid."

"But if you read it in the papers you believe it. It's their way—a form of brainwashing. The newspapers are our only contact with the outside world; that and the radio. And these days even that is limited; propaganda, government regulations and restrictions; walls have ears and all that shit. Wendy was close enough to something or to someone to get information. Do you know if she had any regular clients?"

Fin thought for a moment and slowly began to shake her head.

"Nobody comes to mind," she said. "She was pretty much on her own and paid Pierce a percentage; the ones she admitted to. Apart from the monthly bashes at Pierce's house, Wendy would pick and choose who she fucked."

"Bashes?" I questioned as I slowly turned the pages of Wendy's diary.

"Yeah, bashes. You know, parties. Once a month Pierce would hold these orgies for special clients, rich fat cats, usually foreign, where they could drink and fuck the night away for a price."

"So . . ." I said, turning back to the list of strange names, "could these be the prostitutes Pierce used? Isn't it a possibility they used exotic names like Morgana and Marley—to protect their identity? Couldn't 22 girls be the number required for such orgies?"

"It's a possibility but hardly unlikely," returned Fin. "True, Pierce would recruit a lot of girls for those parties; sometimes up to thirty, but the names are too ridiculous to be taken seriously."

"But prostitutes do change their names, don't they?"

"Some do but not to any great extent. They're prostitutes' not porn stars! Nobody's interested in your name."

She finished her drink and signalled to the landlord for another round. Puzzled by Wendy's list I turned my attention to Peter's notebook. There seemed to be hundreds of short notes, half-written stories and cryptic references, but it occurred to me that when Peter wrote the original story of police corruption, in which he threatened to release the names in the following edition, there must be a story, or at least the genesis of a story to accompany it, and I think I found it—*'A Maiden Tribute to Modern Babylon.'* In short, Peter had cribbed from an original story dating back to 1885, which first appeared as a series of articles in the *Pall Mall Gazette*, which by all accounts shook the nation. It brought to light how women and children were forcibly abducted into brothels at home and abroad, and that the debauched rich used their influence to protect the procurers and brothel-keepers. It sounded remarkably like what Wendy had tried to explain to me, and most probably, the reason for her death. My eyes flashed back and forth between Peter's story and the list of names in Wendy's diary.

"Vincent Pierce was a scout, right?" I said, thoughtfully. "He procured runaways and then took them to some storage facility."

"So the story goes," replied Fin with a shrug of her shoulders, "but he doesn't do it anymore."

"Then why the monthly orgies especially designed to entertain foreign dignitaries?"

"They pay good money. And the things they do here they probably can't get away with in their own country."

I wasn't convinced and shook my head as I turned back to Wendy's list.

"I can't make any sense of it," I said.

The landlord brought over two refills and placed them on the table. He took a moment to glance at the list and nodded with considerable authority.

"Co-ordinances, that's what they are," he said. "2015North—1.3843 West."

I snatched up the diary at once.

"Are you sure they're a co-ordinance?"

"Been in the merchant navy man and boy; I know what a co-ordinance looks like. Give me a nod when you want another drink."

"Wait, wait. Where is it—the co-ordinance, I mean?"

He looked over my shoulder for a second glimpse and shook his head.

"I'm not much with geography, but it's a long way from the equator, I can tell you that much."

He waltzed off to the bar, to talk to the locals, leaving me staring at Wendy's diary in absolute bewilderment.

"Any ideas?" I said to Fin.

She shrugged as if it meant nothing, and probably did.

"Wendy could be obsessive," she said.

"Meaning?"

Again she shrugged.

"Meaning I haven't a clue. Meaning she could be crazy at times. Sometimes when we had been out for a drink she'd drone on and on about how women were being manipulated by rich men."

"And . . . ?"

"And, so what? Tell me something I don't know. Opportunities for women don't come that often, so we take it when it comes. We have to. We'd never survive otherwise. A man can spin a story and we'll believe it. We believe it because we want to. Women need to believe in the fairytale; it's all we have."

She spoke as if she were speaking on behalf of womankind; as if she were an authority. Her replies were spat rather than spoken. And she observed me as if I were an alien rather than a man. Her mood dramatically changed in a matter of seconds.

"Sorry I upset you," I surrendered.

She stared hard into her drink, slowly shaking her head and sometimes muttering to herself.

"Do you know what it's like to be me?" she said. "Do you know what it's like to be Wendy?"

"No, I don't, and neither do I need to. But I do know this. You and Wendy had a choice, and the both of you chose to take the easier route. You chose prostitution."

Fin did no more than sling her drink in my face. She was enraged, her eyes burning with hatred, her body tense. The landlord, observing the fracas from the bar, sighed with exhaustion and bolted over, tossing me a bar-towel. "Fresh drinks?" he asked. Fin dropped her head into her hands while I wiped my face. "We always keep a good stock of towels when Fin comes in here," quipped the landlord. Eventually my fiery attacker looked up sheepishly. "Well—this is fucking embarrassing," she said as she surveyed the staring faces. "Sorry. I overreacted."

"You think so?"

She smiled shyly. "I'm really sorry."

Dry but stinking of scotch I mustered a smile.

"Listen to me," she said. "Girls like Wendy never had a choice; they're manufactured; systematically driven in one direction by their guardians, even by their parents. When Wendy refused to conform, she was beaten. The only way to ease the pain was to conform, to do what they told her to do. With refusal comes pain—lots of it. With conformity comes reward. In Wendy's mind there was no other way. It was all she knew."

Inwardly I cursed myself for my callous remark earlier, and if there was anyone in the room who deserved to have a drink thrown over him—it was me.

"And you? What's your story?"

She sat kind of huddled, her legs crossed and her elbows on her knees, her glassy eyes staring aimlessly at the floor.

She shook her head. "I don't want to talk about it."

And so she didn't. Instead she spent the next two hours talking about Wendy or the intricate skills required to be a tattooist. Occasionally she drifted back into her past life, when she too was a prostitute, but she never lingered there too long, as if she had a sensor inside her brain that activated into 'Shut off' mode if ever she spoke on the subject in any great length. When it was time to leave I paid for the drinks and we both stepped out into the dark street. Walking back to the car Fin never said a word, but when I took the car keys out of my pocket she looked nervously at me.

"Stay with me," she suddenly said.

I was taken aback, for if I had reached any conclusion as to her opinion of me, it was she didn't trust me, or she didn't like me, or both. Certainly she engaged in polite conversation between launching drinks over me, but any exchange was solely alcohol induced—until total saturation left us picking words out of the air.

"You can't drive home; you've had too much to drink," she argued. "And I . . . I'd rather not be alone—not tonight. Sleep here."

"With you?"

She started to laugh. "Not with me, silly. I meant on the settee. Don't get me wrong—a couple of years ago I'd have jumped all over you. And for free. I just don't do it these days—with anyone. So stay."

She was right. I was the worse for ware and agreed.

The house was small, sandwiched in the centre of the street amongst a long terrace of identical, grimy houses. The door opened straight into an extremely untidy front room with clothes strewn everywhere and damp climbing up walls and a one bar electric fire sat in the hearth of the fireplace. A small table was cluttered with American magazines on tattooing, and on the arm of a chair was a drawing book with sketches awaiting transfer to the human anatomy. Fin took an armful of clothes off the settee and dropped them to the floor. "Make yourself comfortable," she said. "Can I get you anything?"

"No, thank you."

"I'll get you a pillow and some blankets."

"Really, I'm fine."

"Okay," she nodded. "Then I'm going to bed. Thanks for staying."

I sat for a while taking in the squalid surroundings, and eventually picked up Peter's notebook to read, and make sense of everything Wendy tried to explain to me.

A Maiden Tribute to Modern Babylon.

William Thomas Stead (1849-1912) was, perhaps, the father of newspaper sensationalism. A publicist of crimes and renowned journalist, he worked for the *Northern Echo*, 1871-80; was assistant editor of the *Pall Mall Gazette*, 1880-83; editor between 1883-90; and started his own *Review of Reviews*, 1890; drowned on the Titanic in 1912. He came to prominence in 1888, when he used the Whitechapel Murders in a radical campaign against the Metropolitan Police for failing to capture Jack the Ripper, also highlighting the living and social conditions of the East-End. He pursued his own personal campaigns for the rescue of General Gordon in 1884, and dangerously put his own reputation at risk with the Criminal Law Amendment Act (1885) restraining child prostitution by raising the age of consent. His scathing articles on the respectable Victorian establishment were a subject of outrage, reporting that the vices of the affluent were just as depraved as the poor, and that their sexual indulgences and instincts went far beyond sexual desire. In 1934 Robert Ensor wrote in his book *England 1870-1914, 'it is very significant that when the well-to-do Victorians gave way to vice they commonly went to Paris to indulge it'.* In 1885 a series of articles about child prostitution appeared in the *Pall Mall Gazette* in which they claimed that children and young women were being abducted into brothels in England and abroad and exploited by the debauched rich who influenced the government and the police in order to protect the procurers and the brothel keepers.

The East-End of London was a breeding ground for vice and sexual exploitation, an immense rookery filled with vicious criminals, squalid houses and prostitutes, who were so unruly and so degenerate, the authorities were content to leave them to their own devices, neither having the manpower to police them nor the authority of which such miscreants would recognize. Foreigners poured in daily from the nearby docks and took up residence in the cheap lodging houses, and desperately poor mothers would sell their children into service or into prostitution for as little as five pounds. Gangs of ruffians rose up out of the squalor to wage war against one another, often resulting in fatal stabbings or sometimes shootings. Such was the obscurity of the protagonists, the problematic issue of language differences, the absence of reliable witnesses, procured alibis by bribes or violence, the police, if ever they were called, could do little to enforce law and order in a place that was ostensibly lawless. Likewise prostitution was outside the law and remained an old age problem, and such was the enormity of the profession, especially in the East-End, that whatever regulations were imposed by the authorities, loopholes ensured guaranteed freedom and only minor fines. The word 'prostitution' was taboo in middle-class circles, never a subject for suitable discussion and only as a form of coarse amusement for the men over cigars and brandy in the drawing room. The East End therefore became the lost part of London, an area neither the authorities nor the middle or upper classes wanted any association with, where the police were powerless and the government rarely intervened. The inhabitants were solely reliant on charity or forced to work in many of the sweatshops and factories for a meager wage.

But as much as the upper echelon detached themselves from East-End vice, pleading ignorance to its very existence, it was blatantly clear that they were very much part of it and, in many cases, reaped the benefits. The toffs indulged in *'Slumming it'*, coming to the East End to drink and copulate away from their opinionated West End friends, to use their wealth as leverage. The master having sex with a young servant girl is not a new story and still continues today. Money is the key to it all, and money is power. The wealthy used that power to satisfy their sexual appetites; appetites that could not be fulfilled by their respectable wives—or even their respectable mistresses. As in life a certain amount of decorum had to be applied in the bedroom, and certain restrictions adhered to. Far from condemning and passing laws to stamp out child prostitution the rich, forever ready to profit from the misery of the poor, did everything in their power to play the whole epidemic down, but the series of articles published in 1885, entitled *A Maiden Tribute to Modern Babylon,* was so disturbing that the problem could not be ignored any longer. Prior to the publication there had been a handful of organizations whose cries of the plague had fallen on deaf ears; the *Society for the Suppression of Vice,* for example, and in the wake of *A Maiden Tribute*, a catalogue of books on the subject began to educate the problem so many were blissfully ignorant of. But there had been some writers willing to take up the cause. As far back as 1839 *Michael Ryan*'s book *'Prostitutes in London'* highlighted the true extent at that time. He estimated that one in five women, between the ages of fifteen and fifty was a prostitute, and that a staggering eight million pounds was spent on prostitution.

Such books had little impact on the public conscience; serving only to be hit-and-miss estimates, lacking both the brutal facts and the punch to be anything other than a reference book. The problem was, and still remains, the definition of a prostitute. A woman would not necessarily consider herself to be a prostitute if she supplied sex for gifts and money in return. Likewise a woman did not consider herself a prostitute if the money paid for her for sexual favours was not her primary source of income. Therefore the lack of definition hindered reform. Yet what the authorities failed to acknowledge was that the epidemic was not the volume of prostitutes within the city—it was the aftermath. In 1850 the *Westminster Review* published an article by *William Rathbone Greg* called *The Great Sins of Great Cities* which, at last, drove home the full extent of the problem. Greg argued that prostitution spread venereal disease and also that prostitution was so deeply rooted in and so much a part of conventional society that abolition was impossible. His radical thinking and opinions would help to entice the government to lay down guidelines and impose new laws, suggesting that venereal disease could only be controlled by the state regulations of prostitutes, that they only be allowed to operate if certified by the government, that they be imprisoned if they are found to prostitute themselves without certification, that they be subject to regular medical inspections and if found diseased detained in a special hospital called a Lock Hospital. Although Greg's article brought to notice the ever increasing problem of venereal contagion, his proposals on monitoring prostitution only served to remind the British government what many other countries had already adopted.

Sexologist *William John Acton* picked up where Greg left off. A recognized authority on venereal disease, he released his book *Functions and Disorders of the Reproductive System*, and although the book was considered 'hugely influential' it was not without its failings. He believed that—semen was a rare and valuable commodity; that women are *'not much troubled by sexual feeling of any kind'* and that male masturbation led to insanity. He does however advocate state-regulated prostitution by providing fact and figures derived from police returns. Furthermore, in his book *Prostitution*, he considers the number of working prostitutes in the city to be considerably higher than originally estimated. He states that in 1839 there were 6,371 prostitutes within the Metropolitan Police area and by 1841 that number had swelled to 9,409, and by mid 1857 the number had decreased to 8,600, but he emphasizes that those figures did not include casual prostitutes or suspected prostitutes. He claims that if these women were included, *'the estimate of the boldest who have preceded me would be thrown into the shade.'* The topic that for so long had been ignored was now on everyone's lips. In 1858 the *Lancet* reported that venereal disease was rife amongst the military—one-fifth of the fighting force of a country. It appeared that when it came to the military the government had to be seen to be doing something.

On June 20th 1864 the *Contagious Diseases Act* was the first of three *Contagious Diseases Acts* to be introduced to Parliament. According to Gladstone, it was passed *'almost without the knowledge of anyone.'* Within six weeks it became law and was applied to the garrison and dockyard towns of Portsmouth, Plymouth, Woolwich, Chatham, Sheerness, Aldershot, Colchester, Shorncliffe, Cork, Queenstown, and the Curragh. Two extensions of the Bill passed in 1866 and 1869 included Canterbury, Dover, Gravesend, Maidstone, Winchester, Windsor and Southampton.

The Act ruled that if a woman was suspected by the police of being a prostitute she should be brought before a magistrate and on his authority be subjected to a medical examination, and if found to be diseased she should be forcibly detained in a Lock Hospital for treatment for a period of up to nine months. The law proved to be successful within the restrictions of garrison and dockland towns as diseased women were relatively cheap to treat and, when locked up, could not deplete our fighting forces. Its success however worked only within the designated areas but soon, supporters of the Act who wanted the law applied to the country as a whole would prove to be its failing. This meant that any women suspected of soliciting could be arrested and brought before the courts, subjected to humiliation, the destruction of her reputation and even divorce from her husband.

W.T. Stead was fighting his own cause—concerning the same subject but for different reasons. On April 11th 1882 policeman and newly promoted Jeremiah Minahan met a brothel-keeper named Mrs. Jefferies who attempted to bribe him. She owned four brothels at 125, 127, 129 and 155 Church Street, Chelsea, and according to Charles Terrot, a flogging house at Rose Cottage in Hampstead, another house catering for perversions in or near the Gray's Inn Road, and a white slave clearing house for the continent near Kew Gardens. Her brothels, it was said, were exclusively patronized by the rich and famous and had made Mrs. Jefferies a very wealthy woman, and it was through bribery she was allowed to continue her operations unchallenged. Minahan, apparently, was a remarkable officer, honest and a man with principles who worked with unwavering zeal. He made a point of keeping the brothels under surveillance and thereafter, in April 1883 submitted a report to his superior in which he claimed fellow officers were accepting bribes. He was immediately demoted to sergeant for making unfounded allegations. Minahan complained to the MP of Chelsea *Charles Dilke* who then sent a report to Home Secretary *Sir William Harcourt.* The reply came January 28th 1884: *"After most careful enquiry by the Assistant Commissioner and District Superintendent into a series of charges which he (Minahan) brought against the superintendent of the Division and other officers, all of which were proved to be without foundation, I see no ground to review the decision of the Commissioners."* Outraged, Minahan resigned and sent copies of his investigation to three newspapers, none of which were interested. *Alfred S. Dyer*, a man who believed that the government and the police were in collusion with the brothel-keepers and the white slavers, took up his cause with the help of *Benjamin Scott's London Committee for the Suppression of Traffic in English Girls.*

Unbelievably neither white slavery nor catering for sexual perversion was illegal at the time, so Minahan, now employed as a private detective, could only prove that Mrs. Jefferies was a brothel-keeper. Minahan was able to obtain evidence from former servants and neighbours of Mrs. Jefferies wealthy and famous clients who included *Lord Fife, Lord Douglas Gordon, Lord Lennox, Lord Hailford, Leopold, King of Belgians, and Edward, Prince of Wales.* The trial against Mrs. Jefferies opened on May 5th 1885, and was a sham. In order to save her clients further embarrassment Mrs. Jefferies pleaded guilty and was fined £200, which she paid in cash. The day after the trial ended the *Criminal Law Amendment Bill* received its second reading in the House of Commons. *Benjamin Scott*, the chairman of the *London Committee for the Suppression of Traffic in English Girls,* knew that with the adjournment for Whitsun the Bill would probably evaporate if it didn't receive support, and on the 23rd May 1885 went to the offices of the *Pall Mall Gazette* and told *W.T. Stead* how young women and children were being abducted into brothels and kidnapped from the streets and the police and government would do nothing about it. Stead turned to *Bramwell Booth*, son of Salvation Army founder *William Booth* for verification of Scott's claim, knowing that *The Salvation Army* had been saving fallen women since 1884, having set up their first refuge in Hanbury Street where *Annie Chapman* was murdered. Booth showed Stead three children who had been used for prostitution. The newspaper editor thundered at Howard Vincent of the CID, *"Do you mean to tell me that actual violation, in the legal sense of the word, is constantly being perpetrated in London, on unwilling virgins, purveyed and procured to rich men at so much a head by brothel-keepers?"* Howard Vincent replied he was fully aware of such violations but never proffered a solution.

William Stead's next port of call was *Benjamin Waugh*, Honorary Secretary of the *London Society for the Prevention of Cruelty to Children.* Waugh was experienced in such matters, having been a Congregational minister in the East End slums where he had witnessed the cruelty and deprivation that children had suffered. He introduced Stead to two little girls, one of which was aged only seven years old and had been abducted to a brothel and had been raped. The other was just four and half years old and had been lured into a brothel and raped twelve times in succession. When Stead approached her she began to scream hysterically and pleaded with him not to hurt her. Stead broke down with emotion and vowed to wreak revenge on the offenders. He also realized that time was of the essence if the Law Amendment Bill stood any chance of surviving. On June 8th 1885 *Gladstone* resigned and *Lord Salisbury* formed a minority government. A general election would cancel any outstanding bills not yet passed by parliament, so there remained half a chance that it could get through the House of Commons and become law. Leaving nothing to chance, Stead set out to prove that children could be bought and sent into prostitution. He sought legal advice before taking action, and thereafter arranged a meeting with reformed prostitute brothel-keeper and procuress *Rebecca Jarrett*, who was reluctant to take part in the operation, but Stead claimed, "*I was ruthless as death.*" Rebecca Jarrett was guilty of all the things Stead was out to prove. She was born March 3rd 1846, and was probably introduced into the world of prostitution by her mother. By the age of 15 or 16 she was living with a succession of men and drinking heavily, and later became a manager of several brothels specializing in procuring young virgins, for the perverts and for men because they were not diseased. Jarrett claimed that she was once paid £13 by a gentleman to be the first with a young virgin; apparently the equivalent of £900 in today's money. In 1884 Rebecca was a chronic alcoholic who suffered with severe bronchitis and a diseased hip. She turned to The Salvation Army refuge in Hanbury Street, and after ten weeks of treatment and drying out at the London Hospital she eventually became the matron of her own home for fallen women called Hope Cottage. One can understand why the rehabilitated Rebecca was reluctant to take part in Stead's game of entrapment, but after being browbeaten by the newspaper editor for all her past deeds, she agreed.

She returned to her old London haunts and met with old friend *Nancy Broughton*, and in the end settled on a young thirteen year old with dark hair named *Eliza Armstrong*. Stead's plan was elaborate and executed for real. Jarrett and Broughton bought Eliza for £5 from her mother, and both were informed that the child was going into service, but thereafter Eliza was subjected to all the procedures a procured child would go through; examined and confirmed a virgin and moved to an accommodation house where, it is said, Stead entered her bedroom in the guise of a ravisher, after which she was examined by a doctor and confirmed her virginity was still in tact. Eliza was then taken to France. When Eliza's stepfather *Charles Armstrong* returned home to find her missing and his wife unable or unwilling to confirm her whereabouts, a row ensued and Mrs. Armstrong fled for her life and took refuge in the nearest pub to spend her ill-gotten gains on alcohol and was later arrested for drunkenness. Charles Armstrong, commonly known as Basher, eventually learned the truth, but public opinion sided not with W.T. Stead but with him. Nevertheless on July 4th 1885 the *Pall Mall Gazette* wallowed in the glory instigated by its editor. The front page crowed: *All those who are squeamish, and all those who are prudish, and all those who prefer to live in a fool's paradise of imaginary innocence and purity, selfishly oblivious of the horrible realities which torment those whose lives are passed in the London inferno, will do well not to read the Pall Mall Gazette of Monday and the following days.*

Stead was out to prove a point and called the four articles 'the *Maiden Tribute to Modern Babylon*' likening the poor children of the East End to the young men and maidens sent from Athens to be sacrificed on Crete to the Minotaur. He brazenly accused the rich and influential of only caring about themselves and mercilessly exploiting the poor and underprivileged, and stealing their children to indulge in their perverse lusts and passions. Never in the annuls of journalism had a story made such an impact, and by the time the third article appeared the offices of the *Pall Mall Gazette* in Northumberland Street were besieged with crowds and a riot ensued, thought to be bullies hired by the brothel-keepers, and the staff were forced to barricade themselves inside with cabinets and desks. By now Stead was aware the police were considering prosecuting him and challenged them to do so, even putting his defiance in print. '. . . *We wait the commencement of those talked proceedings with a composure . . .*' On July 9th, Home Secretary Cross gave the second reading of the Criminal Law Amendment Bill which then went to committee, and on August 14th the bill passed through the House of Commons and the Lords received the royal assent. Stead had achieved his goal. He also sealed his fate. In the article the *Pall Mall Gazette* called Eliza Armstrong 'Lily', but enough was published to identify her, and an angry mob descended on the Armstrong house in Marylebone where Mrs. Armstrong maintained that she had let Eliza go only because she would have a better life with respectable people in service, and thereafter, to save face she applied to Marylebone Magistrates' court for help in securing her daughter's return. Wheels were set in motion and the courts instructed the police to investigate and return Eliza to her mother.

One week later warrants were issued for the arrest of W.T. Stead, Rebecca Jarrett, Bramwell Booth and anyone else involved in the abduction of Eliza Armstrong. Stead's oversight was the law. It was the child's father who had sole authority to make any decisions on the child's behalf—the mother had none. Whether or not Mrs. Armstrong knew that her daughter was actually being sold to a brothel is immaterial. Lawfully she had no rights over her own daughter, and Stead therefore had no defence. Neither could Rebecca Jarrett save the day for she fell to pieces in the witness box, tried to set the blame on others, lied and generally became confused. Stead had little option but to try and win the jury over. *"Mr. Attorney said, 'We must protect the children of the poor.' Was not this the object which I did all this for? You KNOW it was! You know that was why Rebecca did it—and Jacques did it—and Booth did it—and we ALL did it! It was not in order to abduct a girl, but to rescue a girl from what we believed to be her inevitable doom. And, gentlemen, if in the exercise of your judgement, you come to the conclusion that you can take NO note of interest, NO note of scope of the operations—all I have to say, gentlemen, is that when you return your verdict I shall make no appeal to any other tribunal . . . If in the opinion of twelve men—twelve Englishmen born of English mothers—with English fathers—and possibly fathers of English girls—if they to me you are guilty, I take my punishment and do not flinch."*

William Stead received three months imprisonment without hard labour, while Jarrett and Madame Mourney, another of Stead's participants, both received six months with hard labour—the latter dying in prison. Booth and the other defendants were acquitted. Stead's reputation never fully recovered, and getting the Criminal Law Amendment Act passed was at great sacrifice to himself. *George Bernard Shaw* said of him, *"nobody trusted him after the discovery that the case of Eliza Armstrong was a put up job and that he put it up himself."* Despite the mudslinging that followed, by the Armstrong's, the media, but not least of all by Stead himself, most remained oblivious to the point in question, which was whether or not Stead choreographed the whole charade, it didn't detract from the fact that Mrs. Armstrong willingly handed over her daughter for the miserly sum of five pounds which she immediately squandered on drink—such was the value of her precious little girl. It proved the poor would go to extreme lengths for little money. Rebecca Jarrett continued to work for The Salvation Army until her death in 1928. Eliza Armstrong was practically adopted by The Salvation Army after the trial and never saw her parents again. She grew into a fine young woman and married happily.

The next morning I left before Fin awakened, simply leaving her note, saying, *Good luck and take care.* The Maiden's Whisper . . . was intended to be Peter's second lead story in which he would have published the names of the 247 corrupt officers—had he lived. Making comparisons with Wendy's diary and Peter's file, one word appeared in both—BLANCA. What exactly it represented I had no idea at this stage.

Rachel was giving me cause for concern. What with one thing and another I hadn't seen her for a while, and after Wendy's funeral and my meeting with Fin, I felt the need for someone to talk to, even though she was at great pains to tune into my wavelength. It didn't surprise me that she wasn't at the flat, even though I sat outside for over an hour in the hope she would return home soon. And it was while I was sitting in my car, looking up and down the desolate street and counting the specks of rain on my windscreen, that I noticed the curtains twitching in the flat above Rachel's. When after a while boredom began to set in and all movement of the curtains ceased, the front door gingerly opened and an elderly woman appeared on the steps, staring down at me suspiciously. "You a debt-collector?" she hissed. I rolled down the window and pushed my head out a little, enough to hear her but not exposing myself to the drizzle that was threatening to explode into a thunderstorm. "You look like a debt-collector; poncy car and cheap suit." She was a squat woman, barely five feet tall, with tight, grey curly hair that framed a hard face, and one could imagine that if she had a husband, she devoured him years ago. "I'm a friend of Rachel's," I explained, mustering up enough courage to get out of the protective shell of my vehicle. "Perhaps you would be kind enough to tell her Michael called if you see her," I added. The Harridan looked me up and down as if she was appraising me for a coffin, and with tightly folded arms she shook her head. "Not seen her for a couple of days. Went out of here with a suitcase and jumped into a taxi; that's the trouble with them sort." I was confused, to say the least, and shaking my head looked timidly back at the woman. "Gone? Did she say where she was going?" I asked. Again she shook her head rigidly. "Them sort seldom do," she remarked. "I can spot 'em a mile away. All that pretence, but she didn't fool me. Oh, no, she didn't fool me for a second." I was listening but unsure of her meaning, and after she acknowledged my blank expression, she took a couple of steps down that stairs. "Is that what people like you call yourself these days—friends?" she snarled. "In my day they were called clients, punters. Personally I call 'em perverts, degenerate animals that should be strung up by their testicles. I see the cars pulling up outside in the middle of the night; posh cars like yours, and I see the men going in—sometimes women. Makes me wretch! Filthy sods! And you, in your cheap suit and a wallet full of cash, should know better. Don't want her sort living in a respectable street. They shouldn't be allowed to live with decent people. She's gone and good riddance!"

As I drove away, considerably faster than when I arrived I might add, there was only one conclusion to reach, that being that the woman was not only completely insane but also mistaken. Her opinion of Rachel being a prostitute was absurd, as was her story of cars arriving in the dead of the night, but I was intrigued to know where she was and why she was seen leaving with a suitcase. I went directly to the bookshop, where a small, round woman with dark hair and a friendly face was wrapping books at the counter. "Won't be a minute, sir," she said without looking up. "Anything specific you're after?" There were a few people milling up and down the aisles, running their fingers along the spines as if touch would induced them to make a purchase. "I was looking for Rachel. Rachel Porter," I said. Overwhelmed by romance the assistant smiled wistfully and sighed. "Ah, bless her. Isn't it good news?" she said. I shrugged my shoulders. "Isn't what good news?" I replied. She paused from her wrapping and looked up. "You've not heard?" she asked. Obviously I hadn't heard because if I had I wouldn't be asking in the first place. I narrowed my eyes impatiently. "David is back;" she explained, "invalided back a few days ago and put straight into a Portsmouth hospital. As soon as Rachel heard she caught the first train down." My heart fell so hard I thought everyone in the bookshop would hear it hit the floor, and for a moment I felt numb. Secretly I had hoped that David would never return, dead, injured or otherwise; that he would be buried somewhere in Northern France and be just another name amongst thousands on some remote cenotaph. The assistant read the sadness on my face and looked at me with sympathetic eyes. "Did she say when she would be back?" I asked. She shook her head grimly. "I don't think she will be. I think she's looking at it as a new start, you know, away from London, a second chance for her and David." It wasn't what I wanted to hear. "I'm sorry," she added. I nodded and returned a shallow smile. "Me, too."

When I reached the office Penny was sitting behind her desk at reception, slowly turning the pages of one of those glamour magazines that Sylvia was so fond of collecting. Her whole body was slanted, her weight on the desktop and her hand supporting her head, as if she were in bed. She passed me only a cursory glance and dropped her eyes.

"Haven't you got anything to do, Penny?" I said as I passed her.

"No."

I slowed to a stop and turned to face her but she never looked up.

"What about the new cases?"

She turned the page of her glossy mag in a laborious motion.

"Been dealt with," she said, shortly. "Nothing that didn't amount to plea bargaining."

"But there must be commissions outstanding."

"No."

"What? Nothing?"

"No."

I left her perusing an article on Edward G. Robinson and strode off to Badger's office. He was standing at the window, looking out at the light rain sweeping down Blackfriars Road, his thumbs tucked into his waistcoat pockets and his fingers drumming rhythmically on his stomach.

"Ah, Michael . . ." He paused, to look me up and down with an element of astonishment and disapproval. "Been sleeping in public toilets again? You look a mess. And you smell like a brewery."

"I never made it home last night."

He shook his head, moved to his desk and sat down.

"Well, if I were you I'd start making an effort. We have a date."

My mind was addled, with scotch, with Fin, but above all with Rachel.

"Date?"

"For Henderson's preliminary," he said. "Monday."

"What Monday?"

"This Monday."

I collapsed into the chair opposite him and dropped my head into my hands.

"We're not ready," I said.

"Why doesn't that surprise me?"

"Be serious, Badger!"

He allowed me to wallow in my self-pity for a few moments.

"Then I propose we ask the court to assign new counsel," he proposed calmly.

He grinned through the weight of my indignant leer.

"After everything I've been through, you want to assign new counsel!" I growled.

"Have we a choice?"

I dropped my head again. "What day is it?"

"Thursday—until midnight, and then it's Friday."

"Then we have four days. What do you know about co-ordinances?"

His eyebrows arched. "It's my favourite subject. What kind of question is that?"

I flicked through Wendy's diary and pointed to the 2015N-1.3843W, that the landlord of Fin's local assured me was a co-ordinance, and thereafter proceeded to explain how I attained it in the first place, running through the events of the previous day, and even confessing to being drenched in whiskey by an irate tattooist. Badger listened with an air of bewilderment, rarely nodding and continuously shaking his head.

"And this co-ordinance represents what?" he asked tiredly.

"I'm not sure. But Wendy was obsessed with human trafficking, and she clearly lists 22 girls, four or five vainglorious names and the word BLANCA, which appears in both Wendy's diary and Peter's file. Maybe the co-ordinance represents the location of the storage facility."

"Wouldn't it just be easier to write down an address, you know like real people do?"

"You're not helping," I growled.

"Probably because I don't want to," he retorted. "We're beaten, Michael. We've gone as far as we can go."

My eyes narrowed. "Not yet we haven't," I snapped. "We have four days; four days, Badger, to get everything into perspective; to gather all the information and hand it over to chambers as evidence. I'm not giving up now. Are you going to help me or not?"

He observed me from across the desk with hopelessness in his eyes, but eventually he nodded and picked up Wendy's diary.

"What has any of this to do with Henderson?" he sighed.

"Not a clue. Maybe nothing. Maybe everything. But we'll never know until we have all the answers."

Badger started to finger through the index cards on the corner of his desk, and picking up the receiver of the phone, tucked it under his chin.

"Who are you calling?"

"George Arkle, works for the National Geographic; find out what these numbers mean."

I patted him on the shoulder and left his office.

Old Sid was packing away his unsold newspapers and binding them up with string, stacking them next to his newsstand ready for collection and the delivery of the evening papers. "Sold out of The Times I'm afraid, Mr. James," he said. "Might have a Telegraph somewhere," he added. I was preoccupied with the photographs pinned to his kiosk, searching out the young girl he had showed me before. He continued his task vigorously, pausing now and then to acknowledge the passers-by he had served that morning. "Didn't see you earlier," he commented, heaving the final bundle on top of the heap. "Waylaid, Sid," I replied as I scanned the pictures, all to no avail. After observing me for a moment he came and stood by me. "What is it with you and those photographs?" he asked curiously. My eyes were flashing over every picture on the kiosk doors, my hands flapping up the photographs on top to see the ones beneath. "Last time you showed me a photo of a girl. Her friend put it there recently. Remember?" The old man thought for a moment and moved to the other door. "Her?" he said, picking the picture from the mass. I snatched it from his hands as if it was food and I was starving of hunger. "Emily Shaw," I said reading the accompanying note. "Can I borrow this?" Old Sid looked at me as if I had gone quite mad. "Sure. What's this all about?" It was then the front page of a cube of newspapers piled against the kiosk caught my eye, and immediately I tore it from its binding. "Can I have this, Sid?" I asked hurriedly. The old man was dumbfounded but nodded his head. "Of course, but what is going on?" he said.

LONDON EDITOR EARNEST FALLOW ARRESTED ON SUSPICION OF MURDER

I hurried away towards Fleet Street. "A means to an end," I said over my shoulder.

It must have been late by the time I got back to the office because Penny had gone home. Badger, however, was still in his office, leafing through Wendy's diary and jotting down notes. He had obviously thrown his heart and soul into the mission I had set him, for his jacket was off, tie undone and shirtsleeves rolled up. The ashtray on his desk was close to overflowing, and the atmosphere in the office was tainted by a blue, shimmering haze of cigarette smoke.

"And where the hell have you been?" he said, lighting yet another cigarette. "It's all very well taking advantage of my good nature, but I do wish you'd participate in this ridiculous quest of yours."

"I have, I have," I replied as I sat before him.

"Doing what?"

"Research. Call it research." I slapped down the newspaper in front of him and stabbed my finger at it. "What did I tell you, huh? What did I say? Fallow has been arrested for Peter Egan's death. The London Coroner's Court has ordered his body be exhumed for a more stringent examination. Toxins, Badger. They're looking for toxins that may have induced a heart attack. What did I tell you?"

He reclined and drew deeply on his cigarette, and then he exhaled engulfing me in a thick smog.

"I got the answer to your co-ordinances," he said, a thin smile slowly forming on his lips and ignoring my gloating.

"That's good news; seems the landlord was right."

"Oh, yeah, he was spot on," he smirked.

I eyed him suspiciously.

"Something funny?"

"Good grief, no!" he laughed. "The bearings are approximately 57 kilometres south of Southampton."

I looked perturbed.

"I would have thought it would have been London or somewhere just outside . . . Wait! Did you say 'south of Southampton'?"

Badger nodded, still laughing.

"That's right, Columbus, smack bang in the middle of the English Channel. As for the list of names they're meaningless drivel, except for BLANCA, which I'm informed means 'white' in Spanish."

"White? Perhaps it's representative of 'white slavery' or Vassarri—he has Spanish origins," I proposed.

Badger sighed exhaustively. “Perhaps it represents the white clouds you seem to have your head stuck in these days—who knows?”

He lifted the tattered newspaper from the desk and briefly perused it with disinterest.

“You do realise, of course, that if this investigation fizzles out you will look like the biggest interfering busy-body in all God’s creation, don’t you? Undoubtedly Fallow will claim that it is all a conspiracy, instigated by the Metropolitan Police in order to stop him releasing the second part of Peter Egan’s story, and the names of the guilty.”

“But he doesn’t have the story nor the list,” I argued.

“Well, let’s just hope for your sake they find something to incriminate him, otherwise it might be you on the front page of his magazine.”

-29-

I seemed to be moving further away from the truth than closer. That night I took a hot bath and moped around my apartment, and after a sleepless night I got up and moped some more. I was on the verge of losing everything and of becoming a laughing stock. Any answers I had made no sense in their present form, and now they were never likely to. By mid-morning I surrendered to my nagging conscience and resigned myself to informing Thomas Gallagher that we would have to take our chances with what little we had, but in my heart of hearts I knew I wanted out of the whole predicament. I guess now, for the first time since walking out on Sarah, I was feeling lonely, knowing that Rachel had dropped everything to be with her heroic husband and leaving me behind without so much as a goodbye. Still, it wasn’t as if she had kept anything from me. From the start she had made it quite clear that one day she would be back with her precious David, and despite her relentless invitations to ravish her, I did the gentlemanly thing—and didn’t. If I had any regrets it was I should have. Being Mr. Squeaky-clean is all well and good, but it doesn’t fulfil ones needs. Having nothing to do and no one to do it with, I thought I’d take my scotch smelling suit to the cleaners in Fleet Street and probably grab a drink in the Cheshire Cheese in the process. And it was while I was emptying the pockets that I found Eleanor Cole’s Card. I sat on the edge of the bed simply staring at it. As Fallow said, this had government written right through it, and I had to agree. Peter Egan had written her home address on the back, and I thought that as a last resort I should pay her a visit; to find out the truth. But I reconsidered, shut the card in my bedside cabinet and stuffed my suit into a bag before heading off. If I was going to go down in flames, I would do it with honour and in a clean suit.

I did everything I had planned; took my suit to the cleaners and ended up staring into a glass of scotch in the Cheshire Cheese, but there is only so much alcohol a body can consume, especially when one has been drinking heavily the day before and ones liver is going down for the third time. I therefore decided to go to the office. Why, exactly, I decided to go to the office I had no idea, but I headed in that direction anyway. Maybe if I went to the bookshop I might see Rachel, who had suddenly returned from the hospital after finding her husband was a brain-dead vegetable without any chance of a future, and returned to London to pick up where we left off. Fat chance! The streets were all too familiar but the passing faces were different. On Saturday's the city changed. The people I saw every day of the week were now at home—with their wives, with their children, with their loved-ones. I was a stranger, walking like Moses in the wilderness, awaiting a sign. And crossing Blackfriars Bridge, there it was—the answer I was looking for—a miracle.

The following 17 hours were spent scrutinising Peter's notebook and cross-referencing his entries with Wendy's diary, but with the exception of the word BLANCA, that according to Badger meant 'white' in Spanish, there was little else to assist me. Nevertheless, the word had to mean something or represent someone, and had to be important to both Peter and Wendy. Blanca may well be a person, an abbreviation, an organisation or a company, or something entirely different for all I knew. I was tired and frustrated. Time was slipping by me and I had nothing to offer the courts come Monday. I was missing Rachel more than I cared to mention and selfishly felt betrayed. I imagined her sitting at David's bedside, holding his hand and making plans for the future; their new life in the countryside and starting a family; I would miss her. Staring out at the London skyline I could only think of what the future had in store for me—no money, no woman, and only bankruptcy and scandal to look forward to. I watched the sun rising over the rooftops, illuminating the streets and sparkling off the church spires and glistening across the Thames. I would miss this panoramic view, because as sure as God I would be forced to vacate the premises once the world discovered I was a fake. The city was not yet quite awake. Only a few cars moved up and down the embankment, and the odd pedestrian en-route to wherever took a moment to stare into the river and, most probably, contemplate their own future—hopefully with more optimism than me. In my despondent state I dropped my stare to the car park below and to the shiny green Jaguar that once belonged to Peter and had been given to me by his wife as a gift. I smiled, and for a while I thought of Peter and his blatant disregard for authority. And then it occurred to me. I found Peter's notebook in the boot of the car, concealed within the tyre-well, and he said that his reference notes were kept about his person—i.e. his car. There had to be more. Within the hour I had completely excavated the rear of the Jaguar—spare wheel, car-jack and handle, mats and manufacturers accompanying toolkit in canvas wraparound holdall, but no papers, no reference notes and no other books. Yet I knew Peter would never have left to chance leaving such important information in his house, and he could hardly rely on memory, given his insatiable appetite for alcohol. I emptied the glove-compartment, checked the sun-visors, searched the pockets in the doors and behind the seats and prized up the parcel-shelf to peek beneath. Finally I found myself sitting in the backseat, looking around the interior for any nook and cranny where papers could be successfully concealed, and reaching the conclusion that there weren't any I hadn't already investigated, I decided to abandon the search and climbed out. That was when I heard it. That was when I felt it—a slight undulation of the seat, two or three grinding clicks; the sensation that something was not quite right. The leather bench-seat lifted easily, and as if I had discovered the Holy Grail, I cried with glee at the sight of a leather satchel lying on the infrastructure of the flooring.

I spread out the contents of the case on the dining-table; all loose-leaf and all typed. Several were appertaining to Peter's original story, about police corruption, Inspector Carlisle and Sergeant Rawlings, but there were papers obviously destined to make up the second story; the story that would have explained the purpose of the corruption and, hopefully, expose the individuals or organisation behind it. At first BLANCA, or moreover an explanation as to its true meaning, did not seem apparent, not until I started to read what I thought was a brief history of London. Between 100 BC and AD 43 southern Britain was occupied by the Belgae, invaders from north-eastern Gaul, who by all accounts were not primitive by any stretch of the imagination, trading in pottery, minting gold and bronze coins, exporting cattle, hides, metal, dogs and slaves. One particular Belgic tribe, the Catuvellauni became dominant above all others, but the Roman Empire who had been watching Britain most closely never considered them to be a threat and Caesar took a political rather than a military stand to abandon their conquest. Emperor Claudius, however, took a different view and ordered the taking of Britain to inject a little morale into his otherwise unimpressed Empire. And so in AD 43, a Roman invasion of 40,000 landed on the east and south coasts of England, and after winning a battle against the Catuvellauni, made their way across the Thames and set up camp somewhere near Westminster. It was then a nameless and barren marshland, uninhabited by the Belgae or any other race, owing to the possibility of flooding and the hard, clay soil unsuitable for farming. The name *Londinion* was taken from the name of the Roman settlement, derived from the word *lond,* meaning *wild.* Under the rule of Emperor Claudius the Romans set to work building a new empire on foreign shores, constructing a basilica and forum at Cornhill, building roads and a bridge across the river, as well as houses and grain-stores. The layout of the city, or at least the beginnings, were sparse to say the least; a ribbon development where wooden houses and shops hugged the roads only and did not overspill beyond. The project was short-lived, for in AD 60 Boudicca, Queen of Iceni, took offence when her Norfolk kingdom was under threat of Roman rule and promptly waged war on the city and burned it to the ground.

Around AD 80 and 120 Londinium, as it was now called, was under the rule of Flavian Emperors Domitian and Trajen, who were responsible for turning the city into a thriving metropolis. A new basilica and forum was built where the originals once stood—the largest outside Rome itself, and a grand palace for Governor Suetonius was constructed on a riverside five acre site that now lies buried beneath Cannon Street Station. London was governed from the basilica and was run by two senior and two junior magistrates as well as a town council of one hundred men. These officials were responsible for taxation, justice, policing, public order, administration, provincial revenues, the licencing of tradesmen and businesses, water supplies and drainage, market control, public contractors, and the supply and sales of foodstuffs. The great Roman historian Tacitus, who had more than a passing interest in the distant outpost called Britain, wrote vigorously regarding the hostility the British had for their new masters, highlighting brutality, high taxation, the theft of land and houses for ex-soldiers and failing to win the trust of the population. It was Emperor Trajen who inadvertently set the wheels in motion for a secret organisation known as BLANCA. Despite the claims of historians that London was neither a settlement nor a stronghold, Trajen commissioned a 12 acre fort to be constructed to accommodate 1,000 soldiers. Around AD 200, thousands of men were employed to dig a defensive ditch 2 metres deep and two miles long and construct a wall 6 metres high around the city from 85,000 tons of ragstone, incorporating the fort in the north east corner at Cripplegate, encompassing 330 acres—the city.

It was estimated that some 120,000 people occupied the city within the walled area, and the Romans created public facilities including a bath-house at the junction of Upper Thames Street and Huggin Hill which offered a steam room, warm and cold room and cold plunge, serving the purpose of hygiene, relaxation, exercise and, of course, sex. As well as bringing civility to British shores, the conquerors also brought depravity and debauchery. It is believed that the origins of BLANCA was established by several wealthy businessmen who, at their regular meetings at the bath-house, spoke confidentially about the countless accusations levelled at the soldiery by alleged rape victims. Initially the basilica dismissed the claims, associating the indictments as nothing more than unfounded complaints from a minority of hostile natives, but the same problem was emanating from other Roman towns; Camulodunum, (Colchester) Verulamium, (St. Albans) and Lindum (Lincoln); all heavily populated by army personnel. To appease a troubled nation the newly appointed Emperor Hadrian offered up seventeen low-ranking soldiers who, after a brief hearing were found guilty as charged, and had them flogged in full public view in St. Bartholomew's Square. But the accusations still came thick and fast and soon the charges of rape were becoming an epidemic. Barrilius, one of the several businessmen and self-elected leader, had the foresight to realise that thousands of soldiers could not be incarcerated for long periods without repercussions and the need to fulfil their sexual desires. He therefore proposed that girls would be taken to the forts and barracks to indulge the soldiers and take part in what was a degenerate Roman pastime—orgies. The girls would not be allowed to return to their environment in case of reprisals, and after having served their purpose would be sold off into slavery.

Human trafficking are bywords for slavery, a huge and profitable industry that remained unchallenged for centuries and was a contributory factor in fashioning the world as we know it. It was, and in many ways, still is an integral way of life. In ancient times both Rome and Greece, who had an abundance of wealth to lavish on development, relied heavily on slaves to build their cities and roads. Emperor Claudius commissioned Ostia, a vast harbour in which wild beasts, grain and slaves were unloaded from far off continents, and despite the compassionate pleas of great Roman thinkers like Pliny and Cicero, slaves were often cruelly treated, flogged and sometimes crucified. When Rome began to fall to the powers of the church an element of respectability was initiated and slaves were used as serfs and peasants. Slavery was at its height by the 15th century, with explorers discovering new territories and soon the Danes, Spanish, Portuguese and English established themselves as slave traders. At this point in history human trafficking was a global industry. The Atlantic slave trade exploited the people of West Africa, forcing most into service in colonies in the Western Hemisphere, but such was their plight many died—not at the hands of their masters—but by suicide. John Hawkins began the English equivalent in 1562 and set up trade routes to West Africa and the Caribbean, and later the Dutch prospered trading in North and South America. An estimated eight to ten million were taken across the middle passage of America, and English cities such as Bristol and Liverpool were established on slavery.

In Rome the import and export and the selling of slaves was a thoroughly organised business and all slaves were considered the property of Rome. *'Servus Publicus'* were slaves owned by the people of Rome and worked in the public sector—temples and municipalities. Under Roman law a trader was not allowed to sell defective goods and those who purchased a slave and who was not enlightened as to any defects was entitled to his money back within a six month period; slaves with no guarantee were made to wear caps. It was not illegal for a mother to sell her children in lieu of an unpaid debt, and thereafter for the children to be entered into slavery and shipped abroad. So cavalier was the act of selling slaves Julius Caesar sold the entire population of a conquered region of Gaul—53.000—to traders in a single breath. But as distant continents became more accessible a different slave was seen in the market place, and the olive skinned, dark haired Italians bartered for fair, blonde, blue eyed beauties trafficked from Sweden and Scandinavia; these would undoubtedly be purchased for sexual purposes and bought by the older and richer man. The sexual exploits of the Romans have been misconstrued by the west ever since the rise of Christianity and their laws concerning adultery differ greatly from what we now consider the norm. It was not considered perverted for the old, decrepit man who purchased the fair maiden at auction to take her home. Sexual intercourse was not considered adulterous if performed with someone of a lower class, and a wife may allow and even take part if the introduction of young blood helped to rekindle her own sexual relationship with her spouse. It was forbidden, however, for a man to have sex with a freeborn *(stuprum)* a common streetwalker, which was punishable by death. The profile on Roman wives and their sexual proclivities is not well documented, but what is known is most married for wealth and property, which meant an older and affluent husband, and she may covertly be inclined to use a slave to fulfil her own sexual needs. In the same way, slaves were purchased specifically for homosexual purposes, of which history informs us, were plentiful in ancient Rome. Sex slaves, or Comfort slaves as they became known, were targeted and sold at exorbitant prices.

In Pagan times sex was of no value whatsoever, and sharing a meal was considered more intimate than the act of copulation. In a Roman household sex was easily accessible—between man and wife, man and slave, father and daughter or brother and sister; incest was not a crime, and there was no limit to age and gender. As sex with a prostitute did not constitute adultery, so fornication between father and step-daughter was not considered perverted. A master may well sire several children from both his wife and the servants under his jurisdiction, and later perform sex with them. Even though he was the true father, children born outside the 'official family' were not deemed to be related. In the same way a boy from the official family and a girl born to a former mistress could legally have a sexual relationship even though they had the same father. As debauched and depraved as it sounds there was humility in the Romans' approach to sex and it was never spoken of in public; sex for the sake of it was a very private affair even though it was considered to be worthless. They despised the Greeks who looked upon sex as a pleasurable art which Rome considered decadent. Despite the availability and, indeed the temptation, the Romans exercised a great deal of self-constraint as too much sex was frowned upon and seen as a form of weakness, which may account for the subject being taboo. It was believed that habitual copulation was a character flaw and a sign of effeminacy, and even Pompey was looked upon as an effeminate lecher because of his displays of affection towards his wife Julia. This instilled act of self-control may also account for the lack of abuse against their *fides* (servants) and why the Romans sexual exploits were confined to their private quarters. As much as the term 'orgies' has been exploited and exaggerated through literature and film, they were a regular occurrence throughout Rome but condemned by the authorities and performed behind closed doors. A wealthy Roman could afford the luxury of entertainers and dancers, which more often than not transpired into orgies, but the majority opted for simpler and cheaper forms of sexual gratification by joining religious sects like Dionysus or Bacchus from Greece and the Orient in which to indulge their wonton desires. Likewise they would take place in bath houses with slaves and hired prostitutes. The decline of the Roman Empire did not extinguish their concealment of their desires or those they sought to exploit. By the 1700s antislavery campaigns contributed to the decline in slavery, and no thanks to the writings of Voltaire, the preaching of Wesley and the ideals of Rousseau, many nations outlawed slavery, and the British Empire abolished the act in 1833. France freed its bonded labour from all its colonies in 1848, and later the civil war led to freeing its slaves in America.

There is no precise definition of sexual trafficking for the purpose of exploitation but it loosely defines the term as an 'organised movement of people between countries or within countries for sex work by using physical coercion'. Removing the element of 'coercion' and/or 'deception', the definition is dramatically altered and appears only to facilitate those willing to participate. Trafficked women and children are promised work in domestic service but inevitably end up in brothels all over the world, and the laws which exist to protect those who choose to prostitute themselves and the client are somewhat dubious. For instance, in countries such as Sweden, Iceland and Norway, although prostitution is legal it is illegal to pay for sex and it is the client who is guilty of committing a crime and not the prostitute. In Europe the laws on prostitution vary and are commonly vague in their interpretation. A known prostitute cannot be arrested for soliciting on the streets (although in America she can be charged with vagrancy) providing she keeps moving and does not remain static, and should by chance she is arrested and charged, the fines are so minimal that no deterrent exists to prevent reoffending. It is extremely difficult for the authorities to affix a penalty on an occupation that is devoid of intent or whether the act is forced or voluntary. The obscurity and lack of definition regarding prostitution prevents the courts from implicating stronger measures on the offender but, more importantly, on the organisation involved. The word 'prostitute' derives from the Latin '*prostituta*'—'*prostituere*', meaning to '*set forth in public, to expose to dishonour, to prostitute, to put to unworthy use*'. The enormity of prostitution is globally estimated to be $100 billion.

When considering the staggering sums accrued, it is not surprising that slavery went underground on its abolition only to remerge under the heading of Human Trafficking. The principal is unchanged but the procedure is lawless and susceptible to all manner of deviancy. Unlike Rome, who monitored their slaves with impeccable accuracy, traffickers are unrestrained and unaccountable. Organised trafficking by large consortiums impose their own restrictions on those who execute and oversee the process, thus guaranteeing an element of safety for the abductee—at least until they are sold. Statistics account from between 500,000 to 800,000 women trafficked in Europe every year, and is the second to largest illegal trade in the world—the first being drugs. A woman sold into prostitution would be expected to service 30 men a day and forced to live in diabolical conditions. Given the advancement of transportation, the invention of the plane, power driven boats and faster trains, a trafficked victim can be spirited out of the country within hours, whereas in the days of the Roman Empire a journey could take between 40 and 105 days. The recorded victims trafficked vary from one country to another, and contrary to belief they are not transported to the poorer countries on the globe. In the Netherlands the figure is between 1,000 and 7,000 every year, in Germany 775, Greece between 13,000 to 14,000, Switzerland 3000, Belgium 418, Austria 108, and Spain 1,035. In Amsterdam between 8000 to 11,000 prostitutes blatantly ply their trade or display themselves in shop windows for the purpose of selling sex, of which 75% are from Eastern Europe, Africa and Asia, and 70% have no immigration papers. In Asia over 200,000 Nepalese girls are trafficked to India and sold into prostitution, and in Africa, *Trokosi* (Ritual Servitude) forcibly incarcerate thousands of young girls and women in traditional shrines as 'wives to the gods' where priests perform sexual functions in the gods' absence.

The origins of Bonded Labour date back to when a man voluntarily found work in the American colonies and was literally indebted to the owner for the cost of transport and accommodation to which he was expected to work, sometimes for many years, to pay off the debt; thereafter he would be considered the property of the owner—a chattel, a slave. The same rule is imposed on those trafficked and sold into prostitution, thus creating a situation of Debt Bondage in which a person pledges themselves against the loan. The signing of a contract appears, at least on the face of it, to be an amicable agreement between both parties and absolves the traffickers of any wrongdoing. Such underhanded tactics were recognised when trafficking was at its height in the 1880's and the likes of William Stead and anti-campaigners forced parliament to pass the Criminal Law Amendment Act in 1885, raising the age of consent from 13 to 16. Not that this was a deterrent for organised crime; global trafficking is estimated at $31.6 billion. Human trafficking is responsible for the abduction of 1.2 million children who are sold into prostitution and pornography, and a child in Asia can be sold for as little as 10 dollars. Suffice to say the majority are women and young girls who are systematically introduced into the world of prostitution, pornography and strip clubs. They are left in no doubt that escape is futile and work under the constant threat of violence and even death. They are given a basic wage and forced to live in squalid conditions usually thousands of miles from home.

Inconceivable is the fact that today there are 27 million people held in slavery illegally, which means there are more now than were trafficked from Africa during 300 years of the trans-Atlantic slave trade; the most at any time in history. In America a person is trafficked every ten minutes—in the world, every sixty seconds, and half of the abducted 200.000 are children at an estimated age of 13 years old. Of the 2.8 million children who live on the streets, including runaways, a trafficked victim only has a 48 hour window in which to be found. Human trafficking is now a worldwide epidemic but more prevalent in Asia, Europe, Oceania, Africa, Middle East, Central America, Caribbean, and South and North America. Women make up 77% of trafficking cases with sexual exploitation at 87%. In the United Kingdom trafficked victims are from Lithuania, Russia, Albania and the Ukraine, and of the estimated 80.000 women who work the streets, 3 out of 4 started at the age of 21 years old, though many can be as young as 12. The heinous practice covers a wide spectrum of immorality, defined as the illegal activities of child labour, child laundering, comfort women, sexual exploitation, debt bondage, forced labour, forced prostitution, illegal immigration, kidnapping, smuggling and organised crime. The lesser known trade-routes of traffickers are widespread and forever changing, but the main global trade-routes have been retained ever since slavery was officially abolished. Victims procured in Argentina and Chile are transported to the United States of America, and those abducted in Thailand are sent to Australia; Brazil to France and Japan; Russia to Canada, Britain, Japan and South Africa; China to Canada; Britain to America; Germany to France, China and Syria; Africa to Thailand; and Central Africa to Saudi Arabia. From any one of those destinations the victims can be purchased by independent agents and relocated to another country; perhaps even a different continent.

The statistics relating to victims who are forced into prostitution reveal that 87% are reliant on heroin, and 80.000 suffer rape or attempted rape. These measures are purposefully initiated by the pimps and gangs who control prostitution within the towns and cities the victims are trafficked to, and by supplying drugs they ensure an escalating debt that can never be repaid.

By late afternoon Badger was sitting on my settee reading Peter's story with undue concern, occasionally disappearing behind a screen of white cigarette smoke and laboriously thumbing the pages as if every written word was a chore he would rather not undertake. I sat on the chair opposite awaiting his valued opinion, and when at last his eyes looked up and the haze of smog evaporated, he shook his head.

"So—what does it all mean? And why interrupt my precious Sunday with telephone calls and irate ranting's based on an unfounded story? My wife made a roast."

He tossed the story onto the coffee-table as though he was discarding yesterday's newspaper, and thereafter he folded his arms looking decidedly perturbed.

"It proves the abduction of hundreds of young girls isn't the work of a handful of perverts but the result of an organisation dating back thousands of years," I argued.

"But is it true?" questioned my associate doubtfully.

"Of course it's true! Peter wrote it."

"So he might have, Michael, and it is the result of his original story that has got us in this Godforsaken mess. Have you the slightest inclination as to what lies ahead of you? And now—with the world falling down around your ears—you want me to be part of a mad story that may or may not implicate an organisation so secret that nobody alive in the civilized world has ever heard of. Has it crossed your mind that the story may just be pure fantasy? Furthermore, you have less than twenty-four hours before the preliminary hearing and you're focussing on an unfounded fable." He lifted the story and flapped the pages at me. "And what does BLANCA actually mean anyway? Your intrepid hack fails to explain it."

I shrugged my shoulders pathetically.

"My point exactly," said Badger knowingly. "It isn't my intention to speak ill of the dead, but Peter Egan has written a half-arsed story that, as far as we know, cannot be substantiated . . . by anyone. Forget the bloody story and concentrate on the hearing."

I took the typed pages from him and briefly considered the contents.

"It isn't a fable," I disagreed. "Judge Newland knew of it . . ."

"So you said, and without a single shred of evidence to back it up."

"Perhaps BLANCA represents the initials of each founding member of the organisation. There were several, and we know one of them was called Barrilius; it's a possibility, isn't it?"

My friend appeared more concerned with his own future than spending a Sunday afternoon trying to unravel the origins of a secret organisation involved in human trafficking. He stood up and walked to the window, staring out thoughtfully to the south of the river.

"Michael, you're a young man and, it has to be said, a successful young man . . ."

"Until tomorrow," I interrupted.

"I, on the other hand, am ten years from retirement," he continued. "I have no savings to speak of, no premium bonds I can cash, no insurances, no hidden treasures I can sell to stave off poverty in my ebbing years. You will shrug of this unavoidable disaster like water off a duck's back. You will brave the storm and live to fight another day. Any law firm in the city will employ a young and vibrant man like you despite your failings, because you're a risk taker; you thrive on it. I am now at that dispensable age, and after tomorrow's fiasco I will be considered a risk—a junior partner who was foolish enough to embroil himself defending a case that can't be won."

"So we lose. So what? Cases are lost every day. That's the game, Badger. Someone has to lose."

"I'm aware of the implications, Michael. Either way neither you nor this firm is going to survive this. The world's press will all be there tomorrow to witness probably the biggest case of this century and you want to tell stories of government conspiracies and Roman sacrifices. The Law Society will probably have us disbarred and certified as lunatics. And where will I go then, Michael, eh? What happens to me once the newspapers have destroyed us and made us look a laughing stock? If you're right, and I stress if your assumptions are all correct, do you think the government will ever admit to it? And this BLANCA nonsense, how deep does it go? Do you honestly believe that you will discover the identities of the conspirators that have managed to remain underground for two-thousand years? They're ghosts, Michael, and you neither have the time nor the recourses to validate the story written by a dead man."

I thought for a moment, desperately trying to find the words that may offer a valid argument, but there was one overriding factor I could not escape—Badger was right. Had it not been for my father's death and his declaration of guilt, I would not have pursued the Henderson case with such ferocity, which in turn would not have led me to associate with Peter Egan, or Wendy Marshall, or Fin, the likes of Vincent Pierce nor the discovery of the troublesome and elusive BLANCA faction.

"You don't have to be present in court tomorrow," I meekly suggested. "You can disassociate yourself entirely from the case."

"But I can't disassociate myself from you, can I?"

I watched him standing at the window, shaking his head and muttering to himself.

"Why, Michael?" he said, snapping his head round. "We had a steady and lucrative business. Okay, it wasn't going to win us any accolades, but it paid the bills and put food on the table, and in one mad moment you . . ."

"Fucked it up," I anticipated.

He returned his stare to the window and resumed shaking his head and muttering.

"I hear Tom and Andy are doing well for themselves. Perhaps they'll give you a job. Rumour has it they have offices in Southwark. Couldn't hurt to call them," I suggested and in the interim broke the long, cold silence.

"The war will be over soon, Michael, and the opportunities offered by the War Office will be gone. Their days are numbered, but I have no doubt they will survive a little longer than us."

I agreed with a nod, for once again he was undoubtedly right and I could offer no defence.

"So what do you intend to do?" I asked.

After a considerable delay he turned and sighed, taking up his place back on the settee.

"I could re-mortgage the house. That might keep us afloat for a while," he suggested.

I shook my head furiously. "Definitely not, Badger! No, no, no! I'll have to see Sarah and beg her to instruct her solicitors' to release my half of the money as part of the divorce settlement. She'll object of course, but given the fact that she was responsible for the breakdown, and that I will give her my solemn oath not to make any mention of it, I'm sure she'll agree."

My friend suddenly appeared overwhelmed.

"Divorce? Sarah is divorcing you? My God, Michael, why didn't you tell me?" he said.

"I thought you knew."

"If I had known I would have said something."

I shrugged my shoulders once again. "I thought you were being kind."

He shook his head grimly, but then his eyes fired with optimism. "You still have that Rachel girl from the bookshop. She might be good for you if you give it half a chance," he suggested.

"Gone," I replied shortly. "Seems her husband was invalided home. Of course he'll be a war hero, or at least in her eyes he will be. My only hope is that his dick was shot off and she leaves him out of frustration—or am I being unkind?"

"I can detect a slight trace of animosity in your tone but only slight."

He picked up the story once again and perused it with considerably more interest than before.

"This BLANCA organisation was instigated by bankers, lawyers and people of high standing; what we commoners consider the elite. My guess is if it is still in existence—which it must be—then it's run by the same kind of people. Have you any history books, Michael, specifically a history of London. Let's verify that what Peter Egan has written is factual."

I smiled warmly. "I thought you weren't interested," I said.

Badger continued to turn the pages without looking at me. "That was before I realised that you're going to come out of this with less than me. Find me those books."

Peter's story took us through the ages, from the Roman invasion and conquest to their decline and imperial disintegration; the Anglo-Saxon takeover, to the medieval period and beyond, and what was clear, was that despite the drastic changes London had undergone, albeit power, wars, invasion, plague and pestilence, BLANCA survived. Indeed, by 1666, when the Great Fire decimated the city, the secret organisation had an estimated 12,000 members, of which everyone had a bloodline originating back to Rome; it was their only remaining foothold on British soil. Traditionally, so the story goes, the nameless confederation trading in white slavery for the purpose of supplying girls for soldiers, expanded worldwide generating millions of pounds of untraceable revenue, thereby injecting capital into the companies and individual members associated with what by this time was colloquially known as BLANCA. Unwittingly Barrilius and his friends were the forefathers of an industry known as prostitution. Of the several historical reference books I possessed—those I accumulated while wondering the market-stalls and even Rachel's bookshop, everything Peter had written appeared well researched, and true to form Badger tenaciously addressed the challenge with pen and paper while filling his lungs—and my apartment—with acrid and putrid cigarette smoke.

By early evening I had read the History of London from cover to cover until I had reached the reference maps of the city at the back of the book, depicting Roman London, Medieval London, The Agas Map, Franz Hogenberg 1572, Frederick de Wit 1666, and up to present day, given a hundred years or so. I pushed my palms against my eyes and yawned.

"Do you think it's plausible that Wendy Marshall was killed by someone from BLANCA, because of what she had discovered? She must have been scared enough. She owned a gun."

Badger considered the possibility and shook his head.

"I wouldn't have thought so," he said.

I must have looked disappointed at his immediate dismissal of my suggestion, for he shook his head again.

"If this is legitimate, then we're dealing with an organisation capable of spiriting literally thousands of young girls out of this country without a trace. You don't think they could have erased Wendy Marshall entirely?

They would have ensured she was never found—dead or alive. If she was scared of anyone it was someone close to her; perhaps her girlfriend."

"Who—Fin?" I scoffed. "She was devastated! And if she had anything to hide why allow me access to her flat? Why help me search for proof?"

Badger shrugged his shoulders resignedly. "Whatever and whomever, none of this is going to help us tomorrow. Our only hope now is that the Luftwaffe fly over the city tonight and drop a bomb on Wandsworth Prison, thus ridding us of Henderson and the indignity we will undoubtedly face in the courtroom. As for me I'm going home to eat what's left of my cold and decaying roast."

Sometimes you can't see for looking, and only when you stop looking do you find it. Throughout the exchange with Badger I was looking at a map of Medieval London open on the table but was briefly distracted when he rose from the table and placed on his jacket. And suddenly I realised exactly what BLANCA represented.

"They're gates!" I blurted as I snatched up the book. "The name depicts the first letter of every gate built in the wall surrounding the city."

Badger resumed his seat immediately and stared intently at me.

"Bishopsgate, Ludgate, Aldersgate, Newgate, Cripplegate and Aldgate; entrances constructed by the Roman's when the London Wall was built. It has nothing to do with white. It's merely an abbreviation of an unnamed organisation. If we prescribe to the adage 'little and often' then everything falls into place."

My associate looked confused.

"It's something Wendy used to say; 'little and often'. Steal a pound from a man's wallet and more often than not it will go unnoticed."

"What!"

"It's an assembly-line, don't you see? It doesn't matter if one man doesn't know what the man next to him is doing—the end result is achieved. Carlisle was part of that assembly-line; all of the 247 were. It's manipulation, Badger, orchestrated from on high—by those in position of trust and power—the so-called elite. If a person goes missing what is the first thing you do? Register them missing. But what if that file is misplaced or intentionally removed? That person ceases to exist. Nobody follows it up because there's nothing to follow up."

"You can't just erase a history," my associate scoffed.

"No?" I questioned. "Last year the fire of the Blitz consumed Court-houses, town halls, police stations, government buildings and entire archives filled with information about us—all gone."

"But why would somebody in a position of power intentionally lose or misplace a file on a missing person?"

"To stop other people from looking," I replied, waving Peter's manuscript at him. "You've read how much trafficking is worth—millions. My father used to say that nobody questions a person in a position of authority—or at least appears to be a person in a position of authority. That's how it's done, Badger . . ."

I hurried to the bedroom and returned with Eleanor Cole's business card.

"Peter must have had this for a reason," I said as I slipped on my coat. "And I mean to find out what it was."

"Do you want me to come with you?"

"No need," I returned as I headed for the door. "Let yourself out."

-30-

A transition had taken place since my last visit—a phenomenal change that only Mother Nature could execute in minimal time and to maximum effect. The surrounding landscape of Judge Newland's smallholding seemed somehow empty and barren now, and fragile leaves of gold and brown tumbled and rolled in no positive direction and settled, quivering like a wounded bird until the breeze animated them once more. Even the house looked gloomier in the insipid autumn light, grey and formidable with its rickety porch, loose slates and broken gutters; one could be forgiven for thinking it had been abandoned. I stood at the perimeter fence leaning on the gate that had long ago served its rightful purpose due to a broken hinge, and now sat at an oblique rake and was partly buried in the muddy track. A cold bitter wind swirled about the confines of the rolling hills, carrying tiny flecks of snow to herald a bad winter and the possibility of confinement within the rustic house until a thaw. Why I never knocked on the door and addressed my concerns head-on I cannot say. Certainly the issues could have just as easily been resolved in front of a roaring fire while sipping hot tea or soup in the Judge's parlour, but for reasons that escape me I chose to stand outside in the numbing cold until he put in an appearance, and after an hour or so he did. Daisy, his faithful collie bounded out the front door and spun in ever decreasing circles and barked with excitement, while the judge sat on the porch threshold and slipped his feet into muddy wellingtons. I was noticed immediately. Daisy thundered towards me with all the power of a freight-train, yapping a warning that all trespassers will be eaten alive, only to roll on her back at my feet as a blatant invitation to be made a fuss of. Judge Newland approached garbed in a green oilskin coat and supporting himself on a long wooden staff, but unlike before, he lacked warmth and common courtesy.

"The preliminary hearing is looming, Michael, and I'm afraid I can be of no further help to you," he said, purposefully avoiding my stare. "That said, you are obviously here for a reason, and I seriously doubt it is to see an old man like me, especially on a Sunday afternoon."

I was unsettled by his tactless demeanour, and without further consideration for my presence or my purpose for standing in artic conditions for over an hour, he ushered Daisy ahead and walked away.

"Thank you for returning my father's book," I said.

He continued to walk without reply.

"You never proffered an opinion," I added.

The old man slowed to a stop but never turned.

"I said I wouldn't. Why would I?"

"Because you have an opinion about everything; as you said; it keeps senility away from your door."

I saw his shoulders rise and fall and vaguely heard him sigh, but suddenly he snapped his head round. "I've read the damn book, Michael! Am I enlightened? Of course I am! So the history books have got it wrong—who cares; it happens all the time. Am I surprised your father played a part in it? No! Some of the greatest men in history have at one time or another made a bad choice."

"Bad choice!" I argued. "You believe that killing four innocent women was a 'bad choice?' As a judge how can you trivialise such an act?"

He turned away from me, looking in the direction of his loyal dog way ahead of him.

"I wish you luck with the trial," he said. And then he set off again.

"Is it because I'm defending Henderson? Or is it that you don't want to associate with the son of a notorious murderer?" I questioned.

He suddenly spun around and shook his staff at me.

"Don't be so bloody childish!" he growled. "You stand there with your law degree and your fancy firm and dare to question the integrity of the very man who made it all possible—never once considering the sacrifices he went through. He wanted you . . . nay, begged you to follow in his footsteps, but you chose the path of a lawyer; a more despicable occupation imaginable. You had that choice, Michael, because your father made it so. He suffered your countless rejections time and time again, lost his only daughter to a foreign country, and lost his loving wife to cancer. And what have you done with his legacy, eh? You shame his name with infidelity and defending the killer of eight women, no less. Yet he, your own flesh and blood, repels you because he played a part in killing four worthless whores. Where are your priorities, Michael? Where's your loyalty?"

Put that way it did sound remiss of me. Nevertheless I paced after him.

"But that's not the reason for your hostility, is it, Judge? Once you were agreeable—more than willing to read the book, and now you despise me. What is in those pages that makes you hate me?"

Once again he slowed to a stop and bowed his head.

"I don't hate you, Michael," he said, quietly. "But there are some things that should remain unsaid. And if you value your life you'll suppress the urge to know."

"Curiosity killed the cat?"

He nodded and the trace of a smile appeared on his decrepit lips.

"Something like that. Fight the good fight, Michael, and win the day with the knowledge you have already acquired. You don't need to know any more."

He continued on several more steps with an unsteady gait, the frigid wind almost unbalancing him, but once again he stopped and turned towards me with an anxious expression.

"Fine," he surrendered. "Walk with me."

We walked in silence for what seemed an eternity, rounding the hill that looked down on the Dog and Duck, and along the gravel path that led down to the river, and not until we stood on the stone bridge expanding the weir did he stop and rest on a shallow wall.

"I've heard talk that you have been asking questions about an organisation known as BLANCA," he said as he looked about him with a reticence I could not understand. "May I enquire as to how you know of its existence?"

To say I was shocked would be an understatement. As far as I was concerned it was not public knowledge, and certainly I had not bandied the name around to all and sundry. The old man sat patiently staring up at me, evidently amused by my perplexed expression, for a grin expanded across his withered features and continued outward and upward until I spoke.

"Heard?" I asked sceptically as I looked nervously about me. "Heard from whom?"

"It doesn't matter how I know. However, it only goes to prove how clumsy and indiscrete you have been during your private investigation. How do you know about BLANCA?"

I was beginning to think I was being interrogated, and fully expected to be ambushed by masked men armed to the teeth with assorted lethal cutlery, who would chop me up in handy bite-size portions and toss me into the weir.

"Wendy Marshall," I replied. "Although indirectly."

"Meaning?" he asked casually.

"She was dead. I found notes, references at her apartment."

"Appertaining to?"

I wasn't sure of my answer but replied just the same.

"Abducting girls," I said.

He nodded in agreement, wearily rose to his feet and walked on across the bridge.

"I was a young man when it happened," he began. "It was the millennium—1900, and I was a prosecutor for the Crown; thirty-years old and ready to take on the world; nothing was going to stop me. Two men,

Henry Parsons and Edward Childs were about to stand trial for their lives, having been charged with the crime of arson on Westminster Abbey, no less. Then such an act was tantamount to treason; a direct insult to the church and the queen herself; punishable only by death. By any standards it was a simple case to try. Both men were captured within minutes of the blaze, which thankfully was extinguished before it could take hold, and their clothes were found to have splashes of an accelerant on them. To their credit they were young—in their early twenties, both came from good stock with impeccable backgrounds, and both held prestigious positions in their individual employments; one in a bank, the other in the exchange. Neither could they blame their actions on alcohol; according to the police they were sober as judges. And so Parsons and Childs were denied bail and taken directly to Pentonville Prison to await trial, where they remained for several weeks. Undoubtedly Henry Parsons was the stronger of the two, showing little or no emotion at the initial hearing, but Edward Childs appeared a broken young man, literally throwing himself on the mercy of the court. In chambers we prepared for the case, and notwithstanding pleas from the defence that these two young men were without previous convictions and were of good standing, nothing was going to prevent them from facing the gallows. Suddenly and without warning the case was withdrawn."

By now we were walking along a thin track running parallel with the river that thanks to the cold weather remained hard and solid as opposed to liquid mud.

"That was the first time I heard the name BLANCA," he continued. "Childs, realising his days were probably numbered, decided to put pen to paper and confess his sins, much like your father did, Michael. After several weeks of incarceration a handful of official-looking gentlemen arrived at the prison, and after producing all the necessary documentation Parsons and Childs were released into their custody. Obviously elated at being given back his liberty in the dead of night, Childs left his confession behind—to be found by a warden the next morning who handed it over to the prison governor, who then passed it on to us believing it may be of use. As far as we were concerned the case had been stricken and we moved onto pastures new; it wasn't a matter for concern. However, and much like yourself, I was more than curious as to what influenced two upstanding young men to resort to such an act of destruction at the risk of losing their own lives. To me it went far beyond the realms of sanity, and one can hardly attribute their reckless behaviour to the influences of alcohol or drugs, or for that matter, because they possessed criminal tendencies; simply they were two young men of impeccable character. And that is why nobody questioned the decision to repeal the case; obviously there was a mistake and Parsons and Childs were completely innocent of all charges—the only rational explanation."

The old man paused from his narrative and wandered off the track to rummage through and scrutinise tiny mauve flowers on a cluster of foliage sprouting from the riverbank. "Amazing; freezing temperatures and still blooming," he said. All of which was all very well, I thought, but what about the subject at hand? I waited patiently with the raw wind gusting through my thin apparel while the judge completed his botany homework. Even Daisy had tired of the long interval and had sought shelter on the windless side of a felled tree. When eventually the old man returned to the beaten path, still assessing a purple bud with great interest, we continued onward. "You were saying?" I coaxed. The judge held the small flower between his fingers. "Astonishing how something so fragile can survive the fiercest winter," he replied, preoccupied with the wonders of nature. "Astounding," I muttered. "But I was referring to Childs."

"Ah, yes!" he cried. "His confession rambled on for some nineteen pages, attributing the charges against Parsons and himself as the coerced influences of a greater power, of which neither he nor his accomplice could deny. He wrote of his inauguration into a cabbalistic organisation whose allegiances ranged from the occult to commerce, and were predominantly influenced by Roman values; an esoteric conglomeration of which every representative possessed a lineage connected to Italy . . . or to be more specific—Rome. That isn't to say that every member was a direct descendent of the actual city, but a descendent of those who lived there; those who were considered powerful and influential. To get a better understanding of the concept we have to go back to the dawn of our great nation, when the Romans invaded our shores and made Britain their own. Great leaders, generals and Caesars sired many children, and not necessarily with their own spouses, and their ancestries have been constantly monitored and the descendants initiated into an organisation in the belief that they will be as great as their forefathers; a cornerstone of Roman ideals never relinquished even after they ceased to be an empire. According to Childs they are a potent influence on our everyday lives—from the banks to the government, and this is achievable by ensuring that those in power stay in power; promoting a fellow-member up through the ranks as a replacement. Entire dynasties thrive because an ancestor gave birth to a Roman child, and all the time the ranks of this organisation are swelling to tens of thousands."

"BLANCA?" I said.

Judge Newland nodded his head, and as the skies began to dull and icy sleet began to pale the landscape, he whistled to his faithful dog and hurried beneath the shelter of the overhanging trees. He shuddered as he stared out over the woodlands growing whiter by the second, and delving his hand in his coat pocket pulled out a half-bottle of whiskey, of which he opened and offered it to me. I declined, and with a shrug he took a large swallow and returned the bottle from whence it came.

"Do you believe it?" I asked. "Doesn't it all sound very Masonic to you?"

His response was vacillating; a half shrug bereft of conviction.

"There's truth in everything, Michael," he replied. "It's simply a matter of how much we choose to believe. Edward Childs referred to BLANCA as being the Genie of the Lamp, or in mythological terms—selling your soul to the devil. In return for your services and dedication you were guaranteed a successful life."

"And all these riches and a lifetime of happiness would be bestowed on you simply because you were the bastard child of some Roman general! It's absurd!"

He laughed unconvincingly as he peered out at the gloomy panorama.

"And they were the sentiments of everyone in Chambers; everyone who read it regarded the writings as that of a lunatic; a man desperately trying to evade his own execution by concocting a story so unbelievable it defied all belief. And I too was no better—till now."

I watched the old man as he surveyed the dark, racing skies above, the branches of the trees waving frantically as they succumbed to the will of the wind, and the dying leaves desperately clinging to their life-source—torn from their moorings and dispelled into the storm. He shook his head grimly, predicting a tempestuous winter that would render him housebound for its duration. "Till now? What do you mean, till now?" I asked him. With a brief look of reluctance he jerked his head in the direction we had come, and murmured, "We should be getting back." We set off back down the riverbank and crossed the stony bridge, slowly ascending into the shadowy woodland until we met the gravel pathway, and not until the local public house was below us and the homestead before us did he attempt to give an explanation. "My position as a judge—albeit a retired one—forbids me to render an opinion on a subject devoid of evidence or motive; for what have we, nought but hearsay and conjecture. It isn't written in stone, of course, but purely habit; a personal indulgence, if you will. According to Childs' testimony BLANCA's membership came at a price—designed to test ones metal; that you can break the law as easily as you can uphold it, that you can embrace suffering as much as you can languish in luxury, that death holds no more fear than life. His reference to 'coerced influences' implies that the act of arson was not executed out of malice or a deep routed hatred for everything sacred but was the result of an order—an initiation."

"So, you're saying they were guilty?"

"Very much so. The baptism of Parsons and Childs into BLANCA involved an evaluation of their characters and, in exchange for Utopia they were set a simple but formidable task, of which they blundered. I think I should mention at this point that I never considered the story to be credible and have never given it further consideration since, but your personal inquiry has reawakened a dormant memory and gives credence to a name I once believed was purely fictitious. Recently I've spent my time looking into it—as much is readily available on the bookshelves, and one thing is certain—you won't find the name BLANCA in any history book or in the listings of any existing organisations."

"Then perhaps we're talking cross purposes. I'm talking about the abduction of young women."

"And so was Edward Childs, although not in so many words," returned the judge. "You see the key to it all lie with Parsons and Childs' release from prison. Who had the power to sanction their immediate liberation and completely erase a trail when every shred of evidence compounded their guilt? That's friends in high places, Michael. That is manipulation on a vast scale. Childs' confession now doesn't seem so fanciful after all. Perhaps BLANCA is what he said it is; 'a potent influence on our everyday lives'. And let us not forget his reference to Roman ideals."

"Roman ideals!" I echoed as I stopped in my tracks.

He turned around and walked back with the beginning of a smile materialising on his frozen features, appraising my confused expression with an air of bewilderment.

"And you call yourself an expert on history? Bah!"

I watched him walk down the long and steady incline, thrusting his wooden staff into the gravel with a gusto that had remained absent throughout.

Roman ideals!

Suddenly I was hurrying after him, but in the time it had taken me to acknowledge his inference the distance between us was considerable, and now he marched onward at a considerable pace.

"Roman occupation? Is that what you're suggesting?"

"It's as good a term as any," he said, "although these days I believe they refer to it in broader terms—exploitation, and it should be borne in mind that slavery was predominantly a Roman domain."

"But . . . But that was thousands of years ago," I rebuffed. "Are you telling me that BLANCA—this clandestine network—has stayed underground since Biblical times and has never been discovered? It's insane!"

And there, back at the perimeter fence surrounding his property, he placed his staff against the gatepost and leaned on the rail.

"I think that must be what I like about you, Michael—your naivety. Let us for a moment clear our heads of all rational thinking. Is it inconceivable that a small part of Rome still exists, albeit secretly, continuing as they did when they first invaded these shores? The very foundation of this nation is built on Roman statutes, and our life now is comparatively the same.

After all is said and done—we are ostensibly Roman; a heritage we are proud of. Indeed, we pay homage to their great achievements. Look at the buildings in the City, Michael; can you ignore the architecture of the Bank of England and the surrounding facades—unmistakably Romanesque by design."

"They could also be barbaric," I argued. "During the Gallic Wars the entire population of Avaricum, numbering 40,000 souls were slaughtered; 800 cities destroyed, 300 tribes subjugated, and a million enslaved."

"And what of us, Michael? What of Britannia?" he said, arching his eyebrows. "Why—not so long ago we were publically hanging children. I'm merely asking if you can subscribe to the concept. Can you?"

"That slavery is alive and well, yes." I huffed. "Judge Newland, I know that since your retirement your world consists only of the immediate landscape, but I can tell you now that there is a distinct absence of slave-ships moored at Victoria Docks. I'm aware that a majority of prostitutes are controlled by pimps and gangs, but by a bunch of Romans . . . Well!"

The old man shook his head in dismay and reached for his crooked staff, and with a high-pitched whistle summoned Daisy from her investigative duties at the threshold of the woods.

"Time to get Martha her tea," he smiled. "You may wish to give my hypothesis further consideration. Let me know of your findings, and good luck with the trial."

I shook his hand and he and Daisy wandered off towards the house.

"You never explained why you were so obnoxious towards me earlier," I shouted.

He turned immediately with a broad grin.

"No, I never, did I? You know, Michael, I despise theorists and conspiracies, and yet lately I have found myself continually falling into the same trap. I omitted to tell you the final act of the Parsons and Childs chronicle. I later found out that two days after their release, a man by the name of Gabriel Squires died while in custody at Camden Town Police Station; a heart attack by all accounts; a result of high blood pressure and a delicate disposition. Prior to his death he made a statement to the effect that he and he alone was responsible for the arson attack on

Westminster Abbey, and being a man of little or no education, he signed it with a simple cross. Make of that what you will, Michael, but it was all very neat and tidy—all tied up with a pretty bow. And that may well have been the way of it; perhaps Squires was guilty, but if we adhere to Childs' handwritten confession then we have to confront the possibility that BLANCA as an organisation consists of some very influential and dangerous people. Do you know how many unsolved murders there are in London, Michael, all apparently motiveless? Take caution with your investigation. And you may wish to castigate your secretary, who obviously has no inhibitions about discussing such matters over the telephone. I called to make sure you received your book and she was quite outspoken about your present research." He paused as if he were carefully considering his next address. "And that brings me to your father. While I'm presently engaged in unsubstantiated gossip, rumour and innuendo, may I offer one last presumption?"

"I'm all ears," I said.

"Isn't it a possibility that prior to meeting his friend Pip, your father was already inaugurated into this secret sect know as BLANCA and his actions were a form of an initiation? Notwithstanding the inevitable events that affect us all, he led a very charmed life."

"Thus furnishing motive?" I smiled.

"Just an estimated guess," he shrugged, "but worthy of consideration nonetheless."

"That being the case wouldn't I have been approached by now?"

He gave the question some thought, rounding his hand about his chin as he searched out the possible alternatives, and then he snapped his fingers."

"Perhaps it's because you're a lawyer. As unscrupulous as this organisation might be they have to draw the line somewhere," he quipped.

I nodded and grinned back at him. "That must be it. Maybe my application is in the post."

"I think it's an absolute certainty, Michael. They may overlook your contemptible profession just this once."

I chuckled and turned towards the raggedy lane that led to the main road.

"Of course, that would make me a direct descendent of some revered Roman; a general, perhaps, or maybe a Caesar."

The judge laughed and raised his hand. "There you go again—setting your sights too high."

My car slowly circumnavigated Regent's Park in a clockwise direction, and as I approached all the side roads merging from the left, I slowed and flashed my headlights, picking out the names on the street signs and then speeding up to the next. Eventually I found the road on the St. John's Wood side of the park; a quiet cul-de-sac close to the Grand Union Canal, consisting of no more than twenty or so three storey houses with shallow roofs and large semi-circular bay windows embellished with Georgian glass. The Jaguar hummed quietly towards the end of the road, where I half mounted the pavement, silenced the engine and extinguished the lights. I turned on the interior light and examined the card belonging to Eleanor Cole and began to look around for a legible house number. As if fate had guided me there, I was parked right outside the address, staring at the dark house where a weak, yellow light illuminated within reflecting on the squares of glass of the front door. Out of the car I took a look around me at the rows of houses either side that appeared devoid of life and that almost melted into the blackness which enveloped them. The leaves of the trees, strategically placed along the avenue, rustled as a soft wind pushed them away from the direction of the park, and the sapphire eyes of a cat surveyed me curiously from a garden wall. I walked the length of the empty driveway, looking left and right of me for any signs of life, and reaching the front door, I knocked gently. My eyes surveyed the silent avenue; no twitching curtains; no curious neighbours with good intentions. I knocked again, harder and louder, and after a few minutes of listening to my pounding heart and the breeze sliding through the branches, I squatted and looked through the letterbox. The dull, yellow light emanated from behind a partly open door at the end of the hall. What drove me to take my next course of action was sheer desperation; to put an end to this matter once and for all and salvage what little was left of my life.

The latch on the back gate yielded easily, and I blindly groped my way down the side passage until the familiar yellow light bled out through the sides of the pulled blinds at the rear of the house. The back door was of the same design as the front, half glazed in Georgian glass that, at least to me, would look better open rather than closed. I could see the door handle on the other side of the glass, the keys dangling in the lock, and I turned my back to look up the garden for any overlooking windows or signs of activity. I could make out a high wall of trees surrounding the garden, swaying slowly against the black, velvet backdrop, where those who engaged in outside activities, at least enjoyed it in intimate privacy. I thrust my elbow behind me, and while slithers of glass tinkled tunefully on the concrete floor, I spun, reached inside and opened the door. I stepped inside a vast kitchen. One wall was fitted out with glass cabinets with chrome handles, the surrounds painted the colour of vanilla of which the insides were illuminated by small lights that burned a lemony yellow. A long counter of black marble stretched beneath the display, the centre of which jutted out to form an island where two stools were positioned either side; in its centre was a bowl of assorted fruit. On the opposite wall was a large cooker where an array of pots, pans and cooking utensils shone chrome and gold, suspended from a deadly looking contraption chained to the ceiling. There was a bulky American fridge in the corner set against a fully laden wine rack of the same height and width, and an oak dresser where every shelf was decorated in souvenirs from all over the world; a grotesque mask of black wood from Africa; an emblem of the American eagle set in solid silver; a terracotta pot inscribed in Spanish baring the name Eleanor; and dolls dressed in their national costume filled the spaces between.

I edged closer, because for all there was to see on the display, only one particular item caught my attention. On the top shelf a blue, paper flower stretched out of an empty glass; the same paper flower given to Rachel by a clown with big feet and a spinning bow tie at Brighton. My eyes were fixed to it, as though there wasn't anything else in the world that mattered. Everything else in the room seemed to evaporate and disappear. Suddenly I heard a sound behind me, of crunching glass underfoot, and I blinked my eyes closed. "Good evening, Michael."

I turned and there she was. She looked like Rachel, had the same stance, the same captivating eyes, and even the beginnings of the same smile, but it wasn't her. She wore a white satin dress and matching shoes, and her hair seemed somehow lighter, almost blonde. Around her neck and wrist were bands of sparkling diamonds that I knew at once were genuine. She moved to the island and placed down her handbag. I was fixed to the spot, my head still but my eyes following her every move.

"You look like you could do with a drink. Pass me a bottle from the rack, will you? Second from the top—the 1931," she said.

I saw her mouth moving but couldn't hear the words, and she appraised me with a smile borne more out of pity than amusement.

"Michael, the wine."

I blinked again and felt feeling return to my body, and then walking to the wine rack, took the bottle she requested and passed it to her. Instead of taking it she handed me a corkscrew.

"Would you mind? Award ceremonies sap my strength."

Even her voice sounded different; softer, intensely articulate, like the whispers of a tune.

"Award?" I managed to croak; "actress of the year?"

She nodded and smiled as if she deserved every venomous retort I could spit at her.

"It doesn't become you," she said.

"What doesn't?" I replied as I twisted the corkscrew into the cork.

"Being an ogre—being spiteful. It isn't you."

"People change; look at you."

She nodded patiently and turned to the cabinet behind her.

"There's something a little condescending about presentations, don't you think?" she said, taking a long stemmed wine glass and examining it for imperfections against the light. "Which office has been more successful; which official deserves promotion; who deserves greater recognition. It makes me squirm."

"I fail to see how they could have overlooked your thespian qualities."

She took another glass from the shelf and examined it without looking at me.

"It wasn't funny the first time, Michael. Why would you think it would be a second?"

The cork popped from the bottle and I placed it on the counter before her.

"So what do I call you—Rachel or Eleanor?" I asked.

She glanced at me and shook her head.

"Don't park Peter Egan's car on my front lawn, break my windows and presume to be an expert on counter-intelligence, Michael. It makes you appear docile."

"You never answered my question."

"Because it is not worthy of a reply."

"So there never was a David?"

She turned, took a third glass and placed it on the counter.

"How could there be if there never was a Rachel?" she replied.

She fixed her stare to the three glasses lined up before her and I took a step back.

"You're wrong. There was a Rachel," I said. "She was funny and insecure, and she couldn't sleep without the hallway light being left on. She was gullible but streetwise, sometimes neurotic and other times damn right infuriating, but she existed and I believed in her. She shared my secrets, my aspirations, and put up with idiosyncrasies. Don't ever tell me she wasn't real."

Her eyes remained on the glasses, stubbornly refusing to rise to mine.

"Did you love her, Michael? Could you see yourself spending the rest of your life with her?"

Words failed me and I spat forth the first reply that came to mind.

"You lied to me!"

I stabbed an accusing finger at her, unconscious of the fact that I was still holding the corkscrew. I suddenly felt a cold, circle of steel push against the back of my head and my muscles seized immediately.

"Put down the bottle opener, Michael," said a voice behind me.

Somewhere in the English dialect there remained the remnants of a Spanish accent. I instantaneously dropped the corkscrew. Rachel stared across and shook her head scornfully, and the discomfort of a gun barrel pressing against my skull eased.

A man in his mid-fifties passed by me and took up a seat at the island; well tanned, steel, grey hair and bearing a wolfish grin. He placed the metallic grey revolver on the counter and patted Rachel's hand.

"Nicolia Vassarri," I mouthed.

He smiled, perhaps flattered that I had recognized him and nodded by way of making my acquaintance. For a moment my eyes flashed back and forth between Rachel and the mercenary. My mind was scrambled. Where was the association between Eleanor Cole and Nicolia Vassarri, unless of course they were lovers? Rachel poured the wine, equal amounts in each glass, handing one to Vassarri and holding the other out to me. I remained static and she smiled.

"No one is going to hurt you, Michael," she said in a motherly tone. "Here, take it."

I slowly approached with all the trepidation of a deer crossing Oxford Street, registering her wedding ring in the process as I picked the glass from her hand and backed away again. She acknowledged the direction of my stare and held her left hand in her right.

"There was a David," she admitted. "A lie is easier to retain when embellished with fact."

"Did they teach you that at the assassination academy? So where is Mr. David Cole?"

"He died. Shot to death in a Paris hotel four years ago; a botched assignment between the British and French governments, and a case of mistaken identity on their part."

My gaze continued to move between them; lovers, relations, friends? As I appraised them alternately and in quick succession, I noticed similarities, especially in their penetrating brown eyes. And then it dawned on me.

"My God, you're father and daughter," I stammered.

Nicolia Vassarri began to clap his hands slowly much to the disapproval of his daughter.

She drew a deep breath and looked at him. "Can you give us a moment?" she asked. He shook his head defiantly. "I'm not leaving you alone with this man," he returned. Her stare hardened and he reluctantly nodded his head. "As you wish, Eleanor, but if anything . . ."

"Nothing will happen!" she insisted.

He picked up his wine and his revolver and smiled over at me.

"Sorry about the . . ." He rattled the gun at me.

"Please. Think nothing of it."

She waited until her father had left the room.

"Sit down, Michael," she said, nodding towards the chair Vassarri had vacated.

I obeyed, like a child under the spell of a commanding mother.

"More lies?" I said.

She pursed her lips with impatience.

"You came here for answers?" she asked.

I hesitated but nodded.

"I'm listening."

She stared at her wine without touching it.

"Look—firstly it was not my intention to mislead you in any way . . ."

"It wasn't your what!" I retaliated.

"Listen to me. I am a government operative working in the War Division of the Justice Department also attached to the Criminal Division; a department specialising in the registration and training of government agents. Our role, such as it is, is to protect and defend our country—the realm . . ."

"Now I know why your business card is so vague; too much information."

"I am what they call a Special Operative; G.S.O. Government Special Operative—Top Secret."

"And here you are telling me all about it; some secret, eh? What do you intend to do, Rachel, once you've imparted all this information—take me out in the garden and shoot me?"

"Don't keep calling me Rachel!" she hissed. "I'm not Rachel! Rachel was an invention; a role I had to play."

"Then you should be congratulated, because she was pretty convincing to me."

"Because you wanted her to be, Michael. Jesus! You're so infuriatingly stupid. Do you know, secretly I wanted you find out about me. I hated deceiving you. I even gave myself a name that even a moron could have discovered the connection. But, oh no, not you. Were you listening when I was constantly humming 'Anything goes', or were you too preoccupied with people following you?"

"Anything goes! What has that got to do with anything?"

She sighed impatiently. "Anything goes is a song written by Cole Porter. Cole. Porter. Eleanor Cole, Rachel Porter."

I stared away from her, trying desperately to suppress the anger within me, until my heartbeat slowed and my breathing began to shallow. Likewise she was looking at the floor, her eyes glistening with tears of rage.

"However was I threat to Great Britain?" I said, adopting a patient tone.

She raised her eyes to mine briefly and looked away.

"You weren't," she replied, "but the situation you were in, and the situation you stubbornly refused to abandon, was. Why, Michael? Why did you persist in delving deeper and deeper into a case that was only going to end one way?"

"I had my reasons," I said, sulkily.

Again there was a lengthy pause; an atmosphere so thick you could write your name in it. Rachel, or Eleanor as she preferred to be addressed, was staring at the black, marble counter, and she suddenly pulled the large bowl of fruit towards her and picked out an orange.

"This is Henderson," she said, placing it down in front of me. She placed an apple next to it. "And this is Carlisle." She continued to place out the fruit in a straight line. A golden pair representing Peter Egan; a bunch of black grapes—the 247 corrupt officers; a lemon depicting Harry Griffin; a heavily bruised banana—the D.P.P. And when she had completed her arrangement she rested against the counter.

"So what do we have?" she asked.

I gazed at the assortment and sighed. "A fruit salad?"

"No, Michael, you have a breach;" she replied, ignoring my wit, "a hole, a chink in the armour that the enemy can take advantage of. Imagine if that list had been published. Any one of those corrupt police officers could have been targeted by German agents. What secrets would they divulge under interrogation? Would they assist them if their families were under threat of torture and death? It was open a door that had to be closed."

I sighed with boredom.

"So it was you who had me freed from the police station," I said.

"The police are an integral part of our national security, Michael, and you and your anarchist journalist were about to undermine it."

"So you had him killed!"

Her eyes ignited with anger. "I've never killed anyone, or for that matter, ordered anyone to kill! For your information I am what is referred to as a Diva," she snapped.

"How apt," I returned sarcastically.

"Short for deviation, Michael—a distraction; a subtle means to extract information. God, I gave you Fallow and you still kept digging."

"And Fallow was working under your instructions. That's why he killed Peter, using your father's deadly bedside manner."

She raised her eyes and shook her head furiously, cursing under her breath, "Jesus, you're so naïve."

I sat motionless, mulling over the heated exchange, collating her words and searching for their true meaning.

"Fallow isn't government, Michael, and neither is he a murderer," she shouted.

I opened my mouth to give a worthy argument but she intercepted.

"You were as close as you could get when you asked me for my father's book, and when you told me your theory on Fallow I gave him to you, hoping against hope that you would let the matter rest—you didn't."

"Then Foggerty was part of the game."

"He was nothing of the sort," she exclaimed. "Foggerty is straight as an arrow. He was given instructions, that's all. In your eyes, at least, you were right and I hoped you would walk off into the sunset and never look back."

"So I was wrong? Peter really did die of natural causes."

Nicolia Vassarri appeared, leaning his weight against the doorframe.

"Should you be saying these things, Eleanor?" he said.

She bowed her head, and then suddenly snapped round like a striking serpent.

"You dragged me into this fucking profession," she screamed. "He has a right to know. Leave us!"

Her father slowly closed his eyes, nodded faintly and disappeared into the darkness of the hallway.

Her breathing was heavy and erratic, her eyes downcast, but after a few moments she lifted her head and gathered her patience.

"Peter really did die of natural causes;" she verified, her voice still trembling with anger, "an unforeseen tragedy, and certainly ill-timed."

I wanted to hiss another sarcastic comment at her but all I could do was sigh huffily. With all the information being hurled at me and my brain's incapacity to place it into any organised order, I concentrated on Fallow and what led me to suspect him in the first place.

"So it was your people who broke into Fallow's Publishing House. You were looking for the list," I crowed, accusingly.

She shook her head. "No. You were right about that one; Fallow faked the break-in himself."

"For what reason?"

Eleanor looked behind her, to reassure herself her father wasn't still lurking in the shadows.

"Peter Egan had always been considered a threat to national security. His insatiable appetite to ferret out every sleazy story of government misconduct, police corruption and the adulterous affairs of government ministers was giving us cause for concern. He tried, and almost succeeded, in infiltrating and acquiring information on the very department I work for. He planned to use it in a glossy expose in Fallow's magazine. Fortunately we were able to crush the story before it went to print, warning both Fallow and Egan that should they persist in their quest to undermine the government and publish information that could jeopardise matters of national security they would be charged with treason."

"Which is a hanging offence; the attempt to overthrow by illegal means the government to which a person owes allegiance."

She nodded. "Since that event Egan has been kept under surveillance, his calls monitored. The night he died he made three phone calls—the first to Earnest Fallow and two to you. He received no less than six from Fallow afterwards."

She took another brief look into the hallway and walked to the dresser displaying her worldly souvenirs, and opening the cupboard beneath the cluttered shelves, pulled out a box-folder and opened it on the floor within the open doors. She returned, glancing again into the hallway as she passed, and placed down four or five sheets of paper stapled together and identifiable with the heading, *'G.S.O.D. CONFIDENTIAL INFORMATION: Case No: 259874/P. Egan/E. Fallow. Transcript Conversation(s) September 22. 1941.'*

She picked up her wine for the first time and leaned her back on the marble counter.

"This will explain things better than I can," she said.

I turned it squarely in front of me. The first call from Earnest Fallow was tabbed by the exact time:

'19h.36m. 41s. ACTUATE.'

EGAN: *Hello. Is that you, Michael?*

FALLOW: *It's Ernie. Who's Michael?*

EGAN: *Nobody. I was expecting a call from someone else. What is it you want?*

FALLOW: *Don't you think I have a right to know who this lawyer is? You said earlier you gave the list to some lawyer. Do you trust him?*

EGAN: *Does it matter? The story is out now and on the newspaper stands. By morning the nationals will have it and then the whole world will know. And yes, I trust him. He's a friend.*

FALLOW: *Listen, Peter, it's my neck on the line.*

EGAN: *And I wrote the story.*

FALLOW: *It wasn't the deal. Either you or I should be holding the list, not some stranger. You obviously don't trust me, Peter. Am I right?*

EGAN: *You're being foolish. Within twenty-four hours the world and his wife will come looking for that list. It's safer this way—for the both of us.*

FALLOW: *What do you think will happen?*

EGAN: *Christ, Ernie, you've read the story—you know the implications—we've been through all this before.*

FALLOW: *And look what happened? I was nearly destroyed.*

EGAN: *And I was the one who stood by you. Just carry on business as usual. We'll meet tomorrow.*

'1900h.41m.43s. TERMINATE.'

Eleanor sipped her wine, her eyes trained on me when I looked up, but she looked away as if to disengage herself.

'1900h.52m.21s. ACTUATE.'

EGAN: *Yes.*

FALLOW: *It's me again. I'm worried, Peter.*

EGAN: *About what?*

FALLOW: *The story—everything. But I'm worried about you. Are you okay?*

EGAN: *Fine.*

FALLOW: *You don't sound fine. Have you been drinking?*

EGAN: *A little—to celebrate the publication.*

FALLOW: *Only wine, I hope. Your going to need your head screwed on tightly for this one.*

EGAN: *Fine. I hear you. Goodnight, Ernie.*

'1900h.53m.31s. TERMINATE.

'21h.11m.12s. ACTUATE.

EGAN: *(Silence)*

FALLOW: *Peter. Peter, are you there?*

EGAN: *Yes. Yes, I'm here. What is it, Earnest?*

FALLOW: *You sound strange.*

EGAN: *A little groggy. What is the matter?*

FALLOW: *Groggy ill or groggy drunk?*

EGAN: *A little of both I expect. What is it you want? I have to go out. Hurry up.*

FALLOW: *Out where? Are you meeting with the lawyer?*

EGAN: *(Silence)*

FALLOW: *Are you still there, Peter?*

EGAN: *(Silence)*

FALLOW: *Peter.*

EGAN: *I'm here. (Erratic breathing) Feeling a little strange—numb.*

FALLOW: *How much have you had to drink?*

EGAN: *Why have you called me?*

FALLOW: What if they come for me? What if they think I have the list? I couldn't go through all that again.

EGAN: Have some conviction, Ernie. Remember your predecessors. Do you think they would have shied away from a little skirmish? (Pause duration 39sec) I have to go now. Tired. Very tired.

21h.22m.04s. TERMINATE.

21h.24m.16s. ACTUATE EXCHANGE. UNOBTAINABLE.

21h.27m.45s. ACTUATE EXCHANGE. UNOBTAINABLE.

21h.41m.56s. ACTUATE EXCHANGE. UNOBTAINABLE.

I remembered then with vivid clarity the night Sylvia and I entered Peter's house; the empty bottle of brandy and half bottle of scotch on the table and numerous empty wine bottles in the kitchen. When I looked up again Eleanor was still leaning against the counter, her arms folded and her wine glass on the island.

"It would appear that somewhere around 9.30 Peter took himself quietly to bed and died. I could furnish you with the original recording if you still have your doubts," she said.

My eyes turned to the bleakness of the hallway in which Nicolia Vassarri had evaporated a short while ago.

"I know what you're thinking, Michael," she said. "My father was in Norway the night your friend died. Would you require proof of that, too?"

I shook my head. "It won't be necessary."

"As you see, Fallow tried to call three more times after their last conversation. Peter was probably dead by the time the last call was registered."

I nodded, staring into nothingness and wishing I could turn back time.

"Fallow was scared," she continued. "He thought that by faking a break-in he would be left alone; proof that if he possessed the list, it had been found by the imaginary robbers. When you came in he knew exactly where the list was. He did report the break-in."

"There is no record of it."

"We went there, prior to your arrival. We led him to believe we were the police. We seized the report from police files."

"But Fallow was arrested for killing Peter Egan," I stated.

Eleanor shook her head. "Earnest Fallow is in a safe-house, Michael. We put out the story to shut you up; to stop you snooping around like some demented bloodhound. But here you are."

I shook my head in disbelief.

"And the bomb; was that purely coincidental?"

Her face froze and remained motionless for what seemed an eternity, and her eyes slowly closed as she faintly shook her head.

"I had no control over the order," she said, almost in a whisper.

"Is that a fact?" I snarled. "Then who did?"

"You don't understand. You weren't supposed to be there."

"But I was, and so was Sylvia. You tried to kill us."

"Nobody was trying to kill anyone, Michael. It was the list that had to be destroyed."

I stood up and walked across the room and stood by the dresser, as far away from her as I could get.

"So, you're telling me that with all your initiative, all your experience in espionage, counter-intelligence, spies and assassins that that was the best you could come up with. Well, you'll excuse me Rachel or Eleanor or whatever the fuck it is you call yourself, but I consider that a tiny bit heavy handed."

"You weren't supposed to be there."

"I know. I heard you the first time. Did you think I would feel better by mentioning it a second?"

Eleanor dropped her head; out of pity, out of exhaustion, but probably out of shame.

"You played along, Michael," she said.

"I did? How so?"

"Box 927; your safety deposit box at your bank."

"Box? What box?"

"You know full well what I'm referring to. The box in which you deposited the list, the reel of 16 millimetre film and the photographs, given to you by Harold Griffin."

I stood there silently observing her until she raised her head. Now the bomb that destroyed my office and almost cost Sylvia and myself our lives, seemed to pale into insignificance.

"How did you know about box 927?" I asked cautiously.

"It's my job, Michael. You were flagged, and that gives us the right to investigate you in any way we feel is necessary. Did you think the bank was a confidential concern? We have laws, Michael, rules that must be obeyed, and if those rules are broken we have more power than any organisation you care to mention. We gained access to your precious box, the box containing the list and film, and what do you think we found?"

I felt a smile beginning to form on my lips.

"A half-roll of sellotape. A small paperweight in the shape of a Rolls Royce . . ."

"Bentley, actually," I interrupted.

"A half eaten cheese and pickle sandwich—inedible and covered in mould; 27 paperclips; a fountain pen with broken nib; 13 cigarette butts with accompanying ash; and 12 pictures of scantily-clad starlets coarsely cut out of an American magazine entitled 'Glamour Gals,' June edition."

My smile expanded but I tried to convey a serious air.

"Peter warned me—nowhere was safe. Once I realised I was being watched I removed the contents of the box and replaced it—with junk."

"So you suspected we'd find it?"

"Given your authority, yes," I replied with a shrug. "This leads me to my next question."

The mercenary's daughter perched her hands on her hips and stared back at me with arched eyebrows.

"According to you I became Britain's most wanted because I was considering taking on the Henderson case, which in turn led to my association with Peter Egan, who would then reveal his discovery of police corruption and furnish me with the evidence that you deemed a threat to this great and wonderful nation."

"And your point is?"

"How did I meet Peter? I was the one who contacted him so, my little femme-fatal, explain to me how you manipulated that."

"We didn't. He did," she replied with a tired expression. "You're not very good at this are you, Michael?"

"I haven't your vast experience in lies and deception."

She agreed with a patient nod, though her eyes retained a glow of sharp anger.

"When your secretary was shopping around Fleet Street for anything bearing Henderson's name, Egan made sure a copy of Fallow's Magazine was amongst them. He knew his piece on the Blackout Butcher would appeal to your inquisitive nature but, moreover, he knew you would accept him as an ally, especially as you were about to embark on the defence of a suspected killer. In Henderson there was Carlisle. And in Carlisle there was the association of corruption in which you became embroiled."

"And you predicted all this would happen?"

"It's . . ."

"Your job, I know," I groaned.

"We already knew about the corruption. Why do you think Carlisle received such a light sentence? We had known for almost a year. He told us some things but not the whole story. Either way we thought we could prevent it being public knowledge. The Met. tried to suppress the story and we attempted to find the protagonists. We didn't foresee the actions of Harry Griffin."

"And what happens to him?"

"Nothing," she shrugged. "Griffin was never the issue. Once he passed his secret onto Egan it was no longer his responsibility. Simply, he allowed others to do his dirty work for him."

My father's diary came to mind; how he had transferred his own guilt onto me; how he must be looking down and laughing at this very moment. I couldn't help but feel he wasn't looking down but up.

"And your father's book? There has to be a complex explanation."

Nicolia Vassarri appeared out of the darkness, like a ghostly apparition in an expensive beige lightweight suit.

"May I?" he asked, looking at his daughter for approval.

She nodded bitterly and retrieved her wine from the counter, facing the glass cabinets without any intention of turning around.

"I officially retired in the early thirties . . ." he began.

"I know, I read your book," I interrupted. "Your sweet, little girl was good enough to furnish me a copy. I think she over did it with the aging process of the cover, though. Had I have known what I know now you could have signed it for me."

"Then, I was working for a number of different governments, including the German government."

"Forgive me, I'm not a reader of spy novels, but wouldn't that have made you a double-agent, so to speak?"

"It was peacetime, Michael, and everyone in the business knew what I was—a mercenary, an assassin. British Intelligence also knew there was a war on the horizon. I was approached to work exclusively for them; for them and no one else."

I was beginning to understand. If Britain knew Germany were about to wage war, then surely every other intelligence service in Europe must have known, and Vassarri, with his vast range of deadly and linguistic skills would have been a prime candidate for any intelligence service.

"The book was a ruse," I said. "You had probably been approached by every government agency in the western world, but we had already made you an offer you couldn't refuse, so you wrote your memoirs, slipping in for good measure that you were retiring to Italy. Ever been to Italy, Mr. Vassarri?"

"Three times, briefly," he smiled. "Venice is very damp."

"And all these countries and their governments had served you well, as you had them, but now your allegiance was with Britain, so you had the book published. Why Fallow?"

The mercenary remained within the shadows of the hall, the yellow mantle of light of the kitchen barely touching his face.

"It wasn't my choice. He was gullible, rebellious in many ways. But we became friends. I liked him and still do."

It was my turn to smile as I remembered Peter Egan's words, and I looked over at Rachel, whose back was still turned towards us.

"So that's why Fallow refused to publish Peter's story on British Intelligence—he was protecting you," I said, staring back at Vassarri. "And when government officials seized all copies of your book, every foreign government was left in no doubt that you couldn't possibly be working for the British, not after causing so much havoc."

Even in the dull light I could see he was smiling.

"You've missed your vocation, Michael," he sighed. "And most of what you say is true as best I can remember it. But my allegiance was not with this country, although I am warming to it. My allegiances lie with Eleanor, of whom this government used against me. The offer I could not refuse was her survival. Unfortunately she was initiated into my world, but she is no longer under any obligation now they have me."

I stood in silence, looking at his silhouette against the grey light of the glazed front door. A heartless, murdering machine had given up his life for his daughter and appeared proud to have done so. My eyes slowly returned to Rachel. Her head was bowed low, and I could see her shoulders falling and rising and the faint sound of suppressed crying. Vassarri smiled sadly and disappeared into the darkness again.

"Were you the pretty tourist with prominent breasts at Lake Geneva—the Weilermann murder?" I asked.

She straightened her head and nodded.

"Jesus, you were just a kid."

She went to her handbag and removed a handkerchief.

"Eighteen," she said as she dried her eyes. "There were many others and in numerous countries. Sixteen months ago I received my thirty-fifth commendation and a promotion as Section Head of the department, meaning I would never have to work the field again. The breasts have lost a little of their buoyancy."

"And Brighton? You kept me there on purpose, probably so you could search my office."

She nodded her head without making eye contact.

"And Wendy Marshall; did you kill her?"

"She had nothing to do with our investigation!" she retaliated. "Listen, Michael, once you told me the list was in the hands of Inspector Foggerty, I was instructed to withdraw, but we still didn't know the depths of the corruption so I stayed around as long as I could, hoping you may discover it. Has it occurred to you that the newspapers were correct and she did kill herself?"

"No, not for a second. She was killed."

"By whom? And for why?"

"For what she knew. For what she discovered while she was working for Pierce."

"So, are you suggesting Pierce killed her?" she asked.

My mind suddenly ground to a halt and I realised I had been so wrong—about almost everything."

"Michael, if it walks like a duck and talks like a duck—it's a duck."

There was a faint suggestion of a smile on her lips. My eyes wandered to the top shelf of the wooden dresser.

"And that?" I said, pointing to the blue, paper flower. "Why keep it?"

She tilted her head and tears began to run freely down her cheeks.

"Something to look at; to reminisce after love has long gone," she returned in a breaking voice.

I walked across the kitchen and stopped short of the back door.

"Why didn't you, Michael?" she asked. "Why didn't you want to love me?"

I paused, staring at the black tiled floor.

"You know, you would think I would have, wouldn't you? Thing is, I didn't want to ruin what we had—or what I thought we had. What do you know about BLANCA?"

She looked puzzled and shrugged her shoulders. "What is it?"

"It doesn't matter. Goodbye, Rachel."

I stepped out into the darkness, blindly fumbling my way down the side alley and groping for the gate latch. I expected at any moment to be shot in the head by Vassarri. Even when I made it to the car, my hands shaking so much that I could barely find the ignition or insert the key, I thought my life would end there and then. The car started and I steered it slowly down the cul-de-sac towards the main road, keeping my eyes on the rear view mirror at all times, expecting to see the mercenary, standing in the road with a gun aimed at me. The house simply evaporated into the night, and I pulled out of the junction, accelerating with so much force I was thrown back in my seat.

Chapter Five

All Roads Lead Back to Rome

-31-

The walls and fences of Vincent Pierce's house were high and flanked on their insides with bushy fern trees that rose up a further thirty to forty feet obscuring the main-house from passing pedestrians and vehicles. The heavy iron gates that secured the driveway were reminiscent of the entrance to a convent or private school and secured with a heavy chain and padlock. It stood quite alone down a private and made-up road, off the main arteries leading to and from Vauxhall Bridge and next to the Thames. I had sat in my car for close to four hours holding the Derringer gun in my hand and observing the main gates for any comings and goings of the occupant, and with each passing minute I felt more and more fearful—of myself and the inevitable confrontation with the pimp. Now, at nearly two o'clock in the morning I was cold and tired, parked out of sight in a side road that ran alongside the walls of the grounds, engulfed in complete darkness. In the hours I had waited, I had made one phone call from a nearby phone-box, and now awaited the arrival of the cavalry, that seemed to me now was never going to materialise. Dimmed headlights suddenly appeared, approaching down the uneven road, weaving towards the gates. I shrunk in my seat. A shadowy figure got out and unlocked the padlock and returned to the car, and moving forward just inside the confines of the walls, got out again and secured the gates. What I could make out by the interior light of his car was that Vincent Pierce was not alone; he had a female companion. Nevertheless I was not prepared to wait a moment longer for assistance, and leaving the comfort of my own vehicle, began to circumnavigate the wall in the pitch black looking for a way in. A tree so close to the wall that it had undermined the foundations and disjointed the immediate brickwork was my ladder. I groped blindly for overhead branches and pulled myself up until I was atop of the wall, in time to see Pierce and his friend disappear through the front door of the vast house.

I crossed the lawn and slipped through an assortment of heavy foliage until I was at the grand, stone staircase sweeping up to the house, and once I ascended to level ground, I made my way to the rear. It would appear the pimp had no consideration for the blackout regulations because the back of the house was lit up like Crystal Palace, giving me a perfect view inside. He was entertaining, or recruiting, or both. His companion was sixteen if she was a day, a mere child who had undergone her metamorphosis into womanhood, had refined her God-given attributes and stupidly believed it was the key to a successful life. Pierce laughed and joked as he opened a bottle of Champagne while she took up a seductive pose on the settee. Perhaps to make herself appear more mature she took a long cigarette and placed it to her lips, but before she could light it the pimp shook his head and pointed her towards the French doors. I backed away to the side of the building. I watched the young beauty standing on the veranda exhaling clouds of blue smoke into the chilly morning air, smiles of anticipation forming on her lips, of what the remaining night would bring and whatever the pimp had promised her. When she returned back into the house I re-emerged from the side to the rear, glancing in at the canoodling couple on the settee. Obviously help was not on the way, so I waited for the pimp and Snow White to engage in their first kiss, drew a deep breath, and entered though the open doors.

When Pierce pulled his face away from hers, the girl was staring wide eyed at me; at the stranger pointing a loaded revolver at the both of them. He gauged her horrified expression and swung his head around.

"Well, well, well," he said, calmly, "if it isn't the inquisitive rat employed by the great Harry Griffin. You know you're trespassing, don't you?"

"At present I would have thought that was the last of your problems," I returned.

He focused on the gun and grinned.

"Do you plan to use that? Do you know *how* to use that?"

I looked at the revolver and then back to him.

"I'm not sure," I said, "but I'm willing to give it a try."

I squeezed the trigger. I felt the firearm jolt and recoil in the palm of my hand and a bullet lodged itself in the wall two feet above his head. Immediately the girl began to scream and the pimp was on his feet.

"Are you fucking mad!" he screamed.

His condescending smile had gone now, replaced only by one of fear as he stared down the barrel of the revolver. I however felt a newfound energy racing through me; a power I had never experienced before.

"Sit down, Vincent," I ordered. "And tell your girlfriend to have a little decorum. Her incessant yelling is making me nervous."

The pimp did as he was told and sat down, taking the girl's hand and hissing at her to be quiet. I sat on the arm of the chair opposite with the gun still trained on them.

"You're making a big mistake," said Pierce. "I can have you killed."

"And just how do you plan to achieve that if I kill you here and now?"

He looked at the girl and then at me, his face turning paler and his eyes blinking repeatedly.

"You wouldn't kill me. You're not a thug," he scoffed.

"Neither was Jack the Ripper, but it didn't stop him killing four women."

"Who! What the fuck has Jack the Ripper got to do with anything!"

"Private joke," I laughed. "Now let me get to the point. The last time we met you categorically denied killing Wendy Marshall."

"So what? It was the truth!"

I shook my head, still grinning. "You're stubbornness doesn't make you any the more convincing. It only serves to underline what you really are—the lowest form of life I've ever had the displeasure meeting. You're a maggot, Vincent, not to put too finer point to it—a cold-blooded killer. So what happened when you received instructions to free Wendy?"

"I told you!"

"No. No you didn't. Did you bring her here? Is this where you brought all the others? You see, I'm guessing that being so close to the river that you have some type of jetty at the bottom of your garden, big enough for a small boat to come alongside. Am I right, Vincent?"

"You're not making any sense," he spat.

"Oh, I think I am. You couldn't let Wendy go, could you? She knew too much about you. She knew what you were doing. She had documented proof. All the time she was under your rule, she didn't present much of a threat, but when it came to letting her go . . . Well, that was just something you couldn't let happen. So you probably brought her here, argued, and you broke her neck, thereafter you dumped her body in the river. Sure, it cost you three thousand pounds, but it was worth it just to protect your little enterprise."

I appeared to be of little consequence to the girl now. The gun no longer frightened her and neither did my presence. Now she was looking at the pimp with a horrified expression.

"I like this house," I said as I surveyed the room. "It's spacious, roomy, and I bet it has a cellar; a really big cellar. Will you give me a guided tour?"

His young companion had snatched her hand away from his and had edged away from him as far as the settee would allow.

"Did he promise you nice things?" I asked her; "a big house in a sunny country, servants, marriage to a rich man?"

Her frightened eyes stared back at me.

"Thought so. What's your name?"

"Michelle," she barely whispered.

I looked at the pimp who had bowed his head and then looked back to her.

"And where are you from?"

Her wide staring eyes focused on the gun once more.

"Essex."

"A runaway?"

She lowered her eyes confirming my suspicions.

"The problem is, Michelle, is you think you're special—we all do. But to this man you're little more than a commodity, a sex object to be whisked away to foreign shores, to be used, abused and never seen again. As special as you think you are, you're just one of thousands that go missing every year—sold into slavery. And this nice man here, who probably bought you that pretty dress, is a trafficker in human beings, a parasite."

The pimp began to rise from his seat, his eyes flashing at me angrily. Likewise I rose from my position and raised the gun towards his head. I could see in his face he was about to challenge my prowess as an assassin and whether I had the stomach to actually kill someone. Fortunately for me, and for him, there was no need.

"This had better be good, Michael. I don't take kindly to being woken up in the middle of the night."

Harry Griffin and the Neanderthal was standing just within the French doors and slowly moved inside.

"Do you want to explain to me what's going on," he said, looking first at the gun and then to me.

The pimp sighed exhaustively and dropped back down on the settee, clasping his hands to his face.

"I was wrong. He did kill Wendy Marshall," I explained.

Harry was without his usual cigar. He would never leave to chance ash, a butt, or even the smell of Havana being associated with him at a crime scene. He nodded and stood over the pimp.

"You've obviously come prepared, Michael," he said, looking at the gun. "Are going to kill him?"

"This was Wendy's," I said looking at the revolver. "She obviously felt the need for it—to protect herself come the day she confronted him."

He nodded in agreement. "Things never turn out the way we plan, do they? You know, Michael, if you weren't so eager to get that girl away from him she might still be alive. Have you thought of that?"

I nodded reluctantly. "It's why I'm here."

"Then get on with it! Shoot the fucker!" he said.

The young girl had pulled her knees up to her chest, her arms wrapped around her legs and her body shaking and trembling with fear. Harry signalled to the Neanderthal to remove her from the room.

"There's something else, Harry; the reason why I called you," I said. "Pierce is involved in human trafficking. He's working with Phillip Heidegger, better known as the frog—something to do with an organisation called BLANCA. The girls are usually runaways or orphans, picked off the streets and put in storage until the buyer arranges the transfer. Wendy has an apartment in Hackney, and I went there and had a good look around. I found this gun and a diary. In it there was a reference to 22 girls, and underneath there were the names Morgana, Hanley, Christabel and Marley. I thought they were names of prostitutes at first, you know aliases."

"And were they?" asked Harry looking intrigued.

"I thought so until one day I was crossing Blackfriars Bridge. And then I saw it."

"Saw what, Michael? What the fuck did you see?" he growled impatiently.

"Morgana."

"A prostitute?"

I shook my head. "A ship. They're all names of merchant ships. Wendy couldn't be specific, but she knew that 22 girls would be put on one of those ships and taken abroad, to be sold into the slave trade, the sex trade."

Harry was enraged and tore the revolver from my hand and pushed it against Pierce's head. The young girl screamed again but she was held fast by Malcolm the Neanderthal.

"You've been doing fucking what?" shouted Harry as he jolted the nub against the pimp's skull. "Abducting young girls! In my manor! Under my very nose! You fucking piece of shit!"

I truly believed that Harry was going to kill him there and then as I'm sure did the Neanderthal and Michelle.

"If you kill him, Harry, you'll undo everything I've tried to do," I said.

"Oh, no, not this time. I let you talk me out of it last time. This bastard's having an accident!" he screamed.

"Harry, this house is the storage, where the girls are brought before the buyer takes them away. They're here, Harry,—twenty-two of them. Kill him and we've got nothing."

Harry's finger tightened on the trigger, and even the Neanderthal winced as he waited for the gunshot to sound around the room.

"Harry!"

The pimp had covered his head with his hands, as if it would protect him from a missile passing through his brain and exiting out the bottom of his jaw.

"Harry!!!"

The small man shook with rage, but I reached over and took the firearm gently from his trembling hand.

"Fuck you, Michael! I owe you friendship but nothing else!" he growled.

I placed the gun in my pocket and patted him on the shoulder.

"Then there is no friendship, is there? Doesn't respect come into that analogy? You said you were my friend."

"I am," he nodded erratically. "I trust you."

"Then trust me to make the right decision. Let me deal with it."

Tears of anger filled Harry's eyes when he looked at me. He backed away a few steps and nodded, grasping Michelle by the arm and nodding to Malcolm.

"It's your party, Michael. Do your search before I kill him."

I looked down on the pimp, and slowly he lowered his hands and looked up at me.

"Where, Vincent? Where are they?"

He reached in his pocket, and with a shaking hand gave me a key. "First floor—rear."

"Not in the cellar?" I said with surprise.

Pierce shook his head. "A dormitory."

"Lead on."

The interior of the house was Gothic, as probably was the exterior had I seen it in daylight. In the hallway Vincent led us up a vast staircase adorned with heavy oak balustrades and high patterned ceilings. It was melodramatic in appearance, at home in a B movie horror flick, cast in long shadows and the air filled with a putrid smell that only time can manufacture. I had confined my gun to my pocket, but the Neanderthal was taking no chances. His Lugar was pushed into the small of the pimp's back as if it were fused to his anatomy. "What was this place?" I asked. At the top of the stairs Vincent paused, looking back over his shoulder. "As far as I know it was a monastery; dates back to the seventieth century."

He continued on down a dull corridor until he reached the end and stood before a door quite unique in comparison with the others. It was steel with a bar straddled across its entrance and secured with a large padlock. "Here?" I asked. He nodded and winced slightly as the Neanderthal pushed the gun harder into his spine. I slapped my hand on the door several times. "Anyone in there? This is the police!" I could hear voices, many voices, whispering at first, but then they grew louder, shouting excitedly. "Aren't you going to open it?" asked Vincent. I shook my head and smiled at him. "And let twenty-two screaming girls out in the open? You must be mad! It's enough I know they're alive. Have you harmed them?" I asked. Vincent shook his head, and Malcolm dug the revolver in a little bit harder. "I swear they've not been touched," he said.

When we returned to the grand living room, Harry was standing by the French doors holding the young Michelle by the arm. "Well?" he said. I took up a seat on the settee and nodded. "They're there—all of them," I replied. Malcolm guided the pimp to a chair by the tip of his firearm and now held it to his cheekbone, smiling as if he were just waiting for the opportunity to pull the trigger. "Then why the fuck didn't you let them out?" said Harry with a bewildered look. I smiled in the face of his belligerence. "Harry, have you any idea what it takes to look after twenty-two frightened young girls? They need feeding, bathing, clothing, reassuring . . . My guess is that within a couple of hours the staff will arrive. Am I right, Vincent?" The pimp reluctantly nodded as Malcolm applied more pressure to his face. "How many?" I asked. Vincent replied five.

"Then I suggest we shoot him and get out of here," suggested Harry. "Malcolm?"

The Neanderthal took the gun away from the pimp's face and took a step back, aiming the Lugar directly at his head.

"No, Harry!" I protested.

"Why not? A pimp found dead in his own house! The police won't even bother with the paperwork. Shoot him, Malcolm!"

"And then what?" I said. "These are your rules of engagement, Harry, but they're not mine. Kill him and all you have is a dead pimp. I want all of them—every one! The trail begins and ends with Pierce. We need the buyer."

"And you want this piece of shit to meet the buyer and make the sale?"

I shook my head. "He doesn't have to. They never use the same buyer twice. In other words they have no idea what Pierce looks like; we can use someone else in his place. In the meantime I intend to get the girls to safety."

I looked directly to the pimp. "What's the procedure, Vincent? How does it work?"

The Neanderthal took a step forward and then placed the gun to his head. Vincent squeezed his eyes closed but said nothing.

"Tick-tock, Vincent. Two choices—stay alive and take your chances or die. Now!"

The pimp shook in terror as Malcolm applied more pressure.

"The buyer comes in a small boat and the girls are taken. The boat meets with one of the four ships in the middle of the channel and the girls are transferred aboard. Each ship is equipped with a room that appears part of the hull, no doors, no port holes, welded closed once they're inside, usually in the engine room . . ."

"So their sounds can't be heard in case of a search?"

He nodded. "The girls remain on the boat two days after it has docked."

"And then they're collected?"

He nodded again.

"And when is the buyer due next?"

The pimp looked at Harry and then to me.

"Tomorrow. Midnight."

Harry growled angrily. "You believe this shit! Listen, I was born and raised on the docks. Any ship coming or going undergoes a stringent search . . ."

"Not since war broke out," Vincent interrupted. "Sure, the merchant ships are searched when they enter the docks, if they have the manpower, and even then they're lax, but they're never searched on the way out. On the way out they're not a threat. And the blackout ensures safe passage along the river. The war and its regulations have created a whole new world."

"You must be proud," snarled Harry.

It was the Victorians who put pay to the endemic of pilfering and illegal activities of London's underworld on the docks, though not entirely, by constructing enclosed docks. In 1850 the accumulated docks covered 90 acres, of which 35 acres was water; The London Dock was built in 1805; the East India Dock the same year; the Surrey Dock 1807; St. Katharine's Dock 1828, and the West India South Dock 1829, had all been built and designed using the latest technology and enforced by their own officers in which to police them. This system worked for a while, but what was not foreseen was the advent of the railways and steam-powered cargo carriers, allowing no room for expansion of the enclosed docks. The Victoria Dock opened in 1855 and was extended, and the Royal Albert Dock, built in 1880 covered 100 acres, but such was the volume of foreign vessels entering London, the once advanced ports were now antiquated and unable to cope, estimated at 40,000 ships a year with six thousand berthed at any one time. The policing of such areas therefore became an impossible task, and the meagre wages paid offered the criminals the opportunity to buy their way into unbelievable riches.

While Harry and the Neanderthal pressured the pimp for information regarding his activities, I took the liberty of using the phone in the hallway. The gentleman I awakened was not pleased to receive a call at 4.30 in the morning but was nevertheless intrigued by what I had to say. He would be there within the hour.

"Time for you to leave, Harry," I said as I walked back into the room. "Could you ask Malcolm to do the honours and tie Mr. Pierce to that chair?"

Harry looked at me indignantly.

"You what? You want me to leave?" he said.

"I think it best, considering the police are on their way."

I unplugged and ripped the cable from a table-lamp and held it out to the Neanderthal.

"Would you mind?" I asked.

Malcolm looked to Harry for approval.

"What are you playing at, Michael?" Harry questioned, nodding to his henchman to carry out my instructions. "And how the hell did you come to this? The last time we met you were in the throes of defending a murderer. Now it's human trafficking!"

"I'll explain later."

"Explain now."

"No time, Harry. Suffice to say I blame you entirely. Once you discover one secret you're bound to discover another."

"I don't understand."

I watched as Malcolm exercised his Boy Scout skills and tie the pimp to the chair.

"Nor do I—entirely, but this is greater than you or I could ever have fathomed."

"So in the meantime, what am I supposed to do?"

I looked at Pierce trussed up like a Christmas turkey.

"Find Phillip Heidegger. His known haunts are outside Charing Cross Station. He's French/German. He won't be hard to find."

"And what would the great detective have me do once I find this Phillip Heidegger?" he returned sarcastically.

I looked at the pimp and thought of all the hundreds, maybe thousands of girls he and Heidegger had abducted over the years, and looked patiently back at Harry.

"I need him unharmed," I said.

I spent the next fifty minutes or so asking the pimp questions while holding him at gunpoint. He sat on a hardback chair, tied by the wrists and ankles with lighting cable, retorting bitterly and resigned to his fate. The greyness of the dawn revealed the immensity of the grounds in which the house was set, and as I had predicted, a small river idled by at the bottom of the lawn where it slowly petered out, less than a hundred yards away from the main artery of the Thames. Through the open French doors I could see statues embellishing the veranda and either side of the stone steps leading down to the garden, and a thin film of morning haze carpeted the lawn. Even inside I felt the chill of the morning air and shuddered. I rose from my seat on hearing approaching footsteps and placed the gun in my pocket, yet still retaining my finger on the trigger. Inspector Foggerty, wearing a heavy overcoat and his hands buried in his pockets appeared within the frame of the door and set his gaze on Vincent Pierce.

"Who's he?" he asked as he stepped inside.

"Vincent Pierce—a pimp."

He nodded and began to look around the room with admiration.

"So what's going on, Michael? I've done everything you asked. Several plain clothed officers outside, no bells, no whistles to fanfare our arrival, and a couple of nurses from St. Bartholomew's. Care to explain?"

"Pierce has been abducting girls and shipping them abroad," I explained as I resumed my seat. "At present there are twenty-two girls incarcerated in an upstairs dormitory awaiting collection tomorrow at midnight. They may or may not need medical attention," I added, passing him the key. "And he killed Wendy Marshall."

"You wouldn't be saying these things just to piss me off, would you?"

I shook my head.

"Thought not," he said. "So who else is here?"

"Nobody. Just us."

Foggerty calmly observed the bullet hole in the wall, touched it with his hand and smelled his fingertips.

"Only I asked, because judging by the severed chain on the gates, I reached the conclusion that someone else must have arrived after you and before me. I wouldn't have thought that a litigator carries the appropriate tools to force breaking and entering."

"I had help. You don't honestly think I would attempt this alone, do you?"

He agreed with a faint nod and smiled. "Okay, I won't ask. Nevertheless, don't you think you should have called the police?"

"I did. You."

"Past tense, Michael, remember? I am no longer attached to the police force in any shape or form."

"And that's why I called you. You have the list. You know who's corrupt and who isn't. Listen, do you plan to discuss the intricacies of your present status in further depth or are you actually going to do something?"

"Not so touchy, Michael."

"It's been a long night," I replied as I looked at my watch, "and I have a preliminary hearing at 9.30. We have an hour before the staff arrives."

The inspector centred his attention between the key cradled in the palm of his hand and the bound pimp in the chair, and as if to shake himself into action, he walked to the open French doors and stepped out onto the veranda. He was immediately surrounded by several officers and the two nurses. He ordered two of his men to accompany the nurses to the dormitory, another two to take up position within the house, and the other three to remove the cars from the driveway but remain within the grounds. He joined me on the settee, and in front of Vincent Pierce I explained everything I knew, receiving confirmation every now and then from him whenever I or Foggerty demanded it. The pimp had little choice but to comply, and it was my contention that he would rather face prison than freedom, to be hunted down for the rest of his life by Harry Griffin. Within half an hour the house was transformed back to normality; the lights extinguished, the French doors closed, and the gates open to allow entry for the impending arrival of the staff. The pimp was untied and taken to the cellar while the nurses tended to the kidnapped victims. The house appeared calm and silent. Needless to say, the illusion was unnecessary. No sooner had a van entered the driveway and pulled up outside the house, the entrance was blocked by an unmarked police car, and despite the five passengers and driver scattering all over the grounds in search of a way out, they were soon rounded up and handcuffed.

Vincent Pierce was taken away, and Foggerty and myself stood in the Gothic styled hallway and watched as twenty-two bewildered girls descended the staircase towards the front door. More police cars and personnel arrived by the minute, until the driveway was a mass of black cars and every room in the house was being thoroughly searched. As the girls filed down, some calm, some hysterical, and others shrieking with elation, I fixed my stare to one in particular and instinctively said, "Emily? Emily Shaw?" I reached out and took her hand but she shied away, taking refuge behind the girl in front of her, but as she walked on down the hall she looked back over her shoulder at me and, eventually, broke away from the line and returned. "Do you know me?" she asked timidly. She was everything her waiflike image conveyed her to be, awkward and slightly gawky. "I saw your photograph once on a newspaper kiosk. Your friend is looking for you," I replied. Her eyes widened and she smiled. "Jenny!" she shrilled. "If that's her name. You're the reason I found you." She smiled sadly and opened her mouth as if to speak, but she was quickly ushered away by a persistent nurse to one of the many waiting cars. The inspector and I followed the last girl out and watched them from the steps being taken to safety.

"How did you get here, Michael?" Foggerty asked me. "How did you get from Henderson to this?"

I looked at my watch and smiled broadly, proud of what I had done and what I was about to do.

"Have you ever been confronted with the prospect of doing something so outlandish that it threatens to jeopardise everything you have ever aspired to be; something that is guaranteed to destroy your whole career?"

He shook his head slowly. "I can't say I have, no."

"Then you should come to the preliminary. You can witness a litigator commit suicide."

He laughed and slapped me on the back.

"I don't think so," he said. "You'll live forever. They Saint people like you. In years to come your image will be on stained-glass windows on every church in the country. You're a good man, Michael James, despite breaking and entering, assault with a deadly weapon, collusion, fraternising with known criminals, possession of an illegal firearm, and whatever the fuck else you've been up to tonight; excuse my French."

"Deadly weapon?"

The inspector stared down at my bulging pocket and then rolled his eyes to the sky.

"Please! Michael!" he gasped.

I smiled at him bitterly, and he smiled back as if he understood. I looked to the brightening sky and nodded my head slowly.

"Do you know, in less than two months I've lost everything? I never thought I'd let myself down, but I have," I said, quietly. "My marriage is finished, I've been unfaithful, I have ignored the sound advice of good friends, ingratiated myself in a world where I don't belong, questioned the impeccable credentials of my own flesh and blood, and lost someone very dear to me. I don't even have the money to pay my rent."

"You still have your dignity," said Foggerty reassuringly.

"No. My wife's already claimed that."

He erupted with laughter again.

"It'll all change once you win the Henderson case," he said.

I moved away from him, down the steps and onto the gravel driveway.

"We're not special, are we?" I said, turning back to him. "And that's the part I find so hard to come to terms with. I thought I was special. I thought I could achieve things that no one else could; you know, do something great. But the truth is I can't. Bye, Inspector."

Matthew Pilinger sat in the plush waiting room of Conrad & Benson Associates located on the edge of the City at Ludgate. He had been there many times before, always taking up the same seat by the window and as usual, passing the depleting minutes eying the pretty filing clerk at her desk with lustful scenarios sliding through his contaminated brain. He excelled in the art of gawking, staring at his chosen victim with such intensity so as to induce uncomfortable fidgeting or to gain a reciprocating glance. The clerk was twenty-one, perhaps twenty-two, but she was too remote to be spoken for, too consciously disengaged to willingly give her heart completely. That wasn't to say she was a virgin. In all probability she had experienced two or three sexual encounters during her short adult life, but all were executed on impulse and were never intended to be long-term, and always after every sordid liaison, both her heart and conscience were filled with regret. Every sexual act she had ever engaged in made her feel cheap and wanton, and although her hormones were sometimes apt to drive her into the arms of anyone who took her fancy, the memory of her past experiences pulled her back to the realms of celibacy and decency. She was moderately pretty with shoulder-length mousy hair, her complexion slightly pockmarked by some childhood illness—measles or chicken pox, and she fought unconvincingly to remain detached from the perpetual leer of the stranger seated by the window. Pilinger drew considerable gratification by watching his intended targets squirm, and the younger the better. For his part it was a form of mental rape—that within the weight of his stare his lewd thoughts were transmitted and infused into the minds of the innocent. Corruption does not have to be physical!

Like the images in his contaminated mind there was nothing real about Matthew Pilinger—not even his name. True, his suits were the best money could buy and his home was in fashionable Chelsea, but his endeavours to appear like those he tried to emulate were misguided. His world was darker than the one he had ingratiated himself into, the world full of high finance and dogged-minded businessmen, who could dismiss millions of pounds on an error of judgement or bad investments. He considered himself to be like them—a captain of industry and a pioneer of a newfound enterprise that had flourished unchallenged for hundreds of years. Slave trading, or white slave trading to be precise, was an activity that few talked about at the dinner table and less acknowledged on the streets. It was a taboo subject—a predicament others found themselves in. It was a well-documented subject that had been debated by government and accentuated by the likes of Booth and Mayhew, but all to no avail. More troublesome was the fact that white slave trading was not a criminal act, and though many lobbied parliament and fought to have the law reviewed and amended, the selling of children continued, thus people such as Pilinger were allowed to conduct business without fear of reprisals. It was the right of a mother to sell her child if she so wished and history recalls that at Haymarket children were selling for as little as five pounds; all of which were entirely legal transactions. There were of course clandestine sales, conducted mostly by the poor who could ill-afford another mouth to feed and were unconcerned as to the child's future or its welfare. The unscrupulous, willing to take advantage of someone else's misery, would make the purchase and guarantee to place the child in a good home for a substantial fee, payable by the buyer. Guarantees such as these were worthless and both parties knew it. Girls especially were a worthwhile commodity and were either sold into prostitution or into domestic service. Parents considered them to be a burden, lazy and destined for the inevitable—pregnancy, whereas boys were retained for the money they could generate the family once put to work. But there were prostitutes who took their daughters onto the streets to 'learn the game', but the life expectancy of a fledgling was minimal, perhaps ten years, before their looks faded or they were ravished by venereal disease. Those sold into prostitution were monitored by the environment in which they were placed and subject to stringent examinations concerning hygiene, thus prolonging their years and their earning capacity.

Even in his expensive suit Pilinger, a broad shouldered, square faced, fifty year old possessed the appearance of a convict. His posture was irretrievably slouched and he lumbered rather than walked, and his vocabulary was slightly slurred by an uneducated upbringing and embellished with a mismatch of accents—French, German or Belgian. The young filing clerk had passed him an indiscriminate glance, seemingly in the direction of the window, and acknowledged his large hands that at once made her feel ill at ease. They were ruthless hands devoid of tenderness. She shuddered at the image of what such hands were capable of, and she sighed gently to herself as his constant gaze began to irritate her, desperately awaiting the moment when Richard Conrad would call him into his office.

"I've seen you before," he said to her, finally. "Do you have a name?"

The sound of his voice scared her. It was brash and inquisitive and she knew any reply could only provoke further unwanted questions. Nevertheless she was a devoted employee to Messrs.' Conrad & Benson, and she would not allow the incessant lecherous behaviour of this man to distract her from her duty. But ignoring a man such as Matthew Pilinger only provoked him all the more. He approached her with a wolfish smile playing on his lips and sat on the edge of her desk, brushing her cheek with the back of his index finger. She pulled away instinctively and he laughed.

"Don't be so squeamish. Do you think you're different from the others?"

The girl swallowed hard, fear debilitated her entirely.

The tip of his index finger clumsily traced the form of her lips, and his eyes shone with an almost impenetrable excitement.

I merely asked your name."

She pulled back again, as far as she could without overbalancing from her seat, and the more she did so the fiercer his smile.

"Tell me your name, pretty. Tell me your secrets."

He began to stroke her hair as if she were an inconsolable child.

"Patricia," she suddenly gasped. "My name is Patricia."

Pilinger nodded his head and his hand slowly slid down her hair.

"A nice name. And you have a man? I bet he's older—much older. Does he give you nice things, Patricia, in return for your undivided attention? Do you please him? Does he satisfy you?"

He acknowledged her trembling body, and after moving his hand down the length of her tresses, it came to rest on her small breast. Her instincts told her to run from the room—to leave and never return, but every muscle within her was seized rigid. He closed his eyes as if to savour the moment and emitted a long, shuddering sigh.

"Give me your hand, girl. I won't hurt you."

He reached over and took her by the wrist, placing her hand on his thigh and sliding it towards his groin. She squeezed her eyes closed and turned her face away, realizing the pain this man could inflict on her if she denied his wishes. She could hear his breathing growing heavier and he began to gently moan as her hand moved closer. 'Patricia," he groaned.

She drew a deep breath and held it within her.

At the sound of a door being opened Pilinger stood up and swung in the direction of a grey suited gentleman standing in the doorway. Richard Conrad observed the scene for a moment; Pilinger's flushed face and his filing clerk's look of relief that he had at last interrupted the situation. He looked scornfully at Pilinger.

"Is everything in order here?" he asked.

Pilinger smiled. "We were talking; a nice girl."

Conrad looked directly to the distressed clerk.

"Patricia?"

She nodded with embarrassment and hastily began to sort through her papers.

Conrad's eyes narrowed with doubt, but with a jerk of his head he motioned Matthew Pilinger to follow him. Conrad's office was palatial—shelves filled with heavy, leather-bound books on law, a grand desk, and a window view looking across the city rooftops. Agitated by what he had seen but moreover by Pilinger's behaviour, Conrad sat at his desk with a look of disdain glowing on his face.

"I expect a little decorum on these premises," he said. "If I ever have to remind you of that fact you and I will never do business with you or Mr. Heidegger again. Do you understand me, Mr. Pilinger? I might remind you that you are already on a short lead."

"As I said: we were just talking."

"No. You were gauging her reaction. Save your little games for the whores you favour and stay clear of my staff."

Pilinger smiled and shrugged his shoulders. "If that's what you prefer then I have little choice."

"You have no choice!" Conrad snapped.

The moment was allowed to pass, for Pilinger to subdue the humiliation of the reprimand and for Conrad to regain his composure. It was purely business. Richard Conrad was a remnant of the Victorian age with staid values, and in his eyes Pilinger was little more than a thug who had made the right contacts at the right time. But for all his opinions, be them misplaced, biased or simply part of his own rigid upbringing, Conrad was little more than a small rolling cog within a large complex machine; he followed the orders of a higher authority without question.

"How many?" he asked eventually.

Pilinger took a pack of cigarettes from his inside jacket pocket and placed one to his lips to which Conrad shook his head. "Not in my office!"

Pilinger muttered an incoherent reply as he returned the cigarette to the packet.

"Twenty-two," he replied.

Conrad sighed impatiently. "The order is for thirty—thirty a month. That is the agreement."

"I'm aware of the agreement," Pilinger retaliated.

"I have people to answer to."

"Ah, yes, your people," the foreigner began to laugh. "BLANCA, isn't it? An organization I have served loyally for twelve years yet have never been privileged to meet; I have no idea who or what they are. And may I remind you that working for you, albeit indirectly, carried with it certain terms and conditions; an agreement you failed to honour. You gave your word to Phillip and myself."

Conrad reclined in his chair and folded his arms.

"You expect me to introduce you to BLANCA when you have continually failed to meet the agreed quota?" he said.

"Not continually! Recently! You may wish to remind your superiors that there is a war on. The specifications of the merchandise they require has been somewhat limited by the present conditions."

The director smiled. "And no doubt your nationality has compounded the situation."

Pilinger glared back indignantly.

"My passport and papers record me as French," he returned.

"Do they?" Conrad grinned. "Have you forgotten you owe BLANCA an allegiance—for extracting you from a Hamburg whorehouse, giving you a new identity and riches beyond your wildest dreams? Yet you have the audacity to enter my office and make demands of those who gave you life. As long as I draw breath I will never arrange a meeting. You, like your partner, are Germans in London. Don't tell me it does not affect the duty you are bound to."

There was no mistaking Conrad's contempt for Pilinger, but it was not fuelled by his nationality or the fact that his country was waging war on Europe, but moreover by what he regarded him to be—an unscrupulous hoodlum who excelled in the abduction of young women. By the same token Pilinger looked on Conrad as a spineless fop who dignified his own lofty position by ridiculing those who took risks, believing he was serving some great cause while maintaining a position of authority.

"I do not abduct the girls personally," Pilinger said.

"No, you do not. You employ 'takers' of which are answerable to you. And you are answerable to me. Do not set the blame on others. Why the shortfall of eight girls? How difficult can it be?"

Pilinger disregarded protocol and Conrad's warning, drawing a cigarette from his pack, igniting it and momentarily disappearing behind a veil of white smoke. Conrad made no comment.

"In peacetime it was easy," Pilinger began. "There were foreign students, families holidaying and sightseeing, runaway girls from all corners of the country coming to London and seeking opportunity. The outbreak of war has put a stop to all that, and the papers and newsreels depict this city as not some great metropolis paved in gold, but just another shit-hole filled with frightened people. After the blitz who in their right mind would want to come here?"

"Nevertheless you have failed to meet the required number."

The foreigner drew on his cigarette and nodded in agreement.

"I could always lie. Would that satisfy you and the elite members of your secret organization? You require prime girls and I get you prime girls. I could easily make the numbers up by throwing in a few bitches but then what purpose would that serve?"

"None whatsoever," replied Conrad with a shake of his head. "Every girl is examined thoroughly—to see if they're intact. Only the purest can be accepted."

"And the merchandise to date has been good, eh?"

Conrad slowly nodded his head. "With few exceptions, yes. But that is not the issue."

Pilinger visibly swelled with pride but stared questionably back at the director.

"You've yet to tell me what happens to those . . . few exceptions. What becomes of them, the ones who aren't virgins?"

Richard Conrad straightened in his chair and resumed an air of confidentiality.

"I have it on good authority that you have lost one of your prime takers;" he said as he turned the pages of a loose-leaf folder before him, "an Elizabeth McCauley. Perhaps that is the reason for the shortfall in numbers. She was, according to your partner Mr. Heidegger, the very best in the business. What has become of her?"

Pilinger shrugged callously and reclined in his chair.

"Who cares what became of her?" he replied bitterly. "Put a woman in a position of trust and it's bound to end in a catastrophe. We'll replace her—simple."

The director's face fell hard and still.

"I don't think you understand the implications. What guarantees can you give me regarding this woman? Can you be certain that guilt has not induced her to repent; that she has not gone to the police to confess all? This woman must be found, Mr. Pilinger, and silenced. Is that understood?"

"We have people looking for her—she will be found."

"I do hope so. Otherwise we shall be forced to dispense with your services. In the meantime twenty-two will have to be acceptable," he stated. "The board shall be informed of your excuses and assured that it is your intention to make up the shortfall of this quarter by the next."

The foreigner looked perturbed.

"You want me to furnish you with thirty-eight girls within twelve weeks?"

"They are the conditions, and I'm sure the only conditions the board will accept. Or I could easily tell them that you no longer serve the purpose for which you were first brought to this country. I could tell them that your nationality and, indeed, your accent is giving me cause for concern—that your counterparts no longer trust you. Believe me, Mr. Pilinger, when I say that you must never underestimate the powers of BLANCA; your survival depends on it. Who do you think you're dealing with here? Do you think you can hoodwink an organization who has been an influence on the world since Christ was crucified? Never forget how insignificant you are. You are merely a supplier of merchandise—an order you constantly fail to meet. We do not deal in half-measures, Mr. Pilinger, and the next time the cost of transportation will be deducted from fee."

Opening a drawer of his desk Richard Conrad took out a large brown envelope and handed it to Matthew Pilinger.

"The address of the new storage facility and the date of the next transportation; I hope I need not remind you of the rules," he said.

"Read and destroy. No, you don't have to remind me."

"Full Payment for the merchandise is enclosed and payable to the usual account-holder; one hundred pounds per girl. I see no reason to alter the amount due to your failure to meet the quota. The price will remain unchanged next quarter providing you amend the default of the eight missing pieces."

Pilinger crammed the envelope into his inside pocket and stood up.

"A word of warning to you," said Conrad as he reclined in his chair. "It wouldn't do for you to fail next time. You must never forget what you are."

"Which is?" challenged the foreigner.

"A Nazi living in London."

"Have you completely taken leave of your senses, dear boy?" responded Thomas Gallagher as he strode off through the hallowed halls of the courthouse. "And when was the last time you slept? You look an absolute sight."

"Tuesday, I think. Look, I'm simply asking that you allow me to make the opening speech," I said as I hurried after him.

Thomas emphatically shook his head. "My dear deluded boy, we're about to defend one of the biggest cases of the twentieth century with the world's media present, and you look like you've spent the night in a dustbin. Don't they have razors where you live?"

"You don't understand. I have new evidence."

The counsellor slowed to a stop and turned to face me, drawing his pocket watch from his waistcoat and registering the time.

"Then you have twenty minutes in which to enlighten me of this new evidence." He set his sight on an anteroom and nodded his head. "We'll talk in there," he said.

I had met Thomas and Badger on the steps of the courts at a little after 9 o'clock and the counsellor, forever flamboyant in his loud suit and embellished with a blue silk handkerchief and thick gold chain and fob hanging from his vest pocket, was full of anticipation—until he saw me approaching, to which he sighed hopelessly, shook his head and walked inside. Badger observed me in much the same way though never submitted an opinion.

"Thomas, there's no time to go through it all," I persisted.

He placed down his files on the tabletop and took a seat, gazing up at the pathetic figure in front of him and slowly shaking his head as if I had deliberately set out to ruin his day.

"Eighteen minutes," he said, looking at his pocket watch again.

The watch was a Hunter, a fashion accessory for the affluent, the pompous, and those who would rather refer to it as a timepiece than a watch.

"Is that an heirloom?" I asked.

"Not especially," he grunted. "Seventeen minutes and thirty seconds. Make haste, Michael, this is crucial to the outcome of the trial."

Badger, who had been loitering in the doorway throughout, closed the door and sat himself on the edge of the table.

"Thomas, if Michael is in possession of information imperative to the Henderson case, and there is no time in which to discuss its intricacies, then what harm could it possibly do to let him make the opening speech?" he said in a calm and soothing manner.

Thomas Gallagher narrowed his eyes and reclined in his chair.

"Kenneth, I regard you as a worthy examiner and a man who can appreciate the colossus of this case, but you know as well as I that an opening speech can turn a trial and can influence a jury no matter what evidence is put before them. The requirements for a convincing speech is in the way it is delivered; with foresight, clarity, detail, and conveyed to the jury by someone with compassion, of breeding, articulate with a grasp on the English language, but above all, by someone who looks a tad more innocent than the accused. Do you honestly consider Michael James to be such a man?"

They both turned their eyes to me, taking in my wrinkled and grass stained suit, my unkempt hair and stubbly chin, my pale and colourless pallor, and after a brief moment of intense scrutiny, Badger cringed.

"Granted, I have seen Michael in better condition and true, he does resemble some rare species that's evolved from living hundreds of years underground, but I'm sure he can do it. There is no jury, Thomas; it's a preliminary. The only person he has to convince is the judge, and you'll be there to guide him if he goes awry."

Badger had intentionally wasted five minutes, and after looking at his Hunter cradled in his hand and acknowledging the passing of those precious five minutes, Thomas resignedly nodded his head.

"I could ask for an adjournment," he said as he rose from his chair, "but the judge would certainly decline the request; seems I have little choice. But heed my words, dear boy, should your escapade here today result in the slightest embarrassment to me we'll never work on another case again. I won't be made a laughing stock in front of that insufferable oaf Robert Humphrey. Is that understood?"

"Completely," I nodded assertively.

He gathered up his files and tucked them under his arm.

"The presiding judge is Henry Harcourt Crane; an elderly man with radical leanings. He can sometimes be lax and may allow you a little latitude during your babblings. At least have the decency to look half presentable," he said as he walked from the room.

Badger observed me from the corner of the desk, his arms tightly folded and his eyebrows perched high on his head.

"Well here we are," he said. "Somehow, God knows how, I've managed to stay with you till the end. It is the end, isn't it, Michael? Tell me this mind-numbing evidence you possess will not take us to trial."

I grinned at him tiredly.

"You have my word; we won't be going to trial," I assured him.

"Good," he replied. "Perhaps now we can set to work on building this business back up and dispense with all this stupidity. I hope this has taught you a lesson. Why you took this case in the first place is beyond me; as a law firm we're technically dead; broke."

"You know about that?"

"Penny told me you're just a postage stamp away from bankruptcy."

"Bah! What does she know?" I scoffed.

"Evidently a little more than you. She cares, Michael. I care."

"I have some money coming from my father's estate—enough to stay afloat. We'll be fine."

He slid his buttocks off the table and walked to the door, patting me on the shoulder as he passed.

"I do hope so, Michael. Time to face the judge," he said.

I inhaled deeply and nodded my head.

"Have you got a comb?"

Every seat in the wooden panelled courtroom was occupied, seemingly by representatives of the press, who sat with notepads on their laps and pencils poised above them. The minority were the general public; armchair detectives and would-be sleuths and those possessed of a macabre curiosity in murder. Henderson was standing in the dock, gazing over the proceedings with an air of wonder, like a child at his first outing to a fairground or some magical experience. I sat at the defence table with Badger and Thomas Gallagher, not daring to look in his direction in case he waved or tried to speak with me. The low volume of mumblings was suddenly silenced when the clerk stood before us and commanded the court to rise. Henry Harcourt Crane, a tall, stony-faced man of thin stature appeared from his chambers and took his place at the bench, nodding to the clerk to read out the indictments against the accused. Pens flew into action as the charges were read out while Henderson shook his head with the mention of every name he had allegedly consigned to a headstone. The judge nodded firmly on the clerk's conclusion and looked directly to Thomas Gallagher. "I understand the defence is to be first to present their case," he said. Thomas gave me a wary sideways glance and reluctantly stood up. "My Lord, in light of new evidence, evidence I am unfamiliar with at present, the defence requests that Mr. James make the opening statement," he said placing his hand on my shoulder. Henry Harcourt Crane expressed his dissatisfaction with pursed lips and a vague shake of his head. "And Mr. James is who?" he asked. I began to rise but Thomas's heavy hand held me down. "Mr. James is working on behalf of the accused, My Lord, and has gathered the evidence in his defence." The judge nodded. "And he feels confident enough to deal with a case of this magnitude?" he asked, looking directly at me. "Sir, Mr. James is a litigator and more than familiar with proceedings. Our request is that he makes the opening statement and nothing more," replied Thomas with a servile smile. Heads began to turn in all directions and the scribbling pens froze above their notepads as the judge considered the motion. "Under the circumstances I will allow it providing the prosecution has no objections," he said looking directly to the prosecution table. Sir Robert Humphrey, who appeared to be swathed by an entourage of legal minds and advisors, bowed to the bench and then looked in our direction. "We have no objections, My Lord," he said.

I would imagine that Sir Robert would rather allow a novice like me to present the case for the defence than the experienced Thomas Gallagher; it could only assist in his victory. Judge Crane stared down from on high and said, "Proceed, Mr. James." I rose sheepishly and looked to the bench. "Some years ago, in 1933, my firm defended a civil case for George Henderson for unfair dismissal from the Great Eastern Railway," I said. "Needless to say the case was settled out of court and Mr. Henderson was reinstated in his job as an engine driver. It was this year, two months ago, when I learned that the George Henderson we defended was the same George Henderson everyone was referring to as the Blackout Butcher; a man who had walked into Camberwell Police Station and confessed to all eight murders. When the case was brought to me by the D.P.P. I was unaware they were the same man; such was the insignificance of the original case. I can't recall having met him back in 1933, and can only assume somebody in my employment at the time undertook his case. Even when I found out that he was once a client, and we were his designated lawyers, I felt no obligation towards him—none whatsoever. What inspired me to pursue this case were for entirely different reasons. It is a documented fact that the accused is illiterate, and therefore in light of the arresting officer's conduct and, indeed, his imprisonment for falsifying statements and perjury, Henderson's statement must be considered inadmissible, whether Henderson made it or not. The case against George Henderson hinges solely on his illiteracy. When Inspector Carlisle took the statement . . ."

"Objection," cried Humphrey. "The trial of Inspector Carlisle is not open for debate, and never at any time was he found guilty of misappropriation concerning the arrest of George Henderson. Defence is inferring he fabricated the statement."

"I am merely stating the facts appertaining to this case and highlighting the obstacles that both you and the defence will face come the trial. The question of Carlisle will certainly be raised," I retaliated.

"Your objection is overruled, Mr. Humphrey," said the judge. "You will have your chance to redeem Inspector Carlisle's reputation in your opening speech. Continue, Mr. James."

"But, Your Honour . . ." Humphrey persisted.

"Your objection has been overruled and noted! This hearing is to establish whether there is a case to answer, and we shall hear from both sides without continuous objections."

The prosecution bowed humbly and resumed his seat.

"I am not here to take part in a mud-slinging competition," I continued. "At this moment in time it is immaterial as to whether Carlisle fabricated the evidence or not. We will face that hurdle when and if we go to trial. But we must never lose sight as to why George Henderson is standing before you. Allegedly he made a statement and confessed to all the killings, and if he did make that statement he's now denying it. Either way it has to be established that he murdered eight women with what little evidence we have. There are no sightings of him in the vicinity of the murders although he was stopped three times by the police. And every time Henderson gave his real name and his real address. If he had just killed someone, can we honestly believe he would have done such a thing? Why not give a false name and a false address? Why leave to chance that he may be associated with those shocking crimes? The answer is pure and simple. He gave his real name and address because he was unaware of the murders! As an illiterate he couldn't read about the atrocities in the newspapers. He may have heard about the killings on his travels but he would not have known the details. He was oblivious to the fact that women were being killed close to where he lived, what the papers refer to as the Death Diamond. Pathology reports suggest that the murderer wore a variation of different clothing at each murder; no two items were the same; tweed, wool, cotton, even an army tunic. The police took an inventory of Henderson wardrobe at his home, and none of the fabrics matched. There was however a surviving witness by the name of Wendy Marshall; she was the first to be attacked. Unfortunately Miss Marshall died before she had the chance to say her piece for justice, but her claim is that when she met her attacker he was wearing an expensive suit; Savile Row, as she described it. Now, George Henderson is a hard working, underpaid train driver who could barely feed his children let alone afford to buy expensive suits and a vast wardrobe of clothing. It renders the case against him preposterous. And with no witnesses, no trace evidence and no sightings it makes the allegation against him even more ridiculous."

Gaining a little more confidence and free from objections, I rounded the table and stood before the gawping audience. To my surprise Inspector Foggerty had taken up my invitation and was standing at the back of the courtroom looking deadly serious. Badger smiled at me, impressed with my conduct so far, and even the staunch Thomas Gallagher managed to look magnanimous.

"However, my quest for the truth was not without its surprises," I told the packed courthouse. "Peter Egan was a gifted journalist who believed vehemently in George Henderson's innocence. He also brought to the world's attention the ongoing corruption case of two hundred and forty seven officers in the Metropolitan Police Force of which Inspector Carlisle was one."

Sir Robert Humphrey's half rose as if to object but was stared back into his seat by Judge Crane.

"Once we establish that the arresting officer is corrupt, and the courts have already have, then we have to seriously question the statement allegedly made by Henderson. Did he make such a confession or was it manufactured? Was an ambitious police officer, eager for promotion and recognition, guilty of framing an innocent man? Only one man knows the truth, and he's standing there—in the dock. Guilty or not he isn't about to confide in me. He wants his life back. He wants everything returned to normality. It doesn't make any difference if he made the statement in a moment of impulse. It doesn't make a difference if he actually killed those women. He wants what he wants—his rights as a human being—to be judged innocent until proven guilty. It is what we all want, what we all deserve in the free world. And Peter Egan believed in those rights. In the short time I knew him I learned there is a greater power that comes into play, a power so great the common man cannot fathom its immensity. And this power is funded by you and by me—the taxpayer. The free world I mentioned just now is a fairytale, a myth we have all come to believe is a way of life . . ."

"You're straying, Mr. James," said Judge Crane. "Please confine your opinions to the case in question."

"I am, sir. Today we are all here for the preliminary hearing of George Henderson; a man who was arrested exactly one year and sixty-three days ago. Why the delay to bring this man to justice? Why was a case of this magnitude ignored for so long?"

"The period is irrelevant."

"The period is completely relevant, sir. The government intentionally shelved this case because of the discovery of Inspector Carlisle's corruption, and in order to have his sentence reduced, he divulged the true extent of the graft, though he gave no names. Before they could proceed with this case, they had to discover what Carlisle knew. They had to know how deep the corruption went. I believe they call it *hedging your bets*, My Lord."

"The public are aware of the allegations regarding police corruption, Mr. James, but they have no bearing on this case."

"They have every bearing, Your Honour. Wendy Marshall was a witness for the prosecution. Her history was questionable, to say the least, and the D.P.P. never really considered her to be either reliable nor credible; her statement was buried for the best part of a year, and when the government realised that neither the prosecution or the defence had any evidence in which to use, they reintroduced her back into the system, to sway it for the prosecution."

Judge Crane sighed impatiently. "The courts are aware of Miss Marshall's late introduction as a witness, as it is also aware of her recent suicide. Again, Mr. James . . ."

"Suicide!" I interrupted. "Would it interest the courts to know that only a few hours ago Wendy Marshall's pimp was arrested for her murder, and that she was killed for what she knew; what she knew about police corruption?"

The judge sighed exhaustively. "I'm tiring of your incessant deviation, Mr. James, and I am seriously considering retracting my decision to let you speak. Perhaps Mr. Gallagher should make the address on your behalf. I'm willing to adjourn for one hour in order for you to inform him of whatever knowledge you have on this case."

"The Coroner delivered a verdict of suicide because that is exactly what the government instructed the Coroner to do," I argued. "Carlisle didn't give the names of his co-conspirators, so the government were left with the possibility that 247 Metropolitan Police Officers were accepting bribes but they didn't know why. Every act has consequences, and usually motive, but in this case they had nothing."

Judge Crane shook his head and cracked down his gavel to silence me.

"I won't listen to another word," he said. "This is a preliminary hearing concerning Mr. George Henderson and eight female victims, and you are suggesting some vague tale of a government conspiracy."

"I'm not suggesting. I'm stating it as a fact."

"Nevertheless, I won't allow you to turn this hearing into a circus. We will adjourn for one hour."

To my surprise, and everyone else in the courtroom, Sir Robert Humphrey suddenly rose before the judge could sound his gavel and signal an adjournment.

"My Lord, we would regard it beneficial to both the prosecution and the courts to hear what Mr. James has to say, rather than be ignorant of the facts come the trial. It would be remiss to disregard any evidence—no matter how incredible it sounds."

"Are you questioning my authority, Mr. Humphrey?" the judge scowled.

The prosecutor bowed humbly. "It is not my intention. Nevertheless, it should be the right of the prosecution to discredit or substantiate whatever evidence the defence puts forth, and this would be unachievable if we are bereft of all the facts, or if the courts intentionally suppress evidence."

It was the word 'Suppress' that took the wind out of the judge's sails, stole the fire from his eyes, and slightly deflated his posture. In light of the subject—government conspiracy—his decision to silence me may, under the close scrutiny of the media in the courtroom, make him appear part of the very problem I was at such pains to highlight. George Henderson's presence, and indeed the crimes he was accused of, almost paled into insignificance, especially now I had whetted the media's appetite for agents and police corruption. Judge Crane cast his eyes over the courtroom, and even in that short moment, more and more people were entering to stand at the back, having heard by word of mouth in the courthouse that a down-on-his-luck litigator was going berserk in court number 5 telling tales of government intervention and perverted justice. The judge dropped his stare to me, and after some consideration, nodded his head slowly.

"Continue, Mr. James. But I urge you to take caution."

I nodded gratefully.

"Wendy Marshall was a prostitute, as were a few of the other victims the Blackout Butcher claimed. What singled her out from the others is that she survived to tell her story to the police. It was all treated very seriously until they realised just how unstable she was. Her past is nothing short of a tragedy. Police were sceptical, and with little evidence to substantiate her story, her case was filed away and practically forgotten. When the spate of murders ended and Henderson was arrested, she was called in to identify him in a line-up. Henderson, she insisted, was the man who took her to a garage, stripped her naked and cut her arms, legs and torso with a cutthroat razor. I met her and she began to tell me a story of human trafficking. Why she should tell me this, I had no idea; it wasn't relevant to George Henderson, but the two are inextricably linked; and even more remarkably so are the 247 corrupt officers."

I walked directly to the defence table and stared at Thomas Gallagher. "May I borrow your timepiece?" I asked. Thomas looked bewildered by the request, but nevertheless disengaged the chain and handed it to me. Before returning to my place I whipped the blue silk handkerchief from his top pocket and placed it squarely on the floor, and then putting the watch in its centre, proceeded to stamp on it several times. Thomas grunted some incoherent profanity while the courtroom howled with laughter. Judge Crane observed me with disbelief as I took the handkerchief and the fragmented watch and spread it out in front of him. "Do you consider this to be funny?" he said, pointedly as he surveyed the mess. I stood almost on tiptoes to get a view of my masterpiece and lifted a tiny spring between my thumb and forefinger. "Could you tell me what part this piece plays within the mechanism of the watch, sir?" I asked. He stared back incredulously as the laughter in the courts began to rise again. "Your Honour? Can you?" I asked. He shook his head rigidly. I raised another piece, a minute cog no bigger then a match-head on the tip of my finger. "And this? Can you tell me the function of this piece?" He cracked down his gavel to silence the constant tittering and expressed a thunderous glower towards me. "I will not tolerate this a moment longer!" he snapped.

"And that is why the government could never ascertain the source of the corruption. They didn't know. And to make matters worse neither did the corrupt officers. The role of each corrupt policeman was so minimal that it could hardly be considered a crime; a lost document here, turning a blind eye there, but culminated they aided a human trafficking organisation that spirited literally hundreds of girls out of London every year. In the early hours of this morning I was fortunate enough to come face to face with Emily Shaw, a girl whose photograph I had seen on a newspaper kiosk and marked as a missing person. Now I knew for a fact that Emily had been registered missing in no less than twenty-three London police stations, so when I visited the same police stations to also report her missing, I should have been assured she was already registered; she wasn't—not just at one station but all of them. The reports had been taken but never filed. Like that broken watch each policeman had an important function in which to make the whole mechanism function, yet on the face of it they hardly served a purpose. Carlisle never divulged what his part was because he had no idea he was part of a machine. The government, eager to get to the bottom of it, put their own people on the case, targeting those who they believed would discover the route to it all. One person was Peter Egan, the journalist who broke the story of police corruption, and myself because I was Henderson's designated lawyer. They knew that once Carlisle was found to be corrupt, the other 247 would be discovered. Foolishly I let myself be taken in by a young lady who I later discovered was a government agent. With hindsight I should have been suspicious, for I met her the very day the Henderson case was dropped on my desk."

Sir Thomas Humphrey appeared utterly dumbfounded, resting on his elbows and hanging on my every word. Thomas's watch seemed of little consequence to him now as he envisaged his future as a barrister slipping down the toilet, and for his part Badger sat with his head bowed, shaking it slowly from side to side as if he had just been told that a meteorite was going to slam into the earth within the next minute and wipe out all signs of life. The journalists were frantically jotting down notes, and the whole court hummed with anticipation.

"I have allowed you to wander into the realms of fantastical speculation, Mr. James, but it is too far removed from our purpose here today," said Judge Crane. "As compelling as they may sound, I cannot allow you to continue with your fanciful tales of covert operations and government intervention."

"Official Secrets Act?"

"I shall give you one last chance, Mr. James. State your case regarding the accused free from embellishment or I *shall* have you removed."

I reluctantly conceded and expressed a knowing smile back to the judge. The hulking frame of George Henderson stood within the dock dressed in grey trousers and a dark jacket that tugged at his shoulders. He smiled when I looked at him, and Judge Crane coughed deliberately to urge me onward. I faced the crowded courtroom and saw familiar faces, one of which was Edward Foster, George's friend. He nodded his head when meeting my gaze.

"Anyone who knows George Henderson will give you the same opinion," I began. "He is a good man, a hard working man, a friendly man and a funny man. It is inconceivable that such a person could carry out the horrific acts we have come to associate with the Blackout Butcher. And I agree. He is also a brave man—certainly braver than I. In 1915 he and his friends took themselves off to war to fight for King and Country, to free us from tyranny, just as our boys are doing at this very moment. Unfortunately George sustained life-threatening injuries when his unit was bombarded by German artillery fire; only he and his close friend survived and soon they were back home in England recuperating. War is a terrible thing. It gives a man licence to kill with impunity. Some come back as heroes, some never come back at all, and some we decorate with medals; medals for murdering another human-being. In the world of warfare it is expected. We spend, and are still spending vast amounts of money manufacturing weapons of mass destruction and training ordinary men to kill. At times such as these, and of then, we move the goal posts. Outside the realms of the military the rules change. If one man kills another in the civilian world, chances are he'll hang, just as surely as George Henderson will if found guilty. There is no evidence connecting him with the murders that took place in the winter of 1940. All we have is a statement that he disputes ever making. Pathology reports say the same thing; no blood or semen traces, no fingerprints, no sightings, no witnesses. The prosecution are correct in saying that Inspector Carlisle was never indicted for fabricating the statement, and as the only witness to the alleged confession was Sergeant Stephen Rawlings, who disappeared soon after Carlisle's arrest, we are left with only the word of George Henderson. In short, this case cannot be proved by either the prosecution or the defence. There is no case to answer."

Badger appeared relieved I had completed my address and had raised his head and was now looking in my direction, and Thomas half shrugged as if to let me know that I hadn't caused too much damage.

"Do you wish to submit a plea, Mr. James?" asked the judge.

"I do, My Lord," I said. "He's guilty."

The gasps and cheers from the crowd was deafening, and Thomas and Badger collapsed in unison. Such was the furore that Judge Crane actually stood up and repeatedly banged down his gavel as if he were driving a six-inch nail into a plank of wood. Reporters began to scurry in and out of the court, conversing with one another to establish if what I had said was actually what they heard. Court ushers waved their arms in a frantic attempt to bring order, while uniformed policemen began to appear at the doors. When at last the roar subsided, the judge looked down on me.

"You say your client is guilty! Is that your plea?" he said.

"Guilty as hell," I returned confidently. "And I would have been none-the-wiser had it not been for my regimented upbringing at the hands of a father whose ways were deeply entrenched in the Victorian age. He despised familiarity. He considered it to be a weakness. In the workplace he insisted that everyone was addressed formally, and this was instilled into me. I adopted the same set of values when I started my own law firm. I would never allow a client to address me by my Christian name, and by the same token I would never refer to them by their Christian name. It is a form of respect as well as creating a barrier. True, when war broke out I relaxed the rules." I reached in my pocket and took out my wallet, taking out a business card. "Wendy Marshall once accused me of throwing around these gold lettering cards like confetti; and she was right. I do it out of habit—to drum up business. I even had my full name put on them. To reiterate, I had never met George Henderson before in my life, and had I he would know me only as Mr. James—nothing more. It was one day, after a lengthy conversation with Inspector Foggerty, that he said something to me as I left. Three words; '*Thank you, Michael*'. It was then I experienced one of those déjà vu moments; an inexplicable feeling of being in the same predicament before. When my associate and I interviewed George Henderson at Wandsworth Prison some weeks ago, I foolishly did what I always do; I handed him a business card. Pretty stupid coming from someone whose client was known to be illiterate, whose whole life was hanging on that very fact; the only reason I was representing him. By then it was too late, and I simply left the card on the table. It was when we left he said the same words Inspector Foggerty said to me that day I left him; *'Thank you, Michael'*."

I looked at the accused and walked a little closer.

"You can read, can't you, George? You read my name on the business card." I said. "Gathering up discarded newspapers from train compartments for your fire was just a ruse. You just wanted to read about your exploits in murder, and feigning illiteracy was a foolproof plan, that should you ever be arrested any statement taken would be deemed inadmissible."

A faint smile began to form on his lips.

"And May, your wife? When you were charged with the murders she couldn't get out of there quick enough. A year in prison and you didn't receive one visit—not one note! She knew what you were, or at least she suspected. As did your good friend Brian Moffett. The nurse killed at the field hospital had to be you."

I looked to Judge Crane. "Needless to say the courts should assign new counsel. We will not be representing George Henderson from this moment on."

Judge Harcourt Crane nodded his head.

"Under the circumstances the court shall be cleared," he said.

"Thank you, My Lord."

"However, proving the accused is literate is not enough. You have overlooked how the murderer had access to the variation of different clothing."

All eyes were fixed to me and the courtroom fell into a stunned silence.

"Ever left anything on a train, Your Honour?" I asked.

He considered the question and nodded. "Once, yes—a briefcase," he replied.

"And did you manage to get it back?"

"Fortunately, yes, at Lost Property."

I smiled at him and shrugged my shoulders.

"Of which every railway station in this country has. It's amazing what people leave behind on trains; coats, hats, expensive suits, army tunics. All George had to do was walk back through the carriages and collect them or take them from lost property. The Defence rests."

"Yes," murmured the judge tiredly. "I think it's just as well."

It was the court-usher who advised us to make our exit through the back entrance. It was sound advice considering half the world's press and most of the public were baying for blood and more than eager to lynch me from the nearest lamppost. I, on the other hand, felt totally absolved of any guilt and cleansed of all conscious. George Henderson was one hundred percent guilty of his crimes and I knew it. We were whisked through a door adjoining the judge's chambers, which dropped steeply down a staircase and into a labyrinth of claustrophobic corridors that jutted left and right and back and forth until we eventually emerged into daylight. Thomas led the way, heading towards an awaiting car with exhaust pluming and a patient chauffeur seated behind the wheel. "Remind me, dear boy, that once we're out of harms way to never speak to you again," he said. I never got the chance to think of a witty retort, for suddenly I was assailed on by four suited gentlemen, two of which took me by the arms while another, a man scarred with dermatitis took Badger to one side and hissed in his ear. "What's going on?" I demanded. Badger looked at me and shrugged his shoulders. Thomas was at the car door, unconcerned and detached from my predicament, and without giving me a second look, climbed inside and ordered the chauffeur to drive on. "Best do as they say, Michael," warned Badger. The man with dermatitis pointed to a nearby black car. "You're coming with us!" he commanded. I was bundled in the back seat, sandwiched between a miserable looking oaf on my left and the man with dermatitis on my right. From the rear of the courthouse the car moved to the front, through a swathe of reporters and popping flashbulbs, gathered on the pavement and spilling out onto the road, nudging its way into the traffic and then accelerating off to some unknown destination.

The city folded in around us, and the cars and pedestrians were dwarfed by the high buildings that squeezed the roads narrower between them, tightening with every twist and turn. My four kidnappers never said a word, never exchanged in idle conversation, or even had the courtesy to enlighten me as to where I was being taken. For reasons known only to themselves the car swung off across Albert Bridge to the outskirts of Clapham, circumnavigated the common, only to remerge back at the bridge some thirty minutes later. "Are you lost?" I asked the driver. He gave no reply, turned off Chelsea Embankment and headed towards Sloane Square. "Don't ask questions, Mr. James," said the man with dermatitis. Like Vincent Pierce I was resigned to my fate—whatever it was. As a defence lawyer I had pronounced my client guilty. Worse, I had exposed the government as a bunch of novices, incapable to protecting a little old lady crossing the road without pulling her dismembered body from the wheel-arches of the lorry that run her down moments later. I would probably spend the rest of my days in the Tower, charged with treason, or be locked up in some insane asylum. Nevertheless I was fearless. "Is it compulsory for all you government agents to be arseholes? I mean is it an attribute you feel the need to emphasise when you apply for the job? And you; doesn't having a severe skin complaint such as dermatitis hinder your occupation as a government assassin? It makes you so unique from the rest of the crowd. That's how my partner identified you the night you and your associates blew my office to pieces. No wonder you were at the scene so fast. You never left. It's a shame George Henderson never had a skin complaint like yours; he would have certainly been easier to identify."

"Be quiet, Mr. James," he warned.

"Yeah, yeah, yeah," I scoffed. "Listen, Mr . . . ?"

"McFadden," he said.

"Listen, Mr. McFadden, I can understand why you're a little miffed. Had I not this insatiable appetite for history, I'd probably be dead now. Knowing what I knew about the Spider's Web saved my life—and Sylvia's, though it has to be said she saved me to begin with . . ."

McFadden shook his head throughout.

"Anyway, you and your idiotic comrades, including the treacherous bitch you work for, must have seriously been pissed off when I discovered why 247 police officers were on the take and protecting a consortium of foreign human traffickers." I laughed to myself as I looked out the window. "And now here I am, in the back of a government car, being driven around

London by a group of incompetents, as if it were a Sunday outing. What have you in store for me, Mr. McFadden? Can you still be hanged for treason, or was that law revoked? I'll have to look it up. I'm sure they hang you for piracy. Not sure about treason, though. But I'd imagine the government have their own form of punishment; something along the lines of crucifixion only with bigger nails and more torture."

"Mr. James!"

"I've always thought torture was a bit like foreplay you know, to get you used to what was to come. Don't you agree?"

The official sighed exhaustively.

After the car had cruised up Park Lane, circled Marble Arch, and cruised back down again, we headed down to the embankment.

"I suppose my little speech today may have jeopardised your chances of promotion," I gloated. "The king will probably be crossing you off his Christmas card list. You'll be lucky to get a job serving vagrants in a soup kitchen. Still, you're not alone. No doubt I'll end up selling extortionate insurance policies to people who are only hours away from death. That is, of course, if I'm not incarcerated in a dark and dingy dungeon beneath the Tower of London for all eternity."

It was when the car crossed Waterloo Bridge and turned into the car park behind Lambeth Police Station that I realised my fate. Inspector Foggerty had stood at the back of the court looking extremely perturbed as I condemned his profession and those who employed him. He had probably received orders for my immediate arrest and to charge me with a catalogue of trumped-up crimes—and a few not so trumped-up. McFadden took my arm and led me though the back entrance of the building and up the staircase to the second floor. "I know the way," I insisted. The dermatitis detective tightened his grip. "I don't think you realise how much trouble you're in," he returned tersely. "I'm beginning to grasp the situation," I said. I was marched through the corridors like a convict being traversed from Newgate to Tyburn on hanging day, with everyone stopping to gawp and point a finger at me. Being public enemy number one brought with it a certain sense of arrogance, of recognition for all the wrong reasons, and while some shook their heads with total disapproval, others winked and gave me the thumbs-up for my endeavours. We stopped outside the door

I had passed through once before; the operations room where twenty or so detectives sweated over the Henderson case. "Say your prayers, big mouth," the detective smirked as he opened the door. A cheer went up and I stood in a stunned silence as I observed everyone I knew and some I didn't. Inside there were the twenty-two girls we had freed that morning, Badger and Thomas Gallagher, Bernie Mansall, Penny and Inspector Foggerty, all quaffing wine from tall, thin glasses with a spread of food adorning the tables. The dermatitis officer laughed and slapped me on the back, pushing me forward to greet everyone and handing me a glass of wine. Sylvia threw herself into my arms and hugged me as if her very life depended on it, as though she had no intentions of ever letting me go. "Can't you do anything right?" she said, tearfully. "I turn my back for five minutes and you fuck everything up."

I smiled and kissed her on the cheek.

"You look great, Sylvia, really," I said, gently touching her face. "The bruises and the cuts have all gone."

"Not entirely. But Selfridges do a great line in make-up."

Penny joined us and smiled at me and took my hand. I gave her a gentle hug.

"I owe you an apology, Penny," I said. "Since that night I was with you I've been evasive, but I want you to know that . . ."

"Night? What night?" shrilled Sylvia indignantly. "Have you two been at it?"

Penny looked away, her face flushed with embarrassment.

"Just once," I assured her. I looked back to Penny. "I need you to know the time was wrong. I was with Sarah and . . ."

"Don't explain," she interrupted with a smile. "I have someone now. He's a good man, a kind man."

"My brother," said Sylvia.

I smiled and nodded.

"I'm pleased for you, Penny, I really am."

She kissed the tips of her fingers and touched my cheek. "You had your chance," she grinned.

Inspector Foggerty put his arm about my shoulder and excused us from the girls. He chortled like Father Christmas as he led me away to the corner.

"I like surprises, don't you?" he cackled. "Not as good as yours, though. Tell me, Michael, was it Henderson's literacy that convinced you of his guilt?"

"Amongst other things. Suzy West was George's childhood sweetheart. She vowed to wait for him when he went off to war. But women being the impulsive creatures they are didn't wait too long—two months. She found someone new and moved out to somewhere near Guildford. She wrote to George while he was in the field hospital and told him. Culminated with his extensive head injuries it triggered something inside him, turned him into a cold-blooded killer. My father defined it is a form of 'Middle Madness', but George can't be held completely responsible. His condition is amnesic, a form of amnesia devoid of recall, caused by pressure on the parietal lobe and cerebrum—like the fragment of artillery shell he's still carrying around in his head. Only the aftermath of the murders, the blood and defence wounds, would make him aware he probably committed the killings, but he couldn't actually remember carrying out the crimes. When it became obvious he gave himself up and confessed. A year on remand changed his mind, plus the news of Carlisle's impending trial for falsifying evidence and perjury. Despite their long relationship George and Suzy never actually committed themselves to having sex. In his mind Suzy was dead which probably gives credence to the necrophilia allegations. In his mind every woman he killed was Suzy, the girl who betrayed him and willingly gave herself to another man. His fantasy was murdering Suzy."

"But he married and had five kids, for Christ sake!" argued Foggerty.

"But he carries Suzy around with him in his head," I replied. "She epitomized everything he thought a girl should be. She was loyal and promised to wait for him. She didn't. He came back to absolutely nothing. The condemning factor is the letter she sent. If George was illiterate—why send it?"

"He still killed eight women!"

I shook my head. "No."

"No!"

"He didn't. His fantasy did. You have to remember that Suzy West was his first true love."

Inspector Foggerty sighed with impatience. "Excuse my French, but that's bollocks."

"It isn't bollocks," I persisted. "Who was your first love?"

He thought for a moment and began to smile warmly.

"Vanessa Robson. She used to sit next to me at school. She showed me her fanny once behind the bike sheds . . ."

I began to laugh.

"What! I was smitten!" he retaliated.

"And I bet there isn't a day that passes when you don't think of her."

"Not every day;" he said with a shake of his head, "four or five."

We both laughed, but I looked to the young girls.

"What happens now—to them?"

"For the past several hours my team have been making contact with their parents, through phone, local police stations, Red Cross organisations; they'll all be home safe and sound shortly. And our mutual friend Vincent Pierce has agreed to go through the motions and meet the buyer tonight. We'll put a dozen or so officers in the house, have the river police ready on the Thames, and nab the bastard. As for Phillip Heidegger, word is he's gone deep underground; a German in London would have little choice at this present time."

Don't worry about Heidegger. If he's in the city he'll be found. I have people on it."

He gave me a wary look.

"Don't ask," I said. "You might want to look into an organisation called BLANCA—been in existence since Emperor Claudius; Heidegger works for them. I'll give you the information."

It was then I saw her sat in the corner of the room staring thoughtfully into her glass of wine, head bowed and face sad. Rachel—Eleanor.

"Don't be too hard on her, Michael," said Foggerty following my gaze. "Everything in life happens for a reason, and this is yours."

"You think so?" I replied bitterly.

"I know this. Twenty-two girls will be sleeping safely in their beds tonight because of you—and her. Would you have made your discoveries had she not driven you in a particular direction?"

"That's not the point!"

"But it is," he sighed. "It's the only point. Never let your occupation get in the way of what really matters. I haven't seen it for a long time but I can remember what it looks like. There's a woman in love if ever I saw one."

"She was just doing her job," I sneered.

"Is that right? Then why is she here? Her work is done now. She's got no reason to be here. So why is she? I've never met the woman before, but your associate and secretary filled me in on the details. It may interest you to know that she's offered her resignation."

"And why would she do that?"

"Because sometimes it takes someone to show how selfish we can be—someone like you."

He patted me on the back as I walked over to Badger, who stood leaning against the wall next to Thomas Gallagher seated on a chair. Thomas shook his head as I approached but managed a meek smile.

"Sorry I ruined your opening speech," I said to him.

"On the contrary, dear boy," he said, raising his glass, "I couldn't have put it better myself. Of course, I'll probably spend the rest of my life teaching English literature to the natives in some shantytown in the outback of darkest Africa, but I'll survive."

Badger laughed. "He's exaggerating. You were right about the press—they all want the story. You'll be a rich man, Michael."

Badger was talking but I was looking at Eleanor Cole, who was glancing at me and fighting over embarrassment for supremacy.

Emily Shaw, who hadn't taken her eyes off me since I walked through the door, finally mustered up the courage to approach. I gazed at her without saying a word, registering a smile I wish I could bottle for when times were low. She undid a pendant hanging around her neck and handed it to me.

"It was my mother's," she said. "I want you to have it."

I stared at the fragile silver coil of chain in my hand without understanding.

"It's St. Jude, the patron Saint of lost causes," she said. And then she leaned forward and kissed me on the head. "God bless you, Michael James."

Through tiredness and fatigue, but moreover through emotion, the tiny pendant blurred as my eyes filled with tears.

"Not special! My arse," howled Foggerty.

After which each of the twenty-two girls filed past to kiss me on the cheek, and with every passing girl and every gentle kiss, I felt my defences crumble to nothing.

Bernie came and shook my hand, informing me that McFadden, the man with dermatitis, was in fact one of the brotherhood who had risked his own life to rescue Sylvia and I from the devastation that were once my offices, to which I profusely apologised to him for my earlier conduct and wished I was dead. As the room began to empty, and the girls had all left to be taken home, Eleanor Cole put on her coat and began to walk to the door.

"It would never have worked," I blurted impulsively.

She stopped, facing the door without turning. "Why, Michael?" she said. "Why wouldn't it work?"

"Why? I'll tell you why . . ." I stammered.

She turned and expressed a faint smile. "I'm listening. Why? Give me a reason."

"Because . . . ?"

"Because of what?"

"You know! Don't tell me you don't know," I blabbered defensively. "You know I know. And I know you know I know."

"Fuck me!" Foggerty groaned.

"Michael! Will you just give me one good reason so I can leave and put all this behind me," she shouted.

Badger, Foggerty, Bernie, Thomas, Sylvia and Penny all waited with bated breath for the reason.

"Because I . . . ? Because you . . . ?"

I felt the ground beneath me giving way. But then it came to me.

"I could never conceive of the idea of living with someone called Eleanor," I finally concluded.

"You liked the name Rachel," she pointed out.

I shrugged and agreed with a nod. "Because that's who you are to me."

"Then from now on I'll be Rachel. Simple," she smiled. "Now are we going home, or is it your intention to embarrass me further in front of your friends?"

Call it what you will, an epiphany, a revelation, but either way I found myself pacing across the devastation of Paternoster Square towards my solicitors', and once through the door I moved directly to his office, dispensing with announcements, introductions or niceties with Mrs. Metcalf. Mr. Lothby was sitting at his desk and looked visibly shocked, appraising me with a look of both confusion and concern. "Whatever is the matter, Michael?" he gasped. "Please sit down, sit down." He rose immediately and walked to the door. "Mrs. Metcalf, bring tea," he shouted, and then turning back to me, added. "You look perturbed. Tell me what has happened." He returned to his seat and assessed me in the same worried manner.

"Mr. Lothby, I received a breakdown of my father's estate and I was wondering . . ."

"I assure you, Michael, there is nothing amiss," he interrupted.

"Please, I am not suggesting for one moment there is anything amiss. It concerns my father's personal account; the funds remaining in his bank after his death—the sum of £120, 000."

Mr. Lothby looked perplexed, his eyes fixed to mine as though he was hypnotized, and I said his name aloud to break him from his trance. "Mr. Lothby!" He shook his head as if awakening from a deep sleep.

"You're questioning the sum?" he asked, indignantly.

"Indeed, I am, sir," I returned. "The amount seems minimal in context with his position."

He looked at me and slowly shook his head.

"It's a sad day, Michael; a sad day, indeed," he said. "Obviously you are contesting the Will and accusing this company of misconduct."

"No, sir!" I said, emphatically. "I am neither contesting nor accusing you of anything, but do you not find the sum a rather meagre amount given his status?"

The anger etched in his face appeared to dissipate and he nodded as if he began to understand my enquiry, and then he walked directly to a filing cabinet and returned with a folder.

"As you know our firm were privy to all your father's transactions," he mumbled as he flipped the pages. "I have never considered or questioned the amount bequeathed to you and your sister till now."

Suddenly he stopped and gazed back at me, his face absolutely motionless, but his eyes ignited as if he recalled some long-forgotten memory, and dispensing with the contents of the folder he moved directly to the last few pages of accounts. He studied it for a few moments and looked up.

"Here it is," he said. "Your father transferred a large amount of his fortune into your mother's personal account; a substantial sum leaving very little in his own account."

"How much did he transfer?"

"Five hundred thousand pounds; I never questioned it. Mary was his wife and it was considered a gift; completely legal."

"When, Mr. Lothby, when did he transfer the money?"

He dropped his stare to the accounts and raised them again.

"March, 1926."

I tried to put the right questions into the correct order, and that accomplished I realised my initial instinct was proving correct and moving me to the final answer.

"My mother was diagnosed with cancer in February and died in August the same year. Why would my father transfer so much money into a dying woman's account?"

Mr. Lothby shrugged his shoulders.

"Michael, people do strange things when confronted with death; especially when it concerns a loved one. The transferring of that money into your mother's account wasn't so much a totally legal act as one undertaken out of despair. Mary was his life; she did everything for him. And may I remind you that you and Caroline inherited every single penny."

"But why? She had her own money. She was the daughter of a wealthy industrialist."

Just then Mrs. Metcalf breezed into the office carrying a tray, and when I turned to face her she smiled pleasantly.

"Good heavens. Michael. Tut-tut-tut. No appointment?" she frowned.

Mr. Lothby, a man who despised familiarity of any kind, especially in the workplace, expressed his annoyance in the form of a scowl, and with a wave of his hand ushered Mrs. Metcalf out of the room, saying only, "You can talk to Michael later. Please leave us," and on the closing of the door I turned back to him.

"Who told you these things?" he asked confidentially.

It was a point of fact. I had never seen any documented proof appertaining to my mother's family or her fortune and, come to that, had never met any members of her family. Her history, as much as I knew, was that she was an only child, daughter of a wealthy industrialist who died when I was very young and whose wife had died two years earlier of the same dreaded disease that took my own sweet mother. Simply it was an historical fact as told to me by my father.

"Michael, I have known your father since we were twenty-five," began Mr. Lothby in a patient tone. "He was living in an apartment in Sloane Street, and the second time we met he took me back to meet Mary; they had married two years earlier. How they met was never conveyed to me in any great depth, but from what I could fathom was she was once a patient and their friendship developed into a romance. Despite the grand location of the address their apartment was sparse, and I got the distinct impression that William was struggling to pay his bills. But then your mother was a beguiling woman and, I suppose, the address was a taste of things to come; that there was a better life ahead for the both of them. At around the same time I started this firm William placed all his business with me; something he probably did out of friendship, but he rose through the years to become powerful and wealthy. Never at any time did your father tell me that Mary was the daughter of an industrialist or that she inherited a vast fortune. To my knowledge she never had a penny, and this office has performed every transaction William and Mary ever undertook. I fear that you have either misinterpreted the facts or have been seriously misinformed."

As my father said, when authority speaks you will believe anything and, given my present condition and frame of mind I began to doubt myself; as if the story was not related to my mother but someone else entirely. But as I stared back at Mr. Lothby's sympathetic smile, I remembered what Mr. Sandpiper had said. "*She came from good stock, a family of industrialists, and her wealth made your father's look like loose change.*"

Within two hours I pulled up outside the Sandpiper residence, and after getting out I took a moment to collect myself, appraising the clear sky above which was in the beginnings of being consumed by darkness, and no sooner had I set foot on the gravel path, Mr. Sandpiper appeared nervously at the door. As I approached, the cold sound of crunching stone beneath my feet was overwhelmed by the warmth of people talking and laughing, a baby crying, coming from within the house, and clearly Mr. Sandpiper was agitated by my presence. He stepped out and pulled the door to behind him. "Michael, I have my family here," he said. I stared coldly back at him and replied, "We need to talk. We need to talk now, Mr. Sandpiper." He stood motionless, gazing at me as if I hadn't understood the importance of his statement, but he registered my anger and reluctantly nodded. "In the park; five minutes," he said. He about turned but I grabbed the doorknocker, holding the door fast. "I said NOW!" His head lowered and his eyes closed. "Is it time, Michael? Has the time come to pay for my sins?" he said, quietly. I motioned him away from the house with a jerk of my head and like a servile dog he followed me, across the street and through the entrance of the park, and without a single word being exchanged we reached the bench before the small expanse of water. When we sat he looked anxiously at the leather bound book on my lap.

"You didn't have to bring it," he said. "In my heart I always knew it existed."

My eyes roamed the still water for I couldn't bring myself to look at him.

"You knew, didn't you? You knew about my mother," I said.

I heard him sigh and slump back on the bench, and as the silence stretched towards breaking point, I turned to face him.

"Why did you protect me? Why, when I'm about to throw you to the wolves and expose you as a cold, blooded killer did you not tell me the truth?"

"Because there are things a son shouldn't know about his mother," he replied. "From the first time he met Maria at the brothel I knew your father was besotted. He would often go missing, but I knew by his mood that he'd been back to see her. I knew his wife Mary and Maria the prostitute were the same person."

"But my mother wasn't Spanish!"

"Neither was Maria. It was a ruse, Michael, concocted by the Madam of the house. Prostitutes are a commodity like any other, and the prettier you dress them up, the more exotic you make them the more desirable they become. As far as I know your mother was an orphan, raised by an aged aunt in the Cotswolds; a true country girl, but when she died Mary came to the city. Now, London can be a dark place, filled with unscrupulous people who prey on the homeless, and one as beautiful as your mother was a prime candidate for a gay-house, but vast amounts of money are invested in them; fine clothes, and to a point, training in the sexual art and being a lady. Perhaps it was a form of guilt that your father chose to marry a prostitute, but he visited her frequently at the brothel and after some years he managed to get her out."

"He bought her?"

"Every penny he earned. You see, Michael, when a fact is so inconceivable, the lie devised to protect the ones you love has to be extreme, to take it as far away from the truth as possible. You were raised believing your mother was wealthy, so when your mother was diagnosed with terminal cancer, he transferred his own fortune into her account to give the lie credence. It was probably the only lie he ever told you. I neither have the desire nor the inclination to besmirch the good name of your mother, and that's why I never told you."

I sat in silence, coming to terms with my discovery.

"Has anyone ever confided in you, Michael? Has anyone ever asked you if you can keep a secret?" he asked.

"What?" I returned, preoccupied with my own thoughts.

"It's a terrible thing to ask someone because the moment you share that secret, it ceases to be a secret, and simply you have offloaded your burden onto someone else; the secret becomes their responsibility. It's a curse, Michael, a spell. Since that book was given to you your life has taken a downward spiral, and by degrees it will destroy everything you are. Your marriage is over; your wife is an adulteress and you an adulterer. Your business has suffered because your reasoning is clouded, and now you have to live with the cold reality that you and your associates were defending a multiple murderer . . ."

"I've handed all my papers over to the D.P.P. and informed them that George Henderson is guilty. He'll have his day in court."

"But not with you? You don't plan to defend him this time?"

"Of course I don't," I snapped. "The bastard should hang! You should hang!"

He slowly nodded in agreement as everything about my past consumed me; that all of it had been a lie. Mr. Sandpiper watched me as I sat shaking my head angrily.

"Michael, what your father and I did was shocking, but the world was different then. The East End was a barbaric place, ostensibly one big rookery, filled with cutthroats and murderers, thieves and prostitutes. I can't begin to defend myself and nor would I try, but those terrible acts we committed contributed to a massive change in London's East-End; better housing and living conditions, better street-lighting, assistance for the poor, the monitoring of prostitutes. For the first time the whole world could see that the streets of London weren't paved with gold. They were filled with starving people. The invention of the camera made the world aware of what Queen Victoria was oblivious to, and in the years following her death the winds of change began to blow. Newgate Prison, probably the most notorious gaol in the world was demolished, as were a thousand other places like it. I went to Dorset Street back in 1929, the day before they were about to demolish it. Did you know that there were three unconnected murders at number twenty-six in just ten years? That is how terrible the place was; murders were commonplace. But your father and I changed all that. We brought about change—for the better."

The stillness of the pond before us began to take on a dullness as the darkening skies overhead reflected on the waters surface. The ducks and geese had disappeared, and the surrounding trees began to throw long shadows in different directions; the whole park began to submerge into a bluish gloom.

"You told me you met my father back in 1912, on the bridge at the Serpentine; was that the last time you saw him?" I asked.

Pip shook his head.

"I received a telegram late 1929, which simply said, 'Our mutual friend is dead,' and gave instructions as to where and when I should meet him.

Obviously I was skeptical and even considered ignoring the request, but once again my conscience got the better of me, and I never underestimated your father's capabilities. I was living under the threat of his confession and had little choice in the matter. And so at the given time and date I arrived at Wimborne Cemetery. It was mid-November, and I remember the train journey down, wondering why I was going to Dorset, so far from the city, wishing to myself that he wouldn't be there and this was just a prank. I entered the cemetery gates and looked over the countless headstones and memorials, some standing white and proud, others grey and lopped to one side, a few lying flat on their backs. A cold chill blew through the grounds, leaves every shade of brown rolling between the graves and rising into the air, lifted on the undercurrent and spiraling back down to the earth; it was like a ballet. There were a few people milling around; widows with flowers, children with vague memories, and gardeners dragging large, brown sacks filled with redundant leaves; such places are there to remind us of our own mortality. I saw a stationary car in the distance, parked on the grass beside the narrow road that encircles the vast graveyard; a grand car beside which stood two figures; one being your father. I knew enough to know that he owned a blue Bentley, and as he never learned to drive, the other figure must therefore be his chauffer. As I closed nearer I saw him standing beside the car, clad in a dark overcoat and smiling back at me. In front of the car was a picnic table on which sat a bottle of Champagne and two fluted glasses, a small wreath on the bonnet, and he mouthed something to his chauffer who promptly walked up the road a way.

"Good of you to come, Pip," he said as he extended his hand.

My own hands remained buried deep in my pockets but he would never outwardly show any sign of embarrassment. He simply returned his hand back into his pocket.

"Why have you brought me here?" I asked.

He looked every bit his sixty years, as no doubt did I, but he had seemed to age quicker. I sensed a definite deterioration since I had seen him last, twenty years ago on the Serpentine Bridge. His thick, sandy hair had gone, to be replaced only by grey at the sides of his head and baldness on top. His face was craggy now, crazed like an aged oil painting, and his posture belonged to a man twenty years older. There was a brief moment

I felt pity for him, given the time and place we were in, and he, too, must have had the same feelings.

"Oh, dear, what have we done, Pip? What have we done to ourselves? We are nearing the end of our lives and what have we to show for it? Naught but hard work and heartache. I truly can't remember where my life has gone, but there are reminders of my achievements scattered here and there; a portrait hanging in the West-Wing of Bart's, a brass plaque on the wall at Guy's, obscured from view whenever the cleaner's cupboard door is left open. I'm surrounded by associates every day and every night. They follow me through the corridors and strike up conversations I have no desire of taking part in. They invite me to parties and banquets to mull over my past or talk in depth about one of my books. They corner me at lectures and treat me like some messiah, instead of what I really am—a stupid, dithering old man. Do you know, Pip, of all the colleagues and associates I know, there's not one I can call a friend. You are the only true friend I ever had. When we last met I was rude and arrogant, and for that I am truly sorry."

I believed that what he said was sincere, and there was a sadness in his eyes I had never witnessed before. I knew his wife had recently died and felt moved to say something.

"I was sorry to hear about Mary," I said.

"A fine woman;" he replied, "a good hearted woman. You would have liked her, Pip, and I know she would have liked you. I never mentioned you to her and that, I feel, is a tragedy. To her I was a great man, a remarkable physician, and she had a right to know who my inspiration was."

"Me?" I gasped. "I was your inspiration?"

"Inadvertently you were. As much as I've tried to blame you for leaving, I can't. I know in my heart of hearts it was the correct thing for you to do; I even considered it myself. I knew the myth we created had to be stronger and couldn't stop at Eddowes. So the last murder had to be so horrific, so indescribably diabolical, that it could not be the work of any sane person but could only be the work of a lunatic; I think magicians call it 'Misdirection' and it worked, for the police were hunting down every imbecile in the East-End. I knew then I could let go and let the myth continue to develop in its own way. It made me a stronger person, a more ambitious person. So obsessed was I to convince the world that Jack the

Ripper was a monster, I was determined to become the total opposite, a respectable physician. I believe now the price was too high."

"So you regret what we did?"

"Not at all," he replied. "I regret not spending more time with my wife, and I regret not seeing my children, Michael and Caroline grow up, but the killing of those whores was essential to our own evolution. Look at you, Pip, you're an assistant commissioner, soon to be commissioner, I'll wager. Whatever you did then has made you what you are now."

"Firstly, my position as assistant commissioner is only temporary and not one I intentionally sought. Secondly, I intend to retire within the next fifteen months. I want to spend what time I have left with my wife, children and grand children."

He nodded his head agreeably.

"Commendable, Pip, commendable. I seem to be working harder since Mary died. I have all the time in the world; time to remember, time to forget. Strange, but you never forget anything, do you? Everything is like it happened yesterday."

He turned and looked towards the gates and then stared across the cemetery, the cold breeze inducing tears in his eyes, the location a stark reminder of his own inevitable death.

"What about the book?" I asked. "Do you still intend to leave it to your son?"

"Michael? I was hoping he would become a doctor, but he's opted for the despicable profession as a lawyer. I so wanted him to follow in my footsteps."

"He might not have wanted to become a doctor! Have you considered that?"

"Why wouldn't he?"

"He may wish to follow his own dreams. Besides, you're a hard act to follow, William. You've achieved great things in your life, and no matter how hard Michael tries, he'll never be what you are, and that will make him a failure. You've done it all. Why would he wish to repeat it? And the book, this so-called confession, will only make him despise you. Why risk the love of a son on a confession?"

He smiled wickedly, the way he used to when we were in Whitechapel, and for a brief moment I saw him again, as a twenty-year old medical student.

"He has to know, Pip. He has to know what I did and why I did it. If he hates me for it then so be it, but this is one secret I won't be taking to the grave."

A hearse slowly entered through the gates, followed by a solitary mourning car that paused momentarily and then turned left, away from us. It drove a short distance along the far side of the cemetery and stopped where a handful of people got out of the mourning car and walked to a freshly dug grave inside the surrounding headstones. William and I had been so engrossed in the past that neither of us had noticed the vicar take up his position at the head of the grave. Four bearers shouldered a pine coffin from the back of the hearse, and William raised the bottle of Champagne from the picnic table and poured it into the fluted glasses.

"This is why we are here," he said, handing me a glass, "to toast our mutual friend."

"Who is it?" I asked, looking towards the gathering.

"That, Pip, is none other than Inspector Frederick Abberline, the man who pursued us in 1888 and probably up until his recent death. It's ironic that the very people who were responsible for his biggest failure should be at his funeral, don't you agree?"

William had retained his macabre sense of humour despite his age, much like the trinkets he stole from the dead bodies, or returning to the scene of the crime the next morning and standing in the watching crowd. I believe it gave him a great feeling of importance; that he knew something no one else did.

"You never could resist gloating, could you, William?" I said.

"On the contrary, Pip. I have nothing but admiration for the inspector. He, too, will become a legend because of Jack the Ripper. What was deemed his failure will in time become his greatest success simply by association with the myth we created. Nobody can blame him for failing to catch Jack the Ripper."

"Jack the Ripper was never captured because he didn't exist!"

"Exactly my point. That is why you and I are still here today, Pip. What we achieved should be celebrated, not condemned."

We watched from a safe distance at the half-dozen or so mourners congregated around the grave that, to me at least, was beyond sad. I wondered then how many would attend my funeral, how many would cry and how many would miss me. Here I was spying on the funeral of a revered detective; a man who had accumulated no less than 84 commendations throughout his career; an outstanding achievement even by today's standards, and the funeral party amounted to no more than six. William gave me a sideways glance, taking in my sad refrain, and perhaps he could read my thoughts because his were exactly the same.

"Sad isn't it, Pip, that no matter what our achievements, no matter how great we become or how great we think we are, we're naught but ashes and dust in the end, committed to the earth to be consumed by worms? That is the value of a life—zero! You carry the guilt of those dead whores around with you like a cross on your back, but didn't we achieve what we set out to do? Didn't we drive them off the streets and back to the stinking hovels where they belonged?"

"It was temporary, William, that's all."

"Perhaps," he shrugged, "perhaps not. What we instilled into them was a sense of danger. Do you know that prostitutes seeking medication for venereal disease more than trebled after you left? Many abandoned the streets completely and returned to their jobs, or went back home to their parents, or found themselves husbands. The four lives we took probably saved thousands. I for one am proud of that."

Eventually the gathering moved away from the graveside, back to the waiting mourning car, and no sooner was it out the gates, three gravediggers materialized from nowhere and began filling in the grave. Even from that distance I could hear the earth hitting the coffin lid that sent shivers down my spine. William raised his glass and swallowed it whole and then breaking the stem from the glass placed the two pieces on the picnic table. Out of respect for the late Frederick Abberline I did likewise.

"To a good man," said William.

"To a good man," I echoed.

Frederick George Abberline (1843-1929) was the Metropolitan Police Inspector in charge of detectives on the ground. Past authors have mistakenly named him as the officer in charge of the case as a whole. He was born in Blandford, Dorset, son of Edward Abberline, a saddler and Sheriff's Officer as well as Clerk of the Market, and mother Hannah (Nee Chinn) After her husband's death in 1859, she kept a shop and raised the three children, Harriet, Edward and Frederick. Prior to joining the police force in 1863, he worked as a clock-smith, and in 1865, he was promoted to sergeant. In 1867, he was in plain-clothes investigating Fenian activities and a year later he married twenty-five year old Martha Mackness, who died within two months of consumption. In 1873 he was promoted to inspector and transferred to H Division (Whitechapel) and remained there for fourteen years. In 1878 he was promoted again to Local Inspector, Head of H Division and transferred to Scotland Yard. He became actively involved in the Whitechapel Investigation when Annie Chapman was murdered (the second victim) and was promoted to Inspector First Class in 1888 after Mary Jane Kelly (the last victim) was killed. In 1890 he was promoted again to Chief Inspector. He retired two years later and worked as a private enquiry agent, after which he worked in Monte Carlo and was employed with the famous Pinkerton Company. In 1904 he retired and moved to Bournemouth, to Methuen Road, and in 1911 to Holdenhurst Road where he died.

William looked back at his chauffer and beckoned him over with a jerk of his head, and then placing his hand on my shoulder, led me a short distance away from the car while his man packed away the Champagne and picnic table.

"I hope this wasn't an inconvenience for you, Pip," he said, "only I thought you'd like to share this moment."

"It's been very nostalgic," I said, sarcastically. "It really wasn't a problem traveling half the breadth of England to attend a funeral of someone I never knew."

William roared with laughter and slapped me on the back.

"I miss those little quips of yours, Pip, I really do. The least I can do is offer you a lift home. What do you say?"

I took a step back, away from his constant tactility.

"Thank you, no," I said, coldly. "I have a return ticket. Besides I like trains. And I'd be obliged if you never summons me again. Next time I won't come."

"Summons is a harsh word, Pip. Look, truth is we could remain friends; see out our ebbing years and talk over old times."

"That would be just dandy, William. You can tell me how you disemboweled Mary Kelly. Maybe we could have friends round for brandy and cigars and discuss how you can slaughter four women and become a famous physician in the process. No, thank you, William. If you want the truth, I think you're certifiable. Never call on me again!"

His smile dropped away in a moment to be replaced by a hard scowl.

"As you wish, Pip," he nodded. "Would you do me one last kindness?"

He walked a few steps back to the car and took the wreath off the bonnet, and when he walked back he handed it to me.

"Would you place this on the inspector's grave?"

I nodded and took it from him. He returned to his car and without another word being said it slowly drove away.

Despite our reconciliation, despite William's efforts to remain friends, the saddest event of the day was when I reached the grave of Inspector Abberline. This man, this icon of the Metropolitan Police Force, was lying six feet beneath me. I felt there and then that I had betrayed him, that I had been responsible for depriving him of his rightful accolade. He should have seen it. He should have seen it for what it was—nothing more than a stupid prank. Perhaps he wasn't that clever. Perhaps, and being the detective he was, he thought it couldn't be that simple. Why should he think that such things are that simple? I knelt by the side of him, and for reasons I can't describe, tears fell from eyes like rain, and I could hardly mouth the words, "I am so, so sorry," as I laid the wreath on the fresh earth, and through tear-laden eyes, I read the number of his allocated plot; No: Z259N.

Mr. Sandpiper was obviously moved by his recollection, for he sniffed and looked away, sadly shaking his head.

"I was reading about your great speech in court yesterday," he said, regaining his composure. "I think your father would have reconsidered his opinion of your chosen profession. I think he would have been proud of you."

"Oh, yeah," I returned drolly. "How many fathers can state that their only son has destroyed his law practice through stupidity?"

The old man smiled. "Not many. But how many can state that they did it for all the right reasons; that they risked it all because they told the truth—just as your father has?"

It was food for thought, and I found myself nodding. After a short moment of consideration I placed my father's book on Mr. Sandpiper's lap and stood up. He looked up at me, his eyes begging the question why.

"Have you ever heard of an organisation called BLANCA?" I asked.

He looked vacant and then slowly shook his head. "No, why should I have?"

"Go home to your family, Mr. Sandpiper," I said.

"But . . . but the book—the confession? You said you were . . ."

"I changed my mind," I intercepted with a shrug. "The book is yours now—a present—from me to you."

The old man's eyes began to pool with tears and his hands began to shake.

"And I can do whatever I wish with it?" he asked in a breaking voice.

I nodded. "It's your book."

He rose from the bench, and with all his strength he hurled the book into the centre of the pond. The ledger plunged into the water and disappeared, only to bob back to the surface amid a hundred rippling circles. We watched it slowly tilt to one side and roll over, until its aged pages and leather binding became saturated. Slowly it sank into the depths, until the ripples dissipated and the surface of the pond fell still.

Mr. Sandpiper exhaled a shuddering breath and nodded.

"What will you do now?" he asked me.

"If I'm not disbarred I'll go back to doing what I did; the boring stuff that life expects us to endure."

He held his hand out, and though I was reluctant at first, I shook it.

"Thank you, Michael," he said. "Thank you for everything. Will I be seeing you again?"

"God, I hope not," I grinned. "Goodbye, Mr. Sandpiper."

"Goodbye, Michael," he smiled.

I suppose, in the final analysis I had unconsciously but systematically weighed up who the greater offender was between the two—Jonathan Sandpiper or my father. Unquestionably it was the latter; a man who believed vehemently that the weaknesses of others should be exploited to their advantage and that when authority speaks or, at least whatever masquerades as authority, the vulnerable will follow. It was all around me; where ever I looked. Thousands of young men were dying every day because someone in authority deemed it so, and although this act was one of war, it really didn't make it any easier to understand. I remembered those nights as a child and as a young man, when I would enter my father's study and see him staring contemplatively into the fire, and where sometimes he would look at me as if he had something important to say. In the case of Mary Jane Kelly the last victim, he slaughtered her alone, with impunity and a madness us normal human beings cannot ever begin to fathom. Was he insane? I think he was, but not insanity as we have come to know it but an insanity imposed on him by his own upbringing, his staunch values and a superiority he believed was supreme. Like the great emperors of Rome he truly judged those below him as inferior and worthless, to use and do with as he wished. His beliefs were seriously flawed, and to this end I think he tried to make amends, with himself, my mother, me and the world. By freeing Jonathan Sandpiper of his obligation, I denied my father his last wish—to use me or anyone else to his own ends; to deprive him his place in the annuls of criminal history as the most notorious murderer of his day. Apart from a few indiscretions I had stayed true to myself, to what I thought I should be and to what I wanted to be, and the indiscretions we all make through life are gauged only by the context in which they are set. My father and Jonathan Sandpiper knowingly set out to create a monster, whereas George Henderson was a monster and didn't know it. With Harry Griffin it was a way of life—the survival of the fittest. The sting concerning Pierce and the buyer was a success, and three days later a large, wooden crate was delivered to Scotland Yard with an accompanying note. Wary of its contents army personnel and the bomb-squad were sent for, and surrounded by a circle of marksmen the lid was prized open. Inside was Phillip Heidegger, bound wrist and ankles with a sign round his neck which read, 'Happy Christmas love from Santa and the boys'. The buyer, a short, fat man of Libyan extraction, admitted to working for a consortium exclusively dealing in white slavery—BLANCA. The Morgana was bound for Port Said, Egypt, close to the cities of Alexandria and Cairo, and the abducted girls would be distributed to brothels in Libya, Syria, Jordan, and as far as Sudan. The reality of the organisation was shocking, for as a worldwide distributor in white flesh, the federation was responsible not for hundreds, but tens of thousands missing young women every year. It took a further eleven months to get George Henderson back into court, in which time Sergeant Stephen Rawlings was located by Interpol in Switzerland and brought back to England. May Henderson and her children were found living on the outskirts of Blackpool; she was not called as a witness. Prior to the trial, Henderson underwent stringent medical examinations and was found to suffer from an amnesic condition in which all memories are erased while in a state of sexual excitement. The condition is one every man and woman experiences during the moments of ejaculation or orgasm; a chaotic but pleasant state of mind where few have recollection of the event but are aware of the experience afterward. The shrapnel lodged in Henderson's brain enhanced that condition tenfold; his recall of the event totally erased from memory. While on remand he heard of Carlisle's plight of fabricating evidence and perjury and concocted a plan to feign illiteracy so as to challenge his original statement. In court his childhood sweetheart Suzy West produced a letter Henderson had written to her from the field hospital in Northern France, and it was the contention of the prosecution that the gathering of discarded newspapers from train carriages was a ruse to keep up on the events that he suspected he was guilty of and a form of enlightenment. In a trial that barely lasted three weeks, Henderson was found guilty of all the indictments he was accused of, and due to the recommendations of the jury, his sentence was commuted to life imprisonment—or in his case—to life in an asylum. *"Despite your condition, you must be considered a danger to the public,"* remarked the judge before sentencing.

The outcome of the 247 corrupt officers amounted to little and nothing; most being suspended from duty, but eighteen received prison sentences, higher ranking officers who directed the lower ranks to either falsify or purposefully discard documents appertaining to missing girls. It was as most suspected, the tip of the iceberg where few were privileged to see below the surface and only a handful publicly appeared in court.

Either way the government did everything in their power to suppress the accusations, even having media stories proof-read and edited by government officials before they were published; hiding behind the threat to national security agenda. Their interference ensured the impact of Peter Egan's story was minimal, to which it simply withered and died.

As for me I continued in business with Badger as an equal partner. Penny was a war bride and married Sylvia's brother, and Sylvia gave up her life of debauchery and settled down with a respectable young man. Rachel did resign her position in government, and after selling the house in Swiss Cottage we moved to the city. Of Sarah, to date I have had no contact, visually or verbally. On the morning after my meeting with Jonathan Sandpiper, I returned to my father's house for the last time, and dragging the wooden chest from its hiding place in the loft, I took it into the back garden and set fire to it. The secret my father had kept all his life was now nothing more than smoke evaporating up in the heavens. It was with a great sense of relief I watched it burn, and when the last glimmering ember dulled, I sifted the ashes with my foot to assure myself there was not a single trace left. That same day I wrote a brief letter to the King.

Your Majesty

It is with a sense of deep regret and sadness that I am forced to decline the prestigious and posthumous honour it was your intention to bestow on my father William James, for reasons too shameful and too painful to divulge confidentially or publicly. Suffice to say, I would regard any decision to the contrary a travesty to the deserving benefactors of such a privileged title, and thereby request my wishes be acknowledged and upheld.

Your loyal servant

Michael James.

THE END

(SEQUEL) SECRET II SYNOPSIS.

The year is 1945 and the war in Europe is over. Michael James continues with business as usual and his life returns to some normality. In the week leading up to Christmas, three separate events transpire; the first—the abduction of five children, the second—the release of Matthew Pilinger from prison, the agent for London trafficking, and the third—the receipt of documented proof concerning the BLANCA faction and its members.

The power behind BLANCA seek revenge on those who attributed evidence against them and put their London operation on hold; Michael James and Elizabeth McCauley, and it is the assignment of Matthew Pilinger to ensure they are found and punished in the appropriate manner.

In the meantime Michael James sets out to discover the connection—if any—there may be in the abducted children, with the help of some new and some old characters.

SECRET II

ONE

Like the war I was soon forgotten. My heroism concerning twenty-two young trafficked girls, the imprisonment of the pimp Vincent Pierce, and the exposure of 247 corrupt police officers held the public's attention for a short while but soon dissolved amongst the ashes of yesterday's news. Indeed, there was little to remind me of the adventure but for a small scar on the bridge of my nose that would forever swell me with pride whenever I gazed at my reflection. The war ended in September 1945, and now just three months later Europe was about to enjoy its first Christmas in peace. The war babies born in the conflict now played in the ruinous buildings and bombsites across the city, hiding in skeletal frames of palatial houses without fear or respect for those who perished inside them. The cost of the damage was incalculable but worse, much worse was the price paid in human lives—61,000,000. Like every other Londoner I celebrated the cessation of the war and wept with joy, knowing that by the skin of our teeth, Churchill's steadfast defiance and determination, and perhaps an element of divine intervention, Britain had not only survived the onslaught but became a nation to be reckoned with should the next despot hell-bent on world domination feel he was in with a chance. It was as if a great weight had been lifted off the city. The days seemed somehow brighter and the air easier to breathe. Like other businesses' in the metropolis I continued in much the same way as I had before, sometimes flourishing but quite often borrowing from the banks to keep afloat. Kenneth Banner or Badger as I preferred to call him, was now an equal partner in the renamed law firm James, Banner & James; the first James being me Michael, and the second being Rachel my wife, whose real name is Eleanor though seldom is it mentioned. Every once in a while my past endeavours undergo a revival and the firm receives a sudden influx in business, whenever a Fleet Street hack with a mental block decides to resurrect the story of police corruption or human trafficking and my name is mentioned. Just one month after the war ended I was the subject of a glossy exposé in a woman's magazine no less, concerning it with multiple murderers and what makes them become cold-blooded killers. I accepted their generous fee and for the next three days was interviewed about George Henderson, named by the press as the 'Blackout Butcher' and a man I defended without much success. The article, which should have had me earmarked as the greatest detective since Sherlock Holmes and infused the firm with much needed capital, was lost to the editor's lethal pen and a lengthy but interesting piece on pre-menstrual tension.

In a perfect world the days leading up to Christmas should have seen London blanketed in snow, with twinkling fairy lights and nativity scenes in shop windows and groups of small children singing heavenly anthems on street corners. Instead it was gloomily miserable with a cold and bitterly wind soaring through the streets as if borne on the wings of Thor himself. Heavy rain lashed the city with impunity, and dark and thunderous clouds skidded across the rooftops as if it were their intention to crush London entirely. Sylvia, my long, suffering secretary and bane of my life, clung tightly to my arm as we pushed our way through the heavy strain of shoppers in search of that special gift for their loved ones. She would continuously stop to behold the displays embellished with artificial snowdrops and threads of tinsel behind the rain-streaked windows, then like a woman possessed she would drag me off to the next shop to appraise their goods, only to lead me back to the shop we had previously left. Finally, and after much agonising and just as my clothes had doubled in weight due to water saturation, she led me into the dryness of a jeweller and began to slowly walk the length of the shop whilst examining the sparkling goods within the display cabinets. As the minutes expired and far exceeded the allotted one hour dinner break, I momentarily secured Sylvia's attention and tapped the face of my watch impatiently with my finger. She ignored my reminder and moved painfully onward towards the end of the shop, stopping at each individual cabinet and leaving a circle of misted glass in her wake caused by hot breath. "Watch or ring?" she muttered as if the future of mankind depended on her decision.

"Michael, you're a man—of sorts. Which would you prefer, a watch or a ring?" she asked. I skilfully followed her gaze, where beyond the glass lay a silver watch nestling in an ornate box of red velvet. Knowing that my secretary was something of a magpie, and therefore attracted to anything that glittered or was presented in such a way it would test the will of even the most hardened of shoppers I replied watch, hoping against hope she would make the damn purchase and we could return to the office and resume business. My hopes were dashed when she shot me a disagreeable look and wandered on. "Well, you're no help at all, are you?" There was a hopelessness to it all, a futility I failed to grasp. Whilst consumed in the excruciating boredom imposed upon me, and being jostled, pushed and shoved by consumers who were committed to spending every penny they owned as if their lives depended on it, it became evident that men were more adept at shopping than women, for by this time I had reticently slipped out of the jewellers and was now standing under the awning and making my observations. A man would walk into a shop and reappear five or ten minutes later laden with parcels, while a woman would walk into a shop and never be seen again. And once a man had made his choice of gift, he would make his purchase without question, bid the assistant a Merry Christmas and go merrily on his way, whereas the female species were more inclined to faff about indecisively, consider the option of one out of three possible gifts, and then strangle the living daylights out of anyone who dare approach one of their choices. Given the season, and that all these people had been used to living only one day at a time, one could forgive them their wild spending and unreasonable behaviour.

From my relatively dry but windy confines I stared out at the bustling Fleet Street, the traffic bumper to bumper, the pedestrians overflowing into the road. In front of me stood the Royal Courts, to the left St. Mary's Church which never ceased to remind me of how Sylvia and I nearly met our end. It all seemed long ago and far away now, when London was ravaged by the Blitz and I was caught up in a world of assassins, espionage and slavery, but it still brought a smile to my lips and tear to my eye whenever it came to mind. And even though my secretary had yet to make her choice and time was ticking dangerously close to a two hour lunch break, I knew I could never bring myself to berate her, being that I owed her my life. That is to say that I could never reprimand her seriously, though God knows I would go through the motions—usually on an hourly basis. As my mind began to wander and my eyes roamed aimlessly up and down the street, Sylvia finally emerged and emanated one of her sensual smiles, and patting her handbag as if her trawl through every London shop had at last yielded the perfect gift, she laced her arm through mine and jerked her head towards the Thames. "Don't just stand there dallying, Michael, we're late!" The wind was cutting, swirling between the buildings as if in search of an escape and gusting through the narrow alleyways, pushing the hordes of shoppers down the steady incline towards New Bridge Road and blowing robust umbrellas inside out. There were places of refuge however, in the deep recesses of shop doorways or in one of the many side streets, but I chose our local coffeehouse, where I first took Rachel when she was a stranger and where I bought my shot of adrenalin every morning. I found a vacant table while Sylvia hurried to the toilets lest anyone recognise her in her windswept condition. I shook the rain from my coat and hung it on the back of the chair to dry and ordered two coffees. For a while I perused a newspaper left on the seat beside me, concerning itself mostly with the Nazi leaders at the Nuremberg Trials or President Truman's elaboration on the Japanese conflict. Every written line positively exuded British smugness, that indefinable spirit that made Britain Great. There existed a party atmosphere, a true sense of pride amongst those who survived it, and though many were not at the forefront of the battle, we kept the home fires burning by keeping London alive; never once abandoning her—to the Germans or any other tin-pot tyrant who thought he could just waltz through Europe and claim the spoils. We were the victors and proud of it. On the other side of the coin, and one I believe which failed to swell the hearts of even the most patriotic of civilians in the western world, was the abrupt ending to America's war with Japan. I suppose if you want to put an end to a war then dropping two sizeable atom bombs should do the trick, but if somewhere in the dictionaries and the history books a true definition of 'Hollow Victory' is elucidated, then surely this must be it. In its entirety the battle fought by Little Boys and Fat Men against the Japanese population was only going to end one way, with zero casualties for America and no less than a shameful

246,000 fatalities to Japan. Anyone who believes in the adage that 'All is fair and love and war' should be certified insane.

When Sylvia returned, flawless as usual in her presentation, she placed her soaking wet coat on top of mine and took up a seat in front of me, and where after rummaging through her handbag she produced a small, red velvet box and flipped the lid to reveal the watch I had recommended to her.

"Well?" she said. "Isn't it beautiful? I'm so pleased I chose it."

I gazed at the gift askance. "But I chose it—an hour ago!" I said. "We could have been back at work by now instead of sheltering in here."

"Oh, be quiet you miserable sod. You're just jealous because you never saw it first."

"But I did, I did!" I argued. "You asked me which I would prefer and I pointed to the watch. That watches."

"You're such a liar, Michael. How can you live with yourself? You may have given it a passing glance but it was me who made the final decision."

"Which took forever and now we're late back for work."

"And whose fault is that? I never asked to come in here; I simply followed you. Did you get me a cake with my coffee?"

"No."

"No? Then how am I expected to work till five thirty without food? An empty sack won't stand, Michael."

"But we have worked to do, Sylvia!" I argued, tapping the face of my watch once again. "We don't have time for cakes and buns."

My secretary narrowed her eyes threateningly.

"You are coming dangerously close to contravening the conditions of my employment, Michael, in which, and I quote: I am allowed a one hour lunch break."

"But you've had two!"

"Don't make me have to take this to a tribunal, Michael. They don't take kindly to exploitation," she warned me.

I felt my shoulders sag and for a moment sat there utterly defeated.

"My fault," I uttered. "Order what you want. I'll pay."

"I should think so, as well."

It was 3.30 by the time we reached the offices, windblown and bedraggled. I left my mutinous secretary showing off her prized possession to the other girls and headed for my office, removing my rain-sodden coat as I walked and hanging it on a hook behind my door. When I turned a woman was seated in front of my desk. She was perhaps thirty-five or forty, with sad, demoralised eyes and a face lined with pain. She dressed frumpishly, not at all one would expect of a woman of her age, and she expressed a timid smile on seeing me. With no idea as to whom she might be, and with my entire staff presently engaged in comparing Christmas gifts, I gently closed the door and walked to my desk, running my fingers through my unkempt hair to at least convey the illusion of acceptability. When I sat down she simply observed me with that same nervous smile, and when the moments turned into an uncomfortable minute, I feigned composure and smiled back at her.

"Forgive me," I said. "But what with Christmas and the forthcoming festivities, my receptionist has failed to enlighten me as to your appointment."

"Christmas. Yes," said the woman, quietly.

I waited for an announcement of some kind; a name or a reason for her presence, but she lowered her eyes and stared into her lap where her fingers fumbled anxiously with one another.

"Ma'am?" I said. "You do have an appointment?"

When she failed to raise her head I excused myself and slid out of my chair. The girls were congregated in reception, gossiping about gifts, wrapping paper and who they had invited to Christmas dinner.

"Sylvia!" I hissed from the corridor. "Why didn't you tell me I had an appointment?"

She shrugged her shoulders and shook her head. "Because you haven't," and then she proceeded to move onto Boxing Day with her colleagues and bitch about all it entailed.

"Will someone please tell me who this woman is in my office?" I growled.

Rachel, who to be fair should have known better than to engage in idle chit-chat when there was work to be done, suddenly emerged through the gathering and approached me.

"She just came in off the street," she explained, as perplexed as I was. "She asked for you specifically. I said you were out but she insisted in waiting. She doesn't say much."

"Yes, Rachel, I know. I've gathered that much already," I replied, looking back at my office and shaking my head. "Could you do me a really big favour?" I asked, turning to face her once again.

"Of course."

"Would you be so kind as to get these people back to work before I'm declared bankrupt?"

Rachel sighed wearily and walked away, murmuring under her breath something about Scrooge and the values of the Christmas spirit.

When I returned the woman was standing by the window, staring out at the driving rain with immense interest and watching as the cars and lorries ran through puddles and sent torrents of water onto the pavements and the passing pedestrians.

"May I get you a tea, a coffee?" I asked as I took up my seat.

The lady shook her head and half turned towards me, her eyes still cast downwards. What I saw was a woman who had suffered great hardship and considerable strain, whose heart had been shattered and who was unable to see beyond tomorrow. I simply observed her curiously and left her to her own devices. After much hesitation and toing and froing, she resumed her seat, staring at me with those sad, doleful eyes.

"Mr James?" she said. "Mr Michael James?"

I nodded and forced another worthless smile.

She paused again and drew a deep, fretful breath. At this stage I was moved to remind her that it was a week till Christmas, and I rather fancied the idea of making it home by then so I could spend it with my family.

"I have no money . . ." she began.

"Well, if it's any consolation neither do I," I wanted to say.

I nodded sympathetically.

Again she paused from her stilted narrative while fumbling in her pocket, and there she produced a page of the glossy article written about me two months ago and ironed it out on my desk with the palm of her hand. Certainly it wasn't the four page spread as promised but more a small piece lost amongst adverts for bras for the fuller woman and water retention pills. She looked at me steadily and tapped her finger on the creased editorial.

"You?" she said.

There were no actual photographs of me though at the interview several were taken, and I can only assume it was the editor's intention to accumulate more readers rather than lose them and promptly consigned my portraits to the bin.

I nodded my head modestly.

Her insipid smile grew slightly warmer and she folded up the paper carefully and placed it back in her pocket.

"I lost my little girl, Mr James," she said in a trembling voice. "She's just eight years old."

There are some things said that leave you bereft of an answer or a response, and this was one of them. I could only look at the poor woman and sigh, knowing that literally thousands of children had perished during the Blitz and the sporadic bombardments which followed. Unfortunately I had witnessed it with my own eyes, when the savagery began and the Luftwaffe started their daytime assaults. I had been to a meeting beyond Leicester Square, and as I left I heard the low drones of the bombers hidden somewhere above the clouds. Everyone around me began to rush to the undergrounds, like a wave of humanity all surging in the same direction. For some inexplicable reason I stood stock still, just gazing up at the fast moving sky, and then I heard it. A few moments later I saw a plume of black smoke rising from the direction of Soho, and like so many others I quickly headed in that direction. A cluster of bombs had completely erased one side of a narrow street, reducing it to a deep scar in the ground buried beneath tons of rubble and splintered timber. By the time I arrived, which I might add was only a matter of minutes, hundreds of men and women were already excavating the devastation with their bare hands, creating human chains in which debris was passed along to make room. Jets of water spurted up into the heavens and arced across the street, ironically creating a rainbow as the spray was captured in sunlight. The first bodies pulled out were three children, one but a baby, white with dust where crimson patches expanded on their limp bodies like ink on blotting paper. They were laid down on the pavement while searching resumed. I remember standing over them and looking down on their lifeless bodies, wondering what they looked like behind that veil of dust and what their names were. Too soon I was pushed aside, by members of the ARP, the fire brigade and ambulance personnel, and being of little help me slowly walked towards my office.

"I'm not sure how I can help, ma'am," I said, gently. "The war claimed many lives."

She smiled at me again as if I was supposed to know.

"My name is Roberts, Mrs Glenda Roberts, and my little girl isn't dead, Mr James—she was taken."

"Ma'am?"

"Two months and fourteen days ago. I saw him from the bedroom window, holding her in his arms and placing her in the back of a van. I won't forget it. It was exactly 10.42, and although the streets were pitch black, a light from the corner house captured his silhouette. Something told me the child in his arms was my daughter. When I got to her room her bed was empty and the window open."

She spoke almost in a whisper, her eyes fixed and staring as she recalled that fateful night, and when she finished she blinked and resumed her soft, angelic smile. I felt a cold chill run down my spine as I envisaged the scene—of a dark, predatory figure cradling a flaccid child in his arms and disappearing into the night.

"By the time I reached the front door the van pulled away. I have not seen her since," she said.

After some considerable silent moments had elapsed, I leaned forward.

"You have notified the police, yes?" I asked.

"At Bishopsgate police station. And the Red Cross," she nodded.

I reclined and observed her sceptically.

"Mrs Roberts, what is it—exactly—you expect me to do?"

Her smile expanded with hope and she rested her arms on the desk.

"Mr James. Sir, you saved twenty-two young girls from abduction and a lifetime in purgatory. You can find her. I know you can."

My heart suddenly began to race and the blood in my veins seemed to heat up. I could only gaze back at her pitiful smile and feel ashamed.

"Ma'am, I can't help you. I am a lawyer not a . . ."

She suddenly produced the magazine article again and placed it on the desk. I stared at it for a lengthy while and shook my head.

"Ma'am . . . Mrs Roberts . . . Please believe me that I would do anything to help, but I'm not qualified. I am not a detective or an investigator. I am a litigator and deal with law. What you have read was an accident, a search into one thing that led to another. I didn't purposefully set out to find those girls. It just . . ."

All signs of hope seemed to dissolve and her posture sank until she looked at me absently and slowly nodded—as if she accepted my excuse. Once again she returned the article into her pocket and stood up, the suggestion of her gentle smile returning.

"There are people, Mrs Roberts, the right people who can help you. I can have my secretary write down their names and numbers for you and you can call them. Or I can do it on your behalf. I'd be more than happy to make an appointment for you to see someone more proficient in such matters if, of course, you feel the police can be of no further help. Sadly that is all I can do. I'm truly sorry."

I registered the hopelessness in her eyes and tried to smile.

"Thank you for your time, sir. Happy Christmas to you."

'Oh, don't do this to me!' my heart screamed. 'Not now. Not this time of year.'

I suddenly leapt up and drew my wallet from my pocket, offering over its entire contents of thirty-five pounds."

"Please. I'd like you to have it," I said.

She smiled again and walked to the door.

"Ma'am?" I said urgently. "Her name. What was . . . ? What is her name?"

She looked into my eyes and tilted her head slightly.

"Emily," she answered softly.

She left me standing there with my open wallet in one hand and thirty-five pounds in the other.

"Bollocks!" I sighed.

Lightning Source UK Ltd.
Milton Keynes UK
UKOW05f0330280813

216059UK00002B/98/P